CHIMURENGA

WENDY WRIGHT

The Book Guild Ltd

First published in Great Britain in 2022 by
The Book Guild Ltd
Unit E2 Airfield Business Park,
Harrison Road, Market Harborough,
Leicestershire. LE16 7UL
Tel: 0116 2792299
www.bookguild.co.uk
Email: info@bookguild.co.uk
Twitter: @bookguild

Copyright © 2022 Wendy Wright

The right of Wendy Wright to be identified as the author of this
work has been asserted by her in accordance with the
Copyright, Design and Patents Act 1988.

All rights reserved. No part of this publication may be
reproduced, transmitted, or stored in a retrieval system, in any form or by any means,
without permission in writing from the publisher, nor be otherwise circulated in
any form of binding or cover other than that in which it is published and without
a similar condition being imposed on the subsequent purchaser.

This work is entirely fictitious and the characters bear no resemblance to any persons living or dead.

Typeset in 11pt Adobe Jenson Pro

Printed and bound by CPI Group (UK) Ltd, Croydon, CR0 4YY

ISBN 978 1914471 520

British Library Cataloguing in Publication Data.
A catalogue record for this book is available from the British Library.

I would like to thank songwriter John Edmond for his kind permission to use some of the lyrics from 'Sling Your Slayer', from John's 'Phase II – Troopiesongs' album.

FRIDAY 18TH DECEMBER 1981

Think.
 Think straight and get a grip.
 You *haven't* gone deaf, you silly cow. Listen. Yes?
 That weird, muted woolliness and indistinguishable buzz in my ears is, here and there, starting to separate into individual sounds. Like strands of yarn, they're unravelling and beginning to register in my senses as something real. Screaming. Someone is screaming. No, more than one person. Shattering and splintering. Glass. Glass falling from many windows in many buildings over many storeys. Going on and on and on. Then your voice. Behind me. Clear and utterly calm, as if you're identifying fruit in the supermarket.
 "That was a bomb."
 I know. I knew even as the air hit me and turned my eardrums to wool. Is that what they call a shockwave? Gave *me* a bloody shock. Probably how I ended up on my knees. As time seems to be standing still, I take the chance to inspect them. Yup. They're grazed, and they sting.
 Actually, thinking straight doesn't seem to be an option open to me. Muddled doesn't come close to describing my world right now. I don't understand. The war is over. It's all supposed to be all right now.
 Time gets going again. It's all happening. People are surging every which way around me, apart from you, with one steady hand against my back, the other one on my shoulder and your presence grounding me and keeping me from joining the frantic, aimless throng. A middle-aged woman in a blue pinafore-type dress appears in front of us, makes contact with her panicked eyes and yells, "It's near that bakery! The bakery's blown up!"

Your voice is still completely calm when you say, "The ZANU(PF) offices are above the bakery."

There's a log-jam of crazily-angled cars up ahead and an acrid sting in my nostrils. A haze of smoky, dusty stuff is drifting along Manica Road from the east, over the cars.

ZANU(PF) headquarters. The North-West Bakery. Dad, and his jokes about the leadership party operating out of a tiny, dingy office over a bread shop. Mum, telling me it sells the best bread in town. Lasts well, no maize-meal in it, if you need good bread, my girl, you go there to get it, yes? I may well have done that this morning if Moira hadn't been grocery shopping yesterday.

While I have this completely inane nonsense rattling in my head, down below a deep chill of pure horror is seeping into my legs. In a matter of minutes, you and I might've been walking past the bakery, looking for a gap in the traffic so that we could cross the road to Meikles. And Mum might've been queuing there today.

But we're all still in one piece, me, you and Mum. Us here on the pavement in First Street and Mum – where would she be now? – probably on the way down to Southampton, trying to get used to the winter cold and totally oblivious to this. For now at least. It'll hit the world news later today of course.

And I told them it'll be fine. I told them, go, I'll be okay, I know what I'm doing. I said that more than once, didn't I? To parents, to Rosie and even to Charles and Moira and Gill. And you.

Right. Come on, get back to the here and now. Think. What do I do? Now where's that guy going?

He's the one who helped me to my feet and, together with you, held me upright. He peered into my face and asked me if I was all right, but now he's let go of my arm and is running across the road, dodging round a stationary car, shouting. He's yelling in Shona; looks like he's recognised someone on the other side of Manica Road.

Christ, when Mum and Dad hear about this they'll go berserk. They're more than likely to command me to leave on the next available flight and join them. Will they try to come back and fetch me?

How the hell was I supposed to know which was the right choice? It's not like I made the decision just like that – snap. No, I did months of agonising, running pros and cons, creating arguments, upsetting the whole bloody family, driving myself crazy. Then I thought I knew. I chose. And now? Now it all, quite literally, blows up in my face.

Well okay, not in *my* face. Not even right near me, thank God.

God?

Come on, you don't believe in God so why do you even say that? Think, think.

PART ONE

LAND OF HOPE

SUNDAY 17TH AUGUST 1975

I need to treasure those memories, because Mushandike's a thing of the past now. We met a hippo and some eland, a family of warthogs and some jackals and we learned how to track animals and about ecosystems. We climbed a rockface near the dam wall and we ate our dinner and sang songs around a campfire in the middle of nowhere. We watched a sheep being dissected and measured the length of its small intestine, and Elizabeth threw up. We imagined ourselves to be a band of Mashona escaping the marauding Matabele by using that natural rock tunnel hidden in a hillside, crouching and scuttling along it in the dark. We just had such a good time. And then, yesterday, it was over. The birdsong woke us early and the dawn was all pink and misty and we ate bacon and eggs around the revived campfire while the sun gradually rose up over the tops of the trees and its light crept down towards the ground. Then we had to go. None of us wanted to leave, just like, I'll bet, so many other school children over the years, but we had to go home. We left a bush school and soon it will be just an army barracks. Maybe Barry will stay there, in the dormitory where Jess and I were. Maybe Nathan will get to go back.

I guess hope is a thing of the past too. This is real, isn't it? There really is a proper war and it's just arrived on my doorstep.

FRIDAY 8TH DECEMBER 1972

"It's what you get after years of, well, exploitation, frankly."

That's what Nathan said. I remember it exactly. He never says very much so I guess that's why I can remember every single word. Even *exploitation*. The dictionary in my lap says this means "*- the act of using for selfish purposes…*" I've re-read it several times. Enough times. I look up, out into the garden through the French doors in front of me.

Elijah's weeding and tidying the edges of the beds. I allow my mind to be absorbed for a while by his steady and methodical progress – take a weed in forefinger and thumb of the left hand, insert the trowel tip into the soil with the right, wiggle it, free the roots, shake off the crumbs of earth, deposit the tiny plant into the bucket, move on to the next one. A peaceful, tranquil activity, and watching him releases a small plug somewhere in me so that some of that gnawing humiliation starts to drain away. And also the anger. Yes, anger. The wanting to scream and throw something across the room and then cry type of anger. But if I throw the dictionary across the room I'll end up breaking something, or damaging the book and how will I explain it? There's nothing I can do but sit and keep it inside and concentrate instead on admiring those straight and squared off edges, the weed-free paving slabs. Elijah's so tidy and thorough, like Daddy tells us a good garden boy should be.

Oh hell, no. Not again.

Those words – those very words I've just said to myself – have dumped me back in time to the roadside by the school. Simple words, they were, but they've brought my peaceful, tranquil thoughts to a grinding halt.

Yesterday, if anyone had asked me, I would've said the words formed a perfectly reasonable compliment. And they did, or at least that's how I meant them to come out. But not now, today. After all that happened earlier, the voice that says those words sounds as if it comes from someone just like the person the policeman took me for. Am I really like that? I never, *ever* thought what he said I did. I wasn't thinking at all. I was just… well, I guess I did ignore him. But not deliberately, like I was mocking him. Why did he get so angry?

I stop watching Elijah, try to clear these thoughts of him from my brain, and stare at the tops of the msasa trees behind him instead.

What a horrible day. Can't I go back to seven o'clock this morning, get up again and start over? Fridays are meant to be good days, whether you're nine or as old as Daddy. He's always more cheery on Fridays, even before he goes to work. If only Jess hadn't been off ill today. If Jess'd been at school with me none of this would have happened.

Okay, so even if Jess is still sick in my new day, if I could start it over again I wouldn't do what I did.

I wasn't being deliberately naughty. Me and Jess made plans back on Monday for this afternoon. We were going to read my new *Beezer*, and the Barbies were going to go on a holiday to New York, which is why I packed Patsy's clothes in her pink suitcase last night and left it out ready to take over to Jess's house. When I crossed the road all this was in my head, plus the new plan I'd just hatched, literally seconds earlier. If my brain hadn't been off in some other universe it would've all been normal and he would never have even noticed me.

So he's been there, at the zebra crossing, every day since I started school and for all I know he might've been there every day for the last ten years. I know nothing about him, not even his name. He's just the policeman who waves us across the road. When he lets us go over, he commands the traffic to halt with his arms raised outwards, a bit like Mrs Morris said Moses did with the Red Sea. Timothy Dunn says he must be a Matabele.

"My dad said – " (Timothy starts nearly every sentence with "My dad said – ") "My dad said we need to get tribalism to work for us so we have Matabele police in Mashonaland and Mashona police in Matabeleland."

Do we do that? Why? Why did I never ask him why?

I'm seeing the traffic policeman in my head. He's tall, and he's very serious, unlike Elijah. He has what Daddy would call knife edge creases in his shorts, and crisp, dazzling white armbands that cover the whole of his forearms and make him look so smart. He never says very much, just like Nathan. He only ever speaks when he's telling one of the boys to dismount and walk over the crossing. For that he always gets the two fingers – behind his back of course.

They're always trying that, the boys, riding their bikes over the crossing. I never even thought about doing it. Until today. Well I didn't *ride* it, did I? I scooted on one pedal, that's all. That idea sprang on me and I reacted. I needed to go the other way and call by Jess's house to see if she was feeling better, so our plans could be back on after all. Jess and Tess together again.

So suddenly I was in this big hurry, because I knew Mummy would do the Tessa-you're-more-than-FIVE-MINUTES-late bit if I took too long.

I just made it worse of course, ending up more than half an hour late and having to tell a lie. If she finds out there never was a traffic accident I don't know how I'm going to get out of that one.

She'll try and talk about it to one of her friends, won't she? I bet she'll say something like, "Tessa told me about the accident near the school on Friday. Was anyone hurt? What happened? They were held up a long time." And for sure the friend will be one of the mothers who pick up their kids, like Mrs Harrison or Mrs Pretorius, and *she'll* say, "Accident? No. No, I was there and it was all fine. Where did Tessa say it was?" And then...

If I can't throw the book then I'll slam it shut and shove it onto the floor in front of me. I haven't had a churning stomach and buzzing head like this, ever. What if I get reported and have to go to Mr Westfield's office? The policeman doesn't know my name but there were enough kids there who do. Good old Tessa Harmand, never disobedient, never swears, always does her homework, and now in trouble with the police. Mummy and Daddy will be disappointed and Rosie will be ashamed of me and I might even get expelled. I might never be able to ride Gill's horses again. And I wasn't even *trying* to be rebellious, or disobedient, or whatever the guy thought I was up to.

Go on, torture yourself. Relive the scene again, why don't you? There I am, dodging round Robert Thacker, who's fiddling about with the straps of his satchel right in the middle of the cycle track, and I get this strange sensation that something's happened behind me. I'd ignored the first burst of shouting and laughing that rose above the general hubbub of voices and traffic, vaguely curious, yes, but in too much of a hurry to care. Then this weird, kind of sixth sense sensation comes to me just a fraction of a second before I hear my name.

"It's Tessa!"

"Wey-hey, Tessa!"

"Tessa Harmand!"

So I brake, stop, look back. Always stop first, before looking round – I know this from experience. There's the traffic policeman, punching the air with one fist and pointing the other forefinger directly at me, and I'm standing like a lemon with my head twisted round, staring at him, wondering what the heck is going on. He's shouting but I can't hear what because my heart is thumping so hard. For a few thumps I'm not even sure he's speaking English. Then I can hear him. And so can everyone else in the world, and they're gawking, whispering, all focussed on me.

"*Iwe!* You! You must wait! I will speak with you."

Elijah's picked up his bucket of dug-up weeds, put his tools in with them and is walking across to the corner of the house, towards the shed, presumably. He disappears from view. There's some clattering from the kitchen that makes me twitch like you see people on TV do when they've been shot. If Mummy comes through and finds me sitting here on the floor in the study she's bound to ask why. I grab the dictionary again, fumble with a few pages, settle on one. If she does, I'll find a word and say I'm looking it up for my English comprehension question sheet. Then all goes quiet, except for the muffled sound of the patio door opening and closing. Me and the dictionary are back alone with my miserable secret.

So when the officer yelled at me, still pointing at me, I had some crazy thoughts, like why, why me, he can't mean me, jump back on the bike and ride home flat out, just pretend this isn't happening, he's not talking to me.

The problems were, a) I couldn't make any of my muscles move, and b) he clearly *was* talking to me. So many interested, excited, delighted voices told me so.

"Ooh, Tessa!"

"What a naughty girl! You rode your bike across the road!"

"It's *Tessa* who's done it! Wow!"

"He's going to arrest you!"

And I was thinking, all I did was scoot on my pedal and since when was that a crime?

Well, of course I know it's not a crime. I know now why he singled me out like that, but I didn't then.

I felt sick and hot and sweaty, waiting for him by that big jacaranda tree where he leaves his bike. The air's always sticky and sort of heavy in November and December, even long before there's any smell of rain. It still is now. My legs, folded like this, are all slick on the insides. The weather forecaster last night was still harping on about the ITCZ bringing storms, but it hasn't arrived in Rhodesia yet that's for sure.

I didn't have to wait long of course. School empties out in no time at all on a Friday. I'd already decided exactly what I was going to do. Be cheerful and say sorry. He would be happy and I could go home. But it didn't work.

I smiled at him so brightly, but he just scowled back. Scowled back so hard he made me feel like something that had crawled out from under a stone. Even when I said, "I'm sorry. I was in too much of a hurry. I promise I won't do it again," he carried on glaring at me, so then I said "I'd make a horrible mess on the front of someone's car wouldn't I?"

I still think that's quite funny. He didn't.

"Why did you not get off your bicycle? I shouted to you to get off. You ignored me."

I absolutely did not ignore him. I didn't. I never heard him shout. Maybe he didn't shout. Maybe he spoke too quietly. I don't know. I told him this. I told him I never heard him. I said sorry again and I still thought he'd believe me, let me go. I never expected him to say what he said next.

He put his hands on his hips. He leaned forward so close to my face that I had to take a step back. He said a lot of things that are still imprinted in me.

"You think that just because I am a black man you can take no notice of what I say. I call to you. I tell you to get off your bicycle and you think, 'He is black. He is just my servant.' Huh? That is what you think? I am a policeman and I have to tell you to walk across the road but you can say 'No'. You can ignore me. I always have this. White children think I am their servant. I'm just a *kaffir*."

I didn't know what to do, or say, or think. I just started crying. It was like I was ashamed of myself, but I hadn't done anything wrong. He was making out that I'd insulted him, but I didn't… did I? He accused me of calling him a *kaffir*. Well, not calling him that, but thinking it, but I didn't. Lots of people do and now he thinks I'm one of them. I'm not. I don't. I've never called anyone a *kaffir*.

Of course when I said nothing in my defence, he started nodding, like he knew he was right. Then he gave up. Walked away, to his bicycle. I got my voice back too late and shouted, "I. Did. Not. Hear. You!"

Before getting on his bike, he scowled at me again, over his shoulder.

"If I was a white policeman you would have heard me."

I don't want to go back to school on Monday. I can't face him again, or any of them, after that. Everyone else who watched him leave me there found the whole thing hysterically funny. I've never, never been so mortified – is that the word? – in my life.

I can't be bothered to try and find it. I'm done with the dictionary. I get up, put it back in the bookcase, hover near the door and listen, and then scuttle to my room across the corridor. I shut the door, but then just stand in the middle staring out of the window again – this time at the driveway and the gate and the view across the valley.

To make things worse – if that's possible – after I thought I'd got away from the scene there was Nathan, popping up out of nowhere on the corner just down from the school. Well, it seemed to me like he came out of nowhere, as he does, but it turns out he'd been standing there all the time, in front of the hibiscus hedge. Last time I remember seeing him was, what, a week ago? At Makuti Park. Jumping High Time over some ginormous fences.

Why did *he* have to see it all? I hate that he saw me humiliated like that. And what if he tells Gill what happened? She'll be disappointed in me too.

He was looking scruffy as usual. No tie, socks round his ankles, hat on top of his satchel, on the grass. He might be in Standard Five but he hasn't been made a prefect and, to be honest, if any of the prefects had been about he'd have been in for detention for sure. Abuse of the school uniform. But does he care?

He had a hand across his forehead to block out the sun and I was thinking maybe he should've worn his hat. He didn't even say hello. He just started with, "Are you okay? I saw you talking to the traffic cop. He seemed a bit pissed off. I was going to say something to him but he upped and went. What was he on about?"

I really do remember all his words. But then, the last time he said anything to me was the day of the Mushandike exhibition. That was probably even the last time I heard him speak to anyone.

God, how humiliating. He has to watch me get lambasted by that guy, then has to listen to me break down and gabble at him like a baby, explaining myself, justifying what a good girl I am, how I don't ignore people just because they're black, and all because I was so desperate that he should believe me, even if that damned policeman didn't. I wish I'd never… well, I wish a lot of things had never happened today.

It was after we'd stared at each other for a bit, like neither of us knew what to do next, that he said, "I believe you. But he probably doesn't. It's what you get after years of, well, exploitation frankly."

Elijah's back. He's carrying the shears and he's full of purpose, the hedge next to the road in his sights.

Admit it, Tessa. You never normally even notice what he's doing in the garden. He's just there, but you've never seen it as a concern of yours to think any further than your eyes. Have I ever been guilty of thinking he's just a black man, a servant, so he doesn't count? *He's never got angry with me, or even with Mummy, and she's pretty mean to him sometimes.* Like last week when she said to him, "The compost heap is getting rather big now. If some of it doesn't get dug into the beds you'll end up having to dump those grass cuttings you've got there by the garage." So what did he do? He dumped the grass cuttings in a pile – a neat pile – by the garage. She got all miffed and said he'd deliberately misunderstood her but if she talks in backward, obscure sentences like that, what does she expect?

He was nice to me afterwards when I made him up some Mazoe orange squash in his blue enamel mug. He's our garden boy. He has been for ages now. Me and Rosie like him. I am not *like that*. I'm not.

SATURDAY 27TH JANUARY 1973

The day we chose Cleo was almost exactly like this. Then too, we had a thunderstorm that crackled and grumbled its way across the city early in the morning and then vanished leaving wall to wall sunshine and steaming vegetation. That day too, Daddy wore his dark glasses and whinged about being dazzled by the fierce glare from the shiny, wet roads and me and Rosie had an argument in the back of the car, but I don't remember what it was about. It was two years ago, but it might as well be the same day. Even this place looks the same. Over there – under the stately, arching branches of those two flamboyants – that's the run of cat pens where we found her. Cleo, who was this tiniest scrap of black fur amongst so many cats and so many dogs, and so many Eyes. That's what I do remember most vividly. All the Eyes, watching me, all the way round, pleading with me to rescue them.

Dad maintains control of the inspection – up this row of pens, down the next, repeat – to ensure it's methodical. When we're nearly back to where we started, I tug on his sleeve.

"I'm so excited because we're going to get our dog, but sad too. Whichever one we choose, all the others will have to stay here."

He goes, "Yes?" like he means, *have you just realised that?*

Rosie's bouncing around impatiently, going, "Come, there's more!" and Dad says, "We're not taking them all, Tessa, so don't even think about it."

Mummy's in a hurry to push us past the next pen. She calls, "Listen! Puppies!" and I only get to glimpse a lone Rottweiler standing at the back in the shadows. I'm sure Daddy had Rottweilers on his original list of suitable dogs. He lingers slightly, but she's going, "Here we are – look! Aren't they sweet, girls? We're looking for a *puppy*, aren't we Bob?"

The plastic notice fixed to the wire mesh door with black cable ties reads *'LULU. Rescued in Hatfield. Long haired Alsatian bitch approximately five years old. Good with children. Puppies can be adopted with her or separately'.* The puppies making the noise are a yipping, snarling huddle of three, involved in some kind of catch-me-if-you-dare game of black and tan fur, tiny teeth and hairy paws. There's their mother in the corner and lying next to her is one other puppy. He has his front paws outstretched and his back ones tucked under, just like the Sphinx, and he's watching us. He tilts his head and his little puppy tail starts waving about like he wants to be friends but isn't too sure. He – or is it a she? – is lighter in colour than the others, a sort of a reddish-tan with just a little bit of black. When me and Rosie crouch down to get on the same level, the other puppies ignore us and carry on squirming about in a heap, but the Sphinx one leaps up, waddles to us and rolls over, so close to the fence that its furry coat pushes through the mesh. He's definitely a he.

I stick my forefinger through a hole to tickle his tummy and croon, "Ooh, you are a *skellum!*"

Rosie's giggling and scratching the top of his head as best she can without actually trying to force her hand through the fence.

"Yes?" she whispers in my ear. All I need to do is nod.

She's on her feet, throwing her arms around Daddy.

"We'll have this one, and his name is Skellum."

That's Rosie for you. She's only seven but she considers herself a maker of family decisions.

Daddy says, "Are you asking me or telling me, my girl?" and Mummy says, "What about that chocolate Labrador puppy you said you would call Coco…" but me and Rosie are giving each other that Look. It's not questionable. Skellum is the one.

He doesn't look like much of a guard dog to me. Maybe Daddy will get him a spiked collar when he's big enough and send him for attack training like they do with the police dogs. Thing is, it'll be my fault if he does. I was the one who suggested getting a dog after we had the bars put on the windows, but only because me and Rosie've always wanted one and I figured it was clever of me to put the idea in his head right at that time. The Yellands down the road bought that Dobermann just after they got burgled, didn't they? I don't like that dog. I won't go in their garden without Mum or Dad now.

Dad disappears and comes back with a ginger-haired girl in a blue coat. She's thin and pale and she has a key attached to a purple plastic tag. We now have the avid interest of all the puppies and it takes some crazy minutes for the girl to separate Skellum and gather him up in her arms while we keep the others at bay. I'm the one left in the pen when the gate's slammed shut in front of three eager snouts. Now Lulu's ambled over to me and she shoves her cold nose into my left hand.

"Here, let me…" Dad, bending over to see under Skellum's furry body, eases the key off one of the girl's fingers. Rosie and Mummy are off, trotting in pursuit of her, and he's watching me expectantly. But I can't just walk away from Lulu, having taken her son.

I crouch beside her and wrap my arms around her with my face in her coat because it's the only way I can avoid those soft, deep brown Eyes.

"Don't make me cry. I'll take care of him, I promise."

Daddy's hovering and I can feel his impatience. We'll have to leave it here. I stand up and walk away from the dog.

"I wonder if she understands what I'm saying? Look at her. Does she trust us? There must be some way we can communicate without words."

He's doing just that now. His thumb and his head are all telling me "out". Then he says, "Don't be silly, sweetheart. It's just a dog."

Sometimes there's just no point.

*

The air in the office is sharp and tangy with disinfectant. Daddy signs the form that says we can adopt Skellum and the receptionist lady with the lilac hair says, "Vet in six months' time for the booster vaccinations and he has to be neutered as soon as possible and you can make your donation here."

She taps the plastic dog sitting on the desk with the end of her pen. It has sad eyes that are boring directly into mine. The Eyes again, even if they're not real ones.

Daddy stuffs a ten-dollar note into a slot in the box that the dog is wearing round its neck, but that's not the end of it. We can't take Skellum home just yet because all of them – Mum and Dad, the receptionist lady and the fat man in the white coat – get to talking on and on, the way adults do.

I wanted to ask if neutered means the same as spaying, but the moment has gone. Fifteen minutes go by, then twenty, twenty five. Rosie's sitting on the red, shiny bench seat under the window, paging through an old copy of *National Geographic* she found on the counter with one hand while the other one is down deep in the cardboard pet box, scratching Skellum's ears. I read all the notices about lost dogs, pedigree cats for sale, guinea pigs free to good homes, pet-sitting services, dog grooming services and puppy training classes and am just sighing internally while thinking the very white walls look like they were only painted yesterday, when I notice Daddy performing those moves the grown-ups do when they don't want us kids to hear something. He checks us out over his shoulder, shuffles round to present his back to us and lowers his voice.

I haven't registered a word they've said so far, but of course now I prick up my ears and start to listen, sliding down slowly to perch on the end of the bench seat closest to them. Skellum's fallen asleep and Rosie's making cooing noises and managing to talk to me at the same time about where we're going to take him for walks, which toys we're going to give him first, what games we're going to play. It's hard to blot out her nattering and catch snippets of what Daddy's saying:

"Pursued… unexpected… Centenary… other gangs… isolated attack… I mean, it's not the first time… skirmishes…"

If I move a little to the left, I can see past him to the old man in the white coat. He's leaning against the frame of the door that leads to the surgery, with his arms folded like he's getting comfortable and his round glasses halfway down his nose. He has very red cheeks and a big toothy smile, but he's one of those people who can smile and look a bit nasty at the same time. His voice is louder than Daddy's.

"Well, these *munts* are so poorly organised, hey. They just don't stand a chance against the security forces. Good thing. It's just one of those half hearted attempts at being rebellious."

Rosie's gone quiet so I get all of Daddy's reply. He shakes his head. He says, no, he's heard this was different. Apparently planned. And, he's heard there are gangs still active in the area.

He's right, because Timothy said his dad said they're still causing.

The vet's laughing. He scratches at a mosquito bite on his arm. "Well I reckon we should leave them alone and let them fight each other up there, all these different factions, hey? Incompetent bastards."

By 'them', I assume he means the gooks. Timothy told us it was the gooks that carried out the attacks, but he never mentioned any factions. What are those? And why are we calling them gooks?

Rosie chooses this moment to reach out and prod me and go, "Oi. Did you hear me?"

I hiss at her, "Shhh!", and all four of them jerk their heads round. The vet says, "Oh, sorry. Pardon my French."

They all say that when they swear. It's so stupid. Bastard isn't a French word anyway – even I know that and I've never learned any.

And I'll bet even if they knew I was listening to their conversation they'd never guess that I know exactly what they were on about.

*

Rosie's being her usual annoying self, pacing around, everywhere at once, twitching nearly as much as Skellum's nose.

"Look at him, Tee," she says, and I go, "Aw, Skellie," because he's there, fast asleep in his new bed with his little nose resting on his little paws, eyelids and whiskers busy.

Cleo's a bit freaked out; she's still in the spare bedroom, where she's been since we came home.

I jump to my feet. "I'll go see if Cleo's eaten her food. She'll need to go out too. I can let her out the patio doors."

Daddy's in the doorway. "Good girl, Tessa. And it's bedtime, Miss Rosie."

He's leaning against the frame, with his arms folded, smiling, just like the red-faced vet was earlier. I'm not quite sure why I say it; it just comes out.

"We heard about those farm attacks at school you know. Timothy told us on the first day of term."

I can't tell the story like Timothy did. He rambled a bit. He said, "So these gooks attacked a farmhouse, right. Did you guys hear about it? Up at Centenary, hey? They came over from Zambia. They ran away, but then came back again to shoot up the next door farm as well. The family from the first farm had gone to hide there so they got revved twice. Revved *twice*, hey! Revved big time. And this little girl got hurt. Not bad. She's still alive. She didn't, like, get her head blown off or anything. No, so those gooks ran away, man. My dad says the army okes chased them off with the RPGs, blam, blam, blam!"

When Jess asked, "What's an RPG?", Timothy sighed several times and rolled his eyes and said, "I don't believe... you don't... really?"

David said, "Rocket propelled grenade," to Jess, then, to Timothy, "I doubt that Tim. It's an anti-tank weapon."

I tell Dad this now. "Timothy said they used RPGs. But they're anti-tank weapons."

I'd be willing to bet he doesn't know how to use one. Timothy does. He showed us – well not literally of course, but by waving his hands around a lot. Predictably all the boys immediately conjured up some imaginary RPGs and charged off to kill gooks, making explosive noises as they did so.

Dad's looking at me as if I've just told him I've seen an alien spaceship in the back garden.

"Timothy told you this?"

"You never said anything about it. It happened back in December."

"Can't I sleep in the kitchen?" asks Rosie.

Mum stops scraping the lamb chop bones off the plates into the bin and looks utterly incredulous.

"Of course not! Teeth, please. Now."

Dad pushes away from the door frame and heads off in the direction of the lounge. "Don't worry Tessa. It all happened way out in the sticks where there's a few problems sometimes with infighting. The army has some guys out there. They'll sort it out. It's a one-off, like the vet said."

Pursuing him, I can't believe he knows so little about it.

"Oh, but no, it wasn't. The people whose farm it was moved to another farm and then *they* got attacked. And then, some soldiers were killed by landmines in the area. And you know you said last week that our border with Zambia has been closed? Well I know why. Timothy's dad says it's because of the insurgents, come over from Zambia to fight against our government. So Mr Smith closed the border to make a point."

I did have to consult the dictionary to find out exactly what insurgents are, but I don't tell him that.

"*Insurgents?*" He whips round and paces back towards me, shouts loudly with laughter, then clamps a hand over his mouth when Rosie pokes her head round the kitchen door and hisses, "Skellum's *asleep*, Daddy!"

"Rosie... Teeth!"

He beams at me. "Where did you learn that? Timothy's dad? Look, they're not a problem, my girlie, just a bit of a nuisance. Mr Smith has had an argument with Mr Gorilla, so that's why he closed the border."

I sidle past him. I'm beginning to wish I'd kept quiet.

"I'll go to Cleo now."

He thinks I've got a problem with it but I haven't. I'm not the least bit worried. I've got no idea why those farms were attacked in the first place. I just remember being mightily relieved that something so exciting had happened during the Christmas holidays because it meant no-one was talking about me. There may well have been lots of gossip about *Tessa-And-The-Policeman* in the last week of school of course, but with me getting Jess's chest infection I don't know and I'm hoping I never find out.

Now the angry face is floating in my mind again. If I've got any problem, it's because that horrible Friday last year and gooks up in Centenary and closed borders and parents who tell me not to worry about something they're clearly keeping quiet all seem to be connected up somehow.

Mr Gorilla. He reckons Kenneth Kaunda looks like a gorilla. Thanks Daddy. Now I really do have the feeling that my traffic policeman is watching this from somewhere and thinking to himself, *See how the father talks? That's why the girl ignores me when I speak to her.*

TUESDAY 6TH MARCH 1973

"How come *you* got invited to a *braai* at Makuti Park? How do *you* know the Owens?"

Lauren says it like she suspects I've spread this rumour in order to improve my status in the world. Like I've finally realised I'll never attain Somebody status by simply getting good marks in class, because the concept that I wouldn't aspire to be a Somebody doesn't exist in her universe.

This is seriously bugging her. Miss Nobody Tessa, who's taken to pushing her bike across the road in the middle of large groups and keeping her hat pulled down over her eyes in the hope that she'll be all the more invisible has shaken the social grapevine and got Lauren Collingwood keeping pace with her along the gravel track to the playground, trying to start a conversation with her. Lauren doesn't bother herself with Nobodies as a rule.

"Gill teaches me riding. And I help her exercise her horses."

This last statement isn't strictly true, but I like to think that by having lessons on First Foxtrot I'm helping to exercise her.

Lauren starts sniggering so she can encourage me to feel appropriately silly.

"I expect you'll get to eat *caviar* there."

She says 'caviar' as if she has an extremely hot potato in her mouth, then she comes over all sly and goes, "She teaches you riding? I thought you knew how to ride, Tessa."

Now I know full well I'm being mocked, and that I shouldn't take the bait and shouldn't feel this need to explain myself to someone who, frankly, doesn't care, but I do anyway.

"Oh yes, I can *ride* a horse in all paces, but there's so much more technique to it..."

"Oh Tessa! All this time saying you know how to ride. You won't admit that you can't!"

She gives Jess an elbow in the ribs and Jess gives her one of those looks that fires daggers, but daggers bounce off Lauren. Her cocksure, spiteful face is radiating her delight with the situation.

All right, Miss Collingwood. Get this.

"I had champagne at the Christmas party there. *And* caviar. Did you know that caviar is fish eggs?"

Now all I have to do is keep a straight face while Jess is making a face that's both amazed and offended, and rightly so.

"You never told me you'd had…"

I haven't. I grab her by the hand and pull her away, leaving Lauren with her mouth all twisted round the words, "*Fish eggs? Yuk!*" and wondering how come she never knew I hobnobbed with the Owens at Christmas too. Well, Gill's my friend and I've known her for three years now, so why not? And Nathan too. Well, not really. You could say I've known *of* Nathan for nearly three years.

SATURDAY 4TH JULY 1970

"Okay, that's a good one. Well done. Now do another. I'll pass you a band when you've done it."

I divide off another section of mane and Gill remarks, "That's probably a bit big. You want to aim to get all the plaits the same size if you can."

"Oh."

I start again and halfway through my plaiting process, Fancy grabs a bit of hay that won't come out of the net. She gives it an extra big tug and jerks her head away from me, pulling the hairs through my fingers. I wobble on the stool and Gill's hand shoots out to take my elbow.

"Ha, ha! Whoa!" she giggles, then goes still and fixes onto something over the top of the pony's back.

"That's Nathan and High Time! They must be on their way home. God, he's been out a long time. He went out just before I left to come here."

Beyond the boundary rail fence, a pretty bright bay pony with four white socks is trotting along the broad, browned grass verge adjacent to the road. Riding it is that boy from school. He looks very different out of his uniform and I probably would never have recognised him if Gill hadn't been here with me. Now all the connections click into place like Lego bricks. Gill Owen telling me she lives at Makuti Park, a remark by Timothy not so long ago linking Nathan Owen with Makuti Park ("You'd think, coming from that posh place, that he'd be, like, *brighter*. My dad says the guy who owns the place has a new car, *yet again*") and Gill's occasional mention of 'Nathan's pony'.

I take the abandoned half-plait in my hand again and say, "Oh yeah. Your brother," thinking that perhaps I'd better leave it there because of what they all say about him at school.

Nathan and the pony have passed the gates and are now out of sight behind the dark green Cypress hedge. Miss Ashton and Gill would never let *me* ride without a hard hat, but then I guess he can do whatever he likes on his own pony.

She laughs her gurgling laugh. "No, silly. He's my cousin."

Ah, maybe that's why she's never mentioned him and said what's wrong with him. Odd that he lives with her, but then Makuti Park is a huge *plaas* with a massive house. She's never told me about any brothers or sisters of hers so I reckon she's an only child.

"Here you go," she says, holding out a tiny black rubber band. I roll the plaited section of mane and fix it in a ball with the band. It looks cute.

"How many of your cousins live with you?" I ask her. "I've got five, but they were born in England and they all live there. I've never met any of them, although we get letters and photos from them and my aunts and uncles."

"Oh, only him. My others live in England too. His parents died, you see, so my parents adopted him. It's very sad. Haven't you seen him here before? We both have a lesson together on Sundays. Sometimes jumping, sometimes flatwork, depends really. Right, do one more plait then we'd better let Fancy go out in the field. She's been very patient. Is that okay? You've got the gist of it now."

Fancy's given up munching hay and appears to have gone to sleep.

"Does Nathan go to the same shows as you? And win lots of prizes too?"

"No."

I turn to face her, a bit shocked. She's a sweet and gentle and merry girl and that's a very odd tone.

She's not looking at me. She has one arm over Fancy's back and is staring at the gates.

"High Time – that's his pony – could jump the moon, Tessa. But no, he doesn't ever compete. And believe me, he's a damned good rider. Much better than me. Much more intuitive than me. A waste. Still, look, let's finish up shall we?"

I don't believe that. No-one can be a better rider than Gill.

MONDAY 6TH JULY 1970

He's walking right towards me, and Mrs Anderson.

This is crazy. I only ever spot him occasionally in Assembly. He's never out there at breaktime, he doesn't play in any of the teams, I've never come across him in the bike sheds, or anywhere else at school. And now I've encountered him twice in three days. Saturday, when he rode past Turnpike Stables and now *again* here today, literally on a collision course.

I'm a hundred percent certain Mrs Anderson doesn't know I'm following her. Stupid thing is, I wouldn't even be here if I wasn't feeling cold, and I wouldn't be cold if I'd taken my blazer out to the playground like Jess did. This is what Daddy would call a fluke.

Nathan is just passing the lucky bean tree and is getting closer. So does he hang out behind the classrooms at breaktimes? No matter. If I'm going to say something to him, I'd better start thinking exactly what.

Hello is a good start. Then I could move on to *My name's Tessa. Gill leads me at the riding school.* First is true of course, but the second isn't. Not anymore. I ride by myself and Gill just tells me lots of things about horses. Next, I could say *I saw you riding your pony on Saturday,* or *You don't look like Gill.* Or is that rude?

It's true though. Gill has a face shaped like a heart and it's always bright and laughing. She has gold hair and blue eyes, and she's thin and willowy, like an enchanted princess from a story or maybe a flaxen-haired Barbie doll. Nathan is thin, and I've never been close enough to see the colour of his eyes, but he has dark hair and that floppy forelock that falls over his face, like one of the ponies in Mr Thelwell's books. His face is quite squarish and sort of nice but it doesn't do much smiling. It doesn't really do anything.

He's walking along the path like he owns it, his hands in the pockets of his shorts, but he'll have to step off in a second as it's too narrow for both him and Mrs Anderson. She must be wondering if he's even seen her, surely? He's looking straight past her to me and this is causing me a problem. I was right in the act of winding myself up for conversation and now my brain is backtracking. *Don't say anything,* it's telling me. *In fact, don't even be here at all. Turn around and scarper.* My legs ignore the recommendation and just keep on walking.

He hops off the path. He doesn't take off his hat, like the boys are supposed to, and say, "Good morning, Mrs Anderson," and he doesn't even take his hands out of his pockets. He just, like, *ambles* past her as if she doesn't exist, still with his eyes on me.

So when she stops dead, I have to grind to a halt behind her with nowhere to go. My legs really should've listened to my brain and run away.

I can't see her face but everything else about her is giving me a warning of what's coming. She grows a little taller. She turns to stone, her fists clenched at her sides. Her voice, when it comes out, is like one of Miss Ashton's lunge whips cracking in the air.

"Owen! Where are your manners?"

He pauses in mid stride and there's a second or two in which nothing happens. It's like I've got glue on the soles of my shoes, because nothing will move, not even time. At least he's dropped his eyes from me now.

Very slowly, he says, "I don't know, Ma'am. I may have left them at home."

I have three simultaneous reactions to this. One is apparently totally oblivious of the circumstances and tells me, *Hey, Monty Papadopoulos was wrong. He can speak. Isn't it curious how he has a boy-version of Gill's kind of refined Rhodesian accent?* Another one is stunned because everyone knows you simply don't say things like that to teachers. The third one is so impressed it completely overturns the second, and Miss Goody-Two-Shoes-Tessa, who should be shocked into silence, goes, loudly and clearly, "*Wow!*"

After the word's come out my jaw stays hanging open like I'm some gormless idiot. If she's heard me, she's ignoring me for now.

She's dithering about like she's on hot bricks, which makes me give out this ridiculous snort. Nathan's mouth is doing something strange, almost like it's going to laugh, but it never quite gets there.

Then he does take his hat off and tilt his head towards her, but he says nothing and starts walking again, back on the path. He dodges in the same direction as me and we both have to sidestep again, and again.

Don't look at him. Clamp your lips together and make an effort to concentrate on those little baby weeds between the paving slabs at your feet. Your left shoelace is coming undone. Don't look at him.

Above all, don't wait to find out what Mrs Anderson is going to do next.

I take off across the lawn and skid into my class locker room. Signs saying *Don't walk on the grass* are all very well but I need the shortest escape route possible and I'm still cold. Or I thought I was. As soon as I get my blazer on I realise I'm roasting hot.

After nearly five minutes of lurking behind the door, feeling stupid, I creep back to the playing field by the gravel path along the back of the building.

Jess has given up on me and is with Heather and the Barnes twins.

"Well here she is!" she says. "Did you go home to fetch your blazer?"

I should tell her what kept me so long, but is there any point? On the face of it, it's a simple story, but it has complications behind it somehow. A string of connections that won't make much sense to her.

So Timothy says he's a loner, with no friends, and no-one who wants to be friends with him. Richard says there must have been something wrong with his brain at birth and he must have had to repeat either Standard One or Standard Two because he's ten already and most of the others in his year are only nine. And Michael Palmer, who's in Standard Three with Nathan, reckons he won't ever be any good at anything and should be in a special school. Well, he doesn't come across weird, or special. He looks perfectly normal to me. Did he laugh just now or not?

"Don't be silly," I tell Jess. "Of course I didn't go home."

THURSDAY 26TH NOVEMBER 1970

"Mr Westfield's putting the *whole* school in detention for two hours? What? All of you? Every single one?"

This is not the reaction I expected from him upon being informed his daughter's lined up for serious punishment at school. In only her second year of school too. Astonishment, yes, disappointment, yes, but what looks suspiciously like delight, no. It's not funny.

At least Mummy reacted to the news suitably, and predictably. Shocked eyebrows, frowns, pursed lips, words like no, awful, serious, distressing, innocent ones, not to blame, don't worry. I worried what Daddy would say and she told me not to, that she would explain it to him in her own time, and then she said to me and Rosie, "Don't tell him the minute he walks in the door. Let him relax a bit after work. It will all be all right."

Well of course Miss Big Mouth was never going to be able to contain herself, was she? Daddy was on the top step, still actually *outside* the back door, when she yelled her usual, "Daddy's home!" and then, "Tee's going to get detention and so's *everybody* at school! If I was there I'd have it too!"

His face was blank, so she added, "That means *everybody* gets made to stay after school for *two hours!*"

When he still looked like he didn't understand, she had the nerve to turn to me for reassurance. "That's right, isn't it Tee? For punishment for what happened at the gala?"

What was I supposed to say? She's just plain unbelievable sometimes.

So now it's all been explained to him, and he still hasn't got any further than the kitchen. He's clearly not taking the situation seriously at all. Mummy has her hands clasped in front of her and is wearing her Bothered Face as if she's in trouble as well.

"Tessa says he told them he's never done it on this scale before. He gave them all a lecture in Assembly on Monday, didn't he, love? And he said he wanted the guilty party, or parties, because he thinks there's more than one child involved, to own up by Wednesday. But no-one did, did they, Tessa?"

I shake my head.

"He told them that any confessions could be made in confidence, but today he called a special Assembly. It was early this morning, wasn't it, Tessa, so you all missed your first lesson?"

Nod the head this time.

"He's really upset no-one's admitted to it. So this is what he's decided to do. They all have to go back to the school tomorrow from two till four."

And keep quiet and write lines, he said. He made us sit on the floor and he moved his lectern so that it was right at the edge of the stage, and then he brought out that wooden box thing the really little kids like me stand on when we do a reading. When he stood on it and beat his cane on the lectern in time to his words he wasn't tubby, friendly Mr Westfield any more – he was giant, severe and distinctly unfriendly Mr Westfield. You will all write lines, his deepest voice and the tapping cane told us, that will impress upon you the importance of honesty and the dangers of silly pranks.

"It's not a good sign," Mum's saying, "that he feels the need to carry out collective punishment. I do wish those naughty kids who were responsible would do the right thing. It's so unfair on these little ones who've done nothing wrong."

My mother is doing what mothers do and defending her young, but my father is chortling, grinning, picking up his briefcase from the floor and then squeezing my shoulder as he passes. "Well, I'm going to get changed and have a beer on the verandah. You have to admit the incident was a class act and that that gala will be one that goes into the annals of history. Don't worry love. Those who know who it was will put pressure on the culprits, or split on them, then you won't get the detention after all. It's a tactic."

Maybe. I hope so, because Mr Westfield won't find out anything from me for sure.

Mum has turned her head to immediate, pressing matters and is identifying suitable potatoes in the vegetable rack and Dad's whistling one of his non-tunes down in their bedroom and Rosie's bolted off and is practising cartwheels on the lawn and they're all confident I know nothing more than they do while the whole thing plays over and over in my mind.

SATURDAY 21ST NOVEMBER 1970

I can't believe I was stupid enough to get roped into participating in this gala in the first place. It's okay for Jess. Jess lives for swimming, gets herself into every race it's possible for her to be in, wins every one and loves it, but me, I've got zero interest at the best of times and sub-zero interest when I've had to go and miss my riding lesson just to be in a bloody breaststroke relay to make up the numbers. *And* pretend like I've been supporting Msasa House all afternoon.

Give us an M...
M!
Give us an S...
S!
Give us an A...
A!
Give us an S...
S!
Give us an A...
A!
What have you got?
MSASA!
Who are the best at work and play?
Who are the best in every way?
We are the best and we all say MSASA!
And we're WINNING!

Yeah. Do I look like I care? Sorry if that's the wrong answer.

Now I've been dragged into this heaving marquee packed wall-wall with every single mum, dad, aunt, uncle, sister, brother and associated hanger-on. Dad's complaining he can't hear himself think and Mum keeps changing her mind about which is the best side to get the teas while we traipse around behind her like her ducklings. We're like a bunch of zombies with our aimless, slightly demented wandering and our greenish ghoul-like faces. Only zombies don't breathe, and this mob is using up all the available air and generating more heat than the sun is outside. And those ginormous enamel vats of tea and coffee are probably helping stack up the temperature too, if Mrs Parker's bright red face is anything to go by. She's usually pretty laid back but I'd say now she's losing the race to keep up with the demand for little beige cups. Not much tea in one of those – hardly seems worth the hassle.

"Do you want lemon or orange squash?" Mum shouts in my ear, handing one of the cups to Dad, who lifts it high above his shoulder level to prevent it being jolted. A large woman in a strappy orange sundress, with frizzy blonde hair and pinkish shoulder flesh bulging either side of the straps, knocks me forwards towards the trestle table with her hip and says "Oh sorry dear."

I'd rather just get out of this over-crowded sauna. I'll go find Jess, if I can worm my way out. My feet in my open sandals are looking very small amongst all these male *veldskoens* and female heels.

"Nothing thanks. I'm going to..."

"Going? Oh, tell you what... can you get my sunglasses out of my tartan bag and bring them to me? You know my tartan hold-all? It's up where we were sitting – last stand on the right hand side, top row? I can't find them in my handbag so think I left them there."

She presents a clear plastic container of lemon squash to Rosie, who grabs it and promptly spills most of it on her own sandals because she's not watching what she's doing with her hands as usual.

"I'm not going to the stand," I assure her, backing away. "Jess might be still in the House lines so I'm heading back over there. I haven't talked with her all day because she's in a different House to me."

She's not buying it. "Well you can see her after you bring me the sunglasses. Quickly now."

My sister is wailing that her feet are wet and I no longer exist.

The red and white striped plates of sticky cakes and sweet biscuits have been decimated by the hordes and the equally stripy plastic table cover is encrusted with bright crystals of sugar and an assortment of crumbs. I snatch up the last custard cream off the nearest plate seconds ahead of a plump toddler's sticky paw and wriggle away under the orange-dress woman's arm.

I was right. Everyone who was in the spectator stands is now in the marquee. The stands are deserted, strewn with heaps of possessions – raincoats, hats, bags, umbrellas, binocular cases, even a few shoes – and the strings of red, yellow, green and blue bunting that are like the tendrils of some bizarre climbing plant are draped across the back of them and down both sides. Some of this has even crept up over the green canvas judges' tent in its strategic position at the deep end. I'm surprised the tent is so small, considering it's the nerve centre of the gala. Like the stands, it's deserted. The table at the back of the green-glowing, dim interior is laden with the trophies – silver cups and shields, copper shields, small badges to be sewn onto blazers and a thick ream of cream coloured certificates – and the one at the front is strewn with entry lists and other assorted papers, paper-weights, whistles, stopwatches, various coloured biros and some lever arch files. Mr Westfield's beige Peugeot station-wagon is reversed up to the side wall furthest from the stand Mum and Dad were on; against the inside of this wall is the First Aid cabinet surrounded by some coiled cables that must be part of the PA system.

Someone is behind the tent. I swear I can hear movement, a brushing, like a person walking through the longer grass. I stop, cock my head, hover immobile in the middle of a walking stride but nothing reaches my ears.

Probably hearing things. Never mind. Sunglasses, quick.

Take off again, scramble up the rows of seats to where Mum, Dad and Rosie were sitting earlier, grope around in the depths of Mum's gaudy tartan hold-all, pull out the pink pouch and hold it aloft, congratulating myself like Jack Horner did with his plum. Straighten up, ready to jump back down again, and a sudden breeze puffs strands of my wet hair across my face. While I'm paused, peeling them away from my nose, Nathan Owen appears from behind the judges' tent down to my right. He's wearing a light grey T-shirt and school swimming trunks and is barefoot.

I freeze for the second time in just about as many minutes and blink a couple of times like I need to make sure this is real. He hasn't seen me; his eyes are down, surreptitious, glancing right, then left, then right again as if he's about to cross a road. Then he shakes his head fractionally like he's having a conversation with himself and doesn't know the answer to a question he's asked. Then he walks away. Casual.

So now the brushing through grass sounds make sense. And the shock of seeing him appear there is nothing compared with the jolt from my first split second stab at guessing *why* he was there. It's obvious. He's stolen something from the tent.

Why else would he be lurking around when everyone's gone to tea? Why else would he be checking no-one had seen him? Gill's cousin is a thief. All the rumours are fact. He's not only strange – he's also criminal.

Halfway down the long side of the pool, after he's passed in front of me, he hesitates and twists his head to the right towards the tent, then all the way back to his left and to the stand on which I've been turned to stone. *Please don't, please don't, please don't*, I beg someone, but he does, and here I am in full view.

All my blood has drained down to my legs so my head goes light and wafty, but him – he gives no sign of alarm or even recognition. I'm left with his retreating form, forcing myself to breathe again, blinking against the glare of the sparkling, clear pool water. The summer sun is reflected across it and broken up into thousands of golden splinters by the wavelets and ripples and the little white circular polystyrene floats are bobbing on their cords like beads on a necklace. As soon as he's disappeared from view in the crowds round the tea tent, I bolt, leaping down each level like a mountain goat.

When I hand the sunglasses over, Mum squints down at me with doubt in her face.

"Yes? What were you going to say?"

Yes, I'd opened my mouth and taken a breath. Yes, I was about to tell her what I just saw. But…

I get a cup of lemon squash thrust into my hand after all, Rosie's insisting loudly that she wants to go to the toilet and Dad's groaning, "Oh for God's sake, Rosie, why couldn't you say so earlier? We've only got five minutes or so now and we need to get back to our seats again. Tessa, go with her."

Tessa, the Errand Girl. I wish I'd stuck with my plan and refused to get Mum's stupid sunglasses. She'll be back on the stand in a few minutes and surely she could've done without the glasses until then? I should've told her that.

*

It might look like a thick, smooth, green carpet, but kikuyu's pretty prickly stuff, especially when you've been sitting on it for as long as this. The undersides of my thighs and ankles are dented with little red marks and I'm getting the wriggles. How much longer? The only thing that seems to be happening over in the judges' tent is a whole lot of conversation.

No, wait, here we go – Mr Westfield's on his feet, straightening the edge of his safari suit jacket, fiddling with the microphone.

He makes a few odd strangled noises that fill the air over our heads. He should've cleared his throat before he took up the mic, but it's sure had the effect of seizing everyone's attention and causing the swell of human sound to wane into a complete hush. Knowing him, that's probably what he wanted to achieve.

Now he has all eyes fixed on him, he booms at us across the pool. "Ladies and gentlemen, boys and girls. Ahem, ahem, excuse me, sorry, I seem to have a frog in my throat."

He waits for the tittering and a thin burst of clapping to subside, then goes on, blah, blah, we've come to the end of the 1970 swimming gala, thank you all for coming, blah, blah, well done all you competitors for making our afternoon so enjoyable, blah, blah, this brings us to the prize giving ceremony, the climax of this event, hasn't everyone done very well, blah, blah. He nods with satisfaction at the applause and cheering and I think *get on with it.*

Oh he does. This year, he's very proud to unveil a new trophy, to be given to the captain of the House that's displayed the most exuberant House spirit during this afternoon's proceedings. So where is it, we're wondering? No. it's not on display here, so sorry to disappoint you all. He'll fetch it from his office so that its unveiling can be the more dramatic. It's been named after blah, blah. How much longer?

This time the noisy applause is sustained for a couple of minutes and behind me Katie Turpin whispers, "Awful. Do you remember?"

"What?"

"Mike Bester? Got killed in a hit and run? Surely you do? D'you reckon we won the House spirit? Did he say he's got a *frog* in his throat?"

Mr Westfield's voice sounds as gravelly as mine feels after all that bellowing I did earlier. Oh, the trophy. I can't say I knew Mike Bester – he was in Standard Five – but Gill did and his sister Leah rides at Turnpike, so I'm happy he'll be remembered in this way, but I'm not eaten up with curiosity about who's won the thing. I just want to go home. Poor Jess won't be best pleased with Baobab being last. She's been a star performer, but all her team-mates, unfortunately, have been rubbish. The way she won the girls' crawl relay for them was phenomenal, but it wasn't enough.

And the boys' free style relay? That should've gone completely unnoticed by me like ninety percent of races today. He must've been press-ganged into this participation thing as well. He was last to go for Munondo, so Mr Carr must've known he was good. I did wonder if he even knew he was supposed to get in the pool and swim when he was standing like a statue at the back of the Munondo line while all the other boys went crazy, cheering, yelling, jumping up and down. He's got strong arms. When he finished his two lengths he lifted himself up out of the water so high he could put his foot on the edge tiles, and that was from the deep end so he didn't even have the bottom of the pool to push off. I can only get my knee onto the edge and then I have to climb the rest of me out like some sort of clumsy beetle.

They tried to gather round him after he won the race but he blanked them, and they melted apart so he could walk away. He's strange all right.

Is he a thief though? I don't see how. He was only wearing a T-shirt and swimming trunks when I saw him by the tent – it's not like he was dressed in a striped shirt and a mask and carrying a bag marked 'Swag' like all the best burglars in cartoons. And none of the staff in the judges' tent are tearing the place apart hunting for lost trophies and no-one's called the police. I raise myself on my hands a little and stretch my neck as much as it will go, scanning the ranks of children to my left, but the Standard Threes are too far across, and there are too many bodies in between for me to be able to view all of them. I can't find him amongst the ones I can see.

To Katie, I say, "Yes, I remember it. Don't know if we won. Wait and find out. No, of course he doesn't have a real frog in his throat."

Mr Hartman-Davies now has the mic and Mr Westfield is climbing into his car, I guess to go and fetch this House Spirit cup. There's an expectant kind of buzz but I'll bet nothing's going to happen for a while yet. More waiting. Katie behind me is twisted round in conversation with Karen and there's no point trying to talk to Mary-Anne in front 'cause she only ever gives one word answers with a face like a frightened rabbit, so I unfold my legs and stretch them out to one side of her to get grass dents on some other parts of them while I examine and massage the dents I already have.

Mr Westfield's engine fires up and there's a distant clunk as he puts the car into gear, then the attention I'm giving to the wiry grass and my legs is cut short.

A sharp rise in the pitch of the buzz, not around me, but from the direction of the pool, reaches a crescendo that's a cross between a collective gasp and a wail, punctuated with words like "Woah!", "Oooh!", "Loooook!" and "Stop! Stop!"

Around me, kids are scrabbling to their feet, and if I'm to have any chance of finding out what's going on I've got to join in – just in time to see the front table in the judges' tent jerk to the right once, twice and then begin to move towards the side flap, like it's following Mr Westfield's car.

Pandemonium. Spectators jumping, hollering, pointing, Mrs Anderson screaming and stumbling backwards, upsetting some of the prizes on the rear table, all the forms and files scattering and sliding off the front trestle and Mr Hartman-Davies shouting "Bloody Hell!" across all of our heads.

In spite of all this, Mr Westfield starts to accelerate, at which point the trestle table erupts through the canvas flap with a crash. One of the guy ropes is wrenched from the ground by the impact and that side of the tent sags. Then his face, open mouthed, turns towards us and he stands on the brake pedal. There's a twanging vibration and the mystery of the escaping table is revealed. A thin, light cord, identical to those dividing the pool into lanes, has been wound around both trestle legs nearest to the side of the tent and then tied to the rear bumper of the vehicle.

It's like watching a cartoon. Mr Westfield leaps out of his stalled car and capers around on the spot while Mr Hartman-Davies, with commendable presence of mind, tries to prevent the whole tent from collapsing by holding up the roof pole. There's applause, cheering, whistling, hooting. The whole school is on its feet, straining on tiptoe so as not to miss out on any of the action and I'm gasping for breath and wiping tears from my eyes. Then the sight of Mrs Anderson emerging from the remains of the tent triggers off the memory and cuts my hysterics like a switch extinguishes a light.

So where is he? Joining in this hilarity, or hiding somewhere? I'm drawn to try again, searching across all the bodies and faces as I did before. There's a shift and a surge of the bodies forwards, a gap opens and he finds me. He pulls my eyes across to meet with his like he's a magnet and I'm a paper clip. He's standing with his left arm folded across his chest, the forelock of dark hair concealing his eyes, and he's tapping the fingers of his right hand absently against his cheek just like Gill does. With all attention focussed on the drama at the tent, I'm alone in a bubble. With him. His face is utterly devoid of any expression.

I swallow, lick my lips, but he won't release me. He shakes his head twice, with exaggerated slowness, mouths some words at me. Lip reading them isn't hard. He's saying, "Not me."

Then his eyes are gone and I'm free to turn back to the scene of the crime.

Not me. Not him. He didn't do it.

Some semblance of order is restored. Mr Westfield fetches his precious trophy and the prize-giving ceremony is a complete flop.

Applause is thin, barely rising above the chatter and laughter and hubbub and some prize-winners have to be called several times. The House Spirit trophy, awarded to Baobab House, does receive a few whistles if only in recognition of the fact that it's the root of all the fun.

I have a kind of premonition that this spells trouble for us on Monday.

SATURDAY 12TH DECEMBER 1970

Mandy, prattling in over-excited Gobbledegook. Me, catching some of it and thinking, sure, a treasure hunt will be fun. Mandy, squeaking, "Look at this, Tessie! I can't *believe* it! So exciting, hey Tessie?" Me, sighing outwardly and saying inwardly, *God I wish she wouldn't call me Tessie*. Someone else riding into the ménage. Me, not taking much notice because I'm studying the typed list Miss Ashton has just handed me. Mandy, still wittering. Me, deciding to look up and see who's late for the lesson. Him, closing the gate while mounted, turning his pony and nudging her towards the centre of the school and us.

My brain machine clunks all these facts over rapidly, scraps all except the last, and comes up with a single word.

"Why?!"

"What?" says Mandy. "Hey, now, I know where we can find most of these things. We can be partners, can't we? We can gallop round so fast the others won't keep up. That silly fat boy, Simon, will probably fall off anyway. Your pony is really fast, isn't he?"

"She," I whisper.

He's halted. Sitting like a statue, staring at nothing, while Miss Ashton rushes around checking everyone else's stirrups and girths. When High Time shifts her backside to rest a hind hoof, he moves with her like it was his idea. He doesn't appear to have clocked me but my heart is galloping so fast it's going to pop out of my chest and I'm prickling all over my arms and the back of my neck.

"It looks like rain, doesn't it, but I haven't heard any thunder. Have you? A pink wildflower? A fruit? Hmm, don't know. What do you think? Shall we try Fifty Acre Meadow for that? Four horse cubes. Well we can get those from the feed room. An insect, dead or alive… God, whoever typed this was useless. They've put small letters where there should be capitals and capitals where there should be small letters. We'll go together shall we Tessie? Come, we can walk on round the track now, can't we?"

He has private lessons with Gill on Sundays so why is he *here? Now?* He doesn't belong in our class.

Be invisible. Hat brim down, eyes low. But I'm making Peaches walk so close to Mandy's pony that Miss Ashton yells, "Tessa! You'll get that poor pony kicked! Leave a gap!" and everyone looks at me.

What was it Daddy once called her? A sergeant major. A *regular* sergeant major. And he said she'd get us all square-bashing. I haven't a clue what he meant and I never asked.

"Right kids! Pairs. Mandy and… Debs. Elizabeth, you go with James. Simon, go with Richard. Helen and Belinda."

My heart may have been galloping a few minutes ago, but now it's stopped altogether.

I am the only one left. She won't make me go on out my own. I simply cannot believe this is going to happen to me.

And sure enough, pointing at me, she says, "Okay Tessa, you go with Nathan. I know you two know each other because you're always hanging about with Gillian."

Now I don't just want rain, I want an almighty thunderstorm and a hurricane and maybe a tornado for good measure. Desperately. Call this whole lark off. Peaches' creamy coloured mane has a few blackjack seeds in it, so I pick at them like I'm trying to pretend I haven't heard her. I will not cry. I've done nothing wrong.

I never split on you, Nathan. No-one knows what I know. I love Gill, but you scare me. You're invisible ninety percent of the time, but then, when you do turn up, you're good at things. You ride like you're an extension of your horse and you swim faster than any of the other boys. And that time I nearly told Gill how I'd seen you win the race? I chickened out because I knew I couldn't deal with it if she'd gone, *Oh yeah! And what about the judges' tent and Mr Westfield's car? Did you see that?*

"Tessa! Take the cotton wool out of your ears, girl!"

I want to ignore you and pretend you don't exist but you won't let me. You were there too that afternoon, kept in school and made to write out *We must all learn to be honest and admit to our mistakes* five hundred times and then *We must consider the implications of our actions and how they might endanger others* five hundred times and then do homework in silence for the rest of the time, like everyone else. You were there, only two rows in front of me and one desk across to the right, so I was able to keep spying on you sitting there with your dark head down while you wrote your lines – or I assume that's what you were writing – and then reading a book, laid flat on the desk so I never got to see the title. And I watched you file out with the rest of your class, still with your back to me, and by the time I got out of the Hall you'd vanished.

"Come along now! Tessa! Nathan! Off you go!"

She has these really stubby hands and she's rubbing them over the bumpy bulges at the top of her thighs. Her jodhpurs are way too tight.

No heartbeat, and now no breathing. High Time's hoofs are brushing through the grass and my tongue is stuck to the roof of my mouth. What did I expect you to do that day? Refuse to do the punishment or create a scene? Give me some justification to tell Mr Westfield I'd seen you skulking about by the tent during the tea break last Saturday? You know I saw you, of course. You probably imagine that, in spite of your protestation of innocence, I believe you were the one who tied the car to the tent and that I'm just too scared to say anything. But I *am* damned certain you weren't the culprit. And I don't want to be anywhere near you ever again.

I've never actually addressed him. So what am I going to say? *Why are you here?*

So I do. Or not quite like that. My voice, all by itself, accuses him, "You're not in our class."

Stupid thing to say. He shrugs.

"We're off on holiday tomorrow. I wanted to have a go over the cross country practice jumps this weekend, so I came over today instead. But you guys are having a treasure hunt, so Junie here wouldn't let me go galloping around upsetting your ponies. She said she had an odd number of you in the class, which meant you'd have to have one group of three and then she hinted that if I joined in to make up the numbers I could use the jumps afterwards. So here I am. You here every Saturday?"

Junie? I'll never be able to look at her the same way again. Junie, with the thigh bulges. Oh God, Tessa, don't snort or giggle, please.

Yes, I'd forgotten. Of course. Gill did say she was going to Durban, but I didn't know it was tomorrow.

"How shall we go about this, then?"

His voice is so normal, polite and quiet. He hesitates, like he's waiting for an answer, then swings High Time around and I have no choice but to follow him to the gate.

It's so hot that everything is hazy. I'm sweating and so's the world, like the sun is heavy somehow. I can see the stone domes of Domboshawa in the distance but instead of being grey they are shiny and shimmery. There are warm smells like saddle soap and ponies and I have to wave my riding crop around my face to get rid of some very dozy flies.

We do lots of trotting, stopping and turning to find the items – the pink flower from a crop of candy-coloured cosmos, the wild berry from a dark leafed bush, the smooth stone and the three different pieces of bark. I just take them from him and put them in my carrier bag and keep schtum. He speaks to me, but very little. He says things like "Here", "Over there", "Come this way" and he does all the dismounting and remounting. He talks to High Time though, constantly, very quietly, and his moves are smooth, and calm. He touches her often, on the crest of her mane or on the muzzle when he's on the ground, and he scratches her back behind the saddle. I've never seen anyone do that and I copy him, sneakily, so he doesn't see me doing it. I don't know what Peaches makes of it, but it doesn't stop her from trying to grab illicit mouthfuls of grass. I keep the reins short and never once get jerked out of the saddle and am very pleased with myself about this. I hope he's noticed.

Occasionally we spot the other groups, hear child-laughter, someone shouting at a pony. I tag along behind him, and I know I shouldn't just let him do everything, but I do. He finds all the items on the list, even the live insect, and it's only because of this that I end up talking to him. He goes still, staring at the branch of a msasa tree, then his hand shoots out, he plucks something off it and he offers the hand to me. Between forefinger and thumb is a beetle. It's so pretty – shiny yellow and green, like it's made out of metal. It's very frightened, waving its legs and its antennae pathetically, and without even a thought I lean over, take it from him and exclaim, "Oh, don't hurt it!" because in my experience ten-year-old boys often do nasty things to insects.

Then I'm much too close to his face. I snap back upright and retract my hand with a jerk, nearly dropping the beetle. He has brown eyes, again unlike Gill. I can feel my face burning and he gets that very, very small twitch in his mouth, like the one I saw when he was cheeky to Mrs Anderson. He drops his reins and holds up both hands.

"I won't, okay? Well there you are, then. You take it. It's a change to meet a girl who doesn't scream when she sees a creepy-crawly."

He takes up a contact again, nudges High Time and starts to move off, saying, "Gill doesn't either."

We get back to the yard just after Mandy and Debs but they're disqualified because their insect is a spider. Mandy argues, but Miss Ashton isn't having any of it. She tells Mandy to count its legs.

"Eight legs, girl. If it's got eight legs, it doesn't count. And no pulling two of them off!"

She examines the objects in my carrier bag. When I look round, there's no sign of Nathan and High Time. I didn't even see them go.

And he didn't say a single word about the gala.

I hook one of the two red rosettes she hands me onto Peaches' bridle and lead her around to show off a bit. I'll have to give Gill the other rosette when she gets back from holiday and tell her to pass it on to Nathan. Then I let the beetle go in a bush near the gate before I take Peaches back to her stable. I might be Mrs Adams in *Born Free*, releasing animals into the wild. A beetle's not very much like a lion, but that's where day-dreams win. You can make anything into anything.

SATURDAY 24TH JUNE 1972

Mummy tells me I day-dream too much. And maybe I do. I love it. I dream that I ride beautiful horses like Gill's. I dream I'm in show-jumping competitions with her, I walk the course with her and I win lots of prizes like her. This all occurs in my version of Heaven. And now, maybe, my Heaven has appeared as a dot on the horizon.

We've driven past the place loads of times; me, Mum, Dad and Rosie. Sometimes in my day-dreams me and Gill come back here in a big lorry with our horses after a show, but that's where the dream's had to end because the gate is where my knowledge ends. Today I'm going to find out what's inside. I'm going to find out what it might be like to live in a house like this, with stables and paddocks and all those horses. Heaven indeed.

And it was The Nowhere Boy, who came out of his Nowhere, wherever that is, to give me this invitation to Heaven.

I know full well he's in Standard Five, so why did I never even think to wonder if he was in the class that did the Mushandike National Park week this year? But he is, and he was there at the exhibition in the Hall, and I nearly fell through the floor when he beckoned me to come over to him. He must've seen me long before I was aware of him. Seen me discovering his cool photos of the hippo and reading his tidy, very small handwriting claiming *"Pics by Nathan Owen"* and *"Never, EVER get between a hippo and the water!"* and then touching one of the photos with my finger, like I could make it 3D and sweep it round to see where the water was. And seen me standing there gawking at him like a complete numptie.

In the end he had to come over to me. He looked at me with that expressionless face and I've no idea exactly what he said to start. Was it something about the photos? I should've said he was good at taking pictures but I didn't. I did wonder if I should say, *Do you know how much we all hate this annual event? Even me who likes natural history and conservation and stuff, because all we get to look at is a bunch of leaf and flower arrangements, numerous drawings of poo, fuzzy photographs and boring essays and that crummy old* papier-mâché *model of the dam?*

I *very* nearly asked, *Did you see the baboon spider in Miss Foster's bedroom and was it as massive as all the rumours claim?* And I'd no sooner had this thought when he went, "I learned a lot about wild animals. Particularly spiders. I like spiders. Especially big, hairy ones."

"Spiders?" I said, then "You didn't…?" and he said, "Of course *I* didn't. You know I don't do pranks. Poor Miss Foster. The warden's wife did that thing where they feed the traumatised victim gallons of hot, sweet tea. Do you reckon that works? I don't. Mr Westfield says we're not to talk about it anymore and he's banned the whole story. Like he banned *Puff the Magic Dragon.*"

Mr Westfield. The gala. And I *know* he doesn't do pranks?

Then he shrugged, like he was dismissing all these subjects: Mushandike, the gala, Puff, pranks and me.

"Look, I needed to speak to you because I've got a message for you from Gill. Do you want to come to our place sometime and try out some different ponies?"

I thought I'd misunderstood. I made idiotic noises.

"Gill? What? Come? She wants me to… Huh?"

He watched me do this, then as I was about to ask, "When?" he said, "Probably at a weekend. She'll be at Turnpike tomorrow. Ask her then."

Like the beginning of that conversation, I don't remember the end. I do remember yelling at Jess and Jane and Rosie that I was going to ride at Makuti Park and them just staring at me like I'd gone mad. Jess stared past me to where I'd come from and remarked, "I don't think I've seen that guy talking to anyone before. Why was he talking to you?"

Well, the result is that I'm here, about to go beyond these tall white gateposts. Into Heaven.

They each have a black wrought-iron lantern on top and a short, white, curved wing wall that tapers from about a metre in height at the column down to nearly nothing as it extends towards the road. Either side of these are the hedges – dark green hibiscus, with bright red flowers in summer – and grass verges for ever. Driving past, Daddy sometimes says he wants to have our verges mown so perfectly, but he only ever gets Elijah to slash them. These are like a smooth green carpet. A bowling green. Green. It's winter. It hasn't rained for a good while and everyone else's grass has gone brown or blonde.

The lanterns light up at night even though they're like miles from the house.

The driveway is black, like the road, with little gleaming stones embedded in it. I dismount and walk slowly, pushing my bike. On my left is another hibiscus hedge and behind it, about a hundred metres further on, the black and grey tiled roof of a house. On my right is a creosoted timber four-railed fence and a paddock. Three mares and three foals. Heaven.

Coming from behind the hedge are short, sharp clipping sounds and, standing on tiptoe, I can see a garden at least twice as big as ours. A gardener in blue overalls and a blue woollen hat is kneeling beside a flagstone path trimming the lawn edge with a pair of shears. The lawn is as smooth and green and beautiful as the verge outside.

The driveway curves to the left, out of sight, into infinity in my imagination. I mount my bike again to pedal round the bend, but almost immediately here's a gate – matching the fence except that it's got five rails – and the stable yard, right in front of me. The drive turns left again, very sharply, and ends at another gate, beyond which are two double garages and a parking area and the house.

Now I'm torn, don't know which way to go, put my toes down on the ground. There's a plopping and stamping sound; someone walking in rubber boots. A groom, in the yard, with a metal bucket in one hand and a headcollar in the other. The handle of the bucket squeaks a bit as he swings it around. He stops short when he sees me and says, "Hello?"

I jump off my bike and run it to the gate. "Oh, hello. I'm... I'm looking for Gill. Gill Owen?"

He comes towards me and unlatches the gate. He's quite an old man, with a very small amount of beard, like salt, around his chin, and kind eyes. He's smiling at me.

"She says you come, yes. Miss Gill is riding in the school. Go, round there." He points to the end of one of the stable blocks. "Round the corner. She there. Come in."

The buildings are white and the stable doors are dark blue and the concrete yard is pale grey and spotless apart from a few stalks of hay. Ten stables in all, five in each block, at right angles to each other. I push my bike down a paved path that's marked all over with white scrapes from horseshoes, and on my left is a hedge, behind which are the garages I saw earlier.

There she is, in the white railed ménage. And although I've never seen First Foxtrot, Gill has described her to me so many times that I know it's her. Deep, rich chestnut and two socks behind. So... heavenly. Heaven.

She hasn't seen me yet; they're down the far end. I lean my bike against the back wall of the stables, unstrap my velvet hat from the carrier and, looking down, am really pleased I polished my boots today. They're going to get dusty now though. I suppose Gill will want me to stand in the middle and watch her ride.

She's jumped off while I wasn't watching and is leading First Foxtrot towards a gate to my right.

"Come on, then!" she calls, and she offers me the reins. "Let's see how you ride a real horse."

I've been riding for two and a half years and the sum of my experience comes to two ponies; my darling Fancy, who was so patient with Beginner-Me, and palomino Peaches, who is a bit livelier for Better-Me. Fancy really was quite small but I've got so much better at mounting that I can get on Peaches by myself from the ground. Now I'm staring up at Foxie's saddle wondering how the hell I'm going to get up there. Did Gill say she was a pony or a horse? The seat is just about level with the top of my head so this isn't going to work.

"Here." She takes my hands and places them front and back of the saddle, goes, "Bend your left leg and I'll boost you up. Ready? On three. One, two... three!" and I'm there, on top. I gather up the reins as she adjusts the stirrup leathers for me.

"Take her round the school."

I nudge Foxie with my calves, uncertain as to how the horse will react. She sets off briskly, and instead of poking her nose out in front, putting a weight into my hands, like Peaches is apt to do, she drops it and the reins go slack. I shorten up again and her mouth's like a feather on the end of them. She prances a couple of steps, and I feel like her spine is pushing up at me from under the saddle and it's a sensation I could never have anticipated or even explained.

"Into the corners!" Gill calls. "Inside leg!" She's laughing.

Everyone knows Goody Two Shoes Tessa's dotty about horses. Now *she* knows she wants horses for life.

*

"Come and meet Mum and Dad," she says.

We leave Foxie in a field behind the stables with two more of my new acquaintances, Silver Valley and Luna, and I follow Gill back across the yard towards the garden, but not before I've tripped over a root belonging to a jacaranda tree near the gate because I had my head over my shoulder watching the three mares wander off together, reminding myself of what this heaven is like. Now I've got dirty jodhpurs. I'm going to have to meet Gill's parents in dirty jodhpurs. What an idiot.

The garden's a bit lower than the stable yard so we have to go down five stone steps onto a path that's covered in black macadam like the driveway. To the right, the lawn slopes down so the level difference is even greater and the bank that's been formed between the ménage and the garden is steep and covered with rocks of all different sizes, all jumbled together but yet fitting perfectly with neighbours. There must be some good gaps between them though because those spiky-leaved plants can't be clinging to nothing.

"Are those aloes?" I ask, and Gill says, "Yes, they are. Well, you know a lot about plants."

Not really. I wouldn't've known that last week, before I went to the Botanical Gardens with Jess and her folks, would I? I don't tell Gill this.

I scuttle after her to catch up. Out of the corner of my right eye that big rock right on top looks just like a lion, crouching between two of the tallest aloes, with the two flatter rocks in front as its paws. Kind of like the Sphinx.

The lawn here is a little drier than in the front but it still has some green bits. On the left is a black-topped square, with a rotary washing line in the middle and then we're at the house. Two steps up to a kitchen door that's exactly like a stable door, the top half open and hooked back to the white-washed wall, and we're in.

Well, Mummy was super-excited when we got our kitchen fitted out last year and still goes on about it to her friends ("*So* much nicer than having all those freestanding units", "More *cupboard space* than I know what to do with", "The wall units are *such* an advantage", "*So* modern") but believe me, she'd do somersaults if she saw this. It's probably the size of our lounge, which is pretty big, and there are cupboards everywhere, both under the worktop and above it, on three walls out of four. Our kitchen cupboard doors are plain, smooth and pale green, but these are made wholly from decorative panels of dark wood with sculpted brass handles. I doubt even the wooden-looking strips round the edges of ours are real.

There's no cooker. There must be a cooker, surely? I'm looking at the only wall with no cupboards, and there's a breakfast bar, with four stools and a basket overflowing with apples, bananas and grapes, a glass fronted timber cabinet containing more wine bottles than I've ever seen in one place, then an open door into a hallway, then a fridge that's big enough to hold all the ice in the Antarctic, then another door that's closed.

I've been left behind, with all my gawping. I hop forward onto the golden tiled floor behind Gill, take in the double sink by the window, and that's when I spot the glass-fronted ovens, a small one underneath a big one, in a panel between two wall cupboards, and nearby, in the middle of the worktop and under a tiled chimney-like structure, the electric rings that Mummy calls the stovetop. Wow.

"Iwe! Mirai!" It's a woman's voice, with a tone like a knife edge, and Gill twitches, falters, and I walk straight into her back. A black woman has silently opened the closed door and is standing before us clasping a red and white striped flour tin against her bosom. In her maid's uniform of pink, green and blue floral fabric, she's a large, walking flower garden.

"Why do you not wipe your feet? You making my floor dirty!"

Gill leaps backwards onto the thick reed mat, dragging me with her.

"Oh no. Didn't. Of course. Sorry, Amai."

I eye the woman while cowering behind Gill. She can't be as angry as she sounds because she's grinning from ear to ear. Gill's rolling her eyes and shuffling her dusty boots back and forth on the mat so I do the same. The shuffling, that is.

"This kitchen is Amai's domain. Heaven help those who don't abide by the rules."

As *amai* is Shona for 'mother' I take it they're on pretty good terms, so I try a smile, hoping Amai will respond favourably. She does. She's still grinning and chuckling. She takes one hand away from the tin and points at me. "Who is this *mwana*? She looks very scared. Come in, child."

"This is Tessa, Amai," Gill announces with a vague gesture in my direction. "She's come to ride for me."

It makes me sound like some sort of professional, and therefore a fraud, but Amai gives no indication of being impressed. She says, "*Masikati, mwana. Ma swera se?*" and I am suddenly aware that my knowledge of Shona is woeful.

Daddy says that Elijah needs to keep practising his English so there's no need for me or Rosie to learn Shona. And Daddy would never, in a month of Sundays, take orders from Elijah to mind where he put his feet in the domain of the garden. Or think it was any other than *his* domain anyway.

"Hello, um, *masikati*." I whisper the word because I'm not altogether sure I've got it right, and scuttle after Gill.

The vast house is silent. The hush is soaked into the thick pile wall to wall carpets and the luxurious drapes and soars up into the golden pine ceilings and into every corner. A square inner hallway, large enough to be a room in itself, offers me such tantalising views in several different directions – a dining room on the left with quite the biggest table I've ever seen, a living room directly ahead, and on the right an endless corridor. I start trying to count the rectangles of light that cross the carpeted passage from unseen rooms but Gill is talking to me.

"Aah... This way. Come. I bet they're in the garden."

This hallway is a picture gallery. The framed photographs lining the walls are, at a quick glance, mostly of horses and ponies. Makes sense. Gill is jumping them, racing them in gymkhanas, sitting on them and shaking hands while receiving a trophy, standing next to them wearing a winner's sash. She's in both black and white and in colour and at a variety of ages. My eyes are bouncing around like rubber balls trying to take them all in as rapidly as possible but I'm going to get left behind. Among the ponies I get snatches of German Shepherds and terriers and of adults, posed with the dogs and with Gill and... Nathan, I think. He's always the only one not grinning at the photographer. He's looking down at his feet, or off to one side, and in a few of them he's actually turned to face away. Where a dog's involved, he's the one bending down or crouched, cuddling it, his face in its coat.

Gill's already flitted through a wide spanning arch, down two steps into the sunken lounge and has vanished. Quick, one more glance around. Just one. This time I register that, here and there, the rider of the ponies – and occasionally of a horse that seems too big for him – is a boy. They're mostly action shots of the pair flying over obstacles in the ménage out the back and in similar arenas I don't recognise, although one looks like it could be Turnpike Equestrian Centre. That's it – go.

The lounge wall opposite is not painted cream like all the others. It's faced with rough bricks in varying hues from terracotta to pale pink to almost blue and has a central dark grey stone fireplace and chimney breast. The pine shelves on either side are filled with books. No, crammed with books. I have a sizeable bookcase in my bedroom, but this is a library.

Don't, Tessa. Do *not* just head over there and start studying the titles. It's rude.

Among the books are scattered several silver trophies and there's a television set twice the size of ours in the corner.

Gill's been waiting for me, there by the open French doors on the left. She gives me a quizzical grin, beckons and skips through the doors, flicking aside the fine white sun-filter curtain. Outside I can see a roofed patio, *braaivleis* area, the glinting water of a swimming pool and the emerald glow of the garden. A very slight breeze stirs the curtains and slides deliciously into the lounge. Gill turns to her left, smiles her enchanting smile and waves to someone who is out of sight. Then with feet together and chest thrust out, she holds the open palm of her left hand to me and declares, "This, Daddy, is my friend Tessa. I've told you about her. She's just ridden Foxie in the school."

"You've missed your vocation my love. You look a bit Shakespearian there, Gilly."

The voice is deep, and rich. The sort of male voice you just want to keep listening to. I creep through the door and come face to face with Gill's father.

He elbows himself into a sitting position on his lounger and lays his newspaper on his lap. His face is lined and golden brown and in deep contrast to his thatch of dark blonde hair. He's stretched out at knee height, but he feels immensely tall because he's wearing denim shorts and is barefoot and his browned legs are lean. There is something very familiar about his eyes when he creases them up to smile. It's a few moments before it strikes me that he has Gill's eyes. Or rather, she has his eyes.

"Well Tessa, what did you think of the little mare?" he asks and he sounds so genuinely pleased to see me that all my shyness evaporates. He wants to know my opinion, as if I'm an experienced rider. I *am* that professional Gill announced to Amai. I feel taller myself.

"Oh wonderful, thank you. She did everything I asked instantly and Gill even let me canter her."

"My Gill's told me you're turning into a capable rider and she's a good judge. I'm sure next time you come she'll let you do even more. She could teach you a lot, that little horse."

He looks at Gill.

"She could ride some of the others, too."

Next time? Others?

A giant hand has squeezed me about the chest, leaving me short of breath. He's just endowed my future with glorious prospects. Trouble is, I can't come up with a single word. I just grin stupidly at him and all the words I can't say come out as a crimson flush that makes my cheeks burn.

"Have a drink with us," he suggests, casting aside the paper and swinging his elongated legs to the ground. "I don't suppose your father would be too impressed if I gave you a Castle but you're welcome to have a shandy or just lemonade or Coke. Or tonic water. Or cream soda. What would you like? I'm Charles, by the way."

Upright, he towers over me. I squint up at him against the brightness of the afternoon sun and I want to be able to have a proper drink, like a beer shandy, but I've never had one before and can't bring myself to say so. I ask for lemonade instead.

"Make that two, please Dad. Where's Mum?"

Gill leaps down onto the lower *braaivleis* area and trots away across the grass towards the end of the long house. I'm left standing alone to absorb my surroundings, for her father has vanished indoors and I can hear glassware tinkling somewhere. The swimming pool is kidney shaped and is lined with pale cream glitterstone paving rather than the usual tiles. At the deep end the surround is raised into a small dais, lined with stone, and at the shallow end are some broad steps into the water and a rockery. A channel, carved into a flat stone at the top of the rockery, sends an arc of silvery water, glittering in the sun, splashing into the pool with a tinkling sound.

Gill reappears, accompanied by a willowy woman who walks like a ballerina, like she's about to sweep into a curtsey and start to perform Swan Lake. She's wearing a calf-length denim skirt that has some light green stains and some dark brown smears. Up close, she's not quite as tall as she looks, but her fingers, brushing wisps of nut brown hair from her face, are really long and slender.

"Please excuse me," she says, holding out her right hand. "I'm in gardening mode today and I can look better than this. And please, my name's Moira. You don't have to call me Mrs Owen, hey?"

She speaks with a hint of an Afrikaans accent. That's right – Gill told me how her great-grandfather came up to Rhodesia with Cecil Rhodes. He was the one who shot a lion in self-defence, hunted elephant and fought the Matabele *impi*. I can't remember anything I might have been told about *my* great grandfathers. I take the hand I've been offered.

Moira and Charles.

Mummy and Daddy's friends are Aunty This or Uncle That, or Mr and Mrs Something-or-other, and I don't think I've ever called an adult by a Christian name. It like the Owens want to be friends with me, Tessa, and not just be 'Gill's parents' or Mr and Mrs Owen. I grow another inch.

Mrs Owen – Moira – excuses herself and goes back to her gardening. Gill and I perch on the edge of the patio with our lemonade while Charles sinks back onto the lounger and coerces me into talking about my family, riding lessons and school. He doesn't ask me what I want to be when I grow up, like most adults do. Instead, he tells me he's a civil engineering contractor. Well that's a co-incidence. Dad's a civil engineer.

"We won the Firle contract, by the way," he says to Gill, who claps her hands and goes, "Woo-hoo!"

He turns back to me and swills his lager around in its glass to leave a shiny swathe of foam.

"So, you can tell your parents when you get home that you've met a man who builds sewage treatment works."

I hide my smile in the cool, fizzy lemonade, feeling the bubbles tickling my nose as I take a gulp. Then some subconscious part of my brain pulls the words 'parents' and 'get home' out of his sentence and sounds an alarm.

Christ, what's the time? What time did I say I'd be home? Four-thirty?

Wristwatch. Four twenty-five. Okay, panic.

There's no way I'm going to jeopardise future visits to Makuti Park by getting home late. I drain my glass and scramble to my feet.

"I've got to go! My mother will kill me if I'm late."

It sounds so rude.

I wave my wrist in Gill's direction and point at the watch, not wanting to be ungracious but desperate to get away, not wanting to invite myself to come again but hoping someone else will.

"How about next weekend then?" she asks, and I could kiss her. She's just kicked off her jodhpur boots and pulled her damp socks from her feet and is holding them as if she wants to get as far away from them as possible. She stands up.

"Give me your phone number. Here, come inside."

A lifetime later, I'm mounting my bike on the run along the driveway and my feet have wings.

SATURDAY 24TH MARCH 1973

The driver brakes so hard that the car sinks into its front suspension with a light squeal. He then has the nerve to gesticulate at me through the windscreen as if it was *my* fault. Looking for cars, he was, not bikes.

"Look where you're going!" I yell, glaring at him. "*Voetsek!*"

But I'm in too good a mood to dwell on the idiocy of motorists. I'm going to Gill's party.

Pedal on up the hill, past the shopping centre and its Saturday morning mayhem. Waves of warm air from the hedges and bushes at the roadside wind themselves round me as I ride past, like steam from last night's rain. The rush of cooler air on my skin as I turn to freewheel downhill again is delicious.

The left-hand side of the driveway at Makuti Park is already lined with cars, and the area behind the garages is full of them. Voices – many voices – swell from the garden behind the hedge, intermingled with music, and my excitement is gone, just like that, dissolved into shyness.

I stop, hop off my bike. If I had someone to escort me in… but I'm all alone out here, gazing over the closed gate, out of place and not sure what I have to do to get into place. There are plenty of people beyond that hedge, on the patio, in the pool, but they're all strangers. There's a splash, a shout, a clinking of glasses, laughter. The music goes silent, then starts up again – *Mother and Child Reunion*. It sounds so good but I'm rooted to the spot. Then, behind me, Gill's voice.

"Hey! Tess! In here!"

She appears at the yard gate, to my right, a bridle in her hands, her fingers buckling a cheek piece to the head piece. She pulls a snaffle bit out of her jeans pocket and attaches it to the bridle within seconds. And behind her is Nathan, wearing jodhpurs. I haven't seen him since he started senior school in January, even though I'm here every weekend and sometimes during the week. He looks different. I think his legs have got longer and maybe his shoulders a bit wider. He says "Hi," but before I have a chance to open my mouth he turns and walks away towards one of the paddocks, flicking a headcollar over his shoulder.

"Leave your bike in the tack room for now. Come, we've got a new horse."

She unlatches the gate for me, holds it wide.

I've just wriggled out of the cord of my duffel bag and started trying to pull her birthday gift out of it. No matter. It can wait. She slams the gate behind me and I trail after her across to the east-facing stable block.

"He's only just four years old," she's saying as she walks, "Mum and I are going to back him. He's gorgeous."

The stables are empty, as usual at this time of day, except one. Moira's in it, with the horse, and he is just that. Gorgeous.

"Tessa, meet Induna. A Zulu warrior. Like his namesake, he is handsome and full of presence. But actually quite sensible for his age."

Induna is a bay of about fourteen hands, with a rich mahogany coat, a narrow white blaze and no white socks. Led out into the yard, he stands like a statue, ears straining forward and soft nostrils flared, intensely interested in something beyond the far hedge in the paddock into which Nathan disappeared. Gill keeps her right hand on his neck just below the fringe of black, glossy mane and scratches him with her fingertips. After a few moments he relaxes and his ears loll.

"What do you think?" Moira is leaning on the lower half of the stable door. "Would you like to help us with him?"

Gill throws her head back, laughs out loud and gives me the thumbs-up. "Don't say a word! I take it that's a yes?"

I never said a word. Well, I've been looking forward to this day for weeks and it's just got a whole lot better.

The gift is a posh box of imported chocolates that Mummy found in Barbour's department store, but they've been in my bag all morning.

"I'm afraid they may have gone soft. Better put them in the fridge straight away," I tell Gill, who's already torn the wrapping paper off and is turning the box over in her hands while making cooing noises.

"Ooh thanks! You're such an angel!" She hugs me and gives me a kiss on the nose then starts picking at the cellophane wrapper. "Oh no. I'm sorry, but there's only one option open to us. The fridge is too full. We'll just have to eat them before they melt completely."

A third of the chocolates are gone by the time we've made our way through the gate, down the steps, past the rocky slope with the lion on top and through the house. Taking my sticky hand, she leads me into a garden heaving with guests. For several minutes I get introduced to a variety of aunts, uncles, cousins and horsey friends and lose track of all their names immediately. Charles is over there, in charge of the *braai*, and holding court with several of the male guests. Mum would be impressed, if she were here, given that she gets all moany about the way the smoke deliberately follows her so that she can't stand anywhere near a *braai* fire. This one has a monster stone chimney that's drawing all the smoke up into the wide, empty sky.

"Miss Tessa! You must have some of my delicious relish with your *sadza*."

Amai, bearing a tray loaded with platefuls of Porterhouse steaks and lamb chops, sweeps past and beams at me.

Now as far as I'm concerned, *sadza* is just bland, white, lumpy stuff, but I have experienced Amai's tomato, onion and herb relish. My mouth goes juicy, and when I catch a whiff of the meat already on the fire, my insides start to rumble.

"Charles, my man!" a voice hollers from the other side of the pool. "Where do you hide your stash of Castle? And where's the birthday girl?"

Charles spins and shouts "Barry! You're late as usual. We've drunk all the Castle, *shamwari*."

Okay, I'm relieved Mum *isn't* here now. I knew I shouldn't've shown her Gill's invitation the second her eyes started to rove over it and her face started transforming into the Bothered Look. When she said, "I'm not sure it's a suitable party for you to go to Tessa. Gill is sixteen. It's too adult for you," I had to keep up my happy face and do some rapid thinking. Say, "It's not really a *party* Mum. It's a *braai*, that's all. Like, lunch. It's really just lunch with Gill's family on her birthday."

The pictures were telling her otherwise, unfortunately. Entirely my fault for producing a piece of paper with the word 'Party' on the same page as merrily drawn images of champagne and beer bottles and of a record spinning on a lop-sided turntable, whirling out musical notes. I should've just said I'd been asked to stay for lunch after riding.

I got, you can't stay late, blah blah, Daddy and I don't know these people, blah blah, they might be drinkers, blah blah, if you don't like what's going on, you call us and we'll come and get you, blah blah, I hope they don't disturb the neighbours with any loud music, Tessa, blah blah, Tessa are you listening?

God, she makes a fuss. She hopes the neighbours aren't disturbed? The Owens' neighbours' houses are at least half a kilometre away on all sides and anyway, I'm sure I just met a bunch of them five minutes ago. And what would she expect me to *do* about loud music? Tell Charles to turn it down because my mother wouldn't like it?

And after I'd got her over the invitation itself, there was the argument about the jeans.

"*Jeans?* No Tessa. If you're invited to lunch you need to wear something nice and neat. We'll buy you a new dress that will go with your pink sandals."

I won that round too, but I had to wear the pink sandals instead of my tackies. Still, I'm noticing several women in high heels so I guess they don't look too out of place.

So who's this Barry? He's small and red faced and muscly and on closer inspection he isn't bald at all. It's just that his gingery hair is very, very short. I don't believe I've ever seen such a young man with so little hair.

"Barry!" Gill squeals. She shoves her glass of Cinzano and lemonade into my hand and says out of the side of her mouth, "Yet another cousin from one of Mum's many siblings."

She skids round the edge of the pool and into Barry's arms. He's shorter than her by half a head but he lifts her off her feet and swings her around.

She takes his hand and leads him onto the patio and over towards Charles.

There's Nathan, standing behind the *braai* like a statue. First time I've seen him since we were in the yard earlier. He's changed his jodhpurs for shorts and is barefoot and it's as if he's watching everyone from behind a screen. Here, but not here. Well, me too. I don't know all these people milling about and I've never met Barry, so it's weird, like we're both on the outside, looking in. The difference is, I *want* to be on the inside with everyone else whereas he just watches from out there. I used to see him do it at school, then just melt away, so that no-one ever even knew he'd melted away.

I'm still holding Gill's glass. The drink smells sweet and pleasant, and tempting. It *is* sweet, but it has a sharper sting that catches in my throat and next thing I'm spluttering, my eyes are watering, I'm spilling it on the paving stones and frantically searching around to see who's watching me. From his hiding place, behind the *braai*, Nathan is.

He does nothing except raise his own glass of Coke a fraction in my direction, then he moves forward, takes a long-handled fork from a clay pot of *braai* cutlery and starts to poke at the fire Charles has abandoned.

Even with his eyes no longer on me, I really don't know where to put myself. I take a step back, a step forward, I wave both my glass and Gill's aimlessly around as I search in vain for somewhere to put them down before I spill the lot, and then I'm saved by Gill, who returns to claim hers. Barry and Charles are close behind.

"Don't worry Barry, man, I was joking. I'll get you a beer. God, your hair looks awful. Those army barbers are little better than butchers."

"Ja, well, got to be done. Can't get my flowing locks caught in my rifle, can I? In any case, they do like you to know they own you."

The two men vanish into the house.

"Ah, darling Barry," Gill says with something like a sigh. "He's Uncle Graham's son. They used to live in Salisbury when we were kids and he was always round here, but then Unc got a job in Bulawayo and they moved. He's back up here because he's just left school and has to start his National Service. Monday, I believe. They've made it a full year now."

She goes silent, biting her bottom lip. The sun and sparkle has left her and that, together with the idea that Nathan's eyes might still be boring into my back, makes it feel like the temperature's dropped a few degrees.

"What's up?"

She shakes her head. "Nothing. Look, come. Let's help Amai get the rest of the food out. I think we're nearly ready to eat."

*

Tammy's nice. She's shorter than Gill, although they're both sixteen, and she has long, curly fair hair in a high pony tail. Her face is round and all parts of it are moving, like she's on constant high alert, and she talks fast like Rosie. Her pony tail and her fringe are straight right now though, and dripping pool water, and she's hanging onto the tractor tyre tube from the outside, pulling it down under her arms so that me and Gill have to wriggle round a bit and lean away from her to balance it. We bob about on the tube and talk dogs. Gill says she'll visit Tammy's house on Tuesday after school to meet the new puppy and then Tammy asks me about Skellum and Gill admits she never wanted another dog after Captain died. Tammy closes her eyes and sighs, "Oh! Yes. Captain. Darling Captain."

I think these two have known each other for a long time.

Tammy gives the tube a spin to the right by kicking with her legs and the sun is reflecting off the water into my face, the laughter and the music in the air is all around me and the world is good.

Then the water under us erupts, Tammy gets rolled aside and all three of us are dumped, with the tube on top of us. When I surface, Gill is trying to wrestle it from those two tediously annoying boys who were flicking their towels at us earlier. She's laughing, but if I were Gavin or Josh I'd take note of the warning in her eyes that she's far from happy.

Then, from nowhere, Nathan's in the pool with us.

"The girls got it first, guys."

He leaps up over the tube so he's lying across it and his nose is about two centimetres from Gavin's. Gavin slides back underwater and is gone. Josh thinks about it a bit longer but after Nathan's placed a hand flat on top of his head and pushed him down he gives up too and backs off, spluttering.

"Oooh, long lips, boys!" shouts Gill, and gives Nathan a soft punch on the shoulder.

But we've had enough of swimming anyway. Josh and Gavin are back on the tractor tube before my feet have cleared the water, Gill and Tammy ahead of me. Who are these kids anyway?

"Neighbours," says Gill. "Two properties down. Their folks are ever so nice but those boys are a pair of little shits. I didn't want them to come. Shame they didn't have something else to do today hey?"

Is Nathan still swimming? No. No sign of him. The Ghost of Nowhere again.

We eat far too much ice-cream and several slices of birthday cake and then go to help the grooms bring the horses in for the night. Nathan is there in the background again, filling water buckets. Tammy's different around the horses – calm and smooth as silk. I get instructions, but Tammy just knows exactly what Gill needs her to do. She must be a pretty good rider, her father being a racehorse trainer and all. Drifting back to the house, arms linked with Gill and Tammy, I'm on top of the world again.

But, like midnight for Cinderella, six o'clock is the end of my ball. Daddy's appeared in the doorway, seeking me, nodding at people, smiling, but with that slightly blank look you give complete strangers. It's Charles who collects him, guides him over towards me where I've been trying to pretend I haven't seen him. They don't quite make it though. It's a good thing I told Charles what Dad does for a living. As long as they keep swapping stories about roads and dams and piling and stuff I get to enjoy myself a bit longer.

The shadows have stretched all the way across the lawn; the patio is the last place still in the sun. Gill's Aunty Cath, who's very wrinkly but has been whirling about so much she's managed to occupy most of the dance area, puts on *Clair*, turns the volume up, abandons her G&T and grabs her husband's hand. I guess me and Gill and Tammy will have to sit this one out.

Dad's sidling towards me. I can see he wants to keep on talking with Charles but duty is calling and Mum will have given him a time limit for sure. Gill says, "Dad, I can't deal with Aunty Cath and Uncle Rupert smooching on the dance floor for the rest of the night. *Please* put something more upbeat on after this and keep her away from the turntable."

Dad shakes her hand very formally and asks, kind of pointlessly, "So you're Gill?" and wishes her happy birthday and tells me we're ready to go.

"I wish I could stay."

She gives me a hug and whispers in my ear, "There'll be lots of other parties, Tess. And one day you'll be able to make your own decisions about what time to go home."

Aloud, as I'm led away, she promises, "Now I'll see you on Tuesday afternoon, yeah? We'll start on Induna."

Just as Dad's reversing out into the main driveway, Barry emerges from under the open garage door, a cardboard box full of clinking bottles in his arms. I've forgotten where Gill said he was going on Monday. He looks a bit drunk, but Daddy's not paying him any attention.

*

"How was your grown-up party then?"

She's having a tug-of-war with Skellum in the kitchen and I can barely hear her voice above his deliriously happy growls. That puppy lives only to have his chin scratched by an idle hand; I reckon time will prove that Daddy has failed monumentally in his mission to own a ferocious guard dog. Skellie loves everyone and he's perfectly prepared to welcome all of them to our property. He does yap enthusiastically when someone passes by, and more so if they stop at the gate, and Dad points this out to Elijah at every opportunity with comments like, "Always call one of us if any of your friends come to visit. We can control the dog before they come in."

He thinks his new *Chenjera Imbwa* sign is the business and is convinced it guarantees that all strangers, especially black ones, will be very wary of our savage *imbwa*. But I've seen Skellie loving being petted by Elijah's family and friends when Dad's not about. *I* think his bark just says, "I live here! This is me and I see you!" Needless to say, I keep this to myself.

"I wanted to stay," I yell at Rosie. "You should've seen the size of the steaks they were cooking. And the cake! You'd've loved the cake. *And* there was dancing."

At the dinner table I say nothing about the party, Charles and his stash of lager, or the music and tell my family instead about Induna and Gill's programme of work for him. I describe the stages of breaking a horse to saddle. Mum and Dad make out like they're interested but Rosie's staring into space while she chews. I'm in the middle of emphasising the importance of teaching a horse to strike off on the correct foreleg in canter, when she bangs her fork down on the table.

"What *are* you on about? Can't you *ever* stop talking about horses? And don't pout like that. It's true."

"All right, I'll shut up, so there. I don't care."

"It's very interesting, my love," says Mum, and Dad goes, "Yes, I see your point," but I ignore them.

"You're always going on about the rules of hockey, and long jumping techniques! I've even heard you trying to tell Elijah the best way to bat in rounders. I'm sure he was fascinated. Sport is *your* interest. *Mine* is horses."

"Enough! You can carry on arguing later. Eat now. Eat, and listen. I've been hatching a plan. How about a weeks' holiday at Kariba at the end of August, when school breaks up?"

Daddy's looking immensely pleased with himself and I can't think why. Kariba?

"Kariba?" Rosie says slowly. "Why? Oh I get it. So you can do fishing. Mmmmm."

She rolls her eyes. "All my life…"

That's Uncle Dudley's fault. He's not like Daddy. In fact, he's not the sort of guy Daddy should be hanging out with at all. He's very short – not that that's the problem – but he's clearly utterly annoying. Dad says things like,

"I don't know how he does it. Even in October he never undoes his tie or rolls up his sleeves and he never has any bloody sweat patches," and

"The last of the tender drawings was printed off at 4pm and Mike was having kittens. Mayhem. Augustus was hopping around waiting to take the stuff to the post office. Even secretaries got roped into folding drawings and that bloke Dudley went off and made himself a cup of mint tea," and

"His handwriting is so perfectly legible. I can't even read my own calculations. He must be a bloody android or something."

Dad watches rugby and football and wrestling and his office is a mess. He's got no right to tell us to keep our rooms tidy. In summer he'd go to work in shorts and a vest if he thought he could get away with it. That first time he announced he was going fishing with this guy Dudley at Prince Edward Dam none of us believed him. Well, Prince Edward Dam yesterday, Lake Kariba tomorrow.

"I suggested we stay at Caribbea Bay Hotel. Dudley, Andrew and I can do a spot of bream and tiger fishing while you girls do your own thing."

"'*You girls*'?" Mummy is looking a bit too keen. "Still, it does sound okay. I could do with a holiday. I'll ring Pauline."

So I've met the rest of the Foster family only once but I know they're superhuman beings. They manage to fit sessions of every sport known to man into a week of work and school, Uncle Dudley is very active on the kids' school PTA and Aunty Pauline is on committees for all manner of obscure societies and charities. She squeezes all the meetings into her week between ferrying the kids to their various activities. I can't imagine what a week with such whizz kids, all sporty and keen and good at everything they do, will be like and I'm not sure I want to know.

There are so many places in the world… I want to say, but Rosie beats me to it.

"So you get a promotion, Dad, and all that talk of luxury safaris in the Kruger and taking the Blue Train to Cape Town has come down to a fishing trip at Kariba? I don't believe it! Why can't we go to – I don't know – *London?* Visit Aunty Julia?"

It's true. He's an Associate, which means he's more important than before, and he bought Mum a brand new Datsun 1200 and got fully fitted carpets throughout the whole house. He's talked at length about amazing holidays around South Africa but so far he's deflected all our pleas for a trip to England.

"You don't want to go to rainy old England when there's a wonderful country like South Africa next door. England's a dismal place, girlie. It amazes me that Northern Ireland has actually voted to remain part of it. No, you don't want to go there."

"Besides," he adds, setting aside his plate and standing up, "I can pay for all of you to fly halfway round the world but if we can't get enough foreign currency to have a decent holiday wherever we go, there's not much point, is there?"

WEDNESDAY 29TH AUGUST 1973

"No, no, no, don't buy it for that," Aunty Pauline instructs Mum. "You can get it for a lot less than that, my dear."

Mum mumbles something I don't hear and carries on fingering the intricately crocheted table cloth the wrinkly black woman is holding out to her. The younger woman flourishes her own set of crocheted place mats across the gap between the two of them, grinning and emphasising how pretty they are, how brightly red.

Aunty Pauline's clearly up for a bit of bargaining. Straight out of the pages of one of Rosie's fashion magazines she is, with her blow-dried, smooth golden curls, her crisp, beige shorts and cream shirt and her heeled sandals (which are spotlessly white despite the bare, dusty earth underfoot) and the set of gold bracelets tinkling on her arm in time with her gestures. Once again I'm wishing Mum had dressed up a little. I reckon she's had those ghastly floral trousers since the sixties. She insists on wearing them with her various floral blouses, but the trouble is, none of the floral patterns actually go together. Aunty Pauline's even wearing make-up. She has such *style*.

I blame Rosie for putting these thoughts in my head. It would probably have gone right by me if she hadn't been in such a sarcastic mood when they were loading all the fishing tackle and equipment into that gleaming Land Rover of Uncle Dudley's on Monday morning, and if she hadn't hissed at me, "Aunty Pauline's wearing heels *and* make-up at five-thirty in the morning! And those kids look like they're going to a party instead of on a four-hour drive. And look at Mum. Jesus. And I hope that lot don't see inside our car. Thank God Daddy got Elijah to clean and wax it yesterday. I can't believe them. They're just so – I don't know – well ironed and colour co-ordinated."

Rosie knows about things like being colour co-ordinated. But although Aunty Pauline looks like a model, I like her smile and her interest in whatever any of us have to say.

"Let's sit on that stone wall," Julie suggests, pointing. "Leave the mothers to buy the wares. It's boring."

Kariba Town, in the Zambezi Valley as it is, is stinking hot in the summer months from October through to about March. Otherwise, it's just hot. The Heights is a good name for this place. There are several boats on the deep azure waters of the lake far below and the slightly cooler breeze up here is delicious. My Coke bottle is streaming with condensation. Aunty Pauline's voice comes drifting across the dusty paved area from behind.

"Ten dollars? Oh no, I don't think so. I'll give you seven dollars, that's all."

"Yes Madam," I hear the old woman agree, and then she cackles hoarsely. "Seven dollars, seven dollars. But then you can also buy this pink one for only seven dollars too, eh?"

Julie sighs. "I say if you like it, just pay for it. They're hardly expensive are they?"

I take a long swig, savouring the view. It's good how this holiday's turning out so much better than I'd expected. Julie's okay. She's very much like her mother, being blonde – not like the dark-haired twins – enthusiastic, and yet practical. She's only a year older than me but although I've seen her acting the goat with Rosie, like when they were bomb-jumping into the pool yesterday, she talks and acts far more like a grown-up than either of us know how.

"Our mother calls it being thrifty," I say. "Never mind them. Isn't the view from here so vast? It's like being at the top of the world."

I've never thought to question Mum's financial theory and I'm not going there right now. So, I wonder how Induna's getting on with the jumping lessons Gill promised to give him this week?

Catherine's eyes are closed and Rosie's engrossed in tossing small pebbles down the slope to see how accurately she can land them on that ledge about twenty metres below. From somewhere in the distance comes the hauntingly melodious call of a fish eagle.

Squinting up into the sky's a bit pointless. It's just an empty glare of light.

"Isn't that just the most beautiful and sort of lonely sound? It's a weird thing to say, but it almost makes me want to cry."

Julie twirls her empty Coke bottle and traces a finger down its wet surface.

"Me too. Cry, the beloved country eh? Like the book. Have you read it?"

I'm sure I've heard of it. It's quite an old book.

"What's it about?"

"Read it. Mum told us we should because we're living an illusion if we think whites can hold onto this country. Africa will change. It has to."

She shuts her eyes and tips her head back, stretching her legs in front of her. "It's idyllic up here, I agree. Let's enjoy our illusion. It won't last. Dad was just saying last night it's noticeable how many Security Forces vehicles there are around here, in every car park and on every stretch of road. And the place is crawling with troops, don't you think?"

What do I think? I think other kids' parents have superior observational powers compared to those of mine. Or is it just that mine do see these things but don't communicate any of it to us, or in front of us? That utter contentment with the world I felt less than a minute ago? Well, it's just been tipped over the edge of this very cliff. I want to ask Julie, "What won't last?" but I don't want to sound ignorant, or admit that although I've noticed the camouflage-clad troops I never thought to ask why they're here or even to *wonder* why to myself, to be honest. And that book? I could ask Mum what it's about but she'll give me the brush off. I'd hazard a guess it's about racial politics and she'd tell me it's unsuitable for me to read at my age. But the Fosters have shared it with their kids because they think it's important to do so.

There's not a cloud in sight but it suddenly doesn't feel so sunny.

Aunty Pauline and Mum have their new table cloths and want to head back to the hotel.

"We'd do better to save our visit to the dam wall and the crocodile ranch for Saturday, the last day," Mum tells us. "It's too hot. We need a swim."

"We must pace our adventures, ladies," agrees Aunty Pauline.

She's pretty good at manoeuvring the Land Rover and she gets it out of its parking bay and turns it in the tight car park with dainty gear-shift movements that set her bangles jangling. "We'll have much more fun than those boys out fishing."

Mum says it's a long time since Dad was a boy but she's sure Andrew can show him how to do it. I doubt it. Andrew, black haired like his father and Catherine, is literally a miniature version of Dudley, all tidily turned out each day in his khaki shorts, a smoothly ironed, tucked in T-shirt, long school socks and clean *veldskoens*. He pays attention during the adults' conversations about business and engineering and world affairs and contributes with facts I've never even heard reference to. As Rosie said yesterday, the only time we've seen him come close to having fun is when he's swimming and even then he and Catherine compete, diving in together like one entity with barely a splash, keeping pace with each other for several lengths and then eventually racing and comparing notes when they rest. Not my kind of fun for sure. And neither him nor Uncle Dudley come back to the hotel each evening even half as sweaty and water-stained as Daddy.

"How many bream d'you reckon they'll bring back today?" Julie wonders. "Maybe yesterday's two will remain the record. Of course they return most of their catch to the depths, as they'll be so keen to tell us even when questioned separately."

"I don't care," Rosie sighs. "They taste muddy."

SATURDAY 1ST SEPTEMBER 1973

"It's impressive, I'll give you that, but I can't get Dad's pash. It's a concrete wall at the end of the day."

She's hoisted herself up to lie across the parapet and is leaning over so far I'm compelled to make a grab for her right ankle.

"Woah, Rosie! Don't do that, for God's sake. Look, Dad's a civil engineer. He thinks we should know *how* the dam was built."

I've already forgotten most of the detail he rabbited on about last night, although I'm sure Andrew hasn't. All I remember are his stories of the River God, Nyaminyami, and how the engineers and dam builders really annoyed him, so he got back at them. Basically, when the people who lived in the valley said that Nyaminyami was bleak about the intention to flood all their *kraals*, and about the way the people were expected to just pack up their stuff and move out, the dam builders ignored them. The last straw for Nyaminyami was when he got separated from his wife when they started to build the wall. So he got his own back, big time. He sent more rain than anyone had seen in a hundred years (or maybe it was a thousand years?) and he did this twice, so their new dam got washed away twice. I say the engineers really should've taken notice of the warnings.

Rosie wriggles back down from the parapet, fishes Mum's camera from the depths of her rucksack, takes a photo of Nyaminyami's statue and then reaches out to touch it with her fingertips. It's made of stone. He's a short, fat snake with big teeth and fierce eyes.

"I wonder if there really is a River God?"

"Who knows. I heard Aunty Pauline say that there are often earth tremors around here. Maybe he's still here and he's plotting something else."

I lean out over the parapet – not as far as Rosie did – to gaze down at the concrete dam, so solid and so permanent and so twentieth-century. One of the flood gates is open and the lake waters are pouring through in an arc of creamy foam.

Mum yells from behind, "We're moving on now!" but before I turn away, I get this really weird shiver that runs from my hair down into my shorts. Nyaminyami is watching me. In my head I hear Julie say, "Africa will change. It has to."

I'm not sure I'm keen on this. What, exactly, will change? The wall is still separating people, because we're not allowed to go over the centre line now, into Zambia. The Rhodesian troops and the Zambian troops are standing around, watching each other.

Rosie's off, shouting something about the Crocodile Ranch and Big Daddy, who's four metres long. I can't help it – I touch the statue as well. I whisper, "Sorry."

Silly.

*

Mum's trying way too hard to be organised. This family doesn't do organised.

"You should perhaps start packing some of your things you definitely don't need tonight or tomorrow morning. That way there's less to do in the morning, isn't there?"

"True," says Rosie, but only loud enough for me to hear. "But I don't want to. I didn't want to come here but now I don't want to go home. Caribbea Bay's so pretty, don't you think?"

Like a Mediterranean hotel, Dad said. It's all white, rough plastered walls with no straight lines – even the pool is more oval than rectangular – red tiled floors and red, round roof tiles. It has lots of walled courtyard areas to explore and steps everywhere, up to our suite, down to the pool surrounds and the view over the lake. It's haphazard, a jumble of windows and walls and roofs and arched doorways. At night the walls kind of glow pink, as if they've been lit from the inside somehow.

"Yeah," I whisper back. "I'd love to stay longer too."

For another even number of days, obviously. So we both get to have the top bunk equally. She'd be impossible if I had one more night up there than her.

She starts to say something about how she wishes we could've been here for my birthday when there's a resounding rapping on the door in the room behind us. We grab the black iron balcony railing in unison. Rat-tat-a-tat-tat, TAT TAT. Uncle Dudley's signature knock.

"We're going!" yells Dad.

"Okay! God, we're only on the balcony, not the other side of the lake," Rosie hollers back.

Mum winces.

Down at the jetty there's a tall, very skinny, very tanned man wearing a white shirt with blue and gold epaulettes, white shorts, blue deck shoes and a white and blue peaked Captain's cap. He accosts us and takes the tickets Dad hands over.

"Welcome, welcome. Please step aboard."

It's not in a proper boat, like you might think. It's a couple of platforms, double decker style, floating on forty-four gallon drums. From the back end – well, I think it's the back end because both ends look pretty much the same – comes the sound of an engine put-put-puttering away.

We get ourselves a prime position near the rails on the top platform and Daddy and Uncle Dudley waste no time in getting some beers, wine for Mum and Aunty Pauline and Cokes for the rest of us. We get under way in broad daylight but the sun's well on its way down already. The boat, for want of a better word, is full of tourists and their chatter, their clinking bottles and glasses. It's not called the Booze Cruise for nothing, is it?

"Look at that sky," Dad says, not much later. "What an array of colours spreading and intermingling. This has got to be the life, eh? Big skies, big water. Lazy days bobbing on a turquoise lake, that heat, snapping bream, the fish eagle calling through the bare limbs of the Drowned Forest. It was good, Duds."

That's an awful lot of description for Dad to use all at once. He really has enjoyed himself and he really does love fishing. It can't be bad. I want this for him. I don't want anything to change.

They start discussing where to stop for fuel on the way home. Rosie and Julie are talking tennis techniques and I'm not sure where Andrew and Catherine have gone. I turn my attention back to the hippos – three of them, blowing gusts of spray and snorting in the water just fifty metres away to the left.

Dad's sunset colours are deepening. The sky in the east is a dark indigo, while in the west it's the most amazing assortment of colours, running through from that deep indigo and lightening gradually into a series of blues, then cream, pale yellow, gold, orange and finally blood red where the sun is just about to disappear behind the black hills.

I've got horse riding and Dad's got fishing and now Rosie's got tennis. I can't be bothered to try and understand the finer points, but Julie's taught her something every day. I guess Aunty Pauline may've told Mum she's a national junior champion, but I didn't know until that man who got beaten by her on Thursday told me.

*

It's probably nearly an hour since the sun finally gave up for today. We're heading back to shore through blackness; the water gurgling and glugging around the vessel is gleaming like oil as we get closer to the lights at the jetty. They say *night falls* and it does. Just like that, in minutes. Boom. I'm day-dreaming about seeing Induna again when I see that there are five camouflage-painted Land Rovers in a row near the jetty.

FRIDAY 28TH SEPTEMBER 1973

My ladybird alarm clock will go off at six-forty-five but I'm not giving it the chance. I've been awake since around five, squirming about ever since, and I can't stand it any longer. I jam my hand down on the button at six-forty, crawl out of bed and fumble in the cupboard for a clean school uniform. Rosie's already seated at the breakfast table when I arrive there, which is a bit surprising, but I'm desperate so I don't think too much about it. If they wanted to create suspense, they've succeeded, but it will end now. They'll have to give me this mystery gift they've been on about because the day has arrived.

I have this tiny, nasty, niggling doubt that it's all a trick and I'm not going to get anything, but Rosie has a small, shiny gold parcel on her plate and the tension oozing from her is encouraging. She leaps up and holds out the parcel, and an envelope. The toaster pops in the kitchen and Mum calls, "Oh, is she here?"

"Birthday! Birthday!" Rosie squeaks.

"Hello dear." Dad doesn't bother to look round his paper.

"Oh? Oh yes. Oh thank you," I say, cool, like I've forgotten the date.

Inside the envelope is a home-made card illustrated with ribbons and balloons in loud felt tip pen colours. In it, she has simply scrawled, "Happy Birthday Tee" in her excitable handwriting, using a bright pink pen.

I rip at the wrapping paper and pull out a small white box, tipping it as I do so. The lid falls off and a tiny wad of cotton wool drops out onto the checked tablecloth. Hidden in the cotton wool is a pair of dainty gold rose-shaped earrings.

"Oh! Special earrings!" I drop the card and attempt to give my sister a bear hug. She wriggles and tries to get away, but her face is one huge grin, her eyes wicked.

"Let me go! See, now you don't have to wear those boring studs you've had since your ears were done."

As she frees herself, she waves towards the kitchen and declares, "Wait. Wait and see. The big one's coming!"

Mum appears with a rack of fresh toast in one hand and an envelope in the other. The envelope is passed to me and no-one says a word. I glance around at my family and they all stare back, Dad finally putting aside the *Rhodesia Herald*.

This is the big surprise? In an envelope?

Shaken cautiously, it makes no sound. Then, in a flash, I know. Money. I'm considered old enough to receive cash and to choose how to spend it. Not much of a big surprise though. The surprise will actually be theirs because they don't know what I'll do with it.

I start to think what I could spend some money on as I open the envelope. Books probably. It's unlikely to be enough to get a new riding hat. Mine's getting a bit tight. Maybe Daddy can make up the difference.

There's a card inside, but I flick it open without looking to see what's on the front and lay it flat, open on the table. There are no banknotes. Only a square piece of photographic paper, upside down.

I give my parents a cracked smile and still they stare back. I pick up the photo between forefinger and thumb and turn it over.

"That's Induna," I tell them, studying the familiar form. He really does have much more muscle now than he did when I first met him.

Rosie flaps her hands in front of my face and lets out a yell.

"Tessie! *Come on!* Wakey, wakey! You've got a horse!"

They're all applauding, but my brain is struggling. I close my mouth, because it's open, and then burst into tears.

Crying and laughing at the same time doesn't leave much room for breathing. I gasp and get the hiccups.

"Well we couldn't wrap him up and smuggle him into your bedroom," Dad's saying, "so we thought a photo was the next best thing. For God's sake bring her some water before she chokes to death and I've spent good money for nothing."

Mum cocks her head at Rosie. "I'm surprised this one didn't let the cat out of the bag – or should I say the horse out of the stable. We thought we were going to have to tie her up in the garden shed last night."

So they've all been conspiring together. Mum, Dad, Rosie. Gill, who's been vague with me to the point of vexation about Induna's future. Moira and Charles, who must've done the deal with Dad. And even Nathan. Nathan, who says nothing to me except hello and howzit. Then out of the blue, a couple of weeks ago, he said, "Good luck with Indie." He was in his senior school uniform, looking just as scruffy in it as he did in his junior school one. They've all been conspiring. All of them.

We have a group hug and I'm not sure who to hug hardest – Mum and Dad because they've just given me the one thing in the world I wanted more than anything, or Rosie because I don't want her to feel upstaged. I love her earrings – really. Then I sit and stare at my empty plate through my tears, trying to decide what to do.

If I leave right now, this instant, I could go to Makuti Park and see Indie before school...

"Come on." Dad folds the paper and stands up. "You look like you're sitting on hot bricks. I'll take you to school today and we'll stop at the stables on the way. No breakfast for me this morning. And have no doubt about it, you *will* go to school afterwards."

I'm struggling to believe this isn't a dream and that I won't wake up to my alarm and find none of it's happened. Since when have my parents and Charles and Moira ever been in contact? I know I talked about Induna a lot. I know they know I've wanted a pony forever, but they're not interested in horses or riding. Neither is Rosie.

Rosie. Ah, yes. Rosie and her new tennis coach. *She* got all new gear and a year's course at Julie Foster's club didn't she? The parents conspired a bit behind her back too. That evening they were sitting on the patio and I was doing my homework on the lounge floor, I heard them talking about how Uncle Dudley'd said that Julie thought Rosie would make a brilliant tennis player. Natural coordination and ability to read an opponent's mind, she'd said. I'd thought that was pretty funny, Rosie reading people's minds. Then I caught Dad saying he was prepared to arrange it – I didn't know what 'it' was – as long as Rosie was going to take it seriously. "You know what she's like. She tries a bit of this then tries a bit of that. What if it's just a passing phase, like the cricket?"

Next thing, Rosie's presented with this little folder of information about Julie's instructor and his courses. Top-seeded. Yup, sporting terms are utterly nonsensical, although the cricket ones do take the cake.

It *is* true that my sister tries to get involved in everything that's going but she does do it with genuine interest and only gives up on some activities because it's physically impossible to fit it all in. I can see why Aunty Pauline took to her.

So Rosie's staring at my gymkhana rosettes while she listens to Dad's lecture about taking the tennis thing seriously, then she goes, "Well, I love it, a bit like Tee loves riding. Yeah, I'd like to have tennis lessons. Okay. Thanks."

She got a tennis racquet for her birthday from Cleo and Skellum.

I'm bursting to see Gill's face, but when we get to the yard there are only a couple of grooms wandering about.

"Oh no!" I wail. "It's the Umtali show this weekend. I forgot."

This is the thing when you're a champion – you get to miss a day at school to go competing. Well, maybe one day…

I tumble out of the car before it's stopped, ignoring Dad's "Hey! Whoa!" and race into the yard. There, I literally run straight into George, who's leading Induna and Cactus Dan to their paddock.

"Georgie!" I seize him by his elbows and try to spin him around. "Induna's mine! My dad's bought him!"

"I know, Miss Tessa." He's battling to keep the two lead ropes from tangling and dangling. I throw my arms round Induna's neck and bury my face in his sweet smelling mane, oblivious then to all else.

"He's mine, he's mine, he's all mine!"

"Do you still want old George to look after him for you?"

"Of course I do Georgie. You're the best."

So even George has been in on the conspiracy. *When the hell* did Dad get to meet with Charles? It doesn't matter. I want to ride my horse right here and now. All day.

But I have to go to school.

*

This is me – really me – schooling my own horse. I've never tried shoulder-in without Gill being present, but I give it a go. Induna takes advantage of my tentative efforts by merely twisting his neck in towards the centre of the school and humping his back as if to say, "See? I can still buck with my head bent to the right. Aren't I clever? Sorry, what was it you wanted me to do?"

I do actually need Gill but I'm not going to admit that to myself today at all.

SATURDAY 6TH JULY 1974

"Here, look, aren't you cold? Where's your jumper?"

She's got her arms wrapped around her body and her hands tucked under her armpits.

I point at it, draped over the fence where I ditched it after we started the jumping work. Needless to say Induna's barely broken a sweat. He is clipped, though.

"Well, walk him round for five minutes. I'll take it to the yard for you. He went so well for you today, didn't he? That last one was a metre."

She's doing her Cheshire Cat impression again. I know that look.

"I knew it. You put it up while I was cantering my circle down the other end!"

She shrugs on her way to the gate. "You did it, though, didn't you? You've been doing all the work and I've been standing here and now I need some hot chocolate inside me. See you in the kitchen when you've sorted Indie out. Don't hose him off, hey? He's probably only damp under the saddle and there's no point in dousing him in cold water if you don't have to."

She's gone, my sweater flung over her shoulders, hands still tucked in. I give Induna a long rein and let him stretch his neck. I'll get cold again soon enough, but for now I'm fine. It was pretty frosty early this morning. Rosie and I did that thing where we race around the lawn, like, erratically, and then stand back to admire the patterns of our footprints, huffing to see our breath coming out in clouds. Dad was grumpy, as usual, moaning on and on about how much time he wastes having to run the car on choke while it frantically wipes its own windscreen when he could be getting going. It's his own fault the car has to live outside when we have a perfectly good garage. Mum keeps her car in her half but he keeps a load of junk in his bit. He's convinced that one day he'll find a use for all of it. And it *is* junk. Mismatched tools, bits of timber, angle iron, car spares, pieces of carpet, crates, empty tins, full tins of paint from years ago, cardboard boxes, plastic sheeting, rolls of chicken wire, leftover ceramic tiles from when that guy redid the bathrooms. He doesn't think our frosty breath thing is the least bit funny. He appears to have completely forgotten the fact that he once lived in England.

*

Gill hasn't gone back to the house yet. She's still in the stableyard because she's talking to Nathan.

Where did he come from? He wasn't in the house or the yard before my lesson, I swear.

No matter. He must be about to go for a hack because he's got High Time all tacked up, but he's got competition. Kuti is perched on top of the saddle. I leap off and drag Induna over to them.

"Oh isn't she *sweet?*" I coo, reaching out to tickle her throat with my finger. "I love cats. They answer to no-one. They just do their own thing."

I do the obligatory kissing noises and she pushes hard against my finger with her chin, twisting her head so my tickling is transferred to the back of her ear. Her eyes are closed and she's got ecstasy written all over her pretty, pointed face. Her purr is loud and rasping.

Nathan watches, silent. Right then, Induna decides he wants to be involved in my conversation with the cat so he pushes his nose up towards her and huffs noisily through his nostrils. This is too much for Kuti. She's well used to horses but only has time for those who show her some respect. In one movement she hisses, leaps into the air, executes a hundred and eighty degree turn and is gone. Both horses toss their heads and High Time side steps squarely onto Nathan's right boot.

"Ow! Shit! Bloody hell!" He pushes his shoulder into hers in an attempt to make her shift her weight. "Gerrorff!"

"Language, Nathan, language," says Gill absently, staring after the fleeing cat. "You'll corrupt young innocent Tessa here."

Can't say I'm bothered. I just feel sorry for Kuti. She looked so cute, riding a horse.

After some grunting, Nathan manages to extract his foot. He shakes it a couple of times and prods High Time with his forefinger, saying, "Great galumphing lout."

I've seen children, and adults, all too happy to take a whip to a pony for what they perceive as clumsiness. I explore his face cautiously. He doesn't *look* angry, in spite of what he's saying. He's now completely focussed on examining the healing scab on High Time's shoulder, where she got bitten by Floss, probing it gently with the same finger. After what Gill said... his father and his violent rages... it's odd, but I'll bet Nathan never loses his temper.

She's laughing. "Bloody lucky you got steel toe caps, huh?"

He arches his eyebrows, shrugs and withdraws his hand.

"Well, I'm going." He steps back, pauses, and then vaults into the saddle without touching the stirrup. So casual. Just like that. I've tried it. Once. I ended up clinging to the side of Silver Valley's neck with one foot over her back and the other under her belly. I'm sure the grooms thought I'd done it solely for their entertainment. Next time – if there is a next time – I'll do it in private.

*

Mum and Dad are missing, so I guess they've gone to do the weekly shopping, and Rosie's shut in her room. I change into my tracksuit bottoms and carry my weekend homework to the dining table. I get as far as opening my maths exercise book and writing the date at the top of a fresh page when I smell smoke. At the same instant, Rosie comes skipping through from the passageway.

"There's a fire somewhere close over towards the east! I saw it from the bedroom window!"

She vanishes through the French doors onto the patio. I replace the screw cap on my fountain pen and pursue her.

The bushfire's already caused a thick haze that's partially blotted out the sun. Purple-brown, the smoke boils skywards, casting an ochre shadow across the garden, and swirling in the air are the shards of blackened grass that make Mum so furious when she has washing on the line. Within the haze, squadrons of hunting birds are circling.

"Can you see it?" I stand on tiptoe. She's peering into the distance from her vantage point on top of the patio handrail. She has one hand wrapped around the corner roof support column and is using the other to shade her eyes.

"No. I think it's beyond the shopping centre."

She swings round on the handrail and jumps down onto the patio, landing neatly with her feet together. Her eyes flash at me.

"Let's go down and have a look! Come on! Let's get our bikes."

"We're going to see the fire," I inform Elijah as we let ourselves out of the gate. "Can you tell our parents when they come home from the shopping please?"

"You be careful." Elijah sets his shears aside. "These bush fires, they can be too dangerous."

"We'll watch out," I promise, waving to him. I have to pedal fast to catch up with Rosie.

She speaks without looking back at me. "What an old woman! He's worse than an old hen. A *huku*."

She was right. The fire's on the other side of the shopping centre. I scan the parking area on the way past but don't see Dad's car. As we get closer, I start to wonder if the bushfire's on the hundred acres of open ground immediately south of Makuti Park.

And it is. There's a fire engine parked near the perimeter hedge and a mixed crowd of on-lookers on the roadside verges, assorted bicycles lying in the grass. Rosie jumps off and drops hers, but I go, "Uh-uh! We'll take the bikes over there. Chain them to that streetlight."

Dad'll have my guts for garters if they get stolen.

My lock is just big enough to go round the column but Rosie's isn't so we waste some time arguing and then attach her bike to mine.

"Look, there's Timothy and some others from your class," she informs me, but I'm scanning the Makuti Park boundary. The fire hasn't got near it yet, and the grooms are there, manhandling a hose between them and spraying the hedge with water. In the distance, on the western and southern reaches of the open ground, I can just make out figures bobbing in the heat-distorted, yellowish haze. Probably householders and their gardeners doing the same thing, and beating at flames with anything from hessian sacks to leafy branches.

The blaze is sweeping westwards from the road, devouring the tall, dry grass and tinder-like thickets, scorching them within seconds. Behind it is a wide path of black soot and charred sticks, and an acrid smell. A second fire engine is parked at the end of a gravel track that runs through the middle of the vacant land. The track's probably acting as natural firebreak.

The flames in the long grass and the trees are great searing sheets of intense heat. Doused by water from the fire hoses, they're cut short in their tracks, but any nearby scrub or clump of thicker grass needs only a spark to explode it with a roar.

So here are the boys now, being boys, daring each other to get closer to the action. Rosie and I find ourselves drawn cross the road in the small mob behind them.

"It's a *lekker* fire, hey?" Timothy bawls at me. "It was my dad who phoned the Fire Brigade."

"My mum also phoned," someone's small voice protests. There are shouts from the direction of the fire engine; the grass on the opposite side of the track has ignited.

"*Yussis!* It's jumped the road!" Timothy whoops, and we edge on a little further.

"How did it start?" Rosie shouts.

"Dunno." Timothy's not interested, but Alan's keen to enlighten us.

"Probably there was a piece of broken glass in the field. Glass focuses the sun's rays into a point as they are refracted through it and then…"

Timothy brings us all to a halt, arms outstretched.

"Right troopies, let's help the firemen! We need a brigade to grab those beater things over there. Alan, Tessa, Brian… um, me of course and… Kevin… and Ian."

So he's selected me as the only girl? I'm up for it.

Hot on his heels, I can only see five beaters and there are six of us in his brigade. I'm not as fast as Timothy or Ian but I have a lead on the others and I'm keeping it. I snatch one. It's basically just three broad rubber strips, each about a metre long, attached to a stout wooden handle. Right behind me, Rosie's shrieking, "Let me! Let me!" She's not in the Under Tens' athletics team for nothing.

Unfortunately for her, I'm her elder sister and protector, so I go, "You stand well back. I don't want to see you near the fire."

She's crestfallen, so I reconsider. "Well, perhaps you can have a go just now."

I've seen this done before. I can do it. Advance on a bright orange ring of tiny flames that are spreading across some shorter grass, fling the rubber strips high over my head, slice downwards, thrash at the minute ring of fire. Like a lot of things in life, it's harder than it looks, but after a few wildly inaccurate slashes I get into a kind of rhythm. Crisp black shards of burnt grass swirl around me and I can feel the smoke in the back of my throat. My eyes are stinging and watering but the small flickers are dying under my strokes. Immensely satisfying.

I get lost in it. I work my way along, muttering to myself, "Ha! Gotcha! And you, and you!" and get a little smug when I see I'm having more success than Timothy and the other boys. They lost their battle when the wind took their small section of fire into a dense thicket and from there into uncut grass beyond and they've been forced to stand aside for the fire crew.

Squinting through watery eyes, I check out the Makuti Park hedge again. The worst of the fire's headed away towards the southwest now and the grooms are beginning to reel in their hose, a well organised team, each handing the next man a section, chanting as they do so, "*Dhonza! Dhonza!*" Dragging my beater, I stomp through some unburnt tussocky grass and a smokey haze towards the hedge. There's George and Matthew, Lazarus and Mike, and behind Mike is a slim figure dressed in jodhpurs rather than overalls. It's Nathan.

He's pulling, hand over hand, chanting along with them, coiling metres of the thing into the small trailer Charles tows to his sites sometimes. One by one, the grooms gather beside him until it's only George left, bringing in the business end of the hose. George gives Nathan a smart salute, and then he and Matthew take up the trailer's tow bar. With all the others, including Nathan, pushing from behind and on the sides, they roll the trailer back to the open gate and into the five-acre field. Lazarus breaks away to detach the hose from the tap at the trough. He shouts something to Nathan who, incredibly, puts on a kind of circus performer act, twirling a hand in the air and bowing, with one foot outstretched.

No-one sees me standing there at the gate, amazed beyond belief. Lazarus doubles up and slaps his thigh with an open palm. I hear Nathan's reply, but he's speaking Shona and I don't understand a word. The two of them do a high-five and get back to helping the others push the trailer.

My few random Shona words and phrases – horsey stuff I've learned from the grooms – didn't help me with any of that. Now that Mr Westfield's going to make the Standard Fives do Shona classes once a week from next year, I'll be able to up my vocabulary. I'll never be able to speak it like Nathan does though. Not even Gill's at that level. Mum and Dad don't know any, except for *chenjera imbwa*, and that's only because Dad bought that sign. Mum got all bothered when she read Mr Westfield's letter, and said things like, "I don't know why he's made it compulsory. There's no need for the girls to learn Shona. When are they ever going to use it? I don't understand why he's made it compulsory."

Dad, at least, got Mr Westfield's logic. He replied, "Because no-one will go if he doesn't."

Of course Timothy's dad thought it was a good idea.

"My dad says you can't be in charge of them properly if you can't speak their language. You need to know when they're back-chatting you as well."

"Hey," a voice calls out behind me. And weirdly, it's Timothy. He catches up with me, out of breath.

"Howzit? You did a good job there."

Behind him, through the lingering smoke, comes a small figure, struggling with a branch almost as long as the child is tall. It's Rosie, and it looks like she's somehow ripped a young branch from one of the Cypress trees near the road. Or maybe she picked up one someone else had discarded. She's a bit late.

"I was going to help!" Her feet are raising little clouds of cindery dust and the Cypress limb dragging behind her is stirring up more black dust. Her once-white socks are now a murky grey and the tip of her nose is black.

Timothy's hovering. I think he wants to talk, but I'm being torn in two directions – one towards my sister to make sure she's okay and the other in Nathan's tracks to the stables, to visit the horses. The horses will likely win, since Rosie's looking pretty healthy, if disgracefully filthy. I can't work up any interest in whatever he wants.

"Some fire, hey? But we beat it."

"Mmm." I edge towards the gate while holding out a hand to Rosie. He starts to follow me.

"Do you like *Band on the Run?*"

"Um, yes, of course," I assure him, failing to make any connection between the song and our current situation. I kind of wish he'd go away. I've got things to do.

Literally the second I grab Rosie's hand and commence to drag her off to the yard, there's a whole lot of shouting from somewhere behind us. About fifteen kids have gathered around one of the fire engines, making a heck of a racket, and Alan Marchwood's waving to us with both arms.

"Come!" he yells, and he's pointing at the vehicle, again with both hands. The black crew are winding up hoses and opening doors and tossing in bits of equipment, but it's the white officer in charge who's working everyone up into a frenzy. A couple of them are clutching at parts of the engine, staring upwards as though they're about to climb it.

Timothy leaps into the air as if he's been electrocuted. "Wow! *Yes way!* Looks like we might get a ride! Come on!"

He attempts to fling his beater into the air, presumably with the intention of catching it again like a drum major on parade, but the rubber strips get tangled together, and it's heavy anyway, and he nearly falls over.

I can always go back to the stables later. With Rosie's grubby hand in mine, we charge after him. Somewhere along the way she abandons her branch.

Most of us manage to claim a space on the fire engine's running boards and the smaller ones get lifted right onto the top by members of the crew, where they cling to the railings and the ladders. I have a go at climbing up to be next to Rosie but I can't find a foothold so I have to stay on the running board. Timothy's leaning out at an impossible angle and shouting incomprehensibly.

"You will fall off!" bellows one of the firemen above the roar of the engine and the crunching of the gravel under its tyres. Timothy shrugs and moves inboard a fraction.

Where the gravel track meets the main road, we turn right, roll on fifty metres or so and then pull up on the verge.

"Everybody off!" calls the white fire officer, and I swear he's just as excited as we are. We take our time. The crowd of spectators has grown and I for one want to make sure I've been seen riding a fire engine. I've spotted Jess standing on a culvert headwall nearby and can't believe my luck.

"Jess! Hi, Jess!"

Her face goes through confusion and amazement to envy, but she fights it and manages to look disinterested within seconds. Her hair is damp, hanging in ringlets around her shoulders.

Rosie and I jump up onto the wall beside her.

"You haven't been swimming? In *winter?*"

Her eyebrows arch upwards. "*Ja.* Of course. Practice makes perfect. I did fifty lengths."

"You must be *penga.*"

"I'm used to it. I love swimming. You'd go horse riding in any kind of weather wouldn't you?"

Then she winks and gives me an elbow in the ribs.

"So come on. You and Timothy Dunn? You were together over there and then you were next to him up on the fire engine and he couldn't take his eyes off you. Come along, Tessa, have you got something to tell me? Look, he's still watching you."

Sure enough, he is. But my brain has switched tracks with Jess's talk of riding. I was going to call in at Makuti Park to see my horse.

My horse. I still can't get over the fact that I own him. Or does Dad own him? No, of course not. I do.

"I'm not interested in Timothy. Well, we'd better go and see Induna. Quickly now. Come, Rosie."

"That's right, avoid the subject." Jess's looking triumphant.

"Remember Lauren's birthday party?" Rosie's saying, ignoring me. "Kiss catches? Well *I* heard that he really wanted to catch Tess but she was too busy dancing so he caught Debbie Watson instead and kissed her for a full minute. There were loads of witnesses."

"Who told you that?"

Rosie's looking far too pleased with herself. I reckon she shouldn't be concerning herself with things like that at her age.

"Don't remember. The story goes that they were touching their tongues together. Ugh!"

She shudders and wrinkles her nose.

Timothy calls out to me as I march my baby sister up the road towards the main entrance to Makuti Park, ignoring her protests.

"Bye Tessa! See you at school."

I'm about to respond, purely because I've been taught that it's polite to do so, but Rosie's snigger stops me. I look the other way and keep on walking.

Nathan's disappeared, but Gill is there, working Star Point over the cross county practice jumps in the twenty-acre field. That horse is way above my level. He's a Thoroughbred and he's got an impossible amount of energy. He used to belong to Tammy, but Tammy couldn't cope with him and he's too big for her little sister Sherrie. Gill just laughs and calls him over-keen.

"Wow, that was *amazing!*" I call out as she pulls up after literally flying over that ginormous table.

Even Rosie's impressed. She gawps at them and says, "Jesus."

Gill drops the reins and lies flat on Star Point's neck, clapping her hands against him on both sides.

"Good boy! Beautiful. He's so ready for Donnybrook Trials next October. You going to come along to all the trials with us? We'll be doing most of them next season. We might camp overnight at some so hope your folks will let you come."

You bet I am.

"Camping, Rosie! That'll be cool. Want to come too?"

"Camping? In the rainy season? All that mud? No thanks."

Dad makes such a fuss about his precious petrol coupons and about making us choose which outings we do nowadays, but Gill still gets to go to all the competitions she wants, anywhere and everywhere. Charles may've put one of those *Don't Drive Rhodesia Dry* bumper stickers on his Land Rover but the rationing doesn't affect the Owens like it does us and everyone else I know. I said this to Dad, that day he told us he'd either take us to Ewanrigg or the Balancing Rocks for a picnic but not both, and *he* said, "Charles Owen has friends in all sorts of places. I don't."

TUESDAY 26TH NOVEMBER 1974

Right here, in the present, the scene is unchanged, the world seems unchanged. It's the same road that stretches like a dark grey ribbon across our path, the same dry, brown grass under our horses' hoofs, the same petrol station, banners and signs on the opposite side of the road, next to the same invitingly cool copse of trees we'll ride into in a few minutes to escape the heat. I have the same horse under me, the familiar black mane to touch, the feel of the saddle under my seat and of the reins in my hands. We're still standing here waiting for a suitable gap in the traffic.

And as for the future – well, the *entire* future has been altered, even though I still have to do my geography homework when I get back and swot for a maths test tomorrow.

All I did was ask her what she's going to do when she's finished her M Levels. I wanted to cheer her up. When Gill is quiet and won't smile, she's being bad-tempered. She's worried about the exams, I know that, but I thought I could make her feel better by talking about the end of the exams and leaving school.

She's speaking to me now and I haven't heard a word.

"Tessa? Hello? There – the red car. After that one, yes?"

A red car flashes past and we trot over the road and past the service station. Induna shies at a swinging metal Coca Cola sign but I don't react. Gill and Star Point are in front of us, heading into the path through the trees.

I only wanted to cheer her up when I asked her, "Will you teach riding? Start a riding school like Turnpike?"

For ever I've assumed that would be what she wanted to do. And of course I wanted that too, because I could ride at her school. In the future. That future was a good one – the best one.

When she said, "No. I don't think so. I want to teach horses, not people. What I'd like to do is a little bit of breeding so that I can bring on the youngsters and sell them, and also take in livery horses to school for their owners. So then I could coach those people on their horses – you know, like part of the training programme?" I'd thought that was an all right future as well. She could coach me and Induna and I could help her exercise the other horses and her youngsters.

But then she changed that to an inconceivable future.

"I'll have to be qualified to teach at all though, and I can't get any instructor qualifications in this country. So guess what? Dad's promised to send me over to his brother's family in England so that I can take a British Horse Society instructor course. I'll probably take a year out first though, after leaving school, and go over when I'm nineteen. Do the course, get some experience, you know?"

I don't want to know. Go to England? I've got to try and put her off.

Even as I think this, I realise I can't. She needs to go. She'll go, and she'll like it so much she'll stay and never come back. Five kids in my class have left Rhodesia this year and I know they won't be coming back.

Think. Try to remember why Dad reckons the UK is so awful and why we should be so pleased we live here. IRA bombs, rioting, strikes, Labour governments, drugs, pornography. I open my mouth to inform Gill of this line-up of political and social evils I know nothing about, and say, "England's cold! Well, I've never been there but Daddy says it rains all the time."

We drop to a walk. Gill sighs and twists her flaxen pony tail up off her neck with one hand, then tosses it aside and tugs at the brim of her riding hat as if she wants to lift it. Her forehead and fringe, like mine, will be disgustingly sweaty.

"On a day like today I could do with a little English cold. I'm sure it's not that bad. Anyway, it'll be exciting and I'll get to ride some lovely horses. Hunters and warm bloods. We have very few of those here. Our competition horses are mostly Thoroughbreds off the track."

She's really turned into a grown-up now, talking of leaving school and going to study overseas. What happens when school is over? I can't imagine life without school. A very creepy shiver slides through me and grips me and shakes me, and I'm not keen on this unsettled, standing on shifty ground, kind of feeling. I've dreamed up my future as I would like to see it so many times – always involving owning many talented show jumpers and a house and stable yard like Gill's – but this is the first time I've tried to conjure up something real. Everything will change. Julie said Africa will change, but it's not just Africa. I snatch a passing idea that might just keep things more or less as they are. Make a decision. Announce it aloud.

"I want to work with horses too. I could also do a course in England."

She turns on me like she can't believe I just said what I did.

"Don't be silly, Tess. You're so clever. More academic than me. It would be such a waste. You should do a job that will earn you lots of money."

The ground's shifting again. While I'm groping for an answer to that, she carries on as if it doesn't matter. "Did Rosie have her tonsils out?"

Tonsils? Rosie? Oh, yes.

"Last week. She didn't think she'd come out alive, but she did. She won't stop boasting about how much ice cream the nurses in St Anne's let her eat and then she only went and asked the surgeon to keep her tonsils in a bottle and show them to her after the operation."

Gill closes her eyes and makes a face like she's about to throw up. "Did he?"

"No. He promised, but then he said he'd had to throw them away."

We're nearly back at Makuti Park. When we left here just over an hour ago, the white gateposts and the driveway and the paddocks and the house and stables were as they've always been, as they always will be, and they're still all in place, but now there's something different about them. It's an odd, through-the-mirror kind of view, as if they just might not be here for ever after all.

I don't like it.

SUNDAY 10TH AUGUST 1975

The warden – what's his name? – Mr Marsden? He's done this before. This pause for effect after saying, "And lastly, just before you go to your dormitories and unpack your *katunda*, there's one thing I must warn you about. All of you. That includes your teachers. A serious warning."

We all know. Whether he knows we know or not I can't say, but we do. I've been wondering when he'll come up with it and I won't be the only one. He was losing us at one point with his agenda for the week. I'm sure all these lessons will be interesting enough when we get to them, but we've had a long journey. Even Mr Barrie was gazing out across the lake and Mrs King was picking at something under one of her fingernails.

Here he goes.

"We have a hippo in this part of the dam."

Pause. We all react suitably by coming alive again. He goes on.

"She's quite young and she wanders up onto the shore at night to graze so I want you all to be *extremely* cautious. She's never caused any trouble, but hippo can react very aggressively if disturbed. If you want to visit the loos at night, take a good look around before you go across. There are torches in all the dormitories. If you see her, wait for her to move away and whatever you do, don't get between her and the water because that will make her very nervous and a nervous hippo is a dangerous one. Do you all understand? Don't be frightened. Just be sensible and treat any wild animal with the greatest respect."

The hippo – Nathan's hippo. He's learned these things. He wrote a caption under his photos of her, *"Never, EVER get between a hippo and the water!"*

"Oh, and by the way… *Don't* be tempted to swim in the lake just here. There are a few crocs."

I can't recall Nathan mentioning the crocs.

The dormitory's a simple building, long and narrow, just a single large room with a smaller staff bedroom and its own shower room and WC at the end. Mrs King's moved in there and I'm pretty certain it's the same room where the hairy baboon spider was found in Nathan's year.

The long sides of the dormitory are lined with beds and white wooden chests of drawers. Halfway down each side is a pair of French doors, the north facing set opening towards the washroom blocks and the south facing ones giving access to a grassy slope that leads to the dam's edge.

Jess and I choose adjacent beds against the north wall. I've never slept in a dormitory with sixteen other girls before.

"It's like being a boarder, isn't it? At school, from a farm out somewhere in the bush."

Jess is stuffing garments into every last measure of space in the drawers.

"God, why did Mother insist that I bring all this? I took some of it out, you know. She must have put it back in again."

She shakes out a silver and black glittery halter-neck top.

"I'm hardly going to wear this out roughing it in the bundu, now am I? And I can't believe there's going to be a disco anywhere around here."

"Perhaps your mum thinks you might find a boyfriend if you wear your pretty party clothes."

I can't help eyeing the top with some envy. My mother would never've bought me something as daring as that. I don't think you can wear a bra with it. Jess snorts.

"What? One of those creeps in our class? You've got to be joking. Maybe that younger warden though…"

"So stop telling me to show an interest in Timothy then! Speaking of Timothy – look, there he is with his muckers. They're going down to the lake."

Jess drops her top onto her bed. "We can do this later. Let's go exploring."

The shore of the lake is rocky and forms a shallow arc around the bush school complex. The surface of the water beyond the haphazardly piled rocks is a deep blue, almost indigo in colour. Tiny waves lap against the jumbled boulders and leave faint traces of foam before retreating. A narrow arm of the dam reaches out to the west beyond the school and the opposite bank is only a few hundred metres away, rising to form a series of low hills. Broader away to the east, the lake waters heave with a lazy swell and across here the far shore is only a hazy purple line. The sun is nearly at the top of the hills to the west, the shadows are long and the temperature's dropping quite rapidly. We're not quite out of winter yet.

"Nathan told me he wished he could have brought High Time – his pony," I tell Jess just as we reach the others. Timothy's leading, of course, and there's about ten of us in tow. "It sounds like there's fantastic places to ride out here."

She gives me a funny look. "Ride? I sincerely hope not. We can do canoeing, though. On the lake. Who's Nathan?"

I'd wanted to tell him my turn to do Mushandike Week had come at last, but I haven't seen him in at least a month.

I think Dad was quite relieved to drop me off at school this morning. He told me to go and get Mushandike out of my system. To be fair, I've probably been a pain in the neck recently. I even drove Rosie to the point where she wouldn't speak to me. She was huddled in a corner of the back seat when we got there, as far away from me as possible and wearing the mother of all sulks. The coach was waiting and I must have had my nose pressed against the window because Dad said, "Don't you make my glass smeary. I only polished it yesterday."

I was just thinking how cool it was that I was going to get to ride in that huge coach, all shiny black and white and silver, when Mum squeaked, "Doesn't it look splendid, Tessa?"

I impressed myself no end by managing to be both scornful and unconcerned at the same time.

"*Splendid?* What a silly word to use. It's only a coach, Mum."

Actually, it reminded me a bit of a queen termite, surrounded by swarms of ant-kids. There were piles of luggage on the paved car park surround next to it; a haphazard assortment of suitcases, duffel bags, rucksacks, sleeping bag rolls, wicker baskets and supermarket carrier bags.

Dad took just forever to unload my stuff and gave me *another* lesson on how to set the light meter on the camera while I was hopping up and down. Rosie still wouldn't speak to me, even when I said, "Don't worry. You'll get to go in a couple of years." She alternately pouted and looked bored and then bolted when she spotted a few of her classmates with a transistor radio blasting out one of those songs from *Joseph and His Amazing Technicolour Dreamcoat* on the square of winter browned turf near the flagpole.

Jess wanted us to get the front seats, but Mr Barrie wasn't having any of that. Turns out Jess and I weren't the only ones making a bid for them.

"The front seats are for Mrs King and me," he told us, while ticking our names off his list.

Someone in the crowd whined, "But there are *four* front seats!" but he just said, "Well we've got two each then. Aren't we lucky?"

I'll bet they wished they were sitting on the roof when we started singing "*Wo! We're going to Barbados!*" as we left the car park, but none of us knew all the words so it petered out pretty quick.

I'm brought out of the past by Alan. He's highly worked up about something.

"There! What's that? In the water!"

The little wavelets are lapping the edge of the flat boulder we're standing on. About five metres out, between two rocks, I can see a long dark shape just under the water. It's completely still and unidentifiable.

"It's another rock, idiot," says Timothy.

It might be a log or something. It's not moving.

Then it does. It surfaces. It's flat and there are two protruding lumps on each end.

We gasp collectively.

"It's a croc!" Jess snatches at my sleeve. She's right. Two of the lumps are eyes for sure, and the other two will be nostrils.

Before any of us can react, Timothy's stooped, picked up a fist-sized stone and has pitched it at the head, shouting, "Ya! Flat dog!"

Not one of us waits to see what the crocodile is going to do or even whether the stone has landed anywhere near its mark. We take flight as one, and so swiftly that I'm sure the faint ghost images of ten children are left behind on the rock for several seconds. Timothy runs only halfway back to the dormitories with us before slowing to a walk and calling after us, "What a load of yellow bellied cowards you lot are!"

*

The six of us link arms and jostle together to keep on the paved path. Penny has the torch.

"Don't just shine it on the path," Elizabeth hisses. "Move it from side to side so we can see if there's anything around. No, not just down there. Out! Outwards!"

I wander around in our garden at night without a torch often and I've never felt this heart-pumping, hair-prickling, leg-twitching urge to sprint like I have now. Never felt this urge to dive through a doorway into the light. It's Mr Marsden's fault. It was all very well telling us after-dinner stories but he should've left out the one about how crocodiles drown, dismember and then store their prey underwater to rot and get nice and soft enough to eat. Ugh.

FRIDAY 15TH AUGUST 1975

We make our camp around a *dwala* near a river that feeds the dam, in a valley within the gently hilly terrain of the Park. The slope down to the water is punctuated by rocky outcrops and the ground is generally stony underfoot. I notice these things because I'm always imagining myself riding Induna, so I think things like *That would be a nice log to jump* or *If only I could go for a gallop up that grassy slope* or *I'd love to ride along that track into those woods to see where it goes* or *The ground's a bit stony here for too much trotting and cantering*. It's stony everywhere round this park. On the way over here earlier this afternoon, when we met that other National Parks vehicle coming in the opposite direction and the drivers of our three Land Rovers had to pull the nearside wheels off the tarmac strips to make way, the barrage of stones from the gravel shoulder rattling against the underside was so loud I couldn't hear what Jess was saying to me. We left clouds of pinkish dust billowing behind us long after we got back onto both strips. I'm glad I was in the front vehicle – those in the one following had to eat our dust, and the last one – well…

It's a bit – *uncivilised*. The wardens brought tanks of fresh water to drink straight or use to make hot drinks and wash our hands and faces but there are no loos. I'm not very good at going in the bushes. Too exposed. If someone else comes along you can't move very fast with your knickers round your ankles and how do you keep them out of the way, for Christ's sake? Do you have to take them right off? Jess'll laugh at me and tell me I'm a virgin at this. And so I am.

"What are you grinning at?" she says.

"Just wondering how I'm going to break the news to my darling little sister that we had to pee in the bushes. I think suddenly she won't be so keen to come."

"Well it's a good thing Lauren opted not to come out with us for the sleep-out. I don't think any of us would've wanted that now, would we? Messy."

She nods wisely and I agree, "Yes, good thing. Poor Lauren."

I still have no idea what's wrong with Lauren but there's no doubt everyone else does. How come, if she's so ill she's had to stay at the dorm with Mike's wife, no-one's sent for an ambulance or even a doctor? Got to be enteritis or something, surely? Messy. Possibly contagious, even. But no-one's worried. Mr Barrie's oblivious and Mrs King's calm as you like about it after what looked like an initial panic when Lauren went to the toilet in the middle of the ecosystems lecture and didn't come out for half an hour.

"She was so looking forward to tonight. So unlike her to miss out on outdoors stuff," I venture. Come on Jess, say something that'll give me a clue.

"Yeah." Jess shrugs and starts out back to where Mr Barrie and Mike and Dave are piling up firewood.

I give up and follow her.

"Don't you reckon these adults of ours are far more relaxed – well, more human actually – now it's nearly the end of the week?" she asks.

She's stopped and is watching the wardens, Mr Barrie and the cooks unloading packs of steak and *boerewors* from the cooler boxes onto the centre of the *dwala* where it dips a bit into a natural, shallow bowl.

"I mean, Mike and Dave are pretty chilled anyway but take our dear Mr Barrie. Simon. He's turned out to be way more interesting than he ever was in class. He's nice, but he's kind of grey. No personality. And yet, this week, it's like he's come alive. And our Fiona King... well in her checked shirts and her shorts she's really pretty. I hope Mrs Barrie's okay with her hubby spending a week in Fiona's company. And likewise I wonder what Mr King thinks? There, look at him. Now Tess, I ask you again, what do you think of the rugby muscles?"

I had no idea Mr Barrie played rugby before Jess pointed this out to me last Sunday. Now I find myself measuring the tightness of each of his T-shirts and watching his thigh muscles tauten as he climbs into and out of the Land Rovers. I don't tell her though. I'm kind of surprised and a bit embarrassed to find it's actually quite a pleasant pastime, but I'm not going to admit to it.

It'll be dark soon. The flat dining rock is filling up now that most of us have selected our sleeping spots and had a bit of an explore. Only the singing group's still down by the river; the discordant refrains of *Yellow River* are making Mrs King wince. That's another thing I've found out about her this week – she plays the guitar and is a not-at-all-bad singer.

Good thing Joseph and Sebastian have got the fire going in the lowest point of the natural bowl – it's noticeable how jumpers and jackets are starting to make an appearance and how everyone's edging ever closer to the flames. Good thing it's nearly time to eat. I'm starving.

*

Joseph hauls another sack of logs up to the fire and we make way for him to circle it while he inserts four more of the logs into its base. He dumps the sack next to the pile of plastic plates, cooking pots and the frying pans and hunkers down again between Mike and Sebastian.

"Singalong, people," Mike announces, clapping his hands. "A cappella. Come along – what shall we start with?"

A cuppa... what?

We're up for it, anyway. Classic round-the-fire numbers like *Ten Green Bottles* and *One Man went to Mow*, moving on to *Two Little Boys* and *I Never Promised You a Rose Garden* and *Yellow River* again and some other pop stuff and then Mike and Dave sing a few ditties none of us have ever heard, but which have repetitive lines we can learn and join in on. When we started off on these, Mrs King looked like she was squirming but now she's into it, leading on the choruses. Like this one, about this guy whose parachute doesn't open and he has to be scraped up off the runway. It's bugging me that I know the tune so well but I can't remember where I've heard it. I've no doubt these aren't the original words. Elizabeth's looking pretty frigid and shocked and keeps turning to Mrs King and shouting "Hallelujah!" in a very squeaky voice during the chorus but Mrs King's ignoring her like she doesn't care.

Mr Barrie doesn't seem to care very much either. He started off drinking a bottle of Castle every time Mike had one but after a while he slowed down and now I think Mike's had at least four more. But Mike's voice is clear and his eyes are still in focus, while I'm not sure Mr Barrie's seeing anything very well and he's got some serious problems with word pronunciation. That said, each time there's a pause, he insists on trying to explain the lyrics to anyone who'll listen.

"Do you get it? Do you understand?" he quizzes Sebastian, who's managing to be a picture of politeness even though he'd really rather be sitting somewhere else. "It's about a... ahem, a... a... guy who... a *skydiver*, yes, a *skydiver*, whose parachute doesn't open."

I'm sure Sebastian's got that, but he nods and replies, "Oh yes?"

Mr Barrie takes advantage of the current lull to start up again, bellowing about gore and and how the bloke's never going to jump again, waving his arms as if he's conducting a maniac orchestra.

It's all winding down now anyway.

"C'mon." Jess nudges me in the ribs. We creep away to our little hollow and cocoon ourselves in our sleeping bags, pillows touching together on the small, flat rock, reliving the day in whispers while others rustle and shuffle and giggle around us in their own little dens. There are other sounds – strange sounds – animal noises I can't identify. But I'm not bothered. We've got Mike, Dave, Joe and Sebastian to look after us, and although they tried very hard to hide them, I saw the guns. I'm sure we won't get eaten by anything.

SUNDAY 17TH AUGUST 1975

Amai places a rack of fresh toast and the butter dish on the table.

"You want me to bring the strawberry jam or the marmalade, *baas?*"

"Ooh, marmalade I think, please. You're a star."

Charles gestures to me with a sweep of his hand. "Help yourself Tess. Here, take a knife."

"And a plate," adds Moira. "There you go."

I rock up here at eight in the morning and no-one bats an eyelid. They place breakfast before me and involve me in their family time like I've every right to be a part of it. They do know me inside out though and they know I haven't seen my horse for a week.

I'm eyeing up the creamy-yellow brick of butter on the table in front of me.

"We got butter at Mushandike. Real butter, just like you have. Mum won't buy it. She says not only is it expensive, but she wants us to get these poly-un-something-or-others that they put in Sunflower. She says butter is unhealthy."

Charles grins at me and carves off a large slice from the top of the pat, lays it on his toast and starts to work it in with his knife.

"Everything in moderation, my girl. People have been eating butter for centuries and the human race has prevailed thus far. Tell you what, I'd rather eat and drink a bit of whatever I want and die happy than live a couple more miserable years on lettuce and water, thanks. So. How was your week at Mushandike?"

"How long have you got? I gave my folks a minute by minute account yesterday afternoon which I don't think was fully appreciated, although Mum gasped in all the right places. Dad heard most of it, probably. My sister disappeared after the first word. She's furious I got a week off school essentially and she didn't."

"Oh, she'll get her turn," Gill says, laughing. "It's the only reason anyone wants to be in Standard Five. What year is she in now?"

"Standard Three. Well here's the thing though – Mr Barrie reckons there might not be any more school trips to Mushandike. Ever."

She blinks at me, her head cocked to the left. Moira flicks her eyes up, brows arched.

"What? Why?"

"How come?"

Gill and Moira are confused by my surprise news. Charles isn't. His eyes tell me he's already come up with the right answer. His buttery knife is poised over the marmalade jar.

"Mr Barrie said the wardens told him the whole Fort Victoria area's pretty much classified as hot. It's not going to be safe for bunches of school children on a jolly. They're saying they're going to close the conservation school and turn the dormitories into barracks. Soon. So Rosie will never get to go."

Any time spent with the Owens at their kitchen table is never anything other than companionable and comfortable, even when there's a lull in conversation. There's one of those now but it's a long way from comfortable and it has an undertone that almost makes it into a sound. Even Amai has paused her watery clunking in the sink as if she's sensed the altered atmosphere; as if any minute sound she makes might shatter the air. Charles's face, as he lays his knife down across his plate, is for once as unreadable as Nathan's usually is.

"Well, if I'm going to be honest, I'm not surprised. Last week there were three terrorist attacks on lone vehicles along the Fort Victoria to Beitbridge road. That's one of the reasons why the government's in the process of making plans with the Security Forces to provide armed convoys to escort civilians on that route. There's talk of creating several new operational areas that cover the whole country, rather than concentrating on the north and north-east. Now that Mozambique's gone, well…"

Gill sighs. "Fort Vic's where Barry's been stationed lately. They were patrolling out somewhere near Lake Kyle."

Moira snorts and the tension breaks slightly. Amai resumes her washing up.

"When he got himself arrested?"

"Stupid boy!" chortles Charles. "A gallon of booze and suddenly kifing a road sign is a good idea. And God knows where they got hold of the tools to do it."

"You can't blame the troopies for going on benders when they get back into town, Dad. I know he was being a pratt, but heck, he got into three ugly contacts out there. When you don't know when your number's gonna be up you're bound to go a bit mad when you get a weekend pass. And get married ridiculously young. It's happened in every war in history, let's face it."

I wish I hadn't said anything. I've only met Barry the once but he's a part of this family, which makes him a part of my world, and there are no life-threatening situations in my world. It's not right.

Ugly contacts. I know what that means. I've heard the communiqués. Seen Mum and Dad listening to them after the News every night, shushing us if we try to speak while they're on, wearing their serious faces, having muted discussions in their bedroom. But then, when we come home from school with war stories (and there's usually one every other day now – So-and-So's uncle attacked while driving on a lonely road, Whatsisname's brother wounded in a contact or Thingummy's cousins' farmstead revved) we get don't-worry-it-won't-last-long and our-army-is-the-best-in-the-world. That's what they say, but it's *not* what I'm starting to hear in this house. Or at school. We are – and am I admitting this to myself for the first time, or have I known all along? – in the middle of a war.

I mean, just last week, at Mushandike, Timothy told us, "The *kaffirs* want to take over the country. My dad says we've got to fight them off down to the last woman and child. I've decided I'm going to join the army soon. As soon as I leave school."

We're twelve years old. That would mean this'll have to go on for at least another six years. And he can't *decide* to join the army, or not, because it's compulsory. But it won't last that long. It can't.

Charles has been talking all this time and some of his words are touching the periphery of my reverie. Hot areas. A war that can't be won by anyone. More fruitless negotiations between the Rhodesian Front, the Nationalists, Frontline states and the British government. More tantrums, more stalemates. Bloody Smith won't allow the Nationalists into the country to talk terms. You have to give a little if you want to take a little. We need to at least listen to them or we're never going to get anywhere. At least he's had the sense to free the detainees.

He's already explained to me that Robert Mugabe, Joshua Nkomo and Ndabaningi Sithole got set free so we could make a settlement with them, but in the end no-one can agree on how to do this.

Dad calls Mr Sithole, "Ndaba-Nincompoop". He would disagree about this talking lark though, wouldn't he? He would say things like, "You can't talk to these people. They just bang on about majority rule right now. They can't rule the place. It won't happen. Our Smithy knows what's what. Talking's useless. Look what happened when they sent those South African police to parley with a bunch of gooks. Violence is the only language these bastards understand."

The South African policemen went in unarmed and got gunned down. Timothy told us. No negotiations. Not even a battle. Just, well, murder, I guess.

Dad's convinced we'll win the war in no time at all and Mr Smith will be Prime Minister for ever and we'll never hand over the country to anyone. He whinges that the two new black members of his golf club will bring the standards down and it's all doom and gloom and then in the next breath tells us that the economy is booming and the future hasn't looked so good in a long time. I come over here and Charles tells me that the attitude of the whites has to change, move on, and that the foreign currency and import cuts have affected his business pretty badly, and that the rising cost of defence will cripple the economy.

I believe Charles. It's a weird thing to say, but the person I am deep, deep inside my head, and also my body, my core, tells me that *his* version of the current situation, of the past and of the future, is the one that is. I am meant to be a product of my parents. I am meant to be what they want me to be. They have unshakable confidence that I'll believe what they believe, and I'll know without doubt that what they say is true. They trust me to know that they're guiding me through life. And what right have I got to dispute this? But what they don't explain fully enough is that other people have other opinions. That other people believe in their own opinions.

They would say they know this, of course. They're not unreasonable people. But what *would* puzzle them – disappoint them? – is the idea that I should listen to, take note of and consider believing those other points of view. Rather than theirs.

He startles me by scraping back his chair, standing up, announcing, "Right. I need to go to the Farmers' Co-op. You girls coming?"

Everyone's getting up now, taking crockery and cutlery to the sink. Gill's telling Amai not to worry, to go and sort out the laundry stuff; she – Gill – will wash up the breakfast plates.

Then over her shoulder, "No thanks Dad. We can't, because I'm going to give Tess here a lesson. And she needs to commune with her horse. He's missed her."

Moira's saying that's sweet and that I must take a large carrot from the veggie rack down to the yard for Induna, and then the Nowhere Boy appears in the kitchen. I didn't even know he was in the house.

He refuses an offer of the last piece of toast from Moira.

"Thanks all the same. It's already gone cold. I like the butter to soak into it when it's warm. I'll just grab some coffee and then take High Time out for a hack."

That's exactly how I like my toast.

"You're back," he says to me, taking a mug from the plastic basket next to the sink and shaking some drops of water off it. "Did you see the hippo?"

I nod. Manage a smile. "Hannah? Hannah the hippo? Yes, she was there."

"See ya later," calls Charles, exiting, tossing his car keys in his hand and bending down to kiss Gill on the cheek while she's pulling on her jodhpur boots at the back door. She beckons to me, laughter all over her face.

"Hannah the hippo? Classic! Come on Tess. Let's go get tacked up."

He's not looking at me. He's wiping a tea towel over the mug, so I start edging towards Gill and the door and then turn away. Behind me, he asks, "And the eland? Huge, aren't they? Did you hear the way the tendons in their legs click when they walk?"

I did indeed. I remember the day Mike told us to listen to them walking, calling out to us as we stood up in the open Land Rovers, watching the herd watching us. Huge, buff coloured antelope. Not as graceful as some, but magnificent, massive, curious and unafraid. Earlier, Charles wanted me to tell him about my week, and there are so many stories I could recount, especially to Nathan because he's been there too. We could put together a book, couldn't we? *Tales From Mushandike*. But the moment's gone and it's too late to revive it.

I need to treasure those memories, because Mushandike's a thing of the past now. We met a hippo and some eland, a family of warthogs and some jackals and we learned how to track animals and about ecosystems. We climbed a rockface near the dam wall and we ate our dinner and sang songs around a campfire in the middle of nowhere. We watched a sheep being dissected and measured the length of its small intestine, and Elizabeth threw up. We imagined ourselves to be a band of Mashona escaping the marauding Matabele by using that natural rock tunnel hidden in a hillside, crouching and scuttling along it in the dark. We just had such a good time. And then, yesterday, it was over. The birdsong woke us early and the dawn was all pink and misty and we ate bacon and eggs around the revived campfire while the sun gradually rose up over the tops of the trees and its light crept down towards the ground. Then we had to go. None of us wanted to leave, just like, I'll bet, so many other school children over the years, but we had to go home. We left a bush school and soon it will be just an army barracks. Maybe Barry will stay there, in the dormitory where Jess and I were. Maybe Nathan will get to go back.

I guess hope is a thing of the past too. This is real, isn't it? There really is a proper war and it's just arrived on my doorstep.

PART TWO
NO GLORY IN WAR

MONDAY 3RD MARCH 1980

There were no scenes of violence. Television crews and reporters have sent footage and shots of smiling voters in lengthy but jovial queues, under the watchful eyes of our multi-national mentors, all round the world.

So here we are, sitting together as a family on our sunlit patio at the end of a day spent in limbo. Dad is even more morose than he was at the end of last week. He's scowling at the droplets of condensation trickling down the outside of his beer glass. No-one's spoken for a good twenty minutes, not even Rosie. She's reading, rather than trying to talk over me and Mum about her day at school and Alicia's party next week and Heather's dreadful new haircut and Rob's latest, tight-fitting polo shirt. I can't think of anything to say about anything and Mum's intent on mending the hem of her grey skirt. We all know what's going to happen – we just don't know precisely how it will happen.

SATURDAY 27TH MARCH 1976

Halt, make Induna stand for several seconds, tell him he's a good darling. Don't look at the gate.

I love you, Indie. You're so willing and you always give me your all. So I wanted to add a third jump to the grid for you to do, but not now. Not now I'm all flustered and self-conscious, because I'll mess something up for sure. I'll make an idiot of myself. In front of *him*.

Okay, just walk on and slip the reins. I do look at the gate, although I'm still telling myself not to. Can't resist it. He's watching me, caressing High Time's nose as she stands with her chin on his shoulder. One of us is going to have to say something.

"Do you want to use the ménage? I've finished. He's going well. I'll come back and dismantle the jumps for you."

My voice sounds well-controlled, which isn't how I feel. I want to disappear, show off *and* ask his opinion of my beautiful pony all at the same time, but I know I won't do any of these things.

He yanks the gate bolt with a screech of metal on metal and says, "Okay. It's all right. Leave them, thanks. I'll use them too," from behind his impenetrable mask.

Dismounting, I ask, "How's Hightie?"

There was no need to ask that question. I'm getting like my mother, just saying things for the sake of it now. I run up the stirrups, watch him out of the corner of my eye.

"Oh fine." He swings into the saddle. Mounting in the conventional way, but with an agility that's almost liquid.

As conversations with Nathan tend to have abrupt endings, I'm prepared to let it go at that and cluck my tongue to encourage Induna to follow me to the gate, but this time he hasn't finished.

"I'm really getting too big for her now. Uncle Charles has bought me a new horse. He's coming next month."

That pricks up my ears. I turn back to face him, causing Induna to check his stride and eye me expectantly. Nathan is tightening the girth, one leg hitched up over the front of the saddle. Without looking at me, he tells me that the horse is a six-year-old gelding and that after a tricky start he's rapidly gaining dressage points and has recently won a C Grade jumping class.

"What's his name?" I ask, wondering, have I heard of him?

"Oh something complex and ridiculous as usual," he replies dismissively. "It's Red Lane whatsit-whatsit-whatsit. Er, Red Lane Stud's Garden Party. Bloody silly name."

With a slight movement from his seat and hands he persuades High Time to drop softly onto the bit and shift into a perfect square halt. He's watching her ears, which are turned slightly back towards him and it's one of those rare moments when his mask dissolves. All I can see in his face is, undeniably, love.

Then it's gone and he looks over at me, making me flick my fascinated eyes away and pretend I'm not really that interested.

"I shall call him Bravo."

That's so cool. I should tell him. Flick back again.

"Perfect! Much better."

It's lame, but the almost-smile tweaks his lips for a second. He doesn't reply. He just gives High Time the minutest of squeezes and walks her onto the track.

The temperature's soaring now it's nearing lunchtime. I've got some serious hunger pangs that are telling me I had no breakfast. And I need a shower. Indie's rubbing his muzzle up and down my back, pushing me against the gate and through it so now I'll have greenish horse-slobber streaks on my T-shirt. Nathan will see them, but hey, he must empathise with that. If he even notices me go.

I *must* tell George to oil this bolt.

*

Funny how I'd never even heard of a rice salad before Moira asked me if I'd ever made one.

Mum's salads consist of paper-thin slivers of tomato and cucumber hidden in piles of Cos lettuce, unvarying and boring as hell. Everyone else's mother is capable of producing multi-coloured and multi-textured concoctions containing interesting things. Potatoes and eggs, capsicums, fruit, pasta, seeds, nuts, an endless variety of tasty dressings and, unbelievably, bacon chunks. Take Moira's recipe here, with cooked brown rice, spring onions, walnuts, pine nuts, celery, apple and avocado slices, all tossed in walnut oil and vinaigrette. The only purpose the beastly tomatoes serve is as a garnish. Presumably Charles brought the walnut oil back from Jo'burg last month. I didn't like to ask.

She thinks I should write out the recipe and take it home to Mum, but I know all I'll get will be the usual excuse that it's no good her buying all that stuff and then finding she doesn't like it. No sense of adventure.

It tastes amazing, even if I say so myself. I use the spoon to smooth over the dent I've made, pause and munch and stare out of the window in front of me. The back garden's so green, lush and glowing under a mild March sun and the rockery's overflowing with leafy plants that only appear at this time of year. It's how I imagine the Hanging Gardens of Babylon must have looked. I picture that every time we climb up there to sit on the Lion Rock and drink orange juice and eat Amai's delectable shortbread and talk. It'll still be too hot up there today. Best in winter, when it's the warmest place after the sun has slid around towards the north, leaving the front garden in shadow.

I swallow my mouthful and turn to Gill.

"Nathan told me he's getting a new horse. Sounds lovely."

Her eyebrows shoot upwards. "He told you that, did he? Well, well, well. He's not said much about it. Yes, that's right. It's got quite a few issues but I'm sure he can do something with it. Bloody nice horse. It's a belated birthday present and also Daddy's incentive to try and get him to work hard for his O Levels this year, and to be honest he's been a little miffed that Nathan hasn't been displaying much in the way of enthusiasm. Well, nothing new that he keeps himself to himself I guess. Typical going-it-alone. Probably working out a training regime though, if I know him."

"Nathan's birthday was in January, yeah? What date? He never has a party, does he?"

"No. Not interested and the folks gave up trying. It was on the fifteenth. Turned sixteen this year. I can't believe it – him doing O Levels already. And getting his driving licence."

She leans her left hip against the edge of the worktop and folds her arms, staring through the window into the garden. "God how the years fly by. He's not had the easiest time as you know and getting him to take an interest in anything he does, not just birthdays, has been hit and miss. Got no self esteem, but maybe at the back of his mind somewhere he's still the same kid he was *before*. One that still respects himself after all. I'd like to think he'll go on and get his M Levels next year too before he has to go into the army. At least then he's set up for getting a good job. Listen to me, Tessa! I sound like I'm his mother. He'll end up working in Dad's company I'm sure."

"He honestly did sound like he was pleased to be getting his new horse. At least I thought so."

She's moved on though, shifted to another track. She snaps her middle finger and thumb together in my direction.

"Hey, you know I was talking ages ago about enrolling on a British Horse Society course in England? Well, I got a reply from a training yard this morning. They've granted me a place! I'm going over in three months' time. Just three months! It sounds super, Tess. It's at a BHS approved riding school in Surrey and I'll be a student there, a live-in student, and I'll get paid for doing work in the yard alongside my studies. I'll get to compete on their horses and I'll be over there for just over a year."

She's leaning on the worktop now, propped on her elbows, chin on her clasped hands. Her eyes are dancing right in front of me.

I'd forgotten all about that. Assumed she had too. For her, this is my cue to get all enthusiastic, excited to find out more, but the world, seconds ago normal and sunny and horsey and congenial, has fallen flat on its face, sending my belly sliding around with that same sense of disquiet I discovered when she first told me. The opportunities she'll get overseas could, for all I know, be so good as to convince her to stay in England for ever.

And this winter we won't be sitting together on the Lion Rock drinking juice and eating shortbread and swapping stories, will we? She'll be there and I'll be here. I might never see her again. And not just her. In virtually the same breath she's tossed me two feel-good destroyers with no notion of what she's done. It's not just her who will be gone from this, my second home. Nathan's fast approaching the end of his school career. He'll go too. The dreaded call-up.

A chilling mixture of emotions.

"But soldiers are always, like, grown men," I protest, aloud, unintentionally.

"What?" She cocks her head on one side, smiling, unable to follow my train of thought.

I flick a hand in the air to fan away the last few minutes like *braai* smoke, search for the necessary words and fail to find them.

"Nothing."

At least try to sound enthusiastic, Tessa. Ask a few questions. Will she meet any of the famous riders we follow in the magazines – Harvey Smith, David Broome, Lucinda Prior-Palmer? Will Lucinda know who *she* is? Will she go fox hunting?

She laughs, tells me she doubts it, says no, they'll never have heard of Gill Owen from Darkest Africa. And yes, she possibly will end up doing some hunting.

But I'm not paying much attention to her answers. I've gone back in time to some day last year and a conversation we had in this very kitchen, mentally scrolling through the names of some of the boys in my own year at school as though they're credits on the cinema screen; Timothy Dunn, Alan Marchwood, Richard Hall, Mark Hainsworth, Leon Tanner, Mike Groenewald. Seeing Timothy, wanting his piece of the action, his chance to fight. And, maybe his chance to die and get his name on the Honour Roll. Has he thought about that?

Isn't it better to just stay a kid? Peter Pan wanted to. I do. But they won't let us. It's no wonder the boys are already thinking of getting out of school. We're barely three months into the first year of senior school and they've started us on special lessons about how to study for and pass public exams and next term Mrs Parks says she'll be giving us career advice sessions. Career advice? We've only just started on this path and they're prepping us for what's going to happen at the end. Like, this is it guys – you can't be kids anymore.

It's a bit of a shame my last memory of junior school is of that interminable Speech Night back in December. They got the name right okay. Sitting on a hard chair in a hot, stuffy hall all evening while Mr Westfield rambled on and on about how well we'd all done and how much the cake sales and the jumble sales raised and what the money'd been used for and how our teams won this and that and, gosh, we'd got *two* new Governors in one year and then those two Governors followed suit and made more ramblings about... what? I haven't a clue. I'd stopped listening by then. The whole evening was, literally, one monumental pain in the nether regions.

Then the prize-giving. We were right at the end of course, us Standard Fives. Any sense of pride I might've had about winning awards had long gone by the time I got to be passed across the stage from hand to hand, from Mr Westfield to a Mr Thingy with a pompous goatee beard and then to a Mrs Something-hyphen-Something Else with a plum in her mouth.

Like the scrolling names, I'm watching memories of the evening rolling across my mental vision. Jess, dropping an elegant curtsey to the Headmaster as he placed the sash over her head and making the audience laugh, such a long way from the shy, timid girl who cried in the toilets when bullies like Lauren and Karen teased her about her mouth brace and her glasses. Jess, with her hands full of certificates and tokens and badges, collecting the First Prize for Academic Achievement for the third year in a row and the School Colours for swimming and diving. My Rosie, bouncing onto the stage to receive the Most Improved Tennis Trophy, vivacious and vibrant, her unruly dark hair trapped into two curly bunches by strong elastic and wide ribbons. Monty Papadopoulos, tripping on the top step and ending up on his knees and going so bright red he looked like one of the tomatoes on my salad. Mum, watching me exiting stage left, dabbing at her eyes with a square of pink tissue.

I guess she's got issues about this growing up thing too, hey? Probably why she was acting so emotional. She might have also been seeing a string of images running through her head in double-time, like an old movie. Her first baby, then me as a toddler, then a second baby, then growing children turning into gawky teenagers. Flashes of me and Rosie, her and Dad, living our lives. Her, busy raising us and us busy being us. All mothers must do this, surely, and wonder what on earth their kids are going to come up with next, or achieve in five years' time. Was she also thinking, though, that added into this recipe for nostalgia and pride and speculation is the fact that the future of this country seems to be sliding into a wobbling dive? That any hopes she has for a secure life for us are on shaky ground?

Was it last week, when Moira reminded me about the curfew? Must have been last Sunday, when I took Indie for that long hack and got back here just after six. She's never, ever, told me off for anything before. I need to get used to remembering that the limits of the curfew area are only five kays away, because that's nothing to me and Indie.

It's yet another thing that's changing our lives, like how we can't go to Beira for holidays anymore. Jess's been to there every year for the last five. Beaches, seafood, all the stuff we don't have here, and cheaper than South Africa, but now the border's closed. Charles reckons we'll never get those railway engines back and on top of that, South Africa's now our only trade outlet. All our eggs in one basket, he says. Alone, cut off, condemned. Conducting cross-border raids on military camps in Mozambique and taking out civilians in the process isn't helping our case, is it?

Dad says it's too bad. All is fair in war.

SATURDAY 26TH JUNE 1976

Outside everything's sparkling with sunshine and the frost has nearly all gone, so the only crusty bits of lawn are those still in the shadows of the hedges. We sit in Gill's room, face to face, cross legged on the dark rose pink carpet, and try to predict how her year will go. We started off near the window, but we've moved four times to keep in the squares of sunlight.

Gill is as upbeat and sparkly as the day outside. I'm listening, going along with it, adding questions here and there, but I want to tell her to stop it. Stop being cheery and happy and excited. You can't make me be the same, contribute to the jokes, be normal. Not today.

I can't keep my eyes from the suitcase and duffle bag parked in the corner by the door. She's going. Life at Makuti Park without her is unimaginable. I sure as hell don't wish to listen to what she's going to get up to in England. I am *trying*, honest, but I'm not succeeding. No way.

So when she says, "Wow, I can't believe this time tomorrow I'll be in Surrey. D'you know, it might even be warmer there than it is here right now? The days will be long and we'll be able to ride out until, like, I don't know, ten o'clock? I'm kind of looking forward to that. It will be so different, don't you think?" I give up the pretence and blurt out what I'm really thinking.

"You will actually come home next year won't you?"

She blinks at me, then takes me by the shoulders and studies my face with those doll-blue eyes.

"Oh Tessa, don't cry please. Of course I'll come back. This is my home and I don't want to leave it. I'm excited about Star Point's future anyway. I want to ride him again for sure. I need to get this qualification though. You do understand that, don't you?"

I nod, turn away. I'm not crying, but I will if I keep looking at her.

She slips her arms around behind me, squeezes, and rocks me gently in them. "You – we need to think about your riding career too. You should consider putting Induna into the Novice class at the horse trials in Umwindsidale in, when is it – October?"

"What? Without you?" I wriggle out of her grip, shaking my head. No. Absolutely not. What on earth's made her think I'd enter horse trials for the first time while she's not here?

"I need your advice and support at my first go, Gill!"

She thinks that's funny.

"Have you forgotten that my parents exist? That it was them who encouraged me the first time I entered any sort of competition? Who've helped *me* all these years? Come on Tess. Mum and Dad will pull you through it. Induna will do a good dressage test and you know all about the show jumping now. Get Mum to talk you through the cross country phase. She can take you over to Turnpike to practice cross country jumps. Remember how you and Indie did so well the last time we went there? Mum's brilliant with that sort of thing and she'll love it and she'll use you as a kind of substitute daughter while I'm gone. You're family now anyway. I do feel like I have a sister *and* a brother."

Her whole face is glowing at me. "And you and Nathan are neither!"

That's done it. It hits me like a tidal wave and almost knocks me out of breath and I give this odd little howl that I certainly didn't intend to come out. Gill is leaving, which is bad enough, but what really clouts me is the realisation that I love her family quite as much as my own – *and* am loved back. Here I am, seeking more advice and help from the Owens than from my own parents. I *want* their advice and their help. What sort of disloyal daughter does this make me?

"Whatever's the matter?"

Gill gasps, frowns, smiles and frowns again, but I can't tell her. I just sob.

"I *will* come back, honest, my love. Come on."

She rolls up onto her feet and pulls several tissues from the frilly white box on her bedside table. She wipes my face with one of them and pushes the others into my hand.

"Blow your nose. There, that's better. Now let's go out to the yard. We'll tack up Induna and start teaching you some cross country tactics. Tammy's coming at half-ten and she might be bringing her little sister over. You can always talk to her about competition too you know. She's especially good with dressage stuff. Have you met Sherrie, her sister? Pretty little thing."

I allow myself to be led outside.

Nathan's riding Bravo in the ménage. He's a glossy liver chestnut with faint dapple markings, an ochre mane and tail and no white marks – a drop-dead gorgeous sort of horse. An aloof sort of horse. I tried to make friends with him over the stable door last week but although he didn't act like he was going to bite me, he put his ears back and dodged my caresses and my attempts to blow into his nose, then moved to the back of his box and stood there watching me. At least when he did that he pricked his ears forward again. He even keeps a little apart from his companions in the paddock as if he scorns any existing hierarchy and has no desire to be part of it. It's fascinating, because other new horses have invariably just fitted in with what Cactus Dan wants. Dan's been boss for ages and he has issues with Bravo, who's not behaving like he's supposed to. He wastes a whole lot of energy displaying his displeasure, but Bravo watches him with that kind of Do-I-Look-Like-I-Care air about him, and the way the rest of the herd ignores Bravo and Bravo ignores them actually has a kind of harmony about it. It's noticeable now that when Dan tries any of his habitual bullying tactics, the victim hurries over to graze somewhere near Bravo and Dan backs off.

I have this ridiculous notion that if Nathan was to be reincarnated as a horse, he would be Bravo.

Gill rides him well, of course, but he's seventeen hands and with her slight figure she looks a little lost on his back. When Nathan sits on him, however, horse and rider do really become one single animal and Bravo assumes an almost supernatural aura. I'm being whimsical, I know. Bravo has a light, rhythmical cadence to all his paces, as if his limbs were made of elastic rather than of bones, ligaments and tendons, and he has big strides that eat up the ground, and yet he never appears to be moving fast. He has that magical, indefinable quality all my books call 'presence'. There isn't any other way to say it.

They execute a half-pass in trot across the school. The ache of wanting to ride that horse is real and physical, but I'm being over-ambitious here. His type of movement is way beyond any of my experience. I wouldn't dare ask, but if I did I know exactly what Gill would say: "He's too much horse for you Tessa. Maybe one day."

One day… One day.

Nathan is still the same dead-pan, distant ghost flitting into view and then dissolving in a blink, but he must be nearly as tall as Charles now and his sinewy arms and legs have grown hard-edged muscles. His voice reminds me of Charles too, in a way. If Charles were to stand up in front of an audience and read the telephone directory, people would stay just to keep listening.

I keep out of Nathan's way even more than I did before, except when I'm watching him ride, which is when he sticks around the longest. It's like the difference in our ages, not something I've ever thought much about, has, instead of always being constant, suddenly got a whole lot bigger. With Gill in the mix, I'm comfortable, but once she's left the buffer will be gone and it will be just me and him in any of our rare encounters.

I want to like him, but you don't get to like someone really, truly, unless you can get into the sort of twisting, turning conversations that help you find out what makes that person tick, like I do with Gill and Jess. He's too complicated with all those issues and I could quite easily say the wrong thing to him, even though I don't know what the wrong thing is.

Now this is a hard one to figure out: Gill sees him as a brother and now me as a sister and I want Gill to be my sister, but then what will Nathan be to me?

SATURDAY 25TH SEPTEMBER 1976

"So what did your folks think of last night's broadcast?"

Charles springs this on me about ten seconds after Moira's finished running through our lesson plan for tomorrow's cross country schooling. Like he's been itching to do it ever since we arrived in the kitchen.

No need to clarify. 'Last night's broadcast' has been 'The Speech' in our house all yesterday evening and all this morning. Capital T, capital S. Dad sat kind of glum and silent in front of the television last night for a long, long time. I don't think he really knew what came after, although he seemed to be watching it.

I don't particularly want to talk about it but he's expecting an answer.

"My father said, 'Bloody South Africans have got us snookered and they know it. Smithy knows it. We all know it,'" I tell him. "I've heard of snooker, but I had to ask my mother what he meant by that. I didn't dare ask him. We left him alone."

"And?"

Um, can I get this right now?

"She said... She said, like, when two guys are playing snooker, um, one of them can, like, um, get a ball to go... well, actually *place* a ball right in the way of where the other one wants to take a shot to get, um, another ball, like, another colour thing, ball, into one of the holes. 'Cause you have to get all the balls in the holes, don't you? So if you can stop someone from doing that, you..."

He's going to laugh. His face is fighting it. Well, it was a rubbish description. I don't care. I'm not desperate to learn more about the silly game.

Moira's got her serious face on, nodding, but she looks a little *too* serious. Trying too hard.

"Quite right. That's exactly it. So what your dad was really saying is, that whatever he tries now, Smith can't win. Vorster's forced him into a corner."

I guess so. South Africa's going to cut all ties with us unless we get majority rule because if we do that it might take the pressure off them and their apartheid system. Mr Vorster's effectively forcing Mr Smith to give in by threatening to cut off his assistance. Like blackmail. That's what Mum said. And she called them just that: Mr Smith and Mr Vorster. She's always said we should be respectful to adults, who are older and wiser and know better.

The Owens call them Smith and Vorster, and sometimes Charles says "that man Smith" and "bloody Vorster". I have a feeling he doesn't think either of them are very wise at all. They're certainly messing up our lives at the moment. Nobody seems to know what's going to happen next. Actually, that's not quite right. They seem to know now what's going to happen *next*, but not what'll happen after that or whether they're going to like it.

"Have some more shortbread Tess," Charles offers, thrusting the plate under my nose. How can I resist that?

"Kissinger and Vorster hatched the plot when they met in West Germany, didn't they? The Western world must work together to stop the Communists in southern Africa, etc, etc, etc. Achieve an equitable formula in Rhodesia, etc, etc, etc. And bless them, they're prepared to fork out cash for resettlement of all us whites who might want to get out rather than face majority rule. *So* good of them. And I believe it was Vorster who was quite vociferous about that. Has to be seen to be trying to help us, his mates, doesn't he? Only out for himself of course."

"He doesn't want an intensified war here any more than we do," Moira says. "Deep down, he supports the Smith government – same ideals, after all – but Kissinger's forced *him* into a corner as well."

So everyone's snookering everyone else? I've got nothing to contribute so I just watch him while he munches his shortbread and stares into space. Eventually, he sighs.

"That's the thing about politics, Tessa – nobody can really trust anyone else. And Ian Bloody Smith just continues to believe in Gentlemen's Honour. Kissinger makes promises – that sanctions will be lifted, foreign capital will flood in, the economy will boom, we'll rejoin the world in a sense – and our dear Smithy believes him, honestly believes him, and thinks the confidence of all his white voters will be restored. He says that Kissinger was – how did he put it? – 'decent'. He hasn't backtracked on his call for tougher military commitments though, has he, while still reassuring us that all this intensified terrorist activity is only a minor hitch and that a military victory is both possible and probable?"

But my parents *do* have confidence in him. This guy, Henry Kissinger, is blazing round Africa like some sort of fairytale knight trying to find a settlement for us. Dad says he thinks he can please everyone but how often has Charles said you can't please all of the people all of the time? So the compromise is that we'll get a transitional government, which means there'll be two ministers – one black and one white – in all posts. *And*, there'll be a ceasefire.

"He quoted Winston Churchill," I venture, hoping I've remembered what Mum said correctly.

"He did indeed. 'Now is not the end. It is not even the beginning of the end, but it is, perhaps, the end of the beginning.'"

"And what do *you* think?"

He says nothing for a while. Quite a while. Then, "I'm not sure Tessa. I need to think about it. A lot of people are not impressed though. Did you hear? Not an hour after the speech ended, someone – or some people even – took the Rhodesian flag down from its pole in Cecil Square and put up a home-made white one at half-mast. And then nicked a Give Way sign from a junction somewhere and propped it against the base of the flagpole."

And after another pause, "I *am* sort of optimistic. Or at least I'm trying to be optimistic. Smith's trouble, as I said, is that he accepts a man's word as his honour, which is why he experiences such uncomprehending hurt when others, in the nature of humans everywhere, let him down. He and his supporters don't seem to realise we can't have it all our own way. Kissinger has promised the earth to us, but remember that his agenda is to get Smith out. And Vorster's wheedling along with it all, making out he's so happy for everyone."

God, the politicians talk and talk. They even held a complete conference on the bridge over the gorge at Victoria Falls, didn't they? Because it's classed as No Man's Land.

Moira thinks that's funny. "*South Africa* taking responsibility for resolving the Rhodesian problem? That place is hardly a leading light on the march for African freedom. Vorster thinks he's the saviour with all this *détente*, which, my girl, is really just an impressive word to describe the act of going round in ever decreasing circles. What he's actually trying to do is take the spotlight off apartheid. Idiot."

Maybe it will be okay. Mum and Dad think the whole problem will go away and Charles thinks this solution to the problem might work.

Three more kids in my class have gone in the last two months. Helen Edwards to England and James Percival and Karen van Driel to Australia. Helen said her folks are not going to hang around and let her brother, Roger, fight in a war we can never win. Roger is only eighteen months older than us, so, once again, I say – how long is this supposed to last for? How long will it take to lose, if we can't win?

James just said, "Ian Smith will have a lot to answer for."

*

I haven't told Mum or Dad about the conversation in the Owens' kitchen this morning. I won't tell Rosie either, when she gets home from tennis, because she'd tell them for me.

They're stuck in such a deep rut that they're unable to change direction or even see what anyone else is thinking up top. They maintain their convictions: only the whites can rule the country properly, only the whites can maintain law and order and the high standard of efficiency we enjoy, only the whites can maintain the upright morals that we alone manage to have in this depraved world, yes, it's good that the war will end and that the economy will improve, but no, we can't have majority rule.

WEDNESDAY 6TH OCTOBER 1976

She'll come with me. It'll be a laugh. Maybe not for the dressage – she won't get that at all – but the cross country and show jumping're easy to follow. She can cheer me on, can't she? Be one of my team.

So I tell her, "I'm riding at horse trials in Umwinsidale both days this weekend. Why don't you come on the Sunday and watch the cross country and show-jumping phases perhaps? I know you don't like horses much, but you don't have to come too close. It's really exciting and festive and if you wear shorts you'll get a good tan."

Jess hesitates, flicks her eyes around a bit, looks positively shifty.

"I can't," she says.

Oh, right. Well.

This is our weekend planning session, like always. Is she really turning me down? Since when does she refuse a chance to have a laugh and get out in the summer sun?

"You really don't have to go near any horses. Why not?"

"Well, Clive Kenning in Form Two has asked me out. We're going to the cinema with his brother and a couple of their friends."

What?

My happy, horsey train of thought fizzles out, grinds to a halt. I do a kind of mental shake up. Of all the unexpected activities Jess could've chosen to do on a Sunday, going to the cinema with a boy would've been my last guess. This can't be right.

My voice is very reluctant to come out so I end up mumbling, "Oh. All right then."

She's being irritatingly smug.

"Aren't you going to ask what he's like? Never mind, Tess. I'll take a good look at some of these friends and suss out the talent for you!"

Clive Kenning? Never heard the name. He must be new, or come from another junior school. How does she even know him?

I become deaf to whatever she says next, take the sheets I did yesterday's homework on out of my maths file, then put them back in again with a snap of the ring clasps. Junior school and childish exercise books are part of a past life now, although I still haven't got used to this moving around to different classrooms all day. We've got double maths first thing this morning followed by double English and then double science after break. Wednesdays are not good days.

So. Clive. Clive, whom I don't know from Adam, has entered my life and mucked up my weekend with my best friend. We've always been Jess-and-Tess – and I've never minded being second in the name – but how much longer will it *be* our name? Does that all change when you go to high school? When one of you finds a boyfriend?

But *Jess*? My friend, Jess? That's not to say I didn't think she'd ever get a boyfriend, or that I think she's unattractive or anything. Just not yet.

First Rosie, now her. Rosie, my *little* sister, had no fewer than three dancing partners at Angela Walters's party last Saturday, and then she goes and says to me, on the way home, "I can't decide which one I'll marry. What do you think? Who are you going to marry?"

She's eleven, so where's this come from? Planning marriage hasn't yet entered my radar field, but maybe it should. Jess has gone quiet and is gazing absently into nothing with her elbows resting on her school case, so she's probably contemplating it and all.

Is it abnormal to put more of your mental energy into planning your horse's competitions than deciding how and when to get married and who to marry? Have I missed something? I guess I've always kind of assumed it will happen to me at some stage, but…

Jess's brought herself back to reality and is peering into my face.

"Don't worry, Tess. It's just a date and I want to go and I'm sorry I can't come with you to your horsey… jumping… thing."

Horse trials. Has she learned nothing from me?

Then she laughs. "I won't get pregnant from it and have to leave school so I'll still be here. Still haven't started my periods yet anyway."

She sounds almost annoyed, but, believe me, the longer I have to wait for *that* to happen to me, the better.

"My mother only gave me the obligatory mother-to-daughter facts-of-life lecture about a month ago," I tell her. "She cornered me in my bedroom, sat me down on the bed, put her arm around me and told me she had something to explain. Something I might find disturbing. You are growing up, Tessa, she said. Very shortly, I think, you will find things are going to happen to you that you won't understand and I want to tell you about it."

Jess snorts.

"Exactly. I nearly laughed, but Jess, her eyes were so serious and searching. What was I supposed to do? She's obviously forgotten what girls talk about at school. She honestly thought I had no idea."

I've been in touch with the idea since Gill enlightened me five years ago, even though Lauren's 'illness' and behaviour at Mushandike escaped me at the time. I'll never admit to that. But she *was* the first one in our class.

"So what did you say?" demands Jess.

"I thought I'd better reassure her. So I said, 'Oh, I know what you're going to say, Mum. Is it about periods? It's all right. I know what they are and why I'll get them.' She went all disappointed, like I'd stopped her from fulfilling her role."

She's grinning at me. "Have you never told her about your visits to those stud farms with Gill and her mom then?"

"Well yes. But not all the detail. This was her first attempt at sex education, Jess. In her mind I've got no right to know anything prior to getting periods. I'll bet she thinks I still believe in storks. I was diplomatic. Wait till she tries it with Rosie."

"You never mentioned that book then, either?"

"Are you mad?"

I have no idea who brought 'that book' to school and can't for the life of me remember what it was called or who wrote it. I do recall that the protagonists were called Candy and Sherman and that up till then I'd had no clue that any of what they got up to was even possible. Stallions and mares are pretty straightforward animals.

"You could come round mine this arvy and we can play records?" Jess suggests.

So she does feel guilty for turning down my offer. Well, too late for that.

"No, I can't. I've got a training session with Moira. In fact I have one every afternoon this week. Sorry. Perhaps Clive could spend the afternoons with you instead."

She gives me the most pointedly rolled-eyes a person can.

SUNDAY 10TH OCTOBER 1976

The cross country phase is something they'll understand a little better than dressage. I think Dad was the most disappointed of all of them to watch me trotting and cantering in – as he put it – random circles, especially as he's had to miss a golfing session with Uncle Dudley *and* use some of his precious petrol coupons.

He did ask, "So what on earth do all those letters *mean?*" but to be perfectly honest I don't know who dreamed them up, or why, in the first place. I'm sure Gill does. But she's not here.

I told him to wait for the jumping bits because he'll get that.

So now he's cheering as I take off from the start box like a bullet from a gun. Induna's flying, and after the first three obstacles we thunder into the woods, then we'll go over the hill and down into the next valley, so none of them will be able to see us until the finish. I've told them all where to go and stand – I'm sure Moira will shepherd them.

By the time we get halfway round the course I have no breath left. The jumps for the Junior Novice class are only tiny, but the adrenaline surge and the tension and the fact that I'm constantly shouting good boy, oh, what a good boy, hup, whoa, left here, left, left, oh good boy has left me with no air in my lungs. Maybe I need to be fitter.

Moira's there at the finish with her stopwatch and she clicks it with a flourish as we storm past her. I see Mum's, Dad's and Rosie's faces blurred, then we're careering away from them and I'm standing in the stirrups trying to pull up with arms that have far less energy than my horse has. I reckon he could go round again.

"Great time!" she yells after me as I circle round several times. Induna thinks even this is part of the fun.

"You didn't have a stop at the water?"

We finally make it to a standstill, Induna blows and acts surprised that we've stopped, and I'm unable to speak. I shake my head, dismount by sliding down the saddle and fumble with the girth buckles. Moira's holding Induna's head and speaking to Dad.

"There's always one bogey fence, isn't there?"

She's smiling at him, expecting a reply.

"Oh, er, yes," he agrees, frowning. "Always. Bogey. A bogey fence."

Mum hugs me from behind and then recoils ever so slightly from my sweaty T-shirt and number bib.

"You were going *so* fast! I didn't think you'd ride your horse so fast. Really galloping!"

Is she impressed or is she telling me off? I take a few deep breaths and find my voice again.

"That wasn't fast, Mum. It was only a canter. Racehorses gallop."

The results board shows I had no faults across country. I'm in sixth place, on my dressage score.

Show jumping, I let myself get a little too excited by the thought of collecting a rosette and interfere with Induna's stride in the middle of the double combination. He tries to ignore me, but flattens and takes the top pole off the second element. None of those above me get any faults.

I'm irritated with myself that I've ended up seventh, just outside the prizes. Annoyed with myself, adoring my horse, and on such a crazy high. I've done it. I'm an event rider like Gill.

*

Helping Moira and George and the other grooms settle all the horses for the night took longer than I'd anticipated. I never took my bike lights with me and now it's almost completely dark. I'm bloody lucky they haven't extended the curfew zone any further. They wouldn't shoot me anyway. Would they?

Fortunately, Rosie's new tennis coach has just pulled up in the drive, there are shouted greetings going on, the parents are both scurrying about on the patio putting out chair cushions and his

Mazda has blazing headlights. I sneak around the back of it and rush my bike off to the shed before anyone can notice I have no lights.

He's wearing his camouflage fatigues and boots and one of those camo forage caps with the neck-protecting flap that folds up at the back.

"Hi Tessa," he calls out as he slams the driver's door. "Your dad says he's going to pay me some money. Not an opportunity to miss, hey?"

Rosie's waiting for him, also on the patio, and she's waving frantically, jumping around like she's barefoot on an army of ants. Funny, that, after she threatened to give up tennis when her old coach emigrated to South Africa. Since Rob Craddock took over her tuition she's doubled up her lessons and persuaded Dad to buy her a new tennis dress. A shorter one.

He's South African, and is, I think, twenty-six years old. He's a Phys-Ed instructor at St George's College and in the school holidays he inflicts his rigorous physical training on new army recruits. Rosie was in such a foul mood that *first* evening he turned up at our house, to introduce himself and discuss lesson arrangements. He was dressed pretty much as he is now, all camo-clad and dusty and – yes – pretty good looking, with his epaulettes flashing in the dying sunlight, and it was the night she's convinced she fell in love.

I remember her staring down the hill long after his car had disappeared and pushing up the sleeves of her jumper. She sighed. She said, "Isn't he *divine?*"

I was incredulous.

"Go on! It's the uniform. You didn't even want to meet him. He's more than twice your age, for Heaven's sake!"

But she was – still is – completely smitten. She recalls every single word he says to her and she preens herself for an inordinate length of time before each lesson.

He doesn't stay long tonight. By the time I've filled up my bath and am carrying my pyjamas and my book into the bathroom, he's gone and Rosie is wafting dreamily down the corridor to her room.

"Don't worry. You'll survive until the next time you see him."

She pouts and slams her door.

Rob is quite handsome, I have to admit. I reckon I'm unlikely to develop a crush on him, but I've been eyeing up his camouflage forage cap with its back flap because it would be cool to have one to wear at the stables or in the garden. Only trouble is, Dad says civilians are not allowed to wear any item of Rhodesian army uniform so I guess I can't ask Rob to get me one. Maybe I'll mention it to Charles.

FRIDAY 12TH AUGUST 1977

We amble, like we always do, talking, but my ambling is twitchy. I'm too polite. I need to tell Jess, right, sorry, gotta go, things to do, see you tomorrow *ja?* Only knowing about Jess's plans for this weekend, *after* this weekend, would suit me just fine for once.

"So how's Gill? You'll see her today I guess."

You guess right. Need to go. Now.

"Oh fine. I spoke to her on the phone last night. She sounds exactly the same and she didn't utter any strange words or phrases. She says she's had her hair cut and I can't wait to see it. Dad was adamant that we spent nearly two and a half hours on the line and as I had no idea what time the conversation started I couldn't argue, but I know for sure I only strengthened his views about women and yakking. But I don't care. Her letters about her daily life at the yard in Surrey were one thing, but it's *so* much better now we can actually talk to each other again."

We're at the top of her road, but she still wants to stand and chat.

"She survived the winter then?"

"Only just, I reckon. Not impressed. Dad asked the same thing. And given that he's constantly slagging off the British government and the weather and the whole way of life over there, I fully expected him to launch into one of his mud island-striking workforce-degenerate society stories. He didn't, though. Makes a change."

In fact he made no response at all and just started telling Mum about some new road project he was working on. Well, never mind. I have to say I'm kind of relieved she couldn't deal with the winter. At least she'll stay here now. 'Bye, Jess…

I can do my homework tomorrow, or Sunday. Fifteen minutes is all it takes to gobble a sandwich, refuse the biscuits, change into jodhpurs and re-do my plaits. She comes into the bedroom just as I'm yanking the drawstring of my duffel bag to close it and she has that unimpressed air about her.

"So you're off now already? Tell me, what's Jess up to this weekend?"

"Um… I don't… Oh yes, she said she's going boating on Lake MacIllwaine with some cousins and their friends. I got invited, and it's a bit of shame it's the same weekend Gill's back."

It *is* a shame, especially as we're back to being Jess-and-Tess again. No Clive. No more blow-by-blow accounts of *Space: 1999* or *Doctor Who*, no more deep space theories, no more marvelling at the engineering of the Starship Enterprise and no more pointless diatribes on the O Level physics syllabus. No more trying to figure out what she saw in him.

"She spends a lot of time with young people your own age, doesn't she?"

Oh here we go. I spend too much time with the Owens. What's it to her?

She's standing squarely in the doorway like she's trying to block my way. But she hates confrontation and I'm not taking her bait. So I chuck the duffel bag on the bed and waffle on in unnecessary detail about my homework assignments for the weekend and a history test we have next week that I want to swot for and a geography project we've been given and how I want to start this tomorrow. It works. The conversation she wanted has gone and she can't see a way to get it back. She dithers, shifting from one foot to the other and rubbing her hands up her arms and then leans up against the frame to steady herself while she scratches her foot.

That gap is all I need. Grab the duffel bag, go, "Ooh, look at the time. 'Scuse me. Thanks Mum! 'Bye!" and exit.

"I'm doing a roast chicken for this evening so don't be late," she calls after me. "I need you home by five-thirty latest, remember?"

*

An afternoon's not long enough. There's just too much to find out and discuss. I'm okay with Tammy Fletcher being here as well, but it's because of her that I've not found an opening to update Gill on every single detail of Induna's training like I wanted to, and for her to watch me ride him. Nathan's been hanging about on the periphery all the time too, saying little but still competing for her attention along with Tammy. Of course she's had to ride both Bravo and Star Point and she couldn't get enough of either of them, so I'll have to wait until tomorrow now to show off my darling.

So now it's twenty-five to five. I should maybe start trying to take my leave as this conversation between Charles, Gill and Tammy about Tammy's father's racehorses doesn't look like it's going to end any time soon. It developed from a discussion on Gill's new short, feathery haircut and I don't think any of us will be able to explain how that happened.

"I've got to go home," I butt in before Tammy can get any deeper into her description of their Triple Crown hope for next year.

"Aw. Are you sure you won't stay and partake of Amai's speciality lamb casserole with us?" Charles asks me again. "There's plenty to go round and Tammy Stick Insect here doesn't eat much."

"You've no idea how much I'd love to but Mum's expecting me home for dinner."

He inclines his head in deference to my mother's wishes, diplomatic as always, but I just find her wishes galling.

"Well okay, but it'll only take you ten minutes to get home and we've got a little time yet, surely? And I've also got a surprise for you. You're fourteen now, aren't you?"

"Nearly. Next month. Why?"

Nearly fourteen and still a Mummy's girl.

"Well, as good as. Why? Because it's sundowner time. How about a little lager shandy? Tammy? Gill? G&Ts for you girls?"

Why the heck not? Mother instructed me to have dinner at home but she never told me not drink any shandies here.

"Yes? Good girl."

He leaves the kitchen.

"Sorry," I say to Tammy. "I interrupted you. Rude of me."

She laughs and shrugs. "I can go on a bit about horses! It's Gill who should be doing all the talking."

Gill's also stood up and is preparing to follow Charles.

"You might regret saying that. I'll just go and help Dad get the drinks."

Charles's voice comes back to us from the hallway or the corridor or somewhere with, "Nathan? Nathan! Do you...?" There's a pause. Then, "*Ja*, bring it now thanks," and he comes back some five minutes later with my shandy in one hand, his other hand behind his back. He sets the glass down in front of me.

"Gill'll be back with yours in a sec, Tamms," he says. "Right, Tess. You were telling me earlier about how your little sister has learned more words to more *Troopie Songs* than you ever could and still does all her homework and plays sport and comes first in class. But does she have one of these?"

With a flourish he produces a camouflage forage cap just like Rob's, waves it under my nose and then places it back-to-front on my head.

"Charles!" I shriek. I whip it off and spin it round in my hands. "Where did you get it?"

Tammy snatches it from me and puts it on her own head and goes, "Woo hoo! Lucky girl!"

I'm up on my feet and flinging my arms round Charles. He tries to shrug out of my grasp, then gives up and hugs me back.

"I told Nathan how desperate you were to get your hands on one, and he had a word with one of my guys on the Rusape site, unbeknown to me. It showed up in a brown paper bag in my office yesterday."

In a southern drawl, he adds, "If you don' ask no questions, you won' get told no lies."

I don't know exactly what answer I'd expected, but it certainly wasn't that one. Nathan?

I stare reverently at the hat Tammy's just handed back to me and then try to imagine Nathan at work in Charles's company. Does he work in an office? I can't picture him at an office, like Dad's. Of course there's no reason why I should know what he does in between the times I see him.

Tammy, it seems, is thinking the same thing.

"So Nathan's working for the family business at last? You must be proud, Charles?"

"Ja, I've got him involved in doing site tasks some afternoons and in the school holidays. He's doing okay."

"You sound surprised."

"I'm happy to admit I am, Tammy. He'll go full time next year – while he's not in the sticks on duty, that is. Having him working with me was always a hope of mine, of course, but we've battled with his notions of not being good enough so often I've sometimes thought we've lost altogether. It's been tough, on him and on Moira and me. But then he did so much better than we expected in his O Levels, and although he'd never let on, I'd say he shocked himself."

Tammy grins. "Gill did say. Teach him maybe he is good enough, hey?"

"Well precisely," Charles sighs. "But, he passed the lot and is doing geography, economics and maths this year. Bloody hell Nathan, I said to him, you get your M Levels in those subjects and I won't be able to afford to employ you, boy. I'll probably bring him into a different role from what I'd originally planned."

He's staring at the floor, but it's as if he can't actually see it. There's something in his demeanour I've never read before, like a sadness, and it has the same effect on me as any negative emotions in Gill. Those two don't do sad. Like her, Charles is always funny, sunny, full of life, full of enthusiasm for everything, filling every corner of whatever room he's in. Even Tammy's gone still, waiting for him to come back to us.

He looks up at me.

"I may have set out to be a proud father to my sister's son but I ended up with a boy who told me not to bother because he'd been told once that he'd only turn out like his father and bring disgrace on my family."

By one of Gill's other cousins, she'd told me. But she doesn't think he'll be a disgrace at all. And Charles is back to normal – lifted face, big smile and a laugh that's apologetic.

"But, in spite of that, I am proud. My sweet sister would be too, if only she knew. The government will get him next year of course. In the meantime I want him to learn how the business is run, which is why I've started mentoring him part time. Ultimately, I want to train him up first as a site agent and hopefully in the future he can become my right-hand man. Take over when the time comes. I think he's capable but I might have to fight the fact that he doesn't. I'm going to send him to the Polytech to do a course in building studies."

I have absolutely no idea what a site agent is or does. An agent? I get a fleeting glimpse of the guys on *The FBI* and then Roger Moore. Don't be ridiculous. I smile and say, "Oh, building studies? That will be good."

Even Dad's going to get called up now. He'll get eleven days' training. I mean, seriously? Eleven days? He said he'll probably only get duties like riding shotgun for convoys and general patrols around the city but now Charles has made me think about that all over again and it's scarier this time.

Dad made us laugh when he tried to get us to imagine Graham Peakin from the drawing office on a rifle range, balancing on his beer gut and rocking backwards and forwards like one of those wobbly dolls. And Dudley Foster, in an army camp out in the bundu, with an extra suitcase for his powders and lotions and his silk pyjamas and slippers.

Now I'm thinking it's not funny. What if Graham has a heart attack from the unaccustomed exercise? Or Charles? Or Dad? How old is Charles? No, he won't. Of course he won't. Don't be stupid.

Charles is pointing at my half empty glass, raising his eyebrows. I hadn't even realised I was drinking it. It tastes nice, but I'll bet there's more lemonade than beer in there. I shake my head, say no thanks.

"I'm going to have to go. Thanks for the drink and sorry I can't stay for dinner."

Gill reappears in the kitchen and spots me pushing my feet into my jodhpur boots by the door.

"Tess! Don't go yet. I have a Mars Bar for you! Have you ever had a Mars Bar?"

"Oooh, no. Are they nice?"

"Too chewy by half," mutters Charles. "Get stuck in my bloody teeth."

"I'll fetch it... Wait! I brought several back coz I love them, but I wanted to give you, Tamms and Nathan one each. And I got Nathan this Jimmy Cliff single he wanted."

She's speaking over her shoulder as she exits the room.

Nathan will be eighteen next January. This means only one thing to a white Rhodesian male these days. Stints in the bush, six weeks at a time, brief RNR at home, then back for another six weeks to the operational areas, the front line, the killing.

SATURDAY 24TH SEPTEMBER 1977

He doesn't so much wave as lift his right hand out of his shorts pocket and waggle the fingers fractionally then slide the hand back into the pocket.

His companions are oblivious to the exchange, as is Dad, who's caressing the elephant skin briefcase while talking Mum and himself into buying it, but Rosie clocks me mouthing *hello*, follows my line of sight and makes a rapid and expert appraisal of all four of them. It makes her day. She grabs Dad's hand and tugs on it and points and asks the whole of Greatermans, "Did you see that? Tessa can't even wait for her fourteenth birthday before she starts eyeing up potential mates!"

Dad goes, "See what?"

The old couple a few steps away from him temporarily lose interest in the briefcases, simper fondly at Rosie and then at me, shaking their heads and tut-tutting, but so *nicely*, like they think I'm just cute and silly and a bit of an air-head. I'm thinking about how I'll kill her when we get home and how the deed will be carried out slowly.

Mum draws a blank as well and says "Mates?" and Dad insists, "See what, Rosie? What are you talking about, girl?"

"She spots a group of four blokes and starts waving at them. They were not bad looking, I'll give her that."

"I did *not* wave. Stop lying Rosie!"

"Well one of them saw you ogling at them and waved at you and you said hello. Okay, you were lip syncing hello while you were making eyes at them. I saw you."

Her face is bubbling at me with wicked delight at the idea that she might just have caught me out revealing my true self, but at the same time is so full of affection that my murderous self sighs and creeps back into its shell.

I'll have forgotten about her false accusation by the time we get back to the car. What's freaking me out is the notion that there's a scenario in an alternative world in which Nathan and his friends pass across the ground floor of this store just ten minutes earlier. At the time we were standing at the display of matching luggage sets Mum was so taken with, all of us facing out towards the aisle that leads to the Stanley Avenue exit. In this alternative world things happen pretty much as they did in this one, up to a point. He notices me and I notice him in precisely the same second, he lifts his hand out of his pocket and waggles his fingers at me, I mouth *hello* and Rosie observes all of this. But instead of being some fifteen metres away and within seconds of reaching the street outside, they're right in front of us when she hollers, "Did you see that? Tessa…" etc, etc, etc and remain within earshot while we exchange spats about me waving, not waving and making eyes at four blokes because I'm just about to turn fourteen and am looking for a mate. In whatever chains of events led us all to be in Greatermans today, timing was on my side. He's gone, and he heard none of it.

"Rosie, I know him," I sigh. "The one who waved? I haven't a clue who the others were."

Typically, she's decided it's history now and is edging off towards the handbags.

*

I do a final check of my girth, put my leg back down and cluck my tongue so that Induna moves off after Star Point. He's eager and tries to trot to catch up but Gill's told me not to let him do that, so I check him and try to make him extend his walk instead.

She's watching over her shoulder.

"Good walk there, Tess. Well done."

"He knows now, I think, what I want him to do. I'm trying to visualise Bravo's amazing extended walk."

Bravo. Bravo looking amazing. Nathan.

"We saw Nathan in town today. I was in Greatermans with Mum and Dad and Rosie. I don't think I've ever seen him in the city before you know. Only here or at school or at Turnpike."

She doesn't seem surprised and just replies, "Oh, okay," then, "He took himself off fairly early this morning. Was he alone?"

That's the other unusual thing. He wasn't.

"He was with three guys, all a bit older than him possibly? One in camo trousers and a khaki T-shirt and the others in civvies. They were on the ground floor, just leaving through the Stanley Avenue entrance. We didn't speak. He saw me and waved but then they all left."

"Ah, that'll be Jed and Carl and possibly Roland. Was the camo-clad one bushy bearded? A dark beard?"

"Ja, that's right."

"Definitely Roland then. He's in the Selous Scouts. Jed and Carl are two of Dad's guys on the Rusape site at the moment and Roland is Carl's brother. Nath's been on site several days a week through the holidays. He's been hanging out with them a bit lately and they all seem to get on like a house on fire."

She gives her gurgling laugh. "I just hope this new socialising thing doesn't go to his head and lead to him going completely off the rails, getting tanked up and ending up face down in a ditch somewhere!"

"He doesn't drink that much though?"

He wouldn't though, would he?

"Nah, not really. He'll have a beer with Dad in the evenings sometimes but otherwise only at any parties we have. Hey, where do you want to go today? The tracks round the Watsons' farm?"

It takes us twenty minutes to get there, through quiet residential roads basking in the hazy early summer sun and then across the scrubby Crown Land – still brown and dry from the winter – at the top of Milton Close, and into one of the back entrances to the Watson place. Our conversation loops this way and that and Gill's full of her plans for taking in up to three horses at a time for training. Once we start trotting round the white sandy tracks of the farm, with a barrier of tall, tattered gum trees on our left and stalky wheat stubble on our right, she suggests, "Trot twice round the usual three fields, then canter once round all three, trot once more and canter again the final time? That way we build up on what we did the last time."

"Sounds like a plan."

There's a lull while we settle the horses into a rhythm. Five minutes pass, during which both of them snort several times. Then they go quiet and it's just the steady beat of their strides and the faint crunching of Star Point chewing his bit that I can hear. Halfway round the first track, Gill looks over at me.

"It's good to know Nath's arranged something with the boys, even if it's just a trip to town. You probably don't realise what a big deal that is. Well, no, sorry. I guess you do."

It is a big deal for sure. I watch her working on words. Eventually she says, "He just never seems to *need* anyone. Or to want to need anyone. As I've told you, he's dead reluctant to get close to any other person, even us. Especially us, unfortunately. Since he was seven. The fact is, he really is grateful to my folks for all they've given him and for taking him as their son, and I reckon it's because of that that he backs away. In case he lets them down. He can't seem to understand why they'd bother with him."

We're nearly back to where we entered the farm and turn left where the track branches off through a gap in the gum trees, take another sharp left and start on our circuit of the next field.

"Does he remember his parents?"

"Nathan? Hmmm, I reckon he does, to a limited extent. Mum and Dad were always open with him about the fact that he's adopted. But trying to get him to talk about what memories he does have, especially of his mother, really is like getting blood out of a stone. None of us have succeeded. Those kids at school who called him a loner? They didn't know a thing about him. He's been his own worst enemy in cultivating that untouchable, unsociable image, so everyone's left him alone and that's how he wants it."

She puts her reins in one hand and points across the stubble field with the other. "See the tractor over there on the far side? That'll be Leo Watson. We'll have to make sure we don't stop to talk or we'll be here until sunset, bless him. I'll just shout *hi, lovely to see you, we're working on our fitness training* or something and we'll keep going. Whatever you do, don't ask him how he is."

The horses have spotted the slowly moving tractor and are doing passable giraffe impressions, all four ears locked onto it. Star Point's having some backward thoughts.

"Get on!" Gill growls, kicking him in the ribs so that he leaps forward, humping his back, a bit of white foam flicking from his mouth.

Leo trundles his way towards us as we're trotting towards him, sending a cloud of the white sandy dust skywards behind the tractor. That'll make us all cough when we get absorbed by it. He observes us with a wry, closed mouth smile that's lopsided in his long, sun-hardened face, the floppy blue bush hat rammed down low over his eyes so that his round spectacles touch it from below. He has very large ears, which are also up against the short brim of the hat. He draws level with us.

"Gilly Owen!" he shouts above the roar of the tractor's engine. We've pulled the horses off the track onto the stubble by about five metres and there's a bit of waving and a shouted exchange of Gill's scripted greetings.

"Hi Leo! Lovely day."

"Stunning *hachi* you've got there girl."

"He's gorgeous isn't he? I'm using your land for fitness training again, Leo. Many, many thanks!"

"You're welcome, my love. How is…"

"He's very uppity and bucks like a bronc. We'd better get going or he'll have me on the ground. See you soon!"

Now that he's well away from Leo's tractor, Star Point is picking his way carefully through the stony ground amongst the stubble, focused and relaxed and innocent, as if butter wouldn't melt.

*

"Nathan's not back yet," Gill observes, standing at the back door with her arms folded. "Looks like he may be out jawling this evening."

"And ending up in a ditch?"

"Hey, he'll be fine. I do wonder if he's going about with those guys because he knows damned well that when he gets to go into the army he's going to have to be part of a team whether he likes it or not, and that everyone's lives will pretty much depend on that bond. The boys will have plenty of war stories to swap and entertain each other with, so he'll be getting a taste of what army life will be like. Sure, there'll be drinking and getting rowdy but it's what soldiers do. We can't prevent that."

The way she's talking makes it sound like he just can't wait to go and is gearing up for some excitement. Like Timothy.

"Is he looking forward to getting drafted? I can't believe he is."

"God, I don't know. He's never said. It's always been so hard to know what he's thinking. He's stepped up his jogging regime and he's started dragging me down to the squash courts at the Alex club twice a week, so he's trying to get himself fitter. What would *I* feel? Would I be filled with some sort of patriotism, or be dead against it and risk prison as a conchie or just be bloody scared shitless? If I ask him though, I know I'll get nowhere."

As I'm mounting the bike, she giggles, "You never know. Maybe he'll even find himself a girlfriend!"

TUESDAY 21ST FEBRUARY 1978

The tiered seating creaks a bit, someone behind me flips the question sheet over and back again, a Parker biro clicks out and back in. Mrs Walsh opens a file full of papers with a soft thud and picks up her pen. Her green pen. Why she sees the need to mark our work in sickly green when all the other teachers use red is a mystery.

The tall swivel windows beyond the lab benches only reveal a dull, drizzly gloom, the Cypress trees along the boundary fence barely visible. The thunder and lightning have chased each other away and the gutter downpipes have stopped their gurgling.

Right. Let's get on with it. Names and functions of the components of animal and plant cells. I know this stuff. It's my sort of thing.

Question One done. Move on to Two. But I've barely put my pen onto the paper when the air around me is shattered into splinters by a clashing, crashing, nerve-jangling hammering of metal on metal that fills every cubic millimetre in the room. Thoughts come lagging in slow motion behind the action as we, like a single organism, scramble to our feet.

First thought: What the hell?

Next thought: Alarm. Fire drill.

Then: The gong is not the fire alarm. It's the bomb alarm. Bomb drill.

Finally: In the middle of our test. Mrs Walsh won't be impressed.

Mrs Walsh's face is just total confusion.

"Elizabeth! Heather! You open the windows please. The rest of you, come along, quick. Get your cases up onto the tops of the benches, names uppermost, leave them and follow me. Elizabeth and Heather to do the same after the windows. Now! Go!"

The misty veil that's the remains of the torrential rain storm swirls its damp greyness into the lab.

"Oh hell," I say to no-one in particular. "Look at it out there. Why now?"

Jess hefts her suitcase from under the bench, pushes mine towards me with her foot and grabs both of our dripping raincoats.

"Look at her," she whispers, nodding towards Mrs Walsh, who's dithering near the door. "This is for real. She'd have been told if there was going to be a practice."

I have a little curl of fear in my abdomen. We join the line, filter through the double doors. When we had that practice fire drill in the second week of term, it's true that Miss Marston, in that case, was calm and relaxed enough to bring her nail file with her, and she gave out instructions in a conversational tone. When the electric fire alarm bell goes off, girls, you close the windows, leave your suitcases where they are and head out to the playing fields in single file and line up in class order at the Pavilion. Remember though that it will be different for bomb drills, so be prepared. Crispin, the chemistry lab assistant, will beat the *simbi* with an iron bar and in that case you will leave the windows open, leave your suitcases on top of your desk with your name in large white letters in full view and head out to the playing fields in single file and line up in class order at the Pavilion. Any cases or bags without a name that are found by the bomb squad will be destroyed.

The corridors are wet, and slippery with dirty footprints. I hold my plastic raincoat over my head when we get out to the hockey pitch. After shouting us into order, the staff get into a huddle around Mrs Peterson, leaving the Form Captains to carry out roll call. Crispin and the other lab technician are there too. The poor guy's probably a bit shell shocked after his gong-bashing session in the quad. He'll be relieved when we finally get the air raid siren thingy. Eventually Mrs Peterson marches over to stand in front of the lines and opens her mouth to bellow for quiet, but all talking has already ceased. She looks a bit amazed.

"Right, listen! The school has received an anonymous telephone call to say that an explosive device might have been placed somewhere in the buildings. The police will be arriving in a few minutes. Now I want you to all about-turn in your lines quickly and walk across the pitch to the far side in a quiet, orderly manner. There is absolutely no danger if you do as I say. Stop when you reach the goal net and keep your lines. Right? Go!"

Uproar erupts. We turn raggedly and the lines begin to stream across the sodden hockey field.

"QUIET!" Mr Parker roars from behind us and a guilty hush envelopes us like a damp blanket.

"Why did she tell us to move?" Jess whispers to me over her shoulder. "I don't want to stand in the rain anywhere. This is going to be a bad-hair day, I can tell."

"Don't know," I reply, but then, in that instant, I do. "Yes! Of course. A bomb somewhere in the *buildings*. She's sent us away from our usual assembly point in front of the Pavilion. I guess it might be known we always gather there."

"That dilapidated old shed?" Jess squeaks. "Someone ought to blow it up! We need a new one. Anyway, she only said a – what? – an explosive device *might* have been planted."

"She doesn't want to cause panic?" I speculate and Heather hisses "Shhh!" in her Form Captain voice from further down the line. "Jessica Marsh!"

Jess stares straight ahead and pokes out her tongue. She carries on whispering so I have to practically put my chin on her shoulder to hear her.

"I wonder if those two coppers who turned up last term to give us that weapons recognition talk will be here? They were both… mmmm, well, you know. Remember?"

"Yes Jess, we all know you wanted them to arrest you," I hiss back. "Better go do something naughty."

"Tessa! You too!" Heather's getting frantic. Jess snorts and I give her a mild nudge between the shoulder blades.

The police arrive in force and we wait. Thankfully, the drizzle dies out altogether. The sun even starts glimmering somewhere in the grey clouds behind us. For nearly two hours they swarm over the school like a nestful of khaki-clad ants, while members of the

Police Reserve take up station at all the entrances to the grounds, FN rifle butts resting on the ground and eyes watchful from under their navy blue floppy hats. Their presence makes me think of Dad. If he wasn't down at Gatooma on farm guard duty he might've been here.

When we're finally allowed to return to our classrooms it's one o'clock – home time. No bomb, or any other weapon, has been found, or so we're told, so there's a mild collective sense of anti-climax. Someone's idea of a joke, I guess – a pretty sick one after those shoppers were killed in Woolworths last year. Then the terrs blew up that church, although there was no-one in it at the time. Dad said it's like having our very own IRA, and that we have to learn to live with stopped up litter bins and post boxes and criss-cross tape on all the shop windows. And put up with being searched every time we go into one of the shops. Who was it who said that the people will get used to anything? That we all have a tendency to become complacent, even if we don't consciously think, "It will never happen to me"? Like the residents of Umtali, who've got used to being mortared and wear T-shirts with a beer bottle printed on and the words "Come to Umtali and Get Bombed".

We live in a country at war with itself.

I'm so wrapped up in thinking all this dismal stuff that I don't hear what Mrs Walsh says before, "And don't think you've got away with it."

I ram my biology file into my case, stuff my pencil box in a corner and fasten the clasps. The spring's gone in one of them so I'll have to see if Mum can get me a new one. I think we've still got some white paint left in the garage.

In the cycle sheds, a group of us wastes an inordinate amount of time inventing imaginative plots to leave homework and text books in unmarked cases for the attention of the police. Maybe we *are* getting complacent.

FRIDAY 3RD MARCH 1978

They signed an agreement today. It's called The Salisbury Agreement and it marks the beginning of the movement to majority rule, but it's okay because it safeguards a lot of things Mr Smith wants. And what Mum and Dad want too.

The Rhodesian Front says it means the war will end, but then the Rhodesian Action Party says Smith's a dithering sell out and that we should intensify the fighting and win the war on our military strength. Moira reckons the RAP is more right wing than right wing and that Ian Sandeman makes Hitler look like a Communist. I wouldn't support them, if I could vote.

I only want things to get better. Dad now has to pay an extra ten percent tax to help pay for the fighting and Mum moans every shopping day that her groceries are costing more and more. The thing is, the two of them keep telling us everything's going to be okay.

SATURDAY 18TH MARCH 1978

I lick mayonnaise off my fingers and watch the circular washing line rotate a few degrees at a time in the light breeze, like it can't quite decide what it wants to do. One of Charles's old flannel shirts has one sleeve tossed over the line and caught on one of its own pegs. Kuti's sunning herself on one of the steps leading up to the yard gate. Have the rains finally moved off? I thought it was never going to stop raining again.

Like the washing line, we've come full circle. Another *braai*, another milestone. Two years have passed this time. Gill's travelled twelve thousand miles since the last such occasion and a lifetime of history's been made in our country and yet I can still remember it as clearly as yesterday. I was thinking about the war. The same war.

I'd been wondering how much longer it was going to last. Now, two years older and wiser, I know so much more about the politics involved yet I understand the whole situation less. Two years ago I still had some sort of patriotic enthusiasm. I still got a bit teared up when we sang *Rise, O Voices of Rhodesia* in school assembly. Now I no longer know what is right, or what exactly I should be feeling or thinking.

The garden is the same. The washing line, the rockery, the glimpse of the ménage railings at the top, the Lion Rock – they're all still there just as they were before. We carry on regardless with our parties and our *braais* while the fighting and the terror continue in the rural areas and the Combined Forces' Honour Roll continues to lengthen. Three boys who went to our school died within three weeks of each other in January, then Heather's brother was killed in February and now Jess's cousin Mike has got himself added to the casualty list. I've never met him. He'll recover though so I guess he'll end up going back. Not so the others. More and more civilians are getting caught up in it, babies are being bayonetted and motorists are being ambushed on the roads.

Back to the cat. She's licking her fur daintily, one hind leg pointing to the sky, toes outstretched. *Déjà vu*. Or like watching a film second time around.

And I don't want to watch it anymore.

There's a distinctly different age range within Gill's guest list this year. Some of the older relatives I remember are missing. There are fewer aunts and uncles, but more younger men and women like Gill's friends and some of the pupils she's gained in her training business. Tammy's here with her younger sister, Sherrie. She's sixteen now and looks like Tammy did when I first met *her* – short and skinny, long legs in relation to her height and long curly blonde hair, although with a sharper face shape. She has the same sunny smile, but there's something different in her. Her eyes have a slightly harder edge. Tammy manages to find a funny side to almost every situation and has herself a good time no matter what others are doing, whereas Sherrie seems bent on getting everyone else to enjoy themselves as much as she is and bloody well like it. I don't know what she said to that guy from across the road – the one with the tufts of black hair in a circle round his head and a bald patch on top – but whatever it was he didn't get the joke so she actually nudged him in the ribs repeatedly until he thought he'd better laugh.

And, without exception, all the young men are wearing camo in some form. A couple of them are in full uniform – trousers and shirts with sleeves rolled up – and the others have various bits, like trousers, shorts, T-shirts, vests or boots, mixed with civvy articles.

I've run out of food preparation tasks and I don't reckon the meat's ready yet, so I'll go out and park on the paving at the edge of the pool and dangle my hot feet in the water. There's a hubbub of voices and music behind me on the patio and in the emerald garden but for now I'm the only one at the pool. The glitter Slasto paving is wet and will make the seat of my shorts damp but I don't care.

Gill's not far behind me. She says, "Hi," in her warm voice and plonks down cross legged beside me. My friend, Gill. Smiling, sunny, slender, pretty as ever, although more sophisticated now – a woman rather than a girl – and wearing a T-shirt protesting, "Rhodesia Is Super". In that instant, the peaceful moment's gone. We both have to lean back in unison to avoid being soaked by a child as it gallops from nowhere and leaps into the water right in front of us, bouncing up on bright yellow armbands.

"I'm losing track of these kids," she sighs. "Whose is that? Oh, it's Barry's. I'm damned if I can remember his name. Jake? Jason? Jamie? His wife's already got another one on the way. Things move on, don't they? All my aunts and uncles and my parents' friends think I should have had a couple by now. I'm getting old, Tess."

"Don't be ridiculous. You're only twenty-one."

I'm studying her face suspiciously. Gill having babies? That's one that's never been on my radar. She doesn't even have a boyfriend.

We watch the boy doggy-paddle his way across the pool, his armbands keeping him bobbing on the surface. One of the small waves he created when he jumped in comes back and slaps him in the face, leaving him snorting water out of his nose. Charming.

With her elbows on her knees, Gill puts her fingers together in a steeple shape and rests her chin on their tips.

"I've had a couple of phone calls from Nath this last week. He seems to be getting on well in his training. I'm not too sure when the passing out parade is going to be. He'll be in Independent Company number such-and-such of the Rhodesia Regiment when that's all over. During May, I guess."

Ah yes. Back to reality. Nathan'll be off to our borders, to one of our hot operational areas, very, very soon. Maybe to Hurricane in the north, or Thrasher in the Eastern Highlands, or Repulse or Tangent in the south and south-west. The names are harsh and ominous – even Tangent, which up until a short while ago was just maths to me.

"Then they'll send him out to fight the war. To achieve nothing."

I shouldn't have said that. She's got her lips pressed together and as soon as she feels my eyes she turns her head away from me. I'd intended my voice to be matter-of-fact, but it comes out bitter, and that's wrong. While I'm wondering what to follow this up with, she tells me, "Tessa, we're fighting against communism. We have to fight it to preserve what we have, after everyone's let us down. Fight for what we believe in. We must."

There's some exaggerated head nodding, her eyes still averted.

This isn't right, coming from Gill. My parents are the ones who go on about being let down by everyone (the British government, the Yanks, the traitorous South African government). They're the ones who echo the cries of the Rhodesian Front about fighting communism, preserving our way of life, being in the right and refusing to believe this is anything to do with black Africans wanting their country back. I try to compel her to look at me with what Paddington Bear would class as a hard stare, but she won't. My bitter words, spoken half to myself, have had some deep effect on her emotions and I wish I could take them back. It was actually a pretty stupid thing to say because she wants to – needs to – believe Nathan's not here with us today because he's doing something worthwhile. I dig for more words and come up with nothing except truths I know she won't want to hear. Best keep them to myself.

No one's let us down. We've let ourselves down over the years and now we're trying to blame everyone else because we can't have what we want.

She reaches down and drags one hand through the crystal water that's gradually going quiet after Jake-Jason-Jamie has scrambled up the steps on the far side and run off.

"We'll all go to his parade of course. Dad will love that."

The traditional military Passing Out Parade. Inevitably, one or two of the recruits, dressed up to the nines in heavy uniforms and standing to attention for hours in the burning sun, will do just that – pass out before they've officially Passed Out.

Is it a thing to be proud of though, your son going off to war? Your boy? Our Boys On The Border. They're all someone's son, brother, father or husband. Even Nathan, who's as good as a son to Charles and Moira.

"Would his real dad have been proud of him, do you reckon?"

She sighs and wipes her hand on her shorts.

"Him? A stinking bastard drunkard who had an affair and managed to write himself off by wrapping a car round a baobab tree? Nah, he wouldn't have had the sense to be proud of anything. Git."

Oh. Should've known the answer to that one. She's studying my face.

"You still look shocked every time Tess. He never had any interest in his son. It was only about five months after Nathan was born that he started seeing other women. I can only guess it was because they were more available to him – you know what I mean? My aunt did have a bit of post-natal depression and she had some pretty see-saw emotions, and it sure didn't help when the idiot started going out and about spreading himself around. Good riddance, to be honest with you."

He was killed when Nathan was only three. November 1963. A week before JFK. I don't recall much from when *I* was three. If Mum and Dad had died then, would I remember them? What's it like to never know your real parents? I'm thinking of that photo in the hallway of Gill hugging Captain when he was a puppy. She got him for her eighth birthday. Nathan's in it too, sitting on the grass next to her, reaching out a hand that's connected with Captain's tongue and both children are giggling. I remember it especially because Gill loves the picture so much and she told me she wasn't able to look at it for over a year after Captain had to be put to sleep. Was that taken around the time Nathan became her brother? Also, it's one of the few photos in which he's facing and smiling at the camera.

Gill uncrosses her legs and lets her own feet drop into the water.

"I've never shown you any photos of Don, have I? The only ones we keep are the wedding photos and that's only because my gentle, beautiful aunt Annabelle's in them. Dad keeps them in his bedroom cupboard. You'll think that's strange? Yes, I can see you do. I'll tell you why. He doesn't want Nathan to see them. I promise I'll show you and I guarantee that you'll be amazed at how much Nathan is starting to look like Don. But whatever you do, don't *ever* tell him that. I mean it. I can't expect you to really get this, but that's why we keep photos of the guy out of sight. I dare say Nath knows damned well, but he'll be shutting it out for sure."

My mouth must be making the 'oh' shape again.

"He might end up being like his father on the outside, but inside he's turning into *my* father, and maybe our Uncle Richard too. Him and Dad are very much alike. And he has a bit of Annie's artistic side too, I guess."

"Artistic? Does that make you a sensitive rider? He is, as it always seems to me that he's constantly having these subtle, physical conversations with whatever horse he's riding. A quiet, but very effective horseman."

She gives me an appraising stare and purses her lips.

"That's so true. You're very observant and it makes me so proud that you've noticed it. Shows how much you understand what equitation is all about now. I always told you that boy has a gift when it comes to horses and riding. He susses out each horse and instinctively knows which buttons to press and which ones not to press. He's so *not* like his father in that respect. In any respect, actually. I have no real memories of Don that I can recall – it's mainly what my parents have told me. I was a flower girl at their wedding and have snippets of the day still in my head and I do remember Annie. She was a wild child. A free spirit. A painter. She fell head over heels in love with a handsome man and thought all her romantic dreams would come true. Dad says she couldn't see past his good looks and the charm that he could ooze. He detested the bloke from the off and reckons he would never've trusted him as far as he could throw a house. He tried to warn her but she breezed along in good faith and blind love and dated him for nearly a year, had a whirlwind wedding and was pregnant with Nathan after only a few months. That's when the problems started. He began looking elsewhere, and he had no shortage of female admirers. He didn't try to hide it either. The drinking got worse and he started staying away from home. It was…"

"Gilly! There you are! I've been looking for you all over."

It's Moira, and she's harassed, wiping her hands on a tea towel.

"Where's your father? Please can you dig him out from wherever he's hiding and find out how close we are to serving up?

I'll be with Amai in the kitchen. Now, now, please honey." And she's gone again.

Gill sighs, scrambles to her feet, says, "Catchya later," and is also gone.

Her voice floats back to me, "Dad! Mum's looking for ya! Dad!"

Dad.

Dads. They're loving. They're interested in and committed to their children. They're responsible guardians. My dad, Charles, Jess's father. Uncle Harry and Uncle Len. I've never met *them*, but Mum tells us stuff she's read in the letters and what they've been up to and how she loves them both. None of them are stinking bastard drunkards. None of them have had an affair. Or at least I don't think so. I hope not. And they're here for us.

But at least Nathan's had Charles.

*

"That," Charles declares, "is the mother of all birthday cakes."

He's not wrong. Its separate sections are ten centimetres high and form the numbers 2 and 1 and it's thick with pearly white fondant icing, trimmed with gold piped icing and embellished with gold paper ribbons. Moira orchestrates its grand entrance, whisking it out of hiding – or rather, bearing it out of hiding carefully on its gold board with Amai's assistance – glowing as if she's *its* mother. I guess she is, since she made it.

Once cut, it vanishes as magically as it appeared. Dallying to help Amai tip rubbish into the old horse feed bags hasn't helped me in my quest for cake; there are only a few sad looking remnants left, some scattered bits of fruit and numerous crumbs. It's all over for another year – the bones have been disposed of, the *braai* embers are dying to a grey ash and the cake's finished. Never mind. I've eaten too much as it is. I can maybe gather up some of the morsels with my fingertips just to get a taste.

"Oh poor Tessa!"

Gill's voice is ever so slightly slurred.

"Come with us. There's some gorgeously creamy, yummy ice cream in the freezer. Rum and raisin, no less. We'll have some of that and we won't share it with anyone else!"

In her wake, I'm wondering just who 'us' is.

It turns out to be her and a guy I've seen several times today, but only towards evening. I'm sure he wasn't around at lunchtime and I kind of recognise him but I can't quite place him. He's very tall, standing at least a head above Gill, with a thin face and lank fair hair cropped in such a way that it could only have been done by an army barber. He's one of those wearing parts of a uniform – camo trousers, boots and a khaki T-shirt. Slightly older than Gill, I think, but then I do find age hard to judge.

She introduces him in a muffled voice as she dives head first into the gargantuan chest freezer in the scullery area.

"This is Tim Morrison, by the way. Tim, meet Tessa Harmand. You know him, Tess. He rides Serendipity and Electromagnet."

Ah yes, now I know. If Mum is ever unidentifiable as Sheila, she'll be Tessa-and-Rosie's-Mother. Similarly, Tim is Serendipity-and-Electromagnet's-Owner.

It's not just food I've had too much of. I'm ever so slightly spaced out, as if I'm not quite here. It's a very odd feeling.

Gill rears back up from the depths of the freezer with a plastic tub of ice cream in her hands, as smug as a conjurer whipping a silk handkerchief from a top hat.

"*Voilà!* Who wants some?"

*

Tim is laying the attention on thick. I'm having plenty of opportunities to watch him focus all his considerable charm and wit on Gill, sharing a bowl of the ice cream, helping her to move the hi-fi to the French doors so there can be dancing on the verandah, getting very close and staying there, holding her in his arms under the multi-coloured glow of the fairy lights. He lets her go occasionally to dance with a couple of the only remaining elderly relatives but they don't stay the distance. Their repertoire of dance steps doesn't run to disco and one by one they sidle out of the area of maximum decibel count.

Dancing with Charles, trying to ignore his resemblance to a tipsy penguin, I can't shake off the dismal idea that I seem to be the only one without a specific partner. Wasn't I just reflecting earlier that Gill didn't have a boyfriend? After another of Charles's rum and Cokes, the spaced out feeling intensifies, as does the depression.

But now Dad's here. I do recall phoning, as arranged, but not him actually arriving. How long ago was that?

We end up in the car – somehow, don't remember actually saying goodbye to anyone – and set off for home. Dad tells me some stuff about what he got Elijah to do in the garden today. He asks me how the party was and I tell him about the cake. At the end of the road, a brief pause in our chat is broken by the ticking of the car's direction indicator – tick, tick, tick. The one in Gill's Alfa Romeo goes tick, gloop, tick, gloop, tick, gloop. Suppressed giggles come out as a shudder and my eyes start watering. This is no good. I'll get rumbled and there'll be all hell to pay. There's an abrupt return of a clarity of mind as I feel Dad's eyes on me.

I sit up very straight and focus on the tail-lights of the vehicle in front, the dark forms of the trees flashing past, the headlights of another car waiting at a side road junction. These are serious things, interesting things even. They are not funny. The other car's right indicators are flashing orange. Tick, tick, tick. Tick, gloop, tick, gloop.

A strangled noise comes out and Dad jerks his head round again.

"Are you all right?"

Swallow. Stop. It's not funny. It's not hysterical. Stop.

"It was a joke. Gill told me a really good joke."

"Oh? So what was it?"

You would ask, wouldn't you?

"I can't remember it. I'll tell you another time."

"Hmm," he replies.

FRIDAY 14TH JULY 1978

It's precisely seven o'clock. Good timing. Great timing, in fact. The Scout Hall doors are swinging open as we climb out of the car.

"What time, darling?" Mrs Marsh calls across the passenger seat in her toodle-oo voice.

"Eleven, Mrs Marsh," I respond, poking my head through the open window. She gives me a thumbs up, shifts into first gear.

"Same as last time! Seriously? 'Bye Mum!" yells Jess and we're in the throng pushing through the doors into the bright interior of the hall. Its severe, institutionalised layout is as disappointing as it was last month, but at least we now know what's going to happen. The light is harsh enough to make me blink.

We select a couple of the hard chairs lining the perimeter. There are more adults mooching about tonight, stationed around the hall as if they're assuming guard duty. Maybe they've got wind of some of the hanky-panky, as they insist on calling it. Near us is a small knot of girls from our year.

Without warning, the main lights go out and Henry Thorpe's father's voice is emanating from the wall mounted speakers. The tall multi-coloured lighting units take over.

Mr Thorpe talks at us a bit. Welcome, it's Friday night, if you've not been to one of our discos before, let me tell you… and so to stuff about the locations of toilets and refreshment sales and where to assemble if there's a fire. No-one's listening, of course, until he gets to the bit about the refunds for plastic cups. And alcohol's one hundred percent *verboten*, guys.

Staying Alive. Coloured lights synchronised with the thudding beat, falsetto voices filling the space around me, Jess bellowing in my ear, "Come on!"

We become part of a larger creature, a constantly shifting ring of single girls, threading its way through a few couples, splitting up, reforming, in the pulsating music and the colours, jerking puppet-like under the strobe, clutching our sling bags against our bodies or letting them swing in arcs round us.

We dance for about an hour and then take a break, buy lemonades, yell a bit with the other girls about, well, rubbish really, and then get in on the Collection Racket. We missed out last time. It was half-nine before Hannah Brett told us what was going on and too late to really do much about it. Tonight it's going to be different.

There are plenty of the white plastic cups lying around, abandoned by those with no business acumen. We collect a stack each – ten for me and nine for Jess – and take them to the kitchenette, one at a time, over the course of another hour. Find enough of them and you can recoup your evening's expenses or even make a profit. We're not talking long bucks here, but a profit is a profit. Lucky for us, there are far more mothers serving drinks than truly necessary, so we become that much less memorable. Hey, we might just be very thirsty with all that dancing and who's going to know we didn't buy the drinks?

The only trouble with these cup-seeking forays around the grounds is that it's too easy to literally stumble across amorous couples that've left the noise for a little private communication, on varying levels. Heather and Andrew are holding hands, gazing into each other's eyes and murmuring. Roxy and Kevin are stuck fast together in a noisy kiss. Gary has buried his face in Leanne's impressive cleavage – her blouse is undone – and, as I reach into the hibiscus hedge for a lone cup I've spotted, I find Lauren seated on the ground on the other side, giggling while some boy I don't know is groaning and shoving his hand up her skirt.

She's seen my hand and then my face peering at her through the leaves.

"Ag, man, Tessa!" she exclaims, pushing him away from her. I back away from her furious eyes and his vacant, uncomprehending ones, clutching my prize.

"Sorry. Don't mind me. Carry on."

Between me and the hall is a small group of guys passing round bottles of lager from a crate under the same hedge. They must also be from another school because I don't recognise any of them. One of them has noticed the plastic cup in my hand. He produces a large bottle and waves it under my nose.

"Hi there! Want a splash of brandy in your Coke, sweetheart?"

"No, she doesn't."

Jess has grabbed my arm and pulled me around them towards the lights of the hall. There's a whiff of cigarette smoke on the air and also a slightly unusual smell from the white cylinder in the boy's hand.

All the while, Mr Thorpe is still happily DJ-ing inside the hall.

*

My impulsive pirouette on the ball of my right foot works like a charm, balance is maintained, I'm back into the dance and this guy from Saint George's College hasn't noticed my skill. Jess was watching – in the middle of my spin I spotted her perched on her chair with her feet tucked under it. She lifts one hand from where it's gripping the front of the seat and gives me a thumbs up that I just catch sight of as my rotation takes me away from her again.

Another spin. This one wobbles a bit and Jess is no longer alone. That's Gordon Baker. Aka 'Streetwise' Baker. Known as such for the simple reason that Gordon Avenue and Baker Avenue are adjacent to one another in the grid of Salisbury's streets. He's wearing a well studded black leather jacket and although he's quite short and stocky he's a bit better looking than this one I seem to have picked up. Or has he picked me up? I can't make up my mind if I'm liking dancing with him, or just liking dancing. I should be interested in him, shouldn't I? He seems to like me. But here again is that inexplicable almost-wish that keeps trickling through me and alarming me. I can't *possibly* be wishing Timothy was here. Ignore it.

Jess is wriggling through the crush towards us, attached to Gordon's hand, and I give her a thumbs up this time. This action makes Mark stop studying me from the neck down and look up at my face for the first time in a while. He lights up and I can read *wow-she-likes-me* written all over him. I do believe I'm beginning to learn first hand about these wrong impressions and mixed up signals to which boys are supposed to be so prone. I sidle away from him a little.

Three records later, Jess and Gordon have vanished and Mark needs to go to the toilet. Abandoned, I sit in a corner shouting with the two girls from Queen Elizabeth School until he reappears and it's lucky for him I love dancing so much and can't think of any excuses on the spot. It's impossible to talk and dance at the same time without getting uncomfortably close so we grin inanely at one another and Mark continues to watch my jeans. Is it because he's shy or because he really finds that part of me more interesting?

Ten-forty-five and Jess still hasn't shown up. The disco's due to finish at eleven and last month Mrs Marsh was pretty prompt with her taxi service. What will I say to her?

"Sorry, Mrs Marsh. Your daughter disappeared with a young Caucasian male over an hour ago and no-one's seen her since. I think she's eloped. But never mind, I'm here and you can take me home anyway. Just don't mention this to my mother or she won't let me come again."

Which would be a shame after all our efforts to get the approval with the unwitting co-operation of Mrs Marsh herself. When I said, "You do realise my mother will have serious doubts about me being under fifteen and out until eleven o'clock at night with a whole bunch of people she doesn't know?", Jess went, "Not to worry. We'll enlist *my* mother to tell her it's okay. Now, she won't want to tell any lies and we have to get her to say exactly the right things. Leave it to me."

Mrs Marsh has this trilly voice. She trilled, "Oh yes, Sheila my dear, it's quite okay. The Markhams' children have attended some of these di… di… erm, these *events*. You know the Markhams don't you? From a few roads away? John's the Managing Director of Top Marks Animal Feeds? Yes, them. Well these *parties* are reputed to be very well supervised and I've never heard of any nonsense going on. The girls will be fine, just fine, my dear. I'll take them *and* pick them up personally. Yes, that's right. It's run by the Methodist church."

Now my family only ever goes to church for christenings, weddings and funerals but she wasn't to know that and it did the trick. All the same, I half expected a bolt of lightning to strike me through the open patio doors for my audacity in calling on these good Christians in order to get my way with my mother.

"Let's go outside," Mark is insisting, his mouth against my ear. "Away from the noise."

I snatch up my coat and allow myself to be led by the hand into the starlit winter night. After the stuffy heat in the hall, the silken air is at first refreshing. I stare about hopefully at the few others in the vicinity, but of Jess and Gordon there is no sign. Mark slips his arm around my waist, giving me a start that turns into a shiver.

"Cold?"

"Yes. I mean no."

I correct myself pretty rapidly, but it's too late.

"I'll warm you up."

I find myself wrapped in his embrace. No choice. Awkward. Do I want this?

Let's say yes. I put my arms around his shoulders and the wary bit of me gives way to the curious bit, and then the wary one takes over again. This is not kiss-catches. Mark has singled me out from a crowd of girls without knowing me and wants to give me his attentions. It could mean he wants to be my boyfriend, couldn't it? Or maybe he doesn't, and he'll forget me after tonight. What do I say if he asks to see me again?

It's all this not knowing what to expect and yet wanting to find out, but also not wanting to find out that's curdling my brain. And I have questions – about himself, his hobbies, his home and family – although so far he's not shown much inclination towards conversation and the music was too loud in the hall anyway. I was hoping to get to talk to him now, outside, or maybe hold hands and go for a little wander, perhaps not cheek to cheek but shoulder to shoulder. No chance though, and I'm the one who's blown it by reciprocating the embrace. He's now snuggling into my neck and I can feel his mouth against my skin and his fingers are probing the seat of my jeans, pulling my hips towards his.

"Isn't this better than dancing?" he manages to murmur wetly into my ear and all of me swings from the what-will-making-out-be-like end of the scale to the don't-like-the-way-this-is-going-AT-ALL end in an instant.

No. It's not. They're playing ABBA and I want to dance the last dance.

I've had enough of Mark. I don't need this. There's a movement in the corner of my eye. Gordon – the studs on his jacket gleaming dully as he moves into the pool of light cast by one of the harsh sodium security luminaires – with Jess tripping along next to him. Rescue party. I twist out of Mark's clutches.

"Oh look! My friend is here. We have to go home now."

Where the hell has she been? She's spotted me. They draw level and she points a forefinger at me, winks and raises her eyebrows but I just give her my best stony glare and snap, "Oh, *finally!*"

"Um," she says, with a slight frown. "I, well I… I guess Mum'll be here soon."

To be fair, she probably doesn't have a clue what she's done wrong.

"Can I see you again?" Mark is confused by the interruption and he's eyeing the other two with suspicion. "Give me your phone number."

So he has asked. Oh, hell… He has what they call sensuous lips – full and moist – and the skin on my neck is crawling as if there's a small insect on it.

"I have nothing to write with," I tell him, shrugging.

"I'll remember. What is it?"

There's Jess's mother's car. I keep my hand on his chest to make sure he keeps his distance and after a bit of um-ing and ah-ing make up a number. The sensuous lips move silently in a response and my neck prickles again.

"Okay. Got it. I'll call you. 'Bye Tessa."

He's leaning in again. He wants to kiss me, but I've removed my hand and gone. I avoid Jess's eyes as I make a dive for the nearest car door and fall in. It's a long moment before she eventually lets Gordon go and tumbles into the other end of the back seat. We huddle together in the toasty warmth. Mrs Marsh is blasting hot air at us from the dashboard.

Jess gives me a prod in the ribs.

"I heard you, girl. You gave him some random number! He looked really keen on you and you've fobbed him off. Who was he?"

"Mark, from Saints. Mmm, he seemed okay but then he was all over me."

So now, have I done the right thing? I told him I lived in Borrowdale but he didn't seem to twig that the number I reeled off didn't begin with double eight. I started with a six, I think. What suburb has numbers that start with six? I don't know. I can't think. Now I'll never hear from him again unless I manage to contact him through someone who knows someone at St George's College. He'll be hurt and embarrassed and he won't want any more to do with me. I'm not going to come to any more of these discos in case I bump into him. That would be just too awful.

"So what's this with Gordon? I thought you'd eloped!"

Jess stares at the floor and she's trying not to smile, trying to be coy and cool at the same time.

"Oh he's gorgeous, isn't he?"

She leans forward. "Mum. Gordon Baker, you know, Marilyn Baker's son? He's asked me to go and see a movie with Sue Shaw and Alan Trent tomorrow night. Will that be okay?"

Mrs Marsh knows everyone in the city. "Oh yes – Gordon! Marilyn's such a dear. I would think so, love. And Alan's a dear. Does Gordon drive? How long has he had his licence?" She's keeping her eyes on the road and her voice doesn't have the panicky tone I would expect to hear in Mum's in similar circumstances.

"Since his sixteenth birthday, of course," Jess replies, withdrawing sulkily. "He borrows his mother's car and I'm sure he's quite safe on the roads."

FRIDAY 18TH AUGUST 1978

She makes no move to mount her bike. Instead, she leans it against one of the metal bollards along the verge.

"You go on home. Gordon's picking me up in the car and we'll put my bike in the boot. I get to have a car ride home on the last day – fab, huh? We're going to the flicks to see *Grease*, to celebrate later. I wanted to ask you to come along too. We could pick you up. I'll phone you to let you know what time?"

Right. Okay. This is the first I've heard of it and we've been together all day. So I've been working on this idea that we should go to town on the bus one day next week to see *Grease*, but I haven't got round to suggesting it. Too late, I guess.

"Well, um… Nah, don't worry. I don't really want to play gooseberry. Thanks anyway. It's okay. I'll just go home."

"So what'll you do? Wash your hair and watch TV?"

Ha ha.

At our gate, when I dismount, I stand for moment and the world around me is silent. Like I'm the only person left. I can't even hear any birdsong and nothing is moving, not even the brittle brown grass blades along the verge, left a little long through the winter. It's one of those weird moments in which I can't recall anything of my journey to get here. The past ten minutes have been and gone and I've got no recollection of them. I was with Jess outside school and now I'm here, at home.

That's what comes of focussing inwards on yourself with such dedication. I've been tearing my whirling emotions apart and what I'm realising now, as I stand here with one hand on the cool metal of the gate latch and the other on the handlebars, is that I'm jealous. I'm jealous of my best friend.

Not just jealous. Furious. With her. For the first time ever. I have a knot in my middle and tears in my eyes and it's stupid.

There was Clive. And then Clive was ditched and we got on with our familiar little lives. And now there's Gordon and they're calling her Ma Baker already. She clearly isn't interested in me anymore. Well, I don't care. Wipe your eyes with the back of your hand. You don't want anyone to ask questions, do you? What would you admit to?

But it looks like there's no-one home, so it doesn't matter. I *can* hear a few birds now but it's still just me in the world. And actually, I do care.

I let myself in, and the bike tyres and my shoes scraping the gravel and the metallic click and creak of the gate fill the space around me. I do care. I'm alone. I sent Mark-from-Saint-George's packing the night of that disco. He was interested in me but I let him go and now I have nobody. Jess has abandoned me for Gordon and Gill has Tim. They'll be going for evenings at the movies, for weekends out at the lake, to family *braais*. They'll get chauffeured about and have a regular partner for the discos and the parties.

Jealous. Me, who never thinks beyond going back and forth from school, riding horses, reading books, walking for hours with Rosie and Skellum, listening to music and sunbathing in the garden. It's like Clive's back, but worse, because this time my gut tells me Jess is really hooked.

I do bloody care. I don't want to lose either her or Gill. And I also bloody care that, at the age of fifteen – or nearly – I'm apparently on the shelf. I remember now that Mum's taken Rosie to a tennis lesson. Elijah must be on errands somewhere and I can't ride Induna because he had his vaccinations this morning, so I get to mope around the house all afternoon. Alone.

At two-thirty, there's a call from Gill. She just wants to report that all went well with the vet and that Indie was perfectly behaved.

"He's such a poppet," I say, picturing my poor horse having a big needle stuck in his neck. "How was Bravo? Did he have to be sedated in the end?"

She makes a 'huh' sound. "Well, no. His master's back, isn't he? Good timing really. The horse was not happy about it, and the vet had to work quickly, but he was remarkably tolerant. That boy's a wonder and Bravo trusts him explicitly."

It's a couple of seconds before I twig onto what she's saying. She picks up on my hesitation and confirms, "Nath arrived home this morning? Ten days off."

I think she did tell me, but I'd forgotten. I ask the obligatory but rather meaningless question, "How is he?"

"How is he? What, apart from the several days' worth of beard, which looks mighty strange on him? I don't know. He's bloody tired of course. Shut himself in his room now for a sleep. He doesn't ever tell what he's seen out there. He seems a little more… what's the word? Hardened? Cynical, maybe? On his first stint he didn't see any action but this time… I don't want to think about it. Sounds like he's been in at least two contacts. I guess he'll tell me soon enough what happened but I'd rather not know. He said they want him to go on an officer training course."

There's a resigned tone in her voice. We agree I'll ride both tomorrow and Sunday and hang up.

At four-thirty, Mum and Rosie blaze into the house irritatingly full of excited chatter. My kid sister's been selected to represent her club in the under-thirteen group at a national tournament, so I get twenty minutes of that. Then, with a load of unnecessary drama, she produces a camouflage forage cap, identical to the one Charles gave me.

"Look at what I got!"

She's gloating, parading across the living room with the hat at a jaunty angle. She sighs and clasps her hands together.

"Rob gave it to me! Oh he's divine, Tessie. Do you think he'll marry me one day when I'm old enough?"

I'm in no mood to respond in any way kindly to such a suggestion by my twelve-year-old sister.

"I doubt it. I bet he has a really stunning girlfriend he wants to marry desperately. You're being incredibly silly. He won't even look at little girls like you."

"But he *likes me!*" Her voice is choked and she stalks out of the room clutching her new hat to her breast.

Maybe my tone was a little too acid.

I ought to apologise, but instead I pick up the day's edition of *The Rhodesia Herald* and flick through the pages in search of the television viewing schedule. I *will* watch TV actually. Maybe wash my hair too.

At five-thirty, Jess phones. She's made plans and as she talks my matt black mood explodes into glorious technicolour. Once I've finally decided she's not winding me up, that is.

"Tess, your life is due to change tonight. I've fixed you up with a date. Gordon's friend, Danny Proctor, is coming. You know of him, don't you? Gordon's driving, but listen – tell your mother that mine is dropping us off and picking us up. We'll park the car near your neighbour's gate and wait for you. Say, seven o'clock?"

I'm cool and casual in response. After a suitable pause I say, "Okay, cheers. See you later," and hang up.

Sure, I *will* go out with them after all. It sounds okay. So maybe I'll start some preparation now.

I try on my favourite Indian cotton skirt, turning this way and that in front of the mirror to watch the soft fabric and bold colours swirl. It'll do. With a plain white blouse. Then I go through several different pairs of earrings, help myself to a little of Mum's make-up while she's cooking and Dad's in the en-suite bath making untidy-sounding splashing noises, and am fairly pleased with the overall result when I study my image critically in the full length passage mirror. I tie my hair back into a pony tail with a scarf that matches my skirt perfectly, but then after a few moments' consideration I pull it out again to let the hair sweep my shoulders. A small sling bag, containing my purse and a comb, and the light linen jacket I got for Christmas last year will complete the effect. I take it all off again, lay it out on the bed, go for dinner.

I know of this Danny Proctor. Like Gordon, he's in Lower Sixth and wrote his O Levels at the end of last year, passing with, I believe, exceptional results. That's one of the reasons I know who he is. The other is because he's captain of Second Team rugby and rugby is nothing less than a religion in our school. I've seen him. He's one of the tallest in his year and has dark blonde hair, he's a rugby captain and he's clever, and taking all of this into account, I can't believe Tessa Harmand is going on a date with him, even if Jess has set it up. Why doesn't he already have a girlfriend? Maybe he does. Maybe he's a philanderer. Gets about a bit.

My self satisfaction takes a little dip while I consider this possibility but it doesn't last.

At six-forty I get dressed again and go out to wait impatiently – no, calmly – on the patio in the cool, burnished evening light.

Ten to seven and I can hear the sound of a car in the road, slowing, stopping. The engine is cut. I can't see it through the hedge, but the headlights penetrate the thick foliage. It's some distance from the gate.

I leap up, then sit down again. Wait. A female figure appears at the gate and waves at me through the gloom. Jess.

"Jess and her mum are here!" I call, to which my father shouts, "Have a nice time at the cinema. Don't slip on the grease."

"Ha ha."

Although I may appear cool as I walk down the drive, my heart's agitating against my ribs. Silly.

Gordon is behind the wheel of the Peugeot station wagon. Jess's back in the passenger seat and he has a hand resting on her knee. Danny's on the rear seat. We do the *hello-hello-how-are-you-I'm-fine-how-are-you* and he makes complimentary remarks about my skirt and my earrings. Warm smile, green eyes… mmmm, pretty nice. I'm ridiculously pleased. It's a satisfactory start.

*

Karen Carpenter's voice is drifting across the car park. Over the top of her, the driver on our left is having a loud debate with his companions about the merits of the burgers versus the hot dogs.

"Er, *ja*," he shouts into the microphone perched on the pole next to his window, "Three, er, hot dogs. *Ja*, onions. *Ja*, mustard. All of them, *ja*."

The hot dogs are good – I can vouch for that. Gordon and Jess had a similar debate before opting for the box of chips they've got their heads together over. Jess's picking out all the small crispy ones in the silence that accompanies people tucking into food. There's a burst of laughter from the car on the left and Karen's gone quiet. Rod Stewart takes her place.

Danny's finished his burger and is licking his fingers and I need to find something sophisticated to say. I'll ask him about himself and what he does at weekends. Is that suitable? I'll ask as soon as I've finished this mouthful.

"Now Tessa, I'm sure there's more to you than a passion for hot dogs. And how very delicately you eat them as well. So tell me about yourself and what you like to do at weekends," he says.

That's my line gone.

I have a go at mumbling an apology, swallow at the same time and narrowly avoid choking. So much for sophistication and his observation that I eat delicately. I shake my head, point at my mouth and attempt to suppress the stupid giggle that wants to escape.

He's well overtaken Mark from Saints by now. He's charmingly attentive without being overpowering. He keeps his distance, but maybe I wouldn't mind if he got a little closer. He wants to know my opinion about the film trailers we watched and the soundtrack of *Grease* and the American high school system. He's keen to have conversations. My primary objective right now is to make sure I don't put my foot in it and spoil things, like I thought I was going to when he asked me if I like John Travolta. I can't believe I was paranoid enough to assume he was testing me. Now, over an hour later of course, all the right sort of words, the *slick* answers like "Well he can dance a bit but I much prefer the Danny I'm with tonight" are sliding easily round my head but at the time I just went, "He's a great dancer" and Danny said "Do you like dancing then?"

But it was all just fine.

"I ride horses," I tell him around the remains of my mouthful. "Quite dotty about them."

He nods and I'm scrutinising his expression to see if I can identify genuine interest. I reckon I can. That's what I want to see anyway.

He tells me his grandfather was in the mounted police in South Africa, reputedly a good rider who knew a lot about horses. "I've ridden a horse only once I'm afraid," he concludes.

"Well that's a start."

I take another bite. A smaller one this time.

Jess has caught on to our conversation.

"Don't get Tessa talking horses for God's sake. She'll lecture you to death about... trotting and stuff... and describe every one of Induna's hairs to you."

"*Whose* hairs?"

"Induna's. My horse. Shut up, Jess, and get back to your snogging."

I tell Danny that I keep my horse at the Owens' place, expecting him to know of it. He gives me a blank look but smiles delightfully at the same time.

Gordon and Jess declare simultaneously that they both need to visit the toilets.

"Too much Coke earlier," Jess says.

"Yeah, right. Off you two go together, never mind us," says Danny.

They vanish in the direction of the main complex and we're alone.

We talk for a while. This and that, school, his older brother Brian and my Rosie. It's very easy – much easier than I expected. Then he says, "Hey, Tessa, just an idea... look... I wondered... um... My brother Brian's met this girl in the army. Cassie. She's a radio operator. Would you like to... well, he's back on RNR next Tuesday... maybe go out together with them?"

There are a few desperate seconds during which I know I could get this so horribly wrong if I've misinterpreted his words.

My drawn in breath – I didn't mean to suck in like that – sounds like a tidal wave in here with the music, voices and car engines as remote as a soundtrack faded out. Has he just asked me out again? Whatever he's reading in my face has given him some cause for doubt.

"Um... They've been going to Y.F.C.C. on Fridays. I'm not sure it's really my thing, but he's been on at me to go along. It would be so much better if you could come too. I... um... I suggest this because it's like a... a good, kind of safe thing your folks will be happy with us doing? Would they? I hope so. Brian and Cassie will be with us, you can tell them. I can come over and ask them myself if you like?"

The green eyes are only for me, interested and concerned at the same time, absorbing, lit up by the backdrop of electric light from The Gremlin restaurant on our left. How have I ended up being asked out by such a classic storybook Romeo when I'd thought the best I'd get would be someone like mop-haired, unsubtle, boy-racer, gotta-be-like-Dad Timothy Dalton? This guy wants to take me out but is concerned how my parents will react. Oh yes, I'm liking this.

Only thing is, I don't have a clue where we're supposed to be going. It's my turn to look blank.

"Y.F… What? Sorry? Go where?"

"Y.F.C.C. Youth For Christ Church, at Wylie Road Chapel. If you want to?"

Now he's looking at the floor.

The deep part of my core that's been doing back flips with delight at this new invitation promptly sinks down into the heels of my sandals like the original lead balloon. *Church?*

I'm completely mute. The cogs and gears of my brain grind in desperation for the longest moment ever, but no words get churned out. There are some flashing reminders of reluctant attendance at a Sunday School eons ago, a whole lot of stories I never took as anything other than stories, and of me slinking strategically into the back row for R.E. classes so I could make a start on my maths homework from the previous period. We don't do church. We never have.

But, seated in Gordon's car at The Gremlin drive in restaurant, on my first real date, surrounded by the smell of burgers and chips and the sound of piped music, I hear myself tell Danny I'd love to go with him. To church.

Well I'm not going to say no, am I?

"Will you phone me and let me know times etc? I'll give you my number."

I write it on the inside of the torn lid of the box that once held his burger, with a biro we find in the glove compartment. The real number this time.

SUNDAY 20TH AUGUST 1978

Rounding the corner of the garage, pushing my bike towards the shed, I spot Mum framed by the back doorway. She's waving a pink and white striped tea towel at me.

Here we go. I'm a bit later than normal. Like, ten minutes? I shall ignore her and carry on with putting my bike away.

She's not going to let me ignore her.

"Ah, Tessa! Tessa, love! Tessa, you're back."

This is a bit obvious, but I refrain from saying so. Sarcasm absolutely doesn't work.

She's got a slip of paper in her other hand and she's looking at it while still flicking the tea towel sort of in my direction.

"This boy… this… er… Danny Proctor… He called at about three o'clock. He wanted to speak to you and he's left a number. Here it is…" and she starts to read the number out loud.

I drop my bicycle on the grass where I stand and am at the back steps in seconds.

She has curiosity scribbled all over her face and I snatch the note from her in case she refuses to give it to me until I've explained just who *this Danny Proctor* is.

"Oh God, why did he have to call when I wasn't here? I've missed him!"

That came out desperate; I didn't mean it to. But he never phoned yesterday, which not only set my despondency alarm bell off but made it damned awkward when Gill greeted me today with, "So come on – what time did he call you and are you going to see him again?"

She'd only gone and told Moira about my date on Friday night too so I had to describe it all over again to her while wondering if it was actually going to go any further than that. And again, when Charles and Nathan got home, but only to Charles because Nathan did one of his vanishing acts.

"He sounds nice. He was so polite when I spoke to him."

She's positively cooing, sidling up to me. I dodge round her and, on those jumpy sort of legs that want only to run, head straight for the phone.

Act cool. I dial the number with a sweaty finger. As the phone rings at the other end I wonder why the hell I didn't spend a few minutes thinking of things to say to him and nearly put the receiver back. Too late. Someone picks up and intones, "Hello. Proctor household." It's him.

*

"So when are we all going to meet Lover Boy? You talked to him on the phone for long enough."

She's smirking and sniggering at the same time. This is rich, coming from her, after all her wistful and pointless sighings over Rob.

"I don't know when, Rosie. He's asked me to go to the Dairy Den with him on Tuesday morning."

"You're going out with him again on Friday, aren't you?" Mum informs everyone. Mum, the great announcer. "I'm looking forward to meeting him. He sounds ever so nice. Very polite boy. I'm sure he dresses neatly too. Does he?"

Oh please shut up. Why should people only ever be 'nice' if they're 'neat'? Wear your shirt outside your trousers and you clearly have a delinquent temperament and questionable morals.

I give her The Look, while ignoring Rosie's giggling, but she rattles on regardless, dragging me with her.

"Is it that church opposite the shops with the modern flat roof on one side and the funny sloping bit of roof on the other?"

"Lean-to," says Dad.

Rosie swallows her mouthful abruptly.

"*Church?* You're not getting married already?"

I so need to change the subject *right now*, but my mind has emptied. I can't reach her legs with my foot either.

"Don't be ridiculous. And actually no, we're not going after all. Danny says his brother wants him to go to this kind of Christian youth meeting but I don't think he – Danny that is – really wants to go. He said maybe we'll go some other time."

"Wow!" my sister exclaims with some reverence. "It *must* be love!"

We eat for a bit, then Dad asks, "Tessa, did you lock the shed after you came back from riding?"

Did I?

I have a nasty feeling I just left my bike lying on the lawn.

MONDAY 4TH SEPTEMBER 1978

There's normally a day in September when you go outside first thing in the morning and you know the summer has arrived. I can't describe it. It's a feeling, that's all. Something about the light quality perhaps? A smell? A haziness? All of these things in some ways, as well as the soft mauve shroud in the jacaranda trees that heralds the coming of their blooms. Not today though – not yet – but it's still a good day. School's out and summer's just around the corner. It's a sparkling spring morning and we're going to Rainbow Ice Rink and I've got Danny.

Danny. He's a gentleman (he opens car doors for me and helps me put my jacket on) and he's charmed my mother (polite, neat *and* witty). He was keen to meet my family and I'm going to meet his at the weekend. He held my hand under the stars on our patio after dinner last Saturday and we agreed that we want to keep on seeing each other. I've arrived. I've got a boyfriend and a part of me (a very small part) wishes it wasn't the holidays so that everyone at school would know and be amazed that I managed to catch him. Now *I* can talk about what we've done and where we've been, like Jess does. None of this sticking with Mum and Dad's outings anymore and, what's more, they approve of this. I've become part of a group of boys and girls, with Jess, and they've always liked Jess.

She's sitting there in the front of the car and giving off the impression that she and Gordon are the only couple in the world, but now there's me and Danny Proctor.

"Good thing we did manage to get going so early, hey," she says, fondling Gordon's knee. "I'm telling you, it was worth it. Some of those boots are getting a bit crappy and if we're like the first ones there we'll get good pairs."

I get the feeling Gordon's not a morning person. He hasn't said a word since I got into the car apart from a mumbled "Hi."

"You should be able to park right outside the place at this time," Danny adds and Gordon grunts. Jess removes her hand from his knee.

She's right about getting there early. The novelty of having an ice rink in town hasn't worn off yet and it's only the start of the third week of the holidays.

"We'll stay till just before lunchtime, *ja*, coz it'll be unbearably packed this afternoon, don't you reckon?" I suggest. "Go somewhere for lunch in town?"

Gordon's mood lifts visibly. He sits up a little straighter, blinks a few times and goes, "Oh yes! Wimpy? I fancy going to Wimpy," turning his head to look at us on the back seat. "Ice creams after? Dairy Den?"

"Gordon," says Danny, pointing ahead. "Food is important in our lives, but please can you look where you're driving us?"

We spend the morning skating in endless circles to disco music, holding hands, talking, drinking Coke, skating again and laughing at the antics of anyone who fails to remain on their feet. I'm confident now, but I can't help feeling too much confidence is a dangerous thing when it comes to balancing on ridiculously thin blades of steel on a sheet of ice. I have a go at backwards skating, tentatively at first and then faster, crossing one foot over the other at the corners. Inevitably, eventually, it happens. The rear of my left blade was always going to collect the front of my right boot at some stage and it's a soggy thump – the rink is pretty wet by now. Danny's right here of course, blocking other skaters in an attempt at traffic control to clear a space for me so that I can get to my feet again. He takes my arm and looks into my face, pushes my hair aside, says, "Are you okay? Does it hurt anywhere? Shall we go and sit down?" and I wonder if I should kiss him. This could be The Relationship. Jess reckons he's told Gordon he'll be eternally grateful to the two of them for introducing us but she might well be just congratulating herself for making a successful start in the matchmaking business. I better not lean in and kiss him because I can't let him think I'm too forward. But I do want him to know I want to kiss him. Oh, stop dithering – the moment's gone anyway.

I throw myself back into the challenge with, I think, a more stylish technique even if it's just to avoid having to put up with Jess and her lover snogging each other in the tiered seating at the far end of the rink. At least they weren't watching and all they'll ever see of my fall from grace is a wet patch on one leg of my jeans. I'm monumentally well pleased with myself.

In accordance with Gordon's earlier suggestion, we go to the Wimpy where Danny buys my lunch and on the way home we stop at the Dairy Den on Second Street Extension. The slightly crisp morning has turned very warm and it's all just simply perfect. Life can't get much better than this.

As we're arranging ourselves at one of the outdoor tables, Danny says to Gordon, "Liverpool apparently trounced Tottenham on Saturday. I'm going to get a paper. They might have a report on the match."

Jess pulls a face. "English football? Tessa, I feel for you."

I don't mind. I don't get football, but if Danny enjoys keeping up with it I'm happy. He ignores her and disappears into the adjacent grocery store. Jess starts telling Gordon about the last time she was at Mermaid's Pool and how her cousin managed to tear his swimming trunks halfway down the rock slide and then lost them altogether when he dropped off the zipline.

Gordon stretches his legs out and yawns.

"When was that? Closed now isn't it? Hot area."

Danny reappears in the doorway of the store, a copy of *The Rhodesia Herald* in his hands.

"Eighteen months ago I guess," Jess replies, linking her right ankle around Gordon's left.

At this point I glance up because Danny hasn't joined us yet. He's stopped in his tracks and is staring at the front page. Sports results are always at the back of the paper, so that's odd, but what's even more odd is the expression on his face.

"Danny?" I wave my purse at him. "What sort of ice-cream cone do you want? We're going to order now."

He approaches, holding the paper out towards me so that I can see the headline. I give up trying to interpret the expression and switch my eyes to the paper. The words "VISCOUNT FROM KARIBA MISSING", are spanned across the top of a photo of one of the Air Rhodesia Viscount fleet. There's a sub-headline too: "*Search centres on Karoi area*".

I take it from him and place it on my lap; I can feel Jess lean towards my right shoulder. Gordon gets up from his chair and shuffles round to stand behind me. There's a moment of quiet.

I skim through the article. The aircraft disappeared on its routine flight from Kariba to Salisbury yesterday and the last message received from the Captain was a report of the failure of both starboard engines. It's thought that the Viscount crash-landed somewhere in the bush, but no-one knows where for sure. To pick up on the inference that the loss of both engines simultaneously on the same side is a highly unusual occurrence doesn't require much intuition.

Jess takes in a quick, sharp breath and Gordon says, "Oh. My. God."

The heroes in ghost stories often have to put up with the indignity of having their hair stand on end. The words "It was a hair-raising story" once prompted me to draw pictures of startled people with the hair on their heads reaching straight up for the sky. It was funny. It made me laugh. I didn't believe it.

Now I know it really happens, and it's horrible. Creepy. My hair's not literally reaching for the sky of course, but I get this cold prickling along the back of my neck and on my arms, then it starts on my scalp, like my hair has literally lifted. This all comes with the emergence of a crystal clear knowledge that something dreadful's happened and that there's no way to escape it.

A plane crash. Yesterday. So here we are in the middle of a war, surrounded by death and disregard for life – troops here, villagers there, farmers and Internal Affairs personnel in all the outlying areas – but I can only ever remember hearing of one major civilian disaster in Rhodesia. That Wankie colliery. 1972? When some four hundred miners died in a series of explosions. This sort of human tragedy only occurs somewhere else in the world. Aircraft and trains full of mothers, fathers, sisters and boyfriends crash and burn in other places. Not here. I keep my eyes open and focus on lines of print because I don't want to see the picture my imagination is determined I should – bits of broken fuselage and a tail in the distinctive shape of the Vickers Viscount, lying scattered in the tangled bushveld.

It's not just a crash though, is it? Like all the other ones I hear of on TV, predominantly during take-off or landing? Planes rarely just fall out of the sky in mid-flight unless maybe they get caught in a bad storm. Or they get shot down. I'm not a pilot and I know diddly squat about aero engines but a little voice inside my brain is whispering to me that it knows why the two engines failed together and I'm telling the little voice to shut up and not be stupid and not to upset me and that it can't possibly be true.

We go home without ordering any ice-creams.

Mum and Rosie are not in and I go to lunge Induna because it's the only way I can slam the door on those damned images. Makuti Park is quite deserted, which is fairly unusual. There's no sign of Gill, Moira or Charles and there's only one groom in the tack room cleaning saddles. Nathan, of course, is off somewhere in the bush so he's never around now. I think he was back on a pass two weekends ago but that day I didn't ride so I only found out afterwards.

I'm actually pretty thankful there's no one here. I don't want any more news today.

*

I manage to beat Rosie to the phone for once, and it's Danny. We talk a bit of nonsense stuff, then he says, "I've heard there are survivors from the crash. Eighteen, I think. That's great news, isn't it? A group of them were able to set out to fetch help."

I've already heard this from Dad, who was buzzing with the news when he came home from work earlier, and now I'm finally climbing out of the ditch I've been in all day just by the sound of Danny's voice and the way he's called to reassure me. Survivors.

Good. Some passengers and maybe some of the crew survived. He talks me through what he's heard.

I lie on my back on my bed for a while, dreaming up things to do when he comes over on Wednesday afternoon (a bit of swingball, or we could walk up to the granite *dwalas* and take in the view – I could get Mum to buy us a pack of biltong to take up there – or, of course, we could go to Jess's for a swim?) then pick up the Alistair MacLean I got from the library yesterday, open it at the first page and get wrapped up in it.

Survivors. Shocked, defenceless and undoubtedly injured people out there in the middle of nowhere with the crashed aircraft. They're waiting for the rescuers. They'll be taken home or to hospital but in the meantime they have to stay put. The small team that left them to search for help knows where they are; the authorities don't.

It's a ghastly little notion, like a deformed black, demonic imp, and it's wriggled out of the part of my brain that's not focussed on the story in front of my eyes, upward and upward, whispering, scratching at my consciousness until it obscures the words I'm reading. What if? What if someone else – some others – know exactly where they are? Those who saw their prey go down?

I actually say "No!" out loud to myself, shove the book towards the wall, prop up on one elbow and squeeze my eyelids down. How can I even think such a thing? It's absolutely not possible. Not ever. Go away.

There's nothing wrong with Alistair's writing but I can't stay in here on my own with that demon intent on whispering in my head. The bookmark's fallen onto the carpet but I'll find my place again. I bolt for the lounge, and discover Mum, Dad and Rosie watching *Hawaii Five-O*.

Damn, forgot it was on. Danny doesn't know I'm head over heels in love with Steve McGarrett. This is good. If I focus on Steve, I can't think of anything else. Book 'im, Danno. Danny – ha ha, sorry.

Afterwards. The Combined Operations communiqué. The rescue team has reached the site of the crash. During Sunday night, the ten left behind were murdered by Joshua Nkomo's soldiers, who had watched the Viscount go down after taking out the two engines with a SAM 7 missile.

Nkomo openly admits responsibility. His excuse: he'd been informed that there were important military personnel and equipment on board the *Hunyani* and he was only carrying out his duty as an army commander.

FRIDAY 10TH NOVEMBER 1978

"Feel the weight of that. It's *mushe* hey?" says Jess, crowing, pushing the ginormous trophy into my hands. It's silver with a black base like a drum, very curly, twisty handles and has impressive depth. She lets me peer at my own face on the side of the bowl and then into it for all of five seconds before she starts tugging it out of my hands.

"All right, all right. Give it back. There's no champagne in it so stop looking so hopeful."

The stretched out image of my face is broken up by the words *Victrix Ludorum*. The silver shields fixed to the base are engraved with names and dates: *Cheryl Harvey 1975, Elise van Tonder 1976, Sue Tredgold 1977* and a blank one. There are more round the other side but Jess has retaken possession and tucked the monstrosity protectively into her arms.

"That blank shield's for you, look. '*Jess Marsh, Inter-house Gala 1978, Best Diver The School Has Ever Known*'. I can see it now. Although there isn't room for all those words."

I was so proud of her, standing up there in front of the entire school and telling us how she'd be honoured to eventually be a part of a national diving team and represent Rhodesia. I even got a bit teared up. Pride for my friend, yes, but also with this flat, damp sadness that's still lapping around the edges of what's been a celebratory day. She represents the school, she'll undoubtedly represent Mashonaland, and she may well be good enough to get into a national team, but she knows as well as I do that there'll be no-one to challenge except, maybe, South Africa. The politicians have made damned sure that Rhodesians will never play sport against the rest of the world. They nibble away in this manner at our pleasures and our dreams and hopes. They make us all optimistic with small forward steps, congratulate themselves, and then promptly take a massive leap backwards. Look how they officially abolish racial discrimination across the board – okay, admittedly not everyone's optimistic about that but maybe those people should think about leaving – and so now black men are eligible for call up, when they've only ever been voluntarily involved in this before. What a sick irony, or was it a ploy to obtain more manpower to fight their war? Look how they talk about referendums and elections and a ceasefire and in reality the death toll rises, they impose martial law and then scrabble desperately for more men to join up.

Enough of this. I grab Jess's elbow as she turns to inch her way along to the end of the row of seats.

"Hey! Celebration required. How about you guys come out with me and Danny tonight? Why don't we go to Ice Bowl?"

Prizegiving over, the crowd is shuffling, babbling, gathering up belongings, beckoning to family members located across aisles or several rows away. Jess is glowing and still admiring her prize, although she's trying to pretend she isn't.

"So what are you going to buy with your book tokens?" she asks. "A tome on advanced mathematics? Or physics? The History of the World in one volume? Or maybe *The Canterbury Tales*?"

I sigh and say, "Horse books, Jess. What else?"

"Ha ha. Well okay, let's go out to celebrate. I guess we'd both better clear it with our folks though. Speak later, hey?" and she's gone, arms wrapped around her trophy, the sash trailing behind her.

*

It's quarter to twelve when we pull up at the gate. The house is in darkness, but the patio light flicks on as I turn over the gate latch.

"Hah!" I nudge Danny in the ribs. "See, it works. Dad had the system rigged up last week but it's the first time I've seen it put to the test. Look, their bedroom light is out. Does that mean they've developed a total trust in my boyfriend's integrity?"

"Well I hope so. It's important to me that they like and trust me." His squeeze around my waist lasts a little longer than usual and we're there for several moments, still, me with one hand on the gate and the other over his hand across my belly. An intimate moment that's broken by the distraction of a barely detectable twitch of the curtains at my parents' bedroom window. There's a fleeting glimpse of what looks like a face in the gap, then they close and might never have moved. It's the sudden flood of light from outside that's alerted them – as intended – but I'm not so sure it'll have the same effect if they're very sound asleep. How often have we said that only a cattle prod would wake Dad once he's out of it?

"Make sure you call out or something to let us know it's you," he instructed me before I went out, so now, with Danny following, I march with confident footfalls up the path, wiggle my key into the front door lock and clack it open, push the handle down with a clunk, scrape my shoes on the coir mat, call "It's Tessa!", and switch on the hallway light. Danny envelopes me from behind, turns me, kisses me lightly on the lips and I'm over-brimming with contentment. The kisses, his commitment to my happiness and well-being and his arm around my shoulders in the cinema is all I need to make me queen of the world with everything I should have. There's a very odd side-effect of his presence in my life though – I've taken to helping myself to a bit of Mum's eye-shadow and lipstick and perfume and I'm conscious of the scent now. Charlie.

I pull my face back, smiling. His green eyes are not quite focussed.

"Remember I'm giving you a riding lesson on Sunday. Perhaps pick me up at two o'clock?"

He's reluctant to let me withdraw from the embrace.

"You have a one-track mind, Babe. Horse track all the way. I do remember, my Tess, and I'm finding myself looking forward to it more than I expected."

Breathing in the faint smokiness of a *kaya* cooking fire, I wait till the sound of his car has faded into the warm, starry night then lock the door and delve into my delicious fantasy that he'll turn out to be a talented, natural horseman who's never realised his own ability to form a rapport with horses. He'll get his own horse and we'll go to shows together. We'll be together a long time.

Then, as I'm heading down the passage to the sanctity of my room, trying to make my footfalls soft this time, the fantasy evaporates to leave a hollow with which there is nothing to fill. In just over a year he'll be out of school and then what? Not Varsity. Not the path to his career in accountancy. Not a normal start to the rest of his life – our lives. He'll get called up.

The war isn't going to end any time soon, in spite of all these supposed settlements and fruitful (fruitless) negotiations. You can't plan things like life in these shifting, changeable, uncertain times. Not so long ago we were reluctantly imagining that Joshua Nkomo would be our next, and first black, Prime Minister. Dad went on more than once about how much more reasonable he was than all the other Nationalists, internal and external. He even showed some acceptance of the inevitable, deciding that Nkomo was probably trustworthy, and if it's got to happen, he said, *if it's got to happen*, then I guess he should be the one. Well, of course back in September Nkomo went and tore up and threw away forever any shreds of faith the likes of Dad may have had in him. All he did was convince any doubters that the fight must go on and that deaths must be avenged.

How does a mood swing so drastically from contentment and fantasies and lovely ideas to this hopelessness, to this regurgitation of my ghastly premonition all over again? Gill thinks she succeeded in convincing me I'm not some kind of freak or witch.

"Come on, Tess," she told me, "be honest with yourself. Loads of people probably thought the same thing. The plane was obviously shot down. I doubt there were many who didn't guess that. We're at war. It's not weird to speculate that a missile of some sort was involved long before it was confirmed."

"Okay," I challenged her, "so why did I know they were going to be found by the terrs and murdered?"

"You didn't *know*. You couldn't possibly *know*. Your brain sussed out that it was a distinct possibility, that's all. If you shoot a plane out of the sky, you watch it go down. You can follow it and find it, even if it takes several hours. You know full well there may be survivors and if you're a killer… well…"

Whatever, it still frightens the shit out of me.

Rosie's door opens a fraction and her face appears, whitely visible against the darkness of her room.

"Hi," she whispers. "Has Lover Boy gone? Did you fall off your skates again?"

I give her the thumbs-down sign.

"The Ice Bowl was heaving. We went to the cinema instead, but it was trash."

"'Night, 'night." She withdraws and the door clicks shut.

SATURDAY 11TH NOVEMBER 1978

I must have fallen asleep within minutes. Now I have a moment of wild, disorientated confusion. Seconds ago I was in the midst of one of my typically complex dreams that are nothing more than a string of unrelated images. I'd been in the main grandstand at the races for a bit and then I was inside a bus, kneeling on a seat and leaning out of a window to explain to Dad that no, this bus belongs to the Salisbury United Omnibus Company. Can't he see that? If he wants the Express Motorways coach, it's over there on that far stand. He argues with me. In this weird half-awake state I'm becoming incredulously aware that Dad is really talking to me, crouched by my bedside, tugging urgently at my shoulder.

"What?" I sit bolt upright.

"I said, get onto the floor, now, Tessa, and come into the passage. Close your bedroom door and stay on the floor. On the floor, okay? Come on now, quickly!"

He's gone, the door open. Still suspecting that this is just another disjointed chapter of the dream, I roll out of bed and follow him on hands and knees and am further confounded to find Mum, sitting propped against the corridor wall and holding onto Skellum's collar, and Rosie, cuddling a piqued Cleopatra in her arms. Dad closes my bedroom door. All the other doors are closed. No-one speaks. I guess we're all looking at each other but it's too dark to tell.

"Will somebody please tell me why we are sitting on the floor, in the dark, in the passage, at this hour – whatever it is?" My whisper comes out hoarse and cracked. If I get no reply, and this *is* a dream, it doesn't matter because the scene will change just now with no notice.

I do get a reply. An unidentifiable, coughing thump from somewhere in the distance, but close enough that I feel it as well as hear it. My brain starts reluctantly trying to tell me I might really be awake. With eyes now accustomed to the dim light, I stare at Dad. My stare speaks. It says, okay, now for the explanation please?

"Mortar." I swear there are beads of moisture glinting on his forehead. "Three so far. Or three that I've heard anyway."

Maybe I'm the one who needs the cattle prod. And he's only had eleven weeks of military training to hone his reactions and enable him to identify things like this in his sleep.

"You must sleep with one ear open Dad," Rosie sighs, like she's tuned right into my thoughts. "I didn't hear a bloody thing."

"Rosie!" Mum squeaks. "You are absolutely *not* to use language like that."

Clinging to the last shreds of hope for my dream, I visualise a mortar rocket arching overhead and wonder when the detonation will come. A sickness washes over me and turns my limbs to jelly. Rosie is the one who asks, "Why haven't we heard them go off then? Aren't they supposed to explode?"

Nothing happens. In the ensuing silence I hear the muffled sound of a car in the road outside.

"What are we going to do?" Mum's voice breaks a little more. "Shall I phone the police?"

The telephone trills loudly, raucously, and I swear my heart's just leapt clean out of my body. Skellum gives a joyous bark, his feathery tail sweeping Mum's face. Rosie shrieks and the cat springs from her clutch in disgust, vanishing into the darkness at the end of the passage.

"Shit!"

No-one chastises Dad for *his* language. For a brief second he leans his head against the wall, eyes closed, then catapults himself forward onto hands and knees and crawls towards the intersection of the passage with the main hallway. He disappears around the corner; the ringing stops and there's a violent plastic clatter.

"Hello!" he shouts. "Oh, it's you Allan. Sorry. I dropped the bastard phone. What? Yes of course I heard them. Started at about half-past two. What the fuck are they shooting at?"

He pauses. Rosie inches off down the corridor cooing, "Cleo? Cleo? Come, come, kitty."

"Funny thing is, I can't hear any explosions." Dad is still shouting, as though he and our neighbour are not connected by a telephone line but are rather calling to each other across the hills.

"Mortars explode when they hit something. That's the whole idea. Yes. *Ja*. Yes, okay Allan. You let me know what they say, hey? 'Bye."

We hear the sound of the front door being unlocked.

"What are you doing?" Mum yells, pushing Skellum aside and getting to her feet. "Bob! Where are you going?"

There's no reply and, filled with a morbid curiosity, I'm compelled to abandon all common sense and follow. The others feel it too. Rosie and I lead the way with Skellum, who probably thinks this unusual night-time activity has been arranged specifically for his enjoyment. Mum trails behind.

The sky is still completely cloudless. A three-quarter moon hangs in space among the winking stars and the Milky Way lays a faint trail like a pathway across the blackness. Everything is bathed in the faint white moonlight that is so peaceful and silent at three o'clock in the morning. Well, it should be peaceful and silent, but it's not.

Dogs are barking and howling. Human voices are drifting through the canine ones, male and female pitches. Car doors slam and engines start. The broad sweep of the valley up into the hills southwards, usually showing only a few strings of street lights at this hour, is speckled with electric light.

"What a wonderful target," Dad says to all of us in general. "I would have thought a black-out would be more sensible."

I turn to look at our own house, which is in darkness, and as I bring my head back round again a minute coloured movement attracts my attention. I have no idea what it is. In those few seconds it's processed as the blossoming of a dull red tongue, like some evil flower, on one of the hills in the north.

"Dad...?" I break off, mouth open. There's a whispering sound – a soft *whuw whuw whuw* – as a mortar shell etches out its trajectory above us. Only now do I hear the coughing retort of its launch. I duck and I see Dad do the same, and I'm thinking, don't we have stupid reactions sometimes? Then the other sounds come back into focus, intensified, the shouted voices more urgent.

Fascination and fear in equal proportions freeze me. I'm vaguely aware of Mum screaming, "Get inside! Get back!"

It's the sight of Cleopatra wandering out onto the lawn that releases me into a sinking realisation of the danger she's in – that we're all in. I grab her and bear her into the relative safety of the house. Rosie is dragging a reluctant Skellum towards the patio by his collar. Then the practical shuts down and fear has the upper hand. Cold, prickling-all-over fear and there's no room in my head for anything other than a desire to cower behind something solid and a pure horror that any second – any particle of a second – could be when it happens.

It doesn't.

The phone yells again and Dad makes a dive for it.

"Ja? What? Really? Ja. You're kidding me? Ja. Sure. Well I wonder if... Okay. Thanks. Bye."

He turns to face the three of us in our little huddle.

"Allan again. He got hold of the police and they reckon that new station, you know, down at the end of... oh what's the road called?... never mind... east end of the valley... they reckon that's the target. There's cops out trying to locate the spent shells. In the meantime, all of you, back in the passageway. Come on."

Herding us, he's taller, more authoritative, and the fear I'd been terrified to see in his face has been replaced by an electric excitement. "Security Forces are out in active pursuit. They have several units deployed. I wonder if they'll call out us Reservists? I'd better get my kit ready. May have to report to Depot. Right, you lot. Stay there and sit tight. The situation's under control."

"Bloody good show!" I whisper to Rosie, releasing Cleo, who promptly sits down and starts grooming herself. "Everything's ticketty boo, what? It's a good thing Elijah's at home in the township tonight. He'd probably have been scrambled into doing guard duty or patrolling the fences or something."

We giggle hysterically until Mum tells us to calm down.

There are no more mortars. Eventually all the lights go out, the dogs cease their barking and howling and although we wait up for a while, we only hear one burst of gunfire from the direction of the launching site. No-one calls for Dad's services.

I lie awake, my mind buzzing, aware of Mum and Dad talking in the lounge for a very long time. On a visit to the toilet I try to hear what they're saying without actually creeping down the corridor to eavesdrop. I can't, but the gravity of their conversation is unmistakeable and disturbing. I go back to bed, but I still can't sleep.

It's the what-ifs. What if the shells had exploded, wreaking hell and havoc on tidy, safe residential lives, on us, on our neighbours, on friends? I don't like that one and dismiss it. No point. What if there'd been more action? A bit of a shoot-up with the Security Forces, some helicopters or aircraft on a lethal mission and perhaps a few explosions in the hills? That one's more palatable and I spend some time elaborating on it. Always with a good outcome of course – terrorist gang annihilated, Security Forces victorious.

As the dawn seeps its way across the sky, I watch it through my bedroom window and I itch to get out and quiz Gill, Jess and Danny about their take on the drama. I even compose an eloquent description of my version, testing phrases and turning them around in my mind. What's Danny doing now? Why didn't he phone? What did he do when he heard the rockets whispering overhead? Did his brother pray to ask God for deliverance from peril?

Oh yes, God. So, what if some of the terrorists (guerrillas/ freedom fighters?) are Christians and they were praying that their mortar shells would hit the target (did they really have a target or were they just...?) to forward the fight against racial injustice and oppression? To be sure, their Christian targets (victims) would've been praying that they'll remain unharmed in the fight against the evil forces of terrorism and communism. Whose prayers will be answered in the end? Whose prayers *have* been answered tonight? One thing's for sure – if everyone believed in God, someone would always be disappointed.

It's the 11th November. Independence Day. A celebration of the Unilateral Declaration of Independence, signed at the eleventh hour of the eleventh day of the eleventh month, 1965. Look where it's got us thirteen years down the line.

*

Mrs Marsh returns from town about quarter to twelve.

"Guess what I heard?" she trills as she dumps her OK shopping bags on the kitchen table and reaches for the kettle. Her peaches-and-cream face, never usually affected by the highveld sun, is a bit flushed.

"What?" Danny, Gordon and I respond dutifully.

"Stupid question, Mother," says Jess. "Go on, spit it out. We could be here all day guessing."

"Heather Unwin told me her husband said those mortar rockets had not been primed – is that the right word? She said the terrs were aiming for the new police station but they overshot the target by – ooh – probably a kilometre, so the mortars all landed in that stretch of *vlei* down by the river. Isn't that just so hilarious?"

"It's a pity the ones who shot down the Viscount didn't get it so wrong, hey?" Jess pushes herself away from the work top, opens a cupboard and extracts some mugs.

"They used a heat-seeking missile," Gordon tells her. "They would've struggled to get it wrong unless they fired it in completely the opposite direction. Or would it've switched and come back?"

None of us knows the answer.

*

Dad's already heard the story from Allan Parsons.

"Useless sods! Lucky for us they can't use their equipment properly or shoot straight hey, don't you think? Might as well have thrown the damned things by hand!"

His chuckles and his eyes invite us all to respond accordingly. Rosie goes, "Hmm," and I ignore them.

"They might come back and shoot straight tonight," Mum worries. "Or not, and hit some houses this time. With rockets that work."

His eyebrows arch, the left slightly higher than the right.

"What? Nah! They wouldn't dare. This area's hot as far as they're concerned now. It'll be crawling with patrols. They're all just cowards anyway."

Is it all really such a farce to him? Cowards? They're showing no signs of giving up and running away, are they? This is a whole new game now. New targets. They shoot down a civilian aircraft, so then we get our revenge with the air raid on Nkomo's Zambian camp at Westlands Farm, and now we're facing the possibility of being attacked within the capital city limits. Ian Smith talks settlement out of one side of his mouth and then insists we're maintaining and escalating this stupid war to uphold standards and restore the peace out of the other. Well, a little peace wouldn't go amiss.

Mum and I wash up. She piles up the dishes and pots, I run the water and squeeze in some Sunlight and my thoughts escape to horses, as always.

"I'm giving Danny a riding lesson tomorrow. I've never tried to teach anyone before."

"Why don't you ask Gill to give you some tips?"

It's a good point. I never thought of that. She's been teaching me for years and she's damned good at it.

"Mmm. Yes, maybe. She was at a show today, but I'll ask her in the morning."

The telephone cuts across us and my adrenaline levels shoot sky high. Hangover from last night's fun, I guess.

"I'll get it!" Rosie hollers from somewhere. Moments later she appears in the kitchen.

"It's Gill, for you Tess."

I start to laugh at the coincidence, but the look on my sister's face stops me.

"She wants to talk to you urgently. She sounds a bit… strange. Like, upset. Not like her."

I pick up the receiver and manage to say "Hi!" before Gill starts to speak rapidly. I'm more surprised by this than what she's saying. In fact, it's a few moments before my brain clicks into gear and makes me realise what it is she's telling me. It sorts through the snatches of words and the now familiar sensation that something is terribly wrong soaks through me.

"Have to tell you... Tess... I'm so sorry... heard early this morning... contact somewhere in the Hurricane area... injured... six dead in total... casevac'd out by chopper... this evening... the hospital... oh my God... all tubes and wires... unconscious... so many drugs... Tessa? Tessa? Are you there? Say something, Tess! I'd love to see you. Are you coming here tomorrow?"

Nathan.

Oh no. Not Nathan *please*.

It is, isn't it? Oh dear God, why does it have to be you who finally drags this bloody war right up into my face?

I've had enough of this. I can't take any more. I've learned to ignore the faceless statistics but now here is a face. A face and a name I know so well. A member of my friend's family. A friend.

"Tess, please say something!"

I can't. What do I say? Do I ask if he's going to be all right or if... I have no more words. I take a breath. I can feel Mum behind me and I can sense the alarm radiating from her.

"Oh Gill," is all I can manage.

"What's happened?" Mum steps closer.

"Are you coming tomorrow?" Gill insists.

"Yes," I whisper reluctantly. Danny's riding lesson is suddenly of absolutely no importance.

"Well we might not be around. We might be at the hospital but I promise I'll let you know more as soon as we do. Okay? Look, I have to go now. Dad wants me to go with him to the hospital." Her voice takes on a stronger edge as if she's trying to focus on this, a specific requirement, a need.

"Don't worry, Tessa. We are trying not to too. I'll be in touch, okay?"

SUNDAY 12TH NOVEMBER 1978

I knew the house would be totally deserted, and it is. I'm not quite on this planet, still a little spaced out from those tablets Mum gave me last night. Sunday is Amai's day off too, so the place is locked up. They'll be at the hospital. Is that a good thing, or a very bad thing?

I'm thinking the yard is empty too, but no. The complete lack of human sound is all enveloping, soaking into the clammy humidity that clings to us, but over there is George, on the far side, sitting on an upturned bucket in the shade of the hedge. There's a bottle of Coke in the grass beside him and he's intently studying the *Sunday Mail*, eyes flicking between the paper and the Tote betting slips in his left hand.

He only looks up as we approach.

"Ah!" he grunts by way of a greeting, taking a swig from the bottle. "Not one winner again. I have lost too much money now!"

"Well George, you know what the answer is?"

I hadn't wanted to come here in the first place and I certainly don't wish to discuss George's vices.

He reads my mind. Setting aside his Coke, avoiding eye contact, he tears the betting slips into tiny pieces, then stuffs these into the pocket of his overalls.

"Have they told you about Boss Nathan?"

It's all I can do to nod. George does the "Ah!" again and when he does raise his head I see my own fear in his deep brown eyes.

"It has made Amai very ill. She has looked after him since he was very small. What have they told you? Is he going to die?"

"*DON'T* say that!"

I want to punch him for saying the words I've been trying to avoid all night – I mean, *really* want to punch him – and it shocks me.

"Bloody jackals," he grunts. He hawks and spits into the grass a couple of metres away and then studies Danny with an oddly critical stare. I'd better introduce them.

"George, meet Danny. Danny, meet George, the best groom in the country and carer for my horse."

"*Mangwanani*, Boss Danny. *Ma rara sei?* Do you know Nathan?"

Danny doesn't complete the greeting. He nods cordially at George and says, "I do remember him from school George, but he's older than me by a couple of years."

He takes my hand, and his sweat is slimy in my palm.

"Come on, Babe. Lead me to that horse before we bake out here."

He's called me that quite a lot recently. I've liked it, but right now it doesn't seem appropriate. It's too comfortable a word for this fearful, horrible, cruel world. I allow my hand to rest in his and try to convince myself that the distraction of this 'lesson' is what I need.

*

I make us linger at the stables well into the lunchtime feeding routine but, although three more grooms appear to carry out the duties, the Owen family remains absent. Bravo's brought in from his paddock; I have to spin on my heel and walk in the opposite direction because I can't deal with remembering an image I may never see again. Him, riding that beautiful horse. Him, making that horse look like he's performing every move of his own free will. Far too sharp in my mind as well, is the memory of him the last time he was back here on a weekend pass. I was arriving and he was just leaving on some errand in Charles's company pick-up, and we never even greeted each other. It was the first time I'd seen him in his camouflage and army boots and it was so incongruous that the memory jars and hurts somewhere deep within me. He wasn't the boy/teenager Nathan I know, lanky and casual in T-shirts with shorts or jodhpurs. This Nathan was an adult, business-like in uniform and with a grim set to his mouth that I'd never seen before.

And we never even greeted each other.

Maybe that's what jars and hurts more than anything.

This is the point at which I realise I can keep Danny hanging about no longer. I've instructed him on the points of the horse, how to groom, types of grooming tools, parts of the saddle and bridle and even minor equine ailments until his eyes have glazed over. He may have displayed unexpected confidence on horseback and been able to guide Induna in circles and figures-of-eight – admittedly rather odd-shaped ones – while making me smile with some of his comments and silly questions, but he couldn't disguise the fact that his sole objective was distraction.

I tell George I'll phone at four o'clock and we leave.

*

I hover near the phone for a good ten minutes, but I know I'll never make that call. Gill and I have had no end of marathon phone conversations over the years but right now it's the coldest and most impersonal form of communication I can imagine.

"I'll go over on the bike and be back for supper," I call out as I pass the living room door, rattling the shed keys in my hand like they're red hot. I want news, but I don't. My insides are churning and I wish I could run away somewhere – anywhere – or just dig a hole and get in it.

"Are you sure she should be going there?" It's Dad's voice and I pause mid-stride, just out of their line of sight.

"She's upset, Bob. Heaven knows, we get to hear these things every day but don't forget this is someone she knows so it's really hit her. I don't know what I should say to her."

Mum's voice changes in pitch and volume, calling me back.

"Tessa? Tessa are you still there? Dad thinks... I think... Maybe leave them alone darling. It's a very private, family thing and if they're grieving..."

I've reversed and am back in the doorway. I stop her there with, "I am family."

It just comes out. While she's still looking confused, I escape.

Grieving. No, they won't be. They won't.

*

I'm here, but I don't know how I got here. Well of course I know how I got here, but what I mean is… It doesn't matter.

Charles is in the driveway and he's dragging a large sports bag from the rear seat of his Mercedes. He hears my squeaky brakes, looks up at me by the open gate and I look at the bag.

Whose bag is that? What's in it? Has he brought it back from the hospital? Why would he need to bring stuff back from the hospital?

I push my bike into the hedge and, with no warning to either of us, burst into tears with a wail.

"Oh, Tessa!" He runs the few steps to reach me, and I'm in his warm bear hug. In order to do this, he has to drop the bag on the macadam surface and it makes a metallic clinking as it hits the ground. He rocks me several times, kissing the top of my head.

"It's all right, my darling. Don't cry. It will all be okay."

He pulls away a bit, tilts my chin up with a finger and tries a smile. "Now then, Missy. You're making my shirt wet."

I don't know what my streaked face looks like to him or what he can read in it, but I see such affection in his eyes that I start to blub all over again.

"No, no, no!" he protests, pulling me back into his chest. "He's okay. He's okay. He's still very much with us. Look, come inside and I'll tell you everything. Gill and Moira are longing to see you."

He picks up the bag as he leads me to the door. Past Nathan's pale blue Datsun 140J, adjacent to the garage, where he last left it.

"Finally got those two bridles back from Fairmont Saddlery on Friday. Buggers've had them for four weeks!"

When we've all finished hugging each other and I've blown my nose noisily several times, they sit me down at the big kitchen table. Moira shoves a heap of what looks like Charles's paperwork aside, pushes a glass of water into my right hand. Gill pulls her chair close and holds my left. Charles turns one of the chairs around so its tall back is against the table and sits astride it, his thick brown forearms crossed on top of it. He talks.

As is his habit, he doesn't waste words. A routine patrol in a follow-up operation after the murder of some villagers, an ambush, shots taken in the right side of the body and the right leg, blood and tattered uniform cloth, comrades not knowing the extent of the damage, chopper casevac, unconsciousness, transfusions, a list of operating procedures – which I try very hard not to listen to – and then life and a clean, white hospital bed.

"I've no doubt we'll get the full story in time, but he's still drugged up. He's a lucky boy. His vital organs are intact and so's his pelvis and femur. Flesh wounds only, you know?"

Pointlessly, I recall to mind the names of the pelvic bones: ilium, ischium and pubis. I can see the skeleton drawing in my biology file.

"The doctors are saying he'll end up with a bit of a limp for a while due to some muscle damage. What they need to do now is prevent infection. We'll see."

We talk some more and then finally, we laugh. It's a relief. Amai appears from the garden, which means it's nearly dinner time, and there's more hugging. She wraps me in her soft brown arms and clamps my face against her cushiony bosom so I can't breathe. She smells of Palmolive soap. Goodness and safety. Charles eventually prises me away.

"Don't start her crying again, Amai. And you, don't you start either!"

Family. I'm as much at home and as loved here as I am in my own house. This can't be right, but it feels right. Me, Gill, Moira, Charles, Amai – we're good together. And Nathan? Nathan should be here too.

He will be.

SATURDAY 25TH NOVEMBER 1978

Danny's mum is one of those homely, practical, domesticated, arty-crafty types who makes her own everything. My mum cooks okay, and she bakes cakes or biscuits every now and then and they usually come out nice, but Mrs Proctor spends her days up to her elbows in pastry or cake mix or half completed garments, and she's just finished making these – a hundred of them. A *hundred*. I couldn't even find a reason to have a hundred. Who does she send them to?

"Oh wow, those are beautiful Mrs Proctor! We used to make Christmas cards."

She looks up at me with sparks of kindred spirit in her eyes. "We? With your parents?"

"Me and my sister. We thought it would be a good idea, just for family, but I don't reckon they were appreciated."

She thinks that's funny, but I just remember it being a complete pain in the you-know-what. We spent hours measuring with rulers and making faint pencil lines that could be easily rubbed out, then Dad cut the cards with his office guillotine. We then spent more hours folding knife edges precisely and copying pictures from old cards in coloured crayons. My handwriting being far superior to Rosie's, I got the task of penning all the greeting lines (also plagiarised from the previous year's commercial cards) and filling in the addressees' names, and then signing *With lots of love from Bob, Sheila, Tessa, Rosie, Cleo, Skellum and Induna*. Eight times, each year, for four years. Then Grandad Harry died and because he'd so loved our efforts and wrote to tell us how he looked forward to them every year, I couldn't bring myself to send any more home-made cards to Granny Libby in case it made her cry. I don't know if it would've made her cry – I've never met her – but I visualised her alone in her little bungalow in Ringwood, opening an envelope, taking out one of our cards and bursting into tears because Grandad wasn't there to see it. So then, because she wouldn't get any more cards, all of them had to stop in case she felt left out. No more for Dad's brother and his family or Mum's sister and her family or even for Grandad David and Granny Madge. I made the decision, Rosie took no convincing and Mum failed to produce an argument that stood up to that logic, so that was the end of our Christmas card manufacturing career.

Dad's Aunty Julia was the only one who eventually asked, in a letter, "Why don't your girls do their own cards anymore? They were so lovely." Bless her.

I have to say Mrs Proctor's creations are way more impressive than our clumsy attempts, and I wonder where the hell she gets the time to do the measuring and the cutting and the colouring and the gluing and the spraying of glitter and the crafting of the perfect calligraphy, never mind searching the depleted shops in Salisbury for the materials and pens. I'm just about to butter her up with, "Yours are *so* professional!" when Danny's dad appears at the back door, his square face red and a bit sweaty. His nose – which is Danny's nose exactly – is glistening.

"Hi Tessa!" he exclaims, ditching his flip flops one by one. "Lovely to see you today. My, that's such a pretty skirt. Did you make it?"

Did I *what?*

I'm saved from having to make any sort of embarrassing admission, or indeed lie, by Mrs P herself.

"Go and get showered, Roger. Sue said she's serving lunch at one and when Sue says one, she means one. Dan, there's corned beef and salady stuff in the fridge and fresh bread."

When they've gone, Brian and Cassie muck in to help us make sandwiches. My first impression of Brian still comes back to me whenever I'm with him – that he's just a slightly older version of Danny, with a thinner face and a more studious intensity about him. Today he's focussing that intent on finding out how long I'll be staying this afternoon because he's got some friends coming over that he'd like me to meet.

"We're not sticking around Bri," says Danny. "We're off for a walk in a bit."

"Heavy cloud out there. You sure?" Brian leans across the worktop and cranes his neck to study the sky.

"No rain forecast. It'll be fine. Cass, here's your sandwich."

"Well hopefully they'll pitch up before you go. I was kind of hoping I could introduce you, Tessa."

The walk is news to me but I'm okay with it. After a very small amount of time wondering why he's so keen for me to meet these friends I give him the *oh-well-never-mind* noises. I'm sure they're lovely people.

Cassie's an interesting one. She's connected to Brian by a piece of elastic. He takes up ninety percent of her attention, she struggles to move more than about a metre away from him and she agrees with everything he says. She's quite sweet – a bit mousey – but she's so annoyingly In Love and she says "Praise the Lord" and "Hallelujah" after every other sentence. To be fair, I do get that she's going to want to be around him as much as she can while he's back home on RNR, so maybe I'm doing her a disservice. I'll be like that too, I guess, when Danny starts getting called up. We just have no idea what this life is going to serve up to us from one day to the next, do we? Make the most of the time you spend with those you love, Gill told me, and she vowed that if she never did so before, she would do so from now on.

After we've eaten, they leave us alone in the kitchen for a bit and the uncomfortable tension she created in me starts to fade. I wash and Danny dries and puts away and we debate about where to go for our walk. He's in the middle of a story about two small children who've been orphaned because their parents were ambushed on their way back to their farm in Mangula when he's interrupted by the sound of car wheels crunching over the gravel in the driveway and Brian calling from the lounge, "Ah! Dan! Tess! Terry and Nina are here, guys."

"Terry Archer and his wife, who run Brian and Cassie's Christian youth group," Danny whispers. "I think they've come to drop off some newsletters for Brian to deliver. I didn't know until this morning that they were coming today. They're a bit painful. We need to make our escape as soon as possible."

Terry is pale and earnest; tall, with pale brown hair and a pale brown wispy moustache that's struggling to make itself known. Nina is probably two thirds of his height, a bit shorter than me, but very roundly pregnant. He's quiet and calm and gently smiley; she's loud and effervescent.

She spots me within seconds of entering the hallway and fizzes at me, clapping her hands. "Ah! So who are you? We haven't seen you before! Danny, you haven't introduced us. We haven't seen you in a while anyway! So nice to have you here!"

I'm a bit bemused. It's his house, after all.

"This is Tessa, my girlfriend," Danny tells her and I come over fluttery and coy and sidle up close to him. Now I'm behaving like Cass.

He winks down at me and says, "She came for lunch today," and Nina is absolutely delighted.

"And we decided to call in! Terry said only this morning at breakfast, he said, 'D'you know what Neens? I think we should drop those papers round to Brian Proctor today and not Monday evening.' Now, my girlie, I have a feeling our Lord has been at work here. He's sent you here today to meet us. Isn't it wonderful? He knew you would be here and He sent us to help you find Him. It's amazing! Amazing Grace – ha ha! Brian, you have to get your brother to come to Chapel and bring his girl. Do you have any brothers or sisters, Tessa?"

"A sister," I hear myself say.

"Oh super! Great! Bring her along too. We'd love to see her, meet her. We're all family here. In fact…" she pats her belly, "we're expanding ours. This is our fourth. We'll bring more people to worship the King any way we can!"

She chortles merrily and then rattles off again, which is fortunate because I can't come up with anything sensible to say.

"So why don't you come along then? You and Danny could also come to our Bible Study sessions so you can better understand the miracle of being Born Again and how you can be baptised when you are ready to welcome Jesus into your heart. Terry and I give classes at the weekends. It will give you something to do on Saturdays or Sundays, won't it? Great! You can combine that with the Chapel service. I'll bet you like lying in on Sundays? Don't worry, we'll keep you busy!"

Give ME something to do on Saturdays or Sundays? Lying in? I wish. I could tell her what I'm thinking, but I don't.

Danny's not doing a lot to try and rescue me after all his talk about escaping. Brian, Cassie and Terry are regarding me just as fervently as Nina. I'm cornered, even though the French doors are open and the world outside stretches before me.

"Right, sorry, but we're off now. Danny and I were going to go for a walk and it looks like rain later."

We fumble to get our tackies on and are out the door in two minutes.

"See what I mean?" he mumbles out the side of his mouth as we make our exit down the drive. "I don't mean to be nasty – they do no harm – but they're so bloody persistent about recruiting. Drives me nuts."

Over the road, we take one of the paths through the open *vlei*, hand in hand.

He tells me what my parents have already been worrying about for the last week – that from next year the government schools will take in all races. Private schools have done so for years now, but parents of government school kids like us have gone into melt-down over what they perceive as a disastrous and unprecedented decision.

"It had to happen, Danny. And about time. Everyone should be entitled to the same education from the start, don't you think? Why does being white skinned entitle us to a better education? I've talked this through with Charles, Moira and Gill quite a bit. We've debated their views versus those of my folks, who, needless to say, tend to be old school."

Charles says an equivalent education process for blacks should've started ages ago and I agree.

"I can't understand how the settlers in, say, the 1920s, couldn't see that the indigenous population would eventually want a good part in governing Africa. And with the right education there's no reason whatsoever why that shouldn't have been the plan. The settlers never contemplated sharing education and, eventually, power. Why couldn't we all have developed this country together? It's so wrong to assume that Africans – the black Africans that is, because I'm African too – would always be content to have the role of servants and labourers. What job you do should depend on your abilities and skills, not on your colour, don't you think?"

He's focussed on the sandy track stretching ahead. He makes no reply, although his face would indicate he's busy making up one. Just before the main road ahead, the path takes a dip through the shallow-sided drainage swale and up to the verge, but also splits here to run both ways along this side of the ditch. Right is the short route back to his place. Left leads us on a circuit perhaps three times as long.

I tug at his hand. "Left? Or right?"

In that moment of indecision he turns to face me and I'm not sure what I see in his face. It could be fascination, but why? Or maybe amazement – again why? Disconcerting.

"Left then? We can go around the copse and then up across the hill at the back of Bertrand Road."

"Okay." Automatic. His mind is somewhere else.

Then he says, "Weren't we talking about black pupils flooding our schools?"

That's how it started. But then I steered it on to wondering how folks came to be worrying about that in the first place.

"Well… So anyway, don't you think that's true? What if all children in this country had had the same education from age five to sixteen, seventeen? Blacks would surely have naturally sifted into those jobs that have become exclusively white years ago and all this violence might never have come about. It shouldn't matter what colour you are, as long as you have the education and qualifications to do a particular job. The only reason we so blithely say the blacks are not capable, not ready for government, is because most of them have been held back educationally for so long. It's our own doing."

We keep walking, one foot in front of the other. Why doesn't he answer me? Come up with some comment? I pluck the head off a stalk of brown grass, kick a stone that's so smooth it looks like it's come from a river, decide maybe I should grope around in my head for a safe subject instead of trying this grown up stuff.

And he starts to laugh. Creased-up-face, delighted laughter. He says, "Do you know you're even prettier when you're all fired up? Don't start getting a guilt complex about problems our forefathers created, Babe. If you're going to look back that far, remember that the colonial, Victorian mentality saw things very clearly in the light of the glorious British Empire that would save the savage peoples of the world from themselves."

I don't know what I expected, but it wasn't this.

"All fired up?"

"You are," he agrees, grinning.

A sharp retort would be good here, but I'm too astounded. The only direction my brain can scrabble along in is towards self justification.

"I'm just putting the case for what I think. I'm fully aware that mentalities have changed, thanks. There must have been individuals among them with the foresight though, surely?"

"Probably very few and their views wouldn't have been popular. Don't forget also that many whites who came to this country from England, Scotland and other countries in the early part of this century, and even as late as the forties and fifties, were not happy with their lot in their own home territory. They were perhaps lacking in education themselves and they lived a hard life after World War Two in overcrowded homes they couldn't afford to own. Think of the opportunities a place like this, or South Africa, or East Africa, had to offer. Those less educated settler whites were the ones who would've had their jobs threatened by up-and-coming, well-educated blacks who might have worked with the higher class whites. The higher class, business-owning whites were more likely to be liberals anyway, and open to this idea. The working class white folks particularly were afraid of educated blacks. Lots still are today. You're in danger of becoming too idealistic, Tess. You've got to take human nature into account. Anyway, it's too late. It's all happened, we can't change it, and it's no fault of yours or mine. Don't be guilty. Besides, I'd have thought you'd be concerned about standards in schools, my sweetheart?"

I'm aware of all that too. And I'm not guilty.

"I'm aware of that too. And I'm not guilty. Why should I be? And why should I be concerned? I support the idea."

He stops and shakes a puzzled head. "I just thought… Don't you want…? Well never mind. Come down off your soapbox, Babe! These people – your friend and her parents – you've let them influence you in ways you probably don't realise. It will never work, Tessa. The place will collapse, just like the rest of Africa, you wait and see."

His voice in this final sentence is flat and terminal. Conversation over. Like he's disappointed, although I'm his sweetheart. He's saying he thinks I should be concerned about standards in schools. I don't know why he would say that.

Well, I do, of course. Now how about that for a little wormy thought I'd rather ignore for now?

"Well, let's hope the place doesn't collapse, but that's not my point. The point I'm trying to make is that we have to have racial equality. It's inevitable and it really always has been. I've grown up in this war, Danny, as have you. I can barely remember what it was like before. All the death, all the restrictions – it's become a way of life. Do you know what occurred to me just the other day? I haven't seen or heard a firework since… when? I have this dim recollection of being about four or five, or maybe younger, in our garden on Guy Fawkes Night – rockets throwing up colours and patterns, Catherine wheels, lots of noise. I'd forgotten all about it. It's hardly important in itself, but it's something we used to have *before*. Before war."

And another thing…

"And another thing. The Owens are *all* my friends and we have many healthy debates about all sorts of subjects. I happen to think their political views make more sense than those of my parents. What's wrong with that? It means I'm thinking for myself."

He lets go of my hand, slides his arm around my shoulders, soft now, smiling, soothing.

"All right, all right. Don't get worried. Family is important and I think you do really support them although I can see what you're trying to say. I've upset you though, Babe and I'm sorry. It's okay if you're angry. I'm just surprised you... well... you don't see the problems Smith's been trying to prevent all these years."

He's making out that I don't know my own mind. Smith. I've been brought up to be fiercely patriotic for Rhodesia and good old Smithy. Would I still be as patriotic and believing if I'd never met the Owens? Never been party to any opinions other than those of Mum and Dad? Possibly. A government at war uses propaganda to its maximum advantage and my parents have faithfully taken on board that we'll really be able to hang on to a Promised Land. A paradise of easy living in the sun and a privileged position in a society with plenty of cheap labour to create an affordable cost of living and to provide an abundance of domestic help. They see it that this is right. That we, the whites, are upholding civilisation in Africa, benevolent guides to a more simple people, just like the Victorians did. That Ian Smith is leading us in a stand against the rest of the world because we are doing the right thing by holding government. That it's the rest of the world that's wrong. That the racial *status quo* is a perfectly acceptable situation.

I do *not* support my parents' views just because we're all members of the same family. Why should I do that?

"I haven't yet figured out how I would argue this with Mum and Dad. To be honest, I probably won't."

"Sure, sure, sure. Probably best not."

We do a hug and he says shall we go back now and I nod against his shoulder but I'm thinking I won't get back on my soapbox in front of him again. I'm not having my soapbox kicked to pieces under me.

We don't go back straight away. We wander up in the hills for nearly two hours talking comfortable subjects. Finally, he says he thinks the coast is probably clear now, but when we arrive back at his house Terry and Nina are still there.

SATURDAY 2ND DECEMBER 1978

That *is* Julie Foster. I'm absolutely certain now. I wasn't, at first, but I've been watching her all afternoon.

I'd probably never have spotted her if she hadn't been with the Girls' High School team. They're making such a racket it's impossible to ignore them. So I saw her sitting halfway up the stand in the middle of all her noisy team-mates and wondered, idly at the time, why this girl wasn't joining in all the hysterical war cries and arm waving, and then I noticed Lisa Donovan in the row above her. Lisa spoke to her a few times, over her shoulder, and that's when some of her gestures and head movements started distant bells ringing.

It's exceptionally irritating when you realise that someone who's effectively a complete stranger is actually familiar, and you know you've seen them before, but you can't think where. Around three o'clock, just after GHS had won yet another race, a cog clicked over inside my head and that Kariba holiday from eons ago popped up. 1973, it was. Five years ago. Julie Foster. Dad's colleague's daughter who introduced Rosie to tennis. I've seen her maybe three, four times since? Dad did say both Julie and Catherine go to Girls' High School.

What on earth's happened to her? My remembered image of her is cheeky and precocious, with a round, rosy face and glossy, bouncy gold hair. It *is* her though. And now I want to know why she looks like death warmed up.

God, I don't want to be here. We've got no chance now and I'm bored stiff watching these endless relays. I don't know how much chlorine they've been putting in this pool but the smell is so overpowering I'm amazed the competitors aren't coming out green. I'm not sure what's caused this delay in the proceedings, but I don't care. It's a perfect excuse to sneak off. I can always say I've been to the toilet.

Jess has her back to me and is giving our diving team a pep talk. Brilliant. I wriggle off the end of the stand and nip round the back, then make my way to where the GHS team and supporters are wetly and noisily waving banners to make sure everyone knows they're winning, even when nothing's happening. Lisa's on the end of the second row up and she looks as bored as I am.

She wants to talk horses but for once I won't let myself be tempted. I say, "Mmm. Yes, it was a good show, wasn't it? Tell me, isn't that Julie Foster?"

I tilt my head towards the girl with the ashen and vacant face.

Lisa nods. "*Ja*. You know her?"

"Kind of. My father works with hers. I haven't seen her in a long while so I wasn't sure. She looks ill. Is she all right?"

Lisa leans into me conspiratorially and whispers, "Well no. Not really. It's the first time in over a month she's joined in any kind of group activity. Her boyfriend, Tommy, was killed over near Cashel on a weekend home. His folks manage one of the tea estates up there and he drove over a land mine in one of their roads. He was seventeen, Tessa! It's horrible. He was at Prince Edward School. She'd known him for about five years and had been going out with him for two, and it's absolutely destroyed her. She doesn't know what's hit her. They were like two peas in a pod, as they say. We've got to try and get her on her feet again."

Lisa's quite a loud and tactless girl as a rule, but her stricken concern is infectious and it's making me feel slightly nauseous. The ugly fingers of this liberation campaign are reaching for all of us now. Not just servicemen in battle, but civilians too. Direct attacks – missiles and mortars – and now a schoolboy has died at the hands of a murderer who had planted his container of death and been long gone.

*

Six o'clock, and this melancholy is still simmering away. It's changed shape, or rather identity, at times, especially since I got home and have had nothing in particular to distract me. It's been fear, it's been despair, it's even been anger. I've never felt so pointlessly angry before. I'm not even sure I've known real anger, if that's what this is. I've had annoyance, with a reason I can identify or a person I can blame, but this is more akin to helplessness, like an inability to change the course of a future I no longer want to experience. It can't go on, but it is going to go on.

Halfway through my dinner I stop eating and continue to stare at the remains, unable to keep my imagination from attempting to visualise Julie Foster at her boyfriend's funeral, inwardly cursing myself for being morbid. I'm damned lucky I haven't had to attend one.

"Come on Tessa," says Dad, waving his fork at me. "Try and look happier. What's wrong with the food?"

"Did you know about Julie Foster's boyfriend?" I challenge him, stirring my peas with my own fork as if they are to blame. "I saw her at the gala today. She looks ghastly. One of my friends from the horse society told me the story."

He did know, he confesses. He'd said nothing because he hadn't wanted to upset us. His demeanour is crestfallen, caught-out.

Should I be furious with him or sympathise with his predicament? He thinks it's his duty to rinse our minds of any nightmarish worries about bodily harm and mortal danger. He's a father, a protector – who can blame him for that? The knowledge that Nathan's just come within milliseconds of losing his life has shaken me to depths I never knew existed and my reaction to this has upset Rosie and undoubtedly heightened Mum's awareness of the perils Dad is facing on military duty. At every opportunity he's been stressing that he's never in any danger of coming into close contact with the enemy. His role in Dad's Army, he's told us over and over, is mainly that of the 'bright light' – a live-in guard to an absent farmer's family or to the more elderly farming couples attempting to produce crops and manage livestock with some semblance of normality. Plied with good farm food and fresh air, it's a bit like having a holiday at the government's expense, he says. He thinks I believe him, but his unsubtle attempts at propaganda cannot not undo what's been done.

He changes the subject. Well, sort of.

"Hey, well, sounds like, um… whatsisname… um… Gill's brother… is going to be all right anyway? Will he be going to Tsanga Lodge for rehab?"

Rosie jumps on this opportunity to throw a Teenage Moment. She pouts and folds her arms across her chest.

"*Ja*. Tsanga Lodge. I might have gone there, to Tsanga, or to Mushandike like Tee did. But of course that's all spoilt now. They had to stop it before I got to go there, didn't they?"

"Oh don't be so petulant, Rosie," Mum chips in. She laughs because she thinks it's the best way to deal with Teenage Moments and Dad laughs because he's being cheery. I feel like there's a rubber band inside my head that's being strained to breaking point.

"Count yourself lucky, you silly little girl. You lot may have gone to Mushandike and been shot to bits, or all murdered in your beds by gooks. Or blown up. Then *you* might have needed rehab. Or a wooden box. Nathan's not that badly injured anyway Dad. He just needs time to get better."

Gill's been telling me what it's like at the hospital; her world has been centred around her daily visits, either alone or with Charles and Moira. I've never once asked if I can tag along. I know I should, but I keep shying away from asking the question and then cursing myself for doing it, and then justifying it because it's such a personal mission for her. Nathan *is*, in all respects, her little brother. She's seen him through the usual variety of childhood ailments and a broken collar bone, when he fell out of their treehouse, but there's always been life and a future after these minor hiccups. Now, when he got sent out to kill or be killed for his country, another soldier, acting for someone else but under similar instructions, has deliberately tried to rob him of that life.

Rosie's shut up and is scraping her knife across her plate to gather up morsels onto her fork. I'm in trouble now for snapping at my sister and for being petulant myself. To be honest though, I'm just a coward who really has no desire to visit any hospital to view at first hand the damage done by war. I can't face young men, not much older than myself, whose lives have been cruelly altered by what is considered to be their duty. Can't face their anger and frustration and terror. My petulant anger that *my* life is being disrupted is nothing in comparison. What is one supposed to say and how is one supposed to react? I've stayed away. Nathan wouldn't want me there at his bedside anyway.

I can kid myself that I'd been there when he was still drugged and plugged into drips and Gill was reading to him ("I finished reading him *Airport* today. He started it when he was home the last time on RNR. Do you know, he asked me to bring in *Great Expectations*! Dickens! Miracles never cease. I know reading to him is stupid, but I used to do that when we were kids and he always loved the way I tried different voices. Not sure how I'll cope with being Magwitch though!"). I picture this and then wonder if I can imagine the two of them together, Gill aged, say, ten, reading to Nathan, seven or eight. It's intriguing.

I can kid myself that I was there when he started to feel up to moving about. ("He's sitting up now! The doc's delighted with his recovery. Put on a bit more flesh in his face. Much better. I'm going to take some board games from now on. I'll have to dig them out of the spare room cupboard. We can put them on his bed table.") I picture this and then guess at a scene in which they're sitting at the kitchen table together engrossed in Monopoly or Scrabble.

I can kid myself that I was there when he walked up and down the ward and then the corridor for the first time. ("They gave him a stick, which he's unimpressed about – you know him – but I said it's only for now, and it will help, so at least you can keep your muscles toned. Silly boy's saying he can't wait to get back in the saddle. Well, we'll have to see about that hey? We took Amai along today so she was there too. She cried all over him and he was patting her head and saying come on Amai, stop blubbering, I'm fine, can't you see? Brought tears to all of us, I can tell you!")

That's the phone. I bolt from the family and my uneaten food to answer it.

"He's due to come home on the sixteenth, Tess!" she tells me with her triumph oozing down the line. "Home in time for Christmas! Hey, but you won't be here will you? When are you going to Cape Town?"

I'd like to kid myself that I'll be there for his homecoming, but no, I won't.

"Thursday, then back late on the twenty-sixth. I get to miss the last day of school."

"Oh that's right. Christmas in the Cape – you lucky thing! Oh, I can't describe to you the... what's the word?... euphoria almost, that I got when he told us the news today. Like the light at the end of the tunnel has suddenly really turned into a way out, you know? I'm so lucky, so blessed. He was so nearly taken from us but we got him back."

"Danny's brother's got a mate who says Nathan's life was spared so that he could spend the rest of it serving God. This guy's his pastor or something. He evidently thought it would be of great comfort to me to know this."

She breaks into peals of delight. "What? Really? I'll tell him. Should he be honoured?"

"Terry Archer. This is the bloke who also said that the missionaries up at Elim were slaughtered because God wanted them returned to his services. He wanted them back and we must rejoice in this. We must remember that God knows what is best for us and that he has plans for us all, so we mustn't question his motives."

I can see the newspaper images hovering before me now, as I listen to her expletives. The splayed bodies, slightly out of focus, in such gruesome, unnatural positions. Those poor sodding missionaries had been liberals, followers of Christianity and its associated doctrine of peace, and they got rewarded for their sentiments and for trying to help and educate rural communities by being raped and bayonetted to death. Including that baby girl. They must have prayed, begged and pleaded, but it was no good and they suffered unimaginably horrible deaths. Their God was away doing more fun things like setting up a complex chain of events that would lead to me hooking up with Danny so that I could meet Brian, and then Terry and Nina, and be saved.

Man's inhumanity to man, it's becoming apparent, knows no limits. I'm learning this, but it's not something I want to learn. Danny insists on calling the terrorists animals, but they're only displaying human characteristics. Which other animals are known to kill others of their kind out of vindictiveness, or for the hell of it? Chimpanzees. Our closest relatives. What does that tell you?

Gill sighs.

"Sorry. Excuse the language. I don't understand these people who resign themselves to what they say is God's will, Tess. It's actually a complete abdication of responsibility isn't it? Anyway, look, gotta go, but I just couldn't wait till tomorrow to update you. See ya – byeee!"

They'd welcome me at Nathan's homecoming because I have no doubt that to them I'm part of the furniture. As I only realised barely three weeks ago, I'm part of the family. But I'll be in South Africa and anyway, he wouldn't care.

If there's one good thing going to come out of this though, it's that he'll be out of danger for a while. They can't take him back until he's fixed.

WEDNESDAY 27TH DECEMBER 1978

The horse is cantering – no, floating – away from me. It's right at the far end of the field, a good two hundred metres away, but I have no doubt that it's Bravo. The rider must be Justice. A man, so not Gill, and Justice is the only groom who's been exercising him, because he's by far the best rider. And also, Justice often discards his overalls when he's riding; this man's wearing a long-sleeved shirt and jeans. And a wide brimmed safari hat. Justice doesn't have such a hat. Wait a minute…

The horse checks, sinking from that light canter into a perfect halt with no apparent intervention on the part of the rider, who sits relaxed and still in the saddle. The pair turn back towards the gate, but before I even see the white-skinned face, I know. I know only one person who can ride like that.

I drop my bike on the ground and clamber up onto one of the gate rails, waving my arms over my head.

"Nathan!" I yell at the top of my lungs, and have to grab the top rail as I lose my balance.

He's seen me. He slips the reins and lets the horse stretch his nose nearly to the ground then leans forward, circles his left arm in exaggerated waves and gives a whoop of greeting and for one confused second I'm genuinely convinced that I'm mistaken – that this is some stranger. I squint. No, there's zero doubt. What's he doing up and riding anyway? Gill said he was resting either in bed or on the sofa.

I'm still clinging to the gate – suspended, my brain assessing this novel situation – and the distance between us is closing. His face is thinner than I remember, but there's no doubt it's him and he's still eager and waving, although now just the left hand.

About five strides out from the gate he says, "Hello you" and when I don't react (still figuring out *how* to react) he goes on with, "Back from SA? Gill told me you'd been on holiday. She's gone into town with Charles and Moira. I thought I'd haul myself back into the saddle while they weren't about, as I've been expressly forbidden to do so for at least another week. Maybe I shouldn't, but it's been far too long and I was getting withdrawal symptoms."

Is it…? Am I sure…? It *is* him. Lots of words. A lilt I've never heard before. It's very pleasant. From what I can see under the hat, his hair has grown a little from the crew cut he had the last time I saw him. He slides his boots out of the stirrups, takes a deep breath, tenses, makes a move to dismount, but then changes his mind.

"Actually, would you mind opening the gate for me, please? I'd better get off onto the mounting block I think."

Snap out of it. Mental shake. Come on now, stop gawping.

I make an ill-considered backwards leap off the gate and my right ankle twists and twinges as I hit the ground. Hopping, I swing the gate wide for them, latch it closed again once they've passed through and experience a sinking sense of disappointment at the sight of the old, veiled, guarded expression creeping back over his face. It's my fault. I'm not giving these unprecedented greetings or approaches any feedback.

Heaven knows, conversations with Nathan have always been short-lived. Necessary things have been said, we've moved on, walked away. It's never changed since that first encounter outside my classroom and even now his time in the Rhodesia Regiment's as much of a mystery to me as his life has always been. Occasionally there's been a weird unspoken communication but then his shutters have come down again and I've been dismissed from his world.

How to deal with this? Now I'm the one who's closing the shutters. What do I ask someone I don't speak to who's just come back from hospital after being shot up in action? When I've not seen him since well before that even happened? When I haven't made any attempt to visit him, to tell him what's been going on in the normal life he's nearly lost or to reassure him that he'll be back to enjoy it? Gill's done all these things – so have Charles and Moira and even Amai. But I have not. I've pretended to myself that I've made up for this failure by sending inane messages with Gill, like, "Tell him I said hi."

The right phrases aren't making themselves available to me. No stupid questions, for God's sake, like "What was it like to be gunned down?" or "Did it hurt?"

My brain offers, "How's the recovery going?" and I grab it.

He gives no indication he's in any way disillusioned to find I'm such a half-wit. He halts Bravo and turns to look at me.

"Oh, pretty okay. It could've been worse. At least I didn't lose too many bits. I can't claim it was some sort of near-death experience. There was no bringing me back from the brink. All they did was sew me up and pump me back full of blood."

That's not what Gill told me.

He's running his left hand along Bravo's crest, fingers scratching. "I feel that much better for having ridden this beauty again."

Another offering comes, sliding words onto my tongue, and this time they're perfect. I know as soon as they take shape that this information will be vital to him.

"You haven't lost your touch."

I was right. The mask slips, the spark flashes again somewhere (where?) and he inclines his head fractionally in that familiar – that wonderfully familiar – gesture. There's an uncanny sense that the unfathomable schoolboy has been spirited into an adult body and then undergone a transformation I'm incapable of grasping. It's a subliminal understanding that he *wants* to have a conversation with me, but that's not all. There's more – underlying, complex, unidentifiable.

"Are you going out for a ride?" he asks.

"I am indeed. I need to catch myself a horse first though. I'll go grab a headcollar."

I gesture towards the tack room, but then it comes back to me that he's just said he wants to get off onto the mounting block. Of course. He's sore. I can help. Should I help?

Now I'm in dither mode. What do I do, Nathan? Volunteer to hold Bravo's bridle for you? Or just take hold of it? Will that be insulting? You need to ask. Come on, help me by asking me to help you.

Just before I left home earlier, I twisted my hair up on top of my head and secured it with a tortoiseshell clip, but several strands have escaped. To prevent them from tickling my face in the breeze while I'm dithering, I reach up with both hands and try in vain to tuck them under the clip with my fingers. Bravo's starting to get restless, shifting his backside around. Nathan's ignoring him, moving with him, but with his eyes down at me. The oddest feeling I've ever experienced starts with a notion that the space between us is crackling and then generates a swooping in my chest that washes all the way down into my legs.

Swooping? Well that's the only way I can describe it. Maybe it's more like a squeezing.

Nathan snaps his face away from me. He nudges Bravo forward far more abruptly than is necessary, so that the horse gives a grunt and tosses his head. I stay absolutely still for a moment with my arms still raised above my head.

What have I done? It was all going so unusually... different. Well, even. And now? Oh, what the hell. I've never been able to work this guy out.

"Come with me," I call after him. No sooner are the words out when I get a desire to kick myself. Too late. Can't retract it. The only other time we've ridden together was on the day of the treasure hunt at the Turnpike Equestrian Centre centuries ago. That afternoon, my dread of being alone with him ended up being totally unfounded.

Well, I've done it, so I've got to deal with it.

"I'm only going for a short hack. The weather doesn't look too good. If you want to. Maybe you've had enough now?"

When he speaks back to me over his shoulder, his voice is again as light and pleasant as I've ever heard.

"Oh, are you sure? Well yes, okay. Why not? I'll stay on board while you get ready though. Can't face climbing off and then climbing back on again."

I leave him and Bravo by the mounting block and head for the tack room, trying not to limp too much on my dodgy ankle. It'll come right in a few minutes anyway.

*

It's overcast now. The wind is keen, and its cool touch and whispered gusts are making the horses skittish.

Okay, let's try and get this silly animal to stand properly. Second time lucky.

"I didn't think I was going to be able to catch him, you know. He's normally easy but Foxie and Silver Valley in the next paddock were having a funny five minutes and were winding all the others up. I eventually managed to cajole him into a corner where he stood like a lamb. But now… Stand! Indie! Come on, behave. This is naughty."

God, how embarrassing.

"Looks like he's enormously excited at the prospect of going out with a companion, especially on such a blowy day."

Nathan touches the right side of his torso and then the thigh with fingertips, a shadow of doubt momentarily in his expression. Self-doubt.

"I hope they don't jiggle about too much. I'll be in the shit if I bust open the wounds and they've got to stitch me up again."

"He's not likely to buck, is he?"

"Bravo? No. Fortunately."

I am indeed tempted to believe Induna's anticipating the fun of helping a friend to find new horrors lurking in the bushes – dragons and the like – which will be excellent excuses for a bit of shying and for showing me up. Nathan and Bravo are cool and calm to look at, but Bravo's nostrils are flared wide and his ears are pricked so far forward they look like they're going to pop off his head.

My horse isn't going to stand. I have to act fast and I arrive in the saddle with an ungracious bump, fumbling for my offside stirrup while jogging towards Bravo. We set off down the drive and the two of them start conspiring together immediately, shying in unison at some imagined predator skulking in the hedge. Induna collides with Bravo and my right leg is pushed hard up against Nathan's left. Something like an electric shock shoots through me, not unlike what happened earlier, but this time a primeval, hard-wired instinct I never knew I had tells me exactly what is happening.

A brief confusion of thoughts. Nothing very coherent and yet undeniably connected to a fierce ache I'm experiencing in a part of my body I'm not used to thinking about. Just how he's reacting to this unplanned physical encounter I can have no clue. I keep my face averted and hear him comment, matter-of-factly, "Thankfully that was my good leg. It's going to be one of those days, isn't it Bravo?"

You. Oh my God, Nathan. Don't say that. You shouldn't have anything other than two good legs. Knowing you've been hurt, that you're not the perfect whole you've always been is… Shit, if I'd been on the other side when we collided I would've hurt you more. Now I've got that squeezy chest feeling again. This isn't going well.

We cross the road and head down the dirt track opposite. It will take us directly to the *vlei*.

Forget about what's just happened. Concentrate on the riding and the conversation that's developing. It's taking little or no effort on my part, which is good, if a bit unreal. We revolve around how the horses have been and then the oil depot fire everyone's been talking about.

"Did you hear any explosions? My friend Jess said she didn't. The first they knew of it was the next morning when her father saw this huge tower of black smoke on the horizon. Her mum swears her washing got discoloured and there was a greasy film on her car for days. Her dad was one of the Wombles called up to do guard duty. After the event of course. Bolting stable doors after horses have gone. Bit pointless."

With a minute shake of your head, you reply, "No, we didn't hear anything either. But one of Gill's friends who lives in Belvedere said it was pretty spectacular when it all kicked off. They clobbered the tanks with rockets. Bit of a debacle really, with all the reports contradicting each other. First we get told not to worry, it's all okay, there's plenty of fuel in the country and this is some sort of minor hiccup, then Smith's declaring it's a national disaster. They get some sort of specialist fire-fighting bit of kit in from South Africa and then say, oh no, it wasn't really necessary, our lot had it all under control. Rubbish. Most of what happened's being kept hush-hush of course because it's about the most effective attack on us yet. Oh *ja*, Charles also did his Dad's Army bit as a guard. Guess your father would've been with them too, if he'd been here."

"Probably," I admit. "He says both ZIPRA and ZANLA are claiming responsibility so I wonder if we'll ever find out. It's yet another stage we've reached isn't it? A new platform in the war in the city. A new warning that this can't go on."

You lift yourself up from the saddle and sit back down again as if to ease some discomfort, upper teeth briefly bearing down on the lower lip, fighting something in yourself. Then you're back with me.

"So, you missed all the excitement. But how was your holiday?"

"It was the longest family holiday we've had for some time, what with one thing and another. Mum and Dad packed as much into it as they possibly could."

"Just Cape Town, or more of the Cape Province?"

"Cape Town and the Garden Route. We hired a car and drove via George to Knysna and Plettenberg Bay. We also went to Oudtshoorn on the way back. It was stunning. They don't call it the Fairest Cape of Them All for nothing. Every view had the most breath-taking backdrop and Dad was permanently attached to both his still and his cine cameras."

"It's a magnificent part of the world to get away from it all. I took literally hundreds of pictures when we were there… what? Three years ago?"

A distant memory of the Mushandike exhibition of 1972 surfaces. Your surprisingly competent photos of the hippo and other game, the school buildings, sunrise and sunset over the dam.

"Charles whinged about the cost of the film and the developing. I kept expecting him to dock my pocket money, but he never did."

Did you and Gill stand to attention in the kitchen to receive pocket money like Rosie and me, I wonder?

"Oh, Charles would never be that mean. Yes, well, it did kind of make life seem normal again. My dad lost that forced, overbearing cheerfulness that's become his habit and was simply… I don't know… content, I guess. Mum's nagging dwindled and died altogether and she was, for once, oblivious to any of Rosie's hormonal shenanigans. They were more at ease than they've been for… well… for ever, it seems."

Somewhere buried in my brain are memories of them just like that though. The problem is, I can't work out exactly when that was.

"Yeah."

You say it with a sigh, and we're silent for a few strides. Bravo's relaxed now and you're holding the reins in your right hand, your left tucked behind you on the cantle of your saddle.

"You were home for Christmas, then? Gill was so excited about the possibility."

"Ja. Got back on the twenty-third in the end, a bit later than we first thought because the infection I'd had in one of my leg wounds flared up again. There was a welcoming committee laid on for me outside the back door. All the grooms lined up like they were on parade and Amai was poking them from behind to make sure they were all standing to attention properly. She's brilliant. All she was missing was a bugle. And as for Christmas, I told Moira not to make a fuss but she and Gill, and Amai as well, had clearly been planning this massive feast for a week. We had the lot. Roast turkey, ham, about five different varieties of vegetables as well as roast potatoes, hot Christmas pudding with cream, mince pies, cheese and biscuits. We all struggled to walk away from the table afterwards. Ridiculous."

You place your left hand across your eyes, thumb and middle finger on either side of them, massage your temples briefly and sigh again. "I don't mean that nastily. It was unbelievably generous of them to go to all that trouble, especially after I've been running from them for so long. We did have the best time, all together again. As you've probably reasoned, there was a period of time – a short one admittedly, thankfully – during which all of us might have been forgiven for thinking it would never happen again."

You lift your hand away from your face. "But what did you do for Christmas Day in Cape Town?"

I come so close to saying that you bloody scared the life out of me too, but that's irrelevant. This is about you and your family. I can picture them revelling in the homecoming and a feast and in each other's company and Gill not letting you out of her sight. She told me on the phone about the day you came home and how that afternoon she found you still as death and unresponsive on one of the loungers. How she had a minor heart seizure for a few seconds until she realised it was just a combination of medication and a lunchtime beer.

It's good that the world is right with her now. Her build-up to Christmas this year was pretty shit, what with Tim cheating on her, then you being in hospital and her business grinding to a halt. It's not her fault some fifty percent of her clients have emigrated at short notice, selling off the horses she was breaking and schooling, but the effect has been dismal. The only things that were keeping her going in the days before I left to go on holiday were the ideas that you would be home soon and that you were almost certain to make a full recovery.

"We were with friends of Dad's from work years back. They left and went to live in Stellenbosch in '75. It was thoroughly untraditional for once and I enjoyed it. We had a *braai*."

And as an afterthought, "I like ditching tradition sometimes."

I like that you say, "I think you probably do."

"How are you feeling? Okay to carry on, or would you rather go back?"

"I'm fine. Look, Tessa…"

You start fumbling for words in fits and starts. There's something… something you want to say. That you want me to know. That you don't know how… and you take a long, drawn in breath that makes me think you're suffering sudden pain. You dismiss my, "Are you okay?" with a flick of your hand and launch headlong into a declaration that you're grateful for my company today, and for me carrying out escort duty on this, your first ride nearly seven weeks after you got shot. You weren't at all bothered about riding Bravo in the field on your own, but wouldn't have contemplated going out on a hack alone, and for God's sake that makes you sound so bloody pathetic. You bet I think you're pathetic.

"You do, don't you?"

I won't take credit for playing protector to someone who's a far more competent rider than I'll ever be. I didn't offer to hack with you because I thought you needed supervision. Why *did* I offer?

"No! Come off it, Nathan. Please tell me you don't think I think that?"

No reply. How the hell do I coax that new you to come back out again? The shield is back. The anger is back. The old you has surfaced again – mute, impregnable, defensive. What if I say the wrong words and that… something… in you I thought I was touching with my fingertips melts away? Okay. Let's try this.

"That's garbage and you know it. I reckon you're only coming up with this because you know Charles will have your guts for garters when he finds out you've been riding. In fact, if he finds out I was the one who suggested it, he'll probably want mine. I'll have to go on the run."

Yes. Success. A surprised glance and a twitch of the lips is enough for me but I get more. A real laugh.

"Don't be silly. You'd just better make sure nothing happens to me, hey? But seriously Tessa, thank you."

I mumble some protests, unintelligible even to myself. You go, "Sorry?" and I go, "Nothing," and you say, "Sure."

There's an inevitability about what follows. The surprise is the fact that you've chosen to tell me at all.

"So, if you really want to know, I got myself creased while my unit was out patrolling near a mission station in the north east. You know it's called Hurricane, right? The ops area, I mean."

I signal that I do.

"It was pretty routine. Tedious. There'd been no terrorist activity in the location for a couple of weeks. The mission had been attacked once, some time ago, although no-one got taken out. Left a few bullet holes in the walls. It was just a few prefabricated schoolrooms and other buildings – residences I guess – huddled sort of untidily together in a steamy bowl at the foot of the Zambezi escarpment."

"A bit warm, I'll bet, at this time of year."

"All bloody year. Stifling. It's like having a wet sock wrapped around your face. And the air's full of things hell bent on trying to eat you alive. Enough mosquitos that if they all clubbed together they could carry a man off. But at least we got fairly decent grub there. It might've only been *sadza ne nyama* but it was a whole lot better than the shit in our ratpacks. That stuff should be labelled unfit for human consumption."

A pause, contemplation, then "Mind you, they probably think once you're in the army you're not human anyway."

Now *you're* seeking ways to get the reaction you want out of *me*. There's a query in your eyes, and a hesitancy. You want to know whether to carry on or not. You, who's never needed approval or disapproval from me of anything you've ever done. Fragile. I promise I'll handle with care.

"Ha! That's more or less what my father says. He brought one back to show us and Skellum wouldn't eat the biscuits."

The inclined head again. "That your dog? He clearly has good taste."

Skellum Garbage-Can Harmand?

"So go on. Why were you at the mission?"

"We were to stick around for a while and stage follow-up operations to reports of any renewed sightings. There'd been activity to the south of us. For a few days nothing happened, then one night a gang of eight guys that had attacked a farm near Sipolilo came through on their way back to Mozambique. They invaded a village and demanded food and shelter."

You draw the forefinger of your left hand across your throat.

"The poor wretched villagers get flak from both sides, don't they? If they refuse to give the terrs what they want they get all manner of hideous reprisals, but at the same time they're being instructed to report the gangs to us, or else. What are they supposed to do? This particular lot gave the gooks food but the headman refused to allow them to stay in the village to eat it. What possessed him to do that, I don't know. Anyway, they ate the food and then came back, trussed up the headman like one of his own chickens, cut off his ears, forced his chief wife to cook and eat them and then gang-raped her."

"Welcome to the human race."

It's a poor attempt at hiding the wince, although it comes out sounding suitably unperturbed. But I can't fool you. Those are very worried eyes scanning my face. You say, oh Jesus, tell me you're sorry and that you're an idiot. You got used to talking about these things out there.

"I've become hardened to it in a very short time. I never wanted to get so desensitised but if I hadn't… I won't go on about it now. You change the subject."

This really is a day of firsts in my experiences with you, Nathan Owen. How many more emotions will you give me? Enthusiasm, geniality, wit (well, I have glimpsed shadows of humour in you before haven't I?), pain, self-doubt, vulnerability and now consternation and remorse. I owe it to you to put the lid on my revulsion and try and keep this going.

"No. No, go on. Tell me the whole story."

"Sure? I've learned some very hard lessons in the last few months and I don't know that I should be sharing them with you."

I'm pretty sure you're right but we're in it for the duration now. A gust of wind puffs an empty Willard's potato chips packet out of a thicket in front of us and both horses prop to a standstill, huffing through their nostrils as the packet whirls about with a menacing crackle. Then it's hurled away from us as the wind changes direction. I can smell rain.

We arrive at the edge of the *vlei* and turn right in unison without consulting each other. It's the shortest way back to the main road and home.

"Please. I'm listening."

So, tentatively, you lead me back into the intolerable heat. And the fear. Tracking the gang, nerves on edge, the sweat trickling into every crease. The decision to go around an outcrop because you found yourselves faced with a perfect ambush alley in those very rocks. Backtracking again and then losing the spoor. Waiting in the stickiness and the heat for what seemed like hours, crouched in the vegetation, getting cramp in muscles you didn't know you had, knowing those who wanted to kill you were likely to be waiting for you to move. Every little sound, every movement of the leaves by a breath of wind or a small animal causing a surge of adrenaline because when a camouflaged man stops moving, he simply ceases to exist as his patches and stripes are swallowed by the background.

"None of this standing in lines in bright red uniforms in full view of the enemy, waiting for the order to fire, hey?"

"Jesus, I don't know which is worse. Counter-insurgency warfare doesn't have drawn up battlegrounds and lines. You know damned well they're there but you have absolutely no clue where. I cursed those bloody trackers, to myself of course, until the air around me was blue. But that was totally unfair. They can read the signs of man's passing like you and I would read a large print book. As for me, I might just about be able to track a drunken Tyrannosaurus rex that was laying a paper trail."

You and me, laughing together like this? My God, I'm kind of liking this guy I've never met before. I need to tell Gill what I'm discovering but she's not here.

"Then we were in it. One second to another. All was quiet, Scott raised his arm, we moved forward around the outcrop and all hell broke loose. I simply don't have the vocabulary to describe it to you like it was, I'm afraid. I remember hearing... well no, actually, I don't remember hearing it at all. I remember *seeing* a barrage of rounds from, I assumed, an AK-47 heading in my direction. I say seeing, but of course I couldn't see them as such, only the dirt erupting from the ground and then the bark of a tree on my right splintering, and I dived towards some rocks. I must have thought I could get shelter there, but it was too late."

Probably the last few rounds that got you, as you dived, you think. And maybe the one that hit the inside of your leg was a ricochet.

I say, "I..." and then, "What was...?" and then am completely at a loss to explain why I did. You study me for a few seconds. An apologetic smile lifts your face and touches your eyes.

"I'm really not livening up your day, am I Tessa? I'm sorry. Let's forget it. There's not much more to say. Some part of my mind tells me I thought at the time it was like being torn apart, but to be perfectly honest my memory's drawing a complete blank now. I remember finding two small rocks on top of a larger one that I decided I'd use as battlements, like on a castle, you know? But it was actually all over by then and how I got myself there's a mystery anyway. Then there were blokes running about and binding me up and Scotty saying something about 'his leg's a bloody mess' and then I was in the chopper. I'll have to leave it to your imagination at that point."

"I'm not qualified in any way to imagine that sort of fear or that situation or the sensation, Nathan."

"No. Be thankful."

"Was it the first time you'd actually…"

You've been watching me but now you break contact and look ahead. Bravo is hurrying in his walk and has pulled ahead of us slightly. I prepare to take a few strides of trot to catch up but realise I'm already there because you've halted and we're side by side again. Legs nearly touching. I reach down towards my horse's chest to fiddle with his martingale for no reason.

"Actually what? Done shooting for real? No. It was the third time. Doesn't matter how many cardboard cut-outs of maniacal looking blokes you fire at on the range, doing it for real is a whole new game. Charles has a farmer friend who took us hunting a few times several years ago, you know. I shot a couple of gazelles on those trips. How old was I? Thirteen or fourteen? I suffered a whole lot of guilt initially, but somehow in the end it was just part of a natural order in which we killed for the meat of anything we brought back from the hunts. If we'd been living in a cave we would've utilised the skins and the bones."

"Life on earth. Food chains. Even the scavengers that come in afterwards are playing their part."

"Exactly. But not this. When you're not the apex predator and it's an evenly matched fight to the death, instinct takes over. When I've had another killer in full view in front of me I've made it my business to keep any advantage I've got. Finger round the trigger and down he goes. It helps knowing he'd do the same for me."

There's a kind of haunted fascination about you as if you can't believe what you've just said. Whatever you see in me gives you a need to justify yourself.

"Tessa, I can't expect you to understand. I don't even get it myself. It felt right. It was good. At the time. Not now. I needed to do it. It wasn't only survival instinct. It was also revenge. For the tortured and murdered tribespeople and for that farmer's wife and five-year-old daughter those bloody bastards bayonetted at Sipolilo. And what's more, I then craved another kill. I wanted to gun down another one or blow him to little pieces with a grenade. It's not right. I know it's not right, but I got overtaken by this bulldozer of an emotion. I'm nobody's bloody hero, but I was so... *angry*. Unbelievably angry. It's not called the red zone for nothing."

Your voice is tight, bitter, possibly angry, but yet you only manage to look puzzled.

"And also, I... Gill and my family... I'll tell you now I don't agree with this war at all but... And then this cold, cold, icy cold lack of any feeling when afterwards you see the kill laid out in neat rows – or not so neat in some cases. Floppies, we call them. Although later they become Stiffs."

Floppies that became Stiffs. Brilliant. Funny. But not funny.

You've said all you're going to on the subject. I feel it, and then, sure enough, you dismiss it with a terse, "Bloody hell, Tessa, I've got no idea why I'm even... Look, never mind. It's stupid. It's over. I'm only eighteen and I've killed three men and I'm still here to tell the tale. End of. Shall we trot a bit? Try to beat the rain?"

Bravo is sharply instructed to go up a gear.

Induna needs no persuading; this is where we would normally canter. I let the thudding of the horses' hooves, the ripple of Induna's black mane, the creak of my saddle, absorb me. I long for a blinding gallop to clear my brain and blow away the bits – the chunks – of war. I won't ever be able to understand what you've gone through. The tears that are threatening to leak out are for Danny. Danny, who could – will – end up in the same unimaginable situation in the not-too-distant future. It's fitting that our world has, quite literally, become darker.

I blink and point over my shoulder to the sullen, indigo skyscape behind.

"We should cut the corner off. We'll get home quicker and it's definitely going to drip on us. Very soon. We should hurry."

My question, "How do you feel about cantering?" goes unasked. Your normal text-book riding position has given way to a marginally defensive one, inclined forward and to the right, and you're uncharacteristically pallid against the grey background.

It's ridiculous that *I'm* getting stabs of pain. Imagination. I suggest, "Let's walk now."

The breeze has increased to a buffeting gale. At the far corner of the *vlei* we come across a large gathering, seated and standing, in front of one of the netless goal frames used for informal soccer games. The pitch area around them is well trampled, supporting only short, tussocky turf in contrast to the longer virgin grass beyond. There must be a hundred or so in the group, all black and mostly male and they're listening to a single man who stands before them, within the goal. He waves his arms a good deal and occasionally members of the crowd punch the air in response to his gestures.

"Political rally," you observe. "I wonder which party?"

The orator is shouting, but I can only hear snatches of his words over the distance above the rising wind and I can make no sense from the disjointed sounds. Besides, he'll be speaking in Shona. I wonder if you understand him. The crowd pays us no heed and some of them are also glancing at the sky.

"I think we'd better cut through that lane past the shops to get back. We're in for a soaking."

You've just read my mind and I want you to know, so I say, "I was just about to suggest the same thing."

"Trot again?"

"Are you sure you're up to it?"

"Everything's bloody killing me, but yes. Try anyway. See how far I get."

We trot across the main road, the horses' shoes ringing on the tarmac, enter the lane and continue trotting until we reach the edge of the shopping precinct car park. A few anxious folk are hurrying towards their cars with trolley-loads of groceries from the supermarket, caught in that strange, yellowish light that comes before a heavy storm. Huddled together under the bus shelter are three girls in my year at school. They call out as they recognise me, just as large drops of rain begin to plop all around to speckle the road surface with dark polka dots.

"Well look! If it isn't Tessa, riding her horse!"

Karen's tone is faintly more mocking than friendly, but I've survived enough taunts about my love of horses. I acknowledge them with a few strides of walk and a wiggle of fingers but this isn't a time to stop for polite conversation, so I urge Induna into a trot once more, hearing Bravo fall into step behind.

The rain comes in a sweeping curtain and there's no escape. Within minutes there's a waterfall pouring off the brim of my hard hat and I'm wet through to my underwear. My jodhs squelch in the saddle as I post to the trot. Side by side we clatter up the Makuti Park driveway – on our left the house is almost hidden from view by the sheeting downpour. I dismount into a puddle, feeling the dragging weight of my saturated clothing and wail to no-one in particular, "Oh yuk! Why me?"

The catch on the gate is slippery and it takes me a bit of frustrated fumbling to release it so that we can push our way through to the yard. George rushes out from the feed room with a plastic bag tied over his head to hold Bravo's bridle while you ease out of the saddle and onto the top of the concrete mounting block. George helps you get down off the block and I can't watch.

In the shelter of the stable, I struggle to make my slippery fingers pull the swollen, wet leather bridle straps through their keepers. Induna, happy to be in his warm home, shakes himself after I've removed his tack, showering me with more fine droplets. I leave him to dry off by his own body heat.

"Come on! Come inside."

I dump my saddle and bridle in the tack room and hurry to you, but there was no point running.

You won't be running anywhere, judging by the way you're nearly doubled up and your uneven gait is favouring the right leg. You tell me, "Go on ahead, quickly, go on."

Don't be stupid. I can't leave you hobbling along like that. It really doesn't matter. I absolutely couldn't get any wetter if I were to jump into a river. Racked with guilt, I don't offer you support and you don't ask for any. We just potter along side by side.

Gill's in the kitchen buttering a slice of toast when we arrive in the doorway shedding water. She stares, the knife poised in mid-air and when she laughs, it's in what they call peals. Then her expression flicks to one of puzzlement with a hint of suspicion.

"Did you two just ride out together?"

I look to you and you shrug and say, "I wanted to ride and Tessa insisted on being my supervisor. Right now I need to sit down for a bit to psyche myself up for hauling off my boots so I'm afraid I'm going to make the floor and this chair here very wet. I'll mop it up afterwards."

"You'll do no such thing."

Gill launches into an outraged lecture about daring to get on a horse without letting her know first. You stick your fingers in your ears and shut your eyes, slightly slumped in the chair, elbows on the table.

I'm soaked to the bone and starting to shiver, but I'm happy. This is where I belong. There really is such a thing as being on the same wavelength and we're all on it. Intangible. Impossible to describe. But good.

The rain's not going to stop any time soon. Gill escorts me to her bedroom, raids her cupboards and gives me a pair of tracksuit trousers, a sweater and some underwear and we stuff my saturated garments into a plastic bag for me to take home. Back in the kitchen, Amai is on her knees wiping the floor between the door and the table with a towel. You're there, in dry jeans and socks and an unbuttoned lumberjack shirt over a white T-shirt, swallowing some pills from a couple of brown bottles near the kettle. Your soaked boots are by the door.

Amai looks up at Gill and me. She's wearing her offended face.

"He was cleaning up when I came in to start preparing dinner, Miss Gill! I sent him over there to take his *muti*. He is very pale. You must lock him in his bedroom now to rest!"

"I'm fine."

You limp over to the table, pull out one of the dry chairs, motion me to sit on it and then take the one next to it. Over a couple of mugs of coffee Gill and I talk horses and you sit silently, apparently listening but with no participation. After about twenty minutes, in a lull, you do chip in and tell Gill about the political rally we'd come across.

"Well I hope they got soaked too," she says, inspecting the bottom of her mug.

I grin at her. "That's not very charitable. I don't know who they were. What party, I mean."

"Let's just say, they won't be Rhodesian Front," she replies drily, "and if you didn't hear them chant *that is what the people want* then they weren't UANC."

Her imitation of Muzorewa's slogan as it gets broadcast *ad nauseum* on television is comic genius, but I silently remind myself that the parents will descend into one of their alarm-and-despondency sessions if they hear about the rally and my proximity to it. I won't tell them, but I will tell Danny. When I next see him. Not on the phone when Mum can overhear.

"Well," I get up and take my mug over to the sink. "I'd better go home, I guess."

"On your bike?" Gill gestures towards the window and the deluge beating against it. There's a roll of thunder, not too distant.

Good point.

"I'll take you home?" It's a question rather than a statement from you. You just keep on taking me by surprise.

Amai spins round from where she's peeling carrots and Gill's forefinger hovers in front of your face.

"Uh uh! You're damned lucky I got back before Mum and Dad, mister. You went out riding when you'd been specifically told not to. You're most certainly not driving anywhere now. Go and lie down. I'll take Tessa home in the pick-up. We can put her bike in the back. And no, you're not helping us with that either."

Is that disappointment, or am I reading too much into it?

"Gill's right, Nathan. You should stay indoors and rest now. But thanks. And I enjoyed the ride. It was good, even if we did get soaked."

"Better luck next time." You drain the mug of coffee.

I have a brainwave.

"I could ask Danny to come and fetch me. Save you the bother, Gill. Mum'll probably invite him to stay for dinner. That's if you don't mind if I leave my bike here until tomorrow?"

"Good Lord, no." She's already on her feet and unhooking the keys from the board near the back door. "It's fine. I'll nip into OK for some toiletries I need on the way back. Come on. Do you want anything from OK, Nath?"

But while I've been devoting my attention to her, you've left the room without a word or even any sort of sound. Just disappeared.

My bag of sodden clothing is heavy and lands in the passenger footwell with a thump. The rain politely eases off for us to manhandle the bicycle into the open back of the pick-up but then starts up again almost as soon as we're done. As we dive into the cab from our respective sides, she asks, "So how did he seem, out riding?"

"Fine," I reassure her because I know that's what he would want me to say. "He got tired though, towards the end. He seems to be struggling with his leg muscles and I think he was in more pain than he would let on."

"It probably did him good," she sighs, starting the engine. "Mentally, I mean. Physically? Well, yes, he's got a fair bit of muscle damage on the outside of his right thigh and the… what are they called? Oblique muscles? In the waist area? Lost a bit of those, and they had to do a repair on a small section of his colon. They kept telling us how damned lucky he was not to have lost the right kidney or indeed have any bones smashed. And if he'd been just half a metre to the right… I…"

That's pretty much what he said to me when we made our slow way back to the house in the rain. He wants things to be different from now on. He counts himself lucky to be alive and, more importantly, able to lead a normal life. He saw things in the hospital that sickened him and made him scared of losing what he's got.

I put my hand on hers as she shifts the column-mounted gear lever.

We arrive at my house without uttering another word between us. I've no insight as to what's going through her head but mine is seething with a struggle to accept the idea of a boy I've known since early childhood uprooted from his home, processed in a military machine and presented with this choice of kill or die. It's like I'm running footage from one of those Vietnam newsreels we've seen on TV – images of a man (faceless, but I know it's him) wrapped in pouches of ammo and grenades, cradling a semi-automatic rifle, coughing in the dust and the gunsmoke, wild eyed, furious, and looking for someone to slay. It's in the song, isn't it – *'sling your slayer to slay'*? That's what he was sent up there to do. He isn't a boy. He's a soldier who's been in battle. Shows you how a normal life of horses, family, school, parties, swimming pools and other kids' stuff can be swapped just like that for guns, fear and men who want to kill. And for what?

FRIDAY 29TH DECEMBER 1978

"I don't suppose you did any riding on Wednesday, what with that almighty downpour we had?"

It's a perfectly logical question. Shame I don't have a perfectly logical answer.

Across the room, Rosie's face says she's reconsidering any previous assessments of his mental abilities that she may have carried out.

"How well do you actually know my sister, Dan?"

Mum says, "She came home in Gill's clothes. So there's your answer."

"It wasn't raining when we set out. We just got caught, that's all. It's only water."

Danny's not sure whether this is amusing or concerning. I'm only giving him cause to doubt *my* mental capacity. He'll be telling me I'll 'catch cold', or whatever the saying is.

Will he ask who 'we' are? I told the family that Nathan's home and that he came out with me and that he shouldn't have done so, but Danny isn't aware of this yet.

He doesn't ask.

I turn to Mum. "Are Gill's clothes dry?"

"They're folded up in the spare room with the other washing from yesterday."

This movie starts at two-thirty. So if we leave now…

"Dan, if it's okay with you can we go now? I'd like to drop her clothes off on the way. I've even got underwear of hers."

He blinks a couple of times.

"Well, all right. If you're ready?"

I am. It's important to me to get Gill's clothing back to her but

I also have another motive. *He* wasn't around when I was there yesterday.

*

Gill is in the ménage, lungeing Bravo.

And there he is, sitting outside the railings, near the gate, on one of the plastic chairs the grooms keep in their kitchen.

"Danny, look. Nathan's back from hospital."

"Right?" says Danny. "Oh yes. I recognise him. He was that… Oh well, good that he's okay."

It's very good. It's exactly what I wanted to see. He's looking much better than he did when I left on Wednesday. His right leg is stretched out before him but he's upright against the chair back and is animated in his shouted conversation with Gill.

"I never cease to wonder at the way that horse moves. And his attitude is *so* much better. You've worked on him a lot in my absence?"

"Me, and Justice," Gill shouts back, keeping her face towards him as she turns away, then snapping it back round in the opposite direction as she comes back to face him again, like a ballet dancer. I'd probably fall over if I tried that. "He takes a fair bit of the credit… Oh! Hi, Tessa!"

"Be quick, my sweet," Danny whispers. "We can't hang about."

He's learning, isn't he, that once I'm here at the stables I'm likely to be hard to shift. I start to walk towards the chair.

"You haven't been misbehaving and riding any horses, have you, Mr Owen?"

Squinting against the sun, he looks up at me.

"That's rich coming from you, since you were the one who busted me out."

Gill has brought the horse to a halt and is standing at his head. She calls out, "Hi, Danny! Nice to see you again."

Nathan leans back so he can see past me to Danny. I flash him a smile that he doesn't return. I don't think he saw it.

"Gill, I've left your clothes with Amai. Thank you from the

bottom of my heart. They're all washed. We're going to the cinema so we can't stay."

She gives me a thumbs-up and sends Bravo off back onto the circle, laughing. Nathan tucks his leg under the chair after giving the thigh a quick rub and Danny whispers in my ear, "Done? Shall we go, Sweets?"

Yes. We should. I shout goodbye and Gill yells, "See ya!" then, "Canter!"

All I get from Nathan is that slight incline of the head.

Back in Danny's car, the words that I can't quite arrange into anything coherent come out as, "I wanted to make sure he was okay yesterday because I've never seen him so unwell, ever. He was in a lot of pain but he wouldn't admit it. Gill was out teaching so I couldn't ask her, and I did peek into the house before I left but it was all quiet. I thought he might be asleep and I didn't want to disturb him."

"Hmm, what?" says Danny.

"Nothing."

Nathan doesn't need me to worry about him. Let it be.

WEDNESDAY 17TH JANUARY 1979

"Oh, ho!" says Charles by way of a greeting, eyeing up my uniform. "Back to school already?"

"Well done. Full marks for detective work."

He was half in, half out of the Mercedes when I arrived at the gate – now he extracts himself fully and opens his arms to me, gives me a peck of a kiss on my nose. "Don't be sarky. You hacking with Gill this afternoon? I didn't see you yesterday."

"I couldn't come over yesterday. First day back and we got told we have chemistry practical lessons on Tuesday afternoons this year. I was pissed off, I can tell you."

His big, delighted grin lights up his face under the sunglasses.

"I can believe it. Chemistry? What year you in now?"

"Form Four. O Levels in November. That's, like, eleven very short months away."

New year, new form classroom, new timetable, new worries.

Gill comes flying out of the back door, two laundered numnahs in her hand.

"Ah. You're here. I was just going to tack up. How's school? Got any new students then? Nudge, nudge, wink, wink."

Charles leans an elbow on the top of the car door and flicks quickly back and forth between me and Gill. He isn't quite sure where she's coming from, but I am.

"We've only got two in our class. Alice Chifamba and Chipo Makoni. They're nice. Alice is a quiet mouse, but the sporty girls have already found out she's a damned good basketball player. She was in the First Team at her mission school near Karoi. They're determined to cajole her into going to the basketball trials so she can try for a place on one of our teams and I think they're going to persuade her to have a go at hockey too. And as for Chipo – she's a real chatterbox. She talks *a lot* and sings – off-key – and shrieks when she laughs. She kept talking to herself and made us all laugh. She said things like, 'Now Chipo, you've done it all wrong. Do it again.'"

I tap the side of my head with a forefinger. "She's hilarious."

I knew he and Gill would enjoy the anecdote for its own sake, laugh with me, picture the scene, warm to a girl they've never met without questioning what she even looks like because I said she's funny and likeable.

Not like Mum.

It was just a story, an anecdote. Like, hey, this is what happened to me at school today. And of course she saw straight through it to a problem. I should've known. I didn't even get a "Oh that's nice/interesting/funny/strange."

Just the Bothered Tone: "So where has this girl come from then?"

Me, failing to spot the Bothered Tone and setting off on a helpful explanation: "Um, I think she said her father taught maths and geography at a mission school near Wedza, so she's been there all her life so far. Her mother's a nurse. Mr Makoni has now got a job at Allan Wilson School so they moved to Salisbury. Chipo's got one older sister who's already left school and is…"

The frown, stopping me in mid-flow: "Allan Wilson? So they've started putting black teachers into the white schools? I wonder how many others there are?"

My confusion: "Hey? Well how should I know? He was teaching O Level at the other school. There's no difference in the syllabus. They're not 'white' schools any more though, are they?"

The irritated frown: "You know what I mean. It's a sign of things to come. Eventually all the white teachers will leave and you'll only have blacks."

Me, wanting to yell at her, something like: "Why are you being so negative? We have to live with all these changes whether you like it or not. Things might not turn out to be as bloody bad as you think!"

Instead, chickening out and going for sarcasm: "But of course they *can't* be as good as the white teachers."

Wasted on her, of course, in her fog of worry. She only heard the literal words, relieved that I'd finally understood: "Yes. Yes, you're right. They think differently to us. They won't be able to... um, shall we say, *impart* knowledge so well."

Why did I even start the conversation?

I should stop being so angry with Mum and Dad and try to understand it from their point of view. They've got our futures to think of, as well as their own. But I won't allow myself to accept and condone that sort of prejudiced view. I will not consider my schoolmates, or anyone else, in terms of colour or race. It serves no purpose. I'm moving on.

"As far as my mother is concerned, the planet is going to self destruct any day soon. She says to me, when I get home yesterday, she says, 'Tessa! Do you know Rosie's class is fifty percent black! *Fifty percent!*' It's not even fifty percent anyway. Rosie told me there are ten black girls in her class of twenty-eight. Overall it's two thirds of the Form One intake this year though."

They're in serious danger of being totally irrational over this. Rushing off to parent meetings and debates three evenings a week, arguing in the lounge about what to do if seventeen-year-old black girls who, in their view, might not know how to use the toilets properly, join Rosie's class of thirteen-year-old white girls, thrashing out the pros and cons of setting up a Community School and then panicking and chucking in the towel altogether and investigating the ultimate sacrifice of sending us to a private school. Even more irrational, that is, because the private schools have taken in black, coloured and Asian pupils for years now. And the toilets thing?

"Not surprising. And of course the bloody Rhodesia Action Party's stirring as usual by trying to convince the RF supporters who they think are showing signs of weakness that the entire world is moving too fast in the wrong direction. Like, come on guys, you're being forced to accept the fact that blacks can now buy property in your road, and now on top of that you'll have the uneducated black masses mixing with your children at school. This cannot be allowed to happen, etc, etc, you have to vote no in the referendum etc, etc. You know how it is. Resulted in the mass Exodus last month. And if whites keep leaving, these percentages in schools are only going to go the wrong way for those that don't leave. And believe me, the RF is and always has been very concerned about numbers."

He holds up his left wrist and tilts it so that his watch doesn't flash the sun straight into his face.

"Look, my darlings, I'm going to have to get back to the office. Have a nice ride. And enjoy your new classmates, Tessa."

I leave Gill to close the gate behind his car and head for her bedroom. Moira's voice floats down the corridor when I've just removed my skirt, shoes and school socks and am in the act of shaking out my jodhs. I don't catch all of her words, just, "... with Charles tomorrow?" from somewhere close.

Then Nathan's voice: "I guess so. I'll talk it through with him when he gets home again."

He's in the study. I'm so used to never wondering where he is that I haven't wondered where he is. And here I am in the next room, half undressed, with the door wide open. Got to be more careful now he's likely to be in the house most of the time, recuperating. I reach out a foot and give the door a push, wriggle into my jodhs, pull on the school socks again because my old riding ones must be right at the bottom of the duffel bag, whip off my shirt without undoing all the buttons and replace it with my T-shirt, all in one smooth action, then stuff my school things into the bag and take off for the kitchen. Once there, I'm in my riding boots, unlaced admittedly, and out of the door in about five seconds.

*

The light level's altered; it's fractionally darker in here. I tuck the saddle cover around the knee rolls and turn around, expecting to see George or Justice in the doorway, but it's Nathan. No footfalls, no scraping of a boot on the step, he's just there.

"Hmm, you riding?" asks Gill, hanging Star Point's bridle on the ceiling hook so George can clean it later.

He folds his arms and stares at her.

"No. I thought I'd put my jodhpurs on and mosey on down to the Alexandra Sports Club for a game of squash."

I snigger and Gill rolls her eyes but he doesn't react to either of us.

"Okay clever-clogs. You're not bloody capable of playing squash at the moment, are you? Do you want me to be with you?"

"No thanks."

Bravo's saddle is next to mine. I slide away and he steps through the space I've just vacated, favouring the right leg.

"I'll make this fucking leg work if it kills me," he says.

"We'll leave you to it then. Come on Tess."

She stalks ahead of me back to the house. I just remembered that I wanted to ask her about teaching Induna counter-canter but now doesn't seem to be the right time so I keep schtum. Once in the kitchen, she hitches herself up onto the table next to where Moira's sitting with one of her recipe books and kicks her heel hard against the table leg under her.

"Oh God Mum, this is such an awful thing to say, but although I'm over the moon that he's riding again, a part of me doesn't want him to recover too soon. I can't bear the thought of him going back into the bloody army again. And they will take him back. He might get given some kind of desk job at first but they'll shove him back out on the frontline the instant they think he's capable. Or what they fucking think is capable."

"Gill darling…" Moira closes the book and takes off her glasses.

"Can't you send him away, Mum? To England, to Uncle Richard? Or even to the States, to stay with that guy Dad knows who set up a business over there?"

"You know we can't do that. He's not allowed to leave."

A pause. Then Gill gives the table leg another kick and Moira closes her eyes.

"I didn't tell you, but Madeline Watson's son died last week. He was a chopper pilot. Flying troops into a contact zone, he came under fire and they think both he and his tech got shot from the ground. The chopper crashed and they don't know if the guys were dead before or if they were killed in the crash. It's getting worse. If this settlement and the elections and the new constitution don't solve anything, it will go on."

Moira looks as helpless as I feel. There's another pause.

"We'll have to hope the elections do result in a ceasefire," I suggest. It's just for the sake of saying something. I don't think either of them has heard me.

Gill looks up at me and swings her legs without touching the table this time.

"So. Tessa's got two black girls in her class now. Tess, tell her about the new girl who talks and sings."

Moira arches her fine eyebrows at me.

"Oh Chipo? She's brilliant. Yes, she and Alice joined us for the first day yesterday. I felt sorry for them in form registration because Mrs McGovern got them to sit together at the front and then just left them alone while she ferreted around in the stock room at the back. They were self-conscious enough as it was, without being made to be even more conspicuous. At least Rosie's class is nearly half and half, and they're all new girls together anyway."

*

Gill walks with me to the main road to continue telling me about her competition plans for the year. We must keep on planning, she says, as if everything will carry on as normal.

"Heaven knows, we've lived with all manner of unknowns for ever now and this year is no different. No-one can possibly predict the outcomes of the referendum or the elections. Whether we get international recognition of the settlement or not is anyone's guess. Smith's attempting to get us to vote 'yes' by insisting that the constitution must be good for the whites *because* the rest of the world's rejecting it! We have to say yes though. There's no going back."

She stops walking as we reach the gateway.

"The only certainty seems to be this crazy name we're going to get. I mean, have you ever? Seriously Tess, they must be nuts. Dad says it's absolutely the most nonsensical mouthful anyone could've dreamed up."

Her black mood of half an hour ago has evaporated; my upbeat, optimistic Gill is back.

"He got it in one," I agree. "They should just go for Zimbabwe. Why's Smith so determined to hang onto the Rhodesia bit?"

"Trying to please all of the people all of the time and failing miserably. Ah well, what can you do? Hey, I meant to say to you – we're celebrating an Owen Family First this weekend, d'you realise that?"

I go, "No, really? What's that then?" just like she wants me to.

"Actually having an *event* for Nathan's birthday, no less. He turned nineteen on Monday but we've persuaded him to go with us for a posh meal at Tiffany's on Saturday. He told us in no uncertain terms he wouldn't take any gifts but that he'd love to go for a family meal."

Shit, I'd forgotten he had a birthday in January. I should've remembered. I should've said something. Mental note.

"We've decided we'll all get real dressed up in our posh togs for the occasion. Me and Mum are going to buy new dresses tomorrow and Dad and Nathan will be suited and booted. Oh God, Tessa, you can't believe how much I'm looking forward to that. Or maybe you do?"

"I do, Gill. He deserves it. You all deserve it. I can't imagine Charles, or Nathan for that matter, in a suit!"

I've never even contemplated Charles in a suit and tie.

She chuckles and says, "Oh, Nathan has one, I think. Probably outgrown it. Maybe he'll have to go shopping as well. That'll be another Family First. Dad grudgingly wears them when he meets clients or sub-contractors. He's just got a contract for some excavation works and concreting as part of the rebuilding of the fuel depot. He's taking Nathan over there these next couple of days to help with some setting out stuff."

"He's ready for that, do you think? He's still quite lame."

That doesn't sound quite right, does it? Too much talking about horses over the years.

"I reckon he's up to it, yes, while taking into consideration the fact he's not as agile as he should be and gets tired easily. It's a level site, and the more walking about he does, the better for the damaged muscles. I know I went off on one earlier about him riding but I do want to see him doing stuff he enjoys and benefitting from it. And now he *wants* to enjoy, he *wants* to participate and I cannot let this new positiveness die. It started when he was in the hospital and beginning to get back on his feet."

"There's something… I can't really explain. It's not like I've ever interacted that much with him."

She folds her arms and pokes the toe of her boot at a couple of stray pebbles that are lying on the macadam surface.

"You are right. He and my father had words, you know. In the hospital. Neither Mum nor I know what was said and they're not telling and we figured it's best left between them. But it has had an effect on Nathan's whole outlook. He said virtually nothing after this discussion happened, then a couple of days later it was clear he was trying very hard to lose that impenetrable shell. If it keeps up, you may find him wanting to hack out with you again."

This is a novel idea that occupies me for a few moments on my ride home. Hacking with Nathan? He'll be fully fit again one day for sure and I don't reckon he's into asking for help if it can be avoided, so I doubt it. He's definitely been riding pretty regularly but he's never asked to go with me since that time back before Christmas. When we got caught in the deluge. Karen Melton and her mates were there near the shopping centre. Karen Melton, yesterday, plonked down next to me and interrogated me not ten minutes into form time. Nudged me in the ribs and whispered, "So come on, who was that you were with when we saw you? At the bus stop? Remember? Just after Christmas? You were sitting on a horse? It was chucking it down, remember?"

She has no idea. *Sitting* on a horse?

I was thinking, yes, I remember it well. Two miserable, sodden riders hunched against the driving rain, one behind the mini Victoria Falls coming off her riding cap and the other with the brim of his felt safari hat beginning to droop over his ears.

Clearly Nathan's name didn't ring any bells with her. Perhaps the last tendril of the junior school grapevine that used to bear his name, along with the labels so many attached to it, has died. She fired questions at me, like, "Who's he?", "How do you know him?", "Where does he live?" and "When did you meet him?" then, when I told her, she went, "Oh! Ah! I thought as much. So he's not your boyfriend then? Well if he ever wants to meet a nice girl, you know where I am!"

She got fed up with watching me trying to process this request and said, "Oh Tessa. You are just… Wet shirt? No? Oh never mind."

So she fancies him. But then he's male, isn't he? She'll be disappointed. I don't think he'll be the least bit interested in knowing where she is.

That old hat of his really was in a sorry state by the time we got home. And apart from the downpour and the hat, I recall an odd thing. He'd called me Tessa. I don't remember him actually referring to me by name before.

I must tell Danny about Chipo when I call him tonight.

SUNDAY 25TH MARCH 1979

"Here, look, I've got something to show you."

Gill leads me into the lounge and lifts a multi-coloured Kodak envelope from the coffee table. She tosses the negative strips in their plastic covers onto the surface of the table and draws out a wad of printed photos.

"A load of pics from the Bindura show last month," she says, rapidly shuffling each photo from front to back. "I won't bore you with them. I rode Georgie van Driel's horse and that silly chestnut mare that Patty Kilmer owns in the B Grade and neither of them got past the first round, but here's what I wanted to show you. Look. Tiffany's restaurant. You know we went there for Nathan's birthday back in January?"

The first one was taken in the hotel lobby – Gill, Moira and Nathan bunched together. Gill's dazzlingly pretty in a short black dress and her suede black court shoes; Moira is elegant in her long, burgundy dress. I have never seen her in heels like that and didn't know she owned any. Nathan's wearing a black, or maybe dark grey, suit. The jacket is open to reveal a white shirt, black tie and a waistcoat. My goodness. I'm going to start giggling because this isn't something I'd ever contemplated either. Stop. Don't. I pull a stupid face and partly turn my head away, not least because of the disturbing fact that he's leaning on a walking stick in the photo and I've never seen it around the house.

Gill flicks another one over and there are the four of them at their table, champagne flutes aloft, the table top strewn with the remains of a meal. In this one, both Charles and Nathan have discarded their jackets but not the waistcoats or ties.

"Persuaded the resident pianist to take that one," she says. "It was just the best time ever. It was how it should be, Tessa. The four of us as a proper family. I just wish to God this bloody war would end so that this will be our future too."

There are a few more, taken in the restaurant by each in turn – Gill, Moira and Charles; Gill, Charles and Nathan; Moira, Gill and Nathan again. Then one of the two men back here in the lounge, just about where we're standing now, toasting the camera with glasses of red wine, in shirts and trousers only.

"Some of these need to go on the wall in the hallway, Gill. To mark the occasion and get some up there in which he's actually looking at the camera."

She stuffs the photos and the negatives back into the envelope.

"You're damned right the best ones will end up in the gallery. Okay, let's get out there and lunge this horse of yours."

Charles and Nathan are in the driveway unloading some bags of cement from the back of the pick-up. There are several white hard hats, a coil of plastic ducting and a small cable drum on the vehicle as well.

"Tessa, my darling!" booms Charles. "We missed you yesterday, girl. First time ever you've not been at Gilly's party I think?"

They drop one of the bags on top of another one that's already in the wheelbarrow alongside the truck with a dull thump. Charles wipes his hands on his jeans and extends them to me. Nathan steps back and leans an elbow on the side of the pick-up, massaging his right thigh.

Gripping the offered hands, I confess, "You have no idea how much I wanted to be here. I had no choice, unfortunately. Danny's cousin got married yesterday. It was quite an affair, at the Anglican Cathedral, and we all went to Meikles Hotel after. It was a good bash, but I was very bleak that I had to miss yours."

"Well, you've got your own things to do, sweetheart, and someone else in your life now who deserves all of your attention because he's special to you, lucky boy. And you deserve to have a gallant young man to take you out and show you off. We like him, by the way. You have our approval."

"I do consider myself very lucky indeed to have him and you're only echoing my parents' delight. He scores very highly with them."

He chortles his satisfaction and Gill goes, "Yay! Tessa's in love!" and I'm being all pleased with myself and choosing phrases to use when telling Danny that he's acceptable to everyone who matters to me.

"Charles?"

Nathan's moved back round to the tail gate. He points at the three remaining cement bags on the bed of the truck.

"You wanted to get the slab repairs done today and it's already eleven-thirty. I've told Jed Martins I'll meet him at the Ambassador at six-thirty. I've got things to do too."

"Woo hoo, listen to you!" crows Gill, clapping her hands. "Excellent! Well come on, boys. Chop, chop. We'll leave you to your work."

Charles salutes me and backs up towards the truck, the clown as always, then says to Nathan, "Right, boss. Next bag. Ready? So who all's going to the Ambassador?"

I don't hear his response because Gill's telling me about the new horse coming for schooling next week and then we're out of earshot.

FRIDAY 25TH MAY 1979

Gill sits up, pushing her straw hat back up off her face and onto her head and reaches for her Malawi shandy.

"Aptitude tests? Like, psychometric tests? We did those, I think. A friend of mine who was all set to go into the estate agent business like her dad got told she should never even dream of a career in anything to do with sales and marketing. How did you do?"

I turn my head and squint at her in the sharp sunlight from under my own hat. I've warmed up a bit now, but we've got to come to terms with the fact that it's no longer swimming weather. I'm not keen, like Jess. I only do it in summer.

"Honestly? I don't have a clue. The logical tests were straightforward – either you know the answer or you don't – but there were other questions, designed, we were told, to find our hidden strengths. I just gave the answer I reckoned would show me in the best light. I thought I was being clever, but then when Mrs McGovern got me alone during the individual discussion time afterwards she said my aptitudes are – how did she put it – *diverse*, as far as careers are concerned. So she asks me what career appeals to me. I mean, seriously Gill, I'd been rather hoping *she* would tell *me* what I wanted to do. So I mumbled something about working with horses, like you, and that was obviously the wrong answer. She acted like she was so disappointed it made me feel like a complete idiot. I walked away with a bunch of leaflets on accountancy, cartography, computer studies, nursing, teaching and, get this… air traffic control. I can do what I want. Isn't it great? What a fat lot of bloody use when I don't *know* what I want. None of them sound appealing, except for veterinary nursing perhaps. I think I'll join the Foreign Legion. Do they let women in now?"

She snorts and has to put her glass down on paving slabs quickly to avoid spilling the shandy. "Tessa my love, I don't think you're the right type. Have a word with my dad. He's out of town at some site or other but he said he'd be home round about four and it must be nearly that now. He knows someone who's an employment consultant in town, who might be able to tell you more about different careers. This guy deals with all sorts of people in all sorts of fields. What do your parents think? Haven't they discussed it with you?"

"Well of course they have, and so have all their friends over time. *What-do-you-want-to-be-when-you-grow-up?* is a question I've been asked so many bloody times I've given up bothering with genuine answers. The parents are lining me up for junior school teaching. Probably my own fault for never claiming any particular vocation and for showing a desire to teach my teddy bears and other animal toys anything I was learning at the time. Now with O Levels around the corner Mum's got me some brochures for Teacher Training College. By the results of those tests today it looks like it's an option. Not."

"You wouldn't want to teach then? So what about university?"

"Me, teach kids? I'd end up getting done for murder. As to varsity – maybe. I don't know. I don't think I'm capable of doing distinct careers that come out of a university like medicine or law or engineering so it would just be a case of doing a BSc in some subject I fancy then try and find a career to suit it. But I'd rather have more certainty. I have no idea Gill, honestly. It's worrying me now."

That day she first told me her plans for a career with horses was the day I got jolted into realising that there would be life after school. And jolted into realising I should've realised it. Now the time has come to panic.

The sun's starting to slide towards the tops of the gum trees along the western edge of the garden. My swimming costume isn't going to dry any further. I lift myself up on one elbow.

"Vet nursing appeals most. It might lead to working with horses. It seems to involve getting a job in a surgery that provides training. Or, I could join the Grey's Scouts couldn't I? They take on quite a few women as re-mount riders."

She drains her glass. "The army? Funny you should say that though because we've heard there's a possibility Nathan will be able to get posted as a riding instructor when he's fit enough to go back. Not as a career for you though. You're better than that. And what if they don't carry on with the Grey's in peace time?"

"Peace time? Will there be? I'd like a bit of that."

Another Viscount down back in February – this time with the loss of all on board. Numbers of insurgents up significantly. The past seven years have cost an estimated twenty-seven thousand lives and there's no guarantee Muzorewa's victory in the April elections will bring about the end of the conflict. Dad says Margaret Thatcher's on our side and is going to sympathetically solve all our problems, but she won't. She isn't on our side. The fighting won't end until the Patriotic Front are in power. Zimbabwe-Rhodesia is not the ultimate destination for this country. It's temporary. Nothing with a name like that should be allowed to last anyway.

Gill starts rolling up her towel. "Dad's here. I heard the car. It's time to go in anyway. I'm freezing now."

My sentiments exactly.

We change in her room and she lends me a jumper. I can hear Charles whistling in his tuneless fashion somewhere down the corridor.

"Let's go find Dad. Have you got time? Are you seeing Danny tonight?"

"Not tonight. Only tomorrow. He's actually agreed to go to the races. Jess and Gordon asked us because they're going with some of Jess's family. It's very strange. Neither of them are interested in horses, but then I guess it's the betting that attracts."

"Ah, probably. Jess and Gordon are still an item then. Are they sleeping together yet?"

What?

"Um…"

Gill's walking ahead of me, laughing. "You mean you don't know? You should ask her. See what she has to say for herself. You might be surprised."

Ask her how? They're not. Jess wouldn't do that. Would she? No.

Charles is on the patio, dragging his lounger to the last sunny spot near the front edge.

"Yo, Tessa! What's new?"

"Where's Nathan?" Gill asks. We sit together on the edge nearest the pool.

"He's staying up in Bindura. They're pouring the first lift for the last silo tomorrow so he needs to be there for that."

She shrugs. "Oh okay. Tess was talking about going to the races and I'm thinking I might go along tomorrow too. Tammy's dad's got runners in most races and I can get into the trainers' circle with her. I haven't been for ages. I was also thinking Nath might like to go so it's a shame he's not about. Sherrie will be there…" She breaks off and behind me Charles guffaws.

She catches my eye and prompts, "Sherrie Fletcher?"

Oh, her. I know. I've met her a couple of times. Pretty, with blonde curls.

Jess isn't sleeping with Gordon. She's my best friend. She'd've told me.

Gill squirms round to face Charles.

"So, Dad, listen. Tessa's had to do some career aptitude tests at school and they've shown up that she can be anything from a road sweeper to an astronaut so she's completely confused and wants advice. Can, whatsisname, Steve… Steve is it? The recruitment guy. Can he help?"

"Astronaut? What? No, Gill, that's stupid."

Moira steps up onto the far end of the patio, pruning shears in one hand and says, "Hello love, where's Nathan?" so the conversation is repeated and Charles tells her he didn't win the Gwelo sewage treatment works extension contract. She makes sympathetic noises and asks him some questions I don't register.

Jess was as adamant as I was when we swore we'd never let any guy persuade us to get into bed before rings got on fingers. When was that – three years ago? We were raised to be good girls. No babies and no reputations. Save yourself for your husband. This is Rhodesia, Mum says. We have morals the rest of the world should envy.

It's getting late.

Moira's vanished indoors. Gill looks at me looking at my watch and leans backwards, tilting her head towards Charles, who's shifted the lounger a bit further away, chasing the sun. "Come on Dad. Will you call Steve for Tessa?"

"Tessa," says Charles. He sits on the edge of the lounger, leans forward, elbows on knees, his huge hands clasped together. "I can speak to Steve Young at Top Ace Recruitment on your behalf, no problem. But listen to what I have to say before you decide whether you want me to or not. You see, your career dilemma isn't that much of a dilemma if you'd care to hear me out."

That expression on his face? That's smug. He does smug when he's delighted to be withholding some gem of information his listeners want or need.

I offer a very cautious, "Yeees?"

Gill knows as well. She's more direct.

"Dad? Come off it. What are you plotting?"

"I can offer you a good job, Tess. A job that starts with book-keeping but could lead to much more and a hand in the running of the business. Scope to get involved in every aspect of my company. It can be as interesting as you want to make it. Don't look so puzzled, sweetheart. It's true – I'm offering you a job. Well, not right now of course. I should say I'm offering you the opportunity to come along and see if you want a job with me."

Gill twists her head from Charles's direction, to mine and back again so rapidly she's in danger of dislocating something. My jaw is on my knees. He's loving this.

"My accounts department is run solely by a good lady called Megan Trent. She also does general admin, keeping everything where it should be. You know Megs, don't you Gilly? She's hyper-efficient and is a stickler for detail and she makes it all work but she's well over sixty now and her husband is an invalid. He's suffered a stroke and will soon need constant nursing. Megan works mornings only now to give her a chance to attend to their own affairs in the afternoons. So I'm pretty sure old George Trent's civil service pension and other investments will keep them well provided for and

I don't know how much longer she'll be with us. I think you might be the ideal person to be her assistant, eventually take over her role and also become generally involved in the company. What do you think?"

What do I think? Is there really an answer to that?

"Don't decide here and now." He raises a forefinger then taps it against his temple like both Gill and Nathan do. "Go away and sleep on it. Talk to your folks of course."

If he knew what my pulse was doing he'd be calling an ambulance. But I love him. He's taken me from quandary to security in two minutes.

He's right though. I can't make a decision like this in a snap. And anyway, words of advice from teachers over the years are rearing up now to disappoint me with cold common sense.

"I was hoping to do some kind of college training. And I've got my O Levels at the end of the year."

Now I've probably blown it. He wants someone straight away. He won't wait, and so I'm back to Square One.

But he beams and claps his hands onto his thighs. "Excellent idea! What about a course in book-keeping then? Find out about these day-release things. You know, where you go to college on one day a week? Book-keeping, typing, business studies, economics…"

He gestures expansively. "I may even get you doing stuff on the construction side of my company, on the job so to speak."

Now we're getting silly again. Might as well pursue the astronaut idea.

"I don't think I'd be any good at that sort of thing."

"Mmm. You never know. Nathan can tell you all about the construction sites. I've got him going out on his own now to supervise the grain silo contract at Bindura. He still struggles a bit with some of the physical stuff like getting into and out of excavations and being on his feet all day, but he's making excellent progress on the whole. He'll be pretty much fully fit eventually."

He carries on speaking. Something about the administrative procedures involved in running a civil engineering contracting company, but it means nothing to me. Come on, put the brakes on your racing, fantasising imagination. Don't get ahead of yourself or you'll jinx this.

After a couple of minutes I realise he's talking about Nathan again.

"I want him to take over as Contracts Manager eventually so I've just bought a Toyota Land Cruiser for him. I admit I used to have doubts, but he's turning out to be a real asset. Mature. And a decision maker. I really think I can make something of him. You don't drive yet, do you?"

"No. I'll be sixteen in September and Dad's promised to send me to a driving school straight after my birthday."

Total independence is like a beautiful mirage on my horizon. Assuming, that is, Dad buys me a car. But if I have a job…

"Well, never mind. You would only be starting the job next year anyway. Right? Well I'll have to give you a formal interview if you want to go on with this. Nothing to worry about, but it's ethics. Talk it through with your folks and let me know?"

"I won't have my O Level results until January next year," I remind him and he draws his head back slightly with that *are-you-being-serious?* face on.

"You'll do okay. You'll call, yes, and let me know about getting an interview sorted?"

I wish I had his faith in me.

*

Out in the yard Gill grabs me and, with hands on each other's shoulders, we impulsively perform a sort of polka, to the intense — if confounded — amusement of the grooms.

"I haven't got the job yet," I gasp as we finally break hold near the tack room, but she's undaunted.

"After work you can come back here and help me school horses. You'll see — the Owen family will exploit you to the full."

She plonks down suddenly on the mounting block and pulls me down beside her.

"Hey. Have you thought any more about getting another horse?"

A second horse, ready for entering Adult classes once I get to eighteen. It's the right time to start looking, and of course I've thought about it. Never got any further than thinking. Couldn't face asking Dad to spend even more money on horses for me. But now, today, it's not difficult to guess where Gill's thoughts are heading.

A car *and* a horse. And this is without knowing how much I'm even going to get paid. What's next? A ten-bedroom mansion? I'm blissfully oblivious to what Dad pays for Induna's keep, his shoes, his vaccinations and the endless replacements of rugs, tack, fly fringes and headcollars that are standard in horse keeping. Moira said once that horse ownership is all about standing in a muck heap and burning twenty dollar notes. I need to shake myself up and get a grip on things.

She's talking about the type of horse I'll need. Across the other side of the yard, Induna pokes his handsome head over his half door and the guilt washing over me is crushing. It's like I'm plotting some despicable act of betrayal or treason. He's the best pony a girl could have, but Gill's been trying to convince me that I'm outgrowing him, that he simply is not substantial enough to take me through the Adult grades. I know this, but I can't come to terms with it yet.

"Stroller was only a pony."

"What? Stroller? He got to the top Tessa, yes, but he was one in a million. Much as you love Indie, he's not going to be the Stroller of the 1980s."

I must not contemplate pushing Indie on over big show-jumping courses just to suit my own ends. He'd throw his heart into it, I know, but I could break him and then how would I feel?

So what will happen to my beautiful bay pony? He's got years left in him to compete at the level he's reached so I have two choices as I see it. One, put him out on loan to a younger junior rider or, two, carry on at this level myself and forget about being more ambitious. Oh, and there's a third option. Retire him from competition but keep him and get another horse anyway.

Yeah, money again. Horses are expensive pets. Nathan's long outgrown High Time, but she's a mare and has made her contribution to the family's breeding business with two foals so far. She has a job and a home for life.

You grow up, you get these decisions.

You get to know things. Gill and Tim used to spend nights together at his flat in town, Rhodesia or not. Gill's not a wanton, immoral girl. There was no showing off, no daring me to be shocked, just an assumption that I knew that's what people did. But Jess? No, she'd never sleep with Gordon, or anyone.

SUNDAY 29TH JULY 1979

It's a blood red winter sun that's hovering just above the horizon in a sky devoid of clouds. I wiggle each of my hands up into the opposite cuff, fingers and then knuckles. It's okay. Mum can't see me and tell me off for stretching the sleeves of my sweater again. A dove somewhere near the bottom of the garden fills the air with its soft 'Koo-koooroo'.

The patio door behind me clacks and there's a bit of shuffling. Twisting round, I watch him operating the handle with his elbow, his eyes fixed on the contents of both mugs. By the time I've freed my hands and scrambled up he's through the door and is closing it with his left foot.

"No, no, stay there," he says, but he's too late. I take my mug from him, along with a deep breath.

"Mmmm, nothing like the smell of roast beef."

The aroma lingers even after the door's been closed.

We settle back down on the step together, close, him pushing against me in his gentle way. I stretch my cuffs even further so I can give my hands some form of insulation while hold my steaming mug. Now I can come out with what I've been itching to say since he arrived.

"I've got my interview on the twenty-fourth of next month. A new path in life to tread. I was always a little afraid of leaving school because it's all I've ever known but now I have something definitive ahead of me it doesn't seem so bad. Dad's given me a lot of advice on job interviews. It's been quite useful."

"Oh, what did he tell you? How do you see it going?"

"Well my plan is to show Charles the prospectus from Speciss College first off. You remember I told you about the book-keeping and general secretarial studies? It's two full days a week as a day-release course but I think he'll be okay with that. Dad went on about having questions for the interviewer about the company, like what it's business is, where it's going, who's who, etc. I had to laugh. He's clearly forgotten that I've practically lived in Charles's house over weekends for years. When Dad's been interviewed, like when he got the job here, he got asked technical questions but I've got zippo experience to talk about so I asked, 'What then?' He said I need to demonstrate I've got sound integrity and am keen to take on board any role assigned to me."

I search his face. "Do you think I've got integrity and can do that? Dad's been helpful, sure. But he ended up sounding a bit too much like a text book – all full of theory and with no thought of how I personally will deal with it all. I'll kind of need to know Charles believes in me. Would you believe in me if you were interviewing me?"

He blinks at me.

"I can't believe you're asking me this. Of course, Babe. You'll get this job. And then because you'll be all grown up and stuff and I'm going to be a poor university student from next year, you can take *me* out with your fat earnings."

One of the things I enjoy so much about us is the way I can counter with, "Don't you worry. When you're a rich accountant, I'll bleed you dry!" and somehow mean absolutely nothing.

Intuition is a damnably funny thing. It hits you out of nowhere and offers no explanations, but you know it's telling you the truth. It tells me now that something in his eyes has changed. The jolly humour has gone and has been replaced by the softest, sweetest emotion I've ever seen in him. It tells me that whatever he's feeling is good to him, pleases him. It tells me that, to him, I've just said exactly the right thing. The trouble is, it also tells me that I've just said the wrong thing. Reason unknown. Intuition doesn't need a reason.

I can't un-say it. Too late.

He places his mug beside him on the step, shifts so that he's facing me and his arm goes around my shoulders.

"Of course I'll support you, my little girl. For ever. We'll have been going out for a year on the eighteenth of August, you know."

Will we?

Rapid mental time travel. Jess, Gordon, the cinema, The Gremlin, hot dogs in the car. What was I wearing? Nothing wintery, but the evening had been cool. I vaguely recall wearing a light jacket. August sounds about right then. It's nearly the end of July, so why am I not counting the days to our anniversary? It's the sort of thing girls are supposed to remember, and to the very minute.

The correct response is, "Yes. Yes, we will."

He lowers his voice to a whisper. "Have you enjoyed it?"

"Oh yes, so far."

That *really* doesn't sound sincere. Can't un-say that either.

"I mean, it's been wonderful. We've had fun, haven't we?"

And that really was added too hastily. And not delivered quite right.

His eyes are still in mine in the rapidly fading light.

"I shall claim it as the best year of my life so far. I leave school at the end of the year. The Bachelor of Accountancy degree is four years and by then this stupid war will be over, although I don't know what this country will be like to live in. At least now I know I won't get conscripted. I'd thought of eventually emigrating down to South Africa to work after I'm qualified. I have family Down South as you know. What would you think of that, Tess?"

He wants to emigrate. Is he breaking it to me gently that if he does, we'll be over?

But that's not what he's saying. Look at his face.

This water's too deep. Back-paddle. Misunderstand his question.

"Sure. You'd get an excellent job in SA. Better paid than here and maybe with more international prospects. South Africa's not without its problems though. The whole world's attention will focus on them once we've got independence."

The enchantment dims – fractionally but noticeably.

"I… kind of thought… I meant would you…"

Would I? Well I would, surely? It's right. We are, here and

now, sharing the closeness, the darkening patio, the setting sun, the romance. Rosie would be in raptures if she could see us.

Where is she, anyway? I quell the urge to look round and try to see if she's watching us from her bedroom window. It would be difficult while he's holding me so tightly anyway.

No, seriously. We get on well. He makes me laugh and he's fun. I'm complete. A girl with a boyfriend. I have someone to share life and parties with. Someone to kiss me on the lips, and I *so* wanted someone who would kiss me on the lips. I trace my forefinger down his arm the way they do in the movies, because that seems like a fun thing to do. He tenses, and intuition is back, tut-tutting and saying you-shouldn't-have-done-that-Tessa. You've waded straight back into the deepest water and you're giving him the wrong ideas. Say something, quick.

"Do you know, I'd love to do lots of travelling one day. I've never been out of Africa and I want to see more of the world."

He clears his throat. Sits straighter and composes himself.

"Well, so much is possible. Not the same foreign currency restrictions in SA and a better salary for me. But you know, you and me, we've a way to go yet before we'd be free to do globe-trotting. I know you've got yourself lined up for this job and you'll need it for a few years while I get qualified, but then we could go Down South and get set up there and I'd like to do that as quickly as we possibly could to give ourselves plenty of time to have... I mean..."

Yes. Have children.

Way too deep now. Marianas Trench deep. How is this running away so fast? I haven't even actually got my first job yet and my entire future is being mapped out. And not by me. I can't possibly respond to that. End this right now.

"I haven't a clue what to wear to the interview, you know? Mum's telling me I should wear my school uniform."

He blinks, smiles, hides his confusion remarkably well and then, with unconscious perfect timing Mum is at the door behind us.

"It's ready!"

He says, "We can go shopping for something for you to wear if you'd like?" as we cross the patio together.

TUESDAY 31ST JULY 1979

"You should have asked me if you wanted to get some new clothes, Tessa. It's not appropriate for Mrs Owen to buy you things anyway. Some sort of suit is good for an interview but you have no use for a suit at your age. You're only fifteen. You could wear a skirt and blouse, and sandals? No, not sandals. Perhaps your tackies or your school shoes. I could buy you some flat pumps?"

She has zero dress sense. I have very little, to be honest. Rosie has it in abundance, and she's just itching to get involved, but there isn't a hope in hell Mum would see any of her suggestions as appropriate.

"But I didn't go with them. It all came about because I told them Danny said he'd like to buy me an outfit. Moira thought she and Gill would be more useful and offered to take me to get some ideas in town on Saturday. I said I needed to ask you first, and here I am, asking, and you've said no. *She* wasn't going to buy me anything, just take me for a look around."

What Moira actually said was, "Good God! Never, ever, ever go clothes shopping with a man in tow, girl. We can help you out, can't we, Gill?"

Mum sighs. "We'll go into town on Saturday then and I can buy you a blouse and maybe some lace-up shoes that are a different colour to your school shoes."

I can hear Rosie sniggering, even though she's in the dining room, doing her homework.

"No, forget it, Mum. I'll wear my uniform. At least all the parts actually go together and are, well, 1970s instead of 1940s."

Less than a month to go until my job interview. It's all a bit... odd.

FRIDAY 24TH AUGUST 1979

"This is Hood Road. Tessa, how far along did you say it was?"

"Exactly halfway to Highfield Road. I've no idea how far that is I'm afraid. We'll just have to keep our eyes peeled."

She's slowed to a crawl. It's a good job no-one's behind us.

"Gill says the façade is all face brick and glass, and that… There it is! On the left."

Mum flicks the indicator on. A black youth in a red T-shirt and khaki shorts, about to cross the car park entrance, hesitates, mid-stride, one foot extended. She waves him across, turns into the gravelled area with much crunching and brakes in front of a set of broad concrete steps. They're flanked by brickwork flower boxes, but they're empty. I guess they're awaiting re-planting for the new season. There *is* a lot of face brick and glass, just as Gill described, and 'Concrete Structures Ltd' in bronze letters that stand proud of the brickwork over the main doors. My hands are clasped together in my lap, palms sweaty.

"Well this is it. Wish me luck."

"You'll be all right." She leans across and gives me a peck on my nose. "At least you know your interviewer. Not many people get that chance. He'll put you at ease I'm sure. I'll be waiting for you here."

I'm sure I should be carrying something – a file or a folder or a briefcase. People who go for interviews on TV or in movies always carry some sort of important documents with them. But I have nothing. And I *really* wish I'd stood up to Mum and insisted on a proper outfit. I just hope I look suitably employable. Mind you, knowing Charles, I doubt he'd notice anything unusual if I turned up in my jodhpurs, boots and show jacket.

With one foot on the lowermost step, I take a second and try to visualise myself arriving here every morning for work. The image eludes me. I can't quite get round the not-going-to-school-anymore thing.

The main entrance doors and side panels are made of that ochre smoked glass that you can see out of but not into. My own reflection and that of Mum's car as she parks it on the far side of the gravel area are sharp and clear, if ochre coloured. I tug on the chrome handle but the door's heavy and I have to take a couple of steps backwards to swing it open fully. Once inside, I try to pull it closed again but it resists me until I realise that if I just leave it alone it'll close itself. Okay. Faux pas number one.

Don't look at the receptionist behind her desk against the far wall yet. Don't acknowledge that you're making a spectacle of yourself. Take your time and survey the surroundings like you're doing a critical appraisal. Like you've done this before.

The reception room is high ceilinged and bright from the light coming through the large glass panes. The entrance directly faces the sun so the room has a welcoming warmth after the cool winter air. A dark sage carpet stretches wall to wall, complementing the pale sage upholstery of four black-framed easy chairs. Similarly coloured vertical blinds clack together either side of the door following my entrance. In summer, they'll be necessary to reduce the temperature in here, make it less like a greenhouse.

The plants in their low, black containers are dark, large-leafed and abundant Delicious Monsters, and they're impressive, but it's the oil painting above the reception desk that's a magnet to my attention. It must be a metre high and more than that in length and its gilt frame is slim and unobtrusive, drawing the eye directly to the African highveld scene within. The artist has captured the infinitely subtle summer colours and has given the view such depth that I want to step through the frame into its inviting world. I want to know what lies around the bend in that soft, sandy road. There are wheel tracks in the sand. Someone's been there already.

I drag my eyes away from it. The girl behind the desk is attractive, with long dark hair. She jingles a collection of silver bangles with a flick of her wrist and extracts a sheet of paper from her electric typewriter with long fingers that terminate in perfectly shaped, peach varnished ovals. I curl my own hands together in front of me to hide my clean but disgracefully stubby fingernails.

At a guess, she's probably a few years my senior. She doesn't return my smile; instead she inspects me from head to toe and back up again.

"Can I help you?" she drawls, and when I inform her that I've come for an interview, her expression rolls over quickly from apathy through amazement to deep suspicion.

"Are you sure? This is Concrete Structures Ltd."

She's pretty; the scowl hangs badly on her.

"Yes?" I make it a question because I'm not quite sure what her issue is.

"Interview for what?"

What, exactly? I've no idea what sort of description applies to my potential new job. What did Charles say to me?

Megan. I'm to start off by assisting his book-keeper, Megan Trent.

"Book-keeper."

The head to toe and back up again inspection has a voice this time. It gasps, 'In a school uniform?'

She sighs. "What's your name?"

The flawless manicured hands lift the switchboard receiver and punch a two digit number. After a brief pause she announces, "A – er, Tessa Harmand – is here to see you, Charles."

Her telephone voice is earnest and contains silk with no trace of her irritation. She keeps her mascara and shadow framed eyes directly on my face as she speaks and I wonder why it never even occurred to me to put on some make-up, today of all days.

"Mr Owen is coming now," she tells me and then I cease to exist. She folds the sheet of paper she took from the typewriter into three and slides it into an envelope.

I'm more than happy to be non-existent. She hasn't offered me a seat, but I perch on the edge of one of the chairs. Within a few moments a door on the right opens and Charles fills the room.

"Tess!" he booms around his habitual encompassing beam. "Through here, girl. Through here. God, Debs, I'm so sorry. I should've told you she was coming. But you know how disgracefully disorganised I am. Forgive me please!"

Debs flutters her lashes at him and silkily declares it's no problem at all, while he ushers me towards the internal door. His body is between me and the reception desk so I'm able to scuttle past in its protective lee.

Only now do I realise I've forgotten all about Dad's advice to bring an A4 pad and pen. That would've been a good substitution for the important documents I don't have. Oh well. I'll have to remember what he tells me and ask questions as they arise. Or just forget everything and have to ask him again later.

The sage carpet overflows into a short corridor and beyond into Charles's office. This room is also furnished in pale sage and black but here the illusion of space ends, for very little of the carpet is visible around the stacks of box files, cabinets and pile upon pile of folded construction drawings. The drawing prints are neatly stacked and bound by rubber bands, but they're everywhere – on the floor, on the long tables down each side of the office, on top of the metal filing cabinets and all over Charles's huge desk. He shifts several bundles onto the floor before sitting down, so that we'll be able to see each other across the desk.

"Sit! Sit!" he commands. "'Scuse the mess. You know how it is."

I don't yet, but I'm sure I'll find out.

"Now then. Where did that blasted pen go? I only had it seconds ago. Oh, never mind. There's another one in here, somewhere…?"

He opens a drawer by his side and, after much rummaging and rattling, produces a black Parker biro.

"Now then. When I interview someone for a position here, I normally start by asking them to tell me a bit about themselves. But I know all about you, what you do, how you ride a horse. So it's not exactly relevant, is it?"

How I ride a horse?

"This doesn't involve riding, does it?"

I must sound pathetically bewildered, because he spreads his arms wide as if he wants to take me into them.

"More like riding a desk, unfortunately, my love! But have no fear. You can tailor your working hours to get away early and get to your horse. No, what I meant is, I think I know enough about you as a person. You tell me you like maths, so that's fortunate, although it's good old fashioned arithmetic I need you to do I'm afraid. None of this calculus and trigonometry stuff."

He stops and turns thoughtful eyes to the ceiling, then back to me.

"However, I did say you could ultimately have a go at different things within my business and work on site involves a fair bit of the old trig. Setting out and that. Nathan's enrolled on a civil engineering course at the Polytech from next January that includes surveying. He's pretty good with the theodolite already though."

He smiles. I'm nonplussed.

The theo… what?

"So would you fancy that? Having a go at anything? We can get you trained, but it's up to you. Keeping the books, getting involved in preparing tenders, site work, ordering materials. The sky's the limit. The only things not available to you are reception work and making tea. Debs and Sylvester would kill me."

I'm pretty sure Debs thinks I'm here to take her job anyway.

"Perhaps we'd better start with the book-keeping. At least I know more or less what that is."

"Of course, of course." He pulls a copy of the college prospectus across from the edge of the desk. It's the one I gave him last week and it's open at the page I dog-eared. He glances over it then pushes it aside.

"So, let's see." He makes a scribbled note on the desk calendar while intoning out loud, "Tessa. Lectures on Tuesdays and Thursdays during terms."

The calendar itself is barely visible through the jumble of scrawled messages in his large, bold handwriting. There are notes in various colours of ink and at all angles, including some telephone numbers written upside down from his point of view so that I can read them from my side of the desk. Does he realise that he's written the note on the present year's calendar?

"I would have to enrol for January 1980," I tell him, "so there's quite a way to go yet."

"Mmmm," he replies. "Well come on and I'll show you around the premises. Megs has already gone home but you'll meet her soon enough. Sylvester should be doing tea about now. Want some?"

Sylvester is in the post room. His crissy hair is beginning to show a dusting of white, yet his features, in that ageless African way, are those of a much younger man.

Charles herds us both towards the kitchenette.

"Sylvester's a retired police constable. He's sixty-five this year, aren't you Sly? This is Tessa."

"Welcome Tessa." His voice is deep, warm. "Tea all round, Charles? Will you be coming from next week, Tessa?"

"Oh not till January, Sylvester. She doesn't have sugar – just milk. We'll have the tea in my office please *Bwana*."

Charles sweeps me out and back to his office.

"Sylvester comes from Kenya, you know. Hence the *Bwana* bit. He's the boss in the back office, y'see. He also does the posting and spends bloody hours in queues at Southerton Post Office, poor bloke. As you see, we're all on first name terms."

That's just so Charles Owen.

Over tea, Charles suggests a starting date for me in the first week of January and casually informs me that my salary will be five hundred and fifty dollars a month, less PAYE and a small pension and medical aid society contribution.

"Is that okay?"

It's five hundred and forty dollars more than I already receive. I have a stupid urge to giggle, my brain boggling at the thought of having all that money to myself and I start pulling some odd faces trying to suppress it. Charles doesn't appear to notice. He swallows the last dregs of his tea, produces a few A4 sheets from a drawer below the one in which he found the pen and hands them to me. They're stapled together and the heading states "Conditions of Employment".

"Read the blurb – and you must, Tessa. Let your folks read it too. Talk about it. The position is for an Administrative Assistant. I hope you accept it all. If so, I'll get an offer letter typed up. Sign and date the last page there and get it back to me sometime next week. There you go."

So that's it? Short of a signature, I'm employed?

He holds up a forefinger and goes, "Oh, no, wait. I'm afraid if you refuse to join in our annual Christmas meal at the Bombay Duck I can't take you on."

"My God, Charles, I'm in, in that case. My parents have never taken us there because my mother will never know what it's like to be curious about foreign food, but I've eaten there with Danny's family."

"That's it then."

He escorts me back into the reception area. Debs ignores us both, her typewriter keys rattling with astonishing speed.

"I love the painting, by the way."

I point, but he's already looking up at it. At that tantalising road leading to who knows where. "Don't you think the best paintings are the ones that make you want to get into them and be in that scene? Find out what else is there?"

He's still for a few moments, his eyes roving over it. When he talks, his voice is softly un-Charles-like.

"My sister Annabelle. Nathan's mother. She was only twenty when she did that one. Talented artist, that girlie. She got it from my father, and others in the family before him. I didn't get it though. Like so many artistic people she struggled with herself – finding out who she was, what her purpose was, but she *was* interested in finding out. Then she never picked up a paintbrush again after that bastard married her and started knocking her about. The artist in her faded away."

Debs has stopped typing and is watching Charles. He's still absorbed in the painting. Then Debs has the grace to look embarrassed, stand up, gather some files in her arms and escape through the door leading to Charles's office.

"I was hoping she'd get back into it eventually, once she got her life back, after *he* was gone. But then she was gone too. Brain tumour.

She was dead within six months of the diagnosis so I suspect it had been present for some time and probably accounted for some of her irrational behaviour they put down to post-natal depression."

"Does Nathan paint?"

Sometime in the distant past I've seen him painting fences, a large creosoting brush in his hand and black, sticky stuff all over his shirt.

Charles is once again the recognisable, jovial man I know. He guffaws and places a hand on my shoulder.

"No. But he used to draw horses very well as a child. He would draw them with everything correct – the positions of the legs depending on what pace they were supposed to be in, lines showing muscles and tendons, then colour them in. They were good – very lifelike. You should get him to show you sometime."

I unlikely to ever do that, am I? We drift towards the entrance.

"Thank you for showing me round. And for interviewing me."

"I'll see you over the weekend, *ja*?" He winks and pushes open the glazed door for me. I wave at him as it begins to close behind me and skitter across the gravel to Mum's car in the grip of a seriously weird mix of apprehension, excitement and sheer, utter relief.

*

It's all a bit unreal, and the Chardonnay I'm managing to force down in between mouthfuls of veal in some sort of creamy sauce probably isn't helping. The bottle is hovering over my glass again, the waiter's eyes questioning. I cover the top of it with my hand and shake my head.

Rosie's smiling and looking keen but Dad shoves his own glass out under the bottle.

"One's enough for you, my girl."

She doesn't like it any more than I do, but unlike me she wants to be doing the done thing.

"Thanks for the meal, Dad." I raise my glass and we all clink together.

"No problem, my love," he says. "Next year you're paying."

SATURDAY 6TH OCTOBER 1979

So Mrs Longbenton claims Tansy is a 'strong, but brilliant jumper', but I'm not sure I'm going to get to assess the athletic ability that's supposed to make her brilliant while I try to contain her strength.

She carts me along the far side of the paddock in the sort of trot a diesel engine might do if it was a horse. I employ my best tactful horsemanship to slow the pace but in the end it's only the gag snaffle that has any effect. She pulls up sharply with a half rear and then plunges forward, puts her nose level with her knees, and tanks off again. I try again and again and get the same reaction again and again and we do two more circuits in a series of leaps and bounds. I suppose from the audience's point of view we're providing an interesting and spectacular display but it's not getting us anywhere.

Ignoring my screaming sense of self preservation I point Tansy at the yellow and white oxer that looks a bit smaller than the other jumps and she flies it like a hurdler. I catch up with her and, with the perimeter fence approaching at terrifying speed, I drag her to a halt in that leaping, plunging kangaroo fashion.

Enough is enough. I keep her on a tight rein and jog back over to the others. Gill's eyes are like saucers.

"Well she's keen, but I'm not ready to find out if there's life after death."

Mrs Longbenton pouts and folds her arms.

"But she's only learning! Hannah's been schooling her, but she's not that long off the track. You'll have to work at it a bit, you know."

Behind her back, Gill is shaking her head and waving her fingers across her throat.

By the time we get back in the car, I know my shoulder muscles are going to give me grief tomorrow.

"You rode her damned well. I don't think I could've done any better," Gill says cheerfully.

"Don't you dare ever tell my mother what that horse was like," I warn her. "She's seen me ride the Turnpike ponies and Induna and she now thinks all horses are safe. Oh, and don't tell Danny either!"

"Well, that mare was a complete non starter. I would say that anyway, even if I wasn't having a fifty percent stake in this venture. I don't want to train that thing and I'm certainly not letting any of my non-owning pupils ride her. She'll put them off riding for life. Sorry, she sounded like she was going to be good, being a half-sister to The Prodigal and all. No, we'll check out the grey Anglo Arab near MacIlwaine next week shall we?"

As days go, it's one of those best forgotten, what with my alarm clock choosing this morning to go into its last decline, twisting my ankle on the path as I ran to the shed, the flat tyre, and then leaving my hat behind on the kitchen worktop. Dad was remarkably calm about wasting his precious petrol so I'll have to tell him we had a good time and the horse was fantastic, but we'd like to see at least one other.

SATURDAY 13TH OCTOBER 1979

Out of earshot of Rosie, I whisper to Gill, "I wonder what this one does? Headstands? Somersaults? Do you think I ought to've brought a motorcycling helmet or just taken some hefty tranquillizers with a bottle of gin?"

"It'll be *fine!*" she croons, patting my arm. "I thought you said you'd told Rosie what happened?"

"I did. I swore her to secrecy. It's probably why she agreed to come along so readily and isn't whingeing now."

We pile into Gill's Alfa Romeo at ten-thirty.

"Now, girls, here we go. These people are called the van Rooyens. I don't know them at all although Tammy says some branch of the family was involved in racing many years ago. Seems they've bred this horse from one of their old racing stock."

Mr van Rooyen's son, Piet, meets us at the entrance to the main yard.

He's a bear. A massive, hairy, friendly bear. A semi-tamed ginger beard and moustache cover most of his freckled face and the hirsute arms and legs that protrude from the sleeves of his T-shirt and his shorts are solid with muscle. The T-shirt is tight fitting over his wide shoulders and chest but loose where it hangs over his flat belly. No typical Rhodie farmer beer gut in sight here.

His sockless feet are jammed into a pair of *veldskoens*. He walks directly up to me, smiling out at me with sharp green eyes and a wide mouth from under the brim of a battered leather bush hat, and when he speaks he does so with an accent that is refined, with only a hint of Afrikaans.

"You must be the lady come to try the horse, since you're the only one wearing jodhpurs. Are you Gill? You sounded so lovely… Um… We spoke on the phone."

I tear my gaze away from that beard and stare at the hairy paw he's offered. If he decides to give me a bear hug in those arms I'll be lucky to walk away from it.

"Well guessed. But I'm Tessa Harmand. This here is my friend and mentor when it comes to horses, Gill Owen, and my sister Rosie."

"Three pretty young ladies. How delightful!"

From any number of men this may've come across as chauvinistic and even lecherous, but not from Piet van Rooyen. All three of us blossom coyly. My hand, having been completely enveloped in his, is still in one piece.

"Stables over there." He points towards a lop-sided iron gate, beyond which are some low timber buildings with asbestos-cement sheet roofs. Then he adds, "But would you like some coffee first? Tea?"

We decline in unison and he leads the way. My innards are churning with anticipation as I follow in the tracks of Piet's swinging *veldskoens*.

There's a reputedly infallible phenomenon known as the 'gut reaction' and now, looking at Encore, I know he is the horse Gill and I will end up owning. He's an iron grey gelding of about sixteen hands, built along Thoroughbred lines but with the typically dished face and gracefully arched neck of the Arabian. He's good looking all right, but in a strangely ordinary way. Not flashy. But I like his eyes. They're large, inquisitive, warm, generous and sensitive.

Piet is gentle with him, slipping a snaffle bridle over his head and scratching the slim grey ears while Gill runs her hand down each of the gelding's legs and over his back.

"Try him out, Tess. I like him."

"I can assure you he's never bucked with any rider or done anything else dirty," Piet tells me and I believe him. No good reason – I just do.

Piet trots him up in hand first and he's totally sound, and calm. With me up on board, he feels a little green but he moves well. He has a tendency to lean onto his forehand as most young, unschooled horses will, but there's no resistance to my aids and when I direct him at the small, makeshift jumps of rough poles balanced on motor car tyres, he takes them fluently and quietly, steady and focussed.

Glancing towards the paddock gate I see Gill and Piet deep in conversation while Rosie is gazing at the thickly vegetated ridge of the Hunyani range, beyond which lies Lake McIlwaine. The paddock is probably ten acres or so of good dairy grazing land; smooth and slightly sloping up away from the gate. I feel so in tune with this horse that I can't help myself. I squeeze him into a trot, then a swift canter, then lean forward and move my hands to either side of his neck, inviting him to increase speed. At the same time, I click with my tongue and push my calves into his sides. He bounds on eagerly up the incline. We pass the farmhouse – a bungalow clad in creeping plants, its peaceful prettiness marred by the glinting diamond mesh of the three-metre security fence and the lighting columns – and sweep around in a wide arc across the far end of the field. When I ask him to slow, calling "Ooo-ooo" in a low tone, he's surprised, but responds. By the time I turn to head back towards the gate, he's in a walk, although he jogs a few steps now and then.

"Did he run away with you?"

I laugh, because Piet sounds so incredulous.

"Oh no. No, not at all. I asked him for that. He's great! What does he look like, Gill?"

"Good. Good." She's grinning broadly, her eyes sparkling in the sunlight, and I conclude that she must be particularly impressed. I'm about to suggest that we take him, when she forestalls me with, "Yes, we'll go away and think about it, thanks, and I'll get back to you. Eight hundred dollars, you want?"

Piet shrugs and rocks his right hand back and forth, palm down, fingers and thumb outstretched. Gill is bubbling like a child that's just been promised all the chocolate cake and Rosie is… well… frankly, smirking. Furtive. I'm suspecting I've been left out of some conspiracy.

We turn Encore out into a smaller paddock behind the barn at about one-fifteen.

*

"Look at that," Gill says as she starts the car. "It's just after four-fifteen. Will you be in trouble, ladies?"

"Nah," Rosie drawls from the back seat. "The folks said they'd only be back home six-ish. I'm *so* glad I didn't have to go with them. Vic and Mary talk boring stuff a lot."

I could say, "*Uncle* Vic and *Aunty* Mary, Rosie," but I don't.

"Pot, kettle, black, my dear! For the past two and three-quarter hours you've been gassing away with us and Piet and his parents through all those rounds of biscuits and fruit cake with not an inkling of your grumpy teenage persona or any gripes that you missed Lyons Maid Hits of the Week. What did Mrs van Rooyen do to you?"

She giggles. "Yeah, well, it was just one of those conversations wasn't it? Morphs from one topic into another each time you say, 'Well we really must go now…' She's so sweet. They all are. And then it goes on another half an hour. I was having fun watching anyway."

Watching?

I shrug it off and enthuse about Encore for a bit. Not getting much in the way of a response from either of them, I shut up and drift off into a world in which I invent the conversation that will take place when I inform Dad we've been able to procure the new horse for less than he'd anticipated. He'll be pleased as punch.

Gill startles me out of it by apparently reading my thoughts.

"Leave all the price negotiations to me, Tess. Don't you worry about it. I think I can get us a good deal. Do you like the horse? Do you want him?"

The pleading tone is odd.

"Oh *ja*. Yes, that's fine," and I whip round at what sounds like a stifled giggle from behind me. My sister is gazing out of the side window at the scenery with uncharacteristic interest.

*

"Coffee?" Gill tosses her car keys onto the kitchen table.

"We'd better get home. Mum'll freak out if we're not there when they get back. Besides, I've had so much tea this afternoon I'll spend all evening on the loo. I'll come and ride Indie tomorrow."

"Okay. I'll have some though." Gill snatches up the jug kettle from its stand and goes to the sink to fill it. Her hand slips on the tap handle as she tries to close it, so that she opens it further instead and a powerful torrent of water gushes over the top of the kettle.

"Ooops." She's staring out into the garden, eyes vacant. She dances her feet back a step from the splash and says, "'Byee! I'll call Piet, don't worry."

Ahead of Rosie, I free-wheel down the driveway and start to swing left out into the road without checking for any traffic. There's a squeal and I swerve in an instinctive reaction to the appearance of the metallic blue Mercedes Benz on my right. It slides to a halt and I'm off, hopping to keep my balance on one leg, and to keep the bike upright.

Oh God. I'm such an idiot. A lucky idiot. Thank God it's Charles. The car's left-hand indicator lights are flashing the driver's intention to turn into the gateway. If it had been someone else, carrying straight on…

As I approach, pushing the bike, the tinted driver's window slides down to reveal not Charles, but Nathan. I blink at him, aware of Rosie by my side by this time, but I can't gauge just how angry he is. His eyes are hidden behind a pair of aviator sunglasses.

"Got a death wish? Was this horse even worse than the last one?"

I latch onto the trace of amusement in his voice and make a supreme effort to pretend my heart isn't doing a dying bird impression. I swallow, shrug.

"You do realise that if you manage to hit me while I'm moving you get twenty points instead of ten? Besides, I thought you might want to test your brakes."

He pats the top of the dashboard. "Well, lucky for you they work well, and I wouldn't dream of trying to score points at your expense. Gill would skin me alive."

He waves and is gone, the Mercedes accelerating smoothly into the long driveway.

"I *do* like that car."

I stand in the middle of the road and watch it with longing. I've never really longed for any particular car before.

"Who was that? Watch out!" Rosie gasps and grabs my arm, trying to tug me and my bicycle towards the immaculate verge.

Another car is rolling down the hill towards us. Its driver gives us a wide berth and it's time to get home. It's clearly not my day for being out on the roads.

"Well, who was it?"

"What? Oh, Nathan. He's home on RNR now for a few weeks."

"Mmm. O-*kay!*" Rosie swivels back towards the Makuti Park gates but there's no longer any sign of the Mercedes. "The one who got himself shot up? So he's back in the sticks now?"

Back in the sticks. Like the song.

"He is. Charles knows a lot of the right people and he's now an instructor in the Grey's Scouts. Spends his days giving new recruits, and some not so new ones, crash courses in riding. Literally. Well come on. Let's get home."

"I fear your friend Gill has utterly flipped. Don't you think?"

I'm well used to jumping sideways to catch up with her and keep track of the conversation, but right now I'm defeated. I remount and start pedalling. I'm starving. Trying to remember what Mum said she would make us for dinner.

"What are you talking about? There's nothing wrong with Gill."

"No, I know there's nothing *wrong* with her. Didn't you notice? I can't believe you didn't notice!"

"Notice *what?* Rosie, these endless questions are getting us nowhere."

I push on ahead, tired of the game.

"That guy, Piet," she insists, standing up on her pedals and drawing level with me again. "She's completely fallen for him. You know, you really are so wrapped up in your horses you don't see anything else."

Curious little things, inconsistent things, from the day line up before me. I see Gill being vague, indecisive, devoid of concentration on my assessment of Encore, insistent that she must haggle for the horse and that she must contact the van Rooyens again, over-keen to get me to consent to buying the horse. I see her splashing water all over herself, the sink and the floor and hear her cheery "Ooops" as if she'd dropped a pen.

"See? So sweet! Don't you think it's like Beauty and the Beast?"

The great hairy bear and the coquettish and pretty Beauty.

"You're being fanciful. Gill wouldn't lose her head just like that, Rosie. Love at first sight only happens in movies and Mills and Boon novels. Maybe she thinks he's nice – well, he is nice. I like him. But she hasn't fallen in love with him. She's not like that. You're the romantic."

"You wait and see."

She overtakes me as we turn into our road.

*

After I've described the day's events and my new horse, omitting irrelevant references to any strange behaviour by Gill, I spot Rosie wringing her hands and making kissing noises from the end of the hallway. I ignore her.

"So what did you do this morning, Dan?"

He sighs and still doesn't speak immediately.

"Oh, this and that. I went into town with Mike Carney and his girlfriend. You know, the one from Queen Elizabeth School? Sally, is it? Or Sandy? Anyway, it was okay. We bought some LPs and looked at the stereos in Radio City then we had coffee at Barbour's and some of those little chocolate cakes you like."

Ah yes. Barbour's tearoom. A throwback to elegant colonial establishments, where discreet white-jacketed waiters serve tea, coffee and cream in tall silvered pots and lay trays of scones, pastries and dainty cakes on starched white linen tablecloths.

"Oh, they're bad for the hips and thighs. I'll have to give them up!"

"You don't need to," he laughs. "You're really slim."

Then, "I missed you."

I open my mouth for the obligatory "I missed you too," but he hasn't finished talking, so I'm not given time to ask myself if I'd really rather've spent the morning looking at stereo equipment.

"Do you want to come over tomorrow afternoon? I've taped those *Troopie Songs* for you."

"Well… I've got to find out whether Encore *has* been bought and I must ride Induna because I didn't today. Why don't you come to the stables? You can have a ride on him if you like."

There's a kind of a slightly wrong pause. I change tack.

"Oh no. That's all right. Don't worry. I'll ride him in the morning quickly and come over to your place for the afternoon. Can you help me with that Standard Deviation stuff again? Oh, and those stupid Laws of Indices?"

"Oh *ja*, fine. Yes, of course I'd love to. Come as soon after lunch as you can."

As I put the phone down, I'm as relieved as he sounds.

TUESDAY 6TH NOVEMBER 1979

"Now, Sunday," he says. "About Sunday, my sweet. I'll have to pick you up quite early because we want to get the fires going by ten."

Sunday. Ten. Fires. I've missed something. I go, "Oh, okay. Yes, that's fine."

He's laughing at me. "You didn't remember? Family *braai* at Ewanrigg National Park?"

He did say something about it. Excellent, I love a *braai*.

"Yes, yes, that's right. Ewanrigg. Sure."

Then my brain kicks in. He's talking about *this* Sunday. He's asking me out *this* Sunday coming, all day.

Shit. Encore's being delivered.

"Oh, whoops, no, wait a sec, I can't. I'm getting my new horse on Sunday. At about ten actually."

Well he's half mine, but that's still mine nevertheless.

There are times when you just know you've said something that changes everything. Bad feeling. The deep hurt in his eyes burrows way down into my soul.

"Can't this horse come another day?"

Can he? Maybe, if I speak to Gill? No, of course not. What am I thinking?

"It's all been arranged with the other people – Gill, Piet, Mum, Dad. He's not just 'this horse' either. He's my birthday present from my folks and he's been paid for. We can't change it now. But I'm seeing you on Saturday? We're all going out to The Cellar for a meal, remember?"

"Oh. All right. Yes." He swings a leg over the saddle of his bike. "Well I don't think I want to go to the *braai* now. I was really looking forward to showing you off, you know."

He gives a gusty sigh and says, "I'll see you tomorrow then. Or call you tonight?"

"Call me tonight."

We hesitate briefly and I wonder if I should touch his hand, resting on the handlebars of his bike. I'm sorry, and I don't really know how to say it. I just wave goodbye.

"What's up with you?" Jess demands when she finally arrives. "Shall we go? Where's Danny?"

The bad feeling is like the chilliness you get when a cloud passes across the sun on a winter's day.

Ridiculous.

"Oh, he couldn't wait, I don't think. I'll speak to him later."

We cycle off home in the energy-sapping humidity. The sun is blazing, intense, sky encompassing, but my shadow lingers.

SUNDAY 11TH NOVEMBER 1979

"Has she seen him since that day out at the farm, then?"

"I don't know, Rosie."

"Well she must have spoken to him on the phone. How did she sound?"

"I don't know, Rosie. I wasn't there."

"Is she still acting strange, like? Does she sigh a lot, talk about nothing but him, wander about in a white nightie with flowers in her hair?"

"Don't be stupid, Rosie. She's perfectly normal. You make it sound like she's on LSD or something. She hasn't mentioned him, apart from telling me the price she'd negotiated for Encore and that they'd agreed the date for his arrival. Eleventh of November. UDI anniversary, um… fourteen years on? Maybe it's a portent. Of something. I don't know what."

It's a year to the day since Nathan got injured. Charles had this thing a while back about teasing him, saying he was attention-seeking and only got himself in the way of a Kalashnikov for effect as a protest against the Rhodesian Front.

Rosie snorts. "Now you're being stupid. Oh yes. The horse. It's all about the horse. You're no good. You don't notice anything about anyone else."

Well it's hardly surprising. I spent most of my week worrying about last night and looking forward to today in equal measures. I don't know what I would have done if Danny had backed out of the dinner because I'd turned him down for today, or how on earth I would've explained it to Mum and Dad. But he didn't and he was just his normal, sweet self.

Encore's here now though and I'm high again. He steps out

beside me on the way to the stables and I'm only partly aware of my parents making what sounds like appropriate noises of approval to Charles. Then Rosie's voice cuts through with "Well he looks the same as that other one of hers, but just a different colour."

At least she's being honest about her lack of interest and knowledge. I guess Mum and Dad would love to be interested of course, and they do try.

*

Piet really is a just like a big, benevolent bear. They all love him. And Moira's been smirking just like Rosie did that day.

"I've absolutely got to sort out stuff at the farm and get Howard's trailer back to him, but if there's something good on at the cinema I can come back at six-thirty and pick you girls up?"

He's such a gentleman, which such soft, old fashioned manners, but he shouldn't be saying that. No need. We all know he only wants to be with Gill.

"Mum's planned dinner and what have you, but thanks for the invite. Me and Rosie will have to decline I'm afraid."

Piet is relieved. Rosie is disappointed. Gill's face is totally neutral but her unnatural tenseness betrays her.

After the pause she says, "Well, okay then. I suppose. Yes, I'd like to. Thanks."

We all act cool while Piet climbs into the cab of his pick-up, his groom in the passenger seat, and manoeuvres the horse trailer around so he can drive out of the yard. The pick-up is meant to be cream but it looks pink under its film of red earth dust.

"Where's Nathan?" I ask for the sake of something to say while this is happening and Gill tells me he's gone to the stallion viewing day at Moonfields Stud.

"We're considering putting First Foxtrot in foal to Opal Light. He's got another week left at home then he's back to Depot."

"Oh," I reply, then as Piet's vehicles disappear out onto the road Gill punches the air with a fist and cries, "Yes!" and we all fall about in something close to hysterics.

"I thought he'd never ask you, then he asked *all* of us! Do you think he fancies me and Rosie as well?"

She ducks away from my elbow, laughing.

"Well no, but he couldn't just ask me. That would be rude."

She sighs, her eyes distant. "Isn't he just such a complete *gentleman?*"

She herds us into her bedroom to help her choose an outfit, throws open the doors of her built-in wardrobes.

"I bought stacks of dresses in England but I've worn hardly any of them. Haven't really had the opportunity."

"What was it like, you know, coming home after being in the UK for a year?" Rosie asks, her eyeballs on stalks as she takes in the array of clothing on show.

"Fantastic! You have no idea. Oh, I enjoyed my time over there, don't get me wrong. The first few weeks I was there I would go into supermarkets for pure entertainment – I hadn't started earning and I couldn't afford to buy much on my pitiful holiday allowance. I would just hang out gawking at all the variety of goods and wondering what I'd buy if I had lots of money. It was better than TV. I'm sure I had a troop of store detectives following me around going, there's that blonde again casing the joint, keep an eye on her."

She pulls out a few hangers, lays the garments on the bed – a peach coloured chiffony evening dress, a blue and white striped mini dress, a jade silky blouse, a pair of Levi's. There's a pile of shoes on the floor of the right-hand wardrobe. Rosie's shoe-radar has located them and she's craning her neck to get a glimpse past Gill.

"These are like two and a half years old now. I'd be well out of date if I was still there. Yeah, lots to like – not the weather – but I didn't realise how much I'd missed Africa until I stepped out of the plane back here."

She can't describe it, she says. She talks about scenting the air like some sort of primeval animal the way I react to the first days of summer. Neither of us knows what it is and we can't possibly describe it but we're delighted to find we both know it. It's like a smell, but not a smell. Dust in the air? The lingering woodsmoke? Or the particular pollens from indigenous plants and trees?

"The area of Surrey where I was living is lovely and pretty well-heeled so properties are larger than normal and there are tree lined streets, but it's not like here. There's an overall impression of a distinct lack of space. Mostly houses crammed in on top of each other, terraced and semi-detached. The roads are narrow with no verges and each town or village runs into the next like one vast conurbation. Not everywhere, to be fair. There are open spaces, moors, forestry land, heath land, but, yeah, space was what I missed most. And African people. And African music. It's odd, but it was on hot, sunny, dry days that I felt most homesick. Good weather brought back the memories and the feelings. Weird."

I hold the mini dress up to my shoulders and pose in front of the full length mirror. It looks stupid with my jodhpurs and yellow socks poking out below it.

"Nice," she says. "Hey, look, if there's anything you fancy, just ask and you can probably have it. You too, Rosie."

So what does Rosie do? Within a split second she's effectively dived head first into the wardrobe and my attempt at grabbing her by the belt loops of her jeans fails.

"Rosie! Stop behaving like an orphan *piccanin*! Anyone would think you had no clothes of your own."

She's clutching a pink and navy knitted beret when she comes up for air. She places it on her head at a jaunty angle.

"I saw one just like this in Mum's *Woman* magazine once. It's fab!"

"Have it." Gill drops down on the bed and leans back, propped on her elbows. "It suits you and I'll never wear it. Now choose me something for tonight."

*

"Wind your windows down girls. It's like an oven in here."

Dad jerks the transmission into second and then tugs at his collar, presumably to let some air down into his shirt. A delicious draught slides through the car and Rosie sighs, "Oh yes," and shifts the bag of clothes off her lap into the gap between us.

I lean back and close my eyes. I can come over tomorrow after school. It's going to take some organisation now, with two horses to ride. The sharing arrangement with Gill is undoubtedly the best way; she'll do at least fifty percent of the work.

Why is Dad in such a huff? Perhaps he's hungry. It must be nearly six o'clock.

And he proceeds to let me know. Says, "Honestly, Sheila, I'm not sure what Charles was saying is right, you know." Admits that Charles is a very shrewd businessman who's in with a lot of people who are in the know, but can't agree with the conviction that life will just tick along as before once we get this black government.

"They want to pursue this idea of a mixed economy, like stirring socialism and capitalism together in a pot? Mmmm, not so sure."

Oh right. That's why. Someone's disagreed with his political views.

Mum doesn't respond. Good. Lord Carrington, Margaret bloody Thatcher, Lancaster House conference. I'm sick of hearing about it. The only thing I'm interested in hearing about is the ceasefire. That's what I want now and I don't much care how they get to it.

I drift back to my riding plans for next week.

Mum's unlocking the front door by the time I get back from closing the gate, Dad and Rosie hovering behind her. She wiggles the insert out with its tiny key then jingles the bunch as she swaps to the main door key.

"What a palaver, all these security measures," she mutters, half to herself, but Dad's heard her.

"Life in this country I'm afraid. Case of like it or lump it really, and it won't change now."

He pursues Mum through the door, still talking.

"It's like I was saying earlier. About those rumours? Our house boys and garden boys being told they can take over our houses and our cars after independence? Being told it's their right. Their *right*, for Christ's sake? After all we've made this country into! And the one about it becoming law that only Zimbabwe citizens can own property? We'll be forced to either give up our British passports and take up this citizenship or get out."

Rosie and I hang back, although I know she'll be itching to let Skellum out of the kitchen and play with him.

"And how many of us can just simply leave when we're financial prisoners in this place? Faced with a choice of risking getting our money out by illegal means or starting out in a new country with nothing? Nothing! After owning a home and working so bloody hard we get to leave with nothing. It's all right for the likes of Charles Owen. He's probably got business connections overseas to fiddle the system. He'll arrange things so that he can leave and have enough funds to keep going. We can't do that."

They head down the corridor towards their room. We throw open the kitchen door and make a pile of human legs, dog legs, human hair, dog tail and dog tongue on the floor, laughing. First part of the ritual over, I get his feed bowl out of the sink and a pack of meat from the fridge while Rosie and the dog exit through the back door for a quick game.

Dad didn't mean that, about Charles doing shady deals to get his wealth out of the country and then following it to vanish without a trace. Dad can't know about anything about Charles's business plans. They don't really know each other *that* well. I've no idea what they've been talking about all afternoon while I've been with Gill but it wouldn't have been plans to leave the country. Dad's a director now, I've got a job and I've got a new horse.

It's okay. It's a rant and it will blow over like it always does.

SATURDAY 1ST DECEMBER 1979

He squeezes me so tightly round the waist that I gasp and then he tickles me so I try to wriggle away shrieking, but he has my wrist in a soft clutch.

"Come here. I've missed you so much. That sounds crazy, but it feels like we've both been away on different holidays for a month. I know we've seen each other, talked to each other, but not been, like, *out*."

"Well this hardly constitutes as a date! Here, if you don't let me go I can't go catch Induna, can I? I'll show you how to tack him up then we'll get you on board."

Truth is, I reckon he's as desperate to please me as I'm desperate to please him. We never got much chance during the exams to well and truly make up for me standing him up for his family get together, so today's the day. We'll be okay together again. He wants me to give him another riding lesson. It's all good.

The last few weeks have been lost in a continuous cycle of writing each paper and swotting for the next. Crossing through the rows on my exam timetable with a thick black marker. Avoiding the post mortems.

"What did you get for Part (ii) of Number 4?"

"That angle? It was sixty degrees. Why? What did you get?"

"Sixty? No, I got forty-five."

"Yes, she's right. So did I."

"Forty-five? How?"

Whenever I've had the chance I've been disappearing off on either Induna or Encore for up to four hours at a time, soaking up the solitude of the bush, the solitude soaking up my stress. But it's over. I've crossed a line I never knew existed until now. School is finished.

It's all good.

It's baking hot, and still. Not the merest breath of a breeze anywhere. The flies are a damned nuisance and Induna virtually mugs me and tries to shove his nose into the headcollar before I've had a chance to sort it out. He's lost his fly fringe again and I can't be bothered to search for it. Maybe we can scour the paddock later when it's cooled down a bit.

There's what looks like a vague haze of dust hanging in the air above the stable block. I leave Danny to carry the tack to the stable and peek round the corner. It is dust, and there's the reason – Nathan and Bravo. Okay, this is good. If Danny wants to learn to ride, he needs to watch this pair a bit. I'll go tell him.

"Ménage is occupied right now. Here, look, we'll leave Induna in the stable for a bit. Leave the saddle on its pommel on top of the numnah outside the door and hang the bridle there. That's it. We can go and watch until he's finished."

"Who?"

"Nathan. He's riding Bravo."

"Oh."

As we make our way along the paved path to the gate, I nearly take Danny by the hand, but then don't. He's not looking at me so he hasn't seen me reach out and withdraw. I should want to hold his hand, so why I stopped myself I can't quite figure.

"Here we are," I say. Unnecessarily. "Watch and learn, my boy. Here's how to ride a horse properly."

"Hey? But you're a brilliant rider, my sweet."

He's studying the horse and rider. He says, "Oh him. He's back in the army then?"

Nathan's seen us. He brings his horse back into walk, more by telepathic means than by any visible aids, turns up the centre line and halts at X.

"Hi," he calls, kicking his feet out of the stirrups. He's wearing camouflage trousers and his army boots.

"Finished and celebrating? Gill said you had your last paper yesterday."

"Yes! Biology, done. All done! We're both free coz Danny's

finished his A Levels as well. Yippee!" I punch the air with both hands and nearly clout Danny in the mouth. This time I do grab him, pull him close and whisper "Sorry!" in his ear. He gives me a kiss on my cheek.

"If you knock me out I won't be able to ride your horse Babe," he whispers back and tickles me in the waist again. This time I wriggle downwards out of reach so he's bending over me.

He lifts me back up by placing his hands under my arms, then his attention shifts away to over the top of my head.

"I think someone wants to speak to you."

Nathan's dismounted and is right by the gate. He glances from Danny to me and back again then unlatches it and swings it into the ménage without having to move, so he and Bravo are standing in the gap. He offers me Bravo's reins.

"There you are." He's staring at the sandy track under my boots. "I'd like to see you ride him. Would you do that? So I can watch him from the ground?"

Unbelievable. How many times have I dreamed of an offer to ride this horse from either Gill or Nathan? And so now that it's finally been bestowed upon me I'm wishing it hadn't because I'm scared of being totally inept, hashing it all up and making a fool of myself. He looks up to see why I'm dithering and with an air of puzzled amusement proffers the reins again encouragingly. Then he glances down as I uncurl my right hand from around Danny's left to take them from him and the smile that was developing becomes fixed at a point just before reaching its full potential.

"Hello Danny," he says.

"Hi." Danny adjusts his dark glasses.

Nathan widens the gap for me as I pass through and step up to Bravo's head. While I'm scratching the horse on the neck and backing him up away from the gate post, he says to Danny, "You coming in?" then, "No?" and the gate clacks shut behind me.

So with one guy who thinks I'm an amazing rider and one who *is* an amazing rider watching me and my heart fluttering in my chest, I shorten the stirrup leathers, climb onto the lowest fence rail and, mercifully, execute a graceful mount. Bravo, for his part, stands like a statue. Only when I'm on board do I realise Nathan's holding his bridle.

"I was going to give you a leg up but you beat me to it."

He steps away and tells me, "Walk him round then, Tessa. Take up a contact straight away because he's already worked in. When you feel happy, do a bit more. Trot some circles or something."

Bravo is instantly and acutely aware of the fact that he has a new rider. He lifts his back under the saddle and dances his hind legs as if threatening to buck.

"Don't throw the reins at him. Leg on, sit deep and move with him. Don't stick your legs forward like that. Relax. Don't forget you've got sixteen hands of muscle under you that's likely to develop an attitude problem. You have to ask him nicely to work with you."

I flash a grin at Danny, who waves one hand then folds his arms to watch.

This is so cool. Bravo's trot actually seems to hover in the air fractionally between each stride. I circle him a few times on each rein like Nathan said, trying to get used to the feeling, then ask for a bit of shoulder-in. He's flexible and willing on the left rein, but kicks out at my inside leg pressure on the right rein.

"Aha! He doesn't want to step under with that hind leg does he? I've been working on that but he thinks he can get away with it with you. Try it again."

"You should smack him when he plays up like that," Danny suggests as I trot past the gate. "He looks as if he wants to buck you off."

I've never seen Nathan even carry a whip, let alone use one.

Nathan uses his emotionless voice. "Oh, we don't do it like that. We want him to do these movements willingly, not because he thinks he's going to get punished if he doesn't."

The dust had begun to settle but now I've stirred it up again. It's like talcum powder and it's hanging in the humid air like a smog. I ride for fifteen minutes and I want to stay on this lovely animal for ever, but Bravo's fine, dark chocolate coat is becoming lathered and I'm starting to flag. I can't keep Danny waiting like this. I must get him up on Induna soon or he'll completely lose interest.

I leap off at the gate, wipe the perspiration from my upper lip and lift my arms in an attempt to let air circulate under them.

"Horses may sweat and gentlemen may perspire, to quote that old saying, but this lady sure doesn't glow. I sweat with the best of 'em!"

It's Nathan who laughs; Danny doesn't react at all. God, that was such an unladylike thing to say. Am I destined to always be dusty and sweaty and horsey? I unbuckle my chin strap and pull the hard hat off, running my fingers through the lank, wet hair of my fringe. I've no doubt I look like I've been dragged through a hedge, and maybe part of a lake, backwards.

"Horrible things, these skid-lids."

"Better a ruined hair-do than a cracked skull, my sweet."

Ruined hair-do. So it really does look that bad.

I turn to Nathan.

"Thank you. He's stunning. So light and… I don't know. I can't find the words. I had the feeling up there a couple of times that he would have simply done whatever I'd asked at a mere touch. Yes, stunning."

He inclines his head. "You must ride him again for me. I like to watch him from the ground because it gives me a different perspective. Just say when."

Through my haze of euphoria and incredulity I catch sight of Danny's face. He's bored out of his mind and it's my fault.

"Let's get Induna ready. We'll only do a short session because it's so hot and we're going out tonight. Do you still want to ride him?"

"Yes. Okay, let's." It's a commendable attempt at enthusiasm and he takes my hand to show he means it.

With the intention of taking my leave of Nathan, I look back over my shoulder, but he's leading his horse around the track. When I do say, "'Bye," he doesn't turn.

*

Mum's taken Rosie to a tennis lesson and I've no idea where Dad is. I wander aimlessly about the house, unable to settle down to read my library book or to listen to the radio or to my records. The mere idea of making a pot of tea is taxing to the point that I just pour myself a glass of cold water from the jug in the fridge. I don't like plain water very much.

There's some half-hearted thunder and a bit of rain and when Mum and Rosie get back I'm sitting on the storm drain culvert headwall outside the gate, scratching the top of Skellum's head and staring into space. The rainwater's gurgling away beneath me, flattening the tangled bright green grass that lines the sides of the ditch. The wet macadam road surface is steaming in the sun.

"What are you doing out here?" Mum asks through the driver's side window.

"Just thinking. It's weird that it's all over and I don't have to go back to school. Except to get the results. It's only really hit me now."

"You wouldn't reconsider going back to do M and A Levels?"

She's asked me this before. I stop my absent minded scratching and Skellie turns his reproachful brown eyes onto me while tentatively waving his feathery tail in the damp grass.

"Sorry." I place a hand on each of his ears and pull at them gently. He grunts and closes his eyes.

"No. I've already accepted the job with Charles and I don't think A Levels would be much good to me personally. I'm not clever enough. Rosie should do A Levels, but not me."

She irritates me a lot these days but I'm pleased she's come home. I'm pleased both of them are home. I need the company. I stand up and follow the car through the gate, the dog at my heels.

Climbing out of the car, she says, "Would you like to go out for a meal tonight to celebrate? You choose where. Dad won't mind. He's at the office finishing some design thing, but I'll phone him."

"Oh no thanks, Mum." I clap my hands at Skellum, who races dizzily round his own tail twice before bolting off across the lawn in search of his well-chewed tennis ball. "Jess and Gordon are taking us to the Mabelreign Drive-In tonight. We've all finished exams now."

Jess is the only one going back to school, to do Matriculation Level in chemistry, biology and maths. Then in 1981 she'll be gone, to university in South Africa. She dropped this bombshell on me on Friday. I've always known she would go to university, but her revelation that she's chosen to apply to the University of Cape Town was a slap in the face. She's been quietly morphing into an emigrator behind my back.

*

Danny collects me at five-thirty and drives us to Gordon's house. I'm still in a daze and he glances at me several times out of the corner of his left eye. We barely say a word to each other on the journey.

"Gordon's folks have gone to Bulawayo for the weekend and his sister's staying with friends," he tells me as we walk from the car to the house. "I think Gordie intends to make this the mother of all parties so he's been out shopping."

"Oh good, I'm quite hungry."

There's a long row of bottles on the worktop. Red wine, white wine, gin, vodka, mixers. And two crates of Castle on the floor. No food, of course. You idiot, Tessa. You should be crowned Little Miss Naïve 1979.

A number of them are empty by the time we leave for the drive-in.

*

It's midnight, unless that clock I can see in the lounge is wrong. I squint at Danny's watch as I whirl under his arm. Well okay, it is midnight. We've been back an hour already. The edges of everything are a bit blurred, but that's not a surprise.

It's a wonder we got back at all. I'm sure I would've been a lot more bothered about Gordon's ability to drive if I hadn't had those G&Ts before we left. Dear Charles has never been stingy with his rum portions, but after a few too many Castles Gordon's judgement of alcohol measurements wasn't up to much. The first one was vile but the next two did gradually taste much better.

"What's so funny my sweet?" Danny rocks me from side to side and we both nearly fall over. He's remarkably sober, so he keeps me on my feet. He wants to stay in Dad's good books and he won't if he puts the car into a ditch on the way home with me in it.

"Just remembering… Funny… Gordon gripping the wheel with both hands and saying 'Ah, now there's a red light. I'd better stop.' I really thought he was gonna rear-end that car. He was being so… *sober*! And then he stalls it. And then we all ran round the car once before the lights changed. Why did we even do that? Who dreamed that one up?"

He chuckles. "Jesus! He wasn't at all sober and you're not now. Here now. Calm down and hold me close. We can dance. There…"

The telephone jangles from the depths of the hallway and we freeze in position and stare at each other. Jess is nearest to the hi-fi. She steps into the lounge, lifts the stylus and the music dies abruptly. My ears continue to throb.

"What the hell?" Gordon lurches indoors. Jess totters back out, drapes herself over the patio handrail and clings to a brick column for support.

"I bet it's his folks," she manages to say between sniggers. "They've decided to come back and are phoning from the petrol station at the end of the road."

This doesn't make any sense and she knows it. She gives a huge snort and collapses into a sitting position on the slabs with a sigh.

"I don't feel well."

Two minutes later Gordon reappears.

"Neighbours. Complaining. They're okay – not bad for old folks. Henry and Dad are pretty good friends. I told him we'd finished our exams. He said we should enjoy ourselves, but do it more quietly."

His face works its way from indifference through to indignation. "I say we turn the volume up some more. *Ja?*"

Danny leads me over to him, grabs his arm, turns him around and directs him back into the hall.

"Nah. They're not worth worrying about. We'll go indoors now. Come along, girls."

"You should have invited them over," Jess says, making a clumsy effort to get up, then pausing on her knees. "The more, the merrier, as they say."

Danny decides I'm capable of standing on my own, puts his hands under her armpits and lifts her to her feet.

We leave the French doors open to capture the few cool breaths in the dark, still air. Conversation ebbs and flows. This and that, a bit of school gossip. There's a pleasant drowsiness and then a companionable lull. The room recedes. Gordon's voice invades suddenly, loudly, with renewed energy, making me twitch and wonder where the hell I am for a split second.

"So, are we all set for majority rule next year? Revert to being a bloody British colony and then have the elections like everyone's pretending the last fifteen years have never happened? Ridiculous."

Is it normal for drunkenness to drain away in an instant? The blue and green swirls on the carpet come into crystal clear focus along with my thought processes. If the exams were good for anything, it was forcing me to forget the political mire that surrounds us and sucks us in, encompassing every day of our lives. Now in two sentences it's all back. Thanks, Gordon.

It's time to go. I straighten up against Danny and open my mouth to speak, but Jess beats me to it. She's not speaking so much as mumbling.

"There might be violence you know. Remember the Mau Mau? Well, we don't remember it of course – too young, wrong country…"

She sighs and starts probing her fingers into a crisp packet she just picked up off the sofa for any remaining shards.

I jump into the gap. "Perhaps it's time we should…"

Too late. Danny's sensed an interesting debate.

"I've already said to Tess that I'm thinking of starting out Down South when I've got my degree. It will be a better life down there. I don't care to be ruled by a bunch of gooks, thanks. I don't agree, Jess. I don't think we'll get that sort of violence. What we will get is plenty of propaganda about how terrible the white settlers were. All sorts of lies. Don't you think, Tess? You're being quiet."

I should carry on pretending to be drunk at this point. But some annoying urge in me won't let this one go. You're forgetting that we've been fed propaganda all our school lives, I tell him. History books are always toned to suit those in power. We get told how the Empire was great, but nothing from the side of the indigenous people of the countries the Empire absorbed. We get told the Allied Powers in World War Two were right and good but get told nothing from the German side. Our books hail Cecil Rhodes as a hero, Jameson too, but now we're finding out neither of them were heroes to many in this country or South Africa. We believe what we've been told because we're taught to do so and no-one tells us there are other viewpoints.

"Steady on, Tess."

Jess crumples the packet in her hands and tosses it towards a small basket-weave waste paper bin in the corner. Opening itself up in mid-air, it misses its target and lands amongst a few others on the carpet.

"Damn!" she says and closes her eyes.

"You're a right, rolling Leftie, aren't you?" says Gordon, eyeing me as if I've been brought in by the cat.

Well, question something we've been taught to believe and dare to suggest that 'the other side' may have a point, and get immediately branded a Leftie?

Danny only looks disappointed. "You don't think they'd be *right* to rewrite history to suit themselves, do you?"

Yeah, should've kept the mouth shut. Don't care what Gordon thinks, but Danny…? Do I? Actually, not really.

"It's what they will do, Danny. I'm stating fact. Yes, it will happen and that's why. Shall we go? Please?"

"Come along then, Sweets. We'd better go, Gordon."

"Mmm." He's caressing Jess and looks a bit flushed.

I totter over to where I left my bag. "What about Jess? Can we give her a lift?"

But she's asleep now and, weary beyond words, I let Danny lead me away and out into the balmy night.

SUNDAY 2ND DECEMBER 1979

I miss her, of course, but it's a good thing she stayed over last night at Piet's farm, so she didn't see me moping around in my dark glasses looking like death warmed up. George and Lazarus have been displaying only the utmost respect but I know they know. As for Charles and Moira and Nathan – I don't know where any of them are today and for once I don't care. They're not here.

"You," I whisper to Induna, "have had a reprieve today. I was going to lunge you but I feel like shit, so think yourself lucky."

He sighs, bats his eyelashes at me, and starts ripping grass with small flicks of his head, ambling off as he does so. He, at least, is incapable of saying to me, "Yeah, you're well hungover, aren't you Mummy?"

"Georgie, Miss Gill will ride Encore when she gets home."

He fetches my bike from behind the stable block and presents it to me.

"I will make sure, Miss Tessa. Don't worry. You go home and sleep, yes? Don't fall off your bicycle."

The world's a little less harsh now, thank God. I say, "What? Why would I fall off?" and he closes his lips demurely.

I'll call in at Jess's place, I think. George is convinced I'm drunk, but I'm not. Not now. I just feel sick. Or I did. I'm okay now, except for the headache.

She's lying in the sun in her bikini by the pool, also wearing her sunglasses. She sits up, grimaces at me, and we sit side by side for a while, me cross-legged in my grubby jodhpurs and idly splashing in the sparkling water with my fingertips. After a while, I say, "So what time did *you* get home last night? I couldn't believe it – my mother had actually gone to sleep and didn't hear me come in. Thankfully. I was barely conscious. It's funny how the brain works though. Danny offered to put me to bed but the importance of having to lock up the house properly after he'd gone over-rode this rather nice thought. I don't remember anything after bolting the door and setting the alarm. I woke up this morning fully clothed with the sheet over me. I'd managed to take my shoes off though."

She doesn't reply and I look up at her.

"I got back at half-past seven this morning," she says at length and, when I raise my eyebrows, goes on, "I stayed the night with Gordon."

There's another pause. An awkward one. A conversation with Gill comes back to me.

"Well go on then!" she snaps suddenly, almost viciously. "Ask me what happened!"

"If it was nothing you wouldn't react like that. So I assume something did happen. Tell me if you want."

At least I know now for sure that this was the first time. Call it intuition, call it what you want, but I'm sure. What sort of reaction is she expecting from me? I'm damned if I'm going to display shock. I wipe my wet hand on my T-shirt and peer into the darkness of her glasses.

"You know me. I don't pry or make hasty judgements. I'm your friend. If you want to tell me, I'll listen. Now, or later."

"I didn't want to, you know. Really, deep down. I never wanted it to be like that. I was drunk and half asleep and he persuaded me that I wanted to. I believed him and I thought I believed myself. But now I regret it. Deeply."

She sighs, opens her mouth as if to go on, but then closes it again. I know what my next question has to be and when it comes out I can't believe I'm asking it.

"Are you taking anything? I mean, like, well, the Pill?"

My cheeks are burning. Surely she would've told me if she was? Told me if she'd been contemplating sleeping with Gordon? Or maybe she thought I was too naïve to discuss these things with and deliberately left me out of it? I hope not. I really hope not.

"Nope. Why should I? I didn't intend for this to happen yet."

Her mouth twists as she watches me struggle with the implications of this statement.

"And no," she adds, "my mother doesn't know, and she won't unless I tell her."

"Will you go on the Pill now?" My voice is hoarse and I have to clear my throat several times.

Her reply is instant, cutting over the end of my question. "No. It's not going to happen again. Believe me. Not with Gordon anyway."

"Hello, Tessa!" Mrs Marsh's voice trills from close behind. Too close, and we both twitch.

Jess's mother has a cream silk complexion rarely seen on a white woman who's lived under the sun of the tropics. She worries constantly about her daughter's obsession for spending long hours sunbathing by the poolside, even though the only effect this has is to produce more freckles and the lament, "It's not fair! Look at how your skin tans. You always look healthy and brown, not speckled like me."

It's a shame none of us are satisfied with what we've got. We white girls go home and stick ourselves out in the sun to go brown while our brown classmates go home and layer on skin-lightening lotions.

Still smoothing moisturising hand cream between her fingers, Mrs Marsh breezes around a large plant tub to face us.

"Tessa, dear. So nice to see you. I'm just putting together a cold lunch for us. You do eat polony, don't you?"

"Oh really, Mrs Marsh, it's very good of you but I'll go home for lunch. I just popped in on spec to say hello. I need a shower now. I smell of horse."

"Aw, are you also feeling a bit fragile then? Jess says you all fell into a sort of stupor and only woke up early this morning."

She giggles and says, "Tut, tut."

Jess sighs and covers her face with her hand. Mrs Marsh wants to talk but for once I'm desperate to get away. I can't sit across the lunch table from Jess, making polite conversation with her parents while sharing this guilty secret. I stand up.

"I'll be in touch."

Not two roads away, I dismount to walk a bit. Need the thinking time. I amble along under shady and flaming red Flamboyants, balancing on the kerb, my bike in the road.

Jess. She's taken an almighty step in her life. In *our* lives actually. Gill was wrong – this was Jess's first time. It's such an almighty step that it's left me on the other side of a chasm. I am both naïve and childish, and virtuous and smug all at the same time.

I never asked her what it was like. What it felt like before, during and after. I should've asked. These things should interest me. Danny. He may well start asking… pushing…

No, he won't. He's wonderful and kind. He kisses me and cuddles me and calls me pet names. He's never suggested we go any further, but he's considerate, that's why. He wants to – I'm certain – but he doesn't, because it's not right.

Is it right or not though? Am I right to be virtuous and smug, or just plain missing out?

Question is – so many questions – does his kissing and cuddling make *me* want to go further?

It doesn't. But it should. Everything I've read or heard about sex tells me it should. I'm supposed to feel *desire*. I know what desires are. I get these. They come out of the blue some nights, but it's normal. And what about Rosie? She goes on and on *ad nauseum* about how Rob Craddock makes her weak at the knees. She lets me know she desires him. No qualms whatsoever. Happy to admit it. Normal.

And Gill. She adores Piet. She spends nights with him regularly. She's chosen him as her life partner and it's normal.

So, I'm not normal.

Although… No, you will *not* think about that.

But why am I trying to dodge the memory? Trying to pretend I didn't feel what I did that day? Why am I puffing out my cheeks and going all crawly and flushed even though I'm all alone on the side of the road? The only other living thing in sight is that stray mutt, trotting along the opposite verge on a mission. No cars, no cyclists, no pedestrians.

Forget it. It was nothing. It was a fluke. It means nothing.

My scene has been invaded. Three cars, all at once, one from a side road and two from around the bend ahead of me. Come on, remount, get on home. Look at the glorious view across the valley and appreciate the sunshine radiating from the clear dome of the sky.

A hundred metres down the road and I'm *still* feeling the electric shock, the tight ache, the lightness and tremor running down my legs. It was one touch of leg to leg. With *him*, of all people. No, I don't know what caused it. I was probably just having one of those random hormonal moments. Co-incidence.

Was *he* feeling the same thing?

I said, forget it.

I'll start that new book when I get home. I also need to write my Christmas list.

FRIDAY 25TH JANUARY 1980

She doesn't even say hi.

"Tess, listen. The results are in. We've been told to tell you guys who've already left that you can go to the school office today or tomorrow, or you can wait and they'll be posted to you."

My heart's just flopped into the pit of my stomach with a thud.

"Hello? Hello Tess? Are you there?"

"Yes. *Ja*, I am."

They're here. After all the stupid rumours. At best, all public exam results got received back in December and got held back for some obscure reason by all the schools' administrators (were they all too good to be true, or so bad there must be some mistake?) and at worst, the plane carrying them had gone down in the high seas. Or maybe in the Sahara desert somewhere. The same rumours that get regenerated every year.

She'll know her results already of course.

"So, how was it then? Tell me."

A gasp at the other end of the line, then, "Okay! Yes, okay. What a relief! I got eight As and a B for French."

"Well I'm *really* disappointed in you. A B for French? Well, I don't know, Jess Marsh. Not good enough."

But my heart isn't in the joke. There's a pause.

"Phone me as soon as you know yours," she says quietly. "Go on. Go down there now."

This really isn't like me, but I'm going to have to forget about Encore's jumping exercises. Back in my room, I peel off my jodhpurs and put on a pair of shorts, kind of in a hurry to get going, but yet moving as though engulfed in treacle.

"The O Level results are here," I tell Mum. "I'm going down to the school."

She looks nearly as sick as I feel.

"Do you need a lift?" she asks, then titters nervously. "Sorry love, of course you can drive yourself. Borrow the car?"

"No thanks. I'll cycle."

I don't want to have to concentrate on driving right now. Still pretty new to me.

School feels like an alien planet now. Lessons over for today, but there are a few pupils milling around, including an A Level geography group about to embark on an afternoon's field study. Black girls and white girls are mingling, chatting. So different from my early school days. It's good.

The black lady in reception is new as well. How long did it take her to coil her hair into those beautiful braids? It looks stunning but I wouldn't have the patience. Two thick plaits is all I'm willing to deal with.

"I've come to see the Deputy Headmistress," I tell her. "Exam results."

"Oh yes," she replies, pointing along the corridor. "She's free now. Go ahead. Good luck!"

Mrs Fincham looks up at me from over her half glasses and under her floppy grey fringe. "Hello dear?"

"Tessa Harmand. O Level results. Told to come."

Correct sentence construction, a subject of one of Mrs Fincham's little assembly sermons on the necessities of life some time in the distant past, is quite beyond me today.

"Oh yes."

She has a lever arch file on her right. She opens it and runs a forefinger down the dividers, chooses one – presumably 'H' – and flicks all those above it over the arch mechanism. She lifts the lever, extracts a narrow flimsy sheet and holds it out to me.

Why's it so near the top? Oh – maybe 'HA'.

I take it as though it's about to explode in my hand. It's a computer print-out, a page filled with words and letters that make no immediate sense. My name is at the top – 'Harmand T.L.' – with my candidate number, and the subjects I took are listed below, each with a grading letter adjacent. I allow my gaze to slide slowly downwards, each letter popping into focus and then fading away before the next. There are nine of them: four consecutive As, followed by five Bs.

I run my eyes up and down the column several times. I have read it right. Only now do I refer to the subject list, to discover what the A grades were for: maths, biology, English language and English literature.

"Maths?" I say aloud, filled with wonder. "An A for maths?"

Mrs Fincham smiles but says nothing.

*

Danny chuckles. "Those innocuous little paper slips are our tickets to freedom or to university, aren't they? Like airline tickets, hey?"

I pull a face at Rosie, who's doing her kissy-kissy noises through pursed lips and hugging herself. I thought it was funny once and she made me feel smug, but now it just hurts.

"Well the destination's not that exotic but I'm happy. Relieved. All of us – we've got what we wanted, haven't we? You, me, Jess, Gordon."

"A celebration coming up? Shall we all get together?"

Like the one when we finished the exams last year? I don't think so. It started perfectly fine but I didn't care for the ending and the ground has shifted since then.

I avoid a direct answer, we chat a bit more and then end the call with a promise to see each other on Sunday. Just Danny and me. Jess and Gordon are involved in some family do at Jess's place.

I'm not entirely sure how much longer there'll be a Jess-and-Gordon. She's still acting like she's all lovey-dovey with him but something's not ringing true. Certainly since Monday, when she turned up unannounced simply to tell me she wasn't pregnant, I've felt vibes that she's not willing to divulge and I'm not willing to question. And I'm not the only one. Rosie, of course, without knowing any of the facts, is convinced they've split up. I never said a word to her, I swear.

"Jess is looking a bit crushed, I reckon," were her words. "Seems like it's all over, yeah?"

We've all passed the exams and are moving on. So what about Chipo? Impulse drives me to look up "Makoni" in the directory. There's only one in our area and I hold onto the impulse and dial before I can chicken out. A cultured male voice answers in English. His tone contains surprise until I explain who I am.

"Ah, Tessa? Yes. Chipo has talked about you. Please wait. I will call her."

She comes to the phone breathless, her tone pitched to incredulity.

"Tessa! What a surprise! How did you do? Did you pass?"

I give her my results in as neutral a voice as I can muster.

"Well…"

I get the feeling this pause is for dramatic effect, and I'm right. She squeals, "Eish!" and I move the receiver a little further from my ear, grinning like I'm about to burst.

"I passed too! Seven Bs, but I failed French. I knew I'd fail French! I don't need French. Hey, you're going to college aren't you? Which one?"

"Speciss College. My new boss has already enrolled me to do book-keeping and business studies and I start the first week in Feb. Day release, Tuesdays and Thursdays."

"Me too!" Chipo shrieks. "We can sit next to each other and compare notes."

A new friend. I have a new friend. The day just keeps getting better.

When I skip into the lounge, clapping my hands, Dad smiles, but doesn't look up from his paper.

"Was that that Jess-person again? It was a short conversation for her, wasn't it?"

He's always maintained that Jess was born with a special ear attachment for a telephone receiver.

"No. Chipo Makoni." I flop down onto the sofa.

"Who?"

"Another girl in my class last year. She passed her Os too."

"Makoni?" Dad laughs. "A jungle-bunny, eh?"

Oh yes, Dad. How amusing for you. You'll be thinking she shouldn't have come out of the jungle in the first place, huh? I can't be doing with this. I really don't see why I should explain that she's my friend. I have other calls to make anyway. To Gill – and Charles of course. He needs to know his newest employee is at least in some way qualified now.

As I stalk out of the room I hear Dad sigh behind me. He'll reflect briefly on female moodiness and then return to whatever he was reading in his newspaper.

Charles answers the call.

"Excellent, Tessa! That's my girl! So you'll definitely turn up on the fourth of Feb then?" Once again I move the receiver away a fraction.

"I most certainly will, Charles."

"Do you need a lift? You're most welcome to come with me, but I go in very early sometimes."

"No, thanks. Dad's offered to be my chauffeur. It's only a five-minute detour off his own route. On college days I'll catch a bus into town."

"You need a car, girlie."

School finished with, major exams passed, got a job, the war has ended, but my future's not quite complete. He's right. I need a car.

"Dad did say once I've earned a few months' salary he'll help me find one."

"Well let me know too when you start looking and I'll see what I can find out. You want Gill? Hold on, don't go anywhere."

"Gill!" he bellows away from the phone.

There's some very pleasant daydreaming to be done on used car dealers' forecourts but unfortunately Dad hasn't yet specified exactly how this car will be paid for. The notion that my new salary was going to make me rich beyond belief has taken a nosedive after the calculations involving PAYE tax, pension contributions and medical aid society payments I did this afternoon. Maybe I've just got expensive taste in cars.

THURSDAY 28TH FEBRUARY 1980

The grooms are back.

I dismount and start running up Encore's stirrups. He's watching me out of the corner of his left eye. He studies me a lot, especially when I've tied him to the baling twine on the ménage gate while I rearrange poles and jumps for him, like he's curious about what I'm doing, hauling stuff around. Probably thinks I'm crazy dragging two jump poles across the school like a carthorse between the traces. Role reversal.

Induna would've stood there gazing into space, probably dreaming about acres of grass, but Encore watches me. I like this. I find myself waving to him and calling out a running commentary.

"Shall we put this cross pole here? What about if we set up a grid over here of trot poles that lead into a cross and then a nice little oxer?"

If the Karen Meltons and Lauren Collingwoods of this world could see me at it, they'd know they were right after all. I can hear them: "She actually *talks* to her horse like it's a person – can you *believe* that?"

George approaches, holding Encore's headcollar. He doesn't look me in the eye.

"So Miss Tessa. We have done our votes and now we are here again. You didn't need to go because you have voted already, yes?"

"Only my parents, George. Two weeks ago today. I'm not old enough to vote."

"Ah, shame," he says, shaking his head and tut-tutting. "Well Mr Owen said we could have the afternoon off but it only took us two hours. The queue was quite short. I went into the booth and I put my cross on..."

"Don't tell me, George! You don't have to tell anyone who you voted for, remember? Where's Gill today?"

"Ah!" he grunts, with something approaching irritation in his tone. George is never irritated.

"She is neglecting her horses. She has gone visiting again, Miss Tessa. This man, Piet? *Eish*, but I think they are now very good friends."

I can't do anything but laugh at that pretend scowl.

"What's the matter George? Don't you approve?"

He tries very hard not to smile, twisting the scowl, but he won't answer my question.

Moira appears in the yard after I've turned my horse out. Confirms what George just said, with the exact same whimsical aura Gill has about her when she mentions a certain Mr van Rooyen.

"Oh yes. She's at Piet's farm. You know what she said to me, Tessa? She said that Piet came with your horse and went away with a part of her. We like him so much. He runs that farm totally for his father, who's got a bad heart, you know. It's good to see Gilly happy. She was so down after she split up with Tim. Now she's got her spark back."

"Sounds like you've all been captivated by him. Although Gill tried very hard to pretend not to be after he took her to the farm the first time. Said things like oh, *ja*, he showed me around the farm, I particularly wanted to see the farm, you know how I like all animals, they have some nice dairy cattle."

Her face creases up with delight. "That's Gill through and through. Come, walk with me back to the house. You going home now?"

On the way we come to the conclusion that it's just a plain weird situation. Rhodesia now officially never existed. We're Southern Rhodesia again and we have a British Governor, at least until the elections are over. That's what this place was called at the time I was born. We're going backwards to go forwards. And it's a sad fact that everyone, even those in favour of majority rule, knows the elections will be a farce.

"There can be no doubt," she says, "that intimidation will be rife. The rural folk in this country have a deep suspicion of the secret ballot. It goes against all their traditional beliefs and the inheritance of power, of kingship. They won't believe it's secret. Some will, of course, but not enough. Think about it as if you're someone from a remote village. If a man slides up to you in the dark and tells you that if you don't vote for the right party the spirits will know and that they'll tattle, then you vote for whoever he says you should. I would, if I believed in ancestral spirits, wouldn't you?"

It's more or less what Charles told me two weeks ago. He reckoned, "The United Nations think they can control intimidation with their Monitoring Forces, but none of those guys *understand* Africa, or the Africans. New Zealanders? Well maybe they understand the Maoris. I know little about Maoris. And Fijians? All full of wanting to do a good job and keen to visit a new country I'm sure, but hell, no clue. *British Bobbies?* Seriously? Well trained and efficient in their own country, but they have no notion of what they're dealing with out here."

When he left the office on that day to vote in the so-called 'White Roll', along with Debbie, Nathan and one of his site guys whose name escapes me right now, I said, "Careful now. Your ancestors are watching you. Make sure you vote the right way!"

I was being neither scornful nor disparaging. We whites have turned it into a joke because it scares the hell out of us. We don't understand it, but we know it's real. Very real and very intimidating.

Mum and Dad queued the same day to cast their votes for the twenty 'white seats' in the new government's parliament. That's all we're allowed. There's been much talking, more arguing and plenty of wailing. We've been sorry for ourselves, we've blamed the whole world for our predicament. We've ignored what was staring us in the face then we've woken up and fought it tooth and nail. We've done lots of dying, trying to hang on to something we could never keep and simply wouldn't accept that we could never keep. But now we've arrived here and, like the power of the ancestors, it's real.

Yet the ever-sardonic humour of the Rhodesians has risen again. Christmas 1979 will always be known as The-Last-White-Christmas.

PART THREE
FREEDOM

FRIDAY 6TH NOVEMBER 1981

I put my pen down. I haven't told her the half of it but I'm incapable of putting most of the roller coaster emotions I've discovered in the last few weeks into words. The way I've been on such a high – a scudding around in the clouds, life is just the best, nothing could possibly go wrong ever again kind of high – only to come crashing down minutes later into a black hole from which nothing can ever go right again. The way I've endlessly questioned my own decisions like never before and like I never realised was possible. I can't write all that in a letter – I don't have the literary skills. But one of these days we can spend hours talking about it.

Or maybe not. Maybe by the time we get to meet up again it will all seem irrelevant and part of another life. Water under the bridge, as they say.

MONDAY 3RD MARCH 1980

There were no scenes of violence. Television crews and reporters have sent footage and shots of smiling voters in lengthy but jovial queues, under the watchful eyes of our multi-national mentors, all round the world.

So here we are, sitting together as a family on our sunlit patio at the end of a day spent in limbo. Dad is even more morose than he was at the end of last week. He's scowling at the droplets of condensation trickling down the outside of his beer glass. No-one's spoken for a good twenty minutes, not even Rosie. She's reading, rather than trying to talk over me and Mum about her day at school and Alicia's party next week and Heather's dreadful new haircut and Rob's latest, tight-fitting polo shirt. I can't think of anything to say about anything and Mum's intent on mending the hem of her grey skirt. We all know *what's* going to happen – we just don't know precisely *how* it will happen.

Dad is the one to break this crackling silence. He makes his declaration.

"Tomorrow will be a sad day for us all. It's going to be Mugabe. This country is finished now, absolutely finished. These *kaffirs* can't run a country to save their hides. Look at what we've given them: modern technology, a civilised form of government and infrastructure, the *wheel*! Ungrateful bastards."

The rest of us raise our heads – in indignation, like the librarian does if you drop a book or laugh too loudly. We were all happy *not* talking about it. Now we'll have to. My stomach churns and something gives way inside my head with a crack. I've kept quiet about his insults to Chipo but I'm not going to sit here and swallow his petulant political pessimism this time, on the eve of a day that will mark a monumental change in our lives.

"Leave it out, Dad! After all the time you've lived in this country, you still don't really understand Africa, do you?"

Anger, fear and guilt all serve to leave me breathless. Anger, because his prejudice is not something we need – not something *I* need. Fear, because, whatever the election result, the violence could well erupt tomorrow. And guilt, because I've finally dared to openly challenge my father. He could probably shut me up with a curt command to mind my manners, but he doesn't. His mouth is hanging open as though the idea that his opinions are questionable has never occurred to him.

Well, I need him to know that I can, and will, question his opinion. I force myself to keep looking at him.

"Can't you see? It's the only way. We *have* to have majority rule. How much longer do you want to keep on fighting a futile war? We can't just hold out and trust it will all come right. Believe me, these people would fight forever – they won't give up. I don't want to live in a war zone for the rest of my life. Do you?"

Mum puts down her sewing and I switch away from Dad and watch her biting her lip, her eyes flicking between the two of us. I don't give her a chance to chip in. She'd be on his side anyway.

"Yes, we brought all this so-called civilisation to Africa, Dad, but we've been very reluctant to share some of it. We might've brought the wheel with us, but we thought they'd just be content pushing wheelbarrows for us. They were always going to want a piece of the power, surely? Isn't that human nature? Now, in fact, they've got all of it."

Now I've done it. What sort of analogy can I think of? I've just launched myself off a cliff? Pulled a plug out of what could be a very active volcano? There's no going back. I'm actually shaking, so I tuck my hands under my thighs.

He's more amazed than anything else, like I've just got hold of the wrong end of the stick, or perhaps even the wrong stick in this case.

"Where have you got these crazy ideas from, Tessa? You've been talking to your little jungle-bunny friend. She's telling you a load of nonsense." Then the frown spreads from his eyes down to his mouth. "She'll have you siding with the gooks next. Why are you doing this?"

"Tessie please…" Mum is trying to get me to focus on her but I've been stung now.

"Chipo's got absolutely nothing to do with this! How dare you call her a jungle bunny? She's a friend of mine with the same education I've had, thanks to the mission school system. Don't accuse her of stirring. You've never even met her. You know nothing about her. My ideas are my own, Dad!"

That's not quite true. I would probably be agreeing with him if it wasn't for the Owen family's influence in my life. But then, isn't that how we should get a balanced view of this world – by learning what other opinions are out there? You can't just listen to your parents for ever.

"And I'm not siding with any gooks. I could never condone terrorism of any kind, anywhere in the world. Are they even terrorists? Sure, they've been torturing and bombing, but at the back of it all they've just been an opposing army. It's us who have put the term on them. I just find it sad that we've all followed the route away from realising that blacks would always have wanted to be involved in governing Africa at some stage. Thinking that only white is right. We've kind of brought it on ourselves, haven't we? Now we have to give Zimbabwe a chance. I'm not saying it will be easy but I want to try, yes?"

He clicks his tongue and bangs the empty glass down onto the wrought-iron table. Mum winces and clutches her skirt to her chest.

"She's calling the place Zimbabwe already," he says to the glass. Then he looks at me, and with utter shock I realise he's about to cry. "Whatever happened to 'Rhodesians Never Die'? You wore the T-shirt. You seem to have forgotten all about what we've been fighting for. All those stints I did in the bush. I don't understand you."

I've really pushed my spear in now and I hate myself.

"No… Dad, I'm sorry…"

He practically leaps out of his chair and stalks through the French doors into the living room.

"Oh Tessa!" Mum's thrown her sewing onto the table and has pursued him in a flash. "Bob! Please! Please wait darling. Let's talk…"

As her voice fades into the interior, Rosie, who's sat like a statue through all of this, bolts across the space between us and plonks herself on my lap. Last time she did that she was little more than a toddler; now, even though she's skinny and gangly, she fills the space in front of me. I grunt under her weight, but put my arms around her.

"What does he think will happen? It will be fine, won't it?" she whispers after a few moments.

"Tomorrow will be a pretty historic day for us all," I tell her, and it comes out formal and pompous, like I'm attempting to narrate a documentary. Or rouse a rabble. How does it go? *We should be proud! We should all link arms and go forth together! We must remember and treasure this moment and rejoice in the victory over injustice and over the colonial oppressors. Hallelujah!*

None of us has any idea what will happen and our parents are to be forgiven for facing such an uncertain future with trepidation and the bitterness of regret.

"Will you be able to hear the election results at school?"

"Of course!" The delighted wickedness illuminates her face as she twists it round towards me. My sister is back. "We're going to defy school rules and take our radios in!"

TUESDAY 4TH MARCH 1980

Rosie did take her boombox to school. And that's what we all did today, but the teachers at schools and the lecturers at colleges and the managers in workplaces said nothing. They'd brought their own radios and boomboxes in anyway.

It's said that anyone who was old enough at the time can recall exactly what they were doing the moment they first heard of J.F.K.'s assassination. Zimbabweans now wholly appreciate this ability.

Rosie's class was in the Science laboratory. The lesson was cut short when Miss Riddle turned on her radio and adjusted the volume so that the whole class could hear, and it never got started again.

Rosie says it's the memory of the diverse emotions she saw flickering and changing in the faces of her fourteen-year-old classmates that will remain with her forever. She groped for, but couldn't find, the identity of the emotion that brought the pricking to her eyes.

I didn't even try to analyse it. I sat next to Chipo and toyed with a biro on my desk during the announcement. When I finally looked up, I too saw – felt – so many emotions that a light-headedness washed over and threatened to swamp me. The black girls in the class were as silent as we whites, digesting the news, working out what it meant for each of us, wondering what it meant for the others, and simultaneously not quite able to believe that finally it had happened.

Chipo and I stared at each other while the world got frozen on its axis for a time. Then, amid the babble that erupted throughout the college, we clung to each other.

Jess heard the news during one of her study periods ("We're told they're not *free* periods Tessa, they're *study* periods. We are committed to improving our minds") between maths and biology. The school was eerily hushed, she said. Not just the normal lesson period lull, but a tangible, tense hush. After a brief hope that she'd wake up and find none of it had ever happened, she succumbed to sadness and resignation because her folks declared yesterday that in the event of a ZANU(PF) victory they would pack up and leave for South Africa as soon as the school year was over.

I can't hide from this fact any longer, so I asked her, "What about Gordon?" and she shrugged.

"I think I've finally realised I'm doing too many things I don't want to do in order to keep him. You said you wouldn't do that and I thought you were being immature. Don't look at me like that – I did and I'm sorry. Gordon and I can't be that compatible if I have to pretend to be someone I'm not. I don't want to be Ma Baker and I don't want to sleep with him again. It didn't do anything for me. I don't want him that much. One day I might want someone that much and then I would only feel soiled."

Then she said, "You and Danny though… You really enjoy being together, and so you should. He loves you. He's told me. He respects you and knows that there's plenty of time for sex later. He'll be led by you, and you'll get there because you'll want to. I envy you, you know."

I had no reply to that – I could hardly ask her if her intuition had done a runner. If it was meant to make me feel good, it didn't.

"So what did the others say? About the elections, I mean. What about Tsitsi, or Lucy Tsauro? Were they around?"

"No. No, I think they were in lessons. Lucy would have been in English at the time. Well, Mandy Carstairs – you know what she's like – said something like, 'Bastards. They'll regret it.' and I said to her, 'What's done is done.' Joanne suggested hijacking the school bus and going Down South, which I thought was bloody stupid and I guess she was only joking, while someone else – ah, Liz Laurens – said we must give it a chance. Tell you what, Tessa, I wish you'd still been at school. It was a moment to share with a good friend really. You know – for better or for worse and all that."

That did make me feel good.

Elijah told all of us openly that he'd voted for Muzorewa, which had Mum beside herself fretting.

"We don't want anyone to think we've tried to influence his decision! For God's sake Bob, explain to him he doesn't have to tell anyone who he's voted for. I don't want either us or him to get any visitors in the night."

He was holed up in his *kaya* at the time of the announcement and, with me at college, Dad at work and Rosie at school, Mum had only Skellum and Cleo with whom to share the moment. Not two seconds later she heard the hiccupping that heralds the arrival of a regurgitated cat hair ball. I've not felt much like laughing today but I can just see her clapping her hands and shrieking, "*Cleo!* No! Not on the carpet!"

Poor cat, naturally, bolted and left rapidly via the kitchen door. Mum, never good with that sort of thing, threw up in the toilet and stayed out of the hall until I got home. So now I'm going to have to bin the hair ball and clean the carpet.

*

Moira's alone in the kitchen, washing one of the honey coloured glass casserole dishes Mum would like.

"Hi Tessa! Make yourself at home, love. The others are out getting some drinks for tonight. If I say, 'How was your day?' I guess you'll know what I mean, huh?"

"Well, it's done now, isn't it? The college was in a bit of a frenzy but everything just seemed normal on the way home. No trouble. Was there any trouble?"

She smiles, relaxed and serene, puts the dish aside on the draining board and shakes her head. "No. Mind you, I haven't been out. I was here with Joseph at the time and Gilly came in from the stableyard. We'd just finished trimming the jacaranda near the Lion Rock." She points through the window to where the Lion Rock is now in the shadow of the very tree.

"I will call it my Election Tree from now on. I invited Joseph to stay with me and Gill to listen to the results announcement on the patio, which he did. I'm not sure if it was just out of respect because I'd asked him. I wouldn't want him to think I'd pressurised him into coming."

"I doubt it, Moira. Of course he does have respect for you – for all your family – but he likes you as well. I saw him at the gate when I arrived just now. He said to me he thought it was good news and he hoped I thought it was good news too. He's just such a gentleman."

I wonder if he was also just a bit curious to see his white employer's reaction to the news. Perhaps he was disappointed, or maybe only relieved; I can't believe either Gill or Moira would've displayed much high emotion. I imagine her staring calmly, absently at her jacaranda tree and its delicate green foliage, the lilac blossoms of September long forgotten. She will just want her garden and her life to go on as usual, no matter who's in government.

"The best outcome of it all to my mind, Moira, is that the war's really over."

She doesn't reply immediately, but she doesn't have to. Who would fail to be relieved by that? She dries her hands and turns to face me, her buttocks against the worktop edge.

"Tessa, you have no idea. Not like I do. I absolutely don't know what I would have done if we hadn't reached this stage now and it was all still going on. I never dreamed I'd see the day when I wanted to get out of this country and take off somewhere, anywhere, with my family, but that day was the day I saw my boy lying in that hospital bed."

I stay still, silent. This has come from depths inside her I've never been privy to before. Raw, unbearably painful depths. The practical, efficient Moira I know is exposing another Moira who's run out of the ability to cope. Or at least come dangerously close to running out.

"I would never have be able to let him carry on risking his life senselessly Tessa. You must know of course that, although he's not my own blood son, I have a mother's love for him, every bit as much as I have for Gill. He's been one of my two babies. I would've had to devise some way to smuggle him out. I'd honestly have faced life in prison to save him, if that was the punishment. If the war had carried on he'd have been back in the thick of it sooner or later. He got – we all got – a bit of a reprieve and escaped duty for some time then was lucky enough to get the riding instructor role, but with such a desperate shortage of manpower they'd have found him, realised he was reasonably fit again and shoved him back out there. How many times can you be that lucky?"

Gill said the exact same thing while Nathan was still invalided out, didn't she? We had this conversation in one of the many past lives we've endured.

"In a perverse way, him getting relatively minor injuries, at precisely the time he did, actually saved him from ever going back to the frontline," I say cautiously. Cautiously, because how do you tell a mother it was beneficial for her son to get wounded in action? "He was only actually on active duty for a relatively short time too, wasn't he?"

"It was only about eight months, after he'd finished his training," she replies, with a sort of bewildered surprise. "God, it was more like eight years to us here."

I'll bet it was. During which time he was in several contacts before the final one and she came to realise that coping was never going to be an option.

"I'm sure you can probably imagine that when he finished the training and went off out on real ops we were that jittery here at home that every time the phone rang we, all of us, and that includes Amai, had to peel ourselves off the ceiling. There were times when the sound of it made me just want to run and hide down a big black hole and never come out. Then, after a few months, it did get a bit better but that utter dread was always there in the pit of my belly."

I can rewind my mental clock to that year. I rode, I danced at discos, I cycled to and from school. I met Danny and I steered my way through my little life, facing up to my little trials and tribulations. The fact that there was a war out there disturbed me – distressed me even – but, having said that, I interacted with Gill and Charles and Moira four times a week on average and probably barely gave Nathan a thought because he was turning up in my life even less often than before. It appals me now to find that I had no inkling these friends of mine were living with a dread of phone calls. You never let on to me, I want to accuse her.

She's watching me struggle with my guilt but she won't recognise it for what it is. There'll be no doubt in her that I'll have been acutely aware of their anguish. I'm such a fraud. In the next heartbeat I know she's going to tell me how far that anguish could go.

"And then that day, when the call did come? I died over and over, and yet it turned out that he was going to be okay. I simply have no concept of what it would've been like to find out he'd been killed and to have to go to his funeral. Tessa, I swear to you, I've never seen my husband look so utterly destroyed as he did when he took that call. I was in the hall as well – we were on our way out for the supermarket run. I can relive it like it happened five minutes ago. He said hello and then 'Yes, this is he,' in the way that he does, and then he just crumpled and sat on the floor and I knew the origin of the call in that instant. Of course one's first reaction is to think the absolute worst. And even when we knew he was in the hospital, the only information was that he was in theatre and we didn't find out the extent of the injuries until we actually got seen by a surgeon about an hour and a half later."

She pauses, head cocked to one side, then points toward the back door. "Oh, wait, here they all come."

It's been the calm before the family storm. The sound of a car engine swells then recedes then dies altogether, doors are opened and slammed, Charles guffaws, Piet's voice is straining to be heard over him and Gill is shrieking with laughter. If Nathan's with them he's silent.

"So yes, my love, that filthy war is over," Moira concludes quietly to me as she steps towards the door, presumably to open it. I make a grab for her hand, causing her to wait. She squeezes back and holds on to me until we hear the multiple footsteps approaching from outside and some unmistakeable clinking of bottles.

"It's the past now," I tell her, just as quietly, and she stoops to give me a kiss on the head before extracting her hand from mine.

It's only the three of them and they fill the kitchen. Gill, Piet and I do a group hug before Charles takes me in his arms.

"We missed you at work today, kid! Shoulda been there with us for the moment. It was epic."

"So where were you in the moment then?" I ask from the depth of his embrace. "Me and Chipo were sitting together in Accounting class, but we didn't do any accounting in the end."

Piet says, "Anyone for beer?" and Charles says, "In the fridge," releasing me, patting my shoulder.

"Well now. Me, I go further than simply remembering where I was. I was taking off some reinforcement quantities and I reckon that bloody drawing will be forever burned into my brain. Que Que reservoir, pure water incoming main, valve chamber number four, drawing number 'QQ-RES-VC4-RC-01'. The draughtsman was someone called 'P.B.N.' My eyes were fixed on that titleblock throughout the whole broadcast and for several minutes afterwards.

"So I sat there and I thought to myself, it had to be ZANU(PF). I even considered the possibility that I might have to join the Party soon. If you can't beat 'em… So I folded up the drawing and tossed it into the basket that you kindly labelled Current Drawing Queries for me and went to find my staff. Turns out they'd all been in reception listening to Nathan's ghetto blaster and the over-riding vibe was one of relief. And I guess I felt that way too. The uncertainty is over and something concrete… 'scuse the pun… has been achieved. Sylvester, bless him, said we'll all have to become Mashona now, even him. Sylvester! Can you believe that? I said I couldn't see him kow-towing to the Mashona dogs, and Debbie got all idyllic and told him he should be proud of his tribe and that we're all now Zimbabweans together, black and white… oh you should've been there Tess! At risk of sounding as idyllic as Debs, the camaraderie was just the best. We had cream cakes and Debs started fluttering those mascara-laden eyelashes sweetly at Nathan in the way that she does. You know how she's always making bedroom eyes at him!"

Gill creases up with glee and Piet says "Oh-ho? Really?" and I think who-does-Debbie-think-she-is-trying-to-flirt-with-the-boss's-nephew?

Charles is beaming, basking in his story. "You should've seen her, guys. Nathan bestowed one of those dazzling smiles of his upon her and she went all red and coy and you could actually see her heart-rate double. Hilarious, it was!"

Suddenly alone on a little island, I don't find it even faintly amusing. We were talking about the elections here.

Piet returns from the fridge with two bottles of Castle and sits next to me.

"So, Piet. *Pamberi ne ZANU(PF)*, eh? How did it go down on the farm?"

He takes a swig from the bottle and goes, "Ah!", then, "*Ja*, it was fine. I gave the buggers the rest of the day off but some of them have to come back this evening for milking and stables. They seemed quite happy. We all partook of a few bottles of Shumba together."

Where is Nathan anyway? And I haven't spoken to Danny yet. I'm here swapping election-result stories with my second family and we're bantering and it's all so normal that it's bizarre and I've not even wondered what my boyfriend is doing and thinking and where he was when the results came through.

"How are the plans going for your party?" Piet says, and I go, "Sorry?" but he's talking to Gill. She sighs.

"I can't believe I'm going to be twenty-three. With all this drama of the elections it's got rather put to one side. We'll probably have it in two weeks' time if we can get ourselves organised and if I can be bothered, to be honest. I'm too busy really."

Piet flinches and a strangely perturbed expression flickers round his face. He looks like he's trying to bring it under control.

"Oh," he says. "That would be a shame."

He's looking at me, but when I meet his eyes full on he flicks them away. Gill shrugs.

"Perhaps we'll just make it a very small, immediate-family-only thing this year. Go out for a meal. That doesn't exclude you and Danny of course, Tess. Nathan can bring Debbie."

They all think that's just so funny. Gill yawns and shuts her eyes. "Most of the usual crowd have probably left the country today."

With a sinking rush of dread, I have a brief and horrible fantasy of my parents throwing clothes into suitcases and taking pictures down off the walls. Piet is addressing me over Moira's assurances to Gill that plans for the usual *braai* will be made.

"We'll help, won't we? Will your sister come too?"

"What? Sorry."

"A party. We'll help Gill with all the preparations."

"Oh yes. Of course." I manage to make myself smile at him. "Anyone would think it was your party, Piet."

He actually blushes behind his big, ginger beard, but I'm no longer interested in parties. I have an urge to get back home and make sure everyone's still there. As I stand, the legs of my chair scrape excruciatingly on the tiled floor.

*

No-one is packing. As soon as I've put the phone down after speaking to Danny, Dad tells me how he and Dudley Foster, together in Dudley's office, heard the triumphant cheer swell and roar skywards from the city streets below. We exchange some bits of chit-chat and it's good that we're trying to communicate as though our altercation of yesterday never happened. Then he jerks at the knot of his tie as though he's suffocating and ruins the truce.

"We put our backs into working for this place and now the bloody British government has jeopardised the future for all us whites. I told Dudley that if there's any trouble, the damned Brits will have to get us out. They could have sent UN troops in to sort this lot out, so they're entirely responsible if there's any bloodshed."

Rosie, now National Junior Reserve Tennis Champion, saves the moment by creating a magnificent diversion. She comes into the house bouncing off the walls, clapping and trying to waltz with Mum. Skellum is barking and Dad's yelling "For Christ's sake put that dog outside!"

"Wimbledon! Wimbledon! We're all going to Wimbledon! My God, can you imagine? Wimbledon! Rob's going to try and get tickets for all of us in the junior team! We're going to watch Wimbledon!"

An instant positive outcome from the elections at last. Rhodesia was a sporting pariah but now, as Zimbabwe, we've arrived back in the world.

SATURDAY 29TH MARCH 1980

"Jess and Gordon have split up," he tells me.

He pulls me close, gives me a lingering kiss, pushes me back to an arm's length and stares at me. "What's wrong, love? You're a bit tense."

I do a quick scan around. Surreptitiously. There are voices coming from behind the hedge but it's thick enough not to be seen through. I can't make out anyone in the kitchen although I can't be sure because of the reflection on the windows. Relax. Smile. Kiss him back. You ought to be wanting this, surely?

"I know. Jess told me. How's Gordon?"

"He doesn't actually seem too upset. God, I'd be devastated if we broke up, sweetheart."

He really means it. Instead of trying to wriggle out, I need to give this a bit more. So I kiss him back longer and deeper and more desperately than I ever have before because the intensity and the passion should make all the doubts go away. It will make things be how they should be. How I want them to be.

He squeezes me and strokes my hair and grins and sighs.

"Mmm," he whispers. "We are going places, you and me. And I can't wait." We're in full body contact and I know beyond doubt that he's enjoying it.

I do try to make my push gentle but he looks a bit surprised so I put on my best bright face. "Hey, you! We've got a party to go to, remember?"

I suspect this *braai* won't be the small, family affair Gill was after. Most of the usual crowd are obviously still at large and there are quite a few newcomers – business acquaintances of Charles, I believe, and their wives. Brendan and Sarah Mangwende, Robert and Tanaka Nyandoro, Themba and Denise Ncube. The new neighbours, Thomas and Jenny Mhangiroza and their three children. That must be their kids in the pool.

Piet's been watching Danny watching the kids.

"First black family in the road. They've been over here quite a bit actually. Nice folks. Gill's going to teach the oldest kid to ride."

He greeted us cheerfully enough but now he's reluctant to chat and is backing away towards the lounge doors. I ought to find Gill.

"Can I do anything in the kitchen?"

"Um, don't know. Sorry to rush off. Charles... er, Charles sent me to get more meat."

He bolts without a backward glance.

Danny's arm goes around my shoulders. "Relax a bit. Let's get a drink. If you see Gill, ask her if she wants you to do anything."

Gill is lolling on the new swing seat with Tammy and Sherrie. It's pretty. White frame, blue and green floral upholstery, white fringe around the shade. Makes me think of a song from that old musical Mum likes.

Sherrie's had her hair cut since I saw her a few weeks ago. It's really short with tight curls around her head. If I did that to mine I'd look bloody awful but on her, with her pixie-like face, it looks absolutely right.

They attempt to wriggle up to make room for us but it won't take five so I hold up my hand and stick next to Danny.

"Don't worry about offering help, Tess," Gill tells me. "If you really have the urge to do something, seek out Mum, but I got kicked out and told to come and socialise, so here I am, having a nice time with Tam and Shez."

Tammy reckons it's a pleasure to have her out in the garden for a change and says she's looking forward to seeing Uncle Rupert dancing later. Sherrie says, "Rupert? Is he still of this earth? God, Gill, how old is he now?"

Gill leans back and closes her eyes.

"Year in, year out. Christ, I'm getting so tired of these birthday bashes. It's too much like hard work after all these years. Nathan always refused Dad's offers to do one for his birthday as you know and I'm beginning to think he's been right all along, although it's true that the boy had his own reasons."

"Isn't it his twenty-first this year?" Sherrie asks and Gill snaps her eyes open and passes a weary hand across them, massaging her forehead like she's got a migraine.

"Oh Jesus time flies. Not yet. Next year. We'll *have* to do something for that milestone. You know, I used to love these dos, but I'm fed up, and both Mum and Dad are acting like they're completely stressed out today. Piet's been here since the crack of dawn almost, insisting on helping where he's really not needed. It's sweet of him, but... Where is he anyway? And Nathan's in a funny mood today. I've hardly seen him."

"Piet went into the house," Danny says, "to get more meat."

"*More* meat? Where from? Is he going to slaughter a beast or something?" Gill launches herself out of the seat with some difficulty because Sherrie's pushed it backwards and then allowed it to swing forward just as Gill makes her move.

"Sit still, Shezza, or go somewhere else," Tammy tells her and Sherrie bounces up onto her endless brown legs and walks off without a word. Tammy sighs.

Gill's on tiptoe, and she grabs at my shoulder to keep her balance. "We've had many a fun party, but perhaps we've had too much of a good thing. It's all dragging on today. What's Dad up to?"

Charles is on his own at the *braai*. He places his tumbler of amber liquid to one side and starts offloading his steaks and sausages onto the white enamel tray that Amai is holding and Gill's right – there's enough to feed a battalion. It's so like him to have it all ready – beef, chicken, pork, *boerewors*, you name it – at the exact same minute. Mum could learn a few things from him so that we might never have to face cold vegetables with a roast dinner again.

"Is that *whiskey* he's drinking?" Gill pulls her red baseball cap firmly down over her forehead and lets go my shoulder. "Bloody hell. This party thing really is getting to him."

Amai's borne the cooked meat away, but instead of following her Charles is waving one of his *braai* forks over his head. Then he holds up his left arm and points at his watch with his right forefinger, nodding. I try to locate the person he's communicating with, but no-one in my field of vision is paying him any attention. Gill's wrong. He doesn't look stressed out at all. These occasions are his occasions. I have so many vividly beautiful memories of these parties and now… now Gill wants to end them. Everything comes to an end. Everything changes.

Looking at Charles, I'm trying to work out when he started to go so grey.

Piet, who was nowhere to be seen seconds ago, materialises between Gill and me.

"My God, don't *do* that!"

"Sorry Gilly. Come. Let's go up and help your dad out."

"What? Why? Amai's…"

"He wants to speak to you." He leads her away by the elbow and Danny's peering into my face. "Wine, Tess? Some rosé?"

Do I want wine? Not really. I'd prefer a rum and Coke.

"Quiet, please!"

The hubbub fades, hesitantly at first, but we all know what's going to happen. It's Charles's habit to introduce his meat.

"The food is ready people, so you can delve into the feast." He holds up his fork again. "Soon. But first, I have to let you all know I've been involved in a conspiracy. Besides wishing Gill all the very best for her twenty-third birthday, I have an announcement to make in the best Hollywood style. I have been approached by a certain young man who has asked me for my permission to take on this rebellious daughter of mine for a wife. Let us raise our glasses in a toast to this brave gentleman and hope she breaks him in gently!"

A ripple flickers around as a breath of wind disturbs the grass blades. There are a few cheers, glasses are held aloft – a cluster of dazzling pinpricks in the sunlight. Gill's face is kind of bemused and Piet's is tense behind her. Nathan and Amai emerge from the lounge doors bearing a lavender and white iced cake on a silver platter with Moira close on their heels. I can't stay down here a second longer, separated from the whole of my adopted family.

I reach the patio just as Charles grabs Piet to envelop him in one of those impulsive and slightly awkward man-to-man embraces.

I throw my arms around Gill and my voice comes out as a squawk. "I knew it would happen! It was just a case of when. Oh my God! Is this a complete surprise?"

"Well I had been asked on the quiet," she answers slowly, turning to Piet who has escaped his future father-in-law's clutches and is burning scarlet, "but I didn't expect a public announcement. And now I know what the heck was up with my family today. They've been conspiring together behind my back. Did *you* know about this?"

I shake my head, my attention focussed on the small red velvet box that sits on top of the cake.

Piet is not made for public speaking. He shuffles around and mumbles a few words no-one can make out, not even me, and I'm standing two metres away from him. "Come on Piet!" calls someone. "Have you got something to say and do?" and the laughter is friendly but it makes poor Piet go an even brighter shade. He clears his throat a few times and takes a swig of beer.

"Well, I've planned this and now it's happening, so here. This is for you, Gill."

She accepts the box from him and I think he mutters, "I love you", but I'm not sure.

"*Will you marry me?*" the same voice yells. "Come on man – say it. 'Will you marry me?'"

"She's already said yes!" Piet yells back and he looks as if he's about to burst.

The ring is dainty – yellow gold with a diamond of modest proportions set between two deep green and almost luminous Sandawana emeralds. With a smile that looks like it's threatening to cramp her cheek muscles, she allows Piet to slide it onto her finger and nestles into his arm, quite unable to take her eyes off it.

A lot happens very quickly. I'm jostled out of the way by a queue of congratulators, Danny appears with the glass of rosé, murmuring, "Beautiful, hey?" and Gill is now in Nathan's arms. He looks like he never wants to let her go, rocking her to and fro with his eyes closed, the lock of dark hair nodding against his forehead. I automatically lower my eyes to give them the privacy they deserve. He's wearing shorts and there on his right leg are the puckered scars left by the 7.62mm rounds from an AK47, a deep channel just under the hem of the garment and another equally deep one lower down. There's one on the inside of his thigh too but I can't see it from here, and also a pitted dent on the right side of his body between the hip and the rib cage, which I've only ever glimpsed when he's been swimming. Involuntarily, I draw in a breath and wince and get a physical pain in my core. Over-wrought. It's an emotional day.

Tammy claims Gill from him and Sherrie is here too, no longer sulky, nudging Nathan and handing him a glistening bottle of Castle. He looks down at her and does one of his nearly-smiles. They have a murmured conversation and I catch myself gawking. It's time to whirl away before either of them notices and retreat with Danny to make way for more well-wishers. More drinks pass from hand to hand. It's raining happiness and celebration.

A light-headedness washes over me. A mute button has been pressed somewhere in my head. I float away from them all. Gill and Piet and their ring, Charles and Moira and her over-excited relations, the neighbours raising glasses and toasting each other, Nathan and Sherrie talking over their brown bottles of Castle. I cannot let this I-don't-want-change attitude overwhelm me. I shove my wine glass back into Danny's hand and tell him I'm going to help Amai carry the cake platter back into the kitchen.

Amai's happy prattling is incessant but very comforting.

*

At midnight we're the sole remaining guests. We've danced under both the stars and the strings of multi-coloured light bulbs that festoon the patio area and when Danny's eyelids began to droop I told him I'd just quickly help with some of the clearing up, then we'd go.

Now Moira's gone to bed, my eyes keep trying to close and Danny, with his second wind, is deep in discussion with Charles and Piet, Nathan on the periphery. I'm learning more about the management of farm accounts than I really needed to know, frankly.

There's a pause, and it's my moment to chip in with the right-then-we-must-be-off line, but I miss it. Charles is snapping his fingers together, smiling at me. "Oh, talking about extensions and concrete reminds me of what I was telling you in the office the other day. Nathan, get that booklet from the Cement and Concrete Institute – in my study. I promised to show it to Tessa, because it describes the setting process of cement."

Gill rouses herself beside me and pats me on the shoulder. "There you go Tess – what a treat! You know, it's just about the most fascinating subject I've ever had the joy to discover."

"All right, Gill, my darling. Why don't you go to bed? Tessa expressed an interest and I tried to explain but the author of that article does it better."

It had seemed interesting, I admit. At the time.

I've got up to follow Nathan, but I'm not sure what I can do to help him find whatever he's going to be looking for. Moving around might wake me up a bit I guess. Danny's right behind me and Gill moves across on the sofa to lay her head on Piet's lap.

Charles's study, like his office, bears a certain resemblance to a recently bombed site. Having some interest in antiques, his furniture pieces are examples from the Victorian era – so Gill tells me – but they are only partly visible under the layers of paperwork, books and newspapers, box files and even building materials.

Nathan pauses at the doorway to survey the chaos. "Gill and Moira have often threatened to tidy this hole, but Charles becomes pathetically grief-stricken and pleads that he won't then be able to find anything. Amai mutters dark and evil curses when she has to clean in here."

The wine hasn't worn off yet and the idea of gentle, cheerful Amai involving herself in anything dark and evil sets me to giggling while he steps over a small pile of boxed samples of different coloured granites to sift through a pile of brochures and other publications on the nearest bookcase.

"Ah-ha," he says, extracting a small blue and white booklet from under an old copy of *The Rhodesian Engineer*. "God, that was easy. Maybe the system does work after all."

He turns to me, flipping pages. "Look, here we are. I think this is what he was on about."

Come on, concentrate. It makes very little sense in my fuzzy state but I can't admit that, so I make a few lame comments like *Ah okay* and *I see* and *Oh yes Charles told me that.* Nathan's not struggling. He's not reading it to me – he's telling me stuff about hydration and gels, air voids and aggregates in his own words.

"Are you ready to go?" Danny asks abruptly, from behind me. He leans over my shoulder, his hands around my waist, his face resting against my right ear. "Looks very complicated to me. Too taxing right at the moment."

He gives me a kiss on the neck. An indistinct murmur of voices from the direction of the lounge becomes audible.

I close the booklet. "Well, thanks. At least that's given me an idea."

Nathan inclines his head and takes it from me. He says nothing and there's something – a vibe in the air – that's making me exceedingly uncomfortable with Danny's soft breath against my cheek.

"Tessa, I'd really like to go home."

So would I.

Nathan follows us as we return to the living room. Through a prickling in my spine, I'm as aware of his quiet footfalls on the thick carpet as I would be if he was walking hobnailed boots over corrugated iron sheets.

We start to say our goodbyes, but Charles is asking me if I've understood what I've just read and Gill is now wide awake and bent on attracting her cousin's attention.

"Nathan. Nathan? Gosh, you're miles away, kid. You'll be interested in what Piet was just telling us. You know we've seen those race meetings at Beatrice advertised in the classifieds? Well he knows the crowd who run them – farmers – and he's been to some of the meets. Here, Tessa. You'll be interested too."

She's got my hand and is pulling me down onto the sofa beside her. Charles is saying, "Come on, Piet. Tell Tess and Nathan," and Danny clucks his tongue, letting go of my waist at last.

"Amateur racing on dirt tracks," says Piet. "It's a circuit, with meetings held in various districts at specific farms. They're exceptionally well organised. All the venues are great and the *braais* afterwards are legend. The next meet is in May at Beatrice, then there's another Beatrice one in July, followed by one at Eagle's Down farm near Shamva in September. I've been to a few, but I've never ridden in the races myself of course. I like a fast car but not a fast horse, I'm afraid. No brakes or clutch."

He winks at Gill and we all laugh and I can feel Danny's desperation even though I'm not looking at him. "Tessie, please! Let's go!"

*

It's very dark outside. The moonlight's been blotted out by thick cloud but the night is warm and smells sweet, enveloped in the heavy stillness of the midnight hour. Past midnight now. With our shoes crunching on the gravel path we locate Danny's car only by identifying the dull gleam from its windscreen as it throws back a small amount of diffused light from the stableyard security luminaires. I flop into the passenger seat, tired, but pleasantly so now, my thoughts lingering on Piet's description of the race meets. "That sounds like fun, doesn't it? I'd love to try racing. I wonder if Nathan will give it a go?"

Danny gives a short laugh that's loaded with an emotion I'm not sure I can identify, but that isn't a good one. He starts the engine, revs it a couple of times and pulls away, scattering pebbles from under the two wheels that were on the path.

"I couldn't begin to guess." He slings the steering wheel to the right to turn into the driveway. "I see the boy Owen has moved up in the world. All that technical jargon about cement! I didn't know he could read at all, never mind stuff like that."

He turns and grins at me, and the grin falls off his face. This irritation – this unbelievably intense irritation – is a bit scary, and it must show. He starts to say something but I cut him off.

"Oh Nathan Owen was never stupid. You forget I've known him a while, you know."

"A surly bastard. Someone at school once remarked that when they were handing out brains, he wasn't near the front of the queue and he's never come to terms with it."

"You know sod all about him," I say and we're silent all the way home.

THURSDAY 17TH APRIL 1980

So the Independence celebrations start today. Many are keen to get in on the party, more are scathing and sarcastic, but some are predicting a descent into bloodshed. I'm referring only to the white folks, of course. I guess the black population is just super-excited.

Chipo is. She was beside herself that day all the bunting appeared – miles and miles of it, lining the arterial roads. And those vertically striped panels on all the facades of all the government buildings in red, green, black and yellow, like the new flag. And Robert Mugabe's round, bespectacled face, watching us from every streetlighting pole and any other convenient fixture to hand. The printing business has done well.

Chipo was hoping there would be dancing through the streets. Now I'm all for dancing, but I think we're more likely to get marches of military strength. I told her this. I said, "Perhaps we'll get a fly-past of all six biplanes from our Air Force."

"Biplanes?" she squeaked. "Come on, Tessa, you're so funny! You know we've got more modern aircraft than biplanes!"

Of course I know, but you must admit those Canberras and Vampires are pretty vintage in the world now.

Prince Charles and Indira Gandhi will be at the celebrations and the latest scoop is that Bob Marley will be performing, paying his own way. That makes the scathing and sarcastic doubters even more annoyed.

Me, I'm just thinking I shouldn't be looking forward to it as much as I am.

The hushed atmosphere in the house when I got home from work two hours ago was like a damp blanket. Dad is flatly refusing to have anything to do with any celebrations so my plans for watching them live on TV later have crashed. I don't believe I've ever seen him look so sour and Mum's hiding in the kitchen. Thankfully Rosie's back now so things have livened up a bit.

"Ja, Bob Marley!" she shrieks. "He arrived yesterday! God, how amazing is that? We'll get to watch him!"

She flaps the newspaper at me, I catch it from her and I can feel Dad bristling in the corner.

"Who?"

We both stare at him. She looks as incredulous as I feel.

"Bob Marley, Dad? You know? Don't you?"

"No. And we're not having the television on tonight and that's that. You can read or listen to your LPs or something."

There's this saying about someone getting your hackles up. Well it's true. Odd feeling.

"Why can't we watch it? Some of us are interested, you know."

"Well. I. Am. Not. You *won't* watch it on *this* television."

He stabs a forefinger at the offending appliance and I wouldn't be surprised if it were to start cowering. Rosie's staring at the ceiling with one of her blank faces on, arms tightly folded.

For one or two heartbeats I feel myself psyching up for the argument, but what the hell. It really doesn't matter. There are options. I shrug, stand up, chuck the paper onto the settee.

"I'll watch it at Gill's then. You can come too, Rose. If you want to."

Thinking about it, it's no good calling on Jess – her folks will probably be the same and anyway, I don't think it's her thing. Mum startles me at the hallway door. How long has she been lurking there?

"Ooh, I don't want to hear any of that awful Riggy music," she says. Her giggly tone is deliberate, designed of course to be diffusing, but believe me, her mispronunciation is not. "Is that that hideous pop group from some obscure country?"

Rosie's eyes are still clamped on the ceiling. There's a flattie spider up there and he's staying still as he can.

"Good Lord. REGGAE. Please try to get it right, Mum. And they're not a *pop group* and how dare you call them hideous? From

Jamaica. REGGAE, Mother, REGGAE. It's like, chilled and laid back and feel good. Think sun, beaches, coconuts…"

"I thought it was all about anarchy," Dad interrupts. "It's banned isn't it?"

Rosie sighs and clamps her hands over her eyes. The spider bolts across to the coving.

"That's *Punk*, Dad."

Mum's looking at me as if I'm going to back her up. No such luck. Sorry.

"You are hopeless, Mum. And actually Rosie, not all Reggae is soft and gentle. Tonight will be all about political messages I'm sure."

Rosie nods without removing her hands.

"Well there you go then." Dad singles out the TV again with his finger. "We don't like it and you're not watching it here."

I squeeze past Mum and Rosie is right behind me. "Hang on! I'm coming! Did you say Gill's brother is going to Rufaro Stadium tonight?"

Charles did say Nathan wants to go, yes, but I can't believe he will.

"It was probably just bravado. Him and Paul Loftus, the Contracts Manager, and Dave Hanly apparently told Gill they were going, but Gill says Charles wasn't too happy about it. Paul was joking and saying his life policy was paid up to date but I really don't think they'll go. Whites won't be welcome. It's a shame, but…"

In an ideal world maybe we could've all gone together. And Chipo too. But it's not an ideal world.

SATURDAY 5TH JULY 1980

I am, by now, too experienced a competitor to suffer badly from nerves, surely? Skellum enjoyed my cornflakes more than I thought he would, and he won't tell, but at least I don't feel quite so ill now. The dressage test didn't go too badly, I guess. Perhaps Encore will excel himself over the cross country course and be just as controllable as my darling Induna. Perhaps he won't get himself too wound up. I can handle it, anyway. We'll be fine. I have to give him a good experience because he'll take me so much further than Indie. This is just the start of our eventing career.

George holds his bridle while I mount and Gill comes running from the clubhouse.

"You're lying sixth! Excellent! That's out of some thirty-odd competitors."

I'm over the moon that she came with me instead of going to Beatrice with Piet and Nathan. Selfish, I know, especially as Piet's got Nathan a ride in one of the races. He would be wanting Gill to be there, but I need her more. She'll go with him and Bravo to the dressage show tomorrow in any case and help him like she helps me.

The winter sun has warmed the day up considerably now but she's still wrapped into that pale blue padded anorak she brought back from England. It's actually faintly pale green in places now with three years' worth of horse slobber. She gives me calm instructions on how to warm up for the cross country and my confidence comes groping back a little. Take the small log quietly in trot a couple of times, canter a few circles, bring him into the bigger log, then jump the tyres straight away. Make much of him and then walk and trot him and don't jump again until we're actually on the course. Less is more with Encore.

I often wonder how far I would've got without Gill. I love equestrian sport and I couldn't live without horses but everything I've achieved has been with minimal support from my family and a ton of it from hers. Mine say, "Oh, well done!" and "Congratulations – another rosette?" and "You qualified for the championship again? You are doing well!" and they tell all their friends how lovely my horses are, but they're not really *here*. Not here, with me, sharing the experiences. I guess we all have different interests, but it would be nice if they turned up at competitions more than twice a year. And as for Danny? I wish… well he's got an important assignment to get done this weekend. I understand. So once again, under this endless blue African sky I love and with the faint taste of woodsmoke in my mouth and the dry, blonde winter grass underfoot, I'm out with my second sister Gill and my second father Charles. It could be worse.

Charles is there at the starting point, deep in conversation with George. They both acknowledge my presence with a wave and just knowing they're there rooting for me sends my determination to do this up another notch. My horse is like a coiled spring under me. In spite of the quiet warm-up he knows he's going to get a good gallop and he's fitter than he's ever been so he's not going to run out of stamina. At least he's not a bucker – he just springs around on the spot like a pogo stick. Gill's behind me and I think she calls, "Good luck!" as we prance sideways towards the start, Encore snatching at the reins and me crooning, "Easy now. Easy, boy." She shouts something anyway.

As soon as I allow him to straighten up, when the starting flag drops, he leaps forward and the air is whistling in the straps of my helmet.

The first few obstacles are simple. We sail over them at speed and Encore is jumping cleanly, accurately and with great scope. Now I'm enjoying myself. We're in it, doing it, and this is where I forget I was ever nervous with anticipation. We crest a ridge, some gravel scatters and the view ahead is a long valley filled with trees and scrub. The track leads me to the floor of the valley and to that wide stone wall followed by a spread of timber rails two strides beyond. Encore clatters down the path. These jumps are not high, but I need to get him balanced on level ground. It's a split second decision. I try to give him an extra stride in front of the wall by riding a slightly larger arc but he stumbles fractionally and because he's all heart, he takes a flyer at the wall from there while totally off balance. I'm way behind the movement.

My arms snap out straight in a reflex reaction to give him as much rein as I can instead of jabbing the bit against the corners of his mouth. His whole body is stretched out like he's on a rack but he's not going to get over the wall.

But he *is* over it, and without any scraping noises. How? Now I'm floating somewhere over the back of the saddle and my teeth are clenched tight and I'm just a passenger instead of being his pilot.

He takes one long, gallant stride towards the rails. I've half caught up and he can't possibly get over them from here, but that's what he's going to try. I can feel his body ready for the leap and I'm too late to stop it. Then his common sense kicks in. He stops dead in his tracks, skids.

Like I've been fired from a catapult, I'm over his shoulder, rolling in mid-air and there's a thud that I feel rather than hear. The timber rails are bloody solid.

It's odd, because a period of time has gone missing. I'm sitting with my back against the rails and there are two people in front of me, a man and a woman. I'm not sure when they appeared. I must have been lying on the ground – I've just come off my horse – but here I am sitting up. This pair must be the jump judges. I don't remember seeing them when I came into the wall approach. Wall. Bad jump. Left behind. Encore trying to make the most of a bad situation. Encore. Where is he?

They're both talking at once but what stands out is the woman asking me if I'm able to speak now. Dear, she calls me – "Can you speak now, dear?" She's crouched down beside me and she has a very smiley, lined face, grey hair poking out from under a tweed hat, and very blue eyes that are locked intently with mine. "Can you feel any pain?"

Well of course I can speak. What's she on about? I start to say that no, I don't feel any pain – or at least I think I don't – but only a croak and a gasp come out.

"She's winded." He's got a walkie-talkie in his hand and he's wearing one of those bushwhacker waistcoat things with lots of pockets and pouches and all of them look like they're full of something. I've seen him before. Who's dad is he? No matter – the most important thing is that Encore is standing behind him.

"No, no!" he says then, but it's too late, I've got up. The lady rocks backwards, caught off balance by my sudden movement and puts her hand out onto the gravelly ground behind her. I want to say sorry but nothing comes out. I stretch my arms so that I can pat my horse and take the reins, and there's an odd twinge from my left wrist. It's a peculiar sensation but it's not painful so I ignore it.

A few deep breaths later I'm able to croak, "Can you leg me up, please?" I take the reins in my left hand, the cantle of the saddle in my right and bend my left knee in anticipation.

"Whoa!" says a voice that sounds like it's from the man but comes from somewhere in the distance. Mr Rayleigh-Barnes. That's who he is. Sylvie Rayleigh-Barnes's father. Everything's a bit remote, come to think of it. He's still talking and I get odd snippets.

"Not so fast. Not. For sure. Completing the course. Can. Feel. Arms, legs, back, neck? Sure? No pain?"

I stand still and consider this. My skull cap is still in position and is securely buckled under my chin. Apart from that twisted wrist feeling, I seem to be in one piece. I wouldn't be standing up if I wasn't, would I? Perhaps he's right though. To carry on would be a bit silly. That means I have to retire from the competition. Damn.

"Let her sit on the horse, and you walk back with her." The lady's smiling her smiley face at me but addressing Mr Rayleigh-Barnes. I might be a bit concussed, she tells him.

"I'm not concussed. My hat's still on. I'm fine, really…"

She unfolds a bundle of papers and runs her forefinger down the top one. "Tell them to start the next rider, Will. Yvette Cooper. Number sixteen. Here, give me your radio and you go back with her to hand her over to her connections. Make sure they get her to the St John's van."

This is a bit like one of my dreams. Both of them have disappeared and now I find myself seated in the back of Charles's Land Rover. I do get a vague image of riding Encore under some trees in dappled shadows with someone else walking beside his head, but this might have been yesterday, or maybe last week. Charles is half-in, half-out of the open rear door, holding my right hand. He pets my head while still holding my hand and says "Okay. Good girl," as if I'm a dog that's just learned to give a paw. I feel some giggles coming and swallow them, coughing, and get a couple of suspicious stares from Gill, facing me from the front bench seat with her arms resting on its back, and from the blue uniformed woman on my left. The nurse – she must be a nurse – is strapping my left hand and wrist in an elasticated bandage. I try a cautious flexion and it feels stiff and tight.

They let me get out, but they're all three of them watching my every move. George is under the shade of some gum trees nearby grazing Encore and my horse is all dressed up in his travelling gear. George grins at me and gives me a thumbs up, then in the next scene we're headed for home, passing that new house on the corner plot, not five hundred metres from the Makuti Park gates. They're putting the roof on it now. Charles is asking how my wrist feels and I say it feels fine. I don't ask him exactly what's wrong with it because I don't want him to know that there are whole sections of my day that have gone missing.

*

It's happened again, because now, seated at the table in the kitchen in my own house, watching Charles and Dad sipping from mugs, I realise that in the moment before this very moment I was running my hands down each of Encore's legs in his stable at Makuti Park. He was fine. I recall that clearly, but how did I get home?

"Get that wrist X-rayed," Charles is saying to Dad. I've got a mug of coffee in my good hand. Mum is cutting a slice of Victoria sponge for herself and I have a half-eaten slice on a plate in front of me. "The Red Cross lady – not Red Cross, sorry, St John's Ambulance I mean – thought it was only badly sprained but you must get it checked. If you run her down to Casualty they'll do it."

"Sure, sure." Dad's nodding. "We will."

I have a bit of a headache so I'd like a couple of aspirins before we go. They might take away the dull pain in my wrist as well. So I say, "I've got a bit of a headache," and I might just as well have called "Action!" on a film set. Without being consulted in any way I'm bundled out of the back door and into Dad's car, the mugs and plates left in disarray on the table. That's so not like Mum.

SUNDAY 6TH JULY 1980

I'm fine now because I remember everything in detail from the time we arrived at Andrew Fleming Hospital A&E, although that journey's gone missing as well. The hospital scene is all there – the X-ray room, bright lights, bustling humanity, the bed in the ward where the nurse told me I'd broken a couple of small bones, the setting of this hideous plaster cast and the news that I was to be kept in hospital overnight for observation of suspected concussion. And today too, everything's been crystal clear. It's just bloody annoying I'm being forced to stay here on the settee instead of doing normal stuff.

Danny presses the enormous bouquet of red roses and carnations into my arms and kisses my forehead. I make room for him among the pillows and rugs and he nestles up against me, touching my cast with tenderness and looking as if he thinks I'm about to die.

I tell him not to fuss. Tell him it was a bit of concussion, but my head's fine and the wrist will be as good as new in four weeks' time. I've been lucky so far, to be fair, I add. I've bitten the dust many times – it's an occupational hazard – but I've never hurt anything except my pride and only suffered the odd scrape or bruise or stiff muscle.

"There's a maxim I read somewhere, some time ago, which states that gravity is the law that catches up with all horsemen, and horsewomen, sooner or later."

"Tessa, that's not funny. You are my life, do you know that?"

"I…" I swallow my laughter.

"I worry about you, with all your riding. I've never said because I know you love it so much, but… maybe you don't realise. I guess

I was hoping this little incident – and fortunately it is only a little one – might make you realise how dangerous horse riding is, Tessa. Hasn't it given you a fright?"

"Um, what? No. I mean… A *fright?* No. Why? Danny, how well do you actually know me? Of course I know it's dangerous! I'm not an idiot. Safety is the first rule when it comes to dealing with horses and I learned that when I was knee high to a grasshopper. I've spent hundreds of hours learning about horse psyche and trying to perfect my riding technique in order to minimise the risk of having some sort of accident or injury. If you want to be involved with horses you have to accept that it comes with its hazards. It's not the only risk sport in the world. You've played rugby. If I'd been that frightened I'd never have been eventing in the first place. Come on, please don't treat me like I'm stupid."

He's refusing to meet my eyes so he won't know just how bloody angry I am. He fiddles with the pink paper bow binding the flowers together in their plastic sheath. I've run out of things to say so I sit and wait for him to apologise. He doesn't. He says he can't bear the thought of me being hurt again so would I consider giving it up? For him? For us?

There was that day, not so long ago, when my take on our relationship hit a rock and swung off course so dramatically it could never get back. I've ignored this with dedication ever since. Until now. My involvement with horses was the rock.

He's got no idea how much I want him to un-say what he's just said. Or how much I want to believe I didn't hear it.

"You do realise I drive and I walk across roads in town and I stand a reasonable chance of being hurt doing these things as well?"

He says I should just think about it, and there's something in his tone that states his utter conviction I will do just that. He prattles on, a bit breathless, with some earnest plans for the future, of visions of where we might try living in South Africa, with me in one piece. The chilly shadow lays itself across me, and him, the roses and the carnations and it's here for good this time. I'm numb. Horrified, even.

He doesn't notice my despair or see the shadow or feel its touch.

When he leaves, he smiles, laughs and pets me, kisses me – long and on the lips when he's sure none of the rest of the family are anywhere near – and tells me he'll call me soon.

I lie back on my pillow and clutch the flowers to my chest under a crushing sadness and sense of loss. It's just, as they say, a matter of time.

*

I'm wandering about in the garden when Mum calls out that Gill's phoned. She's on her way over. The dressage is finished.

"Come back inside, Tessa," Mum instructs. "You should be resting. Look, will you be okay for a little while? Me and Dad are going to nip over to the Parsons's place then we'll pick up Dad's new plants from the nursery. Just say, and I'll stay here. Dad can get the plants after work tomorrow. Rosie should be home from Maria's fairly shortly anyway."

"No, no! Go!"

Good God, I've only got a broken wrist. I haven't had a heart attack and I've had far too much rest already today. I'll at least survive until Gill gets here.

I grab my pillow and my book and lie on the carpet by the French doors to catch a patch of winter sun. After fifteen minutes my concentration fails me. I transfer myself to the verandah and itch with impatience for twenty minutes before I see her Alfa Romeo approaching up the hill. When she pulls in and parks in front of the closed gates, I'm there to open them.

She pokes her head out of the driver's window. "What are you doing up?"

"Don't you start."

There's a movement inside the car; she's not alone. The passenger door opens and Nathan emerges, still dressed in his white shirt, white breeches and black leather boots, although he's discarded his tie.

"I'll do that," he says, taking the gate latch from me and waving me aside. "I'm glad to see you bounce okay anyway."

Happiness. Overwhelming. How does a depressing day like this one turn a corner so unexpectedly and become so perfect?

"I'm fine! Just fine. That much better even now good friends are here. I only wish someone would tell me what the hell happened."

Gill drives up to the house and as I watch Nathan close the gates behind her I wonder who first thought of white as a suitable colour for horse riding clothing. The backside and inner thighs of his breeches are a dull browney-grey, there are some horse feed/hay type stains on the outside of the left knee and his shirt has a large dark grey blotch on the back. Gill will tell me what happened, he says, making shooing gestures at me. Then he goes, "Hey, what do you mean, what the hell happened, when it happened to you?"

In the kitchen I fill the kettle and select three of the new smoked glass mugs Mum got last week. Gill perches on the edge of the table while Nathan fights his way out of his boots on the doorstep. I dump three dessert-spoonfuls of tea into the pot, then point the spoon at him.

"So come on, how was the dressage?"

He reaches into the breast pocket of his shirt and withdraws a red rosette. Holds it up. Grins. Widely, joyfully, like a grin should be. It creases all the way up his face and threatens to close his eyes but he's keeping them focussed on me from under that dark forelock.

Gill launches into a tale of how ecstatic the judge was and how he wrote these glowing congratulations on Nathan's score sheet, throwing her hands around her head to imitate this judge's excitement and narrowly missing Nathan's left ear. He ducks. I'm listening, but I'm still taking in that grin.

"Don't exaggerate, Gill," he sighs.

"Well you got two *nines* and the rest were sevens and eights, boyo. They want to see you back in the future, they said. Bravo looked gorgeous, Tessa. D'ya need a hand there?"

She starts to lift herself away from the table edge but I wave her back.

Nathan switches the tracks. "But you asked what happened to you. Don't you remember?"

"Kind of. But not all of it. Only after I got this."

I wave the clunky wrist at him and instantly regret it, tuck it back against my body. Might take a couple more of those horse pills with my tea.

Gill makes a decision, gets up and eases me out of the way to take possession of the kettle, pot and mugs.

"Well the first we heard of your prang was an announcement over the PA system that there had been a fall at jump number whatever and that it was rider number fifteen. To be honest, Dad and I took very little notice. We were fetching those Fantas we had in the cooler bag, ready for when you finished, and talking, and it was George who butted in and said, 'Ah! Ah! You are not listening, you two! That man is talking about Miss Tessa! She has fallen and you must both go now, now. *Zvino, zvino! Mhanyisa!*'"

She's put the tea pot down and is waggling her hands frantically in front of my face in what is a very plausible imitation, and accent, of an agitated George seeking to attract attention to himself. I recoil, laughing.

"So we abandoned any ideas of collecting cans of Fanta and we took off like greased lightning, but no-one at the starting box could tell us much. Then someone confirmed that you'd retired and were returning with one of the jump-judges and that's when we saw you coming up the hill on Encore with Mr Rayleigh-Barnes leading him. We both agreed it was a bit like Mary and Joseph. You know, riding on a donkey into town?"

"Well I'm glad you found it so amusing, presumably *after* you knew I was okay. And by the way, I have no designs whatsoever on Mr Rayleigh-Barnes and Encore is not a donkey!"

"Of course, hun. We got you off the horse and you told us your wrist was sore and when we looked at it, it was all swollen and starting to turn blue. You insisted on trying to unsaddle Encore and we had to physically restrain you. Don't you remember that?"

I'm trying, but she could be making this up, for all I know. I shrug, shake my head. We sit down at the table together and Nathan says, "Eish. That's not good."

He's looking about him – first around at our kitchen, then lingering on the doorway that leads to the hallway, passage and living rooms. Not nosiness, just pure curiosity. Of course – he's never been here before.

"You talked a lot. In fact you seemed quite *compos mentis* so we thought you were fine, but you can't have been with us at all, were you?"

"I remember being back at your place, but then I was here. Like I got teleported or something."

Gill leans forward and peers into my face. "Dad took you in the Merc. God, I thought you'd remember that. You went on and on about how you like that car. Tessa, are you sure you're all right now?"

Enough of me, really. I mean, it's nice to know everyone cares so much, but I'm bored with my Saturday. I butter the two of them up with a bit more reassurance and manage to steer the conversation round to Nathan's Saturday instead. And he's keen to talk. He tells me how Piet managed to secure a mount for him in one of the races and he describes the horse – a chestnut three-quarter-bred that was not considered to have much of a chance and was only being run for the fun of a day out.

Gill nudges me and cocks her head at him. "God, he rode a blinder, Tess. Got up for second place! The trainer couldn't believe it. He hadn't even put a bet on his own horse. This one here came home with a wad of bank notes in his pocket because he did bet on himself. All that race-riding preparation you did with the Fletchers paid off, didn't it?"

Nathan's warm brown eyes are focussed on something behind me. "I am *so* very glad I put in that training. Sherrie's dad was a big help with advice and letting me ride some of his horses on the gallops. It's the most exhilarating thing I've ever done on horseback but the position takes some getting used to. And I was only riding in a training saddle so not as short as the jockeys themselves. I did wonder if I'd be able to do it, given the high strain on the thigh muscles. My right leg definitely isn't what it used to be and I guess I'll never have the full strength back, but it held up. Mick du Preez wants me to ride for him again. On a better horse next time."

Gill's nodding. "Well the more race riding you do, the stronger the muscles will get, even the damaged ones. So yes, I think we'll all go to the next one at Eagle's Down Farm. It's in September, but I can't remember the date. You up for it, Tessa?"

"Absolutely. I'll be as good as new by then."

Bombarding me in equal measures are relief that neither my parents nor Danny are around to be involved in this conversation and disappointment that I've missed out on something here. But there's no reason on this earth for me to have been invited to watch him galloping racehorses at the Fletchers' yard. I didn't even know he'd been there. I'm sure John Fletcher had no qualms about putting a rider like Nathan up on some of his string.

We talk about the race meeting a bit more, and what I should expect at the September one, then Gill announces that she still has to school Star Point so they'd better go.

"Not so fast," says Nathan, snapping his fingers together in front of her face. "Come on. Out with it. Tell her what you've been itching to tell her, or have you forgotten?"

I blink. Look from one to the other. Gill goes, "Oh yes," in a small voice, then takes a deep breath.

"We've set a date for the wedding. The twentieth of December. It's a Saturday. The ceremony will be held at Piet's farm, followed by a buffet supper and dancing."

She holds up a hand as I open my mouth.

"So then we had to make up a wedding party. Piet took me completely by surprise when he asked Nathan to be best man, but I'm thrilled and so's Nathan. Piet also asked if his cousin Sally – who's twelve – could be a bridesmaid. I agreed, of course, and then it was my turn to choose. There's only one person I want to be my chief bridesmaid. Now Tessa, all you have to do is say 'Yes.'"

"Yes! Yes, yes, yes!"

I could tell her that ever since they got engaged I've hoped… But she probably knows. We embrace, we do a bit of a jig around the kitchen, we do a high five, me using my good hand. There's a moment when I think Nathan wants to high five me, but it's gone and he's just sitting there watching us like he's studying the amusing and little-understood antics of another species.

"What about Tammy for God's sake?"

"She won't be here. Didn't I tell you? She's going to work at a stud in Kentucky from September. But if she was able to attend the wedding I'd've had you both, don't worry."

"Well don't keep me in suspense, Gill. Come on. Tell me what colour I'll be wearing."

"Well, Mum and I found this poky Indian shop way down Manica Road where we unearthed a heavenly ivory satin for my dress and a deep bronze coloured satin for the bridesmaids. I'll show you the swatches next time you come over. Have you got some paper and a pencil?"

I nick Mum's shopping list pad from the miscellaneous drawer and one of Rosie's pencils from the case she's left in the dining room. Gill sketches her dress design ideas on the pad: a long veil for herself with identical lace on her bodice and sleeves, a high waistline, similar lace covered bodices for us bridesmaids. She spins the pad round to me and glares at Nathan.

"Don't you *dare* tell Piet any of this! You know the rules?"

He shakes his head, holds his hands up, palms outwards.

"I haven't quite found the right lace. But I will. We've commissioned a friend of Mum's who's a professional dressmaker. Mum will do the flowers. She's very artistic with floral arrangements. We're going to have yellow and cream roses, something in white and also orange – possibly marigolds."

My mind whirls around all these colours and designs and forms a picture. A perfect picture.

"There's such a lot to plan, I suppose."

"Well us girls do tend to have these ideas from quite an early age, don't we?"

She glances at me sideways. "Come on. Don't tell me you haven't planned *your* perfect wedding?"

Of course I have.

"Yes, and it's all lilac and powder blue. But I've got quite a few years to wait yet."

"Aha!" She rubs her hands together, the diamonds on her ring glittering in a multitude of colours in the late sunlight that is diffusing across the room. "When you and Danny get married I'll be your Maid of Honour!"

No. Not that crushing sadness and the sense of loss. I can't let it come back in. I snatch up the three mugs.

"More tea, y'all?"

Gill – you have no idea that you've saved my day by turning up and re-channelling my dismal little mind and giving me something tangible to look forward to – something I can throw my heart into with you. We've always done horses, and I love that so much, but now we've got a wedding to plan. And what a treat to see you and Nathan together so much these days. You've grown up with each other of course, but now I've been getting visual evidence of what that must have been like. Evidence that he really is a part of your life. A part of life, full stop. I want you both to stay here with me.

But you're going.

THURSDAY 10TH JULY 1980

There are days when you learn quite a lot of things you don't give a damn about. Like Chipo's last three dates with her new boyfriend and now Rosie's ball-by-ball account of the entire Wimbledon tournament. Convincing her how I managed to miss the live broadcast of the finals without actually saying how far down tennis is on my list of watchable sports is going to be a challenge.

Her curly ponytails have gone and, like Gill, she's got a short, fashionable cut that takes some of the attention from her round face and rather stubby nose. Much more grown up. Maybe I should get a haircut. Everyone's doing it.

She stops short in her diatribe about the semi-finals, or some match or other, and instructs me, "Wait here! I have something to show you. I'll be back."

Maybe she's finally realised I'm not with her. She bolts from the lounge, lanky, all arms and legs, but tough and wiry rather than frail. She's almost as tall as me now. After ten minutes she comes rushing back in a tiny white mini dress; her new tennis outfit.

"London was amazing, Tee! We did Madame Tussaud's, Big Ben, the Tower of London, the London Dungeon. And – *shopping*." This with a long gusty sigh.

"So, what do you think? It's cool, huh? You know, I could've spent three times the money I had. It's so unfair. You can pay for an air ticket to fly all the way round the world from here but you can't take diddly squat money with you. But I loved England. So much choice. So many things we've never had here! You know what? It's supposed to be summer over there, right? Well the temps were about twenty degrees C max. Sort of pleasant really, but the natives were all stripping off and whingeing that it was too hot! And hardly anyone knows where Zimbabwe is. They all still call it Rhodesia or else they think it's part of South Africa. I can't wait for my first lesson in my new dress."

It suits her, and she's twirling about, holding the skirt out – what little there is of it. She loved England. I knew she would. Flashback to the night she left, with her embracing me like there was no tomorrow, promising me loads of presents, disappearing through the doors to Emigration with her friends and Rob, and me left wondering, as I did with Gill, if she would ever want to return. Flashback to me standing on the balcony with Mum and Dad, overlooking the floodlit apron, half of me hoping the Wimbledon trip would go so wrong she would hate the place forever, the other half feeling guilty as hell for daring to wish that. Flashback to how I'd tried to hide the fact that I was crying as I watched the British Airways Boeing 747 thunder ponderously out onto the runway, bearing my sister away to her future.

She only brought me a London mug in the end, but I don't mind. I'd rather she spent her money on herself.

And she's still madly and pointlessly in love with Rob. He's getting married next year.

Love.

Rosie loves Rob, Gill loves Piet, I love Danny and now Chipo's gone and met the man of her dreams as well, and I'm beginning to wonder if the world's legendary love affairs – Romeo and Juliet, Jane Eyre and Mr Rochester, Anthony and Cleopatra, Scarlett and Rhett – were of any significance after all. This hero is Paul Ndhlovu and he's in the National Army. She goes on at length about his physique, the way he dances and the way he makes her feel, and how she's eternally grateful to her cousin Ezekiel, who was in the Rhodesian African Rifles and who set her up with him.

"Why did you go to college today then?" Rosie asks. "I thought you were off for a week."

"I couldn't stand another day around the house knowing I can't ride. I'm only back to work next Monday but yeah, I got Dad to take me into college today."

The next four weeks are going to go bloody slowly.

WEDNESDAY 23RD JULY 1980

I'm just retrieving my work bag from the back seat when Dad says, out of nowhere, "Shall we start looking for a car for you then? How about next weekend?"

I gallop through the doors, through reception and skid into Charles's office. Debs only ever arrives at 8.30am sharp but Megan and Charles have been in since God knows when, as always. They've got their heads together over the final account from that job out at Karoi and the smell of freshly ground coffee drifting along the corridor is divine.

"Dad's going to buy me a car! He came out with it just now when he dropped me off. Rosie got a holiday in England and I get the car. Can you believe it?"

"And good morning to you too, Missy. Megs, my love, we'll carry on with this a bit later as we have to find a vehicle for Miss Tessa here. What's your budget, Tess?"

"*Dad's* budget. We've only had the briefest of discussions but he reckons perhaps two to two and a half thousand dollars. I can put some in if I need to."

"Knew you'd be good at financial management. Now I do know a few folk who might be able to help…" He starts scratching around in one of his desk drawers.

Megan collects up the mugs and the cafetiere, glances at me and jerks her head in the direction of the door.

"I need a refill and I'm sure you want one, my dear?"

We head to the kitchen together. On the way, she says, "Leave him to search his database of car dealers. I won't get any more sense out of him until he's satisfied that urge. I guarantee that by the end of today you'll have a list of suitable cars to view on an itinerary that will take you on an extensive tour of Greater Salisbury and possibly even further afield. You have been warned."

"I can never quite understand how he knows so many people from every conceivable walk of life," I say as I dump the old grounds in the bin.

Megan is tiny and slim, with an athletic body you don't often see on anyone officially past retirement age. She still has shoulder length, shiny hair, although it's completely grey, that she catches up into a pony tail in coloured scrunchies to match whatever outfit she's wearing. She's always so tastefully co-ordinated; skirt and blouse or a dress – never trousers – with a matching jacket. Always a jacket. On the hottest of days it might be a light linen one, but I've never seen her without. She has an eye for detail that I can learn a lot from. Charles requests an invoice or statement, even from a job completed two years ago, and Megan goes straight to where it is. When he acts amazed, she asks him, how else does he think his accounts will be kept? Certainly not under his messy filing system. If he dares to take the initiative and file, or search out, any document himself, she tells him which way is up. She's a legend.

She laughs. "I think it's more that everyone knows him, or wants to know him. He's one of those rare people you meet on the way through life who just *is*. He doesn't try to pretend to be something he's not because he doesn't see any point in that. He doesn't even try to be himself, if that makes any sense. No, it probably doesn't, but it's how I think of him. He is a leader of men without trying to be a leader. And he'll find you a car, don't worry."

The two of us end up drinking our coffee in the kitchen because Charles is already on the phone. I know Sylvester is off on leave until next week, visiting his family, and I can hear evidence that Debbie's arrived and is setting up her typewriter. Other than that the offices are empty.

"Is Nathan still out at the reservoir site at Shabani? Charles did say he would probably spend a couple of days out there. I didn't see him at all over last weekend."

Once upon a time I would've thought nothing of that.

"Oh I think so," she says, with a degree of doubt. "He did go on Monday for sure and I guess he's staying with Sean Masterson and his wife because they're right in the town. You'll have to ask Charles when he's back."

Her slight frown smooths out to a small, knowing smile. "Of course he was at the Borrowdale races last Saturday with Sherrie. He told me how much he was looking forward to that, and I suspect he spent Sunday at hers."

Of course? Like I knew? Well, I'm not his keeper, as the saying goes.

I pick up a spoon and give my coffee a stir, then put the spoon back in the sink. Pointless actions. I don't take sugar.

"Oh, Sherrie. Yes, I know Sherrie."

"I suppose you would, being involved in the horses etc and Gill having been friends with her sister for years. Charles and Moira have known the Fletchers for ever with all that horse breeding Moira does."

She is wistful, smiling, cradling her mug in both hands. "I do feel like Charles's family is part of mine you know, us not having any children and all. I've known them all since the mid-fifties – Charles, Richard and Annabelle – although I don't know Richard's kids because he'd moved to the UK by the time they were born and they've only ever visited here a couple of times. I was as delighted as any mother that Gill's finally got engaged, and now Nathan has someone too. He seems to have come to terms with himself at last and deserves a nice relationship after all he's been through. Is Sherrie pretty? Sounds like she's quite sassy. Nathan says she's one of her father's regular work riders, out on the track at dawn every day. She must be quite a girl. Well, my dear, I really need to get some stuff done as I'm going out to lunch."

She leaves me in the kitchen and I stare at Danny's signature on my plaster cast and the "Hope you get rid of this soon my darling" that he scrawled in red pen yesterday.

Yes, I know Sherrie. He's been staying at *her* place?

Nothing to do with me.

I put a phone call through to Dad and let him know Charles

will probably have a list of dealers for me by the time he comes to collect me at five. At ten-thirty, Charles calls me into his office.

"Right," he says. "Carlisle Motors in Mount Pleasant has three cars you might be interested in and it's the closest to home for you. There's quite a few around though. Here you go – I've written it all down for you. Call the dealers that have the ones you're interested in and remember to mention my name."

SATURDAY 26TH JULY 1980

"I thought you said there were three cars here?"

Dad likes the Peugeot 304 because he knows several people who've recommended them and I like the Corolla because it's a coupe and it's quite cool, but it has done a lot of mileage. The third car is a red Datsun 120Y, according to my list. Standing on tiptoe, I can see the back of it – or I think that must be it – over there behind the Peugeot 404 station wagon. It's very appealing from this angle and it looks lonely, although I'm sure that's not a good reason for buying a second-hand car.

"Over there?" I say, and we head towards it. A salesman emerges from the office and follows us. On closer inspection, there's no price ticket on its windscreen. I cup my hands about my face and peer in through the driver's window at smart grey and red upholstery, black floor mats and protective black carpeting on the rear window shelf and the top of the dashboard.

"How many kilometres on this one? And, I guess, how much?"

"This one? Sixty thousand kays," says the salesman. "You've beaten me to even preparing a price ticket. It only came in on Wednesday and the guys are going to service it today. Lady owner's husband has imported a new car for her from South Africa. How did you guess it was for sale?"

I could say, well my boss knows your boss and they're very good buddies, but I don't.

Sixty thousand kilometres is well within Dad's specified range, but I mustn't get too hopeful.

He doesn't know the price anyway. "I'll have to let you know how much when my mechanic's given it a going over. At a guess I'd say around two eight? But I'll call you later."

Dad's indifferent. As we get back into his car I say, "Two thousand eight hundred will be okay, won't it? I'll give you the extra three hundred. I've got one I can give you now and the other two over two months."

"Let's see what the man comes back with Tessa. Where's next?"

But I don't want to see any other cars. I'm already picturing myself in the Datsun, which is silly.

SATURDAY 27TH SEPTEMBER 1980

Neither of them are here. I still haven't got used to seeing her around and I can't bring myself to mention her.

"Nathan?" Gill shakes her head. "No, he's going to meet us there. He's had to arrange for some guy to fix the JCB out at Morton Jaffray Waterworks. Broke yesterday, apparently, and they need it first thing Monday."

"*Ja*, I know it broke. I walked into him – literally – in the corridor yesterday because I wasn't able to see where I was going over the pile of files I was trying to balance on my right arm. My left wrist still complains about too much pressure so I was having to bear the weight all on the one arm. I was so locked into watching them for the slightest hint of a slip that I didn't see him until I collided with him."

"You shouldn't have been carrying a load of stuff Tessa. Naughty. I hope he helped you?"

He did, I assure her. He said, "Whoa!", relieved me of the top three files just before they toppled off, carried them to my office for me and told me about the JCB packing up halfway through digging the trench for the seven-fifty diameter pipeline. Called it 'That Infernal Machine'.

"I thought he was looking a bit more harassed than is necessary for a pile of unstable stationery. His jeans were, like, blotted all over with oil stains and there was a streak of oil on his right cheek, like war paint. He said him and Andy Unwin had a fight with the JCB for two hours and it won. Then he rubbed the oil streak on his face and wiped his fingers on his jeans. I'll bet Amai was pleased with him."

"She'll make him wash the things himself," she predicts. "Tell him in no uncertain terms that he should wear overalls. Which he should've done of course. You must've been working late. He only got back from site at half six, he said."

"Monthly valuation certificates," I explain, and she nods. "I don't mind. It's interesting, and Megan's been off quite a lot this month, what with her husband's illness. It's just me and Charles sorting them out and your dad pays excellent overtime rates."

She takes a few steps backwards to the inner kitchen door, claps her hands, head over her shoulder, and yells for Piet. "We'd better go! Where are you? Chop, chop."

She tells us the day's itinerary as we climb into the cab of Piet's pick-up, Gill in the middle and me next to the passenger window. The races will start at twelve and the trainers want to know at least an hour before that what jockeys they've got. Piet will arrange the rides for Nathan if he's not there early enough.

"I just hope he makes the races themselves," she adds. "Or you'll have to take his place Piet. Now that would be entertaining."

Piet grunts and starts the engine. "You know my views on horses darling. Love them from the ground, but don't ask me to get on one."

No mention of Sherrie, I note.

*

Off the main road and it's going to be dust all the way. Ten kilometres of it, Piet estimates. This grey dust streams from the rear end of the pick-up like the tail of a comet. We run into a similar tail that's following a bus.

"Not staying behind you, my *shamwari*," he mutters and he accelerates to overtake the vehicle on a slight incline. Mixed with the dust cloud are stinking black exhaust fumes; the driver will have his foot pressed hard to the floor to get as much oomph as he can before being forced to change gear.

The bus windows are opaque with a film of grime except for the one directly in front of the driver, which has a marginally clearer patch marked out by the path of a single wiper blade. The roof rack is heaped with cases, baskets, cooking pots, unidentifiable sheet-wrapped bundles, one bed minus mattress and a table upside down with its legs pointing to the sky. Right at the front, tied to a rail and dumbly resigned to its windswept fate, is a brown and white goat.

"There. Now you can eat my dust."

Poor goat.

The District Club at Eagle's Down Farm is on a flat, dusty plain beside a flat, dusty car park, the two separated by a flat, dusty pavilion-type building The gymkhana events are still running and the bar counter under the pavilion eaves is doing a brisk trade.

"My God, you made it before us!" Gill cries, and there's Nathan, hurrying towards us, carrying a training saddle, skull cap and whip.

"Greetings. Yup, all sorted thankfully."

We claim one of the few remaining vacant circular metal tables outside the bar, facing the open field and one of the long sides of the track. Nathan stands the saddle on its pommel end against a chair, dumps the skull and whip on the table (Gill objects: "Oi, leave us some space for drinks!") and sets off with Piet in search of their farmer-trainer.

I stretch my bare legs out in the sunshine and push my sunglasses up the bridge of my nose with one finger. So Sherrie's let him down? Well, he'll survive. All is right with the world and I'm here to relax and enjoy the action, which currently is a sack race.

A brawny white youth with a tough bay pony successfully juggles his sack and his reins, avoids being bitten by the petulant pony, ignores the hoarse taunts and insults from the spectators and wins the race. Gill and I join the applause and she whispers that she's sure they're all being friendly really. The final gymkhana event is announced – tent pegging. This should be good. I turn to see who the competitors will be, and promptly lose interest. Trailing in the wake of Nathan and Piet is Miss Sherrie, clad in snow white breeches and real soft leather racing boots, and carrying a helmet and the tiniest racing saddle I've ever seen.

She greets us like we're the two girls she most wants to see in the whole world, all "Hi!" and "Wow fab!" and "So glad you made it you'll love it!" and "Did you see that last race wasn't it hilarious?" She places a small green paper pamphlet on the table. "Programme for you-hoo!"

For absolutely no good reason I can't look at her, much less greet her. She looks so perfect and she's being friendly and nice, which makes my aversion to her all the more uncharitable and unjustified. I pick up the pamphlet and flip through the pages. It's been amateurishly typed and then photocopied, the pages stapled together. I read a few advertisements for local businesses – a motor vehicle and tractor repair shop, a butchery and a store trading in fresh fruit, vegetables and preserves – and then get to the pages listing the gymkhana events and the nine races. It keeps my attention for maybe three minutes. In the corner of my left eye are Piet and Gill with their heads together as always, and I'm compelled against my will to take a glance to the right, to where Nathan and Sherrie are ridiculously close to each other. She's touching him, talking in a tone too quiet for me to hear and he's nodding back. Like a blackout curtain, the world closes in on me. I'm alone and excluded even though I'm with my closest friends. I came out to enjoy myself, be part of the group, but actually I'm the odd one out. Body number five when the others are two pairs.

I could've been part of a pair if Danny'd come along. But I never even asked him. No point. He's never expressed any interest in either the racing or spending a day out with these friends. I look at all of them looking at each other and I want someone to speak to *me*. I choose Nathan and make sure he knows I'm addressing him alone.

"So, Nathan. Tell me. What's the difference between the divisions then – this D, C, B and A?"

I know the answer. Piet told me ages ago.

And damn-me if it's not Sherrie who replies.

"It's straightforward. Listen up. 'A' Division is for ex-professional racehorses from Salisbury or Bulawayo and 'B' is for horses that are Thoroughbreds but have never raced professionally. 'C' is for part TBs or Arab horses and 'D' is for your old farm hacks. The Maiden races here differ from those at say, Borrowdale Park, because they're for first-timers only, not those who have never won a race. An amateur horse only ever runs in one Maiden, then it has to go on to the appropriate division."

Listen up? Really? She's nodding as she speaks, ticking off the divisions on the fingers of one hand, like that will make it more understandable for me. Okay, so my plan backfired and now I have to decide whether I respond or not. Gill comes to my rescue. She twists away from Piet to look at them.

"What races are you two in then?"

Sherrie tweaks playfully at the sleeve of Nathan's T-shirt.

"We're both riding for Mick du Preez in the 'A' divisions. I ride for Mick often, as well as most of the others. They know me quite well here, you see."

Oh they know you quite well, do they? I'm sure they do. I transfer my attention to the far side of the track. Nothing's happening there, but it's more interesting than Sherrie's fame. I wish I'd never come.

Gill rescues me again. She's fished her bag out from under her chair and is up on her feet. "Well I want one of those delectable looking cakes to take home. See you in a bit."

I almost fall out of my chair, clutching my own bag, and she's the one following me. She had no idea I was so keen on cake, she tells me, laughing.

Behind me, Sherrie is giving Nathan instructions. "You'd better not have any cake, my boy. The minimum weight for us is sixty-five kilograms but you'll be over that anyway. I'll have to carry lead of course."

*

The first race is the Reedside Butchery Maiden Plate. Over Piet's shoulder I get a view of the backend of each of the six jockeys as they queue to be weighed in on an archaic set of balancing scales set on a timber plinth. All they have in common is a coloured overshirt and a matching saddle cloth.

"Brilliant! They're like the Seven Dwarfs, except there's six of them and four of those are about six-foot three. Tall, short, fat, thin, shorts, jeans, camo trousers… *Sandals?* Bloody hell, he's brave. The jockeys at Borrowdale all look identical, apart from their silks. Little skinny blokes in white breeches. You wouldn't look out of place here, Piet."

He's grinning at me, opens his mouth and I cut in before he can say a word. "Tall. Well built. Not fat!"

Sherrie's voice comes from behind.

"Well they're only amateurs you know. The set weight for this race is sixty kilograms. Any jockey who's overweight, like that tall black-haired guy, presents his mount at a disadvantage. Anyone underweight, like me, has to carry lead in a weight cloth to make up the sixty kilograms."

Oh God, you again. Yes, I do understand the bloody system.

I duck around Piet to get him between me and her and decide not to say what's just about to come out of my mouth.

"I'm going to have a five dollar bet on number five to win," Piet says, pulling his wallet out of his back pocket. "Looks pretty nippy to me."

"That dark bay filly, number – what's it? – four. Number four. She'll win," Sherrie predicts.

The filly must be seven-eighths to full Thoroughbred. She's delicate and lovely and I had my eye on her, and now I'm desperate for her to come last, poor thing.

It's a bit of a melee. I stick by Piet and Gill in the queue at the Tote stand and concentrate on studying the convivial multiracial punters around me, and the resident Country and Western trio (hailed as 'Our very own *Dixie Boyz*' in the programme) as they set up their guitars, loudspeakers and a synthesizer on the flat bed of a lorry. We head back to the track as they start their first set – me, Gill and Piet linking arms and singing *All the Gold in California*, the other two following.

"They're pretty good aren't they?" I suggest to my companions, and they nod agreement, waving their Tote tickets in time to the music. I'm in the middle so I don't have a spare hand.

The dark filly races a bit green and hangs out from the rail, but in spite of this, and the fact that her jockey is three kilos overweight, she passes the post at least five lengths clear of Piet's choice. So maybe I should've bet on her, but there was no way I was going to take advice from Her. It's stupid. I'm acting like a child.

I put my full attention into being cheerful and enthusiastic about everything, applauding the winners and focussing on how sweet the pretty filly is as she accepts a carrot from her owner, while actually all I can hear and see is Sherrie crowing with delight and thumping Nathan on the upper arm. She starts up with tips about the workhorse-like hacks that are collecting in the railed parade ring for the 'D' division race because Nathan wants her to tell him which one's worth a flutter. Gill and Piet are arm in arm, following her patter, eyeing the runners, making comparisons and jokes and I have never wished so hard for Danny to be right here, right now. The wish is a physical sensation in my chest and abdomen, and it almost overrides the tiny voice somewhere in my head taking me back to that moment earlier when I first realised I was Odd Girl Out here. When I had to admit to myself that Danny's only reason for not being with me today is that he was never invited. By me. Because I didn't want to hear him refuse.

But would he have refused? I've denied him a fun day out. He could've assessed the horses with all of us, decided which way to bet, laughed at the jokes, been arm in arm with me. I'm wrong to imagine him so far out of his comfort zone he would need a passport, having nothing in common with Piet, being cool with Nathan and distant with me.

I'm just not getting this relationship thing right, am I?

*

These 'A' division horses are a long way from the common old hacks. There are eight of them, all fit, streamlined and stepping out, keyed up for the running. Professional. They've done all this many times before, although perhaps they're missing the well watered grass and the suits, stiletto heels and fancy hats in the midst of all this red dust, overalls and steel toed boots.

Except for the guy in sandals. Idiot. And what about the one wearing shorts? He's trying to protect his calves from being rubbed raw by the stirrup leathers by wrapping them in a pair of elasticated support bandages, but I can't believe that'll do the trick.

Then, of course, we have Sherrie in her professional jockey get-up. Everyone else might have flung their numbered overshirts on last minute, loose to the wind, but hers... she wears it tucked into the waistband of her breeches like she's carefully selected it from her wardrobe. Needless to say, she's generating a fair bit of interest. I can feel it around me.

"Number Three," people are saying. "She's got Mick du Preez's chestnut" and "That chestnut, er, what's it called? Huck Finn. It's got the best jockey, eh?" and "She won at Beatrice back in May" and "Mmm, sweet."

I'll watch Nathan instead. He's in his black breeches and ordinary black knee-length riding boots but he does kind of look the part I must say. This Mick du Preez guy is greeting him, shaking his hand, gesturing towards the iron grey colt beside him. I wriggle through a few people to get closer so I can listen.

Mick, Gill told me, has known Piet's father for yonks. He took Nathan on as a jockey the last time solely on Piet's recommendation and has asked for him again. Early fifties, perhaps? Good looking man, in spite of the sun-worn skin, and I like the Stetson. I wonder if he got it here, or if he's been to the States? Judging from the tooled leather boots, I'd say he has.

"Okay, Nathan, he's all yours. Here, I'll leg you up." Soft Afrikaans accent. He flips Nathan into the saddle and puts a hand on the horse's neck, just under the mane, and rubs with his fingers. The colt has worked himself into a bit of a lather but he looks like he's trying to keep calm, flicking an ear at Mick and chewing his snaffle. His eyes are all over the place.

"Keep him out of trouble and hold him until about three hundred metres out, then do what you can."

The groom lets go and the grey moves to the outside of the ring in a series of little jog steps.

According to the race card, if Mick's other entry is Huck Finn, this one must be Waterloo.

"Hey, Tessa?" Gill materialises at my shoulder. "You placing a bet in this one? Sherrie's got a good chance. Piet says Mick told him that's not an easy ride but he's got great form."

Huck Finn's groom is having some difficulty keeping his charge in one spot and is being dragged toward us with Mick and Sherrie following.

"They say he's got this nasty habit of stopping dead, dropping one shoulder and ducking sideways and backwards. He's dumped a few weak or unsuspecting jockeys. Fortunately, Sherrie is neither."

No, I'm sure she isn't. She's just perfect.

"You ready to win, Missie?" the groom says. "You win good on this *hachi*."

Sherrie laughs and fastens the chin strap on her skull cap, then checks the girth and surcingle before Mick legs her up onto the horse's back. The groom leads him while she adjusts the stirrups from on board. She rides as short as a professional, her thighs horizontal along the top of her teeny weeny saddle.

"How good is that horse Nathan's riding then?"

"I'm trying to remember what Mick said," Piet answers. "Pretty good. Think it was that one that won his Maiden and then came third out of ten runners in his next and only other outing but is better suited to a longer run so he might be a bet in the sixteen-hundred metre race later. I'm going to have a flutter on Sherrie in this one though. Both she and the horse have more experience and that chestnut looks like a sprinter. What about you girls?"

The Tote is offering odds of two to one on a win by Huck Finn and five to one on Waterloo. From the queue I can only see one end of the parade ring and Huck Finn happens to be in it. His groom has vanished now and Sherrie looks relaxed but my own horse-sense is telling me she's very focussed on the animal beneath her. He's walking sideways in alternate directions, to the left for a few steps and then to the right. It looks innocent but his tail is flicking up and down wickedly. He's impressive. Pure muscle and well proportioned.

Then he's gone from my view and it's Waterloo I'm looking at. This one is younger – leggy and lightly built. He has strong, angled quarters with carved lines of sinewy muscle, well sloped shoulders and a deep chest. Nathan rides with longer stirrups than Sherrie, but they're still much shorter than I would have for jumping.

He's moulded to the saddle, easily following the colt's every move, holding the reins in one hand and stroking the wet neck with the other. From what I've seen, none of the other six runners are worth consideration. I'm going to follow my gut.

Gill shrugs. "Waterloo to win? Suit yourself. We'd better get ourselves a good position by the finish for this one. Quick, quick. They're already going up to the start line."

With one hand on the rail in front of me and Dad's binoculars in the other, I locate the runners. They're all over the far side of the track, milling about in a sort of a circle around the starting official. He's directing, pointing, then he moves away from them and the riders turn their horses together and begin to walk forward in a line. The line straggles as a couple of horses try to surge forward. Huck Finn is a little behind. He's walking purposefully forwards so it's a total surprise when he puts in one of his party pieces. He drops his right shoulder and in the blink of an eye is travelling backwards so swiftly that Sherrie is almost left suspended in mid air. She grabs a handful of mane but it's her lithe and relaxed body that keeps her with him. In that flash, her feet are out of the stirrups and clamped around his sides. Holding them there she takes out her racing whip and stings the horse across his quarters, ready for the backlash – and there is one. Ears pinned flat, he snaps both hind legs out in a furious buck. No denying it, the way she sits that is impressive.

Nathan circles Waterloo around her and they're having some sort of conversation. She gets her stirrups back (no way *I'd* sit on a horse like that with my knees up round my ears) and the line forms again. This time all the runners break into a canter together and the Starter drops his flag to let them go.

It's hard to tell who's got any advantage through the dust. I can see Nathan about halfway down the field and he looks like he's on the inside; I can't see Sherrie at all, except for a bit of blue between two other horses that must be her shirt. Two bends and now they're bearing directly down on me and it's even harder to distinguish any order. The blue shirt and a purple one are clearly visible now.

"Sherrie and that Number One!" shrieks Gill in my ear, her binos glued to her face. "They must be neck and neck!"

"Come on!" Piet's yelling. The babble around us is of similar mind; voices calling "Number Three!" and "Number One!" repeatedly. The weight of the noisy crowd is pushing me from behind, the rumbling from the stampede of hooves building up and pressing from the front. I try to recall who Number One is and take my eyes off the race momentarily to the Tote ticket in my hand with its large red figure seven under the word "Win".

Oh well. Looks like I've lost five dollars.

Someone close behind me bellows, "Number Seven! Number Seven! *Chenjera!* Watch out for Number Seven!"

I whip the glasses up to my face again; holding them steady against the jostling of my neighbours takes some doing. And here, in the yellow shirt, is Nathan charging Waterloo alongside Huck Finn. Whoever wears the purple – Number One presumably – has vanished from view.

Sherrie has her whip in her outside hand and is cracking it expertly along the length of her horse without actually touching him this time. Nathan has bridged his reins across Waterloo's neck and is pushing with both hands. The colt responds by giving it all he has. They sweep past the finish line and his nose is well in front. The crowd roars. Clapping and the "Pwheet-pwheet-pwheet" whistle of Africa is all around me. Then they're flowing in all directions around me like I'm an island in a river. Piet grabs my arm and I'm propelled towards the winner's enclosure.

The jockeys have pulled up and are returning along the track, walking or trotting. Sherrie and Nathan are together, gesticulating, talking breathlessly to each other. Sherrie lifts the plastic goggles from her face and they leave a clean, skin-coloured patch in her otherwise grey face. Hah! The dust gets everyone in the end. Her breeches are no longer white either. My satisfaction doesn't last. The exhilaration I see in her face turns it into something I identify as envy.

I'll show everyone I'm every bit as good a rider as Sherrie Fletcher. Roll on the next race meeting. I turn to tell Piet that I want a ride from one of his trainer friends too but he's gone, lost in the crowds. The third-placed horse arrives, his connections fussing and cheering, the large farmer-jockey red faced and puffing. By the time I've fought my way back to where Sherrie's describing the finish to Gill and Piet, all the horses have been off-saddled and led away and the punters' collective interest is waxing for the next race, another 'D' division. No sign of Nathan, but then I see him over by the scales handing in the two coloured overshirts to the presiding steward. The Country and Western trio have started up again, twanging chords above the general commotion.

Sherrie's voice slices through the air, "Isn't Nathan just a *star*!" and I see my opportunity. Mick du Preez has just joined Nathan and is probably imparting his congratulations, judging from his dazzling expression. He really does look good in that hat. Never mind Piet. I'll introduce myself to this trainer.

"Hunches do pay off sometimes!" I exclaim, brandishing my winning ticket. "Well ridden! That was so exciting!"

Nathan's face is lit by the delight that still takes me by surprise. He carries out introductions as if he's been cued.

"This is Tessa, my cousin Gill's best friend. She keeps her horses with us at Makuti Park. Tessa, this is Mick du Preez."

I plunge in with, "I've never been to these amateur races before. It looks like great fun. I'd love to give it a go."

I swing from Mick's face to Nathan's and back again. I have absolutely no idea what I'm letting myself in for. I don't care.

"Well there you are, Mick," Nathan says, and he's amazed, but pleasantly so, I think. "Bring another horse to the meeting at Beatrice next May. It looks like you've got yourself another jockey. And a good one."

He simply could not have said anything better to me right now and the world rights itself. Mick takes my hand and bows over it and I have this reeling, bloody stupid brief moment wondering if he's married. What if...?

Be serious, Tessa. "Delighted to meet you," I tell him.

"Well if you have no doubts about her abilities, I'll do my best to provide her with a horse," he says. "Enchanted to meet you too, my dear. Speak to some of the other trainers as well, Nathan. You and Piet and all will definitely be coming to Beatrice then?"

I reply for both of us, "You bet!" (well if Sherrie can, so can I) "And now, if you don't mind, I'm off to collect my winnings."

I imagine them both watching me as I walk away. Nonchalantly. I'm in.

*

The afternoon shadows are lengthening. The horses have gone, the Tote booths and the scales have been loaded onto a lorry and taken away, and the music system dismantled. There's a drift in the direction of the club house. Like litmus paper, the sky is soaking up the purple darkness from the east and in ten minutes or so it will be night. The creeping shadows are sliced by the starkness of electric lighting from the building and the red-gold glow from the fires that are being prepared in half-forty-four gallon drums for the evening *braai*. A few strips of purple cloud lie quietly along the northern horizon but it's going to be a fine night.

Mick is striding towards the verandah. He catches my eye, waves and gives me his dazzling face. He leaps up onto the decking and leans on our table. Trouble is, its legs aren't co-ordinating with each other. We know this – we've been treating it with consideration – but there's no time to shout a warning to Mick. We grab our glasses, Piet his bottle of Castle, and Mick goes, "Damn! So sorry guys!" and lifts his hands away. "Tessa! Have I spilt your drink? I'll get you another?"

Shame I was too quick. "Not a drop, Mick."

He's glancing around the table. "No Nathan, or the little professional missy?"

"Gone to the washrooms to shower," Gill tells him. "Those of us who have nothing to do but wait for our food and the disco are reclining here. We've raided the bar as you can see, don't worry."

He produces two envelopes, looks like he's going to hand them to Gill, and then gives them to me.

"A share of the prize money for the jocks. One for each. I've put their names on there. I put in an extra bit for Nathan, having won both of his races. I'm grateful, of course. Hope to see him again soon."

I'm grateful too. I bet on him again and won again, but on shorter odds the second time. The Tote officials have got wind of Mr Owen.

Sherrie's back first, fresh in a white blouse, jeans and sandals and smelling of talcum powder. Her damp blonde hair is in soft and perfect ringlets around her head. She tucks a duffle bag and her racing boots under her chair. I slide her envelope across the iron-topped table. "From Mick."

"Oh," she says, taking it. She has very long fingers. Didn't someone tell me once that the best riders usually have quite stubby fingers? I've never come up with any good reason as to why that should be so. "Did he leave one for Nath as well?"

"It's okay. I'll give it to him."

"No, that's fine. Give it here. I'll take it and find him now." Holding out her hand.

Oh please, not one of those ridiculous I'll-Do-It, No-I'll-Do-It conversations. To avoid that I'll have to capitulate and give it to her. I'm dithering, and someone moves into the frame from behind me. Nathan, here to save me from myself.

*

Piet is keen to get at the food, herding Gill, Nathan and Sherrie before him. I trail behind, wondering where Mick is and thinking maybe I'll get him to buy me a drink after all. Why I'm pursuing this line I haven't yet figured out. It will get me nowhere. There he is now, over by the fires, his arm about the waist of the woman who must be his wife. They look very pleased with each other. Told you. You've got a boyfriend anyway.

I want to do something rebellious, but I'm not the rebellious type. I slow down even more. Let the others get in amongst the food queue. Contemplate the night sky. It's a three-dimensional tableau of star constellations that I never see within the reaches of Salisbury's lights. I've done this before, allowing my finite mind to be boggled by the concept of infinity. How can it possibly go on for ever? And if it doesn't, what lies beyond it?

Gill's not going to let me get left behind. "Come, Tess! I've got you a plate. You okay?"

"Yeah, yeah. Fine. Just star gazing."

I'm not hungry but I pick up some *boerewors* and a lamb chop. A pile of salad I probably won't eat.

"Baked potato?"

"Oh God, no. No thanks."

"You're never trying to lose weight because you've got some race riding coming up?" Nathan says, pausing beside me, looking me up and down. "You don't have to worry. It's me who should be cutting down."

I'm just not that hungry, but it's nice to be complimented. He smells of after-shave, which I've never, ever detected on him before.

*

Piet's put another drink down in front of me and there's talking, laughing, picking at the remains of food. The Dixie Boyz have turned their musical talents to the operation of the club's disco equipment. I stare at the dancers without registering any of the moves because I'm still being a misery-guts. Well, trying to stop being a misery-guts. I'm done with chasing melancholy thoughts round in circles and now I'm lecturing. Come on, life is treating me well. It is. Think about it:

I've left school, I'm starting to make my way in the world. I have a good job, with prospects – isn't that how the saying goes? I live in a beautiful country with a perfect climate and spend long hours outdoors riding my beloved horses. I have *two* horses and I've won more prizes than I deserve on them. My family is normal. Yes, really. Compared to some. I have a happy home. And a car. I have special friends and to cap it all I have a steady boyfriend. Danny. I love Danny. He loves me. I've had a day out in the sunshine and have been eating and drinking under a trillion stars in congenial company, along with good music, and the food and drinks have been paid for by Piet. He says he's my host. I'm privileged and bloody lucky.

Things are on the up. We've all fought our way through times of conflicting emotions and uncertainty recently. Well, we've been doing that for a long while in fact. And the changeover of government, of power, hasn't proved to be as traumatic as predicted. The see-saw's levelled itself out, at least for the time being, in spite of the bucketfuls of doom and gloom we've been fed.

Maybe that's what's causing me to wallow in this melancholy? It would be justifiable.

Actually – unlikely. I'm willing to bet it's not at all attributable to the politics of men but rather to the hormones of women. When is the next round of The Curse due? Next week I think.

I really shouldn't drink another rum and Coke. Doesn't alcohol make you depressed?

I start on it anyway. Focussing on the dancers at last, I see optimistic older couples determined to perform the foxtrot or the *sokkie* to the music of the seventies.

"Right, come on. Let's do it." Gill drags Piet onto the dancefloor. Sherrie and Nathan seem to have disappeared while I was in my decline, and I'm left alone at the table. A couple of records go round and then Gill comes trotting back, pulling Piet, then pushes him towards me. "Go on, ask Tess. Can't have her sitting here like a wallflower!"

A wallflower. Yeah, that's what I am.

It's a waltz. *Three Times a Lady*. He embraces me in a hairy ballroom hold, rocking his arms to-and-fro in time with the steps, whirling me around the floor while humming to himself. It's like dancing with a giant teddy bear. I never put him down as a dancer but he's light on his feet and easy to follow.

"I knew I should have been a ballroom dancer. Rosie and I had lessons many centuries ago. I wanted to be like the champions on TV in those big net dresses in gorgeous colours."

"You look gorgeous enough in your shorts. And you dance perfectly."

I know he really means it, whatever I look like, however I dance, and I start to feel a bit pleased with myself as he executes a whisk and chasse and my memory and legs do exactly the right things to match him.

Then over his shoulder I see Nathan and Sherrie holding each other close, swaying in time to the music and I trip over one of Piet's feet. Nathan Owen, performing a stilted but passable waltz? Where did he learn that, for heaven's sake? How much more is there that I don't know about him? Sherrie is finding out. She's glowing.

The record ends. Piet holds my hands and bows. "Thank you, my lady. Three times."

I curtsey in response, turning my back on them. Piet is such a darling. A real gem. At least Gill knows how lucky she is, no doubt about that.

They say music moves the human soul in many ways, and it does. It becomes a reminder of an era or of a specific time and place, and it creates moods or enhances those already present. I follow Piet over to our table and the lyrics I've just danced to re-play themselves over and over in my ears. I don't want to hear them. I don't want to even start to think I'm on the downslide towards the end of our pretty, familiar rainbow. Danny's rainbow. My rainbow.

Danny. Oh God, don't start. I am. I'm going to cry now.

I need a distraction. I plonk down next to Gill and prattle away about ballroom dancing and sequins and dance lessons at school and doing a jive with Timothy Dunn and – how the hell did I remember *that*? What's Timothy up to these days? I've never even thought to find out.

The couples remaining on the floor begin to dance again, embracing. *Desperado*. I love this song, but it's bloody romantic and above all sad, and romantic and sad are things I so don't need right now. I know all the words too, which doesn't help. Nathan and his partner are revolving slowly across the floor and those words are like a branding iron on my heart.

It's time he came in from wherever he's been most of his life and gets some girl to love. It's normal and healthy. Gill has her wonderful Piet and now Nathan has Sherrie. She's attractive and talented and she loves horses and riding. For the fiftieth time today, I yearn for my Danny and the longing is a physical pain somewhere in my middle. The tears I've just succeeded in swallowing resurface.

The dance is ending. It's not too late for Nathan. He's got his girl. I should be so pleased for him, but I'm... I hate her.

My view of the hall dissolves and I leap up.

"Back in two ticks," I mumble at Gill. Nathan and Sherrie are approaching, their arms around each other, talking, their heads together, and I'm off, blindly, towards the ladies' washroom. The hall outside is heaving, but strangely, thankfully, I'm the only one in here. I slam myself into a cubicle, sit on the closed toilet seat and sob, so hard my shoulders are shaking. Once again my comfortable world has shifted under my feet. Sherrie is now part of Nathan's world and she'll be part of mine too at Makuti Park. They'll get married and go away, or they'll move in there and Gill will go to live at Piet's farm and they'll all have kids and everything will change and I'll have to deal with it or take my horses somewhere else.

So much anger. I'd never've believed I could be so angry with people who have done nothing wrong.

The main door opens and two women come in, chattering about Nigel and Claire and how their eldest son has dyslexia and how they're coping with it. I sit still and silent and then reel off a strip of paper, bundle it around in my hands briefly, stand up and flush the toilet. While the water's running I blow my snotty nose on the paper. The other women spend a lifetime washing and drying their hands and gassing on – Hannah will be leaving school at the end of this year and going to Teacher Training College and Robin is learning to fly – then at last they leave. After a couple of moments I creep out, patting my face with more paper and blowing again. Splashing with cold water and staring at my red eyes in the mirror. Running my fingers through my dusty hair and re-adjusting a clip. The door opens again and Gill's reflection appears.

"Tessa!" She addresses my reflection and her voice echoes and re-echoes across the stark, white-tiled room. "I wondered where you'd got to. Are you all right?"

There's little point in trying to pretend. I turn to face her.

"Too much sun, I think," I lie. "Or maybe I'm going down with something. I feel a bit off colour."

"Ah!" She puts an arm across my shoulders. "We'll go home now. It's been a long day and we've still got a fair drive back. Piet says we'll take you to your house and you can collect your car tomorrow. Come."

It's a convoy: me and Gill with Piet in his pick-up, followed by Sherrie in her Camry, with Nathan in the Concrete Structures Ltd Land Cruiser bringing up the rear. At some point I doze off to the monotonous humming of wheels on macadam; even the sharp silvery beauty of the bush flashing by, lit by the encompassing glow of the risen moon, can't keep my attention. I only know this because I hear Gill whisper, "We're on our own, Piet. Look at her. Shall I sing to you to keep you awake?" at precisely the point my head drops down onto my chest and I wake up with a start and a grunt.

Piet guffaws. "Good God, no, my sweetheart! Please don't. I'll put the radio on low. Really, I'm fine."

The next thing I know is I'm being woken by a gentle hand on my knee. It's Gill, and we're outside my gate.

"You okay? Piet, walk her to the door won't you? See you tomorrow, Tess honey."

We say goodbyes and thank-yous and hug each other. Standing here, waving them off, I'm sure I can hear the television mutedly mumbling in the background. It can't be Mum and Dad, surely – must be Rosie. The lounge is in darkness, but I can see the soft flickers of light from the screen on the walls from where I stand in the hall.

"What are you still doing up? You go to bed late these days. What're you watching?"

She's curled up on the sofa with a blanket wrapped round her and she extracts a hand from its depths to wave at me.

"Late night movie. It's okay. Did you win anything? Ooh – what have you got there? A cake?"

So I didn't manage to hide the cake box behind my back quickly enough.

"Only from betting. I didn't ride today. Fruit cake. And no, you can't have any now. Wait until tomorrow. Guess what? I've probably got a ride in the next race meeting. Cool, huh?"

"Just confirms my views about your sanity. You seem to have no sense of self preservation." She's craning her neck, as though by doing so she can see around me to the battered box.

"Are you okay? You look like you've been asleep."

I have been asleep and I would've stayed asleep, given the choice. Stop me thinking about how lonely I am and how miserable I am and how much I hate Sherrie. Oh don't start that again. Please.

"I'm going to hide this in my room. You can wait in torment. Nighty-night."

She moans loudly and deliberately as I walk away, pulling the door to behind me.

At one point in my usual complicated tangle of dreams, someone touches my knee to awaken me to tell me something. It's Danny, and he's explaining how to place a bet at the races.

TUESDAY 18TH NOVEMBER 1980

Chipo. Breathless, catching up with me, grabbing my elbow.

"All those days we spent in lectures seem almost worthwhile for the high you get when you walk out of the last exam, hey Tessa? What say we go out and celebrate? You haven't met Paul yet! Friday? Come on, please?"

I feel as drunk on the cloud of freedom we're floating in as she looks. No more evenings spent shut in my room, studying. I can actually watch some TV, read a novel, relax, go out on the town. Good idea.

"Okay. Where?"

"*Archipelago's*. The night club. I like to dance." She does a twirl in the corridor, loses her balance and collides with a concrete column, dropping her bag. "Ouch."

I pick it up for her. "You've already planned this, haven't you? Are you all right?"

She's leaning out over the parapet next to the column, turning her face to the midday sun and the dome of the sky. "Ah, heaven. We'll go there Friday night then, yeah?"

"Be there!" I aim a forefinger at her chest and we both shriek with laughter like silly schoolgirls. "Paul picking you up, or do you want a lift home?"

"He's coming to meet me outside the college in…" She tilts her watch and taps it with her right forefinger. "In fifteen minutes. You go. I'll call you before Friday? Where's your car?"

It's parked two roads away. I'm halfway there when a very odd thing happens. I get a desire to buy myself a posh frock. This is not something I've experienced before. A new show jacket, jodhpurs perhaps, a T-shirt or a pair of shorts, yes. But a dress? That's always been Mum's job: "How about this one Tessa?" or "That one will go with your black shoes, don't you think?" or "That looks nice on you." Or her default, like back when I had my interview with Charles, "Why don't you wear your school uniform?"

And I've let her do it. Well, not any more. It's like I've inadvertently pressed a switch in my head – one I never knew was there before – and something's changed.

I jay-walk across the road and head into the city centre.

FRIDAY 21ST NOVEMBER 1980

Paul and I stand together at the bar counter without speaking for a few moments. Now that I've got myself away from the table – away from Danny so I can think more rationally – I wish I'd stayed. Or that Paul had left. Or that I'd gone to the toilet. Now he's here with me, at my invitation, and I've got my heart rising up my oesophagus and I have to find something to say and I'll truly mess things up. Fan the flames. All I've done is jump out of the frying pan.

Seriously, how can a whole evening out fall over so spectacularly in the space of ten minutes?

In spite of my jitters, this silence is comfortable compared with the crackling one we just left, but then, inevitably, he breaks it. And, to be fair, his face tells me he doesn't know whether to choose the pan or the fire either.

"Did Chipo not tell you anything about me?"

Now think this through. He could well have been a bank clerk or a car mechanic, so let's try and imagine that being the case.

Of course I asked her what Paul did for a living. And she said, "He's in the army." So she might have said, "He's a bank clerk" or "He's a car mechanic" and my reaction would've been the same. I said, "Oh?" and we moved on to other things. Half the country's in the bloody army anyway and has been for quite some time now. It was enough for me at the time and it's never cropped up since.

I search his face for any signs of aggression or arrogance, or even amusement, and find none of the above.

"She told me you were in the army. It was…" I shrug and he finishes the sentence for me.

"Nothing unusual."

He gets the picture.

Why did we have to start talking about work here, tonight? There shouldn't be any need to go into ideals or politics either. People should be able to have an evening together without searching or controversial conversations. A nightclub isn't exactly conducive to in-depth conversation anyway. Chipo and I can dance. Paul can drink beer, do whatever. Does he dance? But then there's Danny.

The sigh that comes out of me is involuntary. It's an effort not to put my head down on my forearms and avoid whatever's coming next. I get a grip and trace a finger along the brass trim at the edge of the counter instead. Bizarre doesn't come into it. I'm on a social outing with a man who, little more than a year ago, I would have classed as the Enemy with a capital E. I would've sworn I'd never do such a thing. What happened to that keen, all consuming sense of outrage that comes with having an Enemy? Now it's just like it was a meaningless dream or a past life. Everyone in this country had Enemies, but in the end no-one won, we're all still here and now no-one knows who's who. There are no victors and no vanquished, like France and Prussia, the North and the South, Britain and Germany. Everyone in Zimbabwe has stepped sideways into a slightly different role and life is going on much as it did before. Three armies have combined – the Rhodesian Army, ZANLA and ZIPRA – and if you listen to the hype it's an unprecedented success against all odds and pessimistic predictions.

So Paul was a terrorist. No, the Enemy was a terrorist. He has to be a guerrilla now, or a freedom fighter. My first impressions of him, earlier, before I knew? I met a quiet and unassuming human being with a pleasant disposition. He has so far treated me with the utmost courtesy and respect. It was he who pulled my chair out for me, at the same time as he seated Chipo, while Danny was faffing around with his shoelace.

Think in the here-and-now and forget the past for the minute. Just because he was in ZANLA doesn't mean… What doesn't it mean? Where was he when Nathan…? Don't go there. Close that door. It's okay. That bunch was ZIPRA anyway.

How would Charles Owen approach this? He would be curious, wouldn't he? He likes to know what makes others tick. He would ask questions.

We're both doing frantic brain work here; I can see my own dilemma reflected back at me. Is this equally bizarre to him? Questions. Right, here we go.

"How has everyone sorted themselves out in the new National Army? Has it been difficult?"

He's taken slightly off balance, but he recovers and eyes me with what I want to interpret as approval. He smiles. A genuine smile, not a smirk.

"In some cases, yes. There are always some who can't, or should I say won't, accept change, but they are the ones who have left. I think they will all go down to South Africa now to join the Defence Force."

He inclines his head towards our table.

"Your boyfriend – was he in the Rhodesian Army?"

"No. He's just a bit too young to have been involved. He only left school at the end of last year."

"Exactly with the ceasefire. He's one of the lucky ones then."

I didn't see that one coming. There's a barman with a quizzical face hovering and he's not sure whether to catch my eye or Paul's or if we're together or not. I lift my bag onto the counter and Paul holds up a hand while groping in a back pocket.

"Allow me, please. Yes. We'll have a brandy and Coke for my girl and a Shumba for me and whatever you and Danny want. Tessa?"

Say whatever comes to mind first. "Rum and Coke and a Castle please. Thank you very much."

My Enemy is now offering to buy me a drink. I have absolutely no guidelines on how to play this. Is there a manual?

Through the gloom and muted flashing lights we both watch Chipo and Danny at opposite ends of our table, avoiding each other and staring fixedly at the gyrating humanity on the dance floor.

"You do realise," I'm obliged to tell him, "that Danny is not going to accept this? I can't offer any explanations or excuses, but I hope it doesn't spoil the evening too much."

Then I add, "Well, it will of course. But you and Chipo can leave us if you want to and whenever you want to. I'm sorry, but I don't want any sort of altercation. I don't want that to sound like

I'm hoping you will leave us though. Please feel free to go and enjoy yourselves by yourselves. I won't be offended."

He collects up the bottles and glasses onto the stainless steel tray that the barman is offering and we shuffle along to allow a group of three girls some space.

"Well, we will if we have to, but I hope we don't. I came out to help you and Chipo celebrate the end of your exams after all. You like Bacardi then?"

Tastes in alcohol. Excellent – a normal, harmless conversation. Must keep this going.

"I do. Only with Coke though."

I give him a brief and pointless explanation of how Charles introduced me to the combination and can't tell if he's amused or not.

"Did you know Africans were not officially allowed to drink spirits before 1959?"

Okay, not so harmless then. What have I said wrong to inspire him to start dredging up racial gems from the past like this one?

"Oh? I didn't. I wasn't around then."

The shock must show – perhaps he can hear the blood buzzing in my ears – because he's put the tray on the counter and is holding up both hands in a surrender pose.

"Neither was I. So it wasn't our problem then and it isn't now, hey?"

"I… um, oh, a-ha, ha…" I try to laugh but it's not like a laugh at all. More like a strangled donkey noise.

"Come on, Tessa. I don't want to argue with you or make life difficult for you. You're Chipo's friend and she thinks so much of you and you seem to be trying hard to accept this situation. I don't blame you for finding it difficult. I'm a career army guy. I've been doing it all my adult life, I'm good at it and I like it. I'm a military man. There are some of us out there who want this all to work. We fought for it and we want it to work. Some of us, well, they may make trouble. I don't want trouble. It's not that easy for me either and it won't be for many ZANLA ex-combatants. Some of us, like me, as I said, want to develop our skills and be a part of

Zimbabwe's defence force and be proud of ourselves. Others will be de-mobbed and find themselves as civilians with no jobs. Some are still languishing in the Assembly Points because no-one knows what to do with them."

None of the men coming out of this war are going to find it easy. In a stroke the unavoidable call-up routines and commitments and the causes that have driven their lives for so many years have gone away and they're going to have to find replacements. Them and Us both.

He pours his lager into a glass while I gawk at him, then raises the glass.

"Yes?"

I reach out and take the glass of Bacardi and Coke, lift it hesitantly towards him, knowing I should be doing this, but knowing I shouldn't, because I can feel the touch of eyes. There, to my left and a chilly distance away, is Danny, observing us.

We touch the glasses together and that sinking gut feeling tells me I've done something that's going to bite me hard in the not too distant future. What was the alternative though?

"What do *you* want, Tessa?"

"I want us to have a good life. All of us in Zimbabwe. And I want us to start with this evening. Can we just, like, dance to the music? And I *don't* want to sound patronising. I *don't* want to be arrogant. I mean it."

"None of us has any right to be arrogant."

He picks up the tray and starts weaving around people and tables and chairs and I follow him. Well, my girl, you got through that one but the worst is yet to come.

*

Chipo is sorry – she whispers as much in my ear – but she can't be nearly as sorry as me. I wanted to dance the night away in my new dress. When I was standing in front of the mirror earlier, admiring it, with Rosie in ecstasies behind me, I'd been so surprised and well pleased with myself. I have a Little Black Number. Me – horsey, tomboy Tessa. Short and glovelike it is, but it's a perfect fit and I'm delighted I have no bulges to spoil the image. I pointed my stockinged feet out to either side while I tried to visualise Danny's face when he saw me in it, ignoring Rosie's pleas to tell her how much it cost because Mum was standing in the doorway. There's no need for *her* to be in possession of that sort of information. My spending is my business and I'm fully aware I'll have to be careful next month.

Mum didn't ask how much it cost. Her concern was that she just couldn't understand when I would get to wear it. How does she always manage to put me on the defensive? I asked her, "Don't you think I'll ever get to go to a function which calls for a fashionable evening dress? Maybe look grown up?"

"Yes – well – I know – maybe, but it's not the sort of thing you usually wear."

No, it's not, but here I am, in my perfect dress and I can't have the perfect evening I wanted. Trying to play the diplomat to both sides of a conflict is exhausting and not worth the effort. Conversation was unsustainable, which is why me, Chipo and Paul ended up dancing in a threesome with an agitated Danny hovering nearby. I thought this might just work, but I was wrong.

She clings to my left hand while Paul shakes my right, solemn and stiff with some emotion – embarrassment?

I like him, but this is just doing my head in. Now I know exactly how Alice must have felt in Wonderland.

Danny all but marches me towards the car, a firm grip on my left hand like he thinks he should be holding it but doesn't want to. Anything I say will be taken and used as evidence against me, as the cops on TV would say, so I keep my lips clamped together. He won't look at me trotting along next to him in my heels. My mind bounces around between making a mental note that a fast walk in a narrow skirt is impossible and wondering why I don't just pull away and ask him what the hell he thinks he's doing?

The air is hot and humid and heavy, soaking up the grumble of the Friday night traffic. Only when we reach the car does he release my hand – throws it away in fact – and asks me if I knew Paul was a sodding gook.

His tone is brutal and my mouth is like a mini Sahara. Come on, I'm not in any physical danger. Not from Danny. One hundred percent for sure. But I never dreamed he'd ever talk to me like that. Or be so angry.

I grip the handle of the locked passenger door and shake it ineffectually.

"No. Chipo didn't tell me. It never occurred to me to ask how her boyfriend came to choose his career. She said he was in the army. So what? I'd never met him and I never expected to meet him so it didn't matter. I kind of assumed he'd been in the RAR or something. I don't know. I never stopped to analyse it. It's not like I'm short of things to think about in my life."

"But he's a Captain, Tessa. And she said he's *just joined*. Even in our black regiments all commissioned officers are white. You know that. How could he have been an officer in our army?"

Well now, why did I never think to ask what rank he holds?

"*Our* army is gone, Danny. It's the Zimbabwe National Army now so maybe some of those black guys who were in *our* army will get promoted in this one."

"Well it was obvious to me immediately that he was One Of Them. You seemed very pally with him I must say. Didn't you mind?"

I picture Chipo, queen of the table, formally introducing us to ourselves, bursting with pride, then the strange transformation in her pretty, round face as the crinkled grin fled for, I thought at the time, no apparent reason. The reason came to me probably a fraction of a second after it came to Danny. She must have clocked it in his face like it had been scribbled there with a marker pen.

"No."

He stares at me over the roof of the car for a few moments. I watch the headlights and tail-lights of passing vehicles, drifting along Baker Avenue in blissful ignorance of our state of tension. Baker Avenue. Gordon Baker. What a long, long time ago it was that I first saw him hauling Jess by the hand across the church hall grounds, when I was barely aware my country was at war with itself. Now that war's over and I've just been socialising with someone who, at the time, was likely planning attacks on us, the Rhodesians.

On me, in a way. What was he up to while these two teenage white girls preened themselves at a disco, never knowing their way of life would come to an end?

Danny dives into the car and flicks up the button on the passenger door. I slide in sideways but I can't pretend I'm not here. He drives. He's calm. The calmness is stretched almost to tearing point by the physical tension in the space between us.

I force my focus onto very specific things. Pleasant things. Like every detail of Gill's last dress fitting. The conversations we had, the feel of the heavy satin against my body and the girlish delight of posing in front of the mirror to watch its sheening rainbow colours. The sight of Sally trying to cross the room in Gill's pearly three-inch heels and ending up in a giggling heap. Keep replaying this scene.

We're nearly at my road when he breaks the mute barrier. He still wants to know why I just ignored the fact that that man is a gook. He can't let go of this. He doesn't understand me. He wanted to walk straight out as soon as he knew but he got stuck there with me. I put him in a horribly difficult place. Why did I want to stay?

I have no answer, or none he'll accept anyway, so I offer nothing. He clicks his tongue and stands on the brake, scattering stones at the gate.

When I lean across to kiss him and murmur goodnight, his lips are pressed together in a hard line and the effort of persuading him to soften them is a step too far. He'll come round. We can talk, and things will be back to normal soon. This shouldn't make any difference to our relationship, should it? He could've stormed out of the nightclub but he didn't because he's too well mannered and polite. There's no need for him to ever set eyes on Paul again if he doesn't want to. This shouldn't make any difference to our relationship, should it?

Tessa, girl, you *know* there is no relationship left. Give it up.

He's staring out of the side window, waiting for me to go.

"I'll phone you tomorrow, shall I?"

"Okay. If you want."

FRIDAY 5TH DECEMBER 1980

It's only nine o'clock and I'm still on the first mug of coffee and here's Charles, clattering his way into my office, plonking himself on the front edge of my desk and wanting to know how I'm doing.

"I'm sorry, *Baas*. I haven't done my work for today yet so I've failed you and I don't have time for idle chit-chat. If you'd care to come back at four-thirty…"

His laugh threatens to blast the paper out of my in-tray.

"Well I don't know. You can't get the staff these days. Never mind the work. How would you like to spend the day out? Friday's not a day to be in the office and I'm sure anything you have to do can wait until Monday. There's nothing too urgent, is there? I've cleared it with Mistress Megan by the way."

There're those invoices from Bentley Pipework to pay, I tell him, and I don't get much further than that and a quick glance around at my shelves, a flip through the contents of my tray, before he's up and rubbing his hands together and leaning over the desk to give me some sort of inspection.

"You used those size six safety boots last time we went out, didn't you? They're in the cupboard in my office. And grab a hard hat too. How're you dressed today? Trousers? Good."

"Lots of ladders to climb?"

He grins. "Let's just say skirts can be a bit awkward on a construction site. There are some pairs of socks in the cupboard too. They're all freshly laundered. Good. Right. The sooner you get going, the sooner you can be back and then you can go home early if you like. I'll catch you later…" and he's off towards the door.

I'm poised halfway out of my chair, in the act of trying to tip my bag into the bottom drawer on my right. "Wait a minute. The sooner *I* get going? Where am I going and how do I get there? Not with you?"

"Oh. Sorry, yes. You're going with Nathan. I've got too much to do. The pumping station site at Hartley. Thought it was a great opportunity for you to get out and see it. Look, I'll go with you to his office."

He likes me to see the jobs for which I handle the accounts. It's fine by me; these days out are a kind of perk to my job. I've never been to site with Nathan though. The edge has gone off the idea a bit.

The boots are still muddy from my last outing so I hold them away from my clothing. Debbie is rattling her typewriter and clinking her bracelets as we enter the reception area. The look on her face says it all as she eyes me – boots in one hand and the Concrete Structures Ltd hat in the other – up and down.

"Nathan's still in his office?" Charles asks her and she nods in reply.

"Go through," he says to me, "and tell him to pull finger. He's probably still asleep."

Nathan is, in fact, reading *The Herald*. The flash from his eyes as I push open the door is loaded with guilt. He looks like he was just about to flick the paper aside but he holds onto it instead and gives a short, self-conscious laugh.

"Oh Tessa. It's you."

"Just me. I caught you. You should be more crafty, like me. I keep my paper on the table in the corner among open files. I could be doing any number of things over there if Megan walks in."

"I'll remember that. I won't tell on you if you don't tell on me."

He doesn't quite succeed at being serious. He closes and folds the paper.

"You're coming with, I believe. You ready?"

I hold the boots and the hat out towards him.

"Fully equipped."

"Okay, let's roll. Where've I put the damned car keys?"

He shakes the blazer slung over the back of his chair. It jingles encouragingly and he fishes a bunch of keys out of an inside pocket. The Mercedes emblem on a leather key tag glints in the light from the window. I haven't been in the new one yet and I'm like a child that's been promised an ice cream.

Charles has vanished and Debbie's clearly waiting for us to appear; she's sitting to attention and must have been staring directly at the doorway to Nathan's office.

"Oh, hello Nathan!" Her blouse is straining at its buttons and her smile is luminous. She touches her thin gold necklace and moves her manicured nail down to the vee in her neckline.

She must know he has a girlfriend now, surely. Has Sherrie ever visited the office? I can't recall her being here, unless she's come on one of my college days.

"We'll be back early afternoon," Nathan says from behind me. "Please take any messages. Mike Black of Costain might phone."

"Of course," she simpers. "Just call me from site if you need me to do anything for you. 'Bye now."

She does tend to use that little-girl voice when she speaks to Nathan. How many times has he been treated to a tantalising peek at her bra, I wonder? Assuming she has one on, of course. I have a good look, and she does; I can make out the faint shape of straps under her thin blouse.

"'Bye Debs darlin.'"

He pulls open one of the glass doors and motions me through and then from close proximity he gives me a wink that touches every possible area of his beautiful face. My legs stop moving on the top step outside and he passes me.

I'm looking at a rear view of faded blue jeans, *veldskoens*, an open necked shirt of pale blue striped cotton, sleeves rolled up. I'm looking at muscular forearms and a lean body inside the shirt. And inside the jeans. Tessa, you complete ninny. How come you're just admitting this to yourself now? Have you always known this in some corner of your soul, been blind through sheer naivety and now, today, this instant, you've put Debbie's, Sherrie's, Karen Melton's and Rosie's eyes on like a pair of glasses?

The morning sun reflected off the polished bonnet of the car is dazzling me. He's waiting by the driver's door, wondering why I've stalled. I force my legs into gear and run.

He drives easily through the traffic of the city, relaxed but watchful, eyes flicking from the road ahead to the mirror above him, to the side mirrors, and before he changes lanes he glances over his shoulder like a motorcyclist. I watch every move out of the corner of my right eye, watch his hands caressing the leather steering wheel and the gear shift and have thoughts I absolutely shouldn't have. Oh yes, I do reckon I've always known. Well, not always. Since that day we hacked out together, the physical contact, the electrocution and the ache. I've buried it without even realising I'm doing so because there's been no sense in reflecting on it. It can't be acted upon so best to ignore it and move on. And that's what I'm going to do now.

Turn. Look out of the passenger window. Don't let him see, or even sense, that something's going on in your head. Those hands are spoken for. You can't have them. Sherrie Fletcher has them. You have Danny's, if you want them.

If he wonders why I've gone silent, he doesn't show it.

Salisbury is thronging with people going about their business. Pedestrians are threading their way amongst the traffic with single-minded determination and apparent lack of self-preservation. It's like nothing has changed since Independence and it's hard to believe this is a brand new country, painfully born with a bloody struggle and now falteringly taking its first steps in the world.

My car and Dad's car have handle operated windows. This one doesn't. I probe a button in the arm rest beside me and admit a blast of warm, fresh air that lifts my hair across my face so that I have to catch it and clutch it in my left hand. Out on the open road, beyond the city's limits, the air is scented with the sweet smokiness of farm compounds. The rich, red loam has yielded good crops for these farms; the tops of the maize plants are already out of reach of a tall man and the cobs on them are fat.

He turns his head and looks at me but I don't respond. He fumbles in a compartment in the console between us without taking his eyes off the road and extracts a cassette, which he flips over with a brief glance and slides into the stereo unit. We get The Jackson Five, and they're competing with the road and wind noise coming through my open window. I know I'm messing up the effect of the air con but I need this rush of wind. It lifts my depression, just fractionally, but enough to make me want to keep it going. I want it to blow my eyelashes and my hair while I lean against the head rest and take in the unlimited, empty blue sky of Africa, the lush summer vegetation, the ochre and grey rock formations that have scattered themselves on either side of the road like the abandoned building blocks of a giant child. The Hunyani hills are blue and mauve on the horizon.

The Mercedes hugs the tarmac, whispering past the smoky compounds that are dotted between the stretches of cultivation, past rich paddocks grazed by prime Friesland herds, and the hills creep closer. Between two tracks on the tape he asks if I'm thirsty. I am, and we pull into the petrol station at the junction with the road that leads over the hills to the western reaches of Lake McIlwaine. He parks to one side, away from the pumps. A middle-aged woman standing beside her Toyota pick-up while the pump attendant cleans the windscreen watches us walk past her to the kiosk and I fancy that she's admiring him and wondering if we're an item. I step a little closer to him because I want to enjoy this. Why not? It's harmless, even though I said I was going to ignore it.

She's paying the attendant when we come back out with our bottles of Fanta and in her line of sight I get all impulsive and clink mine against his in a toast – "Here's to a good day out!"

"Oh yeah, cheers!" He looks surprised and pleased but I hope to God he doesn't think I'm just real strange. We get back into the car. I'm foolish. I shouldn't have done it.

The pumping station site is just north of Hartley, on the route of the new pure water pipeline to a reservoir in the town. Some sections of the line have already been laid, Nathan explains, and so far only the floor of the structure has been cast. Labourers are tightening props on the barricade of steel formwork that surrounds it and there's a lot of shouting coming from the direction of the concrete batching plant.

"It's deep. Are they going to do the walls now, then? The crane looks ready for action."

"Four metres below ground level. And yes. They're doing the first lift today. Oh, there's Mike…"

Mike is in the shadow of the tower crane, yelling something up to the driver. He reacts to Nathan's hollered greeting by holding up a hand, and carries on yelling. I'm sure the crane driver can't hear what he's saying. I'm not keen on Mike. He's loud and full of himself and he sometimes comes into the office wearing a T-shirt identifying himself as a Chick Magnet. I don't think so.

I recognise the resident engineer too but his name escapes me. Small, wiry, fair haired and red faced, he comes galloping out of one of the site huts with an A4 hard-backed book in his hand and is breathless as he congratulates us for coming at just the right time. Mike chooses to grace us with his presence and the three of them talk at length about mixes and slumps. Now Charles has told me about such things so I act all knowledgeable but there are far more interesting things going on down in the gaping hole on my left.

The crane has hoisted up a skip of fresh concrete and it's swinging towards us. Two labourers astride the formwork grab it and jostle it and one of them jerks its base open, allowing the liquid concrete to spew out and rattle down into the cage of reinforcement. Together they give the skip a good shake, one of them raises a thumb and it soars aloft to be returned to the mixer. A third man hauls on a buzzing poker vibrator and drops its nose into the wet mass, lifts it out, drops it in again. I can't imagine what sort of sensation travels up his arms when that thing hits the steel bars in there. It sure as hell produces a ghastly screech and I must be pulling a face because Mike says, "Sets your teeth on edge, huh?"

Nathan is also watching the vibrator man. "Fingernails on the blackboard. By the way, Mike, you need to tell that guy with the poker to wear a hard hat, hey. Get someone to fetch him one."

Mike shouts with laughter and slaps his right knee with the open palm of the same hand.

"I wouldn't worry about him. That *kaffir's* a long way from being the sharpest knife. I'd be more concerned about the damage to my skip if it drops on his head!"

He sniggers, beams, waits for us to appreciate his joke. The RE has gone an even brighter red and Nathan's face is a still, expressionless shield like it always used to be. When he speaks, his tone is not expressionless – it's acid.

"Don't give me that bullshit. You *will* be concerned about damage when it's your head that rolls if there's an accident. Get the man a hat, Mike."

The foreman pouts and withdraws and we're left staring after him. Nathan catches my eye and when he speaks his tone is once more engaging.

"Let's show Tessa some of the drawings Tom. Then we should talk about the calcs for the thrust blocks and that fuel issue."

Tom, that's his name. Tom.

Tom is keen and rushes ahead of us into the timber site hut. It's like stepping into a sauna and even when he's flung open all the windows, the stagnant, soggy air doesn't move a millimetre. He distributes iced water and I rest the insides of my wrists against the glass before drinking any. Cools the blood, I was told once, but I reckon it's an urban myth or a tall tale spawned by one of my grandmothers. Half an hour of engineering drawings and bar bending schedules passes and I can confirm my interest is inversely proportional to the amount of sweat I'm producing. I can feel it trickling down my lower spine and along the insides of my arms. This isn't something a girl should admit to, but I do in the hope that the information will serve a purpose. It's not cool outside, but it's the better option.

"Bloody disgusting," Tom agrees. "At lunch times and afternoon break times when I was on the sewage treatment works site at Gwelo I used to take my book and sit inside one of the ten-fifty diameter concrete pipes we'd laid for the incoming line from the intake works. It was about ten degrees cooler than on the surface and there always seemed to be a breeze drifting through."

We down the glasses and make for the door. Nathan says, "Good one, Tom. I'd never have thought of that. Right. Come, Tessa. Let's check on progress here and then get back to Salisbury."

A pathetic waft of air lifts my hair fractionally away from my neck and stirs my blouse. The sunlight is achingly bright after the interior of the hut so I move my sunglasses down into position from the top of my head. The workforce is still busy with the concrete pour and all the men are wearing hats, including Mike.

Next to me – very close next to me, so the hairs on my forearm tell me – he reads my mind.

"Don't take any notice of that idiot, Mike. He's only been with the company a short time and at the rate he's going his time will remain short. I don't care for him and neither does Charles. Did you find the morning interesting, though? Useful?"

It was interesting, genuinely, but how to phrase it so it doesn't sound like I'm just trying to be polite? I turn a few words around in my head and catch myself staring at his body and wondering why he can't undo the buttons on his shirt a bit. He might feel cooler. I'm on the brink of saying, look, I'd like to come out here again with you, soon, so I can see how the work's progressing, when that grating, angry vibrator-hitting-steel-bar sound slots his words onto my tongue instead of my own.

"Ouch. Like fingernails down a blackboard at school. That's what you said."

The present can so easily, with one word, be shoved aside by another time, another place. It happens to me now. Blackboard. How do I link Nathan Owen with a blackboard at school? Lines. Lines we had to write.

We must all learn to be honest and admit to our mistakes.

We must consider the implications of our actions and how they might endanger others.

Ten years ago, but so like yesterday. Mr Westfield and the momentous collapse of the judges' tent. The ensuing chaos, and me staring directly into Nathan's eyes across the heads of the other children and almost hearing his thoughts:

I know you think I did it!

Before I have a chance to register what I'm doing, I've halted and reached out for his left arm. This time it's not some silly, concocted attempt to pretend he can be mine. It just happens.

"Hey! That makes me remember… You… Oh God."

He's hindered by my clinging and is by turns uncomprehending, amused, amazed and then concerned.

"What? Tessa? What's up?"

"I have a question for you. Why has neither of us, in all these years, ever once made reference to that gala? You must remember *The Gala* – capital T, capital G? The day the tent... Yes. You do, don't you?"

You. I can see that you do. The vision is dancing between us. When you draw your forearm in closer to your waist, I get pulled in with it and of course I do nothing to resist. Your voice is so soft it's like a whisper, your eyes over the top of my head.

"You know, when things went wrong in class, like someone got hit by a piece of rubber flicked from a ruler, or perhaps a stink bomb got let off or something went missing and turned up in an odd place, the teachers always suspected me. I don't know why, because I never had any such inclinations, or even thoughts about such inclinations. And I didn't care about myself enough to protest my innocence."

This isn't what I'd intended with my dredging up of the past. I wanted us to have a laugh but the memory has hurt you.

"I'm sorry."

You lower your head and search my face.

"Sorry? Why?"

"For making you remember things you might not..."

We're both trapped against each other, knowing there's so much unsaid. So much unknown. I don't understand your past fully, I'm afraid, but I do know that I understand you. You're whole to me now, not a series of disconnected, unfathomable parts and disjointed, meaningless exchanges of dialogue.

"I didn't care about myself or anyone else in those days so why would I try to make trouble? I would've had nothing to gain by playing pranks. No-one ever proved I was the culprit and usually the whole class was punished by having to write lines in detention, or whatever, just like the whole school after that gala debacle. I knew who tied the car to the table but I couldn't be arsed to do anything about it because it was nothing to me. I can't blame the teachers.

I didn't do anything to help myself, did I? Always the one no-one could figure out. It's because…"

Both of us know you're not going to finish that sentence.

"I saw you near the tent, but…"

"You didn't think I'd done it."

A statement, not a question.

"No. Even then, when you were a complete stranger to me. I couldn't imagine you doing such a thing, if you must know. When the Headmaster demanded information from anyone who had seen anything I didn't squeal."

"I know you didn't. And I was more grateful than you can imagine. I said no-one could figure me out, but you saw something nobody else did, didn't you? I mean… I don't… it's just… Well, that's what I always thought. Maybe you didn't and I was imagining it."

"No. You weren't."

For a few beats you're silent and I'm conscious of the dampness of your shirt against my forearm. You give me the gentlest of pushes and we disentangle.

"I know whodunnit if you really want to know?"

All traces of the uncomfortable recollections have been wiped from behind your eyes. There's a daring, conspiratorial twist to your mouth.

"Go on then. Who?"

"It was twin brothers who were in Standard Five at the time. Robin and Edward Napier. One of their classmates… er… oh God… no, his name escapes me but I can see him like it was yesterday… was in on the conspiracy as well and I spotted Robin and this other guy standing in front of that tent whispering. They stayed there for some minutes and there was something very shifty about the way they kept looking behind them. Edward appeared in between them and then they all scarpered. It was the mid afternoon break, wasn't it? I was all on my own and I couldn't resist a quick scout around the tent to try and find out what they'd been up to, but I was actually petrified that I would be caught so I didn't hang about. I didn't spot that they'd tied the table to that car. I wasn't on my own though, was I?"

No. You found me up there on the stand and I remember wishing myself a long, long way away from the school.

"To be honest I never saw you as the letting off stink bombs type. Although Mr Parker was. Were you there when he prepared some hydrogen sulphide on Parents' Day and placed a beaker of the stuff near the lab doors so that the gas permeated the entire corridor, or was it after you left?"

"Did he, the old reprobate? No, I don't remember that."

You're edging towards the car.

"Come on, you. Let's get some lunch."

This is turning out to be the oddest of days. We make small talk on the short journey back into Hartley. You tell me that Barry and his wife and kids, including a new baby daughter, have left for Australia, did I know? I did, I say, Gill told me last week. I can conjure up that day I met Barry for the first time. It would have been after the infamous gala, but when, amongst all these memories? Memories of the 1970s, one of Gill's many birthday parties, Barry starting National Service in the RLI. You, Nathan, there but not there, watching me watching you. And the spectre of the war – a spectre that somehow wasn't quite malevolent enough to make us realise just how far gone the situation was.

Barry survived the war, unlike so many. Unlike Julie Foster's boyfriend, who never even got to be drafted.

"A work friend of my father's emigrated with his family back in September. Dad used to call him The Android but they were good mates. Uncle Dudley and Aunty Pauline, I call them. Uncle Dudley got offered a job in Klerksdorp, which is sort of west of Jo'burg, I think. One of his daughters had a boyfriend who died in a land mine incident in the Eastern Highlands while he was still at school."

You cluck your tongue. "Senseless. Utterly senseless conflict. Lots leaving now though, like some sort of Exodus. Rats and sinking ships come to mind, although to be fair the ship hasn't actually started sinking yet."

"Lots think it will. Jess Marsh has gone. She got a provisional place at the University of Cape Town, subject to the results of her

M Levels. Did you meet her? She wants to teach maths. She was my best friend at school and I never thought we'd be separated. It's the end of an era."

"Will the last person to leave the country please turn out the lights."

You move your left hand down to the gear shift and for a crazy second I think you're going to put it on my knee. You've taken your watch off and there's a pale band on the skin of your wrist where it normally sits.

"I've heard you talk about Jess. She was the swimming champ?"

Swimming champ and academic and friend. We helped each other, learned from each other, fell out sometimes, but always knew the other was always there.

"Jess-and-Tess, we were known as. I don't mind admitting we cried like babies together the evening before she left. How stupid is that? She's only gone south of the border."

"Of course you'll see her again," you reassure me. "The world is getting smaller. Travel is easy."

True. But nothing in Africa is certain, is it? She was certain that we'd see each other again at my wedding, but I'm not going to tell you that. It's a step too far. She was bemused by my lack of comprehension, giving me what's known as a searching look.

"When you and Danny get hitched? Come on Tessa, it must have crossed your mind, surely?"

When I changed the subject I could see her thinking about dragging me back to it, but she didn't.

Your hand is still there right next to me and I tuck both of mine under my thighs to remove any possibility of me taking hold of it. Not that I would do such a thing. I babble on a bit about Jess's letters, her descriptions of the Cape coastal scenery that made me ask why she never considered a career as a travel writer, her curiosity about the mixed up, muddled up South African politics.

"We've debated the Rhodesians-never-die-they-just-fade-away-and-become-South-Africans thing at home many times, Tessa. I'm not sure why so many Rhodies are flocking Down South, to be honest. South Africa's a pariah as far as the rest of the world is concerned. Don't you think its time as the last white-ruled bastion in Africa is nearly over?"

Precisely. And it's where Danny wants to go, with me.

"What about you? You're not going to disappear Down South are you?"

My eyes flick up to your face, but you're only focussed on the road ahead. Expert horseman and expert driver and expert reader of thoughts. Your hand goes back to the wheel.

"Me? No. No chance."

Just outside Hartley there's a small, untidy roadside store. The pale blue paint is flaking off its walls in between tattered advertising posters to reveal the grey-green plaster underneath and there's a collection of mismatching, tired looking trolleys in a log-jam amongst dented railings next to the entrance.

The interior is dark after the glaring brightness of the car park, and it's busy. Shoppers are threading round and stepping over both upright and flattened cardboard stock boxes. We've arrived at shelf filling time, but most of the shelves appear to be empty. I blink, trying to accustom my eyes to the gloom and nearly bump into you at the head of an aisle.

Looking down at me over your shoulder, you ask, "Ideas for lunch?"

In here? It's not a very inspiring place if you're thinking gastronomy. We come out with a couple of packets of Willards crisps and some chocolate bars. Back in the car I declare that maybe the chocolate wasn't a sensible choice.

You watch me lick my fingers and the palm of my hand, then announce that you're still famished.

"I'll go back in and get some pork pies. Do you like them? Provided they're actually in the refrigerated section of course. If not, I'll give it a miss and eat back at the ranch."

I'm not going to sit waiting in this oven of a car, so I get out and lean against the passenger door. There's no shade; the sun's directly overhead, but, as I discovered when we left the site hut, the heat's marginally more bearable in the open. Away to the north there are ghost images of thunderclouds, just visible through the bluish haze.

Ten minutes later, handing me a Colcom pork pie in a box, you tell me, "I apologise that it's not a particularly nutritious lunch. Let's eat these on the road. No point hanging about here when we can have air conditioning."

Sometimes life throws up such simple pleasures. I get to slice your pie, crudely with the penknife from the glovebox, and hand the pieces to you. My lid is well and truly flipped.

For a while you drive and I watch the world go by without actually registering what I'm seeing. Then, just as I'm inventing a conversation I'll hold with Danny tonight on the phone that will get me out of seeing too much of him this weekend, you ask, "Are you still going out with Danny? I haven't seen him for a while."

How does this keep happening? I get elation and despair in equal measures, bombarding all regions of my head and body and respond rather stupidly, shrugging, opening and closing my mouth, studying my hands because I can't look at you. I use up a few moments by wiping the knife with a tissue from my pocket, pulling open the glove compartment and replacing the knife.

What am I supposed to say? Launch into an analysis of all that's wrong with my relationship and conclude with a jolly account of that disastrous night club affair two weeks ago? I haven't even told Gill or Jess about that debacle yet. Patching things up with Chipo in the Dunking Donut last Saturday was bad enough. I've never seen her so tongue-tied or dejected, determined to prove she'd never set out to deliberately deceive me, telling me how scared she'd been of my reaction to Paul's background. I sat there thinking, how can friends be scared of saying things to each other? Remember me and Jess and sex? We didn't know what to say to each other about that did we? The older you get, the more complicated your relationships, for sure.

Danny did try to make it up to me when he invited me to that *braaivleis* at Eric Blakey's place, but I had show jumping at Lewisham Riding School the next day. He asked me why I was refusing his invitation for Saturday when the show was on Sunday. I tried to be patient. I explained my training regime of giving each horse a couple of hours of nice steady exercise the morning before. I said, why don't we go to the *braai* later in the afternoon? But no. If he couldn't go at lunchtime he didn't want to go at all. He didn't go as far as saying my plans were a damned nuisance, but that's clearly what they were. I tried to decide if it was his intolerance or my selfishness that was the issue. I didn't come to a conclusion either way.

No reason to recite all this. I stutter some words like oh, um, yes, well, it's. Then I dry up.

"He'll be coming to the wedding?"

An age ago, when I accepted Mr and Mrs Charles Owen's formal invitation to Miss Tessa Harmand and Mr Daniel Proctor, he said of course he'd be there. It was exciting to receive the invite even though I'm chief bridesmaid and my attendance is obligatory. I assume Mr Nathan Owen, best man, was an invitation item with Miss Sherrie Fletcher.

My defensive self wants to say, "Yes, of course," but my cold-light-of-day self butts in and comes up with "I really don't know."

You don't reply. After five minutes or so, you flip the cassette in the tape deck. Jimmy Cliff and *Stand Up and Fight Back* is followed by Steve Harley pleading to someone, somewhere, to come up and see him and make him smile.

"You can't say I don't have a variety of music on my tapes," you say to me.

Smile? All I want to do is cry.

*

This hot stillness is flat and unyielding. Why do air conditioning units break down when they're most needed?

I'm not sure how much more of this I can tolerate – my clothes sticking to my skin, my hand damp against the paper as I write. I don't think I could sweat any more if I tried. I close the blinds to keep the searing glare off my paperwork but that makes the office even more claustrophobic and oven-like. This depression I can't shake off isn't helping.

I push back my chair, get up and sidle over to the window. Pulling the blinds apart a crack lets in a band of dazzling white light. Squinting, I see a few lethargic pedestrians, no traffic and a whitish sky with a couple of small, woolly clouds suspended above the south-eastern horizon.

Maybe a cold drink will do something for me. The remnants of the coffee Sylvester made for me this morning have well and truly dried on the base of my mug.

It's a bit cooler in the green-tiled corridor, and silent. The kitchenette is empty. Poor Sylvester is most likely sweating in a queue at Southerton Post Office. After I've had something to drink I'll go home because, unlike him, I'm lucky enough to get flexi-time.

The hot water doesn't seem to be working again. I'll boil some in the kettle to wash out my mug. With a glass of orange squash in my hand, I lean against the counter to wait for the battered white enamel kettle to do its thing, my brain in idle-mode, roving around the tiny room. The surfaces in here are spotless; there's not a trace of a drop of spilt tea or coffee nor a ghost of a mug ring anywhere. Sylvester must work at it twenty times a day.

Idle-mode gaze gets round to the north-facing window and takes a sharp snap back into reality-mode. The sky out there is nothing like the one I've just seen from my office. My dark mood and foreboding feelings are all out there, piled up. Squadrons of them. Tall, dense cloud masses, black with silvery crests, are billowing up into the clear sky across the field of my vision and merging together at their bases into a dark grey haze that reaches down to the horizon. They're very distant, but it's impossible to tell how fast they're travelling.

Check my watch. Three-thirty. I flick up the wall switch and the faint hissing from the kettle subsides. The water will be hot enough. A squirt of washing-up liquid and nearly-boiled water will do for now. Back in my office, I shove papers into a flat file, put that and another few files away on the shelf and gather up my bag and my holdall. The weekend has begun.

I'd better tell someone I'm going. Charles is out and said he's not coming back here today, Debbie will see me go but won't care or be bothered to pass a message on, so it will have to be you, Nathan. Honestly, I'd rather slink out without seeing you. You're inextricably linked to my miserable turmoil through no fault of your own. No choice, though.

I ease open the door to your office and poke my head around it. You're engrossed in adding up a string of numbers, punching at the buttons of a calculator with one forefinger while following the lines of figures with the other. As soon as you become aware of my presence, you glance up briefly from under your eyebrows and I get the silent message, "Hold on, I'll be with you in a sec."

I hover near the door until you jab at the equals button and exclaim, "Ah!" in a tone of deep satisfaction, then raise your eyes to me.

"It must be an omen."

"An omen…?" With black clouds matching black moods still in my mind, I leave the question trailing.

"I have added up all the prices on this monster Bill of Quantities twice in a row and got the same answer each time. It's a miracle. A sign."

It's difficult not to laugh at your awed expression.

"A sign of what, do you think?"

"A sign that, er… well… how am I supposed to know? I'm not an *nganga*."

I jerk a thumb over my shoulder. "Well I've just seen a sign. Distinctly ominous thunderclouds heading this way. I shall foretell that there will be an almighty storm in the near future. I thought I'd go now, actually, to try and beat it home. Okay?"

"Of course." Your eyes and voice are soft. "See you over the weekend?"

"Probably. At the stables. 'Bye."

I'm just closing the door when you call out, "Oh, Tessa, wait." Leaning back into the office I watch you come around from behind the desk and lean one elbow on top of a steel filing cabinet.

"This should've been said so long ago and never was, but thanks for not splitting on me after you'd seen me behaving suspiciously at that gala. I can still see you now, up there on the stands. A little blonde girl with an absolutely horrified expression and eyes boring into my brain. I did try to tell you it wasn't me."

Simultaneously we both make a fractional move towards each other and then both have second thoughts.

"It's a good thing I didn't split on you, Mr Owen, since it turns out you were innocent all the time. It still remains The Greatest Mystery That Ever Was. I'll bet old Mr Westfield still has nightmares about it."

"Mr Westfield!" you breathe, almost in wonder. "I'd forgotten his name. God, that was a long time ago. Like a past life. Well, there was always going to be a storm today I guess. It's been building up all day. Off you go then, Tess."

Out in reception, Debbie ignores me as she clatters away on her typewriter with customary speed. I reciprocate, and my eyes are drawn to the painting above her. It's been thrown into relief by the afternoon sun and I visualise the footprints of my imagination treading along the dusty road in the centre of the scene. What *does* lie around that corner? Is it the answer to my dilemma?

I turn my back on it and Debbie and get out.

Opening the door of my car releases a blast of super-heated air that hits me with physical force. I throw my bags across onto the passenger seat and slide in, gasping as my hands touch the burning, black leather steering wheel cover. I've been known to aspire to having leather upholstery in the past, but right now I'm being thankful this is linen.

Holding the wheel with finger nails only, I start the engine and ease into reverse by gripping the gear shift itself instead of placing my hand over the top of the knob, so I don't get 1-2-3-4-R branded onto my palm. I don't have the luxury of either air-con or electric controls in this one so I have to lie across the passenger seat and wind down that side window, then my own. I set all the air vents wide and join the traffic stream, laying my head back against the headrest.

The northern sky is even darker than it was fifteen minutes ago. I'm sure I'm not imaging things. The traffic is light at this time of the afternoon, so twenty minutes later I'm home, although even that was too long in this Datsun Greenhouse.

Rosie's out at her tennis club. How frighteningly energetic of her, I think as, clad in shorts and a sleeveless top, I take a glass of granadilla juice out to the patio and settle in one of the loungers. My ice tinkles satisfactorily, it's shady here, and relatively cool in a faint breeze that's found its way under the eaves.

"Are you all right, dear?" Mum calls from within the house. "You're very quiet."

"I'm fine thanks. Just hot," I shout back, and close my eyes.

*

On such still air, the storm takes its time coming. Dad and Rosie come home in turn and it's only when the red-gold sun has sunk below the horizon and the daylight is fading with customary swiftness that the first low rumbles of thunder reach out from the north like a bass note to the shrill song of the cicadas. After sunset, the indirect heat is pleasantly warm and enveloping and I stay outside until the mosquitoes emerge, whining for my blood in the enclosing dusk.

The grumbling voice of the storm is, for a long time, infrequent and muted, although lightning plays continually at the cloud bases. As the evening wears on the thunder rolls begin to follow each lightning dagger with an ever-diminishing time delay, booming endlessly into the distance.

"Are you sure you're all right?" Mum persists again later.

"Yes," I lie again.

What can I say? She's so locked into the idea that her daughter is happy with her perfect boyfriend that the concept of any real conflict in the relationship will be beyond her. She has no clue that I knew this has been coming; I've never told her of any of my doubts, any of the tensions. She won't believe I'm learning to accept the fact that my first serious romance is simply fading away. She'll try to reassure me, tell me that we'll get over it. She's delighted with him and so should I be.

So what do I do? If I let Danny go I'll have no-one, and to cap it all I've fallen prey to a ludicrous crush on someone I can never have. Am I doomed to an embittered spinsterhood, forever mourning lost love? The Miss Havisham of Salisbury?

Over and over in my head, like a stuck record, I keep telling myself I've known Nathan Owen for a little over ten years. Why do I now suddenly think I'm in love with him?

I'm not. It's just that – a ludicrous crush.

In bed, I snuggle into the pillow and relax, but sleep won't come. The storm is still grumbling away, threatening but never any closer. Perhaps it will go away. A cooler breath of wind feels its way through my window into the warm stillness. Fitful at first, the breath becomes a steady flow that rustles the leaves of the trees and then, during a brief lull, I hear the first large raindrops seep from sodden clouds and splash onto the earth.

It goes on for a while; intermittent plops on the roof tiles and in the trees outside. Then it all ceases and after a few minutes the cicadas tentatively start up their shrilling again. With one eye I watch the merest hint of a breeze caress the curtains. I close the eye and all is peaceful.

Next second I'm upright in bed, clutching the sheet, heart pounding, the blinding flash and the single whiplash of lightning and thunder together gone before I even open my eyes. There's a hissing roar from outside. The curtains billow like sails and through the gap the trees that should be visible at the edge of the garden have dissolved behind a misty veil.

Fall out of bed, slam the window shut against the deluge. From the rest of the household, voices, footsteps, metallic banging, laughing, swearing.

At each thunderclap the rain intensifies as if the violent movement of air has squeezed the clouds like sponges. A new sound; the gurgling and splashing of the rainwater pouring through the downpipes from the roof gutters onto the concrete moulds before being channelled away to the stormwater pipes. Together in Mum and Dad's bedroom we watch pools of water forming on the lawn and in the flower beds. The drainage ditches each side of the road will fill and become miniature raging torrents, pouring through the culverts and emptying into the natural watercourses down on the *vlei*.

It passes. Back in bed, I can't believe the drop in temperature and haul the blanket back up over me. Cleo materialises out of the darkness and purrs and kneads next to my shoulders. She plonks down and yawns expansively, extending one paw to sink her claws into the blanket. The deluge has eased to a drizzle, leaving the spluttering gurgle of the drainpipes that much louder. The ripping brilliance of the lightning has died to a soft flicker, only occasionally followed by a rumble.

*

How long have I been asleep? Cleo has gone. I slide out of bed and re-open the window, setting it as wide as it will go. There's a fresh smell and the drizzle has stopped, but something's still dripping somewhere outside. A car swishes past in the road. The omen has run its course and my mind is as clear as the sky, which is now awash with bright stars after the last of the tattered clouds has trailed away.

SATURDAY 6TH DECEMBER 1980

She can't believe what I've done.

"What, temporarily or permanently? Tessa, my love, have you thought carefully about this?"

Now why would I do that? I can't come up with an answer to the latter question so I stick with the former.

"Permanently, I reckon."

She's struggling for words. "Well. Well, he's clearly upset. He did leave in a great hurry. I've never seen him drive like that. He must be hurt. I think… I want you to… You must… Oh, Tessa."

Then she says, "He hasn't… well… I mean… tried to put… er… pressure on you to do… well… something you'd rather not?"

Oh Mother Dear, if only you knew. If only you knew the thoughts the daughter you brought up to be chaste has been having about someone else. But you don't, and I'm not telling.

Rosie's still lurking outside the door. She'll be more than a bit interested in my reply to this one, so when I say, no, not in the slightest, not ever, I can feel her disappointment. What's eating both of them, of course, is the fact that I didn't consult with, or confide in, either of them before doing what I did.

"It's not working with me and the horses. He's not been happy about it for some time now. He feels I should be more committed to him and his plans, but I am, and always will be, committed to my horses."

Her face says everything she feels about that and yeah, I know. It's all very well for me as a horse-mad girl/teenager but what about when I'm married and have a family, blah, blah, blah?

Well, what about it?

It's not just the horses of course, but that's the simplest reason.

There are people who need to lay out all their affairs of the heart before family and friends and seek guidance/support/approval. I'm learning that I'm not one of them. I didn't need any help to make the decision I made last night. I also know I don't want to be married to Danny or have his children and it's just such an awful, awful, sad thing to know. He's a gem, and I want to be his friend, but I don't want to marry him.

"Don't think it was easy, Mum. I psyched myself up for several hours before calling him to come over. When he arrived, I wavered and panicked and we sat on the patio and chatted in such a normal way, and it was all exactly as it had been before. I very nearly didn't tell him I wanted to end it. I nearly chickened out."

My heart, which had been hammering behind my ribs when I started on my speech, threatened to stop altogether when he all but broke down in front of me. All my planned setting out of my logical reasons fell in tattered shreds around me.

"He pleaded with me. He said he was prepared to work on it. And I was hard. I had to be hard. I'm sorry."

I'm apologising to them when I should be apologising to him.

FRIDAY 19TH DECEMBER 1980

"That's it. Everything's done. Now all we have to do is mark time until tomorrow."

I'm not sure if she's heard me. She's unwrapping tissue paper from her pearly shoes and setting them out next to the wardrobe. Then she does mine, then Sally's bronze satin ballet pumps.

Tomorrow. A day I've looked forward to for so long, am still looking forward to, am also now dismally sad about because I was going to share it with Danny and now I have no partner.

"Did Rosie get her new outfit?" She sits back on her heels to admire the row of shoes. Her face really shows how the weight's dropped off her in these last few weeks; no wonder the dress had to be taken in a couple of inches. It's a massive upheaval for her and I can't imagine what it's like. Her eyes are glowing though. She's living a dream.

"She did. And Mum. It was a successful Shopping Day for the three Harmand women. We set out early, took lunch at Barbour's and only got home at about five. We treated Dad to a cat-walk parade and he made all sorts of impressed noises, but he never asked exactly how much money had been spent, I noticed."

"Gilly!"

Moira, calling along the passageway. "Nathan's on the phone. You coming?"

She rolls over and gets to her feet in one movement. I follow her to the lounge and sit watching TV with Charles while she gets the low-down on how her horses travelled out to the farm.

I'm not taking in what's on TV. Where's Sherrie? Is she out at the van Rooyens' farm with him and Piet? Or will she be coming with us tomorrow? I don't know which would be worse. Actually, what *will* be worse is tomorrow night when I stay over at the farm. And Nathan. And Sherrie. They might be in the room next to mine. Mrs van Rooyen's probably expecting me and Danny to be together in the same room; she won't be thinking I'll be on my own.

Well, I'll go home with Mum and Dad in fact. That's a better plan.

"They're fine," Gill says as she replaces the receiver. "Star Point sweated up a bit in the lorry but he was calm when they took him out and Foxy and Leander Bay were cool as cucumbers. Good."

That's good news, considering Foxy's condition and how jittery she's been lately. Maybe her hormones have settled down.

Charles excuses himself and heads for his office. Gill leaps up and grabs the handset he left on the oak side table by his chair.

"Here," she says, grinning. "Let's play with the VCR a bit. You haven't seen it work, have you? Are your folks going to get one?"

"I'm sure Dad would rather chew his arm off than pay such exorbitant customs duties. He'd have to import a new TV too. But, you never know. Go on then, show me."

I pour us each another glass of wine and we huddle on the carpet together in front of the TV.

"Now, on here – in here, even – is last night's news broadcast, right?" Gill holds up a cassette that looks a bit like an audio cassette but much larger. She turns it over in her hands, right in front of my face, like a magician about to perform a disappearing trick. "Watch carefully. You hold the tape like this, see? Then you insert it into the slot. There! Now you press the 'Play' button on the remote control and… *Voilà!* That's last night's news."

It is too. She's eyeing me to make sure I'm impressed. And I am. Without waiting for the drumbeat ZTV news theme to finish, I attempt to take the handset from her.

"Here, let me try."

"No, no! Wait! There's more." The tape is stopped, restarted, fast-forwarded and rewound a couple of times. "Cool, huh?" she asks, smug. "Then, see, you eject it."

She jabs a button and it slides back out. She eases it into her hand and holds it out.

"This way?" I line it up with the slot and the flap on the front of the VCR clacks open. Machinery whirs and the tape is taken from me as though by an unseen hand. It vanishes and the flap drops down over the opening.

I snatch my hand away like I've been bitten. Gill sniggers and nods encouragingly. "Go on. Here." She offers me the handset.

When Charles returns some twenty minutes later he stares at us clinging to each other in helpless hysterics in front of the television, but he's forced to wait several more before either of us can speak.

"You tell him," Gill prompts, before flopping down on her back and continuing her hysterics with one hand over her eyes.

"I just had this mental image of not being quick enough to let go of the tape and being sucked into the machine behind it. Then I could imagine my face appearing on the screen."

"Yes, Tess darling." Charles nods, his eyes on the two empty wine bottles on the coffee table. "Interesting theory. And it's a good thing that's the last of my wine."

SATURDAY 20TH DECEMBER 1980

Gill is seated on the edge of the patio in the new morning air, in solitary contemplation.

I drag one of the wrought-iron chairs over to her and perch on it. After a few minutes she says, "It's so strange. I can't believe I'm moving out today. I've lived here all my life. Or it seems like all my life. We moved here when Annabelle and Nathan came to live with us. I've known this house and garden and the paddocks in every season, in every mood, at every time of day."

The melancholy that was plaguing me all last night deepens. As she's just said, Gill Owen has always been here, at Makuti Park. She went away for a little while once, but she came back. We've schooled and hacked our horses together, she's been a sounding board for all my ideas and an unequalled instructor. After this day, me and the horses will be on our own, with Gill van Rooyen living more than thirty miles away.

For no clear reason, I'm prompted to tell her I've broken up with Danny. Her eyes widen in shock and I'm already mentally cringing from the inevitable questions that will aggravate the raw wound.

"Why didn't you tell me before? I never knew you had a problem like that."

Her voice is full of accusation. But mercifully, here comes Moira, stepping through the French doors and bearing a wicker bowl of fresh fruit. She sits next to us and starts oozing all her ideas on planning the morning.

The forecast is good; it promises to be clear and hot. The freelance hairdresser arrives just after ten with ribbons, flowers and heated curlers. The hours vanish from under us and lunchtime comes and goes, but none of us want to eat. Amai is offended, but she's got to get herself ready anyway and we only get a couple of pointed sniffs from her.

An enthusiastic photographer in a floral shirt with a large collar materialises in our midst. He arranges bride, bridesmaids, bride's parents and Amai in various permutations against a background of Cypress trees, chosen as a contrast to Gill's ivory and the bronze of us bridesmaids. Earlier, the shadows from these trees were reaching out to touch the far side of the garden, seeking to meet the base of the hedge opposite, but by now they've all but disappeared into themselves. The bronze satin of my dress gleams alternately copper and silver in the sunshine and I spend some moments turning myself and shifting the skirt around to watch the colours. My posy of roses, marigolds and carnations – cream, orange and yellow – is dainty and light to carry. I'm starting to enjoy myself a little.

One o'clock. Moira is whisked away to the farm in her marigold-coloured dress by Sally's parents. Their car vanishes from sight and simultaneously George pulls into the parking area next to the house in his olive green Peugeot 404 station wagon. Justice, Matthew and Lazarus are squeezed together in the back seat. The car's been waxed and polished to within an inch of its life since I last saw it and they all look a treat in their suits. George stands to attention beside the car and watches Amai hugging Gill and dabbing at her eyes with her large white handkerchief for some minutes before deciding he's had enough of these nattering, weeping women.

"Come now! *Uyai!* The car is waiting!"

Amai arranges her voluminous scarlet dress of frills and basques and puffed sleeves around her in the passenger seat and George gives us all a salute before sliding in behind the wheel.

"No picking up any stray passengers in this gleaming pirate-taxi of yours, eh?" Charles calls, winking at me and Gill. "I don't care how much they pay you. There won't be enough food for them."

George can't believe his ears.

"This car is *not* a pirate-taxi, Mr Owen. It is too good."

Then he realises he's having his leg pulled and drives away chuckling.

The four of us are left by the kitchen door.

"Well." Gill readjusts her lace veil for the fiftieth time. "This is it. All we need now is our own set of wheels."

There's a dull thud in me and I'm brought back to my hollow reality. Piet is at the farm, and his partner – the bride – is about to set out to join him. Nathan is at the farm as well and his partner – Sherrie – is probably already there. I guess I should submit to the Fate that's provided me with this opportunity to ask the burning question I've been unable to so far.

I pretend to readjust Gill's veil for the fifty-first time, reassure her that they'll be here soon I'm sure, and by the way, how is Sherrie getting to the farm?

It comes out all distressed and uptight. I've betrayed myself. But no, Gill has turned her attention to Sally's dress now and appears to have taken it as a perfectly straightforward query.

"How is? Who? Oh, *Sherrie*? Miss Bossy-Boots? Oh no, she's not coming. Nathan told me on Thursday she'd declined the invitation at short notice. Tessa, I was shocked I have to tell you. I don't know what's happened and he's evaded all my questions. I'll get it out of him eventually I guess. And Tammy's in the States of course so I haven't had a chance to really probe it with her. I feel so bad for him… Oh, look, Tess, Sally, Dad… Here it comes!"

It's a wide, white Bentley and it's purring up the driveway.

I'm not even that keen on Bentleys, but its appearance is simultaneous with a sensation in me that's similar, I suspect, to that of having one's veins drained of blood and refilled with champagne. Filled to the brim with the craziest sense of frenzied excitement, I shriek, "Come! Quickly! We're going!"

I'm back in the wedding. Oh boy, am I back in the wedding!

Everything is beautiful. The whole world is the right way up. Colours are brighter and images are sharper than they were just ten minutes ago and I need to shout and wave at everyone in this amazing world – everyone we see along the way in a car or on a bicycle or on foot. I also need to sing *I Can See Clearly Now*, but I just sit in the back seat of the Bentley and grin so as not to ruin Gill's day with the knowledge that her chief bridesmaid is a raving lunatic.

I've travelled this route out of Salisbury dozens of times but today I watch each scene go by in the grip of a fantasy that I've just arrived from a foreign land and am seeing it all for the first time, taking in every detail of every tree, rock, farm field and track. I don't remember the van Rooyens' garden being so fabulous, or such a riot of colour and of light and shade. In fact, thinking back to the day when I first rode Encore, I can picture only a typically drab farmstead garden with that slightly rebellious appearance that comes when the plant kingdom begins to overcome man's feeble attempts at control. Now it's thick with coloured blossoms, spewing over and around a neatly trimmed, brilliant green lawn that's randomly studded with mature msasa trees. I genuinely don't remember the msasa trees at all.

Morning glory and honeysuckle cover the long front verandah in purple and cream, while both gold and red bougainvillea have exploded over the roof ridge to meet them.

The area immediately inside the security gates resembles a second-hand car dealer's yard on account of the twenty-odd vehicles parked haphazardly along the edges of the driveway and over part of the lawn. There's not a soul to be seen anywhere. It's a peaceful and charming setting and only the diamond mesh fence and the stout gates, although wide open, serve as an ugly memorial to the last bloody decade.

The Bentley rolls in through the gates on cue at twenty-nine minutes past two and halts some distance from the house. The floral photographer skips into view from wherever he's been lurking and sets Charles and Gill up for a pose on the verandah steps, then gets a couple of shots of all four of us. There is no sound from within the house but I'm sure I can make out Amai's red frills hovering in the comparative darkness near the doorway.

There's a moment for me to smooth a few creases in the back panel of Gill's dress before the first strains of the Bridal March start up to herald our arrival. It sounds like it's live, so they did manage to squeeze an organ in there for Aunty Aileen to play. I've no idea who Aunty Aileen is, but she's good. The verandah, garden flowers and even the doorway itself recede, detached and remote, while the aisle formed between the rows of seated guests in the long living room becomes sharply focussed; ranks of timber folding chairs have turned the farmhouse lounge into a temporary chapel. Beyond the figures of Gill and Charles is an Anglican vicar robed in white, smiling into his open Bible and facing him, a little to his left, is Piet. And you.

Piet's back view is tense and exudes nervous anticipation. Beside him, and in contrast, your pose is relaxed, casually more on the left leg than the right. We process down the aisle to turned heads and eyes curious to appraise Gill in her layers of satin and lace. Last to turn, you give the bride a barely perceptible nod, like you're acknowledging your own proud approval.

I'm adjusting to the dimmer light now. There's Mum and Dad, and there's Rosie, in her linen suit of cream and burgundy. She raises an elegantly gloved hand in greeting.

We've almost reached the vicar, who has his back to the stone fireplace. Piet shuffles sideways a little to line up with Gill and Charles. You take your eyes from Gill and we make contact. In that devastating smile I know I'm included in the same approval.

My world still remains sharper and clearer, like all my senses have been refined. Standing close to Gill, I feel the breath in her body as she recites her vows in a timid and wondering voice; the voices behind me raised in *Morning Has Broken* and *Amazing Grace* are rich and enveloping, if slightly out of tune. The bride's delicate perfume mingles with mine and with Piet's after-shave from the other side, I can nearly taste the prepared buffet food, even though the aromas have had to stray through a closed door and along a corridor and the rings that you pass across to the vicar are the brightest gold. And above all I feel you, so divinely handsome in your dark suit, as though neither Gill nor Piet are present.

It's done. The vicar leads Man and Wife into the high-ceilinged dining room adjacent to sign the register and we, the entourage, follow. Moira holds Piet's father's arm to assist his walking; Charles and Piet's mum, Maryna, are whispering together. Viewed through the open floor to ceiling window, the blue Hunyani range dominates the horizon like the back of some great serpent, basking in the warmth. Not a breath of wind stirs the msasas. In spite of the low murmur of the vicar's voice and the scratching of the fountain pen, I feel the stillness out there in the garden. A dove coos sleepily from somewhere – that gentle, peaceful sound that can recreate the African Highveld in the mind whenever it's heard.

"That's all, folks!" calls the vicar and there's a pitch invasion of guests to engulf the bride and groom like a tide. This tide sweeps all of us out over the verandah and onto the lawn. Mum's arm is around me on one side and Rosie's going on about heavenly dresses and gorgeous flowers from the other, and then Charles is grabbing my hand, "Tess, love – photos. Photos! Come, you're needed over here sweetheart."

I'm looking back over my shoulder at my sister as I trip after him. When did she get so grown up, so chic, with her new hat tipped at just the right angle over her dark curls, her short gloves, her heels and the pearls at her throat?

The photographing goes on a bit.

"My cheeks are aching from all this smiling," Gill hisses at me through this same smile and we start giggling and then have to compose ourselves again. "Will this photographer never be satisfied? How many rolls of film did he bring?"

He finally lets us go after trying to get all fifty guests in one shot. Maybe he's realised he's competing with the buffet by now.

*

Apart from that one gin and tonic, I've avoided drinking any alcohol so far because I knew the champagne would start flowing soon enough, and when it did, it was in magnums, no less. I feel Charles's South African business connections have been working behind the scenes here somewhere.

A surreptitious sip is necessary here, although Piet's only just started on his speech, to try and take the level down slightly or I'll spill it and look incompetent, or drunk. The waiters have clearly had no instructions to spare any. He was good though, the guy who filled my flute to the brim. He managed to leave only the merest ring of bubbles, despite having poured it all in one go. I wonder where Maryna hired them from?

Poor Piet's not letting any time-honoured bridegroom tradition down and the vibe pulsing the room is painfully sympathetic. If he has a point he's trying to get to it's not obvious, but he's made certain all here present know just what a lucky man he is etc, etc, around much throat clearing, repeated use of such fundamental words as um, er and ah and with an apparent fascination for the small card on the table bearing his name. In fact he's picked this up, turned it over and replaced it five times during his ordeal. And naturally, in accordance with tradition, he gets heckled into silence by discordant strains of *Why was he born so boo-tee-full?*

Fire hydrant red, he yields to Charles and turns his attention to his wine glass and to cuddling Gill.

Charles, of course, has no such public speaking hang ups and immediately starts sending his audience up and down the emotional scale with his anecdotes of Gill's childhood. Where we were all keen for Piet to finish, primarily to save him from further suffering, we now want Charles to carry on. He's toasting all and sundry and the level in my flute is dropping satisfactorily. To applause and cheers he finally sits and the formalities are over. Or not. Charles is saying, "And now, dearly beloved, I hand you over to the best man of them all."

You were the boy who once wouldn't talk to anyone. Now you've taken off your jacket and tie and opened your ivory shirt at the neck and are standing up in front of an audience, eyes only occasionally flicking to the partly folded sheet of A5 paper you hold. No hesitation, no ums, no ahs. I watch you, loving the way you know you've got all the attention and that everyone wants to keep giving it to you.

Gill's choice of husband, Piet's friendship and the hospitality of the van Rooyens for holding the wedding at their farm all get praise. The vicar and the ceremony get a mention. You introduce yourself and say that those who know you will also know you're Charles's nephew.

"But he adopted me and I grew up in his care. I regard him and Moira as my father and mother and this gorgeous lady I'm so happy to share this day with is, to me, my sister. She has been for as long as I can remember and I hope with all my heart that she thinks of me as a brother. We've grown up together, and I honestly can't imagine what I'd be or where I'd be if it wasn't for her and the best parents in the world."

They're loving this – there's much aaahing and nudging. Gill is seriously threatening her mascara with a paper serviette and Moira is rummaging in her clutch bag with some urgency. Charles doesn't seem to be able to look anywhere except at the uplighter on the wall next to him. Megan once said of Charles, he just *is*, and here, now, so are you. You're not showing off, you're not imagining yourself superior to anyone else in this room, you just are you. You are Charles's son.

"So while the bridegroom is obliged to thank guests and above all his new wife, and the bride's father is obliged to tell embarrassing stories about his daughter, the best man is obliged to introduce and thank the bridesmaids. So here, next to me, we have the delightful Sally, who is Piet's niece. Sally will be starting senior school next year at Oriel Girls' School and she loves ballet and is very excited that she will soon be learning – what was it, Sally? Pointing?"

Sally giggles up at him, nearly as red as Piet. "Pointe work, silly!"

"Ah, pointe work. That's standing on your toes to the rest of us. Sounds painful. Sally has also told me today that although she's only twelve now she wants to have a dress just like Gill's when she gets married. Seriously though, Sal, twelve or even thirteen is really a bit too young to get married so perhaps you'd better stand well clear of Gill when she hurls her bouquet into the throng later."

You wait for the laughter to subside, now focussed on me.

"And over there, we have Gill's chief bridesmaid. The very lovely Tessa is not only one of Gill's best friends but is one of our family as well. Gill and Tessa have been such a part of my existence and a part of the fabric of Makuti Park for so long that I think of them as a single unit – 'G&T.'"

More laughter. Gill is delighted and waves one hand at him, blows me a kiss with the other. I can't respond. I just smile like I'm well composed or something and like I was fully expecting to hear this. G&T? You surprise me more every day. I wonder if I look as stupefied as I feel.

After a pause in which, for the first time, you appear to have lost your place in your notes, "Given that G&T is a creature that wears only jodhpurs and T-shirts and generally always has a couple of horses attached to it, I have to say they've both scrubbed up magnificently today. I've already said how stunning my sister is, and I have to admit that my lady Tessa is quite breath-taking in satin and flowers."

Gill nearly drops her flute and my attention is snatched by her suddenly saucer-like eyes. I see them coming round to me in time and use one of Charles's uplighters as an avoidance tactic. Another swig of champagne. Don't choke, don't spill it and above all, don't giggle.

The audience is clapping again as you clear your throat and announce that you have a gift for each of us.

Sally is called upon. She leaps to her feet, has a brief altercation with her chair, and gives you a pretty bob curtsey. As she sits down clutching her small present, her little face is a picture of the agony of restraint as she resists the urge to tear the paper open immediately.

Now you're beckoning to me and I've got to do something. I abandon the uplighter, extricate myself from behind the table with more grace than Sally, float across the front of it to face you and, recklessly, sweep into an extravagant curtsey that would surely be more than acceptable in a Viennese ballroom. Thank God I don't fall over. You press a similar, paper-wrapped box into my hands. I don't look at you. In fact I can barely get my thank-you out and think, fool, now you've ruined the moment and he'll think you don't care a toss.

Some guests applaud, but the collective attention has wandered and moved on. Most of these people have never seen me before and have never known this best man other than how he appears to them now. They enjoyed the speech but it was, after all, just a best man's speech and they've cheerfully had enough of the talking. There's a good deal of shuffling, chatting, laughing. No-one is paying me any attention. Back in my chair I start scratching at the wrapping paper under the table, peeling it back to reveal a white jeweller's box. Inside is a small, oval, gold pendant, set with a deep blue stone and hung on a delicate gold chain. You startle me by saying over my shoulder, "It's a sapphire. Do you like it?"

I smile up at you and I know that you chose it and why.

"My birthstone. It's so pretty. I love it. Thank you."

I touch the twisted plain gold rope necklace I'm wearing and then the neckline of my dress. It's probably just about the right depth for the pendant.

"I'd like to put it on now, I guess."

When you point at the back of my neck and incline your head in query, my brain spins around and gasps, yes, that's exactly what I wanted you to do.

"Oh please. I can put this chain in the box."

Your fingers move my hair aside to fiddle with the clasp and I have to seek out that bloody light fitting on the wall again because if I shut my eyes, which is what my tingling spine is telling me to do, I'll topple off the chair. I really am having a moment and it's almost unbearable. Your proximity as you reach forward to coil my plain gold chain into the cotton wool in the white box and take the sapphire pendant from my palm is sending my body into a frenzy.

"Perfect," you say, and at that second someone sets *In the Navy* going on a record player outside and I spot Gill bearing down on us on a desperate mission. But she gets thwarted, intercepted by Piet and a rotund and jovial uncle of his and is compelled, very reluctantly, to change direction. Her head's over her shoulder facing me but I pretend I haven't seen her.

We follow, though, onto the verandah, which is big enough to be turned into a decent dance floor. Strings of multi-coloured bulbs I never noticed when we arrived are draped around the intricate patterns of the wrought-iron *broekie* lace eaves. Their spectrum of light pools is just beginning to be visible in the darkening evening.

"Wine?" you ask, and we do a co-ordinated about turn and head back to the kitchen where one of the hired waiters has assumed the role of bar tender. While we're waiting for him to pour two glasses of Chardonnay, you roll up your sleeves to treat me to an overview of those forearms. It follows naturally that we remain side by side to wander back out into the warm, still night and over to the far end of the verandah and that you seem to assume I'll do so. The frenzy's subsided to a pleasurable buzz that I'm more than happy to keep stoked up. We both lean on the iron balustrade facing the darkening garden, wine glasses in hand.

"You *are* on your own today then? I couldn't figure out if you weren't sure yourself, or if you really knew he wouldn't be here."

No need to clarify who 'he' is. I sip at the wine and lick my lips. You must know I'll have the same question for you very shortly.

"I won't give up my horses for him and it's become a source of conflict. I'm very sorry about it but not enough to make me try and resolve it."

That's what I've said to everyone so far and, as with everyone else, I stop short of asking if you think I'm being selfish.

The answer, of course, lies in my heart – or rather, where Danny sits in my heart.

It's no surprise when you answer the very question I've just not asked you.

"I think we're all capable of, and willing to, making sacrifices for people we love but at the same time we should have a right to expect sacrifices from them also. We're all selfish to a point. The question is, do you mind that you're looking after your own interests and not his?"

That is exactly it.

"I don't love him, if that's what you mean. Well, I love him in a way – we had a great time together and he's a good person – but not like that."

The relief of saying those words instead of thinking them is a physical thing. I have no need of excuses or explanations. I've simply fallen out of love and it doesn't seem so awful now that I've made this admission. There's no going back. It can't have really been love in the first place then, can it?

Nothing is said for a while and we sip wine. I want to lift the mood, so I launch into a description of the day I came here with Gill and Rosie to try Encore, pointing out the direction of the stables, relating my first impressions of Piet.

"It was Rosie who noticed the apparent – I don't know – vibes, I suppose, between him and Gill. I was so wrapped up with my thoughts about horses I was quite oblivious to everything else. Typical, really."

"You and your sister are not alike then?"

"No! I love her to bits of course, but she's so… so *conventional*. You know – make-up, fashion, pop charts, boys, nail varnish, hair styles. Following the flock with dedication. And it's not that I don't want to be like her. Sometimes I do. I just never think about it. I'm probably what's classed as an eccentric."

"Not at all. It's you, and it's what makes you interesting."

Then you put in this wonderfully comical back-track, apologising for cheesiness, protesting that you didn't mean it like that at all, flustered and mortified, urgently scanning me for signs of indignation or scorn, looking just as comically relieved when you realise there's none.

"Interesting? What, like a previously undiscovered species or a collected sample of something?"

"Well yes, but far more so."

The arm next to me is lifted from the balustrade and I'm ready for it when it goes around my shoulders, in serious danger of bursting into floods of tears with relief. I can sense your uncertainty, your desperate hope that I'm not going to react badly, pull away or slap you across the face. A desperate hope that you've done the right thing. And I feel you sigh as I put my head back against your arm, close my eyes and shift my weight into the warmth of your body.

"I'm not seeing Sherrie any more, if that's what you're thinking," you say in a barely audible voice over the top of my head.

Of course that was my question. But I knew the answer. Because you wouldn't be doing this if she was still in the frame.

SUNDAY 21ST DECEMBER 1980

What snapped me out of my coma? Probably the birds. It'll be their dawn calls, as bright and urgent as my entire nervous system is now, which has leaped from nothingness to full alert in one. It's a first for a girl who always thought four-thirty in the morning was the stuff of myths.

When I went to bed at twenty-past twelve I thought I'd never sleep again. That seems like about two seconds ago, so I must have gone out well and truly. Odd.

I roll over onto my back and stare at the white ceiling, giving dedicated consideration to the intriguing notion that I could relive the whole of yesterday word by word, action by action if I really put my mind to it.

Last night. On the verandah, with his arm around me. Our talk drifted here and there. We talked of nothing and everything, like never before. During that time I had no idea what was going on behind us; the party whirled on in another world. The nothing subjects I don't recall in detail – weather, farm sounds in the night, the taste of the wine, a bit of politics I guess. The everything subjects were the conversations we should have had over the years, but haven't. Family, friends and life. Gill and Piet, Charles and Moira. My parents and Rosie. Amai and George. Danny and Sherrie and the reasons why. Sherrie, who asked him out, was full of fun, piqued his curiosity and ego by telling him she'd long had her eye on him and with whom he'd hoped he could start a steady relationship. Sherrie, who, after only a few weeks, irritated and needled and alarmed with her bossiness and presumptuousness. Sherrie, whose mother had been persuaded to teach him to dance, with a very specific aim in mind. Sherrie, who had to be told about ten days ago, like Danny, that it was not working.

Tears, highly charged with a flood of so many emotions, force me to squeeze my eyelids down, and they run across my cheeks. It was the hope that I was single that prompted him to take the chance and let Sherrie go. I let Danny go with no such spark of hope to make it justifiable, but he took a gamble for me. He told me he felt like a complete shit for doing it to her, although he knew it would've ended anyway, and then he spent Friday dreading that Danny would turn up with me at the wedding. So then I just had to let him know that *I'd* been dreading seeing Sherrie with *him*, and… oh God, remember how he reacted? That was when he asked me to be his date for the rest of the evening and I swear he was still worrying that even if I said yes I'd then forget all about it and him by the next day. And that was when Tessa here took *her* gamble and kissed him on the mouth and said some rubbish about the best man and chief bridesmaid being supposed to pair up but then got down to business and told him she was perfectly happy to keep him if he'd have her.

And then he asked me, in the sort of voice you use when you're struggling to combat emotion, if I realised how happy I'd just made him. He wondered what I thought of him, he asked, and what I'd always thought of him. He said, "We've known each other for a long time now. You've always been around. If I'm honest with myself, I've always known you've always been around. I haven't a clue how you feel about me."

I showed him how I feel and, I'm so sorry Danny, but your kiss never, ever electrocuted me like that or made me imagine things I didn't know I was capable of imagining. It just seemed right that we left the verandah rail then and abandoned the wine glasses somewhere and got into the party proper. Our first dance. *Everybody's Gotta Learn Sometime*. Him, offering me his arms and me stepping straight into them and resting my cheek against his shoulder, grinning all to myself like a village idiot. Rosie, cornering me afterwards and demanding to know why I hadn't told her what I'd been plotting.

"But I didn't plot anything," I protested, perhaps a touch too loudly.

"Yeah, right," she said. "Well Mum's going to want explanations, I warn you. She's still hurting about you breaking up with Dan. She couldn't hide the fact that she was bothered that you weren't just dancing and having a nice time, but that you'd pulled and were snogging. I told her not to be stupid. I said, 'Come on Mother, you know she's known him for bloody years!' When I asked her if she thought he looks a bit like a young Bryan Ferry and she went, 'Who's that? One of the boys at the tennis club? I don't recall him.' God, she really needs to be dragged out of the fifties."

Bryan Ferry? Maybe. A bit.

And then Gill, deliberately cheating tradition and chucking her bouquet directly at my face. She'd been beside herself to try and get me alone, or Nathan presumably, so she could interrogate either one of us or both but never managed to make it happen. But the bouquet got intercepted in mid-air by a middle-aged relation of Piet's with a daring leap that would've put a Dynamos goalkeeper to shame. Gill and Piet had to leave pretty much immediately after that, and Rosie cornered me again to extract a pledge from me to ask Gill where she got those cream-coloured jeans. She did look divine in them, with the pink and cream checked shirt and the brown leather moccasins and her golden ringlets caught in a brown ribbon.

It's nearly five. Their flight is at eight so they'll be getting up as well.

There's a faint light behind the sunfilter curtains now; it's the longest day today. I roll out of bed and part the curtains to listen to the noises that are beginning to compete with the birds. From the direction of what I assume to be the milking sheds comes the insistent lowing of impatient Frieslands, the clanking of iron handles against iron buckets, the shouts of the milkers calling to each other and to their animals, and then the unmistakeable sound of a horse snorting and the dull crack as a hoof is banged on a stable door in expectation of breakfast. Somewhere a diesel engine fires up, splutters and then runs smoothly. Over it come more shouts and the screeching of gate hinges.

I open my overnight bag and pull on shorts, a loose blouse, socks and tackies. I start to drag my brush through my hair, but then I stop and touch the necklace he gave me, where it's lying on the old fashioned dressing table alongside my earrings and my gold signet ring. I pick it up and pass it around the back of my neck, fasten the clasp in front and then twizzle it to bring the pendant back round to my throat. It's like I can see myself doing it but with someone else's eyes. I did this last night as well, when undressing and extracting the flowers from my hair, watching myself but deliberately avoiding trying to place an identity on this detached eye. The eye is there again this morning and it watches me put in the earrings and slide the ring onto the third finger of my right hand.

The homestead is silent. The living and dining areas are still strewn with debris from the wedding – a confused shambles of full ashtrays, empty glasses, half-full bottles, confetti and bits of flowers. It was a good party.

The French doors leading to the verandah are already open. An unknown and earlier riser than me has passed through here, into the perfectly still, fresh and cool garden air. Apart from a few very distant cloud piles to the north-west, pale pink at their tops in the rapidly lightening dawn, the sky is clear. It has that luminous blue quality that promises light and yet is still sprinkled with stars. It's known as Nautical Twilight, Uncle Dudley once told us.

A small breeze sneaks in and is gone almost as rapidly. It brings me warm smells. Animal smells, wood smoke and fodder crops. I'm not sticking around here. I'm going to go and find out what makes a farm tick so early in the morning and I'm hoping I'll find him.

It's strange retracing my steps from the day I met Encore and Piet. Strange that I've ended up back here after leaving with Gill and Rosie, all wrapped up in my horsey thoughts, and not a backward glance. In the small paddock adjacent to the stable that had housed Encore, are two chestnut colts. They're ignoring the strewn hay and are watching me intently. One of them nickers, his fine ears pricked and curious, but his scrutiny soon reveals the disappointing truth – I'm not carrying a bucket. He loses interest in me and does a half pirouette on his hindquarters, heading in a determined walk to the other end of the fence in search of a more useful human. At my insistent beckoning, the second one is persuaded to come over and submit to some petting, but he's also surreptitiously keeping a lookout for his breakfast.

"I thought I'd find you here, Tess."

Wishes do come true.

"*Mangwanani, Baas. Madam.*" A groom, awkwardly grasping two black rubber feed skips in one hand, swings open the timber gate with his other and is mobbed by the colts. "Hai! *Endai!* Go back you!"

He throws a skip in front of each one, separating them by several metres by nipping in between them and waving his arms. The darker of the two flattens his ears, makes a half-hearted attempt at turning his tail towards his companion, then both their noses disappear and the waffling and crunching begins.

"Was it you who left the house before me? The door was open."

You shake your head; you heard *me* leave and followed. You point to the huge barn further down the track.

"It must have been Piet's mum. She's probably in the dairy. I trust you slept well? Or maybe not. I hope your room didn't spin as much as mine did every time I closed my eyes."

Your face is open and full of something that I hope I'm reading as affection. That saying about the heart soaring? Well it really does happen. In fact, I've got all sorts of soarings.

"I confess that all the booze rendered me unconscious, but like you I was wide-eyed alarmingly early."

"I'm sure the hangovers will hit us later."

You take my hand, a little hesitantly, but I push my fingers through yours and you grin and squeeze back.

*

Rosie's seated cross-legged on a folded travel blanket on the low wall that runs alongside the driveway, book in hand. From that distance she makes a show of consulting her watch and gives me her best disapproving face. I peg the gates open and, before getting back into the car, ask, "Were you waiting for me?"

"No," she lies, giving the blanket a brief shake. Skellum charges in on the scene, barking and racing in circles. Pandemonium rages for a short while. I brake just inside and wait for her to slam the gates closed and tumble into the back seat, along with a dog that is all tail and tongue.

"So? He got you then? How was it? Good day? Where'd you go? Are yous two together now?"

"Which question do you want me to answer first? Yes, I reckon we are together."

I have to pause because it sounds so bizarre when I say the words. We're together. Me, and *Nathan Owen*.

"He took me to the Lion and Cheetah Park and the Spillway then all the way across to Cecil Barrett's stud farm near Ruwa. Beautiful place."

"The Spillway? God, it's *ages* since we went there! Do you remember how we used to have cream teas at the café there with the folks eons ago, on that huge verandah?"

Of course I do. Being there today brought a serious rush of nostalgia that transported me back to another time, tripping over long forgotten memories that are hazy and somehow sharp at the same time. Me and her – very small – and Mum and Dad on the iron-framed chairs wrapped in bright plastic strips on the verandah outside the tea rooms. Chasing each other on the lawns below and staring with fascination at the creamy curtain of water spilling over the concrete weir into a deep concrete channel big enough to drive a bus along.

"The place hasn't changed much."

I don't tell her about that unreal feeling of life coming around in a circle. That feeling that today I returned as the adult to a place I'd known as the child, with my life partner, buying the cream tea and, in conjunction with him, being in charge of how the day was spent.

"Mother hasn't actually said, but I'm convinced she thinks you're being indecently hasty and are on some dangerous rebound. I did warn you yesterday."

Under the car port, I switch off the engine and turn to face her. I'm focussed on her and I'm hearing her words and I'm distantly assessing how I'm going to tackle Mum on this, but all the while I'm wondering what Nathan is doing at this precise moment. It's just after six, so Amai is probably dishing up dinner. After abandoning my family all day with no explanation of my whereabouts, we – that is, the Owens – agreed that I wouldn't stay, although the welcome was there and my whole being wanted to. Charles and Moira displayed no surprise or shock whatsoever when we returned to Makuti Park together after being missing for a little under twenty-four hours and when he said, "I'll walk Tessa to her car," they shrugged and nodded and disappeared. Unlike them, I am still finding it bizarre. Me, and Nathan?

It's not a problem. I'll see him tomorrow and he'll be thinking of me now too. Will he watch TV or listen to some music in his room this evening? Rosie's form disappears momentarily and is replaced by the image of him kneeling beside the elderly, plastic-coated wire record rack in the van Rooyens' lounge late last night, leafing through the albums and studying each cover in turn, and then that fades to be replaced by the one of him and Piet, just before the bouquet throwing ceremony, playing air guitar to *More Than a Feeling*. So much more to know.

"You're blushing," she accuses me.

Well, yeah. I can still feel his lips. He called me Kitten. God, how did I get into this state?

"And another thing… Danny phoned this afternoon."

Bubble burst – bang.

"Danny? What did he say? Who spoke to him?"

"Me. I answered the phone," she says. "I told him you were out for the day and explained about the wedding yesterday. I felt real sorry for him because he sounded as if he knew he'd missed out on the party. He wants you to phone back tonight."

Dread, soaking into my bones. In many ways it would've been easier if we'd broken up with a huge fight and heartfuls of ill-feeling. I'd be able to just refuse to speak to him again. As it is, I feel obliged to make contact for the sake of good manners.

"I'll phone him," I tell her – wondering if I'll really have the guts – and yank the key out of the ignition. "Although I've had a great day with a wonderful companion and I don't know what the hell I'm going to say to him."

She climbs out of the car, hauling Skellie with her and watches me take my overnight bag and plastic-covered bridesmaid dress from the boot.

"Nathan suits you much better than Dan. You have the same silly interest in horses, but it's not just that. It's… I can't describe it without sounding… I don't know. I haven't a clue what I mean. I barely know him so I really shouldn't be passing judgement. Why haven't you gone out with him before? If you're after my approval, Tee, you've got it."

"I'm not after your approval my darling but thank you anyway."

She's grinning and elation is trickling back into my veins, but it rapidly recedes again at the thought of what I have to do tonight. I've no doubt I'll put it off for as long as possible but in the end I won't escape it.

*

The phone only gives three rings before I get the scraping sounds of someone picking up. Mrs Proctor. Damn. Now what the heck do I say?

"Oh, Tessa?" Her voice is not only guarded but accusatory to my guilt-twitching ears. I start stumbling and mumbling, both brain and tongue tied.

She knows what I want anyway and cuts through my indecisive babble. "Hold please. I'll call him."

We exchange a few strained pleasantries about health and he asks about the wedding. I'm safely into a description of Gill's dress when he interrupts, abruptly and breathlessly, in a low voice that makes me visualise him hunched over the phone, his back to wherever his family is.

"Look Tessa, my sweet. I accept all you said about problems we had with you competing at shows and all that, but I realise you have to ride your horses and I can't change that. I miss you, Tess. Can't we see each other again? Just occasionally at first, you know? Break us in gently?"

He gives a short, nervous laugh, presumably at his own use

of the equestrian term, then rattles on. "We can sort of go to the movies, like, you know, and have coffee afterwards, or something hey? Say Friday evenings? Not every Friday perhaps. I do miss you so much. I don't do anything or go anywhere and I have nothing to work for at university now. Oh God, that sounds like I'm sliding into a decline, doesn't it? I still work hard but I get the feeling it's all for nothing. I'd planned so much for us. I'm sorry about that time at the nightclub too. I didn't... I love you. Can't we..." He runs out of steam and I'm in tears and feeing like a right bitch.

There's nothing I can say that's remotely appropriate. After a few moments, he pleads, "Oh Tess, speak to me."

I glance around, brush a finger under my eyes, wipe my cheeks with it and sniff. Mum, Dad and Rosie are in the living room behind a partly closed door, laughing. *Dallas* will be on by now.

It's got to be said. Or rather, whispered.

"Danny. Danny, listen. There's no easy way to tell you this, and it's a line that's been trotted out over and over but I can't think of any other way to put it. I've started seeing somebody else."

Blankness. Emptiness. We've been cut off. Damn again – that's all I need. Bloody unreliable phone network.

Thoughts race. I'll have to call back. Should I call back? What's he thinking? Did *he* cut me off rather than the PTC? I didn't hear a click. I can't blame him. My transition from one boyfriend to another has, in truth, taken place over an indecently short time. He's probably guessing I've been two-timing him.

"It's only since yesterday," I say aloud to myself and a small and pathetic word comes at me out of the emptiness. He's still there.

"Who?"

I tell him. Again he comes back a couple of moments later with just one word.

"Why?"

My only desire now is to put the phone down. My mouth says, "I'm sorry," without much input from my brain.

Now he really has gone, with a soft and sorrowful click. I slink to my room, feeling that somehow I've failed.

THURSDAY 15TH JANUARY 1981

There *should* be room for the box in my car. It's a lot bigger than I expected. Might have to rethink that one.

"So Gilly and Piet will bring the food to the office at about nine?" Moira asks. The sky, seen through the window behind her, is nearly fully light. It's time I got going.

"Yup. And the banner. And, if they remember, some balloons."

I look up at her.

"I confess to being a bit doubtful about this. He's always refused any birthday celebrations or fuss, hasn't he? Even in the last couple of years, since… He still doesn't like to be the centre of attention. What if he hates it? It'll be spectacularly embarrassing for all concerned."

Her habitual gentle smile passes over the top of my head, and I can see that in her mind she's going through a journey in time.

"I'm confident that won't be the case, my love. He will, of course, tell us we shouldn't have bothered, but he won't mean it. Not now. His last two birthdays we've deliberately underplayed with a couple of small gifts and a family meal out so no real fuss has been made. It is true that there was a time when I was resigned to the fact that his twenty-first would slide past unwanted and unnoticed just like all the others before and Charles and I would feel like we'd failed him."

"But you haven't! And he knows that, Moira. He loves you both with all his heart."

"We know that now, sweetie, we know that now. And I have the utmost faith that the past is the past. Whatever demons he lived with for being told as a child that we hated him and were going to kick him out of the family have been laid to rest. And he got this from another *child*, for Christ's sake!"

I know what it did to him. He's already told me. Told me about the weariness and depression that swamped him when he came round from the anaesthetic and realised he was all bandaged up but didn't know the nature or extent of the injuries. The sight of the family gathered around the bed brought him to the conclusion that they'd had to drop whatever they'd been doing and traipse to the hospital out of duty and that he was potentially now going to become a serious burden on them. He lay there and instructed Charles to take the family home and leave him alone to either die or get put in a home. Charles sent Moira and Gill out of the ward and proceeded to inform him of the home truths. Cursed him and called him a stupid bastard and told him if he didn't realise what he, Charles, and Moira and Gill had just gone through and if he'd never realised how much they wanted him in their lives then he was a fucking idiot who deserved to lose his leg. Then he broke down, horrified at what he'd said, and he begged forgiveness. They sat with hands clasped together on the sheet for over twenty minutes until Moira and Gill decided to find out what the hell they were up to.

So yes, now he will love that they, and I, have chosen to celebrate this milestone birthday and his life with him.

Okay. Here we go. We pick up and carry the solid cardboard box between us, using the cut-out hand slots, but once I've opened the passenger-side back door it's very apparent that the two of us are not going to get it in without damaging something, including ourselves.

"Charles should've left you with the pick-up."

Good old hindsight.

"It may be better in the front. The door is larger so there's more space to get it in."

"Here, here, what are you doing?" says a voice. George. He's also carrying a box, but it's a whole lot smaller and it's wrapped in shiny blue and silver paper.

He tut-tuts, places his gift on the passenger seat with exaggerated care, runs around to the other side of the car and kneels on the back seat.

"In here," he says, beckoning with both hands. With him pulling and us pushing, we achieve success. We position the box on the passenger side so I can still see through the rear windscreen. It shouldn't matter really because it's that early there'll be virtually no traffic. And hopefully no cops.

"Thank you George. Much appreciated."

He backs out of the offside door and then stays bent over, his hands on his knees, peering into the interior.

"But what is it?" he asks. "It is a very big box."

Moira says, "A jumping saddle and stand. For when Nathan starts seriously competing with Bravo. Which I've told him he shall do. We had it fitted when he was off on site last week. It was your day off, George."

"What's in your box?"

I pick it up and give it a gentle shake but nothing moves inside. George goes, "Ah!" and takes it from me and places it back on top of the gift-wrapped VCR.

"It is a beer glass and it is called Nathan."

Yes, that's right. I'd forgotten. The grooms and Amai commissioned Gill to get it engraved in town a couple of weeks ago.

My gift to him is in my bag of course.

Is it? Check. I snatch it up off the floor of the footwell and scrabble around in it. Yes.

"What did you actually tell him when he left this morning, Moira? I saw him go. I was parked down the road by the Mhangirozas' place with my car out of sight around the bend while I loitered in the trees opposite to give me a clear view of the Makuti entrance."

"Sneaky. And I thought it was down to your accurate planning that you arrived literally a minute after he'd gone. I'll have Jenny on the phone to me later about a suspicious car parked outside her house. No, I wished him happy birthday of course and said to him that we'd all get together over dinner and give him his presents. He didn't really comment. He asked Charles if *he* was going to the site meeting and seemed a bit narked when Charles said no. Right, off you go."

She gives me a kiss on the cheek.

"I'll see you at the office at around twelve."

*

Piet wants to stick the banner above the reception desk. He's unrolled it and is breaking out the Stickistuff.

"Not over the painting," I object and he goes, "Oh? What?" and glances up at it.

"I wasn't going to cover the picture," he says defensively.

"She means don't even put the banner *above* it."

Gill's behind me and she gets what I mean.

"I love it," I say. "Ever since I first saw it I've wanted to walk into it and follow those wheel tracks. Piet, that needs to go over the door to Nathan's office."

"Oh, okay, boss. Here, Debs, grab that end please?"

Debbie got back from her holiday on Monday. Her over-excitement about the plans for Nathan's twenty-first birthday shrivelled up and blew away at roughly two o'clock on that day when he rolled in from site and took me out to a late lunch, but not before kissing me lingeringly up against the Land Cruiser in full view of the reception area. I don't feel guilty.

At eleven forty-five Charles goes to the toilet, leaving me frowning over the reinforcement supplier's latest invoice and the materials-on-site record submitted by Tom last week.

The phone on the desk gives its polite little three-blip ringtone. After a second's hesitation I snatch up the receiver. I can take a message for him.

Debbie's smooth telephone voice: "Charles, it's Tom out at Hartley for you. I'll put him through."

Good – he's probably giving notice that Nathan has left the site.

"Debbie, it's Tessa. Charles is, um, indisposed. I'll talk to Tom, thanks."

That'll be her indignation crackling in my ear and I swear that's a growl I just heard. The smoothness has gone. She goes, "Oh. Right," and there's a clunk. Tom says tentatively, "Charles?"

"Hi, it's Tessa. Has he left then?"

"He has. About five minutes ago. But, well, look, I'm not so sure he's going back to the office. He was very frustrated with me that I kept him here at least half an hour longer than necessary and said he wasn't bothered about checking the invert levels of the surface water outfall this week because it's not on the critical path and then when I wound the meeting up I specifically asked him if he was headed back to HQ and he said um and ah a bit and didn't answer directly but then he did say something about working a lot of extra hours last week and taking some time off in lieu."

He takes a breath, then, "You might want to give him, what, an hour and a half or an hour and forty? If he's not arrived then, try your house."

*

One-thirty.

"Go on then, Tess," sighs Gill. "Call home."

Amai answers.

"Yes, Miss Tessa! Oh, Miss Tessa! Yes, he is here. He is *here*! Five minutes only. He is supposed to be with you all so why is he home? I said to him are you sick and he said no and I said why aren't you at work then and he thought that was very funny Miss Tessa. He said now Boss Charles has made *me* in charge of him and telling him off for not doing his job and sorting him out. I didn't know what to say, Miss Tessa! He has gone to his bedroom to change for horse riding. Shall I fetch him to the phone, Miss Tessa? You want to speak to him? Have you had the party yet? Was it early? Are you coming home too now?"

Even though they can't hear Amai's side of the conversation, Gill is groaning and Piet's going, "Bloody typical."

Amai lets me talk her down from her high state of excitement eventually. She vanishes for a few minutes. There's a muffled conversation, then footsteps on the parquet floor and movement of the receiver.

"Have I been sacked for slacking? Shall I come and collect my stuff from the office?"

"You're not taking this seriously. I'm disappointed."

"I know, Kitten. You coming home soon? I might be out job hunting, although I have an inkling this is less about me skiving off early and more about some conspiracy I've not been party to. Would I be right? Amai's in on it too. You are, aren't you, Amai?"

"Ah! No!" she exclaims in the background and I hear more footsteps, receding this time.

"She's a dreadful liar and an even worse actress. Moira's not about, so I suspect she's in on it. I'll wait here then, shall I? And you can tell me exactly what's going on."

That's the problem with surprise parties, hey? The most important person involved has no idea that the right place and the right time even exist.

*

You turn the signet ring around your finger a few times. Smile those warm, deep brown eyes at me.

"Are you still pissed off with me?"

"Seething. Can't you tell?"

A burst of raucous laughter from the lounge. My nose comes within a few millimetres of yours on the way round. It's… well… yes.

George, Justice and Matthew are squeezed together on the sofa. Lazarus is cross legged on the floor in front of them and Charles is seated opposite on the armchair next to the French doors. There seems to be a round of toasts going on, clinked beer bottles interspersed with the laughter. In the background, Sylvester's following the discourse between Amai and Moira with his habitual respectful and attentive interest. Behind all this, softly, is Joan Baez lamenting the night they drove old Dixie down.

"Check out poor Sly," you whisper. "I'm sure he'd rather be joining in the beer drinking but he doesn't dare turn his back on Amai."

It's been almost unbearably hot today but now the heat has at least mellowed into something more comfortable. We face the pool again. Elbows on knees, you're tweaking the ring, settling it back with the flat top uppermost and rubbing over the small, diamond-shaped garnet and the engraved lines with the ball of your left thumb.

"It's a bit too big, isn't it? I'll get it re-sized in the week. Blame Gill and Charles. They measured his wedding ring and said I should get the same size."

"Never get Charles's advice on anything anyone would wear, Kitten. Moira's your go-to for that kind of thing. And don't fret. It will be just perfect. It's by far the best birthday present I've ever had and I think you know it."

Moira was the one who told me to check the size with Charles. And who sowed the seeds of the idea by telling me you'd lost the plain gold signet ring they gave you for your nineteenth birthday. So I blame all of them. But it doesn't matter. What matters is that you love it. You chose the sapphire for me and I chose the garnet for you.

"In spite of the fact that you blew our plot out of the water today with your no-show, it's turned out well, don't you think? If we'd had our little office party like we'd planned, the grooms and Amai wouldn't've had the chance to join in and celebrate with us. It would've all been a bit of a flop for them."

You pick up the tankard from the step below and raise it, looking through it towards the soft, gleaming ripples caused by the splashing fountain water, then take a gulp and offer me the last few mouthfuls. The lager tastes bitter to me after the shandies I've been drinking but I drain the dregs anyway. The sky is no longer clear. Some cloud has crept up on us to blot out some of the constellations and to shroud the moon, although the moon's still partially visible as if under a diaphanous and translucent veil. We came to sit on the edge of the patio to get some time to ourselves but we've got company. Noisy company. Hundreds of cicadas shrilling into the warm air in a never-ending chorus.

"Try out the new saddle tomorrow then? I'll come over to watch of course. What time do you reckon you'll be riding?"

It's not too warm that I can't shift up a little closer to watch you close your eyes. A day off work tomorrow, spent together. That's what you're thinking.

"Nine o'clock? Maybe half nine? We can set up the VCR with my TV afterwards if you can stay."

Wide open eyes then, searching my face. "It'll be getting pretty late now. You can stay all night as far as I'm concerned, but what about your folks?"

I could tell you my attitude to that, but it won't be any reassurance because that's not how you want things to be, either between us or between me and Mum and Dad. I've no idea what the time is and my blank left wrist is unenlightening. Why didn't I put my watch on today? I take your left hand and draw it up to the space between us where the light from the living room has a better effect.

"Nearly ten-thirty. It's fine. I told them I'd probably be home around midnight."

I place your hand back down on the knee of your jeans but keep it covered with mine.

"Your parents have been remarkably accepting of my presence in your life and at their home, given that I've replaced Danny at very short notice. Do they like me? I just hope I'm reading them correctly and that they're not freaking out because you've hooked up with the black sheep of the Owen family."

How easy it is nowadays to forget about the lack of confidence and the self doubt. Even after a couple of years it's still there. Under the surface. Well plastered over now, admittedly. There is, in me, this deep-seated, intuitive knowledge that it's up to me now to eradicate it. Of all the people in your life who love you or not, I am the only one who can do it. That's quite some responsibility.

"The truth is, they got taken by surprise, but they do trust me and to them you are a member of my best horsey friend's family. It's that simple. It's taken them by surprise because I guess they were pretty much convinced that me and Danny were set for life, and because it apparently happened very suddenly and also because..."

Because the whole dynamic of this new relationship is so far beyond the one I've just abandoned.

"I just picked you up at a party?"

Oh yes, and it was the best night of my life so far.

"As my mother saw it initially, I suppose. But have no doubt I've set her straight. My father is easy to please. You're able to talk to him about earthworks and foundations and that makes you more than acceptable to him. My mother might appear to require more work but I know she's okay with it. She... But what about your mother? What do you think she would've had to say about it?"

I'm treading on new ground. I hope it's not quicksand.

"I mean, if you want to... I don't mean..."

You shake your head, silent, staring out across the garden. Then turn to me.

"You *can* ask, you know. It's okay because my life is your life, or at least that's how I'd like it to be. There are so many things I've wanted to tell you. Nearly told you. But we didn't ever get close to having those sorts of conversations and when I wanted to tell you about myself I got scared and ran away. Not physically of course. Mentally, like."

Still the hesitancy. *My life is your life.* That's causing my heartrate to hammer all the way up into my throat.

"Truth is, I barely remember her. I can't picture her, even when I look at the photos. But I know she would've only wanted me to be happy. And I am."

You allow your right leg to drop fractionally so it lies alongside my left. I could put my hand around your thigh. No, don't do that.

I sat on a patio with Danny once – was it not so long ago, or centuries ago? – and I was drowning in a situation I'd never wanted to create. On that evening I experimented with touch and ended up floundering in deeper waters because my actions only confirmed to him that I wanted more from him. I didn't. Now, tonight, I'm afraid to use touch again because this time I do want it to go further and it's one of the scariest secrets I've ever had. It's like this every time we sit or stand next to each other. My mother – she knows this. I don't know how, but she does. And how can I tell you these thoughts?

What will you think of me? I'm a nice girl. A good girl. I'm your nice, good girl.

So we just sit like that for a while, like neither of us is sure where to take it from here.

SATURDAY 21ST FEBRUARY 1981

"One for you-hoo!" Rosie tosses an airmail envelope at me.

"Jess, by the look of it. Tell me what she has to say. And these three and the phone bill for the folks. This one's from Uncle Hal. I'd recognise that scrawl anywhere. Moaning about the British winter again, what's the bet?"

She slaps the remaining post down on the kitchen table. I treat the four envelopes to one rapid, disinterested glance and take my mug and Jess's letter out onto the patio. It's going to be a long one by the feel of it.

Before tackling it, I take a brief moment lying back on the lounger with my eyes closed, allowing all the pleasant anticipation for the day to come to seep through my body along with the warmth. I haven't seen Gill and Piet since the day they got back from honeymoon and I haven't ridden with Gill now in two months. Piet won't join us of course but I have a feeling this date will become an anniversary in years to come – the very first time Gill, Nathan and I have ever ridden out together. Worth celebrating.

And talking? There'll be plenty of that. As Nathan said yesterday, G&T has been deprived of its own company since before the wedding, apart from the two minutes' allotted time during the Christmas Day call.

The moment's contemplation is over. I sense Rosie in the doorway behind me.

"What's Jess got to say for herself? C'mon, tear it open."

I sigh, and work my thumb under the flap as a crude and blunt envelope knife.

Opening paragraph: *"Tess, you are one sly little creature. Nathan? What are his prospects? What did Dan say? Do you know what you're* doing? What do your folks think? Did they meet him on Boxing Day then?"

None of this "Dear Tessa" or "Greetings" or "My dearest friend" stuff.

A slight breeze ruffles the thin pages and I smooth them back a few times. Rosie chortles, standing on one leg against the door frame, her left foot braced on it behind her right knee. The next few paragraphs are a jaunty jumble of descriptions of lecturers, students, her lecture timetable and an outline of each subject curriculum. Then she writes, "I see they've started changing the names of everything so maybe Salisbury will become Harare after all? My folks said the hospital's not going to be the Andrew Fleming any more. It's going to be called the Parirenyatwa. Is that a word? What the fuck does it mean?"

Rosie's migrated from the doorway, down the steps and onto the lawn below. She flops down and rolls onto her back, an arm over her eyes.

"I've seen that in the paper. Not a clue as to how to pronounce it. Well done you. Rob says it's already getting to be known as the Paranoia Hospital. Apt, when you consider how all the patients and visitors steal bed linen and food these days."

If I remember my history rightly, there was a Doctor Parirenyatwa on the scene back in the 1960s. He was something to do with the ANC, or was it ZAPU? I inform her of this, adding, "And last night Chipo told me the Lady Chancellor Maternity hospital – where we were born? – is going to be named after *Mbuya* Nehanda, who was a spirit medium back in the last century during the old uprising, or First Chimurenga. There. That's my gem of fascinating fact for today."

"Okay, O Great Fountain of Knowledge," she yawns. "Knowledge is power by the way. Just remember I know you let Chipo drive your car last night and Daddy doesn't."

"Just like you to stoop to blackmail. She's a perfectly competent driver but she's looking to do more practice in different vehicles. Do you want to hear what else Jess has to say or not? Actually, you'll have to wait because I need to get ready to go."

The letter will be something to look forward to at the end of my lovely day.

*

"I've never seen the Falls," was intended to lodge my interest in Gill's idea, rather like, "Hey, *ja* I'd love to go."

Except Piet has frozen with his bottle just short of his lips and Gill's reached under the water to take my hand as though about to commiserate with me on a bereavement.

"What? Never? My God, you haven't lived."

"Nath!" Piet bellows in a voice that's slightly hoarse. He places his bottle on the paving slab beside his lounger without it having touched his mouth. "You have a mission, should you choose to accept it my boy. Take your lady to Victoria Falls! She's never been."

You've only just surfaced and shaken water out of your ears so you cock your head and go, "What?"

In two strokes you've made up the distance and you float in to sit on the step next to me, our hips touching under the water, your eyes flicking quizzically between me and Gill.

"You're under orders to make sure I get to see Vic Falls because my failure to do so thus far is upsetting the balance of the universe."

You lean forward and across me, your right elbow on my left knee.

"I gather it's settled then? You'd better get booking, Gill honey."

She's still gripping my right hand.

"And Wankie? Kariba? Oh, hang on, I know you've been to Kariba but that was some years ago."

"Some years ago? It was 1973. Jesus. Where does the time go? And Dad took us to Wankie Game Reserve even earlier than that. I vaguely remember us living in a little rondavel hut and him saying it was the week all the animals moved out. He's still mentally scarred from being let down by the Big Five and being taunted by the same warthog family and a few scraggly wildebeest every day. He swore he'd never go on safari again."

"Well," she says, encompassing all of the rest of us in her glance around, "I can most certainly investigate the prices, flight times and tour details then. When should we go? Sometime towards the end of May? I could do with a holiday."

"Bloody hell, you've only just come back from a holiday. It's all right for some of us."

"Yes, all right, Nathan. Jealousy gets you nowhere. We did send you a postcard."

Gill lets go of me, launches herself off her step and breaststrokes away towards the edge where Piet is sitting. All the postcards they sent are still attached to the stable duties pinboard with bright green tacks – the lighthouse at Cape Point for the grooms and Amai, a Stellenbosch scene for Moira and Charles and a sunset-tinged Table Mountain addressed to Tessa and Nathan. She didn't waste any time putting us two together.

Together. A three-destination holiday. Three hotels over six nights. There's a buzzing in my head and a shiver of anticipation – or something – in my belly.

Precisely the same thread is running through your mind. We watch Gill clamber out of the pool and take her towel from where it's hanging over the back of the lounger next to Piet's. When you speak, I already know what you're going to say.

"I'm absolutely up for going on a Flame Lily Tour with you and Gill and Piet. Are you? But Tess, look, I need you to consider carefully how… if… Well, first off, do you think your folks will object to us going on holiday together?"

I'm damned sure they will, although to be fair their faith in my morality will be naively unshakeable. The fact that I'm having to contemplate this decision is quite extraordinary. And very intriguing. It's like I'm studying myself from the outside during a behavioural experiment. What will Tessa do? How will her brain respond to these stimuli? She's being given a choice that relies on several other choices. Will the brain short circuit or make a cool and rational and correct decision, or will she just run away?

"Think about it," you say, and I can tell from your eyes that you've been panicked into wondering if all the thought processes you can see in my face are going to result in either the short circuit or the running away. I touch the hand that's resting on my knee.

"It's okay, it's okay. I predict that what they'll object to is me doing it so soon into the relationship. I'll have to do some talking but I can probably get round it as Gill and Piet will be going too. So it's a group of four and they know Gill's been my friend for ever."

You raise your eyebrows and give me a sideways look. "What, all chums together? You can bring your dog and we'll be like the Famous Five."

I'm hardly likely to say no to this, am I, when I can't get enough of delving into your history?

"You read the Famous Five? Did you really? I was more into her adventure series with Jack, Dinah, Philip and Lucy-Ann. Did you have those? What were they called? *The Island of Adventure, The...*"

"Tessa. Stick to the subject. We're grown-ups now."

You don't do stern – that face just creases me up.

"All right, I'll be serious." I sit up straight, remove your hand and place it down in the water between us.

"Good. That's very proper. Now, how do you want Gill to book rooms at the hotel? She can get us single rooms each. Is that what you would prefer?"

I hear myself say, "Frankly, if it's okay with you we can share a room," then, "Oh, no, go back. That came out all wrong. I mean, don't think that… I don't… I've never…"

"What on earth are you two up to over there?" Gill calls, paused with her towel wrapped around her middle like a sarong. "Behave yourselves."

When you laugh at me like that I know you understand me no matter what gobbledegook comes out of my mouth. I'll sort it with the parents. I can't wait to see their faces when I tell them about this holiday.

*

I imagine Mum and Dad will be surprised, and perhaps proud, that I'm making my own vacation arrangements now, all independent.

Rosie will probably be jealous, but she'll get over it. She'll want a detailed itinerary and will try to re-plan whatever I propose. Where I choose to sleep in any hotels, however, will be entirely my own business. It won't be a problem. Mum won't even ask. She'll assume that separate rooms goes without saying.

His eyes were so soft – and I'm still so unused to reading such expression in him – when he kissed me lightly, amicably, perfectly. No need for anything more dramatic. We both know we've got what we've always wanted, even if we weren't aware we did want it. Or at least I wasn't aware. I'm starting to suspect now that he was.

He said, "Of course I won't ask anything of you, Kitten. We'll all have the best time and I'll be the one to show you the Falls for the first time. You've never seen anything like it and you never will, anywhere else. Oh, and by the way, there's another amateur race meeting in May. At the Beatrice track this time. Are you game?"

It's my chance to get a race ride at last.

I chuck my bike in the shed, padlock the door and amble into the house, trying half-heartedly to guess what's for supper from the smells that greet me. The feeling of well-being and fulfilment is whole.

Within a split second of walking through the back door and taking in the scene before me, it's all drained away.

Mother is standing, hands on hips, before the row of fitted wall cupboards. All the doors have been flung open to expose their contents – assorted cookware, crockery and glassware. For a few heartbeats I stare and say nothing. The scene before me is, in many respects, unremarkable, but it sets all the hair on my head and arms into a frenzy and drops a sickness into my abdomen. Something momentous has happened while I've been gone. A voice tells me to turn round, walk out and come in again to make sure I haven't imagined this… this weird, indecipherable atmosphere.

"Oh hello, love!" Mum greets me as though I've just interrupted her from a reverie. She offers no more than that and I slide past her and along the corridor to my room, still prickling all over. Their bedroom door at the end of the corridor is open and Dad's in there, seated at the clumsy, old-fashioned bureau in the far corner. If I can believe my eyes, he's writing on a blue aerogramme letter sheet. Dad, writing a letter?

He senses my presence and looks up, smiling. "Oh, it's you Tessa. Hello."

I'm being ridiculous. They both sound normal, and a letter arrived from Uncle Harry today. Dad'll be writing back to him. It's usually Mum who does the writing, but does it matter? Don't worry about it.

Rosie's not around.

She breezes in half an hour later, just minutes before Mum calls us to the table, and subjects me to a detailed description of the make-up set Helen Gillespie's sister brought back from Jo'burg. I humour her with a show of interest while eyeing up the peri-peri pork chop on my plate. I only had an apple and a packet of biltong for lunch so I'm ready for this.

Five minutes into the meal, Dad taps the side of his wine glass with his knife.

"Ladies! Ladies, listen up. I have news."

A study of his expression gives no clue as to whether this is good or bad news. He places the knife back on the table next to his plate. Mum carries on eating, delicately, like she's trying to be unobtrusive, but then I guess she knows what's coming.

"We had a letter from Hal today. I'm very sad to find out our Aunty Julia has passed away, quite suddenly. It turns out she had a tumour on one kidney that she must have lived with for quite a while without telling anyone she wasn't well. When her doctor found out, it was too late. The cancer had spread to most of her organs and there was nothing anyone could do. She went downhill very fast and died last Tuesday."

"Poor Aunty Julia," Rosie says with a commendable attempt at sympathy. "*Great* Aunty Julia. Shame we never got to meet her."

We've seen photos of her. Sepia pictures of three children in various stages of growing up in the early part of the century – Grandad, Barbara and Julia.

"The last of my father's family – gone," Dad muses. He actually sounds like he might cry. He doesn't, though. He perks up and says,

"Julia was such a character. She used to tell us how my grandad forbade her to dance the Charleston and to cut her hair and to wear short dresses, but she did so anyway. Quite a girl. You'd've liked her, Tessa. Quite keen on horse riding she was."

Yeah, yeah, he's told us this before. I gave up wishing I could meet her because there never seemed any likelihood, given Dad's aversion to holidays in England. It strikes me I haven't thought about her in years.

"She inherited most of Barbara's estate," Mum says, and when I look up at her she quickly drops her head and concentrates on her dinner. Suddenly I know where this is going.

"So she's left you some money?" Next to me, I feel Rosie prick up her ears.

Dad has a distant air about him now. He's focussed on something on the far side of the dining room.

"Me and Hal. Half each. With her property and other assets he reckons her total estate is worth around half a million pounds. Got to go through probate and all that malarkey so we won't know for sure for a bit."

Two hundred and fifty thousand pounds? That's an awful lot of money considering there are nearly three Zimbabwe dollars to the pound. No wonder the folks were behaving strangely earlier. Wow. I open my mouth, but Rosie beats me to it.

"What's that in dollars?" she says, around a mouthful of peas. "Will you buy us a new house? And we could do a round-the-world holiday couldn't we? I'll need a car soon. And we could…"

Dad cuts her short with a flick of his hand. He has a weird grin on his face that's not just happy – it's triumphant.

"It doesn't matter a toss what it is in dollars my girlie, because there's no way on this earth I'm bringing the money here. With the foreign currency restrictions we have now – and they're likely to get even tougher – I'd never get it out again. So the bloody government would get it, or it would have to stay here in a blocked account for ever. No way. The Zimbabwe currency will only devalue so I'd lose out big time on whatever I *could* get out. We made good use of my parents' money and Mummy's inheritance at the time, but with hindsight it was a crying shame we had it all sent over here. A mistake, a big, big mistake. Not this time. Things have altered dramatically now anyway and it's the opportunity I've always wanted. A real blessing, God rest poor Julia's soul. No, we leave it in my account in England and we now have the means to set up home over there."

There's a pulse roaring in my ears.

"Set up home? In England?"

He extends his arms wide as if to embrace us all. "Yes, of course! Not, like, tomorrow though! There's a lot to sort out. But certainly by this time next year I'd say."

He beams again with that far-away look. Mum sighs and leans back in her chair and her face says it all. We've been provided with the means to leave behind the troubles of black Africa. Our future security is guaranteed.

Horror rises up my throat and the mouthful I'm just swallowing catches and goes the wrong way. Through my choking fit and watery eyes I relive the scene in the kitchen; Mum standing in front of the flung open cupboards, her distraction, her not asking me, for the first time ever, how my day had gone. She had only one thought in her mind, didn't she? Packing. What will go with us and what will be ditched?

I'm not stupid. Down deep in my soul I knew this day would come. I've gone la-la-la-la-la and pretended I haven't seen the warnings, haven't heard the warnings. While the *Titanic* has been sinking next to me, I've been sitting on top of the iceberg admiring the view. But I knew. Inheritance or no inheritance, they would've made up their minds to leave sometime. Some event, some political decision, would've pushed them over the edge.

They're all acting alarmed, wondering if they're going to have to do a Heimlich on me. I shake my head, wave a hand, wipe my mouth with my napkin. The haze clears fractionally.

"This time next year?"

I repeat his words in the strangled little voice that comes out of a choked throat and Rosie doubles up next to me. She attacks her dinner again without a care in the world. Says, "Don't die on us, Tee!"

My appetite's long gone.

"Do you mean yourself, or you and Mum, to sort out the affairs?" I ask him. Silly question. Only thing I can think of saying when my whole self is trying to run as fast as it can away from here without actually doing so.

"All of us, Tess," he answers. "I want all of us to leave. Together."

Still that gentle, euphoric smile. The other two are carrying on with their lives, beginning to scrape plates clean. I'm fixing his eyes, but I'm not being aggressive. Not yet. I just can't move a muscle. After the pause has dragged on for a bit, the smile slips sideways and he looks at the sideboard.

"But Zimbabwe is my home. My country."

"*Rhodesia* was your country."

Okay, we'll let that go for now.

"I don't want to live in England. It's alien to me. It's crowded and grey and cold and it rains all the time. You want me to tear up my existence and live in some place I can't call home?"

He's amazed. "You've never even been to England! You don't know what it's like."

"No, I haven't. You're right. Because you've never taken us there. You always seemed to think that we never needed to see England because we lived in such a great place."

He searches hard for a response. Mum and Rosie are paying attention now, although they're pretending not to. The vibes tell me there won't be any back-up for either me or Dad.

"We will be *safe* there," he says finally. "And financially secure. Both of those matter a lot to me, as a father and a husband. Do you realise that? I think maybe you don't. Have you ever stopped to think just what this government might do in the future? They've already turned the tide against the whites and now they're squabbling amongst themselves. There's been rumours that anyone who is not a Zimbabwe citizen will not be allowed to own property. That means people like me would have to relinquish British or other foreign passports — my own birth right, dammit — and take on citizenship of this banana republic. The economy's already showing signs of collapse, just like the rest of black Africa. You'll find that we won't be able to get anything apart from subsistence goods and you'll end up eating *sadza* for all your meals. These price control laws on foods are forcing people out of business and, as soon as this pitiful Lancaster House Agreement period is over, who knows what other ridiculous laws they will dream up overnight to follow their 'New Order' and their Marxist ideals and to cover up for their own embezzlement and corruption. You haven't thought about any of this, have you? Have you?"

I have not. This outrage, and his pride at being the head of his family, have formed a cold shadow that's fallen across my self-constructed platform of indignation. Across my shallowness. Across a reluctant guilty acknowledgment that I don't pay enough attention to the news for any of this to be on my happy little radar. But I can't – won't – lie down and roll over. I'll be eighteen before this year's out and then he can't tell me what to do. I'm staying. It's my decision. Things might never get that bad surely? I mean, this might just all be doom-and-gloom rumours. He takes too much stock of rumours. And as for Rhodesia – well I'm sorry but it is no more. It's gone. This country is mine and it's now called Zimbabwe, and it's not going to ever go back to Rhodesia.

I don't mean to sound wheedling, but it comes out that way when I say, "Can't we just give it a chance, like, two years maybe? My whole world is here. *Our* whole world. This lovely lifestyle. And what about my horses?"

And what about my Nathan?

He doesn't give me the chance to voice this question and he doesn't register the shock as it hits me. He bangs the table top with the flat of his hand.

"Give it a chance? Anything can happen in two years! I've just told you these people make up new laws and rules overnight to suit themselves. Aren't you listening to a word I say, Tessa? And what about the horses? You can sell them, can't you? They're certainly not coming with!"

He ignores, or doesn't hear, the distraught whimper that comes from Mum. Rosie groans, "Oh, God" and shoves her plate aside and puts her head down on her folded arms. As I kick back my chair and leave the room, Mum turns her whimper into a sob.

"Oh for Christ's sake Bob! Let her get used to the idea before you start on that, please!"

She bolts after me down the corridor but I'm much faster. I've slammed my bedroom door before she's got halfway.

She tries all sorts of different knocks; soft and apologetic, loud and demanding, a pleading kind of scraping sound. I think about throwing myself on the bed or onto the carpet and I think about grabbing anything that comes to hand and chucking it against one of the walls, or the window, with all my strength, but I end up just standing in the middle of the room. She'll just have to keep knocking and pleading because I can't let anyone in while I'm on fire, the sweat is pumping out of me and my breathing sounds like a dragon's, or when my mind just consists of woolly strands like this, each beginning and ending nowhere.

It takes twenty minutes. Maybe. Thirty, perhaps? I'm not counting. I come down in stages to settle on a bleak, flat plain that's made entirely of sadness. Not a weeping, grieving kind of sadness, just a calm acceptance of what's inevitable.

"I'm not leaving," I tell the top of her head as I unlock and open the door. The whole house feels empty, apart from us two. I've already turned my back on her so I only hear her struggling to her feet and she sounds like a much older woman.

"Dad's in the garden. I've never seen him like this, Tessa. He's been through a bit of a roller coaster today you know. He wasn't that close to Julia after all these years but it was still a sad shock to hear she's died, that his parents' whole generation is now gone. But he was buoyed up with the relief that her money can help us like this. Our financial future's been on his mind a long time now and he couldn't see the way clear. Now he can, and earlier today while he and I were talking about what we should do next, I thought he looked years younger again. We talked a lot before you came home. Will you talk to me now?"

If she's been crying, there's no sign now. We perch together on the bed and she looks as resigned as I feel, tucking her silvery-blonde hair behind her ears and smoothing down her dress. "Please, Tessa. Talk to me."

I don't wish to, no, but from a sense of duty towards her it comes out of me in awkward fits and starts. That I hear all Dad said. That I accept he has fears about the future here. That I understand. But that *I'm* prepared to give it a chance even if he isn't. I have a job, I have a relationship, I'm perfectly settled. I don't have these fears, only hope. The war's finished, so why shouldn't we hope?

Her angle is this: we whites will have no more privileges.

She tells me how we've led a lovely life up until now. I have a job, as I pointed out, and so has Dad, but this process they call 'Africanisation' is scary. It's a move to let blacks take over everything, step into positions of authority, get promotions over whites, simply as a form of retaliation. Rosie could get bumped off university or college waiting lists, she will have tough competition for jobs from blacks who are not as well qualified or because she's not been able to get qualified. Everything will be against white people and it could affect all of us. There will be whites out of work and where would they live? What would they do? It's not a welfare state, like England. Isn't it dreadful, she asks me, a hand over mine, to think there may, in the future, be destitute whites living in the townships with no jobs?

"No more privileges? Like we have a right to those privileges because of the colour of our skin? So white people might end up living in townships on nothing, like you've assumed black people will always do. When blacks don't have jobs they have to rely on their extended family. Is it only us who have the right to jobs and a decent standard of living then? So we can govern our black people successfully? It's very *Animal Farm*, Mum. Look, I get that the false Africanisation is wrong and a problem. It's your attitude about skin colour that I can't stomach I'm afraid. Everyone has a right to education, qualification and good jobs if they have the ability to do them."

She recoils. She blinks at me as if she's wondering if I'm really still Tessa and not some possessed apparition. Tessa doesn't pick fights or contradict her or sarcastically imply that her opinions and her beliefs are ridiculous. I blink back at her, tight-chested, loathing myself for hacking her concrete ideals to pieces, but she has to know

I don't just believe what my parents tell me to believe any more. She can't go on thinking she – they – can influence me for ever. That I will always accept they know best. They don't.

And they can't influence what I do with the things I love. How *dare* he tell me to sell my horses? *My* horses. He used to pay for their keep but now they take a large chunk out of my salary – my choice because they mean the world to me. They're living creatures; they're my responsibility. Living creatures with welfare rights. He's putting them on the same plane as Rosie's tennis racquets, to be sold if considered past their best, or else conveniently packed and shipped. With a sick, sick jolt it occurs to me that this also applies to Cleo and Skellum, the faithful family pets.

And as for Nathan? There's nothing to debate here. I have a man who is a part of me. We're making up for a lot of lost time and we'll go on doing that for the rest of our lives. That's it. My mind is made up. I roll away from her and face the wall, screwing my face up to stop the tears.

"I'll turn eighteen before Dad's deadline. You, Dad and Rosie go. Honestly. It's your decision if that's what you're so desperate to do. I've made mine, and I'm not going. I'm afraid you can't make me. That's it."

She says nothing for nearly a minute, doesn't move, and we're frozen as if time has stopped. I won't look at her face because I don't wish to know how she's reacted. Eventually time starts moving again. The bed lifts slightly as she gets up. There are light slipper-steps on the carpet and the door opens. Her voice is a whisper.

"We'll talk about it again, darling, when things have calmed down."

I shake my head. Like I said, my mind is made up.

THURSDAY 14TH MAY 1981

She pokes her head around my bedroom door during a pause in her usual cyclonic rush before school, her dark curls still un-brushed and forming a rebellious riot around her face.

"You going to idle in bed all morning?"

I stretch and yawn. "Yup. The holiday has begun."

"Don't be so smug. How *ever* will you decide what to do with your day? The pressure must be enormous."

I study her – cheerfully sarcastic, leaning on the door frame in her winter tunic, her long tanned legs crossed at white ankle socks, her shoes with the laces undone. That familiarity of being a schoolgirl suddenly seems to belong to the dim and distant past. Did I used to look like that in the mornings?

"Oh, I'll probably go riding after I've had a bit of a lie in."

An idea pops up and I lean forward onto one elbow. "Say, do you want to go into town this afternoon? We can do a bit of shopping and have afternoon tea and waffles or something."

How terribly colonial. Why do we hang on to these customs?

She's shaking her head. "I'm going to the tennis club after school. Rob'll be there and I may as well get as much of his coaching while… I can."

There's a pause while we stare at each other, the unspoken words suspended between us: *"Before we leave."* In the awkward pause she turns defensive, pushing herself away from the door frame and folding her arms.

"You will finish school in England now, Rosie. Uni over there. Better opportunities for your marine biology career, if you're still into that."

She takes a deep breath, then gives a short, dry laugh.

"Well it does seem a bit of a pointless career in a land-locked country."

"So you don't really mind going, then?"

"No. No, I suppose not. I'm sure I'll be able to adapt, and you know me – always looking for something different, always wondering what's out there in social circles I know nothing about."

She tilts her head and narrows her eyes. "It's not as easy for you though, is it? You've always been a bush-baby, a real child of Africa."

I like that.

"Yes, I am. But aren't you too, in a way?"

"I love the sunshine and the outdoor life but I confess that now I want to experience something of the rest of the world, big city life perhaps, being able to follow the latest fashions and music. Maybe I'll find I don't like it after all and that it's not for me, but I want to give it a go."

"And you'd have access to better tennis coaching and competitive opportunities."

Why am I encouraging her? Why aren't I trying to bring her down on my side?

She points a finger at me. "Ah, yes! Yes. Exactly. And what about your riding? There'll be the same in England for you. You know how you always drool over those horsey magazines from overseas with pictures of the world-class riders and all those shows. Horse of the Year Show. Badminton. Hickstead. You'd be in your element. You could have lessons with the likes of those champion riders."

She throws her hands up to her hair and pulls a face. "Look, gotta go. I've still got to have breakfast after I've tamed this mop."

And she's gone.

"Enjoy your day at school!" I call sweetly, but I guess she's already out of earshot.

It's an interesting idea. Lying back on my pillow, I tantalise myself. I visualise myself riding at Badminton Horse Trials on a magnificent and courageous horse. I feel every movement, sense the high flood of adrenaline, feel the power in flight and then I switch the viewpoint to that of an unknown eye, watching myself in slow motion. That's the advantage of daydreams.

The agonised metallic shrieking of the gate hinge jerks me back into full wakefulness and my dream disintegrates. God, it's a hideous noise. Dad still hasn't got Elijah to oil the damned thing.

Tumbling out of bed, I part the curtains and watch Rosie reach through the lower bars of the wrought-iron gate to pat Skellum's head, then mount her bicycle and set off down the hill at breakneck speed. A web of aching nostalgic memories ensnares me – memories of the countless times we cycled to school together, quite often bickering and wishing the other wasn't there. An endless procession of crisp winter mornings with sharp blue skies followed by balmy blue or dark, thundery summer mornings (plastic raincoats gaping at the buttons, allowing a deluge to seep in and soak our uniforms) have all passed by and the nostalgia is so precious that it's painful. Everyone's schooldays get left far behind, to be yearned for in later life by all accounts, but it's the dread of ripping up my life and leaving these roots as a part of some previous existence that brings hot tears of despair, and even fear, to my eyes.

Victoria Falls. I will see this, one of the natural wonders of the world, for the first time tomorrow. Will it be the place where I'll do my final bit of growing up? I can't begin to imagine how this is going to pan out. What I'm pretty sure of is that I can put my trust in Nathan and that we'll work it out together.

I prise the flat white box out from the back of my top drawer, snap out one of the pills and poke the box back into place. Swallow the pill with some water from my bedside glass. It's been worth taking these because, if nothing else, they've made me more regular and dulled the cramps to a tolerable level. I had to work at it to get the prescription in the first place, with that stupid doctor going, "Well there you go then, my dear. You feel better after doing your horse riding and some other exercise? You see, it's all in your mind."

Patronising idiot. He's a man so how can he possibly know what it feels like?

Now, four and a half months later, I have periods like clockwork and less agony *and* – an outcome my mother would never have contemplated that day at the chemist's counter – I am fully equipped to start experimenting with sex. I just hope I've been taking them long enough if we should… If I want to. If we want to.

I make up my bed mechanically, re-thinking the same thoughts I've had so many times, unable to be anything other than scared stiff because Jess was so bitter and disappointed with the whole thing. He'll be fully aware that I have zero experience of my own, but what of him?

Karen Melton was fond of hinting at how well Joanna Coetzee knew Nathan Owen. Joanna, the School Bike. Okay, it had taken a while for me to work out what that meant, but I got there. Karen was lying though. She made a hobby of putting out juicy stories about everyone (I've no doubt I was on her hit list, but I never had the urge to find out what my stories were) and besides, she always wanted a bit of him herself, so maybe she fantasised at Joanna's expense. Nathan, seducing girls at school? Nathan, who barely said a word to anyone, had no friends and who confounded and scared both boys and girls? If anyone had known he was pursuing and sleeping with the likes of Joanna, it would've been Gill. And she would've told me. I doubt he ever cared one jot about Joanna or even spent any time in her company. He never spent time in anyone's company except Gill's. Until Sherrie.

It must have happened with Sherrie. Well, I'll find out, won't I?

FRIDAY 15TH MAY 1981

We shuffle to one side to make way for a pair of senior citizens who are squinting at their tickets and faffing with a plastic wallet. There's a brief resurfacing of the early morning stupor among us, a hesitation, like we all just really want to lie down where we are and go back to sleep. The three suitcases are trundling off on the squeaky conveyor to be claimed by the black rubber flaps that are like the tentacles around the maw of some mechanical beast. I get a fleeting fancy that they'll be digested in there and we'll never see them again.

Gill makes the decision that we should be awake and bright and cheery.

"Coffee then? At that cafeteria? Come."

There's some doubt in Piet's mind, judging from the grimace on his face.

"I wouldn't risk it. I've had both tea and coffee from that place before and they taste exactly the same. I'm not even sure what they taste of. I'll have a Coke, thanks."

Outside of the cold barn that is the domestic terminal it's as perfect a morning as can be expected for this time of year and a little on the cool side as late summer slides into winter. There's an expanse of plate glass at the end furthest from the check-in bays and on the other side is our Viscount, its new livery colours flashing in the sun. Gone is the dull battleship grey the Air Rhodesia fleet got cloaked in after the two missile attacks. No more practically vertical take-offs and landings from civilian scheduled flights. One of these days, I guess, all that'll be like part of a past life.

Now, for the present, you have your arm around my waist, guiding me in Gill's wake. She's still determined to have that coffee.

Piet's keeping pace with her and I get snatches of their conversation and his optimism about the outcome of the donors conference and the millions of dollars the World Bank has pledged to lend us.

This is how it's going to be. I'm in love. I have an extended family who are also my friends. Zimbabwe will work. We agreed that in the car on the way here. We praised Mugabe's unexpectedly sensible approach to governing this past year and his hope for moderate and evolutionary changes in society. Unity and hard work – that's what he's asking of us.

On the other side of the coin, my father insists the donor countries and organisations are being naïve if they think they'll ever see their money again. He scoffs at Bernard Chidzero's claims that our economy will boom with the promised foreign investment and he reckons of course they'll bloody nationalise the mines and the commercial farms. He said anyone who believes they won't do this is a fool. Well, I don't think any of us here are fools. We know this could well happen. What we hope is that a workable solution will evolve, to the benefit of most, and the country as a whole.

I know I can tell Gill anything, right? And now I know I can tell this perfect partner of mine anything. But I haven't yet managed to bring myself to reveal my parents' plan to leave Zimbabwe. Since the day the decision was made, I've been compelled by some inner force to shut it out, to keep Great Aunty Julia, her estate and my father's inheritance completely to myself. I can't tell because I haven't quite worked out my own plan. I'll stay in Zimbabwe, but I have to figure out where I'll live, how I'll pay my way. There's an obvious solution but I dare not bank on that just yet. For all I know, Dad might change his mind. Nothing will happen until he's secured himself a job in England anyway, I've been assuring myself. So it might all go away.

Someone did tell me that ostriches are not actually prone to burying their heads in the sand (it was probably Charles) but ostrich-like or not, I'm burying my own head firmly and refusing to come out for now. I'm doing exactly what the folks did in Smith's days. Silly cow. I used to criticise them. But it's what us humans – all animals in fact – do; fight, flight or avoidance. If you can't tackle it or run from it, you deny its existence with all your power. So I'll just revel in what I've got for now.

*

The hostess who threw the plastic trays of cardboard sandwiches at us on the way up is coming around again to snatch them back now that we're on the way down. She has that look in her eye that says, if you haven't finished, tough shit.

"What, we going down already?" I cup my hand to the glass of the oval window and put my face against my palm. I get a slight sinking sensation that's accompanied by a very subtle change in the engine note. The propeller blades form glittering circles with a yellowish edge. You lean across me.

"Yup. Look over there. Can you see the spray?"

The Viscount shudders in an air current, up, then sinks down again. Several passengers utter, "Ooh!", then titter. Rising out of the trees on the northern horizon is a pale misty cloud, small and insignificant enough that I wouldn't have noticed it without your prompt. If I had seen it, I may have thought it was a bush fire.

"Spray? You mean, that's the Falls?"

You nod, and I consider asking you to get the camera from my duffel bag in the locker above us, but actually the cloud is too far away and the window isn't exactly clean. It won't make a good photo.

The runway's completely encircled by virgin bush; Mother Nature is one short step away from claiming it back. We slide in over the top of the trees, bump onto the macadam strip, bounce once, wobble briefly as if all control has been lost and then the brakes are applied and we ease down to a crawl. Behind us, Piet mutters something about a good landing being one you walk away from and Gill tells him to shut up, she's known worse.

*

The air here is humid – nothing like the dry crispness we left in Salisbury. We're in second place in the convoy of three brash, touristy zebra-striped minibuses and the air con isn't working; wedged in like traditional sardines we're probably all starting to feel a bit moist. My duffel bag's making the tops of my thighs sweat already and your body against mine is like a radiator. A very nice radiator though.

"How far?" I ask.

"Twenty kays? Other hotels are closer, but we've got the best. Nearest to the Falls."

The buses disgorge passengers in turn at hotels and motels. Two of them vanish and only ours remains, with us four the only occupants for the Victoria Falls Hotel. The entrance is framed by columns, the foyer hushed, cool, opulent and we make an obtrusive clatter with our shoes and our cases. We get assigned with rooms – two – and I'm committed now. It feels good. Wickedly good. Anticipation and dread vie for priority.

A porter with a brass trolley bearing our luggage leads us across a paved courtyard, following pathways framed by ponds and flowering plants. The courtyard is bright with reflected sunlight; as we enter the lofty olive and white lounge on the far side my vision is momentarily dulled. Ahead of us, the lounge has wide doors that give access to a terrace as dazzling as the inner court we've just left and there, in the distance (through a squinted attempt to adjust light levels), is the iron bridge that spans the chasm downstream of the Falls and links us with Zambia. It's ever so slightly hazy in a cloud of mist.

I'm going to walk into something if I'm not careful, my eyes fixed on this ethereal scene over my shoulder. The others have headed off into an adjacent corridor that probes deep into the structure, following the porter, the wheels of his trolley now silent on the thick pile carpet. The corridor is lined with a succession of paintings and Victorian photographs of the Zambezi in all its moods.

We arrive at Gill and Piet's room first and you and I hover in the passage while their case and bags are off loaded.

"See you in a bit." Gill waggles her fingers at us and closes the door.

"This is yours," the porter says, indicating the adjacent door. He produces a key and ushers us in with ceremony, depositing the luggage on a wooden rack just inside the door. He takes the cash you offer in exchange for the key, claps his hands together with a slight bow and exits.

It's cosy and plush, the two single beds covered in mottled pastel shades of pink, lilac, blue and turquoise. There are matching curtains and a rose coloured carpet. Curiosity drags me to the bathroom door where I get a minor rush at the thought of trying out all those potions and lotions in sachets and bottles and the pearly soap cakes in shell-shaped dishes.

"After all the respectable but merely functional hotel bathrooms my family and I have known, this is stupidly exciting. Look, what's this?" I poke about in a small, flat basket. "Shower cap… nail file… a sewing kit? Good God."

Your hands settle on my shoulders from behind and I raise them into the warmth of your touch.

"So you're going to have fun then? Told you it was a nice hotel."

"Nice? That's got to be the understatement of the century."

You turn me, guide me back into the centre of the room. "Which bed do you want, my kitten?"

Well, yours of course, I want to say. I don't say it but I can't suppress a silly little chuckle. I point to the one nearest the window. "Er, that one."

I stare at it, spaced out, not quite on planet Earth, then look back at my suitcase on the rack. Unpacking is too much to think about.

"I'm not unpacking now. Let's collect the others. I want to see this 'ere waterfall."

*

It's when we reach the thatched gatehouse to the National Park that a whisper of something brushes across my eardrums, registering in my sub-consciousness. It's not a sound is it? Maybe it is. I hear it, then can't hear it, then feel it again. Gill and Piet are involved in some sort of debate on the merits of hiring the plastic ponchos that a woman is trying to persuade them to take. Gill's telling Piet she wants to keep her hair dry, and that I will too, and Piet's laughing at her.

I move a little away to where I can sense the whisper again. It's still there, but then it's not. There's too much interference – cars passing on the road to the bridge and the border post with Zambia, curio sellers calling from the gravel car park opposite where baboons are stalking around the assortment of passenger-carrying vehicles and private cars, tourists in conversation with the ticket officer. If it is a sound, I know what's causing it, and my squirm of anticipation increases.

We set off along the path ahead. I want to visualise, in the time-warp of my imagination, a sweating nineteenth-century explorer and his native guides hacking their way through the bush, listening in wonder to the whisper that becomes a breath and finally a roar and then stumbling upon the unbelievable sight of a river plunging over a seventy-metre high cliff. We're told that David Livingstone had already known for some time of the existence of *Mosi oa tunya* – The Smoke That Thunders – but now I need to pretend that I do not. That I've never seen the photographs or the films, that I cannot possibly guess what awaits me at the end of this path.

"Here we go. Watch your footing, Kitten," you breathe into my right ear. I have a subtle dusting of spray droplets on my face, and a super-sized Livingstone up here on my left, on his rock plinth, is slick and shiny like the paving beneath my feet. I devote no more than two seconds of my time to the good Doctor. Ahead, through the spindly bushes, I can see rushing white foam. You're tugging my hand, urging me on.

"Come."

We are poised above Devil's Cataract, where a part of the broad and hitherto peaceful Zambezi nearest to the south bank is compelled forward in a frenzy down an angled incline. It's not particularly wide. Beyond it is a thickly vegetated island mass.

"This is actually the very head of the falls," Gill shouts at me over the thunder of water. "That island there separates this section from the remainder of the river, and one *almighty* cliff. Come on, we can go down lower and get this stunning view along the whole gorge."

Below the promontory on which Livingstone's statue stands watch is a shelf, essentially just a ledge on the cliff opposite the creaming falls. It's reached by a series of deeply cut, treacherous steps. In front of us, Gill is hanging onto Piet's arm.

"We're below the level of the river here," Piet yells as we reach the bottom.

We're all drenched now. The hoods of these hired ponchos aren't going to prevent our hair from getting wet at all and Piet's beard is all silvery round the edges. Devil's Cataract is thundering and terrifying on our left and the main body of the Falls stretches out before us. The incessant roar of millions of gallons of water, the sound and sight of such enormous power, takes complete command of the senses. There's a rainbow arching through the mist, its bright spectrum so intense that it appears solid enough to climb.

I'm asked what I think, how I feel, and 'humbled' is the only word I can dredge up after some scratching around.

We spend a few minutes being swamped by the magnitude of the sight and sound, then we have to leave as there's a group of six tourists coming down on top of us. The ledge isn't big enough to accommodate everyone.

It takes us nearly an hour to wander the meandering pathway through the rainforest, stopping at each viewing point, photographing, being awed. The path terminates amongst the black, glistening rocks of Danger Point. One step too far, a slip on the wet basalt, and the raging waters in the gorge below are the next stop.

"Some spectacle, huh?" There's a pride in your voice as though Victoria Falls is one of your personal possessions. "Impressed?"

"That's as good a word as any, I suppose, given that no words are really good enough. Yes, I'm impressed."

You stand behind, your arms around my waist, and I allow myself to be mesmerised by the torrent below. A freight train dragging ten or so heavily laden, tarpaulin covered trucks behind it, is chugging across the landscape behind us, having crossed the bridge from Zambia. Piet's turned his back on the Falls and is clicking away with his camera.

I'm aware that Gill's been watching us like a proud parent – it's like she can't get over me and you – and now she's gesticulating to us to follow her.

"Shall we head off? I'm in dire need of lunch. We can come back later for more photos and… train spotting. Piet! Why are you wasting film on a *train*, for God's sake? Didn't you notice the waterfall?"

I've used up a whole thirty-six exposure film already.

*

So the next phase in my life is going back to our shared room. Crowding into my head are thoughts of showering, getting undressed, all the mundane things you and I do, and have done all our lives, every day, but just not together. Like Mum and Dad do together. All through the tribal dance show, while my soul was absorbing the drum rhythms like a drug, we sat with our arms around each other and I focussed on enjoying being so close to your body while shutting my mind deliberately to what was to come. The immediate future will have to unfold in its own way – I have no plans or ideas on what I should or shouldn't do. I wonder if you do. With this blank wall in front of me, we're all planning tomorrow and the next day while sipping gin and tonic on the terrace. The spray is still visible, a ghostly white haze against the night sky.

Gill and Piet are tired, they both admit. They're finishing up their drinks. This is completely normal for them now, to go to bed together, do the mundane things together. Did Gill feel like this the first time she spent a night with Tim Morrison, all those years ago? I never asked her.

"Crocodile ranch tour tomorrow then. What time?" Gill finished her sentence with a wide yawn.

"Nine-thirty," says Piet. "Breakfast at eight, guys?"

"Have a good night," says Gill. She smiles benignly as if I've been married to her cousin for years, but I can feel her prescience, and she's very happy with it.

We take our showers demurely, respectfully even, each one undressing in the bathroom and then redressing before emerging, you in a T-shirt and pyjama shorts and me in a thigh-length plain pink night-shirt. I left the Minnie Mouse one at home.

"Did you actually *tell* your mother about this?" you ask as you click in the security chain on the main door. You turn to face me. "I kind of think you didn't. Are you sure you're okay? I am. I hope you are."

You look quite as flummoxed as I feel and it's very endearing.

I sit on my bed propped on one hand, legs crossed at the ankles, hoping I'm presenting an appealing picture. I deliberately didn't wash my hair because wet hair doesn't seem like a good idea in this situation. It didn't look too bad when I examined it minutely in the mirror. I wasn't sure whether to leave it loose or put it in a pony tail. I've left it loose.

"So she asked me at one point if I was happy I could afford this little trip, as she put it, and I said yes of course, I'm capable of looking after my own finances now thank you, the air fares aren't really all that expensive and we've got a good dinner-bed-and-breakfast deal. She goes, 'All right, all right,' in like, surrender, and then 'It's just that I know they really sting you for a single room supplement.' I still can't make up my mind whether she was probing or being concerned about my bank balance. We never discussed it any further than that."

I leave out the fact that her mind was most likely completely occupied with winding up life in Zimbabwe and emigrating.

You cross the room and sit opposite me on your bed in what appears to be a mixture of amazement and blatant apprehension.

"You look so pretty," you say. "I can't believe how lucky I am that I've finally got you."

The state of limbo lifts away from my shoulders. I cross over and perch next to you, slide my left arm around your shoulders and take your right hand in my right. For a few moments we remain like that and I fiddle pointlessly with your signet ring.

"I thought I loved Danny," I say, my eyes on the drawn curtains in front of me. The room service people closed them, turned down the bed coverlets and left a small box on each pillow. Chocolates probably. Odd that neither of us has thought to open them and find out.

"I've said this before, haven't I? He was such a good friend and we had fun enjoying each other's company. Going out, watching movies, eating ice creams. But then… Then he started to get… How do I put it? He started to get intense. Yes, intense. Not pushy and certainly not trying to force me into anything. It was nothing to do with sex. Or maybe it was ultimately, but he was careful and considerate. But he was full of promises and excited about ideas for our future. No, my future. *He* had ideas for *my* future. We would get married of course. And I didn't want him to map out my life. In spite of what I thought of him, I couldn't bear the thought of him deciding what was good for me and what I should be trying to achieve. He was only doing it because he cared about me. He wanted me to give up riding because I might get hurt. And how can I fault that? That was a good thing, surely? It proved he cherished me. But deep down I knew that one of the main reasons he didn't want me hurt was because he wanted me to be a mother. A mother to his children."

I feel you watching my face and I feel your calm and understanding. I've never voiced this to anyone, not even my mother or my sister. Not to Jess or to Gill. Or Danny. He's the one I maybe should've confided in.

"I knew he was seeing me as his wife and a mother. So many of the girls I know dream of that alone. I don't think there's anything wrong with that at all. But what *was* wrong, was that I didn't want it from *him*. How I could know that, when we got on so well together, I have no idea, but I did."

No, I could not have told Danny that. It would've hurt him so much.

You touch my face as though you're blind, feeling every curve, each eyelid, my nose.

"I thought I was weird." I take your hand away from me, not because I don't like what you're doing, but because it's suddenly of vital importance that you hear me out and I can't concentrate like this. "I thought I was some sort of freak. Why wasn't I falling into bed with him and planning the wedding? My classmates were all wanting sex and marriage in whatever order, or so it seemed. But then when you and I started… When we… when *we* got together… It's so different. We are us. Now I want to… You make me feel so… I want to…"

I can't quite say it.

You wriggle back a little and nudge my left shoulder towards the window.

"Here, turn round so your back is to me. I want you to understand you don't have to do anything to keep me. I'm yours if you want me and we have a whole lifetime ahead of us. Or at least, I hope you think we have a whole lifetime ahead of us?"

"Oh God, yes!" I'm laughing, but in a choked up sort of way.

I hook my right knee up onto the bed and you start to smooth your hands across my shoulders over the night shirt. You massage and knead for a while, then slowly slide your hands under the shirt and continue to do the same, your touch electric on my skin. I do nothing to resist as the massaging moves from the ridge of my shoulder line down to the tips of the scapulae. My eyes close; I succumb to the deep relaxation of it and I have no idea how long we stay like that. At some stage we swap roles with me lying beside you. You take the T-shirt off and I run my fingertips over the tanned skin of your back, down the undulations of your spine and then across your neck at the hairline. I tuck my fingers briefly under the waistband of your shorts occasionally. Your right side is uppermost and I run my fingers over the entry wound scar on the front and the corresponding exit wound on the back very lightly. I never even got to see Danny's torso naked, did I? I can't honestly remember.

We talk on and off. You tell me again how you told Sherrie you wanted to have a break from her after she began referring to Charles and Moira as the in-laws.

"So you see," you murmur, sounding as sleepy as I feel, "it was the same for both of us. Our partners were trying to map out the future for each of us. Which as you say, is not the issue in itself. It's that it wasn't the right thing."

"But this is."

"Yes. For me, for sure."

I grin all to myself into your back.

Entering new territory on the map of your life I probe a little about former girlfriends, but apart from Sherrie there've been none because you never wanted to get close to anyone, exactly as I'd thought. I dare myself to reveal the rumours Karen once spread about you and Joanna Coetzee, and your sole comment is, "What? That slut? I don't think so."

*

It's half-past two when I awake with a start to find I'm resting against you with one arm limply over your waist. Your breathing is deep and regular and I watch your back moving fractionally in time with it for a few moments until sleep begins to wash back into my brain. I can't get over how immensely pleased with life and myself I am. The bedside light is still on but I can't find any reason to be bothered to turn it off.

SUNDAY 17TH MAY 1981

It's the bedside telephone. Deep sleep blasted into small pieces. I fumble in the darkness, locate the bloody thing and manage to find the wit to say, "Hello?"

"Your wake-up call, Madam!"

The guy is sickeningly cheerful and I get the vibe that he's expecting a response.

"Thank you," I croak and he tells me to have a nice day, bless him. Beside me, you stir and run a finger across my shoulders. Your luminous watch is beside the telephone and it tells me it's six-thirty-three.

"Reception?"

"Uh huh." I slide back under the covers where it's cosy and happy and just right. "I'll bet they just love doing that. *Hello, Madam, good morning and welcome to the world! I've been at my desk all night and it's time you were awake too. It's your wake-up call!* And you can't just tell him to bugger off. Well, I suppose you could, but it's not very fair."

"Never mind," you whisper, your lips against my ear. "Gill and Piet will get it next."

You wriggle off the bed behind me and a minute later come the sounds of running water and vigorous tooth scrubbing. When we woke up yesterday it was seven-thirty and the pale gold sun rays were seeking to push their way through a minute gap between the curtains, but it's too dark still for that today. I can smile to myself now, remembering how you appeared in the bathroom doorway, dabbing at your mouth with a hand towel, semi-dressed in jeans only, and asking, "So how was the first night spent with your lover?"

Lover. My God, I've never had one of those before. Only a boyfriend. Poor Danny. He just hadn't been qualified to gain that title.

I told you it was terrible, that I'd thought the earth was supposed to move and you kissed the top of my head and said we'd be in a sorry state as a species if it did move and also then you'd never get to make love to me. Well after the second night with my lover, and what he did to me, I know both of these things can and will happen.

"I have a confession to make," I say, sitting up and speaking to the half-closed bathroom door.

"What's that?" in a muffled voice. You put your face around the door with a toothbrush sticking out of it.

"I asked Gill yesterday to call the Wankie Safari Lodge and the Cutty Sark Hotel and try to change our room to one with a double bed. She said she thinks it's been done. She was, shall we say, absolutely delighted."

I'm still a virgin, but the countdown has begun.

SATURDAY 30TH MAY 1981

Waterloo carries me towards the front of the field, oblivious to my presence. I like to think I'm an effective rider but this isn't a show jumper and I'm clearly no race jockey. The horse is doing it all himself. He takes the line closest to the inside of the track and the urgent drumming of hooves on earth is the only sound that fills my head.

The first-placed horse, the bay Anglo-Arab, pulls five lengths clear. For a time nothing changes and the whole world is dust and drumming and pounding movement. I get a brief moment of panic when my horse's offside hooves cut too close to the small ridge of soil that marks the inner edge of the track. I jerk on the left rein and he does a surprised swerve, like he's just realised he has someone crouched on his back.

We sweep into the home straight. I click my tongue experimentally and discover that, in contrast to poor Sapper in the C Division race, this horse has infinite power in reserve. The surge takes away what little breath I have left but by God, now I know what Nathan meant. That day he made me ride Encore on ten circuits of the ten-acre paddock with my stirrups shorter than they are now, and my thighs were burning and I was declaring I'd never actually wanted to do race riding, he told me, "You'll probably get the biggest adrenaline rush of your life so far when you feel a horse literally sink slightly under you and go up several gears at once. Honestly, you'll understand when it happens."

Well, I do. The Anglo-Arab falls away to nowhere and my way to the finish line is clear.

Pushing the contact back and forth, back and forth like he taught me, I hear my own voice drowning out the hysterical roar from the spectators, "Go! Go! Go on! Good boy!" I should take one hand off to crack my whip like Sherrie did, but I can't bring myself to do it for fear of unbalancing both myself and the horse.

We thunder past the red-painted iron circle mounted on a post.

He wants to keep going. Only when he realises he's left all the other horses behind does he give in and come back to a walk and it's a fair way back to the off-saddling enclosures. A groom rushes up to grab the bridle and Mick du Preez is hot on his heels, puffing more than I am. I can see Gill's face in the crowded spectators and beside her Piet waving a small piece of paper. I'm on the ground stroking Waterloo's slippery, lathered neck, with Mick undoing the girth, when you appear between us and put an arm round me and slap Mick on the back simultaneously.

"You did it! Did you bet on yourself?"

"No."

"Your girl would give you a run for your money," Mick says and I have a private embarrassed moment remembering the last race meeting and how I imagined I was fancying him. He *is* good looking and he's wearing that Stetson again but I don't need him now.

*

"See you in the bar," Gill calls as I shoulder my sports bag.

The community centre washrooms here are posher than the ones at Eagle's Down Farm. That other race meeting filled with jealousy and despair is in the distant past. Today everything is right with the world. All of the shower cubicles are free so I dump my bag outside one of them and dig for my soap and shampoo.

There are a few other women around, standing talking in the washbasin area. One of them, watching me, asks, "Are you a professional jockey?"

I'm wearing my cream jodhpurs and black show-jumping boots – not kitted out in real jockey gear like Sherrie was. I have to laugh.

"No, not me. I'm just pretending."

When I get back to the others where they're seated at a table in the corner of the hall, there's a bottle of Moet on the table and between you and Piet is a man I've never seen before. He's probably thirty-ish – I'm not very good at judging age. Plain black T-shirt and jeans, dark, curly hair and a lop-sided smile.

"Champers in plastic glasses. But who cares?" Gill snatches up the bottle and hands it to Piet. "Do the honours please, my darling. We need to celebrate Tessa's win here."

"I should maybe take it outside to pop the cork," he says, frowning. "Do it in here and everyone'll hit the deck."

The stranger turns his smile into a wide, toothy grin and punches you on the shoulder. "Remind you of something, Rifleman Owen?"

I lean over to drop my bag behind the table, deliberately close to you, and get a noseful of the tantalising, spicy odour of your aftershave. Another flashback to that race meeting evening in a past life.

"Here, Kitten," you say, "I'd like you to meet Scott Romford. I've mentioned him somewhere along the line, I know. Scotty, this is Tessa."

Scott Romford half stands and bows. "Delighted! So you're the one who got him in the end? We were always amazed that he didn't have a girl back home to send him soppy messages on the radio shows."

Piet and Gill have taken the Moet away. You call after them, "Oi! Don't drink it out there!" then pull me down on the edge of your chair, shifting to give me space.

"Scotty served with me – Rhodesia Regiment, 2 Independent Company. In fact, he was the leader of our last patrol and the Florence Nightingale who nearly cut my leg off with a tourniquet and then tenderly placed a pack under my head and a hat over my face. Bless you, Scotty."

He jabs two fingers up in front of your face.

"Do you remember that? Tell you what, Owen, you were lucky we managed to get the chopper in so quickly. You were running out of the red stuff pretty rapidly."

"You wouldn't give me any morphine, you bastard."

He blinks and turns his very well affected hurt and dismay on me.

"He's so ungrateful, Tessa. We had no idea where he was, then we found a blood trail to follow and he was in amongst the rocks convinced the battle was still on and surrounded by a pile of doppies. I got him on the ground and he was wriggling about all over the place whilst I was trying to work out how best to make sure we didn't lose him. You kept telling me you were fine, you stupid git. 'I can walk' you said. 'It doesn't fucking hurt' you said. 'Fucking leave me alone' you said. Then you promptly passed out."

"You have no idea how determined I was to make sure I *could* wriggle about, *boet*. I couldn't really feel much. At the time. In fact, that's what worried me when all I could see when I looked down was blood."

You squeeze me around the waist and your face against mine is inviting me to join in the fun. The two of you are acting like you're sharing a recollection of some ludicrous predicament in a Carry On film.

Scotty sits back and looks us both over with a somewhat appraising eye. "I heard you'd recovered fully and I'm glad. We came out pretty much unscathed, didn't we? You remember Neil Fenton, who was with us? And Edmund Tshuma?"

You have this way of making me feel everything you do. I can sense your mood switching down now and although I quite like Scotty I wish he'd go away. You say to me, "Edmund took a bullet in the head about three months later. And Neil got himself blown up by a landmine."

You have told me about this Corporal Romford, who did a lot to try and save your life. And also about this guy Neil. Not that he'd died, but how you'd watched him take out four of the eight ZIPRA soldiers with the MAG. You told me how, after you'd watched another of them go down under your own fire, you got hit and lay there within touching distance of the rocks but didn't dare move in case one of them saw you and came back to finish the job. You wondered if you might be dead at one point but realised you could feel the heat from your rifle barrel so figured you weren't, and then you crawled in amongst the rocks to try and carry on the fight. I've lived through all this on your behalf many more times than

I've wanted to, but you don't know this. You laugh it off nowadays anyway and I would never dream of upsetting you by telling you how much pain it causes me. It's a thing of the past.

"You weren't in the saddle today then?" Scotty asks. "I seem to remember you were hankering after getting transferred to the Grey's Scouts. That you'd always been a rider."

"I still am," you tell him. "And I did end up in the Grey's as an instructor. I've done a couple of these amateur things, but the trainer I usually ride for only had two horses running today and my Tess needed a chance to try this."

The toothy grin encompasses me. "And she won! Obviously as good as you then."

The return of the champagne bottle saves me from having to get all coy and make denials. You lean across me to take it from Piet and carry out a thorough check of its contents by holding it up to the light.

"It's all there. Come on, Nath," says Piet, lining up the plastic cups. "You have to share. Scott, have some with us."

Scotty holds up his hands.

"You're very kind, but I won't, thanks. I need to get back to Kara and her folks anyway or I'll be in the shit. Very nice to meet you two, good to see you again Nathan, and delighted to meet you, Tessa."

You do the African handshake with him.

"Go well, Corporal. Take care of yourself."

Scotty bows and takes his leave. You start pouring, tilting each cup, waiting for the bubbles to subside and then topping up.

We toast each other and Gill remarks, "He's a nice guy. Does he live around here?"

You give us Scotty's backstory. His wife's folks have a farm. He's not from farming stock but he works together with his father-in-law now. A good bloke but, in spite of what he said, he hasn't exactly come out of the war unscathed; never physically wounded but mentally affected. It's not uncommon and it's not a new thing.

"Shell shock," says Piet.

"Yes, but that implies trauma as a result of having been fired on, mortared, exposed to mortal danger in some way and that doesn't cover it. A lot of guys dealt with all that okay and ended up badly traumatised by the horrific massacres and torture of civilians. We got more than our fair share of scenes of unspeakable violence and cruelty."

Piet stares down into his champagne. "And the Rhodesian Army wasn't squeaky clean."

"No."

"He looks quite normal." I can see him now, over on the far side of the hall, at a table with a pretty blonde woman, an older couple and a dark-haired boy of about four.

"I think he's probably got it under control. I had news about him around eighteen months or so ago that he got very violent, especially when drunk – something he never used to do apparently – and that his wife left him for a period. He was encouraged to take up karate to focus and channel the aggression and it seems he's done very well. He told me just now he's aiming to become an instructor."

You're also watching him, and you raise the small white plastic cup into the air towards him. He's unaware, facing the other way.

"Cheers, Scotty man. You all might've thought he refused the champagne out of politeness, but he doesn't touch alcohol now. Hasn't in about a year."

I raise my cup to him as well in a silent toast. He's my hero. He made sure you came back.

*

You send me on my way with a probing kiss and a "See ya tomorrow" and I float up the drive, reliving how we danced to anything that came along and how, when it became too hot inside the hall, we wandered out into the darkness of the early winter night, then when the coolness started to creep under our skins we slipped back into the noisy, throbbing light to continue where we'd left off. My feet are decidedly tender.

I'm already turning my thoughts to next weekend and the work do with our sub contractors at the Meikles Hotel. The sound of Piet's car's fades away and I spend a few pleasant moments imagining your face when you see me in the turquoise silk cocktail dress. Sweet. I hop up the steps onto the patio into the glare of the security light.

Once in the hallway I realise that the dining room light is on. It's gone midnight. It must be Rosie, although she's normally in the lounge watching TV in darkness.

But no, the rumble I can hear is Dad's voice. No words, just the sound. Don't tell me they're waiting up for me? Nathan's ticked a lot of their boxes but they still haven't quite got over Danny. Mum did have a go at lodging an objection that he's a bit more than three and a half years older than me, until I pointed out that Dad's four years older than her.

"That you Tessa?"

Mum's face appears in the archway. She fumbles for the switch and I blink and turn back to re-lock the door to avoid the flood of bright light.

"Did you have a good day?"

"I won, Mum. I won a race."

This is odd and I'm starting to not like it. Now my eyes have adjusted a bit I see the dining room table behind her is littered with papers and soft cover files.

She starts to say something but then thinks better of it. Good. I don't need another lecture on the dangers of race riding. Keeping me away from extreme sports is one category in which poor Nathan has failed to gain any points so far.

But then I take in her expression and feel guilty. She's a mother; of course she's going to worry. I'm thinking I'll give her a hug, but as I approach her I see the hefty elephant-hide briefcase in which Dad keeps all the Important Papers. It's always kept on the top shelf of the linen cupboard but there it is, open on the floor, its contents in disarray. On the top are our four passports.

A few seconds pass. They're both watching me. Perhaps, just perhaps, they're planning a holiday?

"Dad's been offered a job in Southampton."

Of course. Here we go again. I have myself an amazing day and my life is just going as I want it and I come home and…

She starts to babble on – the name of the company, the position he's been offered, the fact that one of his former colleagues who left eighteen months ago had sent him the advertisement. I barely hear her. A voice inside my head is screaming at her to stop acting like she thinks I'm interested.

She smiles at me but her eyes are fixed beyond me somewhere. "We'll all talk about it together tomorrow."

I find my voice. A voice, anyway. I'm not sure it's mine.

"I don't want to talk about it tomorrow. I don't want to talk about it ever, for that matter. I'm going to Makuti Park tomorrow morning anyway. Good night."

It's okay. I'll just walk away and go to bed. I'll think about what work I'll do with Encore in the morning. Nathan and I will probably hack out in the afternoon. I might get a chance to ride Bravo again.

"We *will* discuss it tomorrow and you *will* be there."

I stop in my tracks towards the passageway, blood thudding in my ears, a knot in my stomach. I've never heard that tone in him before. This is really happening. I don't turn back.

Close the door. Don't put the light on. Creep to the bed. Kick off my trainers. Crawl, fully dressed, under the eiderdown. Put pillow over head.

*

At three o'clock the house is silent and dark. The other bedroom doors are shut and the cold of the parquet floor seeps through my socks as I tiptoe to the bathroom. Good. It's here. I thought I remembered there being a half-used pack on the bottom shelf of the cabinet. Cupping my hand under the running tap, I down four of them. It's not so easy swallowing them with my head tipped downwards but I manage to do it without choking and making a noise. So it's technically a mild overdose. So what? I really do have a thumping headache but I also have no intention of lying awake all night chasing options around in my brain.

SUNDAY 31ST MAY 1981

Twilight. In the evening, this yields a sense of closing, of retiring at the end of the day into the stillness of the night. At dawn, however, it creates its own special feeling of promise, of coming awake and of an expectancy of the day to come. Some of the bird calls began just before the sky showed any signs of lightening. How do they know when to start? When you think about it, everything is timeless. The earth is merely rotating endlessly but we insist on telling ourselves that the sun sets and then rises again, wherever we live, day after day. The pattern of life repeats itself over and over on a daily and a yearly basis while we humans create our own little problems and dilemmas and our wars and consider ourselves to be the highest and mightiest of all life forms.

As the darkness eases, the tops of the eucalyptus trees at the end of the neighbours' garden take form. In between the chains of street lights in the valley is the odd single glow here and there, probably a lighted room behind curtains. The population is stirring. Some of it's already on its way; a vehicle somewhere accelerates through its gears and fades into the distance. These folks are early risers for a Sunday morning, but they are nevertheless getting on with their lives as normal. The pattern of life. The everyday activities. On any other Sunday, I would still be asleep. I would drag myself out of bed at around seven-thirty, drink coffee, eat toast and marmalade and then head off to Makuti Park to enjoy my day.

Instead, I'm here, on the verandah in the chilly dawn. I'm huddled in my tracksuit bottoms, slippers and a thick dressing gown and I probably won't enjoy my day very much. At least Skellum's perfectly happy, lying with his back against me. He doesn't perceive the company of one of his pack at this time of the morning as odd at all. Lucky dog, just living in the moment.

The dawn light is rosy. Almost red, in fact. What was that rhyme about red sky at night and red sky in the morning? I never really got what it was supposed to mean and right now I don't care. It's beautiful. The new light reveals strips of cloud low on the eastern horizon. The air smells sweet and unmistakeably of the earth, woodsmoke and Africa.

Yes, this is my decision. My mind is made up. It's got to be sorted, and now, before anyone else in this house stirs. I'm on my feet and Skellum has scattered aside to make way, his feathery tail sweeping the air behind him, tongue lolling, eyes smiling. I recall with amazing clarity the day we all went to the SPCA kennels to choose him, a dog to be ours for life. A dog is for life, and so is a cat. Cleo.

Hot tears smarting – no, don't dwell on that now. My plan will resolve that. I need to focus on the ideas forming in the deepest recesses of my mind.

The brass wall clock in the hallway says it's twenty-past six. I'll get dressed quickly, quietly, sneak out. Everyone at Makuti Park will be up and about by now. I won't drive. I'll ride my bike and wear mittens and ear muffs against the cold air.

But although I manage to get changed into my jeans and a sweater and tackies, brush my hair and clip it back and get out of my room again in less than ten minutes, Dad's beaten me to it. He's in the kitchen. How did he get there so quietly? I'm now face to face with him as he fills the kettle from the cold tap.

"You're up early. Going out already?"

His voice is guarded.

I feel like a child caught with its fingers in the biscuit tin. Trapped.

"No. Yes! Yes, I was going to cycle over to Makuti Park."

He says nothing while he carries the kettle across to its habitual location, pushes the cord into its socket and presses the wall switch down. I dither on the spot, hating myself for being indecisive. Okay, I'll bolt.

"I shan't be long. I'm not going to ride today but I plan to tomorrow after work so I want to set up a jumping grid in the ménage now. To give me more time tomorrow. You know?"

It sounds entirely plausible, if a bit gabbled.

"Don't you want breakfast first? Remember I wanted to speak to you later."

How could I forget?

"No thank you. Yes." And I'm gone, the shed key clutched in one hand, the mittens in the other. There's a spare key in the drawer if anyone else needs the shed. I'll just take this one with me. Not going back into the house.

*

Charles is seated alone at the kitchen table with a mug clasped between his great hands. Its liquid contents are dark – his favourite strong, sweet coffee – and steaming in the chilly air.

"Tessa? My goodness!" His features snap to attention. "Find a scorpion in your bed?"

"No! Frankly, a scorpion in my bed wouldn't have bothered me today. It would've got tossed out."

He laughs, but his brows are still puzzled.

Faced with a situation I've created all by myself, now I falter. I haven't planned what to say. My newly hatched idea filled me with a desperate hoping back at home but now the time has come to put it into words I'm floundering. Bless Charles. His smile is warm and welcoming in spite of my intrusion on his peaceful early morning solitude – and it *is* a ridiculous time to come calling. It's been normal for me to turn up here earlier than is considered polite more times than I care to remember, but never this early, and today isn't normal. I'm freaked out, and the Owens are more than just friends.

"Charles." I pull out a chair and sit facing him. "I'm so sorry to disturb you so early but I have to talk to you. And also to Moira and, of course, very definitely to Nathan."

He reaches out to cover the hand I've just laid on the table with one of his own.

"You have some sort of problem sweetheart?"

"Yes. I have. You don't mind? I can wait until everyone's up. I'll go over to the stables for a bit."

"Nonsense. Look, get yourself whatever you want for breakfast and I'll go and rouse the troops. I'll be back in five."

My eyes rove over every darling familiar detail of the kitchen of my second home. Snatches of memory bombard me in a series of running visual effects. Returning home from a ride soaking wet. Casual conversations about anything and everything. Serious conversations about horse-training problems and that bloody nonsensical war. Hysterical conversations about the comedy of life at school. Drinking tea and eating buttered toast after a horse show. Gill's traditional birthday parties. I close my eyes and squeeze my hands together.

Charles is back in less than five and resumes his chair.

"Hello, love." Moira appears in the doorway in her gardening gear for the day – a fresh yellow T-shirt, jeans, canvas lace-up shoes. Her eyes flit from me to her husband and back again.

Behind her, entering almost on the run, is you. Fully dressed as well, but with half a face covered in shaving foam, the other half clean, and a razor in your hand.

"What's up?" you demand around Moira.

It's a relief to know my sense of humour hasn't left the country along with half the white population. A fist clenches my heart at the sight of your dear, sweet consternation, but the half-shaved, lopsided, uncombed, dripping image is, I realise in this instant, exactly what I need right now. The stress, which has been enveloping me like a physical thing, like a dense, suffocating blanket, is plucked away. How can I possibly be depressed, worried or tortured by the necessity of making life-changing decisions when you're looking at me like that?

It's that tear-squeezing sort of laughter. Charles and Moira are tittering cautiously – they clearly think I've completely lost it – and I can't see your reaction because I'm holding you so tightly. The razor, which must be hovering in the air above me, is dripping onto my left ear.

"Go and finish shaving, for God's sake, Nathan," says Charles in a small, strangled voice. "You look ridiculous."

You lead me away down the corridor to your room and the blue and white luxury of the adjacent en-suite without a word. I sit on the edge of the bath and watch while you complete the job, savouring every move. As you're chasing away the used water with much swirling and splashing and the cold tap on full bore, you remark, "I wonder if the water really goes down the plughole in the opposite direction north of the equator? It's one of those things they say but I've never seen it myself so I'm not sure whether to believe it or not. My family in England would know, I guess."

You have no idea how close to the bone you've cut. I'm all out of witty or appropriate replies on that one. You dry your hands on a thick navy blue towel then put them lightly on my shoulders and bend down to kiss my nose. You're shadowed by a puzzled worry.

"You're very quiet, Kitten. What's all this then? Charles says you're in some sort of trouble. It wasn't to do with the racing yesterday, was it?"

"No. It's a family problem. Come to the kitchen and I'll explain. I need all of you together."

When I tell them all, they're going to suspect that surely I must've had some sort of inkling this was going to happen, that it can't have come so dramatically out of the blue. If I let on that I've been nursing this burden for months, they'll want to know why I never said anything. And I don't have an answer, except that I've been in classic avoidance mode. That's over now though, and I'm entering fight mode.

Is this what it's like to be interviewed on TV? To be set up in front of people and have to talk to them, not knowing what their reaction will be or what questions they'll ask? Moira has set a plate of fresh croissants from the Greek bakery down the road on the table, along with the butter dish and a pot of strawberry jam. She offers me a side plate and a knife and I take them knowing they will remain unused.

I tell everything in a series of fits and starts and re-groupings. No-one interrupts.

I start with family financial history. 1974, when my father and his brother Harry inherited their parents' estate between them and Dad had his share transferred over to his account here. Fast forward to 1975, when Mum and her sister Patricia got half shares in their parents' money. It was the combined windfall of a lifetime because we were going to live in Rhodesia for ever and they could pay off the mortgage and buy new cars and have a fabulous South African holiday.

I lead on to the intervening years and Dad's political views. His discontent with independence, majority rule, the way forward. His certainty that the country will end up on its knees, that law and order will collapse and that we'll lose our property and our rights. Charles is nodding as I relate this – he knows, of course. He's talked to Dad quite a bit over the years and he will have gathered much of it from me.

Then I come to February of this year. Dad's Aunty Julia, who was a bit of a hoarder of not only her own money but also of what she got from Dad's other aunt, Barbara, passes away suddenly. Dad and Uncle Harry are lined up to get about two hundred and fifty thousand pounds each. Dad realises this is his chance to get the family established in England and is determined to ensure the funds stay over there.

I conclude with my realisation of how desperate they both are to leave Zimbabwe, the tension and the arguments, the gearing up towards leaving going up another notch when he got an offer of employment yesterday.

I say, "I know they're only trying to do what they think is best" several times. I say that the parents of so many kids I knew at school have done just that, by seeking out a secure future in another country, paying for it with trauma – the packing up of possessions, the wallowing in incompetent administrative red tape, the attempts to mitigate financial loss – and ending up leaving behind a world they've built up over nearly a lifetime. I say that I'm guilty of refusing to play my part.

Charles is the first to speak after I've dried up.

"How old are you now, my love? Eighteen?"

"I will be in September. I don't think they can force me to go with them, can they? But the point is…"

Here, this is it. No backing out now.

"The point is, I'm not asking you all what I should do. I'm not asking you to advise me on whether I should go or not or to commiserate with me because I'm being forced to leave with them. I've already made my decision. I'm *not* going. But I will need your help. Mum and Dad might be reassured leaving me behind if my well-being is guaranteed and they know I'm in safe hands. What I'm asking you…"

"Is can you stay here?"

Throughout my speech you've sat next to me and neither looked at me nor moved a muscle but now you reach across and snatch both my hands out of my lap. My train of thought is derailed by the impact of the crushing sense of remorse that comes with the realisation that I've brought you to the brink of tears. I've done this. I've caused you pain. You were always the untouchable soul I could never fathom but now you're the one who's penetrated *my* soul and now here we are, both just about blubbing like babies. What do I do? There's nothing to say so I just raise and kiss one of the hands holding mine.

Moira and Charles are both studying the top of the table intently. Moira just said something but I'd tuned her out, so now she's apparently waiting for a response I'm not going to be able to give. It doesn't matter. I have more to say.

"I wouldn't want to impose myself on you all. I'd move out as soon as I could find my own flat in town. It'd be a temporary measure until my family has gone. It's just that I want the folks to be satisfied I'm safely accounted for, and anyway, I'm damned sure I'll need your moral support because it's going to be, well, kind of difficult."

Like I really need to tell them that.

And of course they tell me I can stay as long as I like, all three of them speaking over each other. Why am I trying to shake and nod my head at the same time?

"One thing we don't want to do is come between you and your family, though," Charles says when I've given up this pointless exercise. "We cannot be seen to be coming down on one side or the other. I can understand your point of view only too well but I respect your parents and their decisions based on the welfare of their family. All I can say is that you are more than welcome to live here and I vouch that I'll take responsibility for you."

"You're absolutely right, and I understand. They're still not going to like it though."

"When will you tell them?" Moira asks.

"Dad wants to talk to us all today. Tell us about his plans I guess. I'll have to play it by ear. Find the right moment."

There's no such thing as the right moment for something like this.

"I'd better go back," I say, more to talk myself into it than to inform the others. "I'm going to say hi to Encore and Induna first though. I can't thank you enough for what you're about to do for me, you know that, right? I'll pay my way of course. I..."

I get told to stop protesting and to go to the stables and to take my man with me before he eats all the croissants.

The horses are still in and the grooms haven't finished their own breakfast yet. It's only when I lean on Induna's half door and watch him munching his hay, his black tail flicking at imaginary flies and his off hind hoof tipped up in rest, that the tears really come.

"How could I leave him behind, Nathan? Do you know what my father said to me? When I asked, 'What about the horses?' he actually said, 'What about the horses? You can sell them can't you?' Sell them! Just like that! Because he doesn't care a toss what happens to them."

Jumbled up. I'm hopelessly jumbled up. It's all indescribable relief, blood pumping excitement and blood draining dread in equal measures. Now with you pressing into me from behind like that, it's the blood draining that steps up and it's only your arms that are keeping me from dropping to the ground.

"Hey, hey, come on, stop. Listen to me. He shouldn't have done that. But it doesn't matter, does it? You won't be selling them and you won't be leaving them. And if they don't think themselves lucky, I sure as hell do. *I don't want you to leave the country and* I've got you coming to stay here under my roof."

Then, after a pause, "If you were happy to leave or had made up your own mind to do so, I'd have to emigrate myself. I stuffed up a lot of things in my early life but now I've done something right I'm not letting it go. I love you."

"I'm not going to go. They can't drag me away from you."

I wriggle round to face him. Our faces are very close and so are our bodies. The light-headedness has lifted slightly.

"Look, I've got to go home now, but will you do me a favour? I want to see Gill later today. Can you phone her for me? I can't do it from home under the circumstances. Ask her if she'll be at home. Explain as much as you like. If she's not going to be in, phone me, but otherwise I'll just drive out there. Do you mind?"

"Don't be silly. Let's go and get your bike. I could go with you to Gill's but I guess you'd probably rather do it on your own?"

You so know my mind. I'll go it alone today but thankfully I'm not alone.

*

Dad's decided on a light-hearted approach.

He needn't have bothered. Mum's happy about it anyway and Rosie's warming to the idea and I have other plans. I sit in unfocussed silence while he gives his discourse on the interview he's going to attend and the consulting practice from which it's been offered. He talks a lot about the plans he's hatching for the purchase of property with Julia's money. He mentions the names of places near Southampton. They mean nothing to me.

"You know a funny thing, girls? Over here any dwelling is called a house, irrespective of whether it has one or two storeys or is split-level. In England, they call single-storey houses *bungalows* and what we would call a double storey they call a *house*. Strange, hey?"

Rosie says "Wow" although I know damned well she knows this fact, as do I. Dad takes my lack of response as an indication that I need further enlightening.

"*Bungalow* is an Indian word."

"Yes. I know."

"Okay."

He pauses, swallows, carries on. Rosie's education is set out next. A list of grammar schools has been sent for and arrived and has been scrutinised. My sister's expression, guarded at the start of the meeting, softens. She's picturing a new and different environment. She's thinking A Levels and university and leaving Zimbabwe way behind. With a despair I've never encountered before, I sense this as easily as I feel her shift several steps away from me mentally.

"So tell me what you think of all this, Tessa."

I didn't want to be asked what I think. I certainly don't want to tell them what I think.

"Please don't. There's just too much to consider right now. How can I take it all in?"

They wait for me. Three times I start to move my hands away from my face, where I seem to have placed them without knowing I've done it, but each time I actually only twitch muscles fractionally. Speaking from behind them, I mumble a bit about what I said to Mum – don't you remember, Mum? – about how you should all take this opportunity to go, a great opportunity, don't you know I support your decision entirely, you're right to move back given the circumstances but I'm going to stay.

When Dad eventually sighs, it's difficult to say whether the sigh comes about through sadness, frustration, anger or helplessness. When I finally put my hands back in my lap, he's leaning forward in his armchair, elbows on his knees and hands clasped together and he's gazing absently out of the French doors down the length of the garden.

"I will never regret coming to live in this country. We came here, Sheila and I, with great hopes and we've had a wonderful life. We've been financially secure, been able to do the things we all enjoy in plenty of space and sunshine, had no heating bills to pay, owned a big house with a big garden and outdoor living area, employed a gardener. In many ways I don't want to go back to England. I've been away for more than twenty years and I've no idea what I'm going back to. But the blacks have got majority rule and we don't know, can't possibly foresee, what will happen here. I've said all this before. You know the reasons why I don't wish to stay. All I want to say now is, I think I'm doing right by my family."

Had he erupted angrily, cursed me for a fool, commanded that, as his daughter, I could bloody well knuckle down to obedience or else, it would have been so much easier to turn solidly against him, to use his bitterness to strengthen my own resolve. Instead, I throw myself across the room and hug him with more passion than I've done in many years.

"Dad! Dad. You *are* doing the right thing. Of course you are. All I ask is that you try to consider my point of view. Understand why *I* don't want to leave my life here. I'm not a hundred per cent certain I know what's right. None of us are. I've just got together with Nathan and I love him, Dad. He's the one I'll always be with. I've known him practically all my life but now I'm in love with him. How can I just leave him? D'you know what he said today? He said if I leave with all of you he will have to go to England as well. He loves me too and he doesn't want this to end any more than I do."

Mum and Rosie are behind me. They haven't made a sound and whatever reactions they've had to this little pantomime I will never know.

"Look, I can stay with the Owens. I've already asked. You must know that. I talked it through with them this morning. They're not strangers to you either. I'll be perfectly safe with them and well looked after so you can set your mind at rest about that."

Only now do I stand up and look around. Rosie's gone – how did she do that so quietly? – and Mum's face is an odd shade of grey.

"You know I can live with the Owens," I repeat to both of them. "I hate to say this, but by the time everything's sorted out and you go I will be eighteen and you can't force me to go with you."

Where's Rosie gone? Mum bites her lip and continues to be grey.

"You talked to Nathan this morning? Did he persuade you to stay here?"

There's just a hint of outrage in her tone.

"No! I had already decided. Today I asked permission of Charles and Moira, is all. Charles has volunteered to kind of be my guardian. What Nathan *did* say, as I told you just now, was that if I was determined to emigrate with you he would be coming with us. I assume you wouldn't object to that?"

The conflict on her face would've been comical under any other circumstances.

Dad doesn't seem to be listening any longer and has closed his eyes. It's time to flee. I close the door between the lounge and the hallway as carefully as I can with shaking hands. For a heartbeat, I consider putting an ear to the keyhole to catch any subsequent conversation, but I've promised to visit Gill and Nathan hasn't phoned to say she won't be at home.

I collect my car keys from my room, hurry to the kitchen, pull open the back door already in flight to launch myself down the steps and there have to skid to a halt, grabbing at the door frame for support as I nearly fall over the crouched form of Rosie. There's a small sound, muffled and indefinable at first and I glimpse Skellum's tan-coloured muzzle – nowadays liberally speckled with grey – over my sister's shoulder.

She's cuddling the dog and making a low moaning, a keening sound that sets my spine crawling. For a few seconds I hover, poised as though flash frozen, then drop onto one knee behind the huddled pair. Skellum laughs up at me and wags his tail, with some difficulty considering the stranglehold in which he's contained. Rosie's face is smeared with her tears and the sticky results of her sniffling, her eyes rimmed with red. She struggles with a great gulping sob and blinks wet lashes.

"My dog. What are they going to do with my dog? I love him so much!"

In the midst of all this emotion, Skellum continues his tongue-lolling smile, although he's given up with the tail. There's a soft and gentle bump against my rear end and a questioning "Brrp?" and when we both squint down over our shoulders Cleo is there, curiosity in her intense yellow cat's eyes. Rosie lets out a howl. She tries to gather the cat up in her left arm but Cleo's not having that. She wriggles free and is down the steps into the garden in a flash.

"Shhh!" I whisper. "Nothing's going to happen to them. I can take them to Makuti Park with me, can't I?"

I have no doubt that if I turn up with my pets – our pets – in tow the Owens will say yes. Love me, love my dog and my cat and my horses. The Owens haven't had a dog as long as I've known them and I know why. Gill refused. She told Charles and Moira in no uncertain terms that although she wanted another dog, she didn't want to *lose* another dog. After both Winston and Captain had reached the end of their lives and the family had performed the ultimate act of kindness, she'd decided she never wanted to go through that again. She's no longer living there though.

Rosie's staring at me, her eyes huge with pathetic relief, still clutching the dog to her bosom.

"Oh yes!" she gasps, her lower lip quivering. "You see, Dad doesn't care about the animals. He would do what some other people have done – just take them to the vet and…"

"No, no, no! Shush!" I give her a shake to avoid a fresh flood of tears. "Daddy does care really. He just doesn't show it."

I hope I'm right, but in any case it doesn't matter.

"Skellum and Cleo will be fine. They'll love it at Makuti Park. There are no other dogs and I'm sure Cleo will get on with Kuti."

Rosie smears the tears across her face with her free hand and pushes back her dark, unruly fringe. As her hold slackens, Skellum backs out from under her arms, half falls down to the next step and stands like a statue, watching us cautiously for any more odd behaviours. The few ragged clouds I saw on the horizon at dawn have been carried across the sky on a cold wind and have blotted out the sun's rays in all but a few fleeting areas. Rosie's clad only in a thin T-shirt and a short skirt and she shivers. She stands, leaning on my shoulder for leverage.

"I'll put on my tracksuit and take Skellie for a walk."

She sniffs hard. "Coming, Tee?"

"No thanks. I'm going to Gill's farm. If I go now I can scrounge some lunch off her."

I leave her there and, as I close the gates behind my car, I catch sight of her waving the thick leather leash at a deliriously happy Skellum.

*

The sun's completely disappeared now. This lawn, lush and emerald at the time of the wedding, is now turning brown, dry and crisp in patches. Maryna van Rooyen is there on the verandah in her old wicker chair and she waves at me as I cruise past, pointing at her tea cup, eyebrows raised. I shake my head and effect a sad face, pointing my own finger at the windscreen in the direction of the cottage.

The walls have been lime-washed and the corrugated roof painted black so it doesn't look nearly as sorry for itself as it used to, tucked away as it is behind the stand of pines, out of sight of the world. New beds have been established along the front retaining wall of the verandah but nothing's been planted yet. Gill's Alfa Romeo is parked on the grass under the lounge side windows; there's no sign of Piet's pick-up. I ease my car alongside hers and turn the engine off, lean back against the headrest, eyes closed. This quiet garden, the evergreen pines, the dying grass under my car, the irrigated grazing paddocks beyond the hedge, the Hunyani range, the lake behind the hills – none of them give a shit about my woes. I so want to sit here and just let everything be perfect. Forever.

But I would be wasting my time. The car door closing sounds like a gunshot in the stillness.

They've made a start, but there's still a fair amount of work to be done. I hover for a few minutes at the crumbling concrete kitchen doorstep, dredging up memories from eons ago of conducting explorations around the derelict farmhouse at the far end of the *vlei* with Rosie and Jess. Like this place, it was probably built in the 1920s. It was most likely a farm manager's home on the old Woodford Estate, which had been sold off and subdivided around the time of the Second World War, but the old house fascinated us because its real history was a complete blank. We wasted hours poking around all the nooks and the remains of the antiquated plumbing system, trying to decide what it had looked like in its prime and which room had been the dining room, living room or main bedroom. The gaudy gloss paint may have been peeling from the internal walls, the window frames may have been empty and the internal doors all stolen but to our imaginations it was complete and alive. It was also alive in respect of the diverse life forms we encountered in there. Vegetation pushed through the most impossible cracks, cobwebs hung in great thick ropes from the decayed ceilings or from the exposed rafters where the lathe and plaster had fallen away completely, lizards and geckos clung to vertical faces or perched on the rafters to observe us and it was there that I came across the biggest, hairiest baboon spider ever. It was lurking in a dark corner and when we disturbed it and it ran out waving its long forelegs at us, we screamed and scarpered and then came tiptoeing back, daring each other to get the closest to its horrible hairiness and defensive aggression.

Gill would be mortified to know that her house reminds me of that old, dilapidated place. Her kitchen renovation project has made some progress since I was last here. The original bright green linoleum's gone and the floor boards have been repaired or renewed and overlain with warm, russet quarry tiles. The walls have been repainted a cream colour that contains a hint of honey. I can't remember what colour they were before, but I do remember thinking it was hideous. She's planned a full range of fitted units but in the meantime the aged Welsh dresser is still there against the wall opposite the door and so are the two mis-matching formica-topped freestanding cupboard units either side of the sink. The pipework under the sink is still concealed by that curtain of coarse material with the particularly violent floral pattern. Sort of sixties psychedelia, it is. First time I saw it, I said, "Hey man. Groovy. Where the hell did that monstrosity come from?" and Gill put on her pained face.

"Don't ask. It was one of Piet's mother's efforts at being hip. And don't worry, its future is bleak."

There's a small paraffin heater in the corner, its concave reflective panel throwing warmth across most of the room, but the open door will have reduced its efficiency to the minimum. I rap twice. There's no immediate response so I step inside, shut the door and cock my head to detect any signs of life.

At first all I get are strains of *The Tide is High* from a radio in another room but then there's a plasticky clatter like something's been dropped and a tap is turned on full. We catch sight of each other simultaneously – me stepping into the short parquet-floored corridor from the kitchen and Gill backing out into the corridor from the bathroom with a wet green cloth in one hand, a bottle of Handy Andy in the other and vexation exuding from the set of her jaw and stony face.

"Oh. Hello."

The vexation gives way to confusion.

"Didn't Nathan tell you I was coming?"

"Yes. Yes, he did. Sorry. Was just doing some household chores. Mercia is off today."

She tries a half smile. "I hope you didn't hear what I just said."

She steps aside and gestures towards the bathroom with the hand holding the bottle. Its viscous contents slosh heavily with the movement and I creep a bit closer at the invitation.

"In there. Honestly, I could *kill* Piet. He's left water all around the basin again, probably more than he can actually get *in* the thing. The top's off the toothpaste tube *as usual*. I found it in the *bath* yesterday, would you believe? And, the facecloth was screwed up and *sopping wet* behind the cold tap. It drives me *nuts*. Why is it *so* difficult for him to clean up after himself?"

She fires this last question at me and tightens the cap of the Handy Andy bottle with an unmistakeably neck-wringing motion. Then she breaks a grin that tells me I look just plain idiotic with my mouth open.

"Listen to me. The old nagging housewife already. Don't look so shocked, Tess. I wouldn't dream of killing Piet – not yet, anyway. I do still love him. Some of his habits just get on my nerves."

She re-enters the bathroom, discards the cloth and the Handy Andy into the basin and dries her hands on a pink towel.

"Mum warned me about this side of marriage but I can't say I actually believed her. And I have to break bad news to you, I'm afraid. Nathan makes the most God-awful mess when he shaves."

"I happen to know this. Remember I've shared hotel rooms with him? *And* I was in his bathroom just this morning."

Her eyebrows shoot up into her fringe. "This morning? Oh, really?"

I don't succeed at not blushing.

"As it happens, I arrived at your house at silly o'clock this morning to talk to everyone. Everyone except you of course, so that's why I'm here now. I had a problem. I'll tell you what I told them. By the sounds of it, Nathan didn't enlarge on why I wanted to see you."

The teasing fun has evaporated from her face, replaced by an uncertainty that's a small step away from trepidation. Dismay perhaps. Something that's uncomfortable on her anyway. Something that makes her take quick steps towards me and say, "Tessa? Oh. What? Tell me. Who?"

Defuse. I make a show of peering past her shoulder back into the bathroom.

"I thought I'd just walked in on some grisly murder scene. There's no body in the bath, is there?"

"No. No, don't be silly. Here, look, let's go to the kitchen and you can pour your heart out."

I do just that and she listens, like the rest of her family, with no interruptions. I relate the details of yesterday evening's events, my visit to Makuti Park this morning and our little family talk.

The radio's still playing to itself in the living room – the DJ's getting all excited about something in an exchange with a high-pitched voice on a phone-in.

"You know what, Tess? I'm not even remotely surprised. It was always a matter of when, not if. I've even talked to Mum and Dad about the possibility. Surely you must know we think enough of you to be very concerned about you. None of us dared to predict what you would do when the time came though."

My laugh doesn't contain one iota of humour. "I guess I knew it was going to happen as well and even I never attempted to predict what I would do."

"Tessa, you're ours. In a way you have been since the first day you visited us. You have no need to worry about not having a roof over your head. I know my folks will welcome you – well they have already – and you can stay here too as often as you like. We've been friends a long time now, my love. You don't need my permission."

My lovely Gill. This unselfish personality, this heart full of unbiased, open-minded views, this fulfilling empathy linking us – these have all been with me since my first ever riding lesson. Her angelic face is, of course, older, but her beauty has bloomed. Older and wiser, the saying goes, but is she any wiser now than before? She was mature and wise even as a thirteen-year-old. She guided my mind with a surety in herself that I'd never come across in another child, and she still does. That's what drew me to her. My life became entwined with hers on that day more than a decade ago and, looking at her eyes now, I see the same light, the same deep and intimate understanding and the same familiarity I've only ever recognised in my true blood sister. We've always understood each other on a level neither of us would be capable of explaining. And, as I now know, I share this very same bond with her cousin. Heaven knows, *that* took me long enough to find out.

"I just feel the need to justify myself. I haven't fallen out with my family but I can't walk away from my life here. To me, the politics aren't bad enough for that."

It's unnecessary to explain this. She's also committed to living in Zimbabwe with her new farmer-husband.

"Piet will be home just now," she says, linking her fingers in front of her face and stretching her shoulder muscles as if to ease the tension in them. "He gets hungry very quickly. He eats like a horse. Little and often. Not too little though and so often it's practically non-stop… who *said* that? Was it a character in a book?"

"In one of those kids' pony-story books. I read it too. What's for lunch then? I'm starving."

"Oh I see. Invited yourself to lunch now, have you? Right then, let's see what we've got. I'll turn up that heater. God, I don't envy your folks and Rosie going to live in England. We get a bit of frost here and go all to pieces. And it gets dark over there in the middle of the afternoon in winter. When I was working in Surrey we did morning stables in the dark and evening stables in the dark. It was awful."

A vehicle roars up the driveway and the driver stands on the brake immediately on the other side of the kitchen wall. The engine is cut, two doors slam and seconds later Piet's frame fills the doorway. Gill slides into his bear hug, her murderous intents history. There's someone else behind him. A smaller man. A whippet compared to Piet, and older, and his complexion is swarthy and sunburned. His grey, unruly hair, poking out from under his khaki bush hat, makes him look a bit like Mum's floor mop.

It's odd how sometimes we can take one look at a stranger and get either like or dislike. This guy has a latent aggression in his features, his posture and even the way he wears the hat. His little black eyes dart between Gill and me. Reaching some sort of conclusion, he swipes it off his head and jams it under his arm, liberating the hair.

"Yo! Tessa!" Piet releases Gill and I get snatched and pulled into him. He lets me go after squeezing all my breath out and gestures with his left arm. "This is our neighbour, Craig Maritz. Craig, meet Tessa."

Craig Maritz takes my hand courteously enough. When he smiles I note that one of his top incisors is broken so that the lower edge slopes at forty-five degrees away from its partner. It's repulsively fascinating.

"Want a bite to eat, Craigy, or is Charlotte going to feed you?" Gill asks.

"Does that mean that if I play my cards right I could get two lunches?"

He's Afrikaans. His thick, clipped accent is deep and guttural.

"Aren't you lucky then? It's only sandwiches, I warn you, but there's cold beef, tomatoes, cheese, Vegex or peanut butter or a combination of them all if you want. You choose and I'll make. Or rather, Tessa and I will make."

She smiles sideways at me.

Chair legs scrape on the quarry tiles. Maritz launches into a conversation that must have started out in the truck. About how the

Pretoria government can really put the squeeze on this place if they want. About how they've already taken back their rail locomotives and they've no intention of renewing the loans. More importantly, how they have Mugabe by the you-know-whatsits because they control all our fuel supplies, and if any of us here thinks we'll ever get that pipeline from Mozambique fully operational we're seriously deluded, what with it being blown up on a regular basis by bastard South African-backed dissidents.

He slaps the table with the flat of his hand and Gill, her back turned to him as she slices the bread, flinches.

"Hey, listen to this. I must tell you a story. You'll love this. Guy gets stopped at a roadblock, see, and the military cops ask if they can search his car. He lets them do it, then says, 'What are you looking for?' and the cop says 'We are looking for dissidents.' So the guy then says, 'Oh, well okay. I have some in the glove compartment if you want to take one.'"

He pauses, makes sure we're all with him. Piet has a suitably puzzled air about him and Gill carries on sandwich-making. I'm still staring at the tooth.

"Well the cops get very excited and tear the inside of the car to bits and then arrest the *ou*. He complains bitterly and wants to know why he's been arrested. 'Because you said you are hiding and transporting dissidents in your glove compartment,' the cop says. And the guy says, 'Oh DISSIDENTS? I thought you said DISPIRINS!'"

Oh God. With everything that's been going on today, I'm not in the mood for this. Piet's the only one of us who appreciates the joke. When he's done chuckling he hauls himself to his feet and stomps over to the fridge.

"I need a beer, man. D'you want one, Craig? Ladies?"

It goes on. They agree that they both thought Mugabe would cut all ties with South Africa directly after Independence, promptly committing economic suicide, and are amazed that he didn't. Piet says Pretoria won't pull the plug on us, and Maritz, his joviality now converted into resentment and the aggression I sensed earlier, says he's not so sure. Piet's wrong. The South Africans won't take much more of the repetitive bombardment of insults from us.

"You've heard them," he insists, casting around and then stabbing a forefinger at me like I'm personally responsible. "Even the weather report goes 'The racist, apartheid, imperialist, Zionist, fascist Pretoria regime is sending a cold weather front tomorrow which will bring rain to Zimbabwe.' Morons. It's not Reds-Under-The-Bed any more, it's *Japies*-Behind-Every-Bush. They're shit-scared that all those ex-Rhodesian military personnel living Down South will master-mind and carry out a *coup*."

"If they were going to do it, they'd have done it by now," Piet claims.

Maritz sighs. "You're probably right, but what they will do is continue to stir up trouble. You know, sabotage a little pipeline here, spark off a little tribal dispute there, plant a little bomb in that store. You remember how at the end of last year a quantity of arms was nicked from Cranborne Barracks? Then they found incendiary devices hidden at KG6 Barracks. South Africa was behind all that, I'll guarantee. Mugabe will still harbour ANC terrorists and allow them to have bases in this country. Ex-ZIPRA forces are miffed that ZANU(PF) has power. They're all back fighting again around Bulawayo, killing civilians etc. They're ripe for shit-stirring, I'll tell you. My boss-boy, Isaiah, reckons he's fed up with this lot. '*Baaz*,' he tells me, '*Baaz*, one of these days I am going to go Down South and join the army to fight against terrorists from *this* country.'"

He cackles at his efforts to mimic Isaiah's accent. "I tell you, most of these buggers knows they was better off under Ian Smith and those that doesn't know will soon find out. They thought Majority Rule would instantly solve all their problems and they would all get big houses and fast cars and a licence to print money. Well, now they find out the hard way that we've all had to work to get what we've got. I worked my arse off to build up my farm and I'm sure as hell not going to hand it to some *kaffir* on a plate. Give them a bit of education and they reckon they can be just like us, but you know, they don't think like us. Throw them into a new situation and they don't have a bloody clue what to do."

That's exactly what Mother said when I told her about Chipo's dad getting a job at Allan Wilson. Time to chuck this conversation in or I'm going to say something I'll regret. I refused the offer of beer and now I could probably do with something stronger, but I've got to drive home.

"Gill?" I nudge her elbow with the plate of sandwiches. "Grub's up. Let's get the guys filling their faces."

I don't add, *"Please!"* but she reads it in my grimace and presumably in the way I barge past her to set the plate on the table.

"So Tess," she says, perching on the edge of the table between Piet and Craig. "As I was saying, you should enter the Zimbabwe Horse Trials Championship run this year. Induna's quite capable of doing the Open Novice class and Encore will go Intermediate. What do you think? I've got two novice horses I want to put through this year. One belongs to the Johnsons over on Narrow Spruit Farm."

She bites into a peanut butter sandwich and we smile at each other with our eyes only.

"Oh? Who's that?"

"Telstar. Lovely bright bay Anglo-Arab with two socks behind. The other is Reckless, a fab black Thoroughbred I've been promised by Melody Cloete."

It's worked. The two guys have lost interest. They're munching their sandwiches with dedication and easing the passage with beer and some sort of internal reflection. Gill and I could, of course, talk Horse all afternoon but, shortly after finishing his food, Maritz starts up with his dire prophesies again. He doesn't appear to be in a hurry to leave.

I guess it will have to be me.

"Sorry about old Maritz," Gill says to me through the open side window. "He's a good neighbour and he means well but he's one of the old school politically."

I put the car into reverse. "He seems to know all there is to know about everything."

"Him? Oh yes. He's one of those. Whatever you've done, he's done it better or seen a bigger one. You can't win. We just agree with him."

Friday 06/11/81

Hi Jess!

Yes, it's me. You remember me, right?

Sorry I haven't been in contact for yonks but it's been a strange time. I'm going to scrawl a few lines and then have to leave it till tomorrow as we're meeting Gill and Piet and Mum and Rosie at the Monomatapa for dinner tonight. Nathan is looking over my shoulder at this point and protesting that I don't scrawl. He says my handwriting is, and I quote, "Flowingly lovely". He's such an unrepentant charmer.

So yes, you've guessed it. I've moved into Makuti Park. This is it. I'm here. The house has been sold. Mum and Rosie are living in Meikles Hotel. Dad's in Southampton. We're officially split up. They'll all get back together, but not with me. I don't really, truly know how I feel about that. I AM the only one who has a permanent home, if that's any consolation.

Mum's keeping her car until the day they fly out, then I'll take it over and sell my 120Y.

Like I said, strange. The day after Dad left, Mum started throwing things away in earnest. I had no idea that would give me such a monumental sense of loss. Bloody disconcerting it was, to watch my entire home being permanently dismantled and packed away in cardboard boxes. Of course you've been there. You never said as much but I guess you felt the same? I tried to remember the day we moved into the house and I actually cried when I couldn't. I have no recollection of it at all. I was only four but you'd think I'd remember something? Thinking about it though, I guess it's better that I can't. Maybe it would've been worse leaving if I remembered the excitement of arriving. If I was excited? I guess I must have been.

So Rosie and I got instructed to dig through our cupboards and THROW STUFF OUT (Mum's words, not mine). Did you find so much junk in yours? I found garbage I'd forgotten even existed and I've zero idea how it came to be in there in the first place. Useless stuff. Salt, pepper and sugar sachets from SAA and Air Rhodesia. A Tupperware box with three moonstone pebbles and some chunks of pink quartz in it. Another box with loads of stubby wax crayons in it. (Okay, maybe they did have some use, judging by the length of them.) What else? Two strips of bright red wool bound into thick plaits (why?), one wing of a tin toy aeroplane, sheared off at the root (where was the rest of it?) and some small containers of model paint, gone completely solid. God alone knows what happened to the models. I do remember making a Messerschmitt 109 and some other WWII fighters with Rosie when I was into my Biggles craze. They must've disintegrated or been thrown away eons ago.

Then there were the old school exercise books. Yup, like you found. Why did we keep them? When we got them, the covers were bright blue, hey? Not any more. All grey and curled up at the edges. I spent a good couple of hours reading through those which was seriously wasted time but entertaining in an alarming sort of way. How the hell did I manage to sneak some reference to horses into almost every conceivable subject? Pony stories in Creative Writing, the importance of the horse in the history of transport and agriculture, a biology essay on the evolution of the skeletal structure of the modern equine, you name it, I found it. And SCHOOL REPORTS! Relieved to discover they clearly didn't think I was that bad at all coz I mostly got nice comments, apart from a few. Let me quote some for you.

In recognition of my lack of potential to be a domestic goddess:

"Tessa's knitting has improved little this year. Perhaps she might be more enthusiastic if she could knit herself a pony."

In recognition of my lack of ability or interest in sport:

"Swimming – Tessa tries hard."

"Athletics – If Tessa put as much energy into House athletics as she does into pretending to be a show jumper at breaktime, she could do very well."

And in the absence of anything encouraging to say:

"Tessa has attended hockey and netball lessons this year."

So I was never going to be any good at sports. Or knitting. I didn't need a special report to tell me that.

Going to disappear off now. Gotta get ready to party. Back tomorrow.

Saturday 07/11/81

Well I have to say that was quite strange meeting up with Mum and Rosie for a meal rather than GOING with them. The times, they are a-changing for sure. We drank quite a lot, or at least Rosie and Gill and I did. I assume Piet managed to get Gill to their car, and Nathan poured me into ours and said I was talking nonsense. I slept like a log and, surprisingly, don't seem to have much of a hangover this morning. In fact, I was the first one up and he's still sound asleep. Next time we go out for the evening I'll drive him.

Mum seems in good spirits, although she said it's all a bit unreal being essentially homeless. The folks have had it tough though. So much to do, to sort out. Dad left late in August to take up his new position but he resigned from Prescott, Jones and Partners at the end of June to give himself the free time to arrange for tax clearances, to organise the air freight and shipping and to deal with the unbelievably complicated red tape. He transferred all his money to a new account to which I have access. Ha ha – I'm rich! Well, I like to think I am anyway. I didn't say that to them of course. It's a bloody ridiculous situation. They get this token "settling in allowance" they can take with them, which is frankly pathetic, and have to leave the rest here. I can use the money for air fares to visit England and draw it out to give to them if they ever come back here for a holiday. They're damned lucky they've got Dad's inheritance over there in England. You have family in SA and your Dad's working so you're lucky too. So many of their generation who've decided to leave have done so with next to nothing, knowing they'll probably never own a house again. It makes me want to spit blood.

Mum and R will leave on 17th December and R will start at her new school in Southampton after the Christmas holidays. It's the middle of the school year over there of course. I'm not entirely sure how it will work with her as she'll be like, six months out of step with the school year. Knowing her, she'll be fine. In several months it'll be like she grew up there. I'm not the least worried about her.

The guy who bought the house is an accountant. The day they completed the sale was bloody depressing. Mum seemed quite happy, but me and R were just plain miserable, wandering about trying to memorise every minute detail of the house that's been our home for the last fourteen years. Like the colour of the walls, the curtains, the plants in the garden. I concentrated on the furniture and ornaments too because they're now gone as far as I'm concerned. The others won't lose all that of course.

R did seem to cheer up a bit when she started packing a selection of her clothes to go by sea with the household container. I had three suitcases of clothing to bring with me to Makuti – I was a bit flabbergasted I had so much. Plus several boxes and carrier bags of personal bits and bobs. Mum offered me linen and curtains but how could I take all that? The Owens are being good enough to put me up and I can't dump loads of junk they don't need on them as well. I'd rather put together my own home when the time comes. I told her that. You know what she said? "You're not going to be in too much of a hurry to move out?" What she really meant of course was, "You're not going to be in too much of a hurry to get married". She's grudgingly come round to admitting that Nathan and I are just the best fit ever. Well, I say grudgingly but it's not as bad as that. She likes him – she just was so convinced that Danny was It. Oh – did I tell you I quite literally bumped into him back at the end of September? It was a Saturday and me and R were in town and she was whining about the fact that I'd made her walk all the way down to the saddlery place in Forbes Avenue and I was trying to ignore her and dodge my way through droves of people – the whole world was in town that day – and get back to the car and get home and it suddenly dawned on me that I was following the back of a very familiar form. I had this moment of horrible dilemma, wondering how I was going to tell R why I suddenly wanted to go the other way and then he stopped and I walked into him! Well, if you'd told me a person could look like he did when he turned and saw me, I wouldn't have believed you. He must've had twenty expressions run across his face one after the other. It was hilarious, when I think about it now, but at the time just plain sad. He was SO excited, I swear he thought I was about to say I wanted him back. Poor guy. I felt so mean. He greeted me as My Girl and tried to hug me and I wanted to hug him but didn't want to give him the wrong idea. One of life's more awkward moments, let me tell you. We asked each other a volley of questions at the same time and then started answering those questions over each other. R said it was like watching a comedy sketch.

Basically, he's fine and doing well at university. He had no idea the folks and R were leaving so that news left him a bit dumbfounded. I think he thought for a moment I was going too and that clearly hit him hard, but then when I said I was staying with the Owens he just went all quiet. He said something like What about you and... er... and I said We're fine and I must've sounded as happy as I felt. He didn't like that.

Did you hear about that UANC bloke who was shot coming out of his driveway? They're pointing fingers at ZANU(PF) and so far they haven't denied it. Well, it happened in the street behind the Proctors' place. He told me this story about how he and his mum were the only ones at home and they were watching Danger UXB, and were on the edges of their seats as old Brian Ash was delicately defusing a monster bomb, when they heard what sounded like someone hammering on a sheet of corrugated iron just outside the back door. AK47 of course. They emptied a whole magazine into him by the sound of it and then scarpered. Danny said all the local residents got out their weapons and started firing at anything that moved so it was a bit hairy for a while, until the cops arrived. I can picture it – a bunch of twitchy, trigger-happy citizens hiding behind hedges and gates, trying to be the local SWAT team. Luckily, no one else got hurt.

Danny's not seeing anyone else yet, by the way. He reckons he hasn't found a girl to match the required standard. I didn't know what to say to that.

It was last Friday when we all left the house. My darling kid sister broke down. God, it nearly killed me. She was inconsolable, shutting herself in her bedroom for nearly an hour. When she did come out, she sat on the verandah railings and stared across the valley at the view – our view – that's just been there every day of her life and that she knew she would never see again. Mum and I left her alone until the Biddulphs lorry arrived, but then I had to enlist her to help me get Cleo and Skellum into my car.

Cleo had, inevitably, disappeared earlier in the morning and as you can imagine we all hit a high level of panic. It was a hard job convincing myself and the other two not to rush about like headless chickens, calling for her. You know what cats are like. She'd have known damned well something was up just from the vibe in the air and panicky running about and yelling would only convince her she was right. So sure enough, I spotted her slinking around in the bushes behind the washing line about half an hour later. R was all for diving in and grabbing her but I insisted we just went out to sit on the lawn, to entice her to join us. Once we'd caught her, we shut her in the empty dining room with milk and nibbles. Both her and Skellum have settled remarkably well here, thank goodness. Skellum absolutely adores Nathan but I'm not jealous. I tell him it's only what he should expect when he keeps sharing his biltong with the dog.

Those packers were super-efficient. I got the feeling that if I'd stood still for too long I would've got packed too. In about four hours our entire household was on a lorry. All that was left was the neighbours' kettle and mugs. I couldn't wait to get out. I didn't want to see it like that – empty and echoing, curtainless windows. It might've been okay if we'd been going to a new house we'd all chosen but it all seemed so final in this case. The Parsons were all out so we left the kettle and mugs with Susan (she's their new maid). I was pretty glad all told. I didn't want to go through the Goodbyes. It's not like Mum was flying out right there and then anyway. She's phoned Cheryl and Alan since and they've called into the hotel a few times.

Mum keeps reminding me how the government is talking again about taking land from the white farmers for 'resettlement'. Not buying it, just taking it. And they've also said that anyone who will not conform to the 'New Order' can go right now. She wanted to know how much land Charles has. I keep telling her he's not a commercial farmer so then she moves on to Piet and Gill's place and seems convinced they'll be kicked off at some stage. Piet says it's all talk and they'll never do it. Well it doesn't make sense, does it? Why would they tamper with an industry that's so vital to the economy and supports so many jobs?

I still can't convince Mum why I want to give it a chance and stay. She's worried about leaving me here – I understand that. She's saying – well, so is Dad, to be honest – that most of the government ministers are hell bent on some sort of revenge against the whites. They keep telling me I'm burying my head in the sand.

The Constitution they eventually managed to draw up at that Lancaster House fiasco can't be changed for ten years. By then things may have settled and we should know which way it's all going. Charles Owen reckons the IMF has a tight rein on the situation and they'll stop financial aid at any violation of human rights. Mugabe's a sensible man. He knows he needs the support of the world for the economy to survive.

So, I'm staying.

Now look – I want an equally long epistle back from you my girl. Get your pen out.

Work hard and don't let the bastards grind you down!

Love 'n' love,

Tess xxx

I put my pen down. I haven't told her the half of it but I'm incapable of putting most of the roller coaster emotions I've discovered in the last few weeks into words. The way I've been on such a high – a scudding around in the clouds, life is just the best, nothing could possibly go wrong ever again kind of high – only to come crashing down minutes later into a black hole from which nothing can ever go right again. The way I've endlessly questioned my own decisions like never before and like I never realised was possible. I can't write all that in a letter – I don't have the literary skills. But one of these days we can spend hours talking about it.

Or maybe not. Maybe by the time we get to meet up again it will all seem irrelevant and part of another life. Water under the bridge, as they say.

Just how I'm going to say goodbye to Mum and Rosie, or how I'll feel at the airport, is one of those unknowns that is so impossible to foresee it's outright petrifying. Saying goodbye to Dad wasn't hard at all, but only because it was like he was going on a business trip, because the rest of us were still together and seeing him off like we've done before, as if he'd be returning soon and we'd be back at the airport to pick him up. When they go… Can I deal with something so final?

Don't be stupid. It won't be final at all. We'll see each other again of course. But what *is* final, what *has* ended, is the way I've lived for the last eighteen years. We won't ever live all together again – of that I'm sure. And that's another thing that puts me in the clouds or down in the hole depending on the direction of the wind, or so it seems.

It was bad enough saying goodbye to Elijah. Mum was calm, business-like, at a distance, thanking him for his services, wishing him well, taking it for granted that he'd turn his back and walk away and put their relationship at an end. Or at least that's how she came across to me, hoping in vain like I was that she'd show at least some emotion. Rosie and I had no such inhibitions. We did the awkward thing first – double African handshakes all round, thank yous, wish you wells – then like someone had pressed a button we all started blubbing and he grabbed both of us at once in a three-way hug. Anyone watching would've thought one or more of us was about to die, even though I knew – I *know* – there's a distinct possibility I'll meet him again. Rosie won't, though. I never saw Mum's face, but she was probably hopping about, incredulously disapproving of our intimate moment with the gardener. Still, nothing she could do about it.

Elijah. In my head right now he's picking vegetables and fruit, hoeing the beds, weeding, clipping edges, mending bike tyre punctures, playing with Skellum (our vicious guard dog), opening the gates for Dad. He's sitting outside his *kaya* of an evening with his family around him and, those times Rosie and I dared to join them, telling us stories of Shona traditions and myths. We're sitting cross legged in front of him and listening and asking questions and sharing jokes. We're playing games with his kids, making roads for our Dinky cars in the sand behind the *kaya*, dressing Mary's dolls in our dolls' clothing.

But the line in the sand that over-rode everything was that line between us, wasn't it? Gardener and The Family. Not simply Employee and Employers, but Black and White. We knew the line existed and we wanted to ignore it, but Dad had drawn it and we minded Dad.

"Don't spend too much time down there in the *kaya*," was the repeated warning. We asked why. Mum said Mary might make the doll clothing dirty, or lose it, or Simeon and Ephraim might damage our cars. She said, did we realise these kids might actually *steal* the clothes, dolls and cars? Sometimes she was more generous – she thought they might just *forget to give them back*. Dad said we might start picking up Shona expressions and learn to speak like Africans.

Hell, we live in Africa. We grew up here. If we'd chanced to live in France, we'd've learned to speak like the French. Or in Germany, the Germans. He wouldn't have objected to that, would he? Of course not. He thinks being multi-lingual in European languages is admirable.

So he drew lines, and good little well-behaved me has respected his lines all my life and only ever picked up a pathetic few words and phrases in Shona. Well, damnit, things have changed and I can learn whatever I want. I'll enrol on a Shona course.

Actually, I don't even have to do that. From now on I'm going to enlist the grooms to teach me more. And Nathan. He's pretty much fluent. Gill not so much, but she understands more than she speaks. There are grammar books here in this house. Charles probably taught them as much as any native speakers.

Mum liked the dividing lines for health reasons too.

"Don't ever eat anything Irene offers you. The *kaya*'s not very clean and they don't eat like us."

To this day I don't know if she ever went into the *kaya* to see for herself. Irene's cooking utensils were kept scrupulously clean and tidy and as all her children were healthy and strong and had perfect teeth, I figured there couldn't be much wrong with her cooking. Rosie and I were well fed, so we never had need to accept any food from her, and nor would the idea have occurred to us I guess, until that hot, sultry summer evening when we saw Mary, Ephraim and Simeon catching flying ants. I can't precisely remember *how* they were catching them – masses of them, clouding around each streetlight even as the thunder died away – I just remember the OK carrier-bags wriggling with life and Mary shouting, in English, "Keep it closed! No, Simeon, look, you're letting them out, man, idiot!" because each time he tried to put another handful of insects into his bag, a whole squadron of them escaped.

There's nothing like a game of dare and double-dare. Of course we goaded each other into following the kids back to the *kaya*, where we spent the best part of thirty minutes persuading Irene to give us a few of the fried insects from her hefty iron pan.

"You should go back to the house. Your mother will be looking for you."

"Nah," Rosie scoffed. "She thinks we're at the Halls' place. Oh Irene, please? Just a few. Come on! Bet *you* wouldn't eat them, Tee."

"Bet I would. Would *you?*"

"Of course! Bet you won't though."

"Bet *you* won't."

"I will. I'll dare you to eat some!"

"I double-dare you to eat some!"

Irene didn't have a clue what to do with us. She giggled a lot and avoided eye contact. Her three children just stared at us open mouthed, watching us baiting each other, their heads bobbing back and forth as if they were at a tennis match.

I really, really didn't want to eat any flying ants. Seriously. But in the end it came down to saving face. I screwed up my nose and stuffed a spoonful of them into my mouth. And I boasted of it to Charles the next day.

"Yeah, course I ate them. They just taste like peanut butter."

He said he guessed they probably did and that will be because they'd been fried in groundnut oil.

Of course.

Just short of six weeks till they fly. It seems like a lifetime, right now. But it'll be over in a flash.

THURSDAY 17TH DECEMBER 1981

It's starting to rain.

"Ah, silence. Blessed silence," I say, indicating to turn into the Makuti Park driveway.

I can feel you giving me what they call a Sideways Look.

"What?"

"Windscreen wipers. Silent. The ones on my dear Datsun squealed at me on every downstroke. Hideous, but there didn't seem much point changing them when I was going to sell her and take over Mum's."

"Her?" You laugh and pull up the hood of your sweatshirt. "So you like your new car then? I'll open the gate."

You salute me as I drive past. Like I do several dozen times a day I fall in love all over again. In love with your abjectness as you hold the gate for me in the warm, soft rain. In love with the way I'm looking forward to walking with you into our home in a few minutes. Oh my God, I've really gone soft.

I park the Cressida directly behind your Land Cruiser, switch off, close my eyes to force the mental images to return. Mum and Rosie. All of us resolutely dry-eyed and standing around like spare parts in the terminal like we had no idea we were supposed to check in the luggage and were trying to work out the system. The two of them disappearing into security and passport control. The lights of the Jumbo disappearing into the night sky. Why do I feel so cold and detached?

You tap on the side window, questioning, your face shining wet in the light from the back porch.

"Let's go and check on the horses," you shout.

I leave my bag and my umbrella in the car and link my arm

under yours. The rain has eased to a very fine mist and we can get under the stable eaves in a couple of minutes.

For a while we just talk to the horses, each one in turn, tickling muzzles, stroking necks, dodging Bravo's teeth and laughing at him. He's not impressed at being disturbed and he's never understood why a human should want to cuddle him.

For once in my life though, these horses are not keeping my attention. I can't let go of trying to reason why I feel so cold, so unemotional. At the end of the row we stand, hand in hand, staring out into the rain – sheeting now – lit into thousands of silver spears by the PIR light on the edge of the eave above us.

"Do you know something? I'm so unsure as to what I should feel at the departure of my entire family that I feel nothing at all. That can't be normal."

"What is normal?"

Good point. It'll hit me soon enough, I'll bet.

We'll visit them next year, together, you tell me and the dark, rainy night brightens, like the end of the tunnel I didn't know I was in has just appeared on the horizon. Yes, of course. You and me together, because that's what we are now.

"I want to travel a lot. All over the world. Do you?"

Silly question. I know you do.

You stick a hand out into the deluge, turn it over a few times like you're fascinated to see it getting wet.

"Yes. Then that's what we'll do. But right now there's a much warmer, drier place to be than this and I'll be the happiest man on the planet if I can travel there with you now."

For the first time in weeks the sky-high has come back and I'm convinced life can only get better.

FRIDAY 18TH DECEMBER 1981

"Didn't you want to go into town for something?"

Your head appears at the half-open door of my office. A welcome intrusion. I'm struggling to concentrate. Several delivery notes for various building materials are missing and I can't work up sufficient enthusiasm to phone the respective site agents and moan at them. It's a week to go to Christmas, so does anyone really care?

"I did indeed. I want to treat myself to a new handbag. This black one is looking a bit sad and frayed."

I extract it from the drawer next to me, hold it up, twiddle the loose thread along the strap. If I play my cards right, I'll get one bought for me.

"I also want shampoo, as a matter of fact."

"Well I'm driving in, in about half an hour. Come with me then."

You vanish, your familiar footsteps receding along the corridor. It's a smug little smile on my lips. It's a distinct advantage when one's boyfriend is the boss's son.

*

Charles's new Mercedes estate smells, well, *new*. The upholstery is cream-coloured and softer than that in the old one – although I thought that was pretty nice. You park in the open-sided multi-storey Parkade, on the side adjacent to Southampton House.

Southampton. Mum, Dad and Rosie will all be headed from Heathrow Airport to another Southampton this morning, six thousand miles away. Is it raining there, I wonder? It's a fabulous day here, under a deep blue sky, and we're high enough up to get a view of the whole city, eye-achingly bright under the summer sun.

You lock the car with the little hand-held gadgetty thingy and the Mercedes blips in response. I make you unlock it, then take the fob off you and lock it myself, just so I can say I've done it.

"Satisfied, Kitten?"

You signal to me to keep the key and add, "I wonder how cold it is in England today."

"Well they were carrying enough coats between them when they left last night and I'll bet they're making good use of them today. We'll find out when they get in contact I guess."

We ignore the lifts and walk down the concrete stairs to ground level, passing a few others going up in the narrow stairwell.

"Try and remember which side we're on," you plead over your shoulder. "It's the Union Avenue side, not Jameson Avenue. There's nothing worse than tramping up and down not knowing what bit you've parked in and quite unable to find the car."

"Mmm. It's okay as long as you know you're lost and that the car is still there somewhere. That it's not been 'borrowed' by someone else."

"Don't worry so much. I'd like to see someone break into that one. The old coat hanger trick won't work."

We emerge into the paved shopping mall below the parking decks and take the steps up onto Union Avenue. The intense reflected heat and dazzling sunlight reverts my thoughts back to my family, far away in another world. What time does it get dark in winter? Gill said it was about four o'clock. How depressing.

Aloud, I say, "They'll phone later."

"Hmm?"

"Mum and Dad. They'll phone from Dad's new rented house."

You take my hand.

"Do you miss them?"

"I will do."

I'm surrounded by my African people, thronging towards me, past me, away from me. People accustomed to space and sunshine in a city that's open and never hostile or threatening. Too bad if they rename it Harare – it's still a great place to live. I spend a few moments indulging in a mental comparison of my new spacious home, with its landscaped gardens, stables and paddocks and the crammed-together terraced houses on *Coronation Street*. I allow myself to feel content with all that I've opted to keep.

"Shopping? Hello? Earth calling Tess."

You're waving a hand across my eyes, dragging them back into focus. "I'm over here, Kitten. What did we come for? Handbag and shampoo, yes?"

"Ah, so you have a head for a woman's shopping list now?"

"No. Just a good memory. What about Meikles department store?"

We cross the street along with scores of other jaywalkers.

Along First Street I start picturing the sort of bag I want. It's black, leather of course, and has lots of compartments. Maybe I'll see a nice one in another colour as well. I'm dodging my fellow pedestrians with ease of practice – a woman on a mission. At the junction with Manica Road, while still in the shade under the overhanging canopy roof, I pause to allow my man to catch up.

For the next few moments the earth falters on its axis, the pavement trembles under me and the walls vibrate. Sound waves hit me in a physical blow. Shying backwards, like a startled horse, I lose my balance, end up on my knees. A black stranger beside me stoops and catches hold of my arm and we stare at each other without comprehension. No fear – only puzzlement, like neither of us can make any sense of anything. And a numbness, a deafness.

Think.

Think straight and get a grip.

You *haven't* gone deaf, you silly cow. Listen. Yes?

That weird, muted woolliness and indistinguishable buzz in my ears is, here and there, starting to separate into individual sounds. Like strands of yarn, they're unravelling and beginning to register in my senses as something real. Screaming. Someone is screaming. No, more than one person. Shattering and splintering. Glass. Glass falling from many windows in many buildings over many storeys. Going on and on and on. Then your voice. Behind me. Clear and utterly calm, as if you're identifying fruit in the supermarket.

"That was a bomb."

I know. I knew even as the air hit me and turned my eardrums to wool. Is that what they call a shockwave? Gave *me* a bloody shock. Probably how I ended up on my knees. As time seems to be standing still, I take the chance to inspect them. Yup. They're grazed, and they sting.

Actually, thinking straight doesn't seem to be an option open to me. Muddled doesn't come close to describing my world right now. I don't understand. The war is over. It's all supposed to be all right now.

Time gets going again. It's all happening. People are surging every which way around me, apart from you, with one steady hand against my back, the other one on my shoulder and your presence grounding me and keeping me from joining the frantic, aimless throng. A middle-aged woman in a blue pinafore-type dress appears in front of us, makes contact with her panicked eyes and yells, "It's near that bakery! The bakery's blown up!"

Your voice is still completely calm when you say, "The ZANU(PF) offices are above the bakery."

There's a log-jam of crazily-angled cars up ahead and an acrid sting in my nostrils. A haze of smoky, dusty stuff is drifting along Manica Road from the east, over the cars.

ZANU(PF) headquarters. The North-West Bakery. Dad, and his jokes about the leadership party operating out of a tiny, dingy office over a bread shop. Mum, telling me it sells the best bread in town. Lasts well, no maize-meal in it, if you need good bread, my girl, you go there to get it, yes? I may well have done that this morning if Moira hadn't been grocery shopping yesterday.

While I have this completely inane nonsense rattling in my head, down below a deep chill of pure horror is seeping into my legs. In a matter of minutes, you and I might've been walking past the bakery, looking for a gap in the traffic so that we could cross the road to Meikles. And Mum might've been queuing there today.

But we're all still in one piece, me, you and Mum. Us here on the pavement in First Street and Mum — where would she be now? — probably on the way down to Southampton, trying to get used to the winter cold and totally oblivious to this. For now at least. It'll hit the world news later today of course.

And I told them it'll be fine. I told them, go, I'll be okay, I know what I'm doing. I said that more than once, didn't I? To parents, to Rosie and even to Charles and Moira and Gill. And you.

Right. Come on, get back to the here and now. Think. What do I do? Now where's that guy going?

He's the one who helped me to my feet and, together with you, held me upright. He peered into my face and asked me if I was all right, but now he's let go of my arm and is running across the road, dodging round a stationary car, shouting. He's yelling in Shona; looks like he's recognised someone on the other side of Manica Road.

Christ, when Mum and Dad hear about this they'll go berserk. They're more than likely to command me to leave on the next available flight and join them. Will they try to come back and fetch me?

How the hell was I supposed to know which was the right choice? It's not like I made the decision just like that – snap. No, I did months of agonising, running pros and cons, creating arguments, upsetting the whole bloody family, driving myself crazy. Then I thought I knew. I chose. And now? Now it all, quite literally, blows up in my face.

Well okay, not in *my* face. Not even right near me, thank God. God?

Come on, you don't believe in God so why do you even say that? Think, think.

You materialise in front of me. Seconds ago you were behind me. You draw my face close to yours and kiss my cheek.

"Look, stay here. All right? Are you listening? Tess? Just stay here. I'm going to see if I can help anyone, if I can remember my First Aid training."

No, you can't leave me here. You can't go. No, please don't go! Oh God, it will be horrible, Nathan, please. I'm not sure if I've said anything aloud or not.

"Stay here," you repeat. "I'll be okay."

"I ought to help too. Do something. But I don't think I've got the guts. No! Nathan, no! What if there's another one?"

"There won't be. Just stay here. I'll come back. You believe me, don't you?"

I fight you to try and stop you moving away from me. Then I'm leaning against the wall behind me, alone in a heaving sea of people. It's impossible to relate the panic-stricken mob before me to the unconcerned, daily-life-driven, bustling crowd we were pushing our way through earlier.

Think in the here and now. Blot out the flickering images of my blissful daydreams of barely an hour ago – the Owens' spacious home, the landscaped gardens, the stables, the paddocks., the feeling of space, the contentment. I close my eyes.

Nathan's gone round the corner. He's going to help. I'm going to have to go and find him. Find him. I need him. He was part of my decision to stay. Part of me now. The others have all gone and I'm here because I said I wanted to stay and now this goes and happens and oh God (God, again?) now what am I going to do?

This is Africa. It's never going to be easy, but we love it. Nathan quoted me a line from a book just last week – "Africa is a cruel place". I think it was *Naught for Your Comfort*. They say it gets in your blood, under your skin, fills your soul. Africa has always been about survival against the odds, no matter what species you are. So we will survive. We will rise. We will Wait And See like we've always done.

Push off the wall, throw the sling strap of the good, old, faithful handbag over the head and set off in search of your Nathan. There he is, ahead of me, that familiar shape, the walk, the way of being. Run! Run after him.

"Nathan! Wait! I'm here. I'm coming. I'll stick with this!"

You hear me in spite of the racket, the screaming, the hooting and the sirens that are just beginning to make themselves heard in the distance. You turn. Smile. Hold out your hands to me.

Nathan, and you, Africa, I'm here to stay, no matter what you've got to throw at me.